PAGAN EYES
COLLECTION

RAYNA NOIRE

CONTENTS

INITIATION

PAGAN EYES, BOOK 1

BY
RAYNA NOIRE

INITIATION
Rayna Noire
Copyright © 2013

To obtain permission to excerpt portions of the text, please contact the author.

All characters in this book are fictional and figments of the author's imagination.

CHAPTER ONE

N ANA HOBBLED INTO the living room, dragging her left leg behind her, waving the evening newspaper. Red-faced and out of breath, she drew everyone's attention. Mother ran over to her, wrapping one arm around her and urging her to sit down.

"Please, Mama, you must calm down. It's not good for your heart."

Father nodded from his place in the kitchen doorway, drying a plate. Leah's brother, Ethan, watched his grandmother with an expectant expression and drawn breath, probably certain she'd fall to the floor, as she'd only a couple of months before. Luckily, they all lived together. She'd never have survived the stroke on her own. The doctor had instructed them to keep her calm, but often Nana demonstrated the high drama associated with a teenage girl.

Leah stood up and walked over to her grandmother, taking the newspaper from her hand. "What is it, Nana?"

Her brother announced from his spot on the couch, "It's the cyberbullying article on the front page. I've no worries, Nana. No one bullies me." Ethan pushed up his sleeve and clenched his fist to display a meager bicep, though probably more than most ten-year-olds could lay claim to.

A smile crossed the woman's lined face. "No, sweetheart, no, this is much worse."

Leah's mother, Maura, managed to get Nana to sit in a chair with some difficulty, since only one leg worked right. Leah looked away. It reminded her of the time she'd watched a three-legged dog lie down. The dog never acted like it minded, but it still made her feel bad watching it.

Crouching beside the chair, her mother took Nana's hand. "Tell me, tell us."

Pointing with one hand to Leah, who still clutched the newspaper, she commanded, "Read it to them. Let them know the barbarians still exist. There's no justice, no fairness, no equal rights, and no protection." Her voice became louder and stronger with each word. Her body shook as she half rose from the chair.

Mother cut her eyes meaningfully at her husband, who nodded at Leah, who paged through the paper.

Leah searched for what could be upsetting her grandmother. "Lead story is local boy signing with the NFL." Both her father and mother shook their heads no. She kept paging through the paper. "A huge storm is predicted for the Northeast?"

Grandmother waved her hand in a circle to keep going.

"Ah." She knew that wasn't the right story, but what could it be? On the back page of the front section near the fold was a small article. She knew instinctively it was the one her grandmother meant. "Yesterday, in Papua, New Guinea, a twenty-year-old woman accused of being a witch was burned alive. The young widow and mother left two small children behind."

Her grandmother shook off her daughter's hand. Stabbing the air with an emphatic index finger, she crowed, "See? See? They're at it again." Her dark eyes darted around the room to make sure she'd everyone's attention. "That poor girl. What was her crime, really?"

Maura sighed. "Just twenty, so young. Could be she was too pretty and attracted a married man's eye. Calling her a witch is always a good way to get rid of her. It worked countless times before."

Her father laid down the plate and towel and walked into the living room to join the conversation. He sat down on the couch on the other side of Ethan. "Something happened in their village. Chickens weren't laying or a goat died. It's always easier to blame it on the evil eye or a hex, than accept it for what it is. Just life, luck, usually both. People always seem to believe life owes them more than they deserve. The only way to rationalize not getting it is to blame someone for blocking it."

Ethan joined in. "Just like calling someone a cheat, a liar, or even a bully."

"In a way," Maura agreed. "But not exactly. People don't feel it is okay to kill people for telling a lie or even being accused of telling a lie. The hatred goes bone deep, associated with fear and helplessness. Even the simple fact she'd no man to stand for her would be enough to persecute her."

Leah stood, silent, thinking that only a few years separated her from the young woman burned alive. Yesterday, her history teacher, Miss Santiago, had grown as animated as Nana talking about human slavery in the US. Her voice had become shrill as she'd spoken of undocumented workers not receiving any pay for their work and being kept in unheated garages, treated no better than animals. After class, the popular girls, Lauren, Brianna, and Alexis, had joked about Miss Santiago's behavior, even pretending to be her, waving their arms and bugging out their eyes, spitting out the words. The other students had enjoyed their performance. Leah hadn't. Besides being mean, she'd had no reason to appease the girls. She already knew she was on their short list.

Yeah, she knew her teacher had gone overboard, but she knew without having it spelled out that it was personal. Often Leah knew things without words, just as she knew someone close to Miss Santiago had died under such conditions. Leah knew all about taking things personally. A woman burned as a witch was personal for her family. How could it not be when her entire family followed the old ways?

Her family circled her grandmother, trying to calm her down without much success. Leah leaned back against the wall the offending newspaper still in her hand, she wanted to throw it to the ground and flee. An image took shape in her mind. It was dark, most likely night. The sound of running, yelling, and then screaming, a long prolonged scream as if whoever uttered it felt absolute terror. A spark charged the night, then caught fire and became a flame, growing into an orb of light. It illuminated sweaty, dark faces with feverish eyes and determined countenances. Two strong men stripped to the waist held a woman between them. Her long hair covered her face as she struggled.

Off to the side, a chair sat on a dais. An almost skeletal man sat there, garbed in a long robe. His lips quirked up as the men wrestled the woman, who wore a coarse, shapeless gown, to a standstill in front of him. A brutal push shoved her to her knees. The sound of weeping almost broke Leah's heart. She was watching what had happened in New Guinea only days before.

No doubt, the man on the dais had caused this woman to be in such a situation. The crying continued as the man ordered. "Let me look on the face of the witch." The surrounding crowd hissed and murmured. Most threw their hands in front of their faces or looked away as if looking at the woman's face might hurt them. She couldn't. The woman deserved her respect. One guard grabbed her long dark hair and yanked, snapping her head up. Despite the tears glistening on her skin, her expression was defiant. Her face was familiar. It should have been, since she saw it every morning in the mirror as she brushed her hair.

HER LEGS, MORE rubberlike than bone and muscle, slid out from under her, landing her on the floor. What did it mean? Nana used to tell her the visions she received were similar to a tornado watch. It didn't necessarily mean the vision would happen, but it was best to get ready for it in case it did. Most of her visions included small things, such as being ridiculed by Lauren and Brianna or failing an algebra test, or slipping on the ice and losing two teeth. It all had happened, except the teeth. Whenever she saw anything glistening like ice, she avoided it, keeping her teeth intact so far.

The image of the man on the dais chilled her, unlike any amount of teeth-cracking ice could. The clothes she wore, the way the man spoke, none of it made sense. Her mother's voice broke into her daze.

"Leah, what are you doing? Try to be of some help, will you? Go get your grandmother a glass of water. Ethan, go get Nana's protection heart charm from the box in her bedroom."

Pushing up to her knees, she watched her brother scamper out of the room to retrieve the charm. Her mother threw her an irritated look, probably because she was still sitting there. Standing, she walked to the kitchen, but she could hear them talking. Her grandmother's shrill voice carried.

"Maura." Her voice had an imperious tone that defied her fragile appearance. "Be gentle with your daughter. Soon, she will be called on to make the ultimate sacrifice."

The ultimate sacrifice? The water splashed over the glass rim as she continued to hold it under the faucet, not seeing it but instead the glee in the man's face who'd called her a witch. She truly hoped her grandmother didn't expect her to become a burnt offering.

Turning off the faucet, she tipped the glass to pour out the excess water. Taking a dishtowel, she dried the glass. Nana could trace her ancestry back to Romany gypsies. She claimed this centuries-old bond allowed her to turn the Tarot cards with surprising accuracy for her loyal clients. Leah had doubts about her grandmother's actual ability, though the fact she'd seen the same clients faithfully for years made Leah wonder. Then there were the crystals and charms strewn about the family home, which kept her from inviting classmates over. All she really wanted was just to be another teenage girl obsessed with drama and boys. Well, only the boys part...one boy, Dylan Torres, if she was honest with herself.

As she handed the glass to Nana, their hands touched. Her grandmother's eyes gleamed dark with intelligence. The brief glance conveyed awareness of Leah's inner turmoil. It was the equivalent of kneeling to bury her face against Nana's shoulder, sobbing out her confusion, her fears, and her inappropriate attraction to Dylan, whose father happened to be a Pentecostal minister. A bad thing about the Pentecostals was the fact they believed witches existed and shouldn't, rather like cockroaches.

As her grandmother's fingers touched hers, the look, the touch, and the sudden knowledge that her legacy was to never be a normal girl caused her heart to plummet. No matter what excuses she might make for Nana's uncanny ability, she recognized Nana was never wrong.

Curious why so many well-heeled ladies would come month after month to have her grandmother tell their fortunes, she'd asked. Nana's answer had implied that knowing helped people shape their destiny and relieved stress. Seeing herself about to be burned at the stake didn't make her feel less stressed. Rather, just the opposite.

✧   ✧   ✧   ✧

NANA EVENTUALLY CALMED down. Adam, Leah's father, talked his determined mother-in-law out of calling the news organizations. Any negative attention might influence her father's engineering job. Nana understood this on one hand, but on another, she didn't since she chose not to hide what she was. Her grandmother had as much bravado as a drag queen in full costume demonstrating for marriage equality. There was a good chance she was pecking out a letter to the editor on her old typewriter. Leah had noticed a few of the letters in the papers, signed as Pagan Philosopher, had sounded exactly like Nana in full rant.

Her father had never mentioned the letters, which meant he hadn't seen them or had realized he could exercise no control over his mother-in-law. For years, the family had maintained a careful balance trying to please both extended families. Father's family was ultra-religious and had named their children Adam and Eve, somehow missing the incestuous connotation in the pairing. Everything that was part of the secular world was not only evil, but also forbidden. How he and her mother had ended up together appeared to be an unfathomable question. It could have been the lure of the forbidden, but more likely, it had started out as lust. Her father never would put it so bluntly, but she'd seen the pictures of them together in college. No doubt, many men had craved her mother's dark, almost foreign, beauty, but she'd chosen instead the shy, short, bespectacled engineering student.

Her mother's reasoning for their romance was he accepted her the way she was. It would be great if someone accepted Leah for who she was. She peered at her own image in the mirror, complete with a disbelieving smirk. It indicated her non-belief of her father's total acceptance of her mother. Nana had chided her son-in-law on numerous occasions for keeping quiet about their religious beliefs. Inquiries from his parents asking if they'd been to church that week were usually appeased by saying they had. He intentionally forgot to mention their services took place on a farm ten miles out of town, often under the light of a full moon. Her father had decided to follow the old ways to humor his wife, but Leah suspected it was mainly to get his mother-in-law off his back.

Setting her alarm clock for the school day, she noted five hours had passed since the news meltdown. Theodora, her cat, jumped on the bed, kneading the pillow with her paws as if preparing it. Leah knew the feline was making her own bed. Grabbing another pillow from the floor, she placed it on the bed. Dropping her clothes on the floor, she climbed between the cool sheets. Locking her hands behind her head, she stared at the ceiling, thinking about her parents' relationship. Her parents got along better than most. Her family life was unusual in that she'd both original parents living in the same house. Still, she wanted more than what they had, something stronger, bolder, something void of the timidity her father demonstrated in hiding from his parents that Maura was a witch, as was her grandmother.

No doubt, they had figured out Esmeralda Hare was a bit different, loving to play up the image of the carnival fortune-teller with flowing skirts, too much jewelry, and always wishing everyone a blessed day or merry meet again. The word most commonly used for Nana was "colorful." Nora, Leah's older sister, had confided once she'd overheard an argument between their parents over her father never telling his parents they didn't celebrate Christmas or Easter. None of the kids had cared because they'd enjoyed the Easter baskets and Christmas presents given to them by their grandparents.

Grandfather had retired from the ministry the same time his wife had divorced him. Instead of warning everyone to stay on the straight and narrow, he'd donned tie-dyed shirts, made home-brewed beer, and attended the concerts of aging rock stars. Nora had pointed out that Grandfather would accept the family's religion since he'd changed so much on his own. Of course, their father chose to say nothing. As much as Leah loved her father, she acknowledged, if only to herself, most of his actions were motivated out of fear of being different or that people might not like him. It wasn't so much that he accepted mother just how she was, but rather she accepted him with his fears, worries, and rules, able to see past everything to the caring man inside.

Scratching Theodora's head, she confided to the cat, "I won't be like that. I'm who I'm. It doesn't matter what people think."

The feline blinked her eyes as if commenting on the bold statement. Leah sighed. "You're right. I know. For all my brave words, I'm no better than my father." Balling up her fist, she pounded her pillow in disgust. "Coward, that's all I'm."

Threading her fingers under Theo's heavy body, she cradled the cat. The cat let out a few plaintive mews, but resigned herself to the cuddling, even to the point of purring. "Theodora, what am I to do? I know I'm a fraud. I talk of nothing of consequence to Dylan. Questions about homework, reactions to pop quizzes, and comments on the weather are another way to spell lame. Brianna, at least, flirts with him."

The popular blonde's flirtatious banter always seemed to switch on whenever she was near a cute guy. It didn't matter that her boyfriend, Marcus, was a senior football player who'd scored scholarships at six colleges. Could be Brianna was looking for a replacement, not that she'd consider Dylan. He was too small a deal for her, too young, not popular enough. His father was a minister, which made him the male equivalent to poison ivy. Brianna only flirted with him because Leah liked him. Worse, she'd confessed to liking Dylan in a brief spate of time when she and Brianna had been friends.

Looking back, she wondered if it had been some elaborate scheme to get information. No doubt, Brianna had relayed to Dylan that Leah had a serious crush on him. If it bothered him too much, he could stop talking to her. Then again, if he did like her, he could ask her out, which he hadn't. The third option was Brianna hadn't told him or he'd chosen not to believe her. If it were the last, then he'd showed more sense than Leah had.

"I can see your light on," her mother called through the locked door.

Leah clapped her hands, turning the light off. As a kid, she'd been so enamored of the clapper lamp that her parents had bought her one. Most people would label it hokey, but she still liked it.

"Good girl," her mother admonished, before tacking on, "Love you."

"Love you, too, Mom," she called back, closing her eyes, easing into sleep. Tomorrow would be another day, just like so many others. The image of the man in the throne-like chair flickered into her weary mind. Sitting up, she shook her head to shake the offending image out. "I refuse to dream about him. I'll think of something pleasant, such as Dylan asking me to the homecoming dance."

Lying back down, she let her eyelids flick closed. Maybe Dylan didn't dance. She'd heard some of those religions had rules against it. Something about if people danced, they'd end up having sex like rabbits. As she drifted off to sleep, her last thought was she couldn't remember ever seeing a dancing rabbit.

✧   ✧   ✧   ✧

THE SMELL STRUCK her first. The acrid, smelly odor reminded her of her fourth-grade field trip to a pioneer village. The candle maker had intrigued her by dipping wicks in what she'd assumed was wax until the woman explained it was made of animal fat from butchered animals. That's what it smelled like, along with the campfire aroma of burning wood.

In the misty night sky, a clouded crescent moon shed meager light on the surroundings. Turning slowly, she examined the primitive thatched hut behind her. In the small front garden, a split log supported by two stumps served as a bench. An oaken bucket sat by a door that flew open. An elderly woman hobbled out, dressed in a black cloak. The woman reminded Leah of her grandmother, but instead of a look of fierce determination, terror pulled her face into an anxious mask. Reaching Leah, she tugged on her clothes, pushing her toward the woods. "Flee, flee, they come. Smell the torches." The woman pointed to a path winding toward the east.

A dim glow was coming from that direction, along with the sounds of voices and snapping branches as dozens of feet marched in their direction.

An overwhelming desire to run after the unknown woman came over her. Another part of her wanted to see who was coming down the path. It was only a dream, right? People couldn't be hurt in a dream, or could they? She struggled to remember what her psychology teacher, Mr. Schaeffer, had said. He'd said either people couldn't be hurt by their fears or your fears could kill you by bringing on cardiac arrest.

A few men came into view, burly men garbed in shapeless garments, with wild hair and ragged beards. Held high, flickering torches illuminating a small circle around them. One held a curved knife, reminiscent of the scythe the grim reaper carried. It didn't bode well. One of the men spotted her, yelled, "Witch!" and charged her way. It was a definite bad sign, causing her to sprint toward the woods in the same direction as the old woman. Sticks, rocks, and briars pierced her feet, reminding her of her shoeless state. At home, she excelled in cross-country, but she'd shoes, sunlight, and a feel for the course with no angry villagers behind her. The running men drew closer. Leah stumbled over a tree root, wasting precious time.

"Here, over here." The voice came from overhead. Staring up into the canopy of leaves, she saw a small hand motioning to her. Of course, hide in the trees. Why didn't she think of that? Grabbing the lowest limb, she pulled herself into the leafy covering. In the dark, she felt for the branches, climbing higher. Eventually she grabbed an ankle or calf, and received a hand up for her trouble, helping her climb higher.

Good Goddess, how many people were in this tree? She held her breath as the light and noise came closer. The men below argued about which way to go, while a woman waded in with her opinion. "Samuel, let the witch get away. Mayhap he uses the witch for his own purposes."

One of the front-runners denied the accusations. "Martha seeks to harm my name, because I did not plight my troth with her."

The argument moved on a little farther away from the tree. Leah exhaled in a whoosh, thanking the stars for the scorned woman and lack of dogs. As if hearing her silent prayer, a long canine bay rent the air.

More footsteps ran underneath their tree, where there was some minor disagreement about which way to go, then they ran after the previous party. The sound of her heart was so loud in her ears she couldn't believe her pursuers hadn't heard it. The barking dog came closer, along with the sound of its handler.

"Ar-roo, Ar-roo." The dog sounded close, very close. Its nails scratching at her tree stopped Leah's heart. Stupid canine. She was history. She was ready to drop out of the tree and give herself up when a hand touched her and stopped her in the dark. A single word sounded in her ear. "Wait."

Two villagers stood under the tree, arguing. "Pull the hound off the tree. You will anger the tree spirits. Misfortune will befall us entering the forest at night."

"Umfrey, still your wild speech. You speak of the old ways. We're now all Christians by order of the king. Such talk will cause the witch hunters to take you up."

"I tell you this, Collin. A decree does not make the tree spirits, the fairies, the mysterious lights in the woods cease to be. Do you think they bow to kings?"

The dog's protest about the lack of interest in his treed prey caused Leah's heart to slow a tiny bit, but not return to normal. Crouched in the tree, like blackbirds on the line, she waited with the still unseen others.

"Morn is coming, and the field needs plowing. Umfrey, I will return, not because of your fears of tree fairies and what not, but because I've land to attend to."

"Good call. Your Mary may have some porridge simmering over the fire."

She listened to them move away. The staying hand remained on her arm. They all crouched in the tree for what seemed like hours as they waited for each group of witch hunters to pass by them. Dawn colored the sky with a pink glow, giving way to the sun's rays.

Finally, the hand released Leah's arm. They dropped out of the tree, one by one, the old crone in the black cloak, a young woman a bit older than herself but not by much, and a man, which surprised her. "I didn't think they took men as witches." She covered her mouth with her hand, realizing she'd spoken the words aloud.

The young woman stared at her, "What manner of speech is this?"

Before she could answer, the weathered-looking man chose to answer her inquiry. "They take whoever has trespassed against the village elders in some form or manner. My sin is I accused the miller of using unfair scales. People like Old Margaret, who has no one to stand for her, also are taken."

Turning to the young woman, Leah touched her own chest with her hand. "My speech is different because I'm from America."

"A Mer Rica." The young woman tried to sound out the name. "Strange, I never heard talk of such a place. My name is Sabina."

"Leah," she answered, pointing to herself.

Sabina cocked her head at her slightly, "Is that your real name or your witch name? It is best you do not speak your Christian name."

Her witch name? Her grandmother had insisted on giving her the witch name Raven, but she never used it. "I assume Sabina is your witch name."

Sabina bobbed her head as if the whole discussion was a no-brainer. "It is and isn't. I didn't have a witch name to begin with, but since we will go to a new town, I will need a new name. Sabina it is. Witches only give out their false name to each other else it will be spoken under the pain of torture."

It made sense. She remembered something about that when Nana had made her watch one of those online videos about the Burning Times, full of grainy black-and-white illustrations of people being tortured in myriad of ways. Guilty or innocent, somehow the people had always ended up dead.

Margaret started walking in the direction of her house. The man grabbed her arm. "No, someone will wait at the cottage for your return."

The old woman struggled in his grasp. "I must save Odo."

"Odo is a creature of the wild. He can take care of himself better than you," the man insisted, turning the woman to walk deeper into the woods.

A whoosh and the sound of crackling caused them all to turn in the direction of Old Margaret's house. A thick plume of smoke filled the air, darkening the morning sky. The old woman cried out, "That is all I have!" and shook in the man's half embrace.

Sabina stepped forward to touch the woman's cheek, wet with tears. "You have life, Margaret. Once the witch hunters come, you can never return home."

Sorrow swept over Leah for the weeping devastated woman. Margaret raised her head to glare at Leah. Pulling herself out of comforting arms, she pointed one bony finger at Leah. "You're the reason they came. If I had not found you in the forest and took you and gave you succor, I would have my home and my beloved Odo."

Found her in the forest? At least that explained how she'd ended up here, but not really. "I'm sorry. I did not mean to hurt you or Odo."

"Margaret," the man inserted. "You're speaking out of your loss. It was only a matter of time before they came for each of us. We all knew it. Why else did we create witch names or assemble our dark clothing so we can vanish into the night? We do not call ourselves witches. We may not worship the new god or practice the old ways to ensure a good crop, but that does not make us evil, or witches. Still, once others call us witches, we have to prepare."

Leah wanted to protest that witches weren't evil, but she listened and considered the trio. The man served as a sort of shepherd, as he managed to get everyone back on the trail through the woods. He nodded to Leah. "You can call me Henry."

Leah nodded to him, aware that Henry probably wasn't his name. "Thanks. This is a new place for me, and I appreciate your help."

Henry nodded and gestured to the path ahead. "Make haste. Many have chores to do. Most fear the monks more who travel to villages stirring up suspicions with their talk of witches and intercourse with the devil. They will head back into the woods in search of people they can *label witches. Their sins might have been lingering in the woods too long or picking herbs for a disorder instead of calling on a physician. I heard an entire town in Germany was taken up as witches, the children, and priests, too. The blood lust is on them, making me wonder if there will be any people left to populate the earth."*

Leah shuddered. Hearing or reading about the Burning Times was something entirely different from walking through the woods with people accused of being witches. Not a good different, either. She preferred the distance accompanying a span of centuries. Still, there had to be a reason behind this. These dreams were more realistic than anything she'd dreamt before. Was the universe speaking to her? Was this something she should understand? In a way similar to her father, she never spoke about her faith. Could be she was having a crisis of faith.

"Sabina, I was wondering what happened to people who practice the old ways."

"Same thing," the woman replied matter-of-factly. "We're all people in the way of the newest religion, government, or what comes down the road. No place for differences. Everyone must be the same. Is that the practice where you come from?"

Just before falling asleep, she'd wondered the same thing. "I thought it was, but not as bad here. Being different or practicing the old ways might keep me from getting a date I might want or hanging out with the popular kids, but I doubt our house would get burned down."

Sabina regarded her oddly. "What is a date or hanging out? Why are these things important?"

Good question. How did she explain dating, especially if these people participated in the practice of arranged marriages? She searched for a way to explain, but a beeping interrupted her explanation.

Leah blinked. Dawn's light peeked through her blinds, dappling her walls. Theodora meowed in her ear, reminding her breakfast, at least hers, was eminent. A loud trio of knocks rattled her door.

Ethan yelled, "Are you awake? Mom said to make sure you were awake so you wouldn't be late to school."

"I'm awake! I'm awake." She gently pushed Theo off her chest to sit up. Placing her bare feet on the floor, she cataloged everything familiar. Yes, she was home. The woods were just a dream.

CHAPTER TWO

LEAH RUSHED TO pull on her school uniform of monogrammed polo and khaki pants. The good thing about uniforms was there was no time lost deciding what to wear. It also eliminated another potential target for the mean girls. A hairbrush failed to coerce her hair into some sort of order. Biting her bottom lip, she tried to clear her mind from her troubling dreams.

Opening her door, she peered down the hallway, checking the possibility of scooting into the bathroom. The closed door wasn't what she wanted to see. Great. A family of five sharing one bathroom made for early-morning headaches. Only a few months ago, before her older sister, Nora, headed off to college, it had been worse. Ethan's vocalizing reached her ears. Her bladder was ready to burst, while her baby brother used the bathroom as his own personal sound booth.

Tired of waiting hammered on the bathroom door. "C'mon, other people need to use the bathroom." Her brother grumbled on the other side of the door but did not open it.

Her mother opened her bedroom door while still buttoning her own white uniform. "Kids, enough, too much noise."

"Mom." Leah turned to complain about her brother, who suddenly opened the door.

Ethan flashed a large grin and indicated the bathroom with a swooping flourish, "My lady, your bathroom awaits."

Her mother glared at Leah as if she'd caused the problem. Pushing past her brother, she slammed the door. Staring into the mirror, she leaned on the sink. Dark circles drew attention to her eyes, making her resemble a silent-movie actress. Today would be a makeup day. Just as well. Wearing makeup often felt like she wore a mask, pretending to be someone she wasn't. Smoothing on cover-up, she considered the distance makeup put between her and the next person. Most of her life she'd rejected primping, but not so much now.

Curling her eyelashes, she wondered who influenced her behavior more, Dylan or the mean girl trio of Brianna, Alexis, and Lauren. She wanted to look nice for Dylan, but then again, she didn't want to attract the attention, either. The three-headed dog of Hades, Cerberus, was the name she'd given to the girls, never aloud, though. Cerberus paid close attention to the other students' appearance, especially the girls, looking for something to heckle. The uniforms protected those who couldn't buy the expensive clothes Cerberus favored out of school. Even a pimple or a wayward booger caught on the tip of someone's nose made the person a minor celebrity in a very bad way.

She swooped up her lashes with black mascara, exacting a fine line between the right amount of makeup and too much. Once previously, her eyeliner had been a little heavy. Alexis had sidled up to her and asked her if she was going Goth. Lauren and Brianna had told a couple of Goth boys, she was crushing on them. While smoothing clear lip-gloss over her lips, she wondered how the girls managed to keep their grades up when they spent so much time taunting others. It wouldn't surprise if they black-mailed other students into doing their homework.

At her mother's brisk knock, she opened the door. "Hurry, Leah, if you want a ride to school with your father."

"Yes, Mom," she answered. Riding the bus would be the ultimate slap to her self-esteem. The recognizable yellow school buses bore the nickname Loser Cruisers. Students who could afford to drive did. There was no extra money in their household for more than the aging sedan her father drove. Her mother rode to work with another nurse's aide, while her grandmother walked the few blocks to Madame Zelda's Magick Shoppe. Only Ethan had no issue with riding the school bus.

Her grandmother handed her an apple and lunch as Leah tagged after her father. As she bit into her apple, she heard Nana call after her. "When you come home, Leah, we'll talk."

She almost said about *what?* Since her mouth was full, she chewed instead.

Nana held up her index finger. "You know what I mean. No worries, it can wait until you return."

Her father opened the garage door for her and asked, "Do you know what she is talking about, Trinka?"

Her father's use of his pet name both warmed and embarrassed her. It reminded her of a simpler time when she used to beg her father for trinkets when he'd returned from road trips. She'd often searched through his pockets filled with plastic jewelry, cat-eyed sunglasses, tiny dolls, and candy. It was never good when he used the pet name in public where people could hear him. Leah usually didn't want to explain, believing it made her sound greedy. To keep from answering, she bit into her apple again and shrugged her shoulder as if she were clueless.

No good would come of telling her father of her dreams and visions. As a practical man who grudgingly tolerated Nana's emphatic Pagan ways and accepted his wife's less showy ways, he persevered to be unremarkable and pragmatic. Her television watching or books would merit blame for her dreams. There might have been some truth in such rationale. Still, it was hard to separate the real terror last night from some boring documentary with shaky camera action her grandmother always urged her to watch.

Her father backed out of the garage slowly, looking over his shoulder at the driveway. "How's school?"

His inquiry indicated he'd forgotten his original question, which worked. Unfortunately, he must have read an article or felt some paternal guilt about not connecting to prompt his latest foray into her life. Most of the time, her father acted as if he were adrift in the waves his family created, not that he yelled or bullied, like some fathers. Unlike other dads, he actually lived in the house with them and helped with chores. He'd occasionally flash a smile or slap her on the back when she'd earned some academic award or made the honor roll. Lately, since she always made the honor roll, it no longer merited a special, "Way to go!"

Unlike Stella's father, hers never told her he wished she'd never been born and his life would have been better without kids. How cold was that? Nope, her father loved all his offspring, but his hesitancy about parenting was obvious. His anxiety about saying or doing the wrong thing made her want to reassure him, which made for an unusual relationship. After twenty years of fatherhood, you'd think he'd have loosened up, but this might have been as loose as he would get. Probably late at night, he combed through the Internet looking for an elusive parenting manual, which included diagrams and flow charts. It was better to honor his attempts.

"Not flunking," she said and took another bite of the apple. It wasn't the largest apple in the world, so she might have to make real conversation if she ate too fast.

He chuckled as he turned out of the neighborhood. "I should say not, not with two intelligent parents."

Leah's lips turned down. There, that was the problem. Yes, both her parents were intelligent, but what about her contribution? The work just didn't do itself. The reason she couldn't connect with her father was he saw her as a product of Adam and Maura, as opposed to an individual. Her gaze flickered to her father, who drove with both hands on the wheel.

Was it harsh of her to judge him? He probably always did as told, never questioning, never rebelling. Leah never wondered if he did drugs when he was younger. She knew the answer was an unequivocal "no." The words popped out before she thought about them. "Dad, did you always follow the rules when you were in school?"

"Yes, as well as I could. Sometimes, there were rules I didn't understand or social pecking order I truly didn't get until I was pecked a few times." He turned his head to glance at her. Oh, he might reveal something of himself. Another reason she felt a tenacious connection with her father. All she knew was his parents had been Sales Reps for Christ, peddling the wonders of religion from both the pulpit and the street corner until his mother had taken up with a visiting evangelist and left. Her desertion had made Grandpa Carpenter transform himself into an aging hippie with talk about meditation, life's journey, and brewing methods. At last, she'd get a glimpse into the secretive man who was her father.

Her lips curved up in satisfaction as she mentally scrolled through all the things she'd always wanted to ask. There were many. A motion at the edge of her vision caught her eye. "Dog!" she screamed, causing her father to swerve, barely missing the small white dog, someone's indulged pet.

His hands gripped the steering wheel with an unnatural ferocity. No doubt, he was internally lecturing himself on what happens when you glance away from the road. It didn't matter that ninety percent of the time there was no one else on Mulholland, a back road to the school. The tension lines around his mouth were obvious, indicating the small window of opportunity to find out more about him had just closed.

Neither of them spoke the rest of the ride. Her father was probably going over everything he could have done differently, a mental debriefing of the near-miss incident. Her thoughts jumped between avoiding Cerberus, seeing Dylan, and wondering about her father. When her grandpa had abruptly turned into this mellow fellow, she'd thought it would allow her own father to relax some, but it hadn't.

How would she feel if suddenly her parents moved to Utah and declared themselves Mormons? The mental picture of herself in a long, unfashionable dress came to mind, along with her father trying to juggle multiple wives. Of course, that was just how Mormons were portrayed on a television show. Mormons were probably about the same as her family, trying to live average lives. People only imagined they were different.

The sprawl of the high school came into view. It was a mishmash of buildings and connecting hallways. Every time the city population went up, they threw up a new wing. There was no organization or planning in the details, which made it close to impossible to get from geometry to civics in the four-minute passing period. The idea was to not allow students time to linger at their lockers or flirt. Flirting was hard when you were jogging through four buildings to get to your next class. Forget talking. Often, she found catching her breath difficult as she sprinted for the open door of her civics class. Mr. Patterson took delight in closing the door and locking it, forcing the tardy students to go to the office for a pass and make the long trek back. Never mind the student returned twenty minutes later, missing a good chunk of the class.

Her father slowed as they approached one of the initial wings. He did her the courtesy of not taking her up to the central drop-off. It allowed

Leah the opportunity to slip into the school unnoticed. Some students, but more likely the parent, enjoyed the big goodbye scene where the mother trilled loudly for her darling child to have a wonderful day and learn something as if he were five. Some even forced their child to publicly kiss them. Did those mothers even consider how their behavior made their child the butt of teasing and bullying? She doubted they thought of it. Instead, the handful of parents with an insane need for attention took any attention they could get, even from the handful of slackers who hung around outside the school as long as they could.

Leah exited the car, turned and waved at her father. Overall, he was okay, just a man trying to find his way in a world that constantly shifted on him. Grandpa changing overnight from a hell-and-damnation preacher to a clerk at the local organic market must have taken some getting used to. What Grandpa had morphed into might not even have been the problem, but the change itself.

A few students she barely knew called out greetings, which she answered. Leah never thought of herself as a popular person, never really made the effort to be so. An incident a few months ago in German class had bought her some notoriety and a small cult following.

Jeremy's father had died unexpectedly, which had forced the high school junior to work long hours after school to support his mother and younger siblings. The result was he fell asleep in class. Herr Vaughn never took that well. He would drop books near Jeremy's head, slap, or kick his desk, jolting him awake. He often grumbled loudly about how worthless Jeremy was, causing the other students to giggle nervously, glad not to be on the receiving end of his ire. One day she'd had it.

Ironically, she didn't know Jeremy all that well, even though they'd passed through various grades together. He was a tall, shy boy in desperate need of braces his family couldn't afford. His determination to help support his family told her even more than his appearance. Stella whispered something once about his mother being handicapped or sick as the reason, she couldn't support the family. When Herr Vaughn had started in on Jeremy, she'd held up her hand. Yes, held up her hand. She was a rule follower like her father and waited for acknowledgment before speaking.

She'd stood and explained in a few short sentences the train wreck called Jeremy's life of long hours, little sleep, and even less pay working as an assistant manager at a local fast-food restaurant. The smirk on the teacher's face had melted away as he'd considered the sleeping boy. The class had burst into a spontaneous applause that embarrassed her. She'd thought for sure she'd get a write-up for her actions, but she hadn't.

Jeremy had slept through her explanation and the class reaction, which indicated his exhaustion. During the next class, she'd overheard Herr

Vaughn tell Jeremy he could sleep in his class, and he would still pass. The story had spread all over the school in two days, making her sort of a giant slayer. A few other teachers had decided to let Jeremy sleep, too.

She noticed Cerberus to her left and nodded to the three. To ignore them would invite their catty remarks. To talk to them might result in them ignoring her. She'd decided a head bob worked best. Her folk legend status protected her some, not that she deserved it. Hard to know what had gotten into her, causing her to act in such a way. All she knew was she hated seeing people accused unfairly. Something deep within her had caused her to act without thinking things through.

The buzzer sounded right when she stepped into the classroom. Good thing she'd decided against darting into the bathroom on her way to check her hair. Dylan looked up at her entrance, smiled slightly then looked down at his paper. Her heart tripped. It had to mean something, right? She thought he liked her. Why would he smile at her otherwise? A voice punctured her thoughts and her ear.

"Move it, will ya? You're blocking my opportunity to accumulate the vast stores of knowledge awaiting me."

A skinny male with thick glasses managed to push around her. Great, she'd Dooran to thank for her major humiliation. Slinking to the back of the classroom, she slid into her seat, fighting the desire to open her geometry book and use it to cover her face. Wasn't it enough she was already one year behind in math due to their moving? Most of the other students were younger. Dooran was only a jumped-up ninth-grader after skipping a grade or something, which might explain why he was so obnoxious.

Still, she glanced at the boy who already had his hand up to answer a question the teacher hadn't asked since the equation wasn't on the white board yet. On the first or second day of school, he'd run into the door, thus earning him the nickname "Dooran." Leah wasn't even sure of his real name. Still, with that type of welcome, you'd think he'd stay low, but he didn't. Instead, he rattled off wordy phrases, sounding like someone from a nineteenth-century novel.

Dooran forgotten, her attention drifted up to Dylan, or at least his back. Since everyone wore the same blue polo shirt, you'd think everyone would look the same. That wasn't true. Many girls tried to make statements with jewelry, wildly colored socks or too much makeup, which lasted about one period until Mrs. Collins caught them. Nicknamed "The Enforcer," the petite biology teacher roamed the halls during passing periods on the lookout for uniform breakers. Girls who had unbuttoned their polo one extra button found themselves not only re-buttoning it, but also earning a detention for their daring display. It never did any good to complain against a uniform violation because The Enforcer's word was law.

Leah didn't worry about censure since her own goal was to escape notice. Doing anything extraordinary would get her noticed. She didn't need or want that, especially after their last move. Ironically, her family must have moved around the same time as Jeremy's had, since they'd ended up in the same schools. His move had probably happened because of his father's death. Hers, on the other hand, had happened for reasons she wasn't totally clear about. Her father had made some comment about the neighborhood not being safe, which was odd since they'd moved into an obviously poorer area.

She resumed her study of Dylan's neck. His hair ended in a square cut right above his collar, indicating his desire to stay with dress code. A large freckle punctuated the uniformity of his light skin.

"Ms. Carpenter, paging Ms. Carpenter." The teacher's words caused all those around her to giggle. Leah's eyes jerked up to where her instructor regarded her with a knowing gaze and folded arms. Dooran waved his hand vigorously, trying to catch the math teacher's attention.

Her father always reminded her: When in a difficult position, use your manners and stall. "Yes, sir, could you repeat the question, please?"

The teacher's pointer landed on the whiteboard where three triangles drawn in different-colored markers, he asked, "Which one is acute?"

Good. She knew this one. "Is not the one in the middle, the green one, because it is less than ninety degrees." Feeling cocky, she added, "The red one is obtuse because it is more than ninety degrees, and the third is a right angle because it is ninety degrees."

Instead of looking pleased with her, her instructor looked disgruntled. "Very good, Ms. Carpenter. I will accept that you may have paid attention the first week of class, but how would you compute the area of a triangle?" He nodded in her direction.

What had she done to earn this spotlight? Not paying attention was the culprit. "Multiply the base by the height, and then divide by two."

"Right, moving on." He returned to the board to write something else, which gave Dylan just enough time to turn and wink at her.

He did like her. Aniyah, who sat beside her, nudged her. "Did you see that Dylan Torres winked at me?"

"Oh, he did?" It was the best Leah could come up with. Who had he winked at? Aniyah was cute, friendly, intelligent, and a star athlete. Who wouldn't like her? Slumping in her seat, she decided she was ready to head to English class, where she hadn't had to worry about Dylan crushing on any of the girls sitting next to her. It felt like she'd swallowed a rock, a big one, which managed to lodge in her throat.

✦   ✦   ✦   ✦

THE STUDENTS REACTED to the buzzer like a floodgate had opened. They rushed to the doorway, pushing their way into the exterior hallway. Leah hung back, unsure what she wanted to happen. Maybe she could talk to Dylan in the hallway. Then again, he might walk right past her or, worse yet, talk to Aniyah. Before she could make her decision, her math teacher called her name, "Ms. Carpenter, may I have a moment?"

What had she done now? Her feet, feeling the pull of gravity, shuffled toward his desk. "Yes, sir," she answered and made eye contact. Convey sincerity, she coached herself, keeping visual contact.

"Ms. Carpenter," he started, stopped, cracking his knuckles. "You're a very bright student, probably one of the brightest in my class. At this point, you can indulge in your obsession with Mr. Torres and still answer any question I throw at you, but the class speed is about to pick up. The material will be tougher and will require more attention on your part. Do you understand?"

"Yes, sir," she answered as her face heated. Obsession? She wasn't stalking Dylan, but if the teacher had noticed, then Dylan must have, too. Students drifted into the room, glancing at her, wondering what she'd done. "Is that all?"

"Yes," he said and reached for a packet of passes. He spoke as he wrote, not noticing the many students who were sitting quietly at their desks, listening. Normally, there would have been chattering, but they didn't want to miss anything. "I've taught for almost thirty years. In that time, I've watched hundreds of girls throw themselves at young men at the cost of their education. Make sure you're one of those." He ripped off the pass and handed it to her.

Refusing to make eye contact with anyone, she scooted out of the room and into the sanctuary of the hallway. Holding the pass prominently in her hand, she made her way to the English wing, hoping to lose her humiliation along the way. She doubted it would happen since there had been so many witnesses who would repeat the scene to infinity. See, she was learning something in math, but that was algebra, wasn't it? What would happen if she didn't go to English class? The thought tempted her. The stairs beckoned. At the end of the stairs, there was a set of double doors, her exit to freedom. All she'd to do was claim a dentist appointment when passing the campus security guard. It all sounded good in theory, except she hadn't have an office pass, someone to pick her up, or a car to drive away in. Might as well head to class. Escaping her embarrassing life would have to wait until latter.

Stella, her best friend, pantomimed wiping sweat from her brow as she entered the room. Leah dropped her pass on Mrs. Barkin's desk and headed to her place beside Stella. Her friend might have been concerned about her absence since they were working on a project together.

Leah managed to relate her personal disaster in hushed tones before their teacher descended upon them with a fluttering of hands. "Good, good, you're finally here. I wanted to address the two of you together."

The woman bent toward them, reinforcing Leah's bird imagery of her as she rested her long wings—make that, hands—against their table, giving the impression she sheltered them under her wings. She blocked the other students from hearing her instructions. "Girls, I think you have a great topic about how people are shaped to be prejudiced by their religious views. Remember this is a persuasive speech. It isn't enough to say prejudice is rampant. Give personal examples. No one can dispute that. You also must have more of a mission here. How is this prejudice ruining the world? Tell me how it can be changed. I want a call to action. Your essay in its present form is lacking that. Do you understand what I want?"

Leah and Stella nodded in unison as Mrs. Barkin smiled and headed on to a different group of students to help. Leah knew how to punch up the essay. Did she dare? It would mean risking possibly even more ridicule, even misdirected hatred. When she'd first started school, she'd been anxious. Her grandmother had bestowed a delicate silver pentacle on a chain upon her to keep her safe and strong and as a reminder of how special she was. Everything had been fine until another student had asked her about her necklace.

As she'd explained about the elements, a small group of students had gathered, interested in the necklace's powers. Unfortunately, she'd caught her teacher's interest, too. The woman had made a grab for the necklace, but had pulled her hand back suddenly, making Leah wonder if Nana had put a protection spell on it. The principal had insisted she could not wear the pentacle, claiming it disrupted the classroom. The necklace hadn't done anything. Leah had known that much at even a young age. First grade had been a hard year for her, but luckily, she'd already known how to read and write when she'd entered school, thanks to her father. It had been just as well because she'd often caught her teacher mouthing the words "devil child" whenever she'd been near.

Could she share this story? Would it make Stella think any different of her? The few times she'd been in Stella's house, no religious symbols had decorated the walls, indicating her mother wasn't overly religious. Failure to attend a church, mosque, or temple didn't stop people from claiming religious affiliation or the prejudices often attached to that religion. "What can we do different?"

Her friend held up one finger. "Well, I thought we might start with a quote from Buddha."

This was interesting. Her friend had never mentioned religion or Buddha before, but she'd also picked the topic for the paper. They could have gone with the easier ones about cloning, nuclear warfare, domestic abuse, or the dangers of GMOs.

"Which one?" She said the words as if she'd a head full of quotes by Buddha.

Gesturing to her pearl choker, Stella's expression became serene and distant, as if viewing an interior landscape only she could see. "We're all pearls on a string."

"That sounds good, but what does it mean?" Leah's experience with other religions consisted of televangelists, billboards, and people trying to shove tracts in her hand outside of movie theaters, warning her that movies were the devil's tools.

Stella blinked. "You don't know about Siddhartha's journey?" The surprise in her voice made Leah think she should have known. She might as well have announced she'd never heard of Abraham Lincoln or Santa Claus.

"You could tell me, but I thought we were talking about Buddha, pearls, and our essay." Leah could feel the tension leave her as her friend explained. "Siddhartha Buddha was his full name. Born a prince and married for love, he decided to see the people of his kingdom by walking through it. He discovered much heartache and poverty, which saddened him."

Stella finished waving one hand with a flourish. "That's why we're all like pearls on a string."

Leah didn't want to ask, but she did. "The man who had everything went for a walk and saw those with nothing. That makes us pearls how?"

Laughing, Stella touched her shoulder. "You almost have it. Buddha found all our actions have a profound impact on the universe. By having great wealth, lavish parties, and huge palaces, he took from people who barely had enough to feed their families. Of course, all the people in the kingdom must give a tithe to the prince to enable him to do all this. In turn, he saw how everyone in the universe is connected. He, of course, changed his ways after learning this. Do you get it now?"

"Yes," Leah answered softly. She thought she got it. It made sense because she believed everything in the universe was connected. This was a side to Stella she'd not seen before. "If Buddha believed everyone was part of a giant pearl necklace, then those folks who believe some people are untouchables, others are going to hell, and still others just shouldn't be sharing the same air as them, they might regard everyone else as being loose pearls, not even on the necklace with them."

Her friend's fingers flew over the keyboard. "I'm getting this down. I believe we're going to have a great paper."

"What if no one understands what we're trying to say? They could be offended." Leah always worried about offending people, especially after the necklace incident. She understood on some level that just by existing on the same planet she offended some.

✧   ✧   ✧   ✧

STELLA SAVED THEIR paper and powered down the computer right before the buzzer sounded. Slipping the computer in its case, she grinned at Leah. "Why worry so much? It's not as if we're going to read it to the class. See ya later."

Her friend turned the opposite way as Leah headed toward the music wing. The hall grew less crowded since all music classes were electives. The higher-level ones required auditions, which was enough to discourage even musically inclined students. Even though Leah didn't like attention, she did like singing. When she sang, everything fell away. She didn't notice people around her. Truth be told, they were probably not paying attention to her, too busy gossiping, flirting, and furtively texting. Thinking about her solo, she didn't notice immediately all the other students were gone. The hall lights flickered and went out.

CHAPTER THREE

N O, NOT HERE, not now! She couldn't have a vision at school. She'd never had one during school. She could count the number of visions she'd had on one hand. Holding her hand high, she spread her fingers, noticing they appeared to be growing more transparent. Dropping her hand in horror, she looked down the hall, which went dark as the lights flickered out.

Great, was it a power shortage or what? Leah knew better as she tried to locate the skylights over her head. Nothing. The whole point of the skylights was to provide light. No light meant it wasn't daytime, or she wasn't in the school hallway anymore. A voice confirmed this.

"Make haste, Leah, before a long-nosed monk takes hold of you."

She recognized Henry, the unspoken leader from the night before. It didn't make sense that she was continuing her dream. Maybe even now she was drooling in her sleep in class, causing the other students to take photos of her with their camera phones without the teacher catching them. The thought caused her to shudder.

A forest formed around her with light filtering through the tree leaves. A few birds called from above her, and something rattled in the bushes near her. Her gaze traveled to her right where someone was coming toward her, possibly a teacher or a staff member to rescue her. Instead, an exasperated Sabina lunged toward her, grabbing her arm.

"No time for you to go simple. The witch catchers will fill you full of needles, claiming they found the devil's mark when they themselves made the marks."

Leah stumbled alongside the woman who held her in a strong grip. Sabina was much stronger than she looked despite, being a few inches shorter and definitely a few pounds lighter than Leah. There was no way to resist Sabina's determination to save her from the witch catchers. Why would she want to resist?

Running beside each other, they reached the clearing where Henry and Margaret waited. The old woman in black wrung her hands, looking all the worse for their unexpected flight. Why shouldn't she? She'd lost everything to a villager's torch, burning her cottage and possibly her beloved pet. Henry's mouth firmed into a straight line as he spotted them. "I've a place we can use for the day to rest and decide what to do next. It is a small hut belonging to my cousin, which will give us refuge."

Moving onward, Leah gave silent thanks for Margaret who could not move as fast as the rest. Who knew people stuck in the middle ages were in such good shape? Leah guessed they had to be when running from people or animals who wanted to kill them.

They stopped only to take a deep drink at a stream. Leah watched all of them drop to their knees, scooping the water up to their lips with cupped hands. "Aren't you worried about...?" The word pollution stayed in her mouth. Instead, she knelt, carrying some of the cool water up to her mouth. It was delicious and refreshing. Dropping to her belly, she managed to get closer to the clear water, even immersing her face in it. Wonderful. A tug on the back of her head brought her face out of the water.

"No need for that. The witch catchers will surely drown you if they catch you." His voice rang with certainty.

Leah thought about protesting. She wasn't committing suicide, but decided against saying anything. Sometimes it was just better to follow orders. Back on her feet, she followed Henry's zigzagging trail. Occasionally he would run off the trail and circle a tree several times. When she caught her eyes on him, he explained with one word. "Dogs."

At last, they reached the small hut, little more than a thatched circular building with a hide-covered door and no windows. The four of them crowded into a space measuring no more than five feet at its widest point. The women reclined against the feeble walls while Henry stabbed his walking stick at the ground as if trying to uncover something. Eventually, he brought up a clay jar out of the ground.

The meager light streaming in from missing thatches and the imperfectly cut door illuminated the man and his find. The container released a vile smell. The other two women leaned forward eagerly as he shook out uneven off-whitish pieces that he passed out. Leah held hers in her hand, unsure of what to do with it, while the others crammed theirs in their mouths. It was food obviously, but what kind?

Her nose crinkled as it passed under her nose. Henry, noticing her actions, urged her to eat. "It is fish, girl. Might be all you get in a good long while. Do not waste time thinking about eating it. Just do the deed." The others nodded their heads in acknowledgment.

Leah placed the bit in her mouth and tried to bite through it with some difficulty. It looked and felt like the cuttlebone she used to put in her old parakeet's cage for him to rub his beak against. It tasted not like fish, exactly, but more like smoke, campfires, charcoal, or the liquid smoke flavoring Mother sometimes brushed on meat. They must cure the meat by smoking it. It made sense with salt being so expensive. She chewed meditatively as the other two put out their hands for more.

"Good fish," Sabina commented.

Henry agreed. "Yes, we're lucky Peter restocked the hut. Ever since his cousin from the next village died from her examination by the witch catchers, he's kept the hut stocked for whoever might need it."

Examination? Leah knew she didn't want to know, but she asked anyhow. "This examination happened when they were looking for the mark of the devil?"

"Yes," Henry answered, then placed a square of fish into his mouth.

"What is this mark of the devil when such a creature does not exist? He's a bogeyman made up by people who wanted to scare folks into accepted behavior." She related what she'd been taught, causing Henry to choke on his fish.

The man used his fist to pound on his chest. Henry stopped coughing but gasped for air a few times. He stood and announced, "I think I might go back to visit the water."

Sabina watched him go and then turned to look at Leah. "Talk like yours will get you branded a witch. No matter what you say, they would call you a witch, just to strip you naked and look upon your form before torturing you. I'm unsure if they hate all women or just the comely ones. It is certain that all those without a powerful family name or a man are certain to be accused."

"Are you saying these priests are pervs?" Leah knew the stories about the Burning Times, but none had suggested sexual perversion, or maybe she hadn't paid attention.

Sabina pursed her lips, trying out the word. "Pervs, I do not know this word. I know They're evil despite calling themselves men of God. That I do know. If they wanted to find the devil, then they would do well to hold a mirror up to their own faces."

Margaret seemed shocked at her words. "Be still, child. They might hear you. It will not go well for you."

Sabina sighed, her shoulders drooping. "It is not going well for me now."

Leah paused in the act of chewing and stared at her erstwhile rescuer, before asking, "What have you done that is so terrible?"

The dark-haired woman shrugged. "I'm a woman alone."

"Why should that matter?" Leah tried to remember what Nana had said, but she usually became so emotional when talking about the Burning Times, you'd think she'd lived through it herself. All her words ended up being indecipherable due to anger or garbled because of tears. Leah never understood half the things Nana said. The family knew never to bring up the topic, because it might cause another stroke.

Margaret answered instead. "An old woman alone has no merit or purpose in the village. With no children to call my own or to look out for me, it is easy to blame me when a cow refuses to give milk or a baby dies. If the village wants a culprit, my absence creates no loss."

Leah remembered being in the woman's home earlier, though she didn't remember when. Various spices and herbs had hung drying from the crossbeams. Margaret had secretly confided that she could even read, a skill usually limited to the clergy. As a young girl, she'd trained to be a nun, but when their motherhouse had broken up, she'd returned to her village. Some had whispered that God had rejected her. She'd used her knowledge to write down various recipes for possets and creams. No matter what the villagers whispered about her, they still came to her house for medicine. "They still ask you for help. I saw the woman at your door."

The old woman nodded in agreement. "That is true. When everything else fails, they seek my assistance." Margaret made some sign with her hand, causing Sabina to chuckle. "Ah, that's what I think of them. Some say I cause the illnesses as opposed to their over-imbibing or gluttonous natures. Those claiming I consort with the devil come to my door when the moon is full, begging for pennyroyal."

Pennyroyal. She remembered seeing a container of it in Nana's herb closet. She'd left it alone, although the name intrigued her. "What do they do with it?"

Both women looked at Leah in surprise.

The old woman rolled her eyes. "It can be used to chase fleas away. Those who asked for it did not overly care about fleas, considering the curs they chose to lay with." Both women giggled at the remark, which irritated Leah.

The language was difficult enough to make sense of without all the archaic metaphors. "Why would they sneak around at night to get some herb to get rid of fleas? Why not ask for it in the day?"

Waving a gnarled index finger, Margaret explained, "Their need was black, which is why they crept around at night. The pennyroyal would rid them of a child not of their husband's seed."

Sabina leaned in, motioning to the old woman with her hand. "For that they call her witch. I think they just want to get rid of her because she holds all their secrets."

"Makes sense," Leah agreed, wondering how Old Margaret managed to survive so long without someone offing her. "How old are you?"

The woman bit her withered bottom lip as her eyes flicked upward in the thin light. "I believe I've survived forty-four winters."

Forty-four! Her mother was the same age. She certainly didn't look anywhere as old as Margaret did. Nana didn't even look as old, and she was dragging her leg, too. Apparently, life had been harsh in the past. What year was she in? Better yet, what century? "Do you know what year this is?" Both women looked confused at her question. "What century is it?"

She thought she could at least pinpoint a general date. The women instead looked at each other as if they didn't understand her words or at least the meaning behind them. Even though she didn't understand every word she'd a feeling the language was supposed to be English.

"Am I in England?" Both women bobbed their heads and smiled.

Sabina pointed to Leah. "Do you be Welsh? I heard the people of Wales be dark."

Leah held out her arm, trying to see it as someone else would. She didn't see herself as dark, far from it, especially compared to some of the other students in her school. They might consider her dark, having no experience with people beyond their small village. "No, I'm American. I told you this before."

Margaret narrowed her eyes, displaying her doubt, while Sabina cocked her head. "You still be foreign and fair, which would be enough to condemn you as a witch."

The sound of footsteps nearby caused the three of them to freeze, casting anxious glances toward the door. The door opened slightly, allowing in enough sunlight to temporarily blind them.

"No fear, it is only I," Henry called out to the sunblind women.

Leah blinked a couple of times to bring her vision back to normal. The familiar outline of Henry began to take shape and solidified once he closed the door behind him.

"Have you ladies been gossiping about me?" he teased.

Shaking her thick hair back, Sabina sighed. "Our tongues recounted the evil of the witch takers and how Leah should take care, being foreign and fair."

Henry nodded, his weathered face taking on a solemn cast. "It is easy to blame the priests, even the church, even the King's soldiers, who allow the witch hunts to go on unabated, but the real evil lies in jealous, voracious hearts. Sabina's only crime is being prettier than all the other lasses in town. No fault of her own that her man died. Many village men cast lustful stares at her. Some less careful ones did so in the presence of their wives. Her beauty and friendliness earned her the witch label. All three of us are people who discommoded someone."

Leah stretched out her hand to touch Henry's shoulder to offer him some comfort, but her hands encountered a cool concrete brick wall instead of a rough woolen shirt. Flexing her fingers, she recognized the feel. It was how the walls in the hall felt. Henry's voice along with Sabina's grew distant as their bodies grew dimmer, like fading images on a movie screen.

Her environment became lighter, until she realized she was in the hallway, fingering the walls.

"There you're," a male voice chirped behind her. The sturdy figure of the school principal, Mr. Sharpe, strode up to her. When Leah had started school, she'd at first thought his rotund belly and handlebar mustache indicated he would be a jolly fellow. Appearances could be deceiving. The frowning man reached her.

"Ms. Carpenter, your choral teacher, reported you skipping. Where have you been?" Principal Sharpe faced her, leveling a belligerent look that dared her to utter some type of falsehood he could denounce to earn her another detention.

"I was here. Right here. I may have been late, but not that late, I think." Skipping didn't happen until you were more than ten minutes late, at least. Until then she was only tardy, which most teachers overlooked.

He folded his arms and sucked in his lips. If he thought that made him look more intimidating, Leah was more than willing to concur. "So, Carpenter, you mean to tell me you were here in this hall for the last ninety minutes? People passed through the hall on the way to lunch, but no one saw you? Is that what you mean?" His voice became louder as he growled the words.

No doubt, he'd never believe she'd just evaded witch hunters and had spent the last period in not-so-merry old England. Instead, she just nodded.

He grunted his disbelief. "Come with me."

That's what she'd been afraid of. Couldn't get a break in either century. In this one, she could expect to live a little longer, though.

✧   ✧   ✧   ✧

LEAH SAT IN the seat placed at an angle to the principal's desk. No one had to tell her it was where all previously nabbed students sat. The residual anxiety, fear, even defiance surrounded her as she adjusted her bottom on the vinyl-covered chair. The presence of so many negative emotions overwhelmed her senses, making her nauseated. A quick look up through her eyelashes showed Principal Sharpe peering at his computer screen, most likely looking up her home phone number. The obvious solution would have been to ask her, not that all students in trouble would furnish the appropriate answer. Then again, some might not even know their parents' number. They were used to having numbers programmed into their cell.

A pair of soft upholstered chairs beckoned to her. From their location in front of the desk and the fact they appeared comfortable, Leah guessed they were for parents and visiting school officials, not for skippers. If she asked to move, the answer would be no. Her excuse for moving could be she'd a psychological fear of puke green as she glanced down at the ugly greenish covering of her chair. Nope, that would just make her sound even weirder.

Residual emotions emanated from the chair, wrapping around her, echoing with the possibility of losing one foster home placement only to go to a crummier one. One boy had realized this was the "one more thing" his mother constantly threatened that would send him to live with his father and his new family. One girl had become so frightened the principal might find drugs on her that she'd wet herself. Yuk! That settled it. She quietly moved to the chair in front of the desk. Forget about asking, she refused to sit in that chair one second longer.

Principal Sharpe merely raised a questioning eyebrow, but continued to hold the phone up to his ear. He probably didn't want to yell into the phone when someone was picking up. Could be he thought she was already in enough trouble. What did one more thing matter? Leah considered the vacated chair with a baleful look. She'd never considered herself empathic with the ability to pick up unspoken emotional responses from others. Nana had concluded once, after watching a Sherlock Holmes episode, that the detective must have a touch of psychometric ability to pick up objects and know so much about the person who used them. Leah had never pointed out his powers of observation solved the crime as opposed to some mystical ability.

THE PRINCIPAL RELATED her crime of missing chorus and apparently lunch. Her stomach growled, confirming the fact. Her hands gripped the soft padded arms of her current chair. A thought seeped into her head of the principal as a jackbooted thug who had never taught a day in his life. Great, now she was receiving parent impressions, but why would a parent know about his lack of teaching experience? Good chance she'd picked up a teacher's reflection. Some staff member called to the office, probably feeling just as victimized as she did.

Principal Sharpe hung up the phone. He stared at her, using what she knew he felt was his most intimidating stare with downturned lips and narrowed eyes. Great Goddess, what was happening to her? How did she know, without a doubt, this was what Sharpe considered his best glare that usually had the kids' knees knocking together, especially non-defiant students like her? The tall, broad-shouldered boys with attitude who enjoyed jaw jacking scared him. She blinked. Had she just read his mind? She was almost sure of it.

"Leah Carpenter," he started in a firm, deep voice. "Your grandmother is coming to pick you up. You're suspended for the rest of the day for your actions."

She bobbed her head in acknowledgment, unsure if a response was expected. Suspension for the day, was he kidding? Talk about stupid punishments. If she'd been the type of student who skipped class, a school suspension would have been a reward. Nana was coming to get her. Good, it would give them alone time to talk about all the weirdness suddenly constituting her life.

The scent of smoke clung to her. Turning her head, a little, she managed to sniff her shoulder. Definitely smelled like smoke, not cigarette, but rather wood smoke. Which didn't make any sense unless her spontaneous trips to medieval England were more real than she'd previously imagined?

Principal Sharpe fiddled with a pen on his desk, and then pushed up suddenly. "I'll have my secretary notify you when your grandmother arrives." He disappeared out the door, leaving behind apprehension of Nana. He'd left to avoid talking to her grandmother. *The old crone gives me the creeps* had been his last thought, which would delight Nana.

Leah stood and walked around his office. If she were the type to snoop, now would be the time. Slowly circling the room, she drew closer to the computer screen displaying a screensaver of the school building. What had she expected? Babes in bikinis? Sharpe would be the type to have a camera in his office to film what the students did after he left.

Opening her senses, she searched for a camera hidden somewhere. No camera. How did she know there wasn't one? Hard to explain, but she'd a sense of certainty, perhaps like what Sherlock Holmes had experienced. Pulling out the corner of her polo, she wrapped her fingers in it and pushed the mouse. Her information popped up. Discipline record was clean except for a bold notation about skipping class with suspension being the consequence. Again, she shook her head at the idea of it being a punishment.

In theory, the teachers were supposed to deprive her of her makeup work so she'd receive a zero for the day. Students normally in trouble never asked to make up their work, so what did it matter? Good students would still ask for makeup work and get it, with a warning not to mention it to anyone. Stella had told her this after her own suspension resulting from enthusiastically welcoming a foreign-exchange student who had mistaken her friendliness for bullying.

A click took her to Teacher Concerns. A small note from Miss Santiago indicated concerns about the trio of girls bullying Leah. Well, she'd that right. Despite the note, there had been no follow-up. Geesh, she'd have received more attention if Principal Sharpe had thought she might turn into an international incident. Good students received suspensions, like herself and Stella, while bullies practically ran the school.

The rumble of a car engine drew her attention to the window in time to see Nana emerging from a cab. Stepping away from the computer, Leah headed to the door. Snatching up her book and purse, she made her way out to the secretary's desk before she called her. Outside in the outer office, she tucked in her shirt, hoping no one noticed her actions. All she needed was a uniform violation added to her formerly clean discipline record. The secretary gave her an apologetic smile. Well, at least one person didn't think she was guilty of the crime.

The tap of her cane announced Nana before she showed. Always one to look at the bright side, her grandmother had announced the stroke that had left one leg weaker than the other was just the excuse she needed to use her ornate silver wolf-head cane. It was an elaborate stick, which looked as if it might have served in a horror movie, which was probably why Nana liked it. While her father avoided attention, Nana treated it as her right.

Her grandmother came in with a smile and headed to the sign-out sheet. She signed Leah out with a jingle of her bracelets. Leah joined her grandmother, taking the arm that didn't wield the cane.

Her grandmother greeted her with a jovial air. "What trumped-up crime have they tried to pin on you?" She said it loud enough so anyone could hear.

Wincing a little, Leah shrugged, not wanting to discuss it in a hallway filled with students. Bad enough they would see her leaving, but most would consider she'd an appointment or was sick. The others wouldn't even notice. Having only her geometry book, she wondered if she should get her other books. Leah abandoned the idea. She'd homework all right, but it had more to do with finding out why she suddenly sensed thoughts and took impromptu trips into the past.

Principal Sharpe was nowhere in sight. Probably a good thing. He would not have to explain in excruciating detail his version of the story. One of the good things about her family was they actually listened to her.

Their former neighbor had accused Leah of terrorizing her overweight basset hound. What Mrs. Higginbottoms, the neighbor, had been unwilling to admit was Theodora, Leah's cat, had chased and cornered the cantankerous canine. Apparently, the dog had had to have extra anxiety medicine that day. Leah had arrived on the scene when she'd heard the woman's cries and the angry snarl of her feline, along with some pitiful whimpering. Her family chose her version of the story over the outraged neighbor's dramatic account.

CHAPTER FOUR

N O SOONER HAD they scooted into the back seat and slammed the taxi door than her grandmother turned to her with a knowing look. "Come into your powers, have you?"

"Nana, please." She angled her head to the cab driver, hoping to convey her need for privacy. A snort answered her pleas as they both settled into the tobacco-smoke-tainted back seat. Wasn't there supposed to a smoking ban in public places? Then again, it might have been her. Turning her head, she sniffed the shoulder of her uniform shirt again. Still smelled like wood smoke, pine trees, and that disgusting fish she'd eaten. How could that be?

Her grandmother leaned over and sniffed her clothes, too. A thoughtful look crossed her face as she pointed to Leah's ankles, which were caked with mud and leaves. Where had that come from and why hadn't the principal noticed? Nana said nothing, honoring Leah's desire not to talk publicly.

The scenery outside the cab window included brown grass and withered leaves on the trees. The drought hadn't dealt well with the area. It took rain usually to make mud. She picked a small green leaf from her mud-encrusted legs. Twirling it between two fingers, she knew it hadn't come from here.

Where would she have encountered mud and green leaves in the few short steps from her father's sedan to the school doors? The flight through the woods had garnered the mud and leaves. It had been real, not a vision or daydream. If her run through the woods with Sabina, Henry, and Margaret had happened, then that meant the man in the throne-like chair existed. Remembering the man's crazed eyes and hate-filled voice caused her to shiver. How could she stop this?

The ride home in some ways was more like a funeral possession, slow and somber. If she couldn't think of a way to stop taking these return trips, it might end up being her funeral. Would her death in the past prevent her from being in the present? All she really knew was she didn't want to test out any theories. She looked at her grandmother for answers, and the woman took her hand and squeezed it.

"Be at peace, my little bird." Nana managed a smile that didn't quite reach her troubled eyes.

The driver coasted to a stop in front of their house. Leah opened the door and waited as Nana painstakingly counted out the fee, plus an appropriate tip. Once out of the cab, Leah turned slowly, peering at the familiar, run-down neighborhood. Most of the houses were older ranch-style homes showing their age with peeling paint, crooked shutters, and crumbling driveways. Most of them were rentals with property owners too penny-pinching to fix the places up. Why should they when a renter might just destroy their efforts? A house two blocks down sported a perfect green lawn and freshly painted shutters. An older couple owned it.

The rental houses served only as a stop on the renters' journey to somewhere else. Leah wished desperately for a house to call home, rather than a rental. She'd never had a tree house or marks on an interior doorframe to show how she'd grown over the years. Instead, her family worked hard not to change anything, from paint to landscaping, because it was not their home. The modest home boasted a basement where a few boards, drywall, and a door suggested the possibility of another bedroom. Her brother slept in the unfinished room with exposed wiring. Even though it was petty of her, she was glad it was him, instead of her.

The neighborhood didn't show any signs of transforming itself into another time.

Nana snagged her arm as she moved her cane to her other hand. "Let's go and deal with your trouble."

Just like that, her grandmother had made it sound like she'd a report to write. She could imagine writing such a report. She could title it *How I Slipped through Time*. The subtitle could be *How I Was Almost Burned as a Witch*. Although, what she could remember about the Salem witch trials from a television special was some girls started it trying to cover their own attempts at divination. They wanted to see the faces of their future husbands. No one had ended up burned at the stake, just hanged, probably their version of being humane.

Nana unlocked the door and pushed it open. The smell of scorched coffee greeted them. Leah rushed to the kitchen to turn off the coffeemaker. Often, mornings were chaos as they all headed off their separate ways.

Following more slowly, her grandmother entered the kitchen. "Aye, the coffee. I guess that would be my fault, even though I never touch the stuff." Nana pulled out a chair and collapsed into it. "Could you make us some tea, sweet pea? I believe we're going to need it."

Grabbing the battered teapot, Leah filled it with water and set it on the stove to boil. Remembering she'd missed lunch, she also got out a small plate, arranged some almond cookies on it and placed it on the table. She picked out two mugs and bent to search for the tea bags. Her grandmother came up behind her silently, startling her when she spoke.

"Not those mugs. I need cups and saucers. I will get my special loose-leaf tea." Nana weaved a little bit as she held onto the counter for balance.

Leah didn't like tea, but usually choked down a cup to please her grandmother, who often treated it like a magical elixir. The loose tea was the worst, with the ground-up tea leaves getting in her mouth, often choking her. If she caught them before they slid down her throat, there was always the issue of spitting them out gracefully. So far, she'd managed to deposit them in a napkin while pretending to wipe her mouth. The loose tea was for fortune-telling.

The ritual was a familiar one. Not that Nana had used it to tell her fortune, but Leah had witnessed some of the regulars having their fortunes told. Some of the ladies liked it better than the Tarot cards, feeling it didn't compromise their religious beliefs. It was more like an elegant parlor trick, since they drank tea while doing it. Nana charged the same.

Her grandmother found the tin of tea and lurched to the table with the tin under one arm. Leah shook her head at her determined grandmother. Why hadn't she stayed seated? Leah could find the tea on her own. The sounds of objects falling alerted her Nana was on the move again. The sound of cursing led her to the living room, where several candles rolled across the wooden floor.

Leaning against the server that had previously housed the candles, her grandmother pointed to a white column candle half hidden by the couch. "I want that one, for protection. I need the purple one, too, to enhance my psychic senses and as an offering to Minona."

Leah preferred not to have the fuss of the whole lighting-candles-and-casting-a-circle thing. For a while, she waivered, not certain she even believed any of that stuff. All it had ever done for her was solidify her loner image. Different wasn't good, especially if she'd to keep re-inventing herself with each move. Her life would have been easier if the Sabbats and rituals fell on the traditional school holidays. Still, at this point, she should take all the charms, amulets, and protection she could get.

Kneeling, she gathered up the candles. Nana leaned against the server, favoring her bad leg and warned. "Don't get old, Leah. Even simple things become impossible tasks."

Leah looked up from her position and noticed her grandmother sported a half smile. "I'll do my best, but I think it's inevitable." She placed the column candle on the server as she bundled the others back into the box from where they'd fallen. "Is that all you need?"

Nana already had the purple candle in her hand. Pushing upright, she walked back to the kitchen. "Yes, it is enough. I'm only going to call on Minona today."

Leah followed her. "Not calling on the elements, then?"

Her grandmother turned suddenly, causing her to wobble a little. Her voice was firm but trembled with something. Leah couldn't decide if it was anger or horror. "I always call all the elements. You'd do good to remember that, young lady."

Of course, Leah knew that. The teapot whistled as they entered the kitchen. "Do you want me to handle the leaves and pour?" Normally, her grandmother fussed with the tea for her clients, making a huge ceremony out of it.

Nana centered the candle on the table, before answering. "It is better if you do it. I want as much of your energy on it as possible, since we're telling your fortune, not mine."

Pulling out a teaspoon, Leah measured the leaves for each cup, and then poured the steaming water into the delicate wide-mouthed teacups. "How come you always fix the tea for your customers?"

Her grandmother snorted as she cleared the table surface, arranging a cup of water, a stone, and an incense cone at various intervals. "I can't depend on any of them to do it right. Secondly, they would consider making tea something a servant does, which would be why I must make it. In the end, it doesn't matter too much for my women since their lives seldom change overly much. They just come for reassurance that they will continue to lead their well-fed, easy lives. You, on the other hand, have much going on."

Leah had always wondered why the same middle-age women continued to come to Nana. They weren't single and looking for love, nor were they businesswomen hoping to start a new project. They were married women who had devoted themselves to a high-earning husband and raising spoiled children and pampered pets. They'd ask about vacation plans, remodeling the house, and plastic surgery, nothing too serious or earthshattering. A few didn't even follow the advice Nana gave, much to their regret.

The image of one of the regulars, with her oversized lips resembling flotation devices, made Leah shudder. Nana had told her not to have the procedure done, but she hadn't listened. Now she'd to wait it out and hope her lips would return to normal over time.

Leah stirred in three teaspoons of sugar then carefully carried the thin saucers supporting the cups to the table, sloshing only a little bit. Probably would have been better to pour the tea at the table.

Nana reached for her cup, took a sip, and sighed. "Ah, just the way I like it."

Leah pulled out a chair to sit down when her grandmother pinned her with a look and an inquiring eyebrow lift. "Since you're up, why don't you cast the circle?"

It really wasn't a request, but rather an order. Leah started to walk around the table, but her grandmother stopped her. "Get the salt, the sea salt. This is serious. We don't want any bad energy or spirits messing with the reading. Come to think of it. It is fortunate you were sent home today so we could have a quiet reading without interference."

Fortunate might not have been the word Leah would have used. It was serendipitous how everything had worked together.

Her fingers fisted around the salt in her hand as she tried to clear her mind of woods, baying dogs, and the skeletal man on the throne. Breathing deeply, she counted to twelve before walking clockwise around the table, spreading a thin line of salt behind her. Nana welcomed the elements as she walked. Turning to the east, she lifted her hands. "Welcome, Air, breath of life." She touched a lit match to the incense cone.

Leah pivoted and raised her hands in a southern direction. "Welcome, Fire, symbol of warmth and passion."

Nana placed her fingers in the cup of water, pulling them upward, allowing the water to trickle off her fingers. "Welcome, Water. Mother, life giver, and nurturer."

A crystal embedded in the stone reflected the flickering light of the candle. Nana placed her hand over the stone. "Earth, Mother Earth, from which all life springs, welcome."

Leah finished walking the circle and stood while Nana held a match to the white candle flame to light the purple candle. Holding up her hands in a beseeching manner, her grandmother took on a majestic and command-ing tone. "Come, great Minona, Goddess of Fortune-Telling, and help us now. As you helped the people of Togo predict the future with palm kernels and cones, help me now read these humble tea leaves. Great praise and gratitude are offered up to you, wise Goddess." Her grandmother sat down.

At least that answered the question of who Minona was. Leah had had her cards read dozens of times but never tea leaves. "What do we do now?"

Her grandmother gestured to her cup. "You drink your tea, but make sure to leave a little liquid so the leaves can flow free to form shapes. We also talk. Cup your hands around the bowl of your cup to give it energy. Tell me, child, all that is happening to you. I've felt a disturbance."

Leah took a sip of cooling tea, wondering where to start. "I've been having these visions that feel real. Look at my legs." She stretched out a leg to show her muddy ankles. Nana reached out a finger to wipe up some mud to hold it up to her face. She rubbed her fingers together, feeling the mud texture.

"This is not from around here." She held the mud up to her nose and sniffed it. "Lots of humus in it, rich soil, probably from a forest with decaying matter. Tell me how your legs got so muddy."

The story of running from the witch catchers tumbled out. Her grand-mother didn't look surprised, only interested. Occasionally, she'd hold up a finger as if counting only to put it down, encouraging her to continue speaking with a gesture. Finally, Leah stuttered to a stop, aware of the fantastic nature of her tale now that she'd said it aloud.

Nana looked thoughtful as she rubbed two fingers against her brow where the third eye resided. "What is your name in these visions?"

"It is Leah, the same as it is now." An odd question. What could the meaning be behind it?

"Do you remember the clothes you wore?"

Good question. Had she spent much time looking down at herself? "The first time I wore rough, homespun garments. I saw myself as in third person. I didn't realize the woman was me until she pushed the hair out of her face. The second time I had on similar garments, but I tried to explain I was from America, but they didn't seem to understand. The third time, I don't remember, but I'm dirty from running through the forest."

"This is odd," Nana said. That was the understatement of the year. "Drink your tea." Leah picked up the cup, sipping and listening. "Many things are going on. It is possible you're returning to a previous life. If so, why are you physically returning? This is something I have never heard of before. If an earlier you held your spirit and existed in the past, why would the twenty-first-century you need to be present, too?"

Another her? Leah loosely believed a person could have several lives, but she'd never bothered to explore any of her past lives. What might this other her be like? She might have a boyfriend or was already married. People married much younger then.

Pointing to her teacup, Nana asked, "Done yet?"

A small residue of tea remained over the leaves. She nodded, waiting for instructions, hoping something useful to keep her safe and guide her while putting an end to her impromptu trips could come out of this reading. Cerberus, her three-headed mean-girl monster, was preferable to the evil man on the throne chair.

Nana held up one finger. "Follow my instructions exactly. Swirl the remaining liquid three times in your cup, then turn it over in your saucer, take three breaths, then lift your cup."

Holding the china cup in her hands, Leah gently swirled the liquid. She placed the cup on the table, placed the saucer on top of it, and inverted it. Taking three shallow breaths, she carefully lifted the cup. Brown liquid oozed across the saucer, leaving stranded piles of tea leaves scattered across the surface. It didn't look like an answer. It didn't look like anything.

Her grandmother must have sensed it and covered her right hand with her own. "Be at peace, child. Let me see what the leaves have to say.

Hmmm."

Leah leaned closer.

With one finger, Nana pointed to lines almost making a loop. "Broken loop means disruption and trouble in your life."

"I got that already." Her top teeth sank into bottom lip as she tried to find symbols in the leaves. A streak with a rounded head caught her eye. "What about that? It looks like a comet. What does it mean?"

"Good eye, Leah. It is a comet, which signals change, even a pivotal event." Nana cocked her head, first one way and then another, searching for symbols.

"Will the change be good or bad?" She feared she knew the answer, but crossed her fingers underneath the table anyway.

"Ah, I see a wolf, a rose, and a hand." Nana looked up. "Change is change. It just is. A man who loses his job thinks the change is bad until he gets a better job, then the change is good." Her bracelet jingled as she waved her hand for emphasis.

Leaving school early was a change that had worked in her favor. "What do those other symbols mean?"

Her grandmother fixed her with one of her enigmatic stares, probably the same look that had had Principal Sharpe running to hide. "A rose means new love."

A smile appeared as she thought of Dylan. It could happen and was certainly not as weird as appearing in a different century. "The hand, what does it mean?"

Nana held her hand open, demonstrating what she saw in the saucer. "That is destiny. Karma. Right now, what is happening to you has a higher purpose you might not understand immediately, but you will." Balling up her fist, she flourished it. "What do you think this means?"

"A fight." She answered without thinking. Even in this, her grandmother was teaching.

"You're correct, or an argument." She pointed to a small symbol that resembled a tiny dog. "The wolf symbol troubles me."

"Are you sure it isn't a tiny dog? A Chihuahua might chase me. Maybe Ethan will finally get the puppy he's wanted," Leah joked, trying to elevate Nana's somber mood.

"No, it's a wolf. This I know. Did I not call on the great Minona to assist me in the reading?" She looked at the white candle.

Leah stared at it, too, waiting for the Goddess to appear in the flame. Fortune-telling used to be a pleasurable activity. Her grandmother was always one to give happy news, believing you would find out the bad things on your own. She'd also pointed out that bad news didn't earn any tips or follow-up visits. A happy customer left on the lookout for good fortune and recognized it when it came. "The wolf?"

"Someone close to you will betray you," Nana said, slowly raising her face to meet her eyes.

"In this century or the other?" She could probably survive a modern betrayal, but she wasn't sure about one in the past.

Leaning over the saucer, Nana traced an outline in the air. "I cannot tell you when these things will happen. My clients only exist in one century, but I think I see a bag in this last pile of leaves."

"A bag? As in paper sack?" Leah wasn't too sure she wanted to know what it meant, but a warning could help. She couldn't fight the enemy if she didn't know what to expect.

Turning the saucer gently, Nana moved the elusive bag closer to her. "I'm unsure if it is open. Age dims your focus."

"What difference does it make if a bag is open or not?" The reading experience was not as fun and upbeat as she'd hoped it would be. An eerie sense of foreboding similar to a wet blanket settled around her shoulders, chilling her and pushing her down with its soaked heaviness.

"It troubles me that I cannot see it clearly. A bag if opened is a form of escape, which means you can escape these odd trips to the Burning Times."

Escape, that was good, which meant no more return trips to the land of scary. Truthfully, the forest was nice and unpolluted, but she'd no desire to stay there. "What does it mean if the bag is closed?"

Sucking her lips in, Nana hesitated, and then said, "A trap."

A trap? Not exactly what she'd wanted to hear, especially paired with someone betraying her. But there was love, new love. In the end, it wouldn't matter if she'd love if she was stuck, or even died, in the wrong century.

"Nana, is that all it says? It's not exactly clear." Leah had expected more since her grandmother's reputation rested on her ability to make detailed and accurate predictions. Part of it was she kept the readings positive, too.

Placing her hand over Leah's, Nana squeezed it lightly. "Tea leaf reading is open to interpretation. Where I see a wolf, someone else might see a Pomeranian."

Her initial impression of gloom and disaster could be wrong, Leah grabbed a cookie, munched thoughtfully and swallowed before giving voice to her thoughts. "You could be wrong, then."

Nana's head came up like a dog scenting a rabbit, her dark eyes narrowed, as she said, "I'm never wrong." With such an expression, it was easy to see why Principal Sharpe had hidden. Even knowing Nana worked hard to create the image of a scary gypsy woman from the horror movies didn't make it any less effective. Her grandmother blinked, as if suddenly remembering to whom she was talking, and managed a weak smile. "What

I meant to say, dear one, is we shape our destiny. These are symbols, road signs, to tell you what is out there and to beware."

That didn't make her feel any better. "Does it tell me what century I need to be looking for love and betrayal?" So far, she hadn't met any potential love interests running through the medieval forest. Henry was too old, although kind. Since people in the past aged rough, could be Henry was only twenty-two. She snorted at the idea. Besides, he did nothing for her.

As far as betrayal, she'd go for the mean-girl trio every time. That's how they normally acted, so how could it be a betrayal? She wasn't exactly friends with them. It wasn't a betrayal unless you trusted someone. That narrowed down the field big time.

Leah had learned early on not to trust people, not early enough, though. Whom did she trust? Her family, of course. They might irritate her, but they'd never betray her. There was Stella and Dylan. She trusted both. Dylan didn't know enough about her to betray anything, and Stella had her own secrets.

If not this century, maybe the dream century? All she knew were the three fellow runners. Old Margaret would probably turn her over in a heartbeat since she blamed her for the loss of her cat and home. Henry had too much character to turn her over. A man who stood up to the mayor and helped them to escape was not the type to stab her in the back. Then there was Sabina. The woman was near her age and friendly. If the twenty-first century had taught her anything, it was to be careful of people who pretend to be your friends. They too often weren't.

Opportunistic friendships, her father called them. People who be-friended you because they thought it might somehow benefit them, from getting on the dance team to hanging out with a particular guy friend. Perhaps they believed your momentary popularity would rub off on them. She'd gathered a small group of followers after her spirited defense of Jeremy, but most had fallen away after she'd failed to do anything else as interesting. The few who had hung on puzzled her. They were people who wanted to know her for something she'd done as opposed to who she was.

Leah needed to know more. Nana could use the Tarot cards, which had to be clearer than the leaves. "Could you…" she started to ask, only to hear the front door slam.

CHAPTER FIVE

E THAN WAS ALREADY home. The clock revealed two hours had passed since her taxi ride. Her brother stumbled into the kitchen, holding his hand to his nose and sporting a darkening, bruised eye. Nana stood. Remembering the circle, she cut a doorway in it, reminding Leah to open the circle properly as she rushed to her grandson.

"What happened?" Nana's loud voice filled the kitchen, causing Ethan to cringe a little.

He reached for a paper towel to hold up to his bleeding nose. "Fight," he mumbled.

Opening the freezer door, Nana pulled out a bag of peas and handed it to Ethan. "Put that on your eye. I can tell you were in a fight. Why?"

Leah guided her brother to a kitchen chair. "Might as well tell all or Nana will take to the neighborhood to investigate. You know you don't want that."

Ethan grumbled something indistinct through his bag of peas and paper towel.

"What? I don't understand?"

Her brother might have been a pain, but he was her pain, and no one should have been slapping him around. Anger bubbled to the surface, making her want to run out the door and find the big bully who had hurt her brother. Probably the hulking kid down the street whose parents had held him back a grade to bulk up for sports.

"Monica." He whispered the name.

Doubting she'd heard right, Leah repeated the name. "Monica? The British girl who moved in after us?"

"Yes," her brother answered, refusing to look up.

"She's a girl," Nana added, stating the obvious.

"A big, angry girl," Ethan added, his cut lip garbling his words a bit.

Yep, she was big, and she did have an attitude. Leah agreed with her brother. It surprised her since she'd thought British folks were happy and polite. Turned out, she'd gotten that wrong too. "Why did she hit you?"

ETHAN SHRUGGED. "EMILY had a book about fairies. It was surprisingly real, as opposed to all the made-up cartoon nonsense. Monica sat behind us making jokes about fairies not being real. I may have told her to shut up. Emily might have, too."

"That set her off?" It seemed like a relatively harmless exchange children and adults often had, without any noses bloodied in the process.

"I dunno. We were getting off the bus, and she pushes into me and calls me a 'ginger beer.' I think she's playing with me, like calling me a Coke or something. I say, 'Same to you,' then she starts swinging."

Nana piped in, "I don't know why she'd call you a ginger beer. Isn't that like a root beer?"

Clearing her throat, Leah got everyone's attention. "I guess it is, in a way. Apparently, it's also a British slur for gay."

Ethan lowered the bag of peas. "She thinks I'm gay, and then I said she was gay?" His eyes flicked up, as if he was thinking. "She is a big girl with a bad haircut that makes her look like a boy from the 1950s. I bet I'm not the first person to call her gay."

Leah didn't correct her brother for going right to the stereotypes. "Then you understand why it might upset her."

"Yeah," he agreed. "Still, it makes no sense why she'd call me gay."

Leah was starting to wonder about her little brother, who had better fashion awareness than she did. Now, she was heading right into the stereotypes. There had to be a better way to make sense of it for her little brother.

Resting one arm on the table, she angled her chair in Ethan's direction. "Remember when we moved and how you had trouble fitting in?"

Ethan managed to bob his head in agreement while the bag of peas still covered half his face. "It was only a few months ago. Yeah, fifth grade is even worse with the gender polarization."

Nana cocked her head like a curious bird. "What?"

Leah tried to explain. "He means the girls only hang out with girls and guys with guys."

Her grandmother pulled the bag holding her deck of Tarot cards from her pocket and muttered, "That's the way it is supposed to be. You're ten years old."

She'd had the Tarot cards all along. It was peculiar she'd chosen to read tea leaves for her. Had she not wanted to see things too clearly or had she been afraid of what she might find? Despite her belligerent nature, Nana wanted people to be happy. The best way to do that was to tell them only the happy things.

Ethan grumbled about the injustice of his place in life, not limited by a swollen lip and a pea bag. At least his nose had stopped bleeding. It was almost impossible to make out his words with the tissue wadded up in his nostril. "Sports. That's all the boys ever talk about. Sports they watch on television, sports they're going to try out for, games they might attend, and sports players' stats. Yawn. I could understand if Monica had to listen to that. Still, she has girls to talk to who talk about everything." Her brother threw out his free arm for emphasis.

Leah was tempted to add that in her experience females didn't talk about much besides boys, other girls, and boys. Stella was an exception, which was one of the reasons she liked her.

Nana shoved the deck in front of Ethan, who automatically cut it, a little sloppy with one hand, but he still managed to stack one-half on top of the other. "Are you thinking of your question?"

For him, she pulls out the cards, Leah complained to herself. What was the difference?

Instead of turning the card over, Nana kept her cupped hands over the deck and asked another question. "Does Monica talk much to the girls in her class?"

Ethan fingered his lip, possibly checking the swelling, before answering. "I don't know since weren't in the same class. I see her outside in the hall or in the lunchroom. When I see her there, she looks just as angry as she did before she punched me. The girls avoid her. Don't blame them. If I hadn't stood so close, I wouldn't be freezing my face with frozen vegetables."

Leah teased her brother, who was starting to sound more like himself. "I imagine those peas are cooked now, considering all the hot air you've been putting out."

Ethan forced out a laugh at the same time Nana turned over a card.

The three of them stared at the Tower card. The old deck was familiar, as was the slightly leaning tower of stones that looked to Leah like it might tumble down at any time. Not exactly a strong symbol.

Ethan touched the card with an index finger and softly mouthed the word, "Turmoil." He looked up. "I know it indicates, but what does it really mean?"

"It depends on the question." Nana flashed a slight smile. "It could mean change is coming to your finances, spiritual plane, love life, or even health."

Lowering the pea bag, he gestured to his darkened eye. "I've already experienced the health change. What else can I expect?"

"This might not be a good time for financial investments. You may have a few revelations or insights. Things are not always as they seem. Those you may depend on to be there for you might not."

Ethan sat with a dumbstruck look on his face, staring off in the distance.

Seeing his expression, Nana hurried to offer, "I can turn another card for confirmation."

Waving his hand, Ethan protested, "Don't bother. I'm not sure I can deal with any more happy revelations." He pushed out his chair and left the kitchen without saying another word.

Leah watched her brother go, troubled at the absence of his usual happy demeanor. Growing up had a tendency to knock your feet out from under you. Her grandmother picked up the card and placed it back in the deck, reminding Leah of her frustration with the ambiguous tea leaf symbols.

"Nana?" She gestured in the direction of the deck. "Why no cards for me? You pulled out the deck as soon as Ethan had an issue."

The deck disappeared into a silk bag and returned to the skirt pocket. "Ethan is a child who needs clearer answers, while you're a woman who needs to find her own answers and make her own destiny."

You're a woman. Need to make your own destiny. Just yesterday, her father had informed her she couldn't take the car to drive to Stella's, despite having her driver's license, because she was too young. "The other day I was too young, now I'm to pick out my own destiny. How's that work?" Her voice grew louder with her frustration. Realizing she was yelling at her grandmother, she tacked on a "Sorry."

Nana reached forward to cradle a hand around Leah's chin. "My child, I wish it were easier for you, but it isn't. Destiny picked you, but you can shape your path somewhat. Something in your past life calls to you, unfinished business your soul must complete."

"What?" Leah shook her head as if trying to remove Nana's words. "How can I have unfinished business in the past? I've never heard of anyone returning to the past to tidy up things. This makes no sense."

Her grandmother's face drooped with sadness. "I wish I could take this trial away from you, but it is yours. It will be the making of you, even though you're already a strong person."

Trial? That never sounded good. She'd an image of the dark-headed young woman, who she knew was herself, being dragged into a courtroom where a skeletal man in dark robes presided as judge and jury. There had to be a way to stop her unplanned trips. "If people travel back and forth through time, why can't they remember it?"

Her grandmother gave her chin a squeeze. "Good question. It shows you're always thinking. There are many reasons why people do not *clearly* remember." She emphasized the one telling word. "Often, they solved the problem in the previous life, so there's no reason to remember. They solved their karmic dilemma. Other times, only sections appear to us in dreams or a sense of déjà vu. Perhaps we see a stranger on the street whose spirit resonates with ours. It is someone from our previous lives in a different body. Our mind doesn't recognize them, but our spirit does."

"Is there a reason we don't remember everything? Life would be easier if you could use past-life knowledge. How can you solve a problem if you don't know what it is?" This time-traveling business was not only frightening her but also making her angry. Why couldn't her old self tell her new self what to do? Of course, her old self didn't seem to be lingering around to be of any use.

Nana stood and carried her used cup and saucer to the sink swaying slightly without the help of her cane. She strained off the tea leaves into one saucer to use in the compost pile. Papa teased her sometimes, calling it magickal compost, which yielded astounding vegetables and blooms. Looking out the window, she spoke. "I often wondered if it was like victims of violent crime whose brains bury the memories since living with the knowledge is too much. Then again, I heard a reincarnation expert speak on karmic destiny at the Spiritual Fair last year. You remember the fair?"

The fair was one of the few times she'd felt normal. Children dressed as elves and fairies had dashed through the various stalls that had sold everything from healing crystals to every type of incense a person could envision. The sheer volume of books addressing everything from reading auras to astral travel had staggered her imagination. A feeling of peace swept over her with the memory. "Yes, I remember it."

Nana continued as if she hadn't heard the wistful quality to her answer, or she'd chosen not to acknowledge it, saving her some embarrassment. "He said most people who try to recall previous lives remember only the moment of death clearly. If it is a violent death, the emotional impact is especially strong. It is also the closest memory to the new person."

"That makes sense," Leah replied, picking up the plate of remaining cookies. Her other self in the other time had had a violent ending. She didn't even have to wonder about it. Would her current self prevent it or had it already happened? "Still, knowing what needs to be done would make things much simpler."

Her grandmother half-filled the sink with water, squirted in some soap liquid and whipped it into lather with her hands. "It should all be that easy. You're not born knowing what you did wrong in the previous life and knowing what you should do with this one. With each life, we encounter other people on their karmic paths, often souls we knew before. Together we have to discover our destiny and learn what we need to know."

Sealing the cookies into a plastic container, Leah asked aloud, "What if you don't do the thing you're supposed to do in your lifetime?"

Grandmother's voice, muted by the running water, still rang clear. "You have to repeat it in each new life until you get it right."

She'd thought as much without Nana confirming it. Her lips twisted to one side. No one needed to tell her this was not her first time reliving this scenario. Apparently, she hadn't gotten it right in previous lifetimes.

Her life depended on her making it this time. If she didn't die violently in the past, would it change her current life? Would she cease to exist? She'd a feeling if she died in the past, she'd die in the now, too. Would her family simply have one less daughter and never even blink when they heard the name Leah? This time she'd to succeed, and to do that, she needed knowledge. This called for a research trip to the library.

A need to have more information for the essay was how she framed her plans to both her father and Stella. He even let her have the car, which was strange since the other day she'd been too young. Had Nana said something? She'd chosen not to trouble her parents with her recent adventures. Not much they could have done. Her mother's mental health already bore too much stress from the recent death of two of her homecare clients. As a health care professional, she tended to take it hard when her patients died.

Her father would have given her a doubtful look if she confessed all. If they had been Jewish, he would have converted to Judaism. It was as simple as that. Or was it that simple? She used to bemoan her Wiccan roots, considering them an insurmountable obstacle to any type of future relationship with Dylan. Maybe they weren't.

No one her age had any use for religion, or anything vaguely like mainstream kind. There were a few born-again kids at school who wore enough cross jewelry to prevent them from ever getting through an airport metal detector. She chose not to enlighten them. Their symbol had come from an Egyptian sun-god culture a mere six hundred years ago. Even if she'd, they wouldn't have believed her. They were so thoroughly entrenched in their Bible studies, contemporary gospel music, and Christian fiction that they refused to examine the very world around them. They took every word their minister said as gospel. Yep, they were the only ones who never had doubts or questions.

Some folks might have called it great faith. On the other hand, it might just have been laziness, the fear of examining life, and all it entails, on their own. She'd even heard once, from one of her Christian friends, that to question anything could result in eternal damnation. That would certainly put an end to any thinking outside the religious box. What would they do if they were to found themselves caught in the same situation?

Would they think they were possessed? Would they call for the priest or run out in front of an oncoming semi? Hard to know, but in the end, this was a fight resting squarely on her shoulders. She might not like it, but that didn't change the circumstances. This sudden knowing people's thoughts would help.

Taking the keys offered by her father, she tried to probe his mind. Nothing. Had her ability gone away as soon as it had occurred? Great, what now? She'd found a magic tool, but lost it a second later?

CHAPTER SIX

L EAH DROVE TO Stella's house, making sure to use her turn signal and come to full stops. Did her father know how to shield his thoughts? In a house full of Pagans, it might have been an important skill to have. She should try to read Stella. Walking through other people's thoughts was wrong, but how could she find out? She could pick a stranger as opposed to losing a friend.

Stella waited on her front step, clutching a notebook. Leah had barely stopped the sedan before her friend vaulted in, slamming the passenger door. Turning red eyes and a tight face her way, Stella said, "Let's get out of here now. I'm not sure if I can put up with those people a minute longer."

Leah reversed slowly out of the driveway. The thought of burning rubber to leave as fast as her friend had suggested crossed her mind only briefly. Such action would have resulted in the cancellation of any future use of the family car. "Those people" had to be Stella's parents, since no one else resided in their house. Besides, most teens battled with the limitations or demanding expectations of their parents, and a few were unlucky enough to have parents who wanted to relive the life they wished they'd had as a teen through their children.

A rock ballad played softly as raindrops pelted the windshield. Rain, just what she didn't need. Oh, well, she'd have to drive in all kinds of weather. She might as well get used to it. Stella sniffled occasionally, probably wondering why her friend wasn't asking her what was wrong. Driving was difficult enough with trying to remember all the rules plus directions to the library. Why had she never paid attention when other people were driving? Then again, the issue of popping out of the current century into another was a bit disconcerting.

Her hands tightened on the steering wheel as she realized she could disappear in a flash, leaving the car driverless and her friend in danger. It would be hard to explain to her father when she returned. Make that if she returned. Stella sniffled again.

Leah sighed. "What happened?"

STELLA WIPED HER nose with the back of her hand. Leah reached for the ready supply of fast-food napkins kept in the car, handing one to her tearful friend.

"Boundaries, apparently my mother has none." She blew her nose, sounding almost like a honking cartoon character. Leah decided against mentioning it. Instead, she waited, knowing her friend would reveal all if given enough time.

Stella jerked at her shoulder belt impatiently as if it was the one guilty of offending her as opposed to her parent. "She snooped through my room. She calls it cleaning. Ever since my mother lost her job as an office manager, she has too much time on her hands. Obviously enough time to root through my room."

Leah would be upset if her mother rooted through her room, mainly because it would merit a lecture on being more organized. What could Stella have that would upset her mother? "So, what did she find? Racy magazines, a suggestive love letter, some weed?" She laughed because she doubted her introverted friend would have any of the mentioned items, but you never knew.

Stella answered with an abrupt one-word reply. "No."

That was it. First, she blubbered until Leah asked, then she clammed up. Kinda hard to sympathize when she didn't know what to feel bad about. She braked for a four-way stop, paying attention to who arrived first to decide when her turn came. Luckily, only one other car was at the stop. He shot through the four-way, not allowing her to question who had the right of way. She'd have let him go first, but the sports car driver wasn't taking chances.

Information signs denoting a library nearby caught her eye at the same time Stella decided to enlighten her. "Hey, Leah, I'm sorry. I didn't tell you because I didn't know how you'd react. Certainly not like my mother, but I want to tell you."

"Go ahead," she encouraged, spotting the library building a couple of blocks down the street. Her friend couldn't tell her anything that would be too surprising.

"Well," Stella started and then stopped. She looked out the window. "I suggested the topic about religious intolerance and prejudice."

Leah flicked on the turn signal and pulled into the library parking lot. "It's a good topic. I've no complaints. In fact, I want to do a little more research on it today."

"Yeah, I know, but I never explained why I picked it." Stella turned a wary expression to her.

Twisting the key to turn the car off, Leah answered, "Okay." Stella's family had never struck her as overly religious. They might make it to church a half-dozen times a year, but she doubted anyone would be guilty of persecuting them. Her friend sat, inspecting her cuticles, probably waiting for her to say something else. "Why did you?"

"I've developed an interest in earlier religions, even Pagan ones. I've been studying them. New religions replaced them sometimes under the penalty of death. Convert or lose your head." She made a slashing motion across her neck. "Were you aware of this?" Stella's raised eyebrows expressed her outrage.

The thought of Nana's lectures on the subject crossed her mind. "I may have heard of it."

Stella visibly inhaled, as if steeling herself for something. "The more I read the more curious I became. Eventually, I started reading Wiccan books. That's what my mother found in my room. It caused her to go berserk, accusing me of being a witch and putting the evil eye on people. Are you shocked? Do you still want to be my friend?"

A genuine smile broke across Leah's face, and she surged forward to hug her friend only to have the shoulder safety belt cut into her neck and shoulder. Releasing the belt, she managed to wrap Stella in a tight embrace. "No worries, friend. I'm not shocked. You won't believe how not shocked I'm."

"Really?" The word tangled in Leah's hair as her friend returned the hug with vigor. "Why is that? Most people might be weirded out or something."

Leah laughed. "You met Nana."

"Right," Stella agreed, then chuckled. "You're the only person I know who has a grandmother who tells fortunes. I guess that makes you open to anything."

"Not quite anything," Leah murmured, easing out of the embrace. They were in a public place. "Too much hugging and we'll be the next girl couple at Silverton High."

"Oh, you didn't know? We already are, thanks to our own mean girls and their campaign to keep you and Dylan apart. It isn't going too well, though, thanks to my romantic interaction with Jacob 'Thinks He's God's Gift to Women' Collins." Stella mimicked polishing her nails on her jacket.

"What? What's this to do with you and Jacob? I thought you guys only had two dates?"

"YOU'RE RIGHT. WE only had two dates. I thought he was okay on the first date, so I agreed to the second. We kissed, but it wasn't anything special, no chemistry. Still, Jacob couldn't believe any lesbo wouldn't switch teams after dating him or at least that's what he'd want everyone to think. He made sure to tell everyone I was hot for him, as opposed to you. He may even give me another chance." Stella pretended to fan herself as if overcome by the thought.

"Lucky you," Leah teased.

Her friend agreed with a chuckle. "What I want to know is which mean girl has her eye on Dylan that Team Evil is willing to put so much work into painting you and me with the rainbow paintbrush."

What Stella suggested was something Leah hadn't considered. Brianna and Alexis had boyfriends, but that didn't stop them from flirting with every attractive male within range. Lauren, she didn't know. It might explain why they'd singled her out, then another thought occurred to her. "I guess I always thought it was me they picked on, but I think it's you. Could be that Lauren has her eye on Jacob."

Resting her hand on the door, Stella grinned as she swung the door open. "Well, she's welcome to him. I'm not standing in her way."

Leah hopped out of the car, making sure to lock it. The last thing she needed was for some slackers to decide to take the family car for a joyride. She waited for her friend to round the car to finish their conversation. "It could be Jacob has no interest in her, but she thinks you're the problem." It was rather like her three newfound friends from the Burning Times who took the blame for sheep dying and crops not doing well.

"Yay me," Stella said. "The bad thing is I can't do anything about it. If I pretend to ignore Jacob for some strange reason, it will make me more desirable. No matter what I do, I'm doomed."

"I know the feeling." Leah hadn't really thought about what she was going to do when she next appeared in olden times. Apparently, she didn't get to take things with her to prove she was not a local. Just as well. Something as innocent as an MP3 player would have been an instrument of the devil.

They entered the library, silencing their voices to escape the head librarian's watchful eye. The somber head librarian appeared to have a special dislike of children in all forms, expecting or afraid they would bully her offspring, the books, with dirty fingers or bent pages.

Stella looked up the books they needed in the online catalog. Most of them were not on the shelf. They managed to find a few books on anti-Semitism, but that was it. It appeared they weren't the only people interested in the same topic. It would be helpful if some of the books came back soon. The list of titles in hand, Leah searched for the reference librarian.

Both girls approached the reference desk quietly. A young woman, probably fresh out of college with her library science degree, looked up. "Can I help you?"

"Yes." Leah placed the list on the counter. "My friend and I are working on a report for school, but we can't find any of these books."

The librarian looked at the list and mumbled a bit under her breath before looking up. "Can't help you. I'm surprised They're still in the online catalog. They were stolen a while ago."

They weren't spell books. "Why would someone steal them? They're only history books."

The librarian nodded her head. "That's true, but they may have presented a more honest and complete picture of the witch trials and persecution. Plenty of people around here don't want that. We weren't even going to order replacements. They'll just be stolen again."

Stella grumbled beside her. "My mother."

Leah turned in surprise. "What?"

"People like my mother are stealing them. I'm not saying my mother stole your books. I doubt she even knew they were here. Someone who doesn't want any diversity in his or her world."

The librarian looked intrigued. "Yes, these monotheists think they run it."

Another one? It always surprised Leah when she stumbled across someone not part of the dominant religions. There were Pagans all around her, or at least people who didn't march with the leading faith. All the same, it wasn't helping her with her report or her more important personal research.

Leah turned away, and the librarian called out, "Wait."

She bent low behind the reference desk, rattled some papers, and reappeared clutching a typewritten page with various Internet site names on it. "Here, this might help. You can use the library computers."

Stella snatched the paper and read it with an avid expression. Leah murmured her thanks, eager to pull the paper from her friend's hands. How weird was it that the woman would have the paper with all sorts of sites printed on it? Could be she'd pulled the paper out of her purse as opposed to a library file while rattling under the desk. Leah reached for the paper her friend held, but Stella slapped her hands away.

"I'm not finished." She hurried to a computer, leaving Leah to follow.

Her friend typed in the words to a site called Teen Witch. Looking over Stella's shoulder, Leah asked, "Do you think you'll get an unbiased opinion from such a site?" She knew the site and felt it was fair, but she wanted to know her friend's opinion before she revealed any of her own secrets.

Stella spun on the desk chair and regarded Leah with a mixture of scorn and surprise. "Seriously? You're asking me if I think the site is unbiased? I'm willing to bet it is more unbiased than any of those Holy Roller sites. Everyone has an agenda or an angle to promote. I think it is to our benefit to check out all angles."

Leah agreed and scanned the paper for any site that might be beneficial to her, finding a registry of people killed as witches. She slid into a chair next to her friend and typed in the site address. What would she find?

What did she want to find?

The site came up with a somber banner featuring old-time people standing on a scaffold, waiting to be hanged. Even though it was only a sketch, each person's face mirrored identical confusion. How had they ended up there?

Leah began to read. *This is an incomplete registry of people who were tortured and put to death due to the evil that often exists in the heart of men combined with the mob mentality, which results in the worst behavior of humankind. Make no mistake. Every bit as horrific as the Holocaust perpetuated on the Jewish race by Hitler. Unfortunately, not every name was recorded, due to the sudden violence of the acts. Often, people killed for being in the wrong place at the wrong time didn't even have a chance to give their names. Other times, no one cared. The surviving relatives worked to piece together a registry of sorts to remember those whose lives ended too soon.*

The search box beckoned to her. She first typed in Old Margaret's name only to find plenty who had died as accused witches. No help there. She typed in Sabina's name and got fewer names than with Margaret, but still considerable. Too bad, she didn't know anyone's last name. Still, Henry might work because not too many men had been witches. About two dozen popped up, obviously more than she'd thought. Looking around carefully, she noticed Stella was intent on writing something down that she'd found on her site.

She let her finger hover over the keyboard, unsure if she truly wanted to know. Then again, she might come up with nothing since the records did not have every name. She typed in Leah Carpenter, then pushed the enter key. An entry came up immediately.

Leah Carpenter, an unknown stranger to the town, sentenced as a witch to be burned at the stake.

She gasped, and her head snapped back, attracting Stella's attention.

"Leah, what is it?" Concern filled her face.

"Um, nothing." She stalled, swishing the mouse to close the window. Her friend might have been open to other religions, but her best friend traveling through different time periods and running from witch catchers would have been a little more to swallow. That she might have to rescue the past Leah if she wanted to exist now would have been even harder. Still, she could use some help, even if it was only moral support.

She maximized the screen and turned the monitor so Stella could see it.

Her eyes flickered over it. "How weird that someone long ago had the same name as you. Creepy, is not it?"

"You have no clue." Despair flavored her voice, making it tired and flat.

Stella's face grew troubled. "You don't mean…" She pointed at Leah and then the computer screen, the obvious question apparent in her eyes.

"Yes, I do think it's me, which is the reason I wanted to find out more to avoid dying in some medieval village at the hands of angry peasants." She attempted a sheepish smile, hoping it didn't resemble indigestion more.

Stella shook her head slowly as if trying to shake something off. "Is this like some ancestor you're trying to get in touch with?"

"I wish." Things would have been a lot simpler that way. "Nope. For some reason I seem to slip into another time unexpectedly. I'm sure you heard about me leaving school today."

"Who hasn't? Gives you a few bad-girl vibes just to keep things interesting. I was waiting for you to tell me where you went. Did you sneak off campus? Go hide in the second gym like most of the skippers?" Stella wiggled her eyebrows at the last question. They'd both previously discussed the stupidity of skipping school only to end up hiding underneath the bleachers of the rarely used old gym.

Leah inhaled. Here it went. It was one thing telling Nana, who believed in astral travel, but she wasn't a hundred percent sure this was what was happening to her. "I wasn't in school today because I was in some hut at the edge of a forest, eating dried fish with three other alleged witches." She watched Stella mull over the concept as her eyes flicked up to the ceiling as she chewed her bottom lip. At least, she didn't immediately call her crazy.

"Bet you didn't mention that to Principal Sharpe."

The interest in her friend's voice indicated she didn't totally disbelieve her. "Nope, I kept insisting I was in the hall. I was surprised how much time had passed. It didn't seem that long. Maybe time moves faster when you're running for your life."

Stella touched her foot to hers. "Hey, what can I do to help?"

"I'm not sure. Believing me helps. I'm trying to find out what I can about that time to protect myself. You could cover for me if I disappear in the future. I can be walking down the music hall and suddenly I'm in the forest." The ability to flash in and out of centuries baffled her. It would have helped if some warning bell would sound, preparing her for the shift, but it never did. How a person prepared for such a thing baffled her. The best she could do was accumulate knowledge.

Stella agreed with a head bob and a somber countenance. "What else? That seems like such a small thing to do. I would have done that without knowing where you were."

Chewing on her thumbnail, Leah wondered what her friend could do. Stella was as good a student as, or better than, she was. Her friend hovered between going into law and becoming an investigative reporter. If you wanted to get to the root of something, you asked Stella to look into it. "I'm trying to find out more about the time I shifted to, thinking I could find something to help me when I do. Henry mentioned something about everyone dying a witch's death in a couple of German villages, even the children and priests."

"Goodness, that's hard to believe. Who's Henry?" Stella turned backed to the computer and typed in "witch hunts in Germany."

"Henry is the man helping us to escape the mob who wants to string us up or light a fire under us. I'm not sure what the prevailing method is." Leah looked over her friend's shoulder at the various sites that popped up. She pointed to one. "Don't bother going there. That man is whacked. Supposed to be a college professor or something, and he doesn't even know that King James deliberately changed the verse 'Thou shall not suffer a poisoner to live,' and substituted 'witch' for 'poisoner.' The prof definitely has an agenda to sow more hate and prejudice."

Stella continued to scroll down the entries, squinting. She'd a hard time focusing on print and refused to put on her glasses in public. She complained they made her feel like a little old lady. Leah figured it had something to do with her glasses making her look smart. Everyone knew smart girls were on the bottom rung of the flirtation ladder, unless some guy wanted to copy your homework. Neither one of them was desperate enough to fall for that obvious trick. Okay, maybe once, but never again.

Stella still stared at the screen. "I think I found it."

Leah leaned forward to see, and everything went black.

✧   ✧   ✧   ✧

THE DARKNESS BECAME gray, but still dark, with a few spots of brightness where torches glowed against stone walls. The rough stone floor chilled her bare legs. Fingering her skirt, she realized it was a rough homespun material. Guess it was too much to come back as a princess in jewels and satin.

Something heavy weighed down her arms. A large hand wrapped around her slender biceps. Make that, one around each arm. An upward glance revealed a pair of muscular brutes. One cracked a grin, showing his rotted teeth. Apparently, dental care didn't rate in this time.

"Bring the prisoner closer," an authoritative voice rang out.

Leah was betting it was her skeletal friend, but she couldn't see him. Expecting to walk, she pushed up with her quads as the thugs pulled her upright. Stifling a moan, she experimentally put her weight on one foot. Her leg crumpled as if it was wet spaghetti. Instead of letting her fall, her guards held tight to her arms and dragged her the few yards.

A pair of lit, tapered candles revealed that once again she faced her good buddy, making her question why the two of them appeared bound together in some type of karmic dance.

"Closer." The guards dragged her a few steps closer. "Now, leave." He clapped his hands, treating the guards as no more than trained dogs.

The men dropped their hold. The sudden loss of support caused her knees to crash into the hard stone, making her wince in pain.

"Not so high-and-mighty now, are you, Arabella?" The man purred the words as if delighted. He put his bony fingers on his knees and leaned forward, attempting to look in her eyes.

Leah wiggled her toes and fingers. They all worked, but why had her legs refused to hold her? It made no sense. The man called her Arabella, which could be her name in this time. He said it as if he knew her, which made it personal. Who knew? Could Arabella have done something bad to him? It might explain why she wasn't already dead. She flexed a shoulder as she pushed up into a seated position. The motion hurt, but she could still manage, which was a plus. Still, there was this man. Truth might serve her for once. She hoped it would.

"Excuse me, sir. I think you mistake me for someone else. My name is Leah." She crossed her fingers, hidden under her skirt.

"Leah." He said the name and laughed. "Taking on the name of the less-favored sister will not save you. You were always Arabella, even though your parents chose to give you an elegant name much above your station. They hoped for something better for you than to be a wife of a farmer or a traveling tinker. Maybe you did as well."

His dark eyes stared into hers without blinking. She turned away, never any good at these staring contests. He wanted something from her, but what? A confession of some sort? It was personal. No doubt about it. Henry thought those accused of being witches had been on the wrong side in political battles. Margaret had declared it was because she'd no husband or family to stand for her. Sabina had blamed her accusation on being too pretty and single. It was enough to damn her in most of the town women's opinions.

She scooted her legs underneath her, ready to rise. Her muscles trembled, spasmed even, reminding her of the time she broke her personal best in the 880-meter run. The way her legs had shaken the entire bus trip back had frightened her. The coach had kept urging her to drink more and eat a banana. She was sure she hadn't run any races now, but she might have. Pressing her fingers into her leg muscles didn't stop the trembling.

"Ah, the shakes usually accompany torture." He stretched out his arm as if to touch her.

Leah jerked back, lost her balance, and fell backward to slam her head against the floor. She lay for a moment with her eyes closed. Could she possibly play dead? Numerous people talked about surviving the Holocaust by pretending to be dead. It might work for her. Breathing in deeply, she held her breath. How long it would take to convince her captor she'd expired?

The sound of the chair scraping against the wood as the man stood indicated her performance lacked some authenticity. She heard the rustle of his robes along with his accompanying footsteps. Leah willed herself not to move, to hold perfectly still. Actors did it in movies all the time. Why couldn't she?

His shadow loomed over her, touching her. "Oh, Arabella," he said softly.

She'd hoped believing she was dead, he might feel some regret for treating her so poorly. A metallic sound echoed off the wall. Her head snapped off the ground, bowing her back into a curve with agonizing pain to her neck, forcing out a gasp as her eyes flickered open. He held a short chain in his hands attached to a cool metal band that encompassed her neck.

Pulling her slowly back into a sitting position, he dropped the chain. "Arabella, you could never fool me, a lesson that never took. You used to call me your own beloved Lionel, but now you pretend we have never met."

It was an intimate matter. Hard to imagine there was anything to love about this malevolent bag of bones, but perhaps there had been at one time.

Should she flatter the man? Tell him how she missed him? Pretend to recognize him?

The decision vanished as she found herself in the rolling chair beside her friend in the county library.

CHAPTER SEVEN

S TELLA SPUN AROUND, looking both relieved and angry. "There you're! I checked the aisles, the restroom, even asked the reference librarian. I wasn't even sure how I would get home if I couldn't find you. I called your phone, but it was here." She angled her head in the direction of the bright lime-green cell phone lying by the keyboard. "Where have you been?"

Leah listened patiently to her friend's rant, holding herself up with one arm resting on the counter. "I think you're going to have to drive. I don't feel so well."

Her friend placed her hand against her forehead. "Your skin is clammy. I'll drive you home, but I doubt your father will be too pleased."

She tried to push her lips into a smile but failed. "Just don't kill us." Stella tried to help her up, but staggered under her weight.

The helpful reference librarian came to assist. "What's wrong with her?"

"Some type of brain fever or malaria," Stella offered. Leah wished she'd be quiet. Unlike most teenagers, lying to adults was a skill her friend lacked, not that she was much better. Still, she knew enough not to make the mistake of elaborating too much, as Stella often did.

"Really?" The doubt was obvious in the librarian's voice. "I considered that more of a tropical disease."

Leah could hear one of the patrons murmuring something about a strung-out junkie. The man was talking about her. The nerve. Just went to show what happened when you made assumptions. She wanted to march back to them and explain that she'd just shifted through centuries and been tortured by thugs for something she couldn't remember doing. Of course, that would only confirm his earlier junkie assessment with such outrageous claims.

Stella opened her mouth. A tale including missionary parents and malaria emerged. Great, just her luck the librarian would ask her parents about their religious outreach when they visited the library next. Her mother would politely tell her she didn't believe in inflicting her religious beliefs on others and would promptly hand her a pamphlet on how to help Mother Earth.

Her eyelids flickered shut as her butt hit the car upholstery. "Keys in pocket." She pushed out the words.

Leah retained consciousness, but she wished she hadn't. The way her friend drove, going up on curbs only to careen back down with a jolt, rattled her brain even more. A cacophony of horns indicated either Stella had stolen a right-of-way or had run a red light. Leah bet it was the former.

The sedan bumped into the driveway, where Stella laid on the horn, bringing out Leah's father, followed by her mother and ever-curious brother. Having reached her limit, her friend babbled as her father opened the driver's side door. "Please help Leah. She went away and then came back. She can barely walk."

Her father hurried to Leah's side of the car. She recognized his voice. How would she explain? He scooped her up in his arms and carried her into the house. Sometimes she forgot how strong he could be until needed. "What has happened?"

She opened her mouth to reply, but her father kept talking. "I hope you did not get in a fight where someone films it and puts it up on the Internet."

Ethan bounced along beside them, opening the front door wide. "Get real, Dad. Stella and Leah are not the type to start girl fights."

Mother hovered close by smoothing her hair. The pinched expression on her mother's face concerned her. She tried to spare her mother grief by not telling her things. She'd not mentioned that their various moves made it hard to fit in at school. Her brother thought he knew it all, but he was unaware she'd been in three girl fights due to being the new kid.

Being new was enough to set some people off. The early altercations had taught her to go in ruthless. Acting insane didn't hurt, either. That should have been her tactic with her medieval tormenter.

Nana pushed her way to Leah's side. "My poor dear, did you travel back in time again?"

She blinked her eyes twice for yes since her throat was too raw for talking.

As her father carried her to bed, her mother's voice rose above everyone else's. It was a tone seldom used by her mother and never when speaking to her opinionated mother. "What do you mean, traveling back in time?"

Her mother's irritation most likely resulted from Leah telling Nana about the time travel as opposed to her. She could hear her grandmother's efforts to calm her mother, which was a turn of the tables.

Her father knelt to place her on the bed. Theodora jumped up beside her and began to knead her stomach, causing her to whimper.

Both Nana and Mother stopped their fussing to look over at her. Their faces were white, bodies frozen, until Leah whimpered again, causing them both to spring like racehorses out of the gate. Mother reached her first and shoved her father aside, but Nana moved fast for a woman with a cane. When they peeled back the shirt sticking to her skin, the two gasped. Pushing up on her elbows, she was able to see the crisscross marks on her torso.

"Damn delinquents." Her father growled the words. "I'm calling the police."

"Wait." Nana's imperious tone cut through the tension enveloping the room. "Only thing that will come of that is they will lock you up for child abuse and send in some social worker who will have Leah removed to some dubious foster family who might actually abuse her. Do you want that?"

A frown pulled at his lips as he crossed his arms. "No, I don't want that. What can we do? She needs to go to a hospital."

"Adam." Her mother touched her father's arm. "I'm almost done with my clinicals. I can take care of her here. At the hospital, she'd get the same treatment plus a call to social services. A whipped victim would receive an automatic referral, which would put us back right to the same place."

Leah forced her eyes open as she watched her family discuss her as if she were an uninterested third party. Yep, her unplanned trips to the past would be hard to explain to any social worker or cop. They'd not only have her family up on abuse charges, but might lock her away in some psych ward. Just the other day, her biggest problem had been getting Dylan to notice her. If only she could turn back the clock.

Nana and Mother exchanged a few words and then hurried off in different directions, leaving Stella and Ethan to gaze at her as if she were a two-headed cow. Their wordless scrutiny made her uncomfortable.

In hopes of breaking the tension, she looked up at her friend. "Not exactly what you were expecting from a trip to the library?" she joked.

"No." Stella shook her head, speaking slowly, no doubt searching for the right words. "In a way, I guess it is a real-life example of religious persecution."

Leah tried for a smile but even her face hurt. "We should get an A on our report for going the extra mile, or three thousand miles. I'm not sure it is about religion. Hard to say. I think it is a love affair gone bad. People always say something is about religion to justify their bad behavior, especially if it is a popular opinion."

Dad stood next to the door with his arms still folded and his brow furrowed, probably chafing at his inability to do anything. "Sounds like you're getting a bit philosophical."

Leah speared her fingers through her hair. "I'm not sure. I guess things aren't always as they seem on the surface. The people I've met in the past are motivated by fear and greed." The trio of Henry, Sabina, and Margaret had run out of fear. What about the villagers? It would have been easy to assume some moral high ground motivated them. They could even tell themselves that as they turned on their neighbors.

Her father's thoughts must have mirrored her own. "In the end, you have to think did turning on their neighbors benefit them? The same person they vilified may have helped with the harvest only months ago. At first, they do nothing out of fear, not wanting to attract attention. Then again, what benefit is it to them? Do they get the goods or land of the persecuted individual?"

Sabina had complained the women disliked her because she was attractive and unmarried. "They might get rid of the competition for the affection of a beau or even a husband."

Leah imagined there were definitely a few women in the village who wouldn't mind seeing the beautiful woman disappear, and they wouldn't care how it happened.

Ethan grimaced. "Girls. They're even mean in the past."

"Yeah," Leah agreed. "You have no clue, little brother. Be glad you're a male. All you guys do is punch each other in the nose when you get aggravated, then suddenly you're pals."

Her brother's hand went up to feel his nose. "I don't want to be punched in the nose again." He displayed some concern about the future of his nose and some puzzlement as to why someone might want to rearrange it. Keeping his hand protectively over his nose, he left the room, passing Nana and Mother on their way in. They laid out the homemade bandages that had cartoon images on them. The old, faded sheet set from her younger years finally been put to a different use.

Mother carried a teakettle with a plume of steam wafting gently behind her as she walked. Leah looked at the teakettle, while hoping boiling water didn't constitute a cure for anything.

"BOILING WATER AND torn-up sheets. Is not this what they always ask for when someone is having a baby?"

Setting the kettle down, her mother shooed her father from the room, turning to a swaying Stella, she asked, "Would you like to help?"

Her answer was a soft, "I guess."

Nana took the lid off a pot that held an aromatic mixture. "Old family secret that will heal your wounds in no time." She shoved the pot in Stella's direction, causing her to stagger a few steps back.

Her mother poured the hot water into a dishpan and began to dip some of the bandages in it. "We may have to soften up your clothes to separate them from your wounds. Pulling them off would only cause the scabs to break open."

Her mother went about her duties with a no-nonsense attitude, which was probably her approach at work. The idea of tearing open scabbed-over wounds caused Leah to shudder. She'd never been a good patient. She'd made it her life mission not to do dangerous things when she'd relatives who were more likely to pull out a needle and put in a few stitches after splashing her with alcohol. Nope, she'd stayed away from anything even slightly dangerous, from skateboarding to rollerblading. Ironic that now she'd to endure pretty much everything she'd avoided.

Even though the water had to have been burning, her mother calmly wrung out the bandages and placed them against her shirt. Steeling herself for the pain by tightening her muscles, Leah felt slow warmth penetrate the fabric, skin, and eventually her muscles, relaxing her. Her eyelids fluttered shut as her mother placed several warmer bandages around her torso.

With her eyes closed, she felt safe listening to her mother and grandmother talk to each other as they moved around her. Her friend asked a few halting, difficult-to-hear questions. Her grandmother gave her the usual cryptic answers she seemed to have for everything that often appeared to answer the question, but on deeper inspection said nothing at all.

Her mother bent over her body, removing the cooling bandages. "I'm going to remove your shirt. I hope it is not a favorite, because I'm going to cut it off you." Flourishing a pair of blunt-nosed scissors, she eased the tip of the metal shears under the material and snipped, pulling the fabric gently away. Nana hovered over her mother, leaning on her cane, probably anxious to offer instruction, but for once, she held her tongue.

Her mother's gasp broke through her stupor. What was it? She saw the blue polo she'd donned earlier that day in strips around her torso. Make that, her striped torso. Her body was a quilt of yellowing, blue and black bruises separated by red lash marks crusting over with pus and dried blood. Not a pretty sight, and apparently, she wasn't the only one who felt that way. Stella darted out of the room with a hand over her mouth, making a retching noise.

The soft sound of Nana's chanting as she moved above her, holding out her hands to invoke a healing protection spell, both frightened and reassured Leah. The words sounded foreign to her, probably Romany. In times of great distress, Nana often abandoned speaking in English, claiming it took too much thought when all one could do was feel. How serious was it that Nana brought out the language of her ancestors? In another way, it reassured her. Nana wasn't above murmuring a few Gypsy words to give her paying customers the feeling they had an authentic fortune-teller. Of course, that was all for show. Leah knew this time the words were not for show, but were serious business, which unfortunately was her business.

Her mother's arms wrapped around her as if in an embrace, pulling her slightly forward. Leah lifted her hands to her mother's arms. How long since they had truly hugged? She could not remember. It wasn't that she disliked her mother. Hugging fell about the wayside, along with evening bed-tucks. After all, she was almost a senior. Too old for such things, they said, "I love you," or "Love you, too," at the end of conversations. It often felt meaningless, rather like a clerk wishing her a nice day with a snarl in her voice. She leaned into her mother's arms, taking solace from the simple action.

The brief embrace lasted only seconds, until her mother whispered in her ear, "I need you to try to sit up on your own so I can cut off the shirt from your back."

Was that all it had been? Not a hug, not a sign of love, but only a way to get to her back to cut her shirt off? Leah didn't want to consider it. Of course, her mother loved her. That's what mothers did. Instead, she willed herself to hold her body erect during the process of the cool metal medical shears moving down her back. Would it be too much to ask for reassurance of her love?

Her mother's voice, clouded with concern, breathed on her neck. "You do realize that if there was a way, I would take your place. I love you, Leah. Nana has explained to me this is your journey, but that doesn't mean I have to like it."

Leah allowed her head to drop to her mother's shoulder. Resting it there, she inhaled her familiar scent of lily of the valley perfume, wondering if this could be the last conversation between the two of them. "That makes two of us. I love you, too." She mumbled her reply but knew her mother heard.

Her grandmother picked up a paintbrush and stirred the pot.

"You're using a paintbrush on me?" What was she, a house?

Her mother cleaned her back as Nana drew closer. "A paintbrush will help provide the solution in an even fashion. Yes, there's much of you that needs to be covered."

Her mother unsnapped her bra. Realizing the action might reveal more marks and require a total stripping had something rising in her throat, gagging her some. She swallowed as her mother swiped down her bra-strap area.

"This area is clean."

The announcement relieved her some. It was worst when she could not remember what had happened.

The smooth slide of the brush on her back was warm and moist, and it smelled strongly of garlic. As it brushed over her wounds, it stung. Probably salt or vinegar in the mixture. Better than alcohol, she reminded herself, and fought against wincing.

"Sit up straight," her mother urged.

Her changed posture allowed her mother and grandmother to work as a tag team, with Nana spreading the unguent while Mother wrapped bandages around her torso. With her upper torso and arms done, her head was lowered to the pillow to rest before they tackled her lower body. It made her feel a bit like a pharaoh being prepared for burial. Of course, they were dead at the time. Still, they were familiar with the process. Closing her eyes, she decided to take a tiny break with no intention of sleeping. When she slept, her mind wandered often into the other century.

✧   ✧   ✧   ✧

IT WAS A warm spring day. A few trees sported blossoms, while others wore new leaves. Birds called to each other in a mating ritual, hoping to find a mate before nesting began. The sun was shining, and she was done with her morning chores. A sense of freedom assailed her as she ran down the hill as fast as her young legs could propel her. Her laughter floated out behind her, as did her homespun skirt.

Reaching the flat land, she spun in circles. Her dull, circle skirt flared out. She'd asked her mother if they could dye their clothes magnificent colors, such as the red and purple of the spring flowers. Her mother had said those colors were not for them. It did not make sense to her. If flowers could wear such vivid colors, why not people?

She pretended not to see him hiding among the trees. Her brother teased her that Lionel, the lord's third son, had feelings for her. Even at ten, she knew the ways of men and women. Being married at twelve, while not common, wasn't rare, either. She needed to look to her future, and Lionel might be that future.

He stepped out from behind the trees and approached with a deter-mined gait. "Ho, Arabella, well met," he called out, as if he'd happened to meet her while walking, as opposed to waiting for her.

She smiled sweetly, her eyes sparkling at the coltish boy. He was handsome with his unmarked skin and thick, brown hair. "Good day, Lionel." Feeling unusually daring, she added, "My beloved Lionel."

His smile was reward enough, but from behind his back, he brought out a fistful of half-wilted wildflowers. "For you."

She took the flowers and held them up to her nose. Why did her father discourage her association with Lionel? He was kind to her. In time, he might even be lord of the manor. How could such an association be wrong?

They walked side by side under the warming sun. Saying nothing, Lionel reached for her hand, and she allowed him to take it, intertwining their fingers.

"Arabella," he started, his smile vanishing while his fingers tightened.

"I'm going to have to go away for schooling. I should have left years ago, but my mother begged my father to let me stay since I was the last of her other sons left at home. Reginald is away at school, while Archibald fosters at another household."

Schooling. She'd heard of it. It was something males did. Wellborn males. Boys like her brother took up the father's trade or were fortunate to be an apprentice to a tradesman. "Where is this school?"

Her heart made a little lurch as if it knew her life was about to change. There were some in the village who had made mention of how her mother thought too much of herself and put on airs, and as the daughter of such a woman, she was twice as bad. Her mother had assured her that such women spoke out of spite. They were not as well favored nor were their daughters.

Their hands still united, pulled her to a stop with him. Facing her, his dark eyes held hers. "Arabella, I know not where this school is. Know this. I will come back for you." He dropped a kiss on her hair from his superior height.

"I will wait," she promised, determined to do just that, despite her initial reluctance.

Later that day, she confided to her brother that Lionel had to go away to schooling. Her brother shook his head, muttering something about Lionel becoming a dress wearer.

"Tomas, you make no sense," she complained.

"Little sister, it is time for you to look elsewhere for a mate. Lionel is too high for you, but even if he does care for you, as the third son, he's for the church. Since his family has popish ways, they will turn him into a skirt-wearing Jesuit. No wife or women in his life from now on." Her brother shook his head, giving her a sad smile as he headed for the barn.

"He told me to wait," she shouted after him.

Her mother, carrying a double-bucket yoke, met her on the path. "Who are you supposed to wait for?"

"Lionel," she explained, knowing she'd an avid supporter in her mother. "Tomas tells me he will be a skirt-wearing priest who will take no wife."

Her mother's still beautiful face took on a reflective mien. "Ah, 'tis so. I suspected otherwise since his mother held on to him so long. Ye best be looking. Make haste as well, as the other girls have sized up the available men while ye been making cow eyes at Lionel."

She wanted to argue. Her mother had encouraged their association, but now everything had changed. Marriage of daughters helped to forge helpful connections. Her family was a moderate one in the village, not too poor, but not over-rich. Her father could cobble together a decent dowry, but her older sister, Helena, needed to marry fast. At fourteen, she was on her way to earning the labels of old and persnickety.

Lionel hadn't even left, and yet his abandonment weighed heavy on her.

✧   ✧   ✧   ✧

A GENTLE ROCKING woke her. She blinked twice and stared into Nana's face. "Did you drift way to the other time?"

Leah blinked, slowly allowing the room to come into focus, allowing her thoughts time to coalesce. "I'm not sure. I may have just remembered something from the past. I understand now why Lionel hates me, or I should say Arabella, so much."

Nana stroked her cheek with her age-freckled hand. "Why is that, sweet pea?"

"He asked her to wait for him while he went away to priest school. Arabella's family advised against it, pointing out she'd miss getting a good husband. Nana, she was only ten. How should she know what to do at that age?" It seemed unfair to expect a ten-year-old to make life-altering decisions.

"Keep in mind that to live to be forty was average for the women. To be an elderly woman was another sign the witch hunters used to point out association with the devil. I'd say it was a sign of lack of association with men in general, since most women died in childbirth or from the difficulties resulting from a birth. It was a hard life for a woman. Yes, Lionel would have expected her to wait. Women generally did what men told them to do. It would be enough of a reason for him to want revenge, especially if he loved her." Nana limped toward her dresser to pour a glass of water.

Her grandmother lurched a little without the cane, sloshing the water she'd poured. Even if the glass were half full, she'd accept it gratefully. The image of Arabella's self-serving attitude was bitter in her memory. Why would a man like such a little brat? Apparently, he'd come back but had not found her waiting. Where had she gone? Why had Lionel felt the need to ring retribution on the entire village?

CHAPTER EIGHT

A LONG, PIERCING scream jolted Leah wake. Had she fallen asleep again? She hadn't meant to. Where was she? It was dark. Who screamed? The gentle purr of Theodora reassured her, along with the glowing red numerals of her clock radio. The sound of tire wheels screeching and her brother shouting, "Floor it, they're getting away!" emphasized it was a normal Thursday with her father and brother indulging in their love of crime dramas.

Who would have thought such things would offer comfort? Occasionally, the local paper would run stories about teens helping in Third World countries or after natural disasters. The central theme was how grateful they'd become for what they had after such an experience. Usually, they joked about things like cell phones, hair dryers, or the Internet. There was so much more to miss, such as basic laws to prevent your neighbor from burning your house down and trying to do likewise to you.

Pushing up in her bed, she gathered a few pillows to plump behind her back and placed Theodora in her lap. The cat promptly curled herself into a circle and began purring. Leah scratched the feline's head as she pondered what made people act in horrific ways.

Some experts would say it was because the villagers were uneducated and easily manipulated by their fear, which was true to an extent. Leah had experienced enough mean-girl spite to want to avoid it, but she certainly didn't consider herself ignorant. Centuries later, people still resorted to genocide, while ethnic groups had been living in harmony, often intermarrying, until one charismatic and driven individual decided it was wrong.

Miss Santiago had explained how throughout history there seemed to be a need for an enemy for people to hate. Politicians, ministers, and advertisers capitalized on it. The enemy kept changing. Americans used to hate the Brits. Now, they were übercool, especially their accents. Before she'd been born, the Russians were bad news. They, too, had morphed into some sort of distant neighbor who was both mysterious and intriguing.

Depending on which group you belonged to, you hated the Jews, the gays, the Democrats, or anyone who didn't claim to be a Christian. The general impression was that different was bad and dangerous. Leah sighed. The more things changed, the more they stayed the same. In a high school of more than three thousand students, most of them tried to be the same.

The school did its part by issuing uniforms. Even if it hadn't, a uniform policy would have happened in a more insidious fashion. The popular crowd would have set the fashion tone, and those who could copy it would. Those who chose not to or couldn't afford the brands, would earn sly insults that sometimes sounded like compliments, but everyone would know better. Without fashions to comment on, the popular crowd liked to ridicule the actual bodies wearing the clothing. No one ever came out well, either.

The door cracked, letting in light as her mother peeped in. "You're awake."

"Yeah."

Leah's sister, Nora, always joked that their mother stated the obvious, which was often true. Her mother slipped into the room, leaving the door slightly ajar. Yellow light spilled in, a slice highlighting her wood floor, leaving the rest of the room in shadows.

Her mother smoothed out a place on her bed before perching on the edge. "Could you use some company?"

Nora would have pointed out to their mother that she'd already taken a seat before she asked the question. "Yes, I could use some company." It would be nice to have conversations that made sense instead of cryptic inferences to a past she did not remember.

Her mother patted her leg under the cover. "I miss talking with you. I know part of it is my fault because I'm gone so much with work and school, but I do remember when we used to sit and talk."

"Me, too." The image of them sitting around the kitchen table preparing a meal and chatting came to mind. They used to work together to prepare supper. Even Ethan had contributed. Somehow, that had slipped away as their schedules changed, and they'd started eating more sandwiches and pizza. "When did that stop?"

"I'd say about four years ago. The same time I decided I wanted to be a nurse. I knew there would be sacrifices to get there, but I didn't realize it would mean cutting out our time." Her voice stumbled on the last two words.

The darkness made it hard to distinguish whether her mother was close to tears or just tired. "It's still our time. Anything you want to talk about?"

Her mother forced a laugh. "Tons. What were you thinking about when I came in?"

Leah's hand stilling on Theodora caused the feline to turn her head into her palm, her way of insisting the petting continue. Message noted, she continued to stroke the cat. "I was trying to figure out why people tend to hate people that are different. Why the kids in our school are so anxious to conform to whatever is the accepted norm even if they think it is BS?

Why does it matter if someone is different?"

Her mother's hand tightened on her leg for a second. "It really doesn't matter if people are different. It's preferable. Can you imagine if everyone were pianists? There'd be no one to play the violin, fix your car, or examine your sick child. Currently, there's a perception that to be different is wrong. The people who resist being different have some strange agenda that usually makes sense only to them. Think about ancient times, when people worshipped several deities at once. You might have been friends with a person who followed Zeus, while you were an Artemis devotee."

The image of Stella and a few other friends in togas amused her. "It's like that with music. A few friends like country, others jazz, and still others classical, and yet we can still talk. I probably wouldn't want to go to a concert with them. Then again, maybe I would just for the experience."

"It does my heart good to hear you say such a thing. Makes me think your father and I did something right." Her voice had started low and melodious. It grew a little thin at the end, as if she was fighting back emotions.

Pushing Theodora out of her lap, Leah bent toward her mother and opened her arms. They embraced, with Leah resting her head on her mother's shoulder. "You guys did a lot right. The fact I don't feel the need to hate any group is a major point in your favor."

Her mother tightened the hug. It didn't hurt. Leah stretched her fingers and toes and flexed her muscles, causing her mother to ask, "What are you doing?"

"Just checking. Nothing hurts anymore. I think I'm well enough to go to school tomorrow." Leah knew she was weird. She wanted to go to school. For the most part, she liked it. What else was she going to do? Hanging around watching daytime television was not an option. Thinking of school reminded her of her friend. "What happened to Stella?"

Her mother released her and leaned back on her hands. "Oh, your father had to drive her home." In the dim light, her exaggerated expression of rolled eyes and wry smile were visible. "I imagine he debriefed her about jumping centuries, magickal healing elixirs, and such. He has a way of making the oddest things sound believable. He convinced me, right? A witch married to a Bible-thumper."

Leah never thought of her father as being persuasive. He certainly was intelligent and rational. It made her wonder what types of conversations her parents had had. Still harder for her to understand was why her father had knowingly dated a witch. "Maybe he thought he'd convert you."

"I doubt that." Her mother shook her head. "We never talked of religion, his or mine. We never even…"

"Hold that thought," Leah warned. "I want to think of you as my parents, not some rebellious, wild college students who did things I don't want to hear about."

Her mother's laughter washed over her, light and lilting. "Leah, Leah, you're being silly. You don't want to hear about how your father and I were crazy mad in love? All we could think of was when we'd be together next. When we were together, we made love so passionate the Love Goddess applauded us."

"Mom," Leah pretended to complain. "Please, you're traumatizing me."

Her mother bounced on the bed a little, overcome with mirth. Leaning forward, she touched Leah's shoulder. "You know, we still do."

"Ugh." Leah covered her ears. This wasn't news to her, since it was a small house, but she pretended to be astounded. "Years of therapy in my future."

Her mother pried her hands off her ears. "Listen, sweetie. I want the same for you. It could happen."

"Yeah, but there's this issue with staying in the same century. What if I meet someone when I'm in the past?" Not like that was going to happen, since most of them weren't big on bathing. They also had all those rules about what women couldn't do, which was pretty much everything except cooking, keeping house, and having babies.

"I've thought about this. This jumping back and forth in time is new to me. I've never known anyone doing it, but I've read about it. You have a mission to accomplish. Most of us get to work out our destiny in our own century, but you're special."

"Yay special," Leah mock cheered.

"It makes me wonder if there's something only you can do. No one in that time will suffice. Could be there's someone you're supposed to meet. If so, I would prefer they'd be here in a new version in this century, too. That's the mother in me talking. I've heard of people passing into other times and staying."

Leah's heart leaped. She even pinched herself with her ragged fingernails to make sure she was not dreaming. It would have to be a dream if her mother spoke utter nonsense. "What? Are you kidding me?"

"While you were sleeping, darling, I've been doing some research. It's difficult. There's the issue of, if a person stays in the past, they will never be born in the future, which means people won't remember they existed."

The words tumbled out in a rush, as if she were anxious to push them out or run them by her fast enough, she'd not make sense of them, but Leah understood perfectly. She speared one hand through her hair, which felt dirty and greasy, as if she hadn't washed it for days. Yuk, somehow, she was already going medieval. "Wait. You think other people disappeared into time, but we don't have any records of it because no one remembered them once they disappeared? Is that about it?"

"Pretty much. Still, the universe places us where we're needed, and right now, it needs you in the past."

Her mother spoke the statement with a mixture of acceptance and bafflement. Probably the same way the ancient Mayan sacrifices had spoken of knowing they were about to be killed and considered it an honor? Wait a minute. She'd be the sacrifice, not her mother. That would make her mother...the mother of the sacrifice.

"I don't want to go in the past or serve a purpose."

Wrapping her fingers around hers, her mother squeezed her hand. "I don't want you to go, either. So far, there doesn't seem to be any way to stop it."

That's what she'd thought. Didn't parents rush in and save their children from things that might hurt them? Goddess knows, her family had tried. Her father had disassembled their metal swing set after she'd taken a header from the sliding board. The swing set hadn't caused the accident. She'd tried to fly.

All the cartoon witches could fly. She'd figured she should have been able to fly, too. She'd never confessed why she'd fallen. She hadn't wanted her family to know she'd failed at being a witch. Often, she'd wondered if she were their natural child. Failure to fly had confirmed her adoption status. "You know I used to think I was adopted, just some ordinary child without parents you picked up one day."

"Really?" Her mother's voice reflected surprise. "You resembled Nora, and were little like me, but you're the mirror image of your grandmother when she was sixteen."

"I never saw any photos of Nana when she was young."

There had been a few in the last ten years. Nana would commandeer the camera and shoot photos, but seldom, if ever, would she be in them. In some ways, she resembled some suspicious tribesman convinced the camera would steal her soul. Her grandmother might have been on the run from the law, too.

Her mother fingered the covers. "My mother stopped appearing in pictures about the same time my father disappeared."

Her grandfather had vanished? She'd always assumed he'd died. There was an understanding among all of them that no mention was ever made of his name. Early on, when she'd started kindergarten and the other children had had grandfathers show up for Grandparents' Day, she'd made the mistake of asking where hers was. Nana had locked herself in her room for the duration of the day with a brandy bottle. The sound of soft sobbing had slipped under the door, which had confused Leah. Nana never cried. Her mother had explained that her grandfather was gone, which she assumed was a euphemism for dead.

Among the other students, a few divorced grandmas had used words like horn-dog and old codger to refer to the missing grandfather. Her mother had shushed her, asking her to never repeat the words. If her grandparents had divorced, she'd no doubt Nana would have had even more colorful names for her grandfather. All she really knew was his name had been Buell. Her mother's voice interrupted her musings, making her wonder how long she'd been talking.

"Before he disappeared, your grandfather was the love of your grandmother's life. Of course, I always thought of them as old since they were my parents, but they weren't, not really. He was as old as your father is now when he went missing. Before that, they were always laughing, playing, even dancing around the house. Nana loved to take photos. Ironically, it was usually her and Dad mugging for the camera. She called him her soul mate, swore she'd searched lifetimes to find him, and to lose him again devastated her. For a few years, I worried she'd never snap out of her depression, but then Nora was born, which started her living again."

A man disappearing off the face of the earth without a sign was a bit bizarre. It sounded like one of those crime shows, except Grandpa would not have been a sexy young woman trusting the wrong people in her effort to be a star. "Didn't you look for him?"

"We did. Called the police, for all the good it did us. They implied he was a grown man who could go where he pleased, and it pleased him to be elsewhere. Nana called in the Pagan community. We did physical searches, posted missing signs, ran ads in the newspaper and on the Internet. Several times that year, Nana went down to the coroner to look at unclaimed bodies fitting my father's description. They weren't him. The search took its toll on her. Eventually she took down all the pictures of him around the house and packed up his clothes." Her mother's voice grew hoarse as she wiped a tear away.

Such a disappearance smelled of foul play or even magick. "Do you think he could have been the victim of a hex or magick gone wrong?"

Sniffling, she shook her head, coughed, and then cleared her throat. "You never knew my father, but there was no one he wouldn't help. He was a jolly fellow, joking with the men, complimenting the women, and playing with the children. He'd to be one of the best-loved men in town. No one would have wanted to hurt him. No one."

"Do you think," Leah hesitated not wanting to give false hope to an old sorrow, "he fell into a time portal?"

Twisting her hair around her finger, she sat, saying nothing for a few seconds. "Maybe."

"If so, what about your theory that no one would remember you if you went back in time?" Leah feared she might have raised hope only to dash it down again.

"Well, uh," her mother started, then looked off to the dark corner. She spoke slowly, more as if she were thinking aloud as opposed to talking to Leah. "I've never known anyone who traveled to the past, except for you. My theory is not much of a theory, because it hasn't been tested."

It had. Leah realized she was the official time-traveling guinea pig. "It has been tested. I tested it in the last forty-eight hours. Did you ever think you only had two children?" The concept of a person vanishing in a second from the memories of everyone who knew her was staggering. What if for a few moments, her mother really did forget her? Then again, if she came back, wouldn't she bring back the memory of herself to all who knew her?

The sound of another car chase carried down the hall and into her room. She couldn't accuse the males in her family of having intellectual television choices. Her mother steepled her fingers and stared into a dark corner. "I can't remember thinking I only had two kids. Could this be because you keep coming back?"

It was the same thought she'd had, but it didn't answer anything. "I don't know what it means. I wonder if it's like a movie I saw once where all those who died went to a city to live, not unlike any other city, with stores, restaurants, and apartments. If people remembered them, they continued to exist, but when people forgot them, they began to fade until they were no more. Your father is like that. He exists because you remember him."

Theodora bumped against her, signaling she was tired of people ignoring her. Leah picked up the feline and cuddled her a little. Too bad people couldn't be more like cats and demanded simply what they needed. When someone ignored them, they went to someone else. Eventually, cats got what they wanted.

The slice of light on the floor widened as Nana pushed the door open. "What are you girls doing sitting in the dark?"

Leah's mother turned to the door and motioned her in. "Come in. We're thinking and theorizing. We've come up with something to consider."

Nana entered the room, using her cane to sweep in front of her as if she were blind. Leah realized the low light must have made it difficult for her to see, but then she decided her grandmother was mocking her lack of tidiness. "It's not that messy."

Nana reached her bed and eased down on the foot of it. "I never said it was. Makes me wonder why you're so touchy."

It was better not to debate with Nana. The woman was smarter than anyone she'd ever met, which humbled her, since Nana had never finished high school. The school of hard knocks and an internship at the University of Experience taught Nana all she needed to know. All the same, she'd a feeling her grandmother would not enjoy their sudden insight into what may have happened to her husband.

"Mother, Leah and I were talking about her sojourns into another century. While she was gone, none of us had a sense of her not with us. We didn't forget her when she physically left us." Her speech slowed as if she wasn't sure of her thoughts or was afraid of mentioning her father.

Nana nodded. "I agree. Never forget my Leah." She reached out to pat her legs outlined by the covers. "Maura, what is your point? I know you must have one, or you wouldn't have bothered with this long, rambling introduction."

"I do." Her head swung to Leah, who nodded a little to encourage her mother to continue. "What if father slipped into another time?"

"Maura." Nana's voice grew stronger as she pushed herself up from the bed. "You know better than to speak of your father. You're just being cruel."

"Wait," Leah called, surprised that she'd be the one to try to make her headstrong grandmother listen. "I know it hurts, but what if Grandfather somehow fell into a different time? I've proved it's possible."

Nana swayed a little as she planted her cane for support. "It could be possible. If so, why doesn't he come back?"

Her mother shrugged. Her grandmother seemed to deflate in front of her. It was up to her to do something. "Maybe he can't. It's not a problem of wanting. I never try to go, but then I'm there. When I'm there, I'm usually talking to someone when I disappear again. Guess that won't do much for my witch reputation."

Nana appeared to think about what she'd said and made two halting steps to the bed, where she eased herself down again. "I assume there was another you there, which allows you to join and leave at will. For Buell, there's only one him, which keeps him there."

Her mother reached for her grandmother's hand. "Dad used to be able to predict better than you."

"Oh yes," she agreed. "All he'd to do is touch someone's hand, and he could tell their future. Other times, just their name was enough."

Leah watched the exchange between the two. She thought she knew where her mother was going.

"What if Dad fell through a portal? He even sought it out because he knew it was part of his destiny," her mother suggested matter-of-factly.

Yep, only in her family did people casually pass through centuries and regard it as fate. Did non-magickal people pass through time and slowly lose their minds due to their inability to accept such a transition? She accepted it, but it was far from easy, especially knowing she could disappear into the past at any time. It sucked, since she almost had things worked out in this century. Not perfect, but she was getting there.

Emotions shifted across her grandmother's face in such a rapid sequence it was hard to catalog them all, but the last one appeared to be hope. "It would be like Buell not to tell me, afraid I might stop him, which I would have, if only to keep him selfishly to myself."

Leah had never seen such vulnerability before, at least on Nana's face. This woman put fear into high school administrators. "He could have gone ahead to be in place to help me."

"That's it." Nana stamped her cane in agitation. "That's exactly what Buell did."

What had she done? The only reason she'd suggested it was because her grandmother had suddenly appeared as fragile as a glass vase teetering on the edge of the table. She didn't think she'd take her seriously. Her mother's contented smile signaled she, too, believed her off-the-wall suggestion.

Great, now everyone believed her. When had she graduated to fortune-teller? Wasn't it enough to try to find a way to convince Lionel she was not the girl who'd jilted him? Now she'd to bring Grandfather back with her, or everyone would be disappointed. She'd never ever seen a picture of him. How would she recognize him if she did stumble across him?

CHAPTER NINE

THE ALARM JOLTED her awake as usual. Leah pushed herself out of bed, wondering why her legs wouldn't bend well. A quick downward glance revealed her bandages. A fading memory of being beaten flickered in her mind. A beating should stay in a person's mind, but it hadn't. Once she'd left the other century, the memories had grown faint. How was she going to succeed if she couldn't remember? Would she have to repeat the same thing over and over again? It was a good chance her body might not hold up to another beating.

A nearby notebook collected her dreams as she wrote down all she could remember, including the image of her and Lionel as childhood sweethearts. Was Arabella a mean girl of her time? What was normal by her time standards could appear mean in this century. The girl tried to make the best of her circumstances. Her writing was almost illegible as she filled several pages with her big, loopy writing. She could read it, but she might be the only person. She could type it later.

It might be a good record, in case she never returned. Not exactly a cheerful thought, but someone should know her story. The second alarm went off, reminding her she only had fifteen minutes to get ready for school. Dropping her notebook, she managed to locate a clean pair of pants and a polo top. Another quick search netted her panties and a bra. Her room could benefit from cleaning.

Her parents and Nana sat at the kitchen table, talking. Odd, but no one was hurrying to get ready for work. Ethan popped out of his room, still wearing his cartoon pajamas. That was going to put a clog in everything if her brother wasn't ready. His bus would arrive before she left for school since he was bussed across town. Eyeing him suspiciously, she inquired, "You're not sick, are you?"

"No, we're all staying home today just in case you disappear again. It might be my last time to see my big sister." Ethan startled her enough to allow him time to dart into the bathroom before she could. Was he making it up? She hadn't put it past her brother.

Giving up on having access to the bathroom anytime soon, she walked into the kitchen. Maps, large reference books, and a few photographs of a younger Nana looking adoringly at a grinning, dark-haired man littered the kitchen table. No one had to tell her she was finally seeing a picture of her grandfather when he'd been very young. Her grandmother had looked surprisingly like her. She picked up the photograph and cradled it in her hands.

The man had an open, trusting face with wide-set eyes and dark, back-swept hair. He reminded her of Dylan a little, not so much in looks, but more in attitude. This man had loved life. Life had done him the courtesy of loving him right back. Even though her grandmother's face was turned so she could look at him, it was obvious she adored him. What must it be like to be that much in love? Wow, she hoped she lived long enough to find out. It also helped her to understand the depth of Nana's sorrow.

Leah carefully placed the photo back on the table, she caught her grandmother looking expectantly at her. Nana waited for her to say something, so she did. "He certainly was a handsome fellow. He looks like he was a friend to everyone."

Nana's resultant smile let her know she'd said the right thing. "He was."

This was the first time anyone had ever opened up about her grandfather. She'd so many questions. "What did he do for a living?"

Her mother answered before her grandmother could. "He was an actuary in his nine-to-five job. On the weekends, he performed as a magician."

How cool was that? Leah looked at the picture again. It wasn't too hard to imagine him mesmerizing the audience with his dark good looks. "I bet he'd a rich, deep voice, somewhat accented, making him even more mysterious."

Her mother and Nana locked gazes, then turned in her direction. Her mother spoke first. "You're right."

Nana turned more slowly. Her eyes took on a slight sheen. "You have his gift. What else can you tell me?" She dabbed at her face with a cloth napkin.

Why was Nana asking her about a man she'd never met? Why would she know anything? She reached out for the picture, which her father placed in her hand. Thoughts poured into her head quickly, crowding against each other. Thoughts she'd have sworn had not been there before. She took on a thousand-yard stare as the thoughts gathered substance and became images in her mind.

Her grandfather was laying out the props for a magic show for a friend's birthday. They joked as they put a coffin on a sawhorse. Leah shared what her mind so vividly revealed. "He'd a close friend named Barney, who helped him set up for the show. His friend used to call him Ricky Ricardo because of his accent and his love of singing and dancing."

"Did you hear that, Adam? Maura?" Nana rotated her head, trying to catch each person's attention. Her fingers plucked a framed picture from the table. "Try this one. What do you get from it?"

Leah accepted the photo, turning it over to see that it was a wedding shot. A tide of passion and love hit her, almost knocking her off her feet. She staggered a little bit, grabbed an empty chair, and slid into it. "Never did a man ever love a woman more than he did you."

Nana gave a little yelp. "That's what Buell always said. Leah has the gift. His gift was the secret of his shows. Most people didn't believe he could read minds and thought the people he brought up were shills. He didn't just read minds, he knew the people. I think that is what made him so likable."

"How is that?" Leah wouldn't have minded being likable.

Nana eyes glowed as she explained, almost as if lit by an internal source. "When he met someone, he knew what they needed to hear to be happy. He gave it to them. I scolded him once when he told an awkward fellow he would meet the girl of his dreams. My mistake was thinking no one would find the man attractive. Buell assured me there was such a woman, and after what he told him, the man would see her as the girl of his dreams. All he needed was a little encouragement."

"Dad really was magick in the best sense of the word," Leah's mother said. "He made our house the place to be. Kids wanted him to guess what they had in their hands or in their minds, which he did. They didn't freak the way adults did. Every day was a party, until he vanished." The jovial mood surrounding the table faded away, rather like the mythical Buell.

Nana caught Leah's hand and squeezed it. "Find him. Bring him back."

Really, how could she? She hadn't even mastered bringing herself back. Somehow, she was supposed to wander through time, pick the man up, and return him like an overdue library book. She opened her mouth to explain why such a task was impossible and noticed they were all staring at her. Their faces reflected varying degrees of optimism. It was easy to understand why Nana and Mother wanted her to bring Buell back, but her father looked just as hopeful. He could want to meet the man who'd inspired such stores. More likely, he just wanted his wife to be happy.

How would she have felt if someone had disappeared out of her life without an excuse or a goodbye? Truth was, she hadn't have liked it if Stella or even Dylan had left in the night. There would have been plenty of rumors, none of them true. She'd never know. Right now, she'd her fingers crossed she hadn't been the person who evaporated into thin air or shifted into another century. They were still staring at her, waiting for her answer. "Never fear, Nana. I will bring Grandfather back."

Why had she said that? Worse yet, they all wore identical expressions of relief, as if they thought she could. Did she need to remind them she was still a kid, a few months short of her seventeenth birthday, but still a kid? The best she'd managed in her lifetime was a science essay about how pigs weren't aerodynamically suited for flying. It had earned her third place in the science *Imagine* essay contest when she was in fifth grade. Truthfully, not too many kids had entered, which explained her third-place finish.

How did she suddenly become so powerful? Why did her family believe she could do the impossible? Ethan walked into the kitchen. He gazed at the adults, then at her, before asking, "Why are they all staring at you like that?"

"Oh, they're just expecting me to do the impossible." she muttered under her breath.

Ethan had a way of de-glorifying everything with a few words. All little brothers did, but he excelled at it. "Better get changed unless you want to shift in your nightshirt."

Leah took the opportunity to change, dashing from the kitchen to the open bathroom. For a few seconds, no one would expect anything miraculous from her. She pulled off her nightshirt quickly. So far, she'd appeared in the past in period clothing, but it would have been just her luck to show up in her Hello Kitty nightshirt or nothing at all. No time to waste while dressing, she removed the bandages from her legs, marveling at the smooth, unblemished skin. Nana's potion had worked. She looked at the back of her leg, where a jagged scar from her failure to become airborne from her flying attempt had existed. Nothing.

The bandages dropped to the floor as she examined the rest of her body. Lifting her arms up, she stretched up on her toes, then twisted one way, then the other. Nothing hurt, until she smacked the shower curtain rod. Their bathroom was not big enough for stretching out. The tub, stool, and sink crowded into a small space left a person barely enough room to turn around. Enough of that, she got dressed in her school clothes.

What if she time shifted today? Apparently, that's why her family had taken the day off. Had her mother called in and made her excuses? *Sorry, my daughter won't be in today. She's in another century changing the world for the betterment of all.* Did time pass the same in the other century? Did a day pass the same? Had it been a week or a year?

If she showed up with her skin smooth and healed, wouldn't it convince them she was a witch? Her plan of action would be not to show anyone her skin. When Miss Santiago talked about women coming a long way as far as rights and status, she'd no clue how far they had progressed from the Middle Ages.

Brushing her hair, she looked at herself in the mirror. With her long, dark hair and tattoo-free skin, nothing noticeably tied her to the twenty-first century. She'd read a novel once where a woman's smallpox scar had branded her a witch. No one her age had a smallpox scar, since smallpox no longer existed and there was no need for the vaccination.

Her pale skin could use some help, though. Some foundation, blush, eyeliner, and mascara might help. She opened up her makeup bag and shook her bottle of moisturizer. Smoothing the lotion on her skin, she wondered about the advisability of makeup. How would her arch nemesis react to it? Sure, makeup had been around forever, but who had worn it? Was it the fast women, the evil folks, those guilty of a crime? Hard to know. It might be better just to be naked face.

Opening the door, she listened. A morning show blared from the living room while she could hear the clatter of dishes and running water in the kitchen. Someone was watching television, although she doubted it was her brother. Mother and Nana were cleaning the breakfast dishes. Her stomach growled, reminding her that she somehow had bypassed her last meal. That wasn't too unusual. Breakfast usually consisted of what she could reasonably eat in the car.

It might do her well to eat breakfast, since she couldn't guarantee when she'd eat again. The memory of smoked, dried fish on her tongue sent her in search of cereal. Her father sat at the table poring over outdated encyclopedias, which meant her brother was watching the morning show with perky hosts and fluffy news that contributed nothing.

She sniffed the milk before pouring it on her cereal. It smelled okay today. She brought a spoon of cereal to her mouth and chewed. Stale, no big surprise there. When was the last time she'd eaten cereal? The only time her family ate breakfast together was when her father made pancakes on Sunday mornings. Weekends were her time to sleep in, even lately when she'd been helping her brother with his lawn moving endeavor. It wasn't too hard since most people didn't want to hear a lawnmower before ten in the morning.

Her father's eyes searched her face. She tried to ignore his staring. It was weird. For the most part, she mainly spoke to her family as they each hurried off to their job or school. Suddenly, everyone watched her, just waiting for her to disappear. Instead of acknowledging his gaze, she read the nutrition facts printed on the cereal box. but that didn't stop his thoughts from coming at her.

Will this be the last time I ever see my baby girl? What kind of father have I been? Always working, staying late to finish projects, and even bringing work home. What type of childhood is that for her? She'll remember me as the father who was never there. Have I told her how wonderful she is? How proud I'm of her? How much I love her?

His thoughts were so strong they sounded like shouts in her mind. It was louder than Principal Sharpe's fears of Nana. "I know Dad, don't worry. You have always been and always will be a good father."

Her father's head snapped up. "You heard my thoughts?"

"Yes." She tilted her bowl to get the last of the milk.

"Damn," he swore under his breath.

Leah looked up. "I heard that."

Shaking his head, he said, "Wouldn't even matter. If I thought it, you'd still hear it."

"Maybe." She shrugged her shoulders. It was peculiar hearing her father's thoughts. Shouldn't some things be private? "It comes and goes. I found out Principal Sharpe is terrified of Nana."

Her father laughed, canted his chair back on two legs. "Any man with sense would be very afraid of your grandma. Not so much that she'd put the evil eye on him, but more that she can see into his soul and know who he really is, as opposed to the face he presents to the public."

It made her think of her grandmother in an entirely different way. "I'm not afraid of her. Neither are you."

"Not too much anymore. I used to be terrified of her," her father admitted with a sheepish grin.

Her analytical father wasn't in the habit of expressing a wide range of emotions. Just last night, she'd been traumatized her with the idea of the two of them being part of a wild, passionate love affair. It wasn't something she really liked to consider. Nana summed it up once by saying every generation thought they were the ones who'd created love and passion. This outlook made it hard to explain the existence of offspring. Leah shuddered at the thought. "Why did Nana scare you?"

Her father lowered his chair. His expression turned somber. "I figure she'd chase me away from your mother. I was the wrong type. One look into her shrewd face, and I knew she'd see I wasn't good enough for her daughter."

Leah pushed up against the table to stand and carried her dish to the sink. "None of that happened, so you had nothing to worry about."

Her father was silent, but his thoughts weren't. *All of it did happen, but Maura chose to fight for me.*

Leah did a double take at her father. Nope, his lips were not moving. Until he said, "You heard that too?"

That was hard to answer. It was like walking in on your parent when they were in the bathroom. You pretended it didn't happen so everyone could be comfortable. She bit her lip, stalling. What could she say? "Yes, it would embarrass him. No would be an obvious lie. She'd never mastered lying. Ah, yes, change the subject, "Do you think grandfather was a ceremonial magician?"

"I'm not sure. What I've heard about the ceremonial magicians is that they were very into details. Their rituals were precise and scientific in nature. Always done the right way at the right time. Might call them the engineers of the Wiccan world." Her father laughed at his joke, before continuing.

"They evolved from a type of priesthood. Some called them witches, but they always considered themselves better. It would be like someone comparing a chef to a cook. They both cook food, but the chef considers himself an artist." He stood and walked over to her, dusted her hair with a kiss. "As for you, I'll need to learn how to shield my thoughts."

"That's okay. I'll try not to listen. What am I going to do if I'm in a room with a whole bunch of people? Better yet, what if I hear someone say in his mind, 'I could kill him for that,' do I notify the police? People say that all the time when they're angry but don't really mean it." Goodness, this was supposed to help her out somehow. Already, it seemed like it had caused more trouble rather than providing any help. She rinsed her bowl and put it in the dishwasher. Her father stood with his mouth half open as he debated what he should say.

"It's okay if you don't know the answer. I don't know it, either," she reassured him.

He gave her a half salute and left the room. His last thought before leaving was about how his daughter reading his thoughts was like her seeing him in his underwear. Oh, Dad. How he'd ever fallen for her mom always amazed her. There had to have been other tightly laced students at college for him to associate with as opposed to her mother. It had to have been the lure of the forbidden. They'd initially met when her father had wandered into the Pagans United office as opposed to the Baptist Union next door. It had been her mother's turn to man the office, or woman the office, as she liked to put it.

If she didn't go to school today, what would she do? Sitting around wondering what might happen to her didn't appeal. She could get Nana to tell her more about her grandfather, maybe show her some more recent photos. Anything she'd would be at least twenty years old.

The house had a glassed-in porch the property owner called a Florida room. Nana liked it for growing the medicinal herbs she often used in medicine and rituals. The landlord, she remembered a man with a scraggly goatee, a receding hairline, and a ponytail. He could have been the poster boy for an aging hippie. She doubted he'd care what they grew as long as they paid the rent on time.

The smell of sandalwood incense met her before she walked into the room. Nana held a crystal in the stream of smoke, before placing it on the table and picking up a snowflake obsidian chunk. "What are you purifying the crystals for?"

"Your protection ritual," she said without turning around. "Your sister is here."

"What?" She hadn't heard Nora arrive. The choppy sound of a diesel engine car as it sputtered to a stop penetrated the walls. How did she do that? And why couldn't she read Nana's thoughts? Being able to tell where people were or when they were arriving might be a more useful skill to have.

Nora's throaty voice rumbled below her mother's and brother's voices. How her sister ended up sounding like some blues singer astounded her since she'd never smoked. She dashed to the living room. "Nora," she called out as she fell into her open arms. They both squeezed hard. Hard to believe she'd only been gone a few months.

Nora pulled back and looked at her thoroughly. Leah could hear her thoughts, not that she was trying to. They were there in her mind.

My little sister, she looks the same, but different. There's wariness about her that wasn't there before. I guess trying to stay alive, running from witch catchers, and being beaten half to death will do that to a person. What else has changed?

"I can hear your thoughts. That's another thing that has changed," she said, just in case her sister might go into some maudlin thought about this being the last time she'd see her little sister alive. She could do without that. The doorbell rang, startling both of them.

Her mother answered the door, recognized the two women, and called them by name. One cotton-topped lady in a colorful wind suit and walking shoes reminded her of the quintessential grandmother. The woman spotted her and wrapped her in a talcum-scented hug.

"Oh, my dear, my dear, I came as soon as I heard."

Leah wondered if she was the talk of the Pagan community. If she remembered correctly, Helena, who was squeezing the daylights out of her, worked with animals. Somehow, Helena communed with them and eased their distress. She was a regular pet whisperer. It made Leah wonder what she'd do for her.

Zaharra, dressed in a colorful caftan complete with headscarf, was Nana's most serious competition. Nana called her faux Romany, declaring she didn't have a drop of gypsy blood, her ancestors were Swedes, and she dyed her hair. Yet, here she was. Her grandmother thanked her for coming. The woman gave Leah a measuring look.

I don't see anything special about the girl. This is all a big scam cooked up by Esmeralda Hare. I wouldn't put it past her.

Leah folded her arms, gave the woman a knowing look, and shook her head. The woman's false eyelashes fluttered, and then she acknowledged her. "Accept my apologies."

She angled her head to her grandmother. "I'm not the one you should be apologizing to."

Hurrying to Nana, the woman offered her apologies, begging forgiveness for any doubts. Her grandmother caught her eye and winked. Being able to hear thoughts wouldn't be a total waste after all. If she went to school today, maybe she'd hear Dylan's thoughts. She thought about who sat around her in geometry and how their thoughts would dribble over into her mind. Connor, who sat in front of her, drew naked women in his notebook. Did she want to hear his thoughts? No, there had to be a way to cut out people she didn't want to hear. She didn't hear Nana's thoughts.

That's because I don't want you to.

Leah looked at her grandmother, who smiled. Yes, Nana had the skill. If only she could teach her. It also explained one reason why she was such a good fortune-teller. She knew the questions her clients didn't ask but wanted the answers to.

Four other older women came to the door. Her mother greeted them as Nana herded them to the backroom. Nora remarked near her ear, "It looks like all the old crones are here."

Her mother overheard them. "Yes, be grateful Nana knows so many. You two will be our only maidens. Some powerful magic will occur here today. Speaking of that, Nana ordered me to prepare you with bathing."

Leah pretended to sniff her pits. "Do I smell?"

Nora put her arm around her shoulder. "I'll talk to you while you soak."

Their mother held up her hand. "Nora can start the bath, sprinkle the herbs, even bless you, but the bath time should be used for contemplation and purification."

"Yes, Mother," they said in unison.

Leah understood the dynamics of rituals. It was like going to church and never listening to the sermon, contemplating the stained-glass windows or bemoaning the lack of cute boys instead of listening, and then one day realizing the sermon was about you. Yep, that's where she was. The ritual was about her.

CHAPTER TEN

T HE WATER SLOWLY filled the tub for the ceremonial bath as Nora pawed through her box filled with colorful silk bags. "I see we still have the same sucky water pressure."

Leah nodded. Of course, as Pagans they never complained about water pressure, never thought they could. People assumed they could put a hex on someone to get them to do as they wanted, or just threaten and that would be it. The law of three would bite them in the butt if they ever thought about doing it. It was like the golden rule, only three times as bad. Whatever you did would come back to you threefold. If you were nice to other people, then other people would be nice to you.

Nora opened a bag, sprinkling some in the water. "Angelica, for protection against negative energy, and it draws positive energy to your side."

Leah quipped, "I can definitely use that."

Her sister held up four bags and waited for her attention. The bath itself was part of the ritual. Nora had changed. They used to joke about being the kids of a witch, but her sister acted as if she took it seriously. It could have been because her little sister's life was on the line. In that case, it was all good.

"Sister mine, these four are for protection: arnica, basil, bay leaf, and blessed thistle. The thistle is especially potent and should aid you, being a medieval herb." The herbs floated through the air before coming to a rest on the water. Once in the water, they steeped, perfuming the air with a rich, earthy aroma that reminded her of the various herbs shops Nana insisted on dragging her through when she needed extra ingredients. She always liked the smell of the shops.

Opening another bag, Nora took a large handful and released it into the flowing water. "Balsam fir for strength. I gave you extra because I figured you needed it."

"Thank you." She did need all the strength and cunning she could get. A troop of well-armed soldiers wouldn't hurt, either. She inhaled the steam filling the room. "It smells like an evergreen tree."

"It does," Nora agreed. "I'm going to ruin all these great smells by adding camphor."

Camphor? Leah's nose wrinkled. Camphor is what they used to keep the moths away from their winter clothes. Unlike cedar, it didn't smell good. "Why?"

"Camphor increases your psychic divination. If you know what you're walking into, then you can develop solutions. That, along with your ability to read people's thoughts, should stand you in good stead." She dropped a small white block into the water.

The smell of mothballs filled the room, making her cough. "I'm not sure I can stand that."

Her sister gave her a sympathetic smile. "You will." Nora lit the white votive candles on the rim of the tub and the toilet back. With each candle, she called on a different entity. "Artemis, give my sister strength." She touched the lit match to the biggest candles. "Isis, guard my sister." All the candles glowed gently, casting a golden light over the crowded bathroom, masking some of its untidiness.

Pulling a bottle out of her pants pocket, her sister placed it on the sink corner. "Sandalwood oil. Make sure you anoint yourself with it when you're finished. It will help seal in the magick. Don't forget to scrub down with the salt first." The bathroom door closed softly behind Nora.

Too bad she couldn't have stayed. It would have been good to talk to someone about everything that was happening in her life. For reasons unknown, Mom chose to talk about how crazy in love she and Dad were, and still are. Then she found out her never-talked-about grandfather was a likable fellow who may or may not have been a ceremonial magician. He also might not be dead, but possibly fallen through time. If she could pick him up on her way back from dark and scary times that would be nice.

As if.

If she could figure out a way to stop going back, she'd. The various herbs' smells mingled, but the camphor dominated. Dropping her clothes, she reached for the salt paste and rubbed the rough mixture all over her body, avoiding her eyes. Not only would it flake off bad energy, but it would do a number on dead skin cells, too. Her skin would be glowing and protected. *Think of it not as a protection ritual to chase the bogeyman away, but as a spa day*, Leah told herself as she climbed into the tub. The water was hot, but not hot enough to burn her.

Her father used to joke that their landlord was smart because he made sure the temperature on the water heater was set low enough that none of them could ever level a lawsuit against him for burning themselves. Leah placed one foot in the water, then the other and gently lowered her body into the steamy broth. It was as if she were part of a stew, the main ingredient.

Leaning back against the tub, she closed her eyes. For a brief second, she worried about shifting in the nude, but she felt safe and protected in the water. Whatever power was in the herbs enveloped her. It probably didn't hurt to have thirteen witches in the house. Since most of them were about Nana's age, it meant they'd have plenty of experience.

How had she called her spirit guide? It had been so long. Something about a beach, she remembered that much. The image of a beach with gentle waves took form in her mind. Seagulls called to one another. The clouds bunched together, filtering most of the sun, but the air was still warm and humid. As she walked, the sand shifted under her bare feet, and the air carried the tang of fish. She tried to make her mind as blank as possible as she observed the scenery around her and simply existed. Suddenly, she was no longer alone. Two beings stood on either side of her. What was this?

"No worries, friend," her guide assured her.

Ah, yes, it was Jamaican Man, as she'd dubbed her guide in earlier times when they'd seen each other. He'd once told her his name was Lowe, which she thought was a peculiar name.

"Why are there two of you?" She was unwilling to look to her left at the unknown presence. It didn't feel hostile. Far from it, she felt warmth, acceptance, and some amusement.

"Sometimes you need more than one. The guides come, as needed. Look at your new friend."

Turning her head slightly, she took in the form of a woman about her height. A sense of familiarity overwhelmed her. It was Nana at a younger age. The features were so familiar. Didn't she see the same ones in the mirror every day? "Are you an earlier version of my grandmother?"

The woman smiled at her. "No, I'm an older version of you. Take heart, Leah, you will make it through this trial, wiser and stronger."

The thought did cheer her some, but spirit guides were often a facet of yourself you reached through meditation. This wasn't an actual older her, which meant she could still die or get stuck in the past.

Lowe clucked his tongue. "Don't be going there, girl. You know as well as I we act as we think. If you think bad thoughts, you'll have bad results. You're a champion. If I was a betting man and you were a horse, I would place my money on you."

Leah imagined herself being a horse in a race, stretching her long neck forward to win by a nose. "Thanks. I will win this race. What do I need to know?"

Her future self spoke. "Number one, things are not as they seem. People might say they do something for one reason, but they don't. Often, the reason is so deep, even They're clueless."

Leah spoke more to herself than her guides. "My ability to read thoughts would be of no help."

Lowe landed a hearty pat on her back that caused her to stumble a little. "What did I tell you, little bird? No bad thoughts. Know this. People do everything out of greed or fear. In the dark times, mostly fear. Fear of not being able to survive, fear of being snatched up as a witch, fear of not being loved, let them go. It was a dark time, not much love going around. Even greed was another way to stockpile against fear. Gold will buy food, protection, or even company to keep the fear at bay. Remember this."

It made sense. She usually reacted out of fear, not greed. She wanted to ask some more questions, but Lowe shimmered and faded. Quickly turning, she discovered that her future self had blinked out of existence, too. She was all alone on the beach. Even the gulls had disappeared into the clouds, and a long, ominous roll of thunder sounded as the sky darkened.

A loud hammering dissolved the beach scene. "Leah, are you awake?" Her mother's voice carried a sense of urgency. The woman would barrel into the bathroom if she didn't answer, pull her dripping body out of the tub, and start CPR. Locks were another thing their property owner wasn't big on. It must be disappointing to her mother to have gotten all this medical training and not be able to use it on her family.

"I'm okay." Stepping out of the tub, she reached for the towel Nora had left behind. She held the unfamiliar towel up and sniffed it. It was new. Hard to miss the symbolism: unused towel for the virgin. She refused to be a sacrifice.

Mother's voice carried clearly into the room. "It's time. Wear the robe Nora left for you."

A quick glance revealed the door not entirely shut. A flowing robe of blues and greens with a touch of silver hung on the back of the door. Nora must have put it there when Leah had been conversing with her guides. She'd certainly have remembered such an elegant garment.

"Just the robe," her mother instructed.

"Got it." First the oil, then the robe. She glanced back at the still-flickering candles. Ideally, she should put them out. Blowing them out would scatter her luck, and she didn't need that. Instead, she made a mental note to send her brother to take care of them.

Her hands smoothed the sandalwood oil down her arms in slow strokes, she thought of all it represented. Nana called it the workhorse of the oils because it aided in spirituality, protection, meditation, and healing. All good things she could use. Her hand stilled as she rubbed it against her belly, realizing it was also a component in spells to induce lust or love. "Not today."

The last thing she needed was for Lionel to remember his childhood crush on her. Nope. She didn't need some medieval lurker to complicate her life even more. Rubbing the oil into her elbows, she wondered, *Would it be so bad if he loved me? Don't you treat people nice if you love them?*

A memory of a recent court case of a woman who'd killed in the name of love played havoc with her theory. Still, had Lionel ever loved her? It was hard to decide what constituted love back in the olden days. The man obviously felt some ownership or rights over her. When she'd moved on, he'd felt the need to punish her, and obviously those who bore any similarity to her. It described more of a psychotic obsession as opposed to love.

As she pulled the robe off the hook, a tingling passed through her fingers. No doubt, as she'd bathed, the robe had undergone numerous blessings. If she'd been in a cartoon, a glow would have emanated from the robe. She felt a tangible presence pulsating inches from the fabric. She slipped on the garment, and it rested in the air instead of against her body. Enchantments lay warm and thick against her skin.

Leah pulled the hair tie loose and ran a brush through her hair. Always best to put your best face forward for the Lord and Lady, her mother would always say. Her grandmother had become a solid Goddess worshipper and had left the Lord behind, probably due to Grandfather's disappearance. Knowing Nana, it was her form of protest.

The face in the mirror reminded her of her older self, but that woman had seemed at peace. Leah envied her. She'd known what she was about and who she was. Then again, she'd already conquered her greatest trial.

Even though it was day, the house was dark, every curtain, every blind pulled shut against the light and possibly curious neighbors. They weren't party throwers, so the series of cars decorated with bumper stickers announcing *Friend of the Fae, Something Wiccan This Way Comes,* and *My Other Vehicle Is a Broom* were bound to attract some attention. The smell of incense and burnt matches wafted toward her. She could hear chanting in the distance.

Her mother waited in the hall with the ceremonial hood of her robe up. Her motionless stance allowed her to blend into the shadows. Leah startled a little when her mother placed a hand on her.

"Come, I will bring you in. The circle has been cast and the ritual started," her mother said in an authoritarian voice, which she never used at home.

Leah stifled her offhand reply and answered instead with, "I'm ready."

Her father stood at the doorway arch of the room and announced, "The maiden approaches."

A flurry of rattling sounds and furious drumming greeted his announcement. Leah knew the group was women only. Allowing her father to participate to such a small extent was a huge concession. Thank the Goddess, because she could use all the good energy she could get.

The chanting resumed, gaining energy with her approach, but she felt a tugging. Her gaze flickered downward. Her mother's hand was no longer touching hers, but the feeling of tugging increased. Her mother sketched an opening in the circle wall. Leah walked through, and the tugging stopped. It was like walking into a sauna of energy, thick, warm, and heavy as it surrounded her on every side. The women turned and touched her, urging her toward the end of the table, where Nana's important occasions white-lace tablecloth covered the rolling desk chair. Leah carefully took her seat, very aware of how the chair could get away from her at inopportune moments. The chair and she did not seem to get along.

Tucking her fingers under the edge of the chair, she held on, least it surprise her once again. One woman called for order, stilling the music. Nana stood, holding her palms up and out. She nodded her head in Leah's direction. "Thank you, maidens, mothers, and sister crones for coming to the aid of my granddaughter. You're all powerful forces to be reckoned with on your own, but united with the Goddess, the force of Mother Earth, the Elements, and the combined forces of honor, compassion, and love, none can prevail." Nana's voice gathered power and majesty as she spoke, ending in a crescendo that would have made many a wizard proud.

The women reached for one another's hands, creating another circle within the original circle. Leah held out her hands, only to have them clasped by her sister and her mother. When had they ended up on either side of her? They must have followed her in. It was reassuring to have them on either side. Nana walked behind her and interwove her fingers in Leah's hair.

The chanting started at the far end of the table and caught as if it were a wildfire burning toward her. "Oh, Great Goddess, Creator of All, watch over your creation. Protect Leah from all harm, evil intent, and those set upon harming her. Open her eyes, so she can see the hearts and intentions of those around her."

Leah closed her eyelids to better concentrate on the spell. The words were similar to what her spirit guide had said. People's words often hid their intentions. Could Henry mean her harm and Lionel want to save her? It made no sense. By the end of the ritual, things would become clearer. The heat, incense, and energy lulled her into a meditative state. Her spirit drifted high in the corner, looking down at everyone. A group of women held hands tightly as if playing a very competitive game of Red Rover. They chanted, some swayed, and a few had their eyes closed as she did, while others looked upward, fixed on other realms.

From the corner of the room, she saw her bent head with Nana standing behind her, her hands resting on her hair. Her grandmother had her head thrown back, calling out in a language she assumed to be Romany because she could not understand it.

Her older self appeared and held out her hand, mouthing the word, "Come." She looked back at the group, wondering if she should leave her own ceremony.

Her other self whispered, "This is your vision. You must know it to succeed."

It made sense in a way that strange things she'd never done before made sense. Reaching out, she grasped her older self's hand. In a twinkling, they disappeared only to reappear in a damp, stone room smelling of mold. Two priests sat at a trestle table.

The younger priest looked up, revealing the young Lionel's curling locks and deep-set eyes. "Abbot, I realize it is an honor to be a servant of Christ, but is it also not an honor to be a husband who sires children? Making even more to follow Christ?"

The older man pushed back his hood, revealing a tonsured head. "It is good you give this much thought before taking your final vows. There are many who are able to be father and husband. There are few who are capable of joining the exclusive brotherhood of clergy."

Her older self hissed, "Expensive," when the man said exclusive. Leah made a mental note to ask her later what she'd meant.

Lionel bobbed his head, agreeing with the older man. "It's a special privilege to be part of the Church, but I believe my place is to walk the ordinary path. I've a girl waiting for me. We have pledged our troth to one another."

The sincerity shining from Lionel's face stirred Leah's heart. He really did love her.

The abbot stood in a hurry, knocking back his stool. "A girl. Fie on her. You have not defiled yourself with her?"

"No, Father," Lionel answered, eyes downcast, while color mounted his cheeks.

Even though Arabella knew he'd never taken liberties with her, it appeared that her medieval lover had strayed from the chaste path. She wondered how she'd feel about this as a woman of that period. Would she expect as much? How would she feel if Dylan confessed to sleeping with Alexis or Lauren? That would be a bit much to accept. It was better not to know. She could not hold anything he'd done before he'd met her against him now. Maybe that was how Arabella felt.

Lionel found his cuticles intriguing as the old man placed a bowl on the table. The abbot poured water from an oaken bucket into a silver bowl. He moved his hands over it several times, allowing some powder to slip from his fingers into the water. The water bubbled once, then became opaque.

Leah whispered to her guide, "What's he doing?"

Her guide whispered back, "The old toad is up to no good. He's using charlatan tricks to fool the earnest lover."

Lionel's head went up to stare at the priest. "Divination is not allowed."

The priest waved his hand as if to shoo away the words. "Divination is not allowed because many cannot control it as I can. Rest assured what you're about to see is best for you."

"Notice he didn't say true," her guide mentioned.

Leah shifted her position behind the priest to see more.

Shapes slithered across the water as the priest questioned Lionel. "Tell me about this girl you love."

Lionel's face took on a dreamy expression. "She's beautiful."

An image of a blonde maiden with blue eyes shimmered in the water. Leah knew that couldn't be her and wondered what game the priest played.

Lionel continued to talk, not looking at the water, "Her hair is dark, as are her eyes."

The priest held his hands over the water, and the image changed as if the old man willed it. Leah could see between his outspread fingers. It looked like her in a vague way that the woman was female with dark hair. "Tell me more," the abbot urged.

Lionel sighed a little, reflecting on his love. "She has a strong chin and straight white teeth and a smallish nose. Dark, winged brows frame her eyes." The image changed as Lionel described her. Leah hated to admit it, but it looked more and more like her.

Smiling a little to himself, the man held his large hands over the bowl. "How long since you've seen the wench?" He coughed, then said, "I meant, girl."

"Two years now." Lionel looked thoughtful. "Soon, she'll be thirteen summers, old enough to wed and bed. She is especially fond of colors and glittery objects, rather like a magpie," he added with a chuckle.

Thirteen was old enough to wed. The sixteen-year-old version of herself hadn't had a real date yet. The man made a few more moves with his hand, dressing the water version in red and turning her sideways, probably to prevent Lionel from recognizing it wasn't her. A man materialized beside her in fine court clothes and a pointed beard. He began to kiss and caress her as Arabella responded to his caresses as lustily as any porn star.

"Look! Look at your beloved and how she comports herself in your absence," the man yelled, pointing to the water.

Lionel looked with avid interest, his brow furrowed, and he bit his bottom lip. "She never lets me kiss her on the lips. Why would she act in *such a manner? Who is this man?"*

The abbot picked up the bowl containing the writhing couple and poured the water back into the bucket. *"The man makes no matter. The important thing is the woman played you false. Women are not to be trusted. Her love for you was turned aside, all for a bag of colorful material."*

Leah looked at her guide in horror. *"I became a slut for fabric? I think not."*

"Remember," her guide pressed her hand against her arm, *"things are not as they seem. That devious man is able to extract people's thoughts and use them to create his illusions. Lionel saw you because he wanted to believe."*

"He wanted to believe Arabella could be unfaithful to him. The girl is barely a teenager," Leah complained, irritated that she could do no more than float about in an ethereal fashion. She was so angry she'd prefer to stride with purpose, kick something or, better yet, someone.

"Twelve is old enough to marry," her guide reminded. *"It is also obvious to Lionel that he won't be going back to you. The church expects noble families to contribute generously to the church coffers when one of their own is behind the walls. Lionel cannot follow his heart. He knows this on some level. To deal with this knowledge, he already believes you will play him false. It doesn't mean it will hurt any less. In your relationship, he was the one who always loved more."*

"Still." Leah felt the need to defend Arabella, but her guide pointed to the drama unfolding before them.

Lionel clutched his chest as if he'd taken a direct hit. *"Why would she deny me for a dress?"*

The abbot shook his head. *"Such is the way of women. Their nature is low and base. God has placed man below the angels, while woman is below the animals. A faithful steed, hound, or an ox can be better trusted than a female."*

Below the animals? Now, that might have been true for some girls she could name, but not her. She narrowed her eyes at the man talking gibberish, fisted her hands on her hips, as she glared at the old fool. Apparently, he couldn't feel her look. He continued to fill Lionel's ears with nonsense.

"Good thing you came into the service of our Lord before you were misled by the lies that fall from honeyed lips. Women cause men to stray from the good way as Eve deceived Adam."

Worse yet, Lionel nodded, agreeing with his statements. Of course, at that time, it was what people believed. She found it hard to believe that the pretty Arabella, who'd refused to let Lionel kiss her, had thrown up her skirts at the first man who'd come her way. She'd no doubt Arabella's *family pressured her to choose elsewhere, but part of her still cared for Lionel.*

"Women are the devil." The man's voice vibrated with hate. "They have intercourse with Satan and hand over their souls to him. Know this now."

Lionel cradled his head in his hands, and his shoulders shook as he wept. Leah watched in surprise.

The abbot frowned at the display of emotion and turned promptly toward the cupboard. Uncorking a decanter, he poured some wine into a wooden goblet. Using his body to block his actions, he shook powder into the cup and stirred it with his finger.

The guide pointed to the cup. "Here it starts. He gets the young priests hooked on a potion he's concocted. They become dependent on him for their supply, willing to do whatever he tells them."

What he'd put in the cup also explained the skeletal, drugged look of the Lionel she'd seen before. "I thought drugs weren't really popular until later."

The older Leah sniffed. "Reading the history books again. The Crusaders brought many types of drugs back with them. Wily men like Abbot Augustus there knew enough to demand a steady supply. He also had a ready supply of guinea pigs to try his potions on. Ever wonder how soldiers managed to kill infidel women and children without their actions sickening them? The drugged wine they consumed before slaughtering innocents could either wipe their minds of the memories or cause the fleeing children to appear to be monsters. It wouldn't be the first-time soldiers went into battle with drug-fogged brains. Watch Lionel to see what symptoms he displays."

The abbot handed the cup to Lionel. "Drink all of it, son. It will help you forget the faithless wench."

Her guide pressed her fingers into Leah's arms, returning them back to the Florida room filled with stoked women whose chants sounded tired and forced. The ritual was coming to an end, which made it the perfect time to return to her body.

CHAPTER ELEVEN

T HE WOMEN BEGAN to sing a song about the circle being open but unbroken. Leah sensed this without seeing it, just as she knew her father had stepped into the room now that the ritual had ended. No one would complain about his masculine energy as if it were a contaminant. Her mother still grasped one hand, while Nora wove her fingers through hers. Nana left her position at her back to herd her fellow witches into the kitchen.

Savory smells wafted from the kitchen as the women removed the lids on dishes they'd brought. Nana rounded up close to every plate they owned amid the clatter of dishes and silverware. Their family was not in the habit of serving more than six, which may have been all the plates they had.

Mother's grip tightened and loosened as she stood. "I should go help."

Nora kept a silent vigil with her in companionable silence. In some ways, Leah was rather like Helen Keller. Adrift in a world none of them knew or could understand. Her eyelids stayed closed as she allowed her mind to examine the revelations she'd received.

The older her seemed to have a deeper knowledge of the myriad things that motivated the human heart. The abbot's motivation puzzled her. Did he truly think women were the source of evil? Sure, there were chauvinistic males now who thought men were superior to women, but that was the extent of it. They might keep mental lists of jobs not suitable for a female. Sometimes they might express their opinions loudly. Overall, though, they posed no danger to her or the way of life of most American women.

The abbot needed to punish women as much as he needed to enslave the young priests. His potion should do the trick. She'd heard about soldiers in various wars becoming morphine addicts. The abbot might just be doing what those in power had done before him and after. Lionel used to be such a sweet, idealistic individual. Leah realized she felt compassion for the boy he used to be. The crazed, angry priest Lionel had evolved into did not merit her sympathy.

Someone in the kitchen called Nora's name, causing her to let go of Leah's hand. Her sister kissed her hair in passing and whispered, "Be safe, little sister."

That's all it took. With Nora leaving and letting go of her hand, the tugging increased, reminiscent of some horror movie she'd watched where tiny people lived under the floorboards. They were not kind, helpful brownies. No, these people were cruel and devious. It felt like they were pulling on her from all sides. She struggled to release the pull of the past. Maybe seeing Nana's plants scattered around the room would help break her trance.

Her eyelids popped open at about the same time that she sank deeper into the chair, dropping into another dimension. Nora's voice echoed as she fell: "Leah's fading. Stop her."

She fell, aware she was passing through time, seeing flashes of color and light. That had never happened before. What was different? Instead of hitting the ground in a clumsy heap, she floated to the ground rather like Mary Poppins, but with no umbrella.

She gently touched the ground with her bare feet settling on the cold-packed dirt. Tall trees threw out intimidating shadows with the setting sun. Once she made full contact with the ground, she shook out her robe. Her hands bunched the wide skirt of the voluminous blue and green robe. She still had it on. That was odd.

From behind the trees appeared a few heads. In the fading light, she thought she made out the features of Henry and Sabina. Henry eased around the tree, checking out her dress in detail. "Your garment is passing strange for these parts."

Sabina, possibly emboldened by Henry's behavior, stepped out from the tree with a swagger, as if she weren't afraid. "You fell out of the heavens like an angel, a fallen angel." Sliding closer, she reached out to touch the richly decorated fabric.

The instant Sabina's fingers touched the cloth, she yelped. "The fabric burned me. It is enchanted. You're a witch."

Ideally, she knew the robe was supposed to help her. Although all it seemed to be doing now was confirming her witch status. Still, she wondered if that was the plan. Instead of cowering and awaiting death, she was to stand strong. Now would be a good time to start as any. "I'm a witch. The gown is enchanted."

Old Margaret stepped out from behind a tree, pointing a gnarled finger at her. "You bear the blame for my house gone."

"Not really." Leah held her hands out in front of her as if she could stop the words and the incipient guilt they carried. "Ignorance and fear are the culprits, not me."

Turning in Henry's direction, she asked, "Didn't you tell me your property was seized for the church after the mayor named you a witch?"

"This is true," he agreed, and then placed a small twig between his

teeth to chew. His brow furrowed in thought. Pulling the stick out of his mouth, he gestured with it. "The mayor had need to put me out of the way. Once I confronted him with the knowledge, I knew he be cheating the townsfolk by only giving them back a percentage of the grain they brought in to be milled. Enough angry villagers would have turned on him as opposed to me, Old Margaret, or Sabina."

Leah listened, familiar with Henry's tale, but she wanted the others to hear it again. Strange how someone else they knew repeating the same premise that she wasn't to blame sounded more believable from lips other than hers. "In my time, they'd refer to Margaret and Sabina as collateral damage. They didn't do anything wrong, but just to have Henry, a man, accused as a witch would appear suspicious, especially if it were known he'd disagreed with the mayor."

Taking a cautious step forward, Margaret slowly circled Leah. Fearing the woman wasn't in her right mind after the destruction of her home and the loss of her beloved cat, Leah turned with her, never allowing the woman behind her back. The woman might have been packing a sharp knife.

Sabina placed both hands on her hips and gave Henry a knowing look. "People knew there was bad blood between Henry and the mayor. The village wanted Henry to be the mayor because he was a fair man, but the title is an appointed one. Rumors were that money changed hands to ensure the title fell as it did."

"Not rumors, 'tis the truth," *Henry said, the anger in his face gathering like storm clouds.* "All the more reason to be rid of me." *Kicking at a rock in the path with his booted foot, he swore something indistinct, most likely directed at the mayor.*

In some ways, Henry was the natural leader of the villagers. It paid to get rid of your strongest competition first. How convenient the church just happened to have these witch trials to help remove the troublesome element. "Why do you think there are all these accusations flying about cattle dying, crops failing, and witches? It is obvious the mayor uses it to get rid of people he doesn't like, but why does it work?"

Old Margaret answered first. "Times have always been tough. The earth makes us work hard to bring forth food. Calves, lambs, and even children die often before birth. Our sin causes bad things to happen, but no one wants to be guilty of causing their own child to die, so it is easier to blame someone else."

The urge to correct the old woman about the true nature of sin died a quick death. These people only knew what the priests had told them. Their minds were not exactly receptive vessels waiting for her to pour knowledge into them. "Still, like you said, Margaret, people have had problems all through the centuries. Why start blaming witches? What does it mean to be *a witch?"*

Sabina cocked her head curiously. *"You call yourself a witch. Mayhap you should tell us?"*

"True," Leah agreed, realizing it was the first time she'd ever called herself a witch in public. She'd gone to the regional meetings where people assumed, she must be a witch because of her mother and grand-mother, but still that hadn't always rung true. It had to be a personal experience. You weren't a witch due to your relatives. *"My kind of witch is not what you think. I'm bound to work for the good of all and the harm of none. I honor both people and nature. Many Wiccans in my time choose not to eat meat, to honor their fellow creatures."*

Henry shook his head as if astounded. *"That is more than passing strange."* Interlacing his fingers, he turned out his palms and cracked his knuckles. *"I've given much thought to all that you have said. I've thought on it before. Those of us who cannot read are at a disadvantage. The clergy say the Bible tells us to do this witch killing, but we cannot read to see if it is so. Scripture translation suits whoever is in power. Heard tell in France and Italy, the clerics meet to vote on which Scriptures they will believe. King James, a powerful man afraid of witches, put out the edict for the last rewriting."*

"The man is trying to deny his destiny." Margaret cackled. *"Rumor was a fortune-teller told him a witch would cause his death. Seems fitting that he rid himself of all."*

Sabina strutted in a circle until she gained everyone's attention. *"A visiting tinker I happened to strike up an acquaintanceship with had been up to London. He told me all about the king."*

Margaret gazed at Henry and Leah. *"That explains the new pots you acquired."*

Sticking her nose in the air and ignoring the old woman's remarks, Sabina continued. *"King James' favorites are all men, three especial men."*

Henry and Margaret gasped in response, but Leah couldn't figure out what was special about having friends. Didn't kings have friends? Then it hit her. Special friends. But that wasn't okay in these times. *"Aren't there laws against having special friends if you're a man, and those friends are men?"*

"Yes," Sabina answered, smacking her fist into her hand. *"Kings don't follow laws like we do. Who will punish them?"*

She'd a point. *"Do you think this whole witch hunt is a smoke screen to keep people from finding out about his boyfriends?"*

Henry stroked his chin. *"I hope not. I imagine that, besides his wife, most folks do not care what James does. It has been the way of kings to blame others. There's also word of Jews, lepers, and gypsies bringing plagues and pestilence. Then again, most people do what benefits them the most. Right now, chasing us out of town benefits them. I do not believe they even want us to go to trial. It is best that we vanish. If we went to trial, I would say all I know, causing questions to grow in the minds of fellow villagers."*

Leah understood what Henry was proposing. "You're saying we should just pick up and go elsewhere? What about your property?"

"It is the best solution. I believe my townspeople do not want to put me to the test and have me die in the testing. When I saw which way the wind blows, my cousin and I traveled to the next village to have a deed drawn up that transfers my land to my cousin. My land stays in my family, instead of going to the church. If the mayor moves against my cousin, then he'll do it with scrutiny, because all will remember how he was with me. I do not think the move too difficult." Henry shrugged his shoulders as if it were nothing.

The man had to be one of the most easygoing she'd ever run across. He reminded her of her father in some ways. Margaret didn't share his attitude. She stomped her feet, ignoring the pain that must have been resonating through her bare feet. "Easy for you, Henry. Your cousin has pledged to take care of you. In one fell swoop, he has all he ever wanted. I've nothing. Nothing, do you hear me? What little I had burned to the ground." Her eyes cut to Leah, letting her know she still blamed her.

Henry strode to the trembling woman and wrapped an arm around her shoulders. "I will take care of you. I feel beholden since my initial charge may have compounded the accusations leveled against you and Sabina."

Sabina folded her arms and tapped her toe, as if waiting for Henry to say something. She cleared her throat when that didn't work. Henry let go of Margaret and threw up his hands.

"I suppose you want me to offer to care for you, too." Henry said the words as if put upon. Sabina smiled, looking up through her lashes, in an expression that may have garnered her more than new pots. "I'm not sure what good it would do either of us. A new town will be full of new prospects for you. They won't approach you if they think you're under my care. On the other hand, I doubt I want to go to the trouble to look after you to have you take off when someone more to your taste arrives."

Sabina bit her lips, and then concurred. "You're right. You can be my brother wherever we stop."

Leah watched all this interaction and wondered what it meant for her. She wasn't here to be part of a traveling band of misfit would-be witches. Still, until the universe made her path a little clearer, she'd follow along. The sunlight streaming through the leaves reminded her it was daytime. The breeze chilled her slightly, making her wonder what month it was. Both Margaret and Sabina sported shawls, although Sabina wore hers wrapped around her hips, cinching her skirt closer, no doubt to emphasize her curves. Margaret huddled under hers, shivering as if she'd never be warm again.

Henry, on the other hand, wore a loose tunic-like shirt and a rough vest over it. He didn't act cold. Leah was sure men somehow stayed warmer in archaic times, unless it was uncool for a guy to act cold. In the mornings when her father drove her to school, there were plenty of jacketless boys at the bus stop, who acted as if they didn't have a care in the world. Some of them did look a little on the frozen side.

If things went well, somehow, she'd bump into Grandpa, recognize him despite the twenty-year gap since his last picture, grab him, and return home. It sounded like a good plan to her, with only a few possibilities of going very wrong. She hadn't found Grandpa. There was also the chance he liked it just fine here, which could be the real reason he'd never come back. Nope, she did not want to tell Nana that. Some people might think her grandmother was already in the angry mode, but currently she just lingered in the strong-willed and opinionated department. Leah never wanted to see her move up to angry.

There was her mission, as well, or the mission her family thought she was on. Was it a heroic mission like Joan of Arc's? She doubted it. Was it a personal mission, more like solving something in her past so she could return to her present? If so, what did she have to do? Lionel figured into it somehow, but that was the limit to her insight. That, and someone she trusted would betray her. Her eyes drifted to the three figures in front of her.

Sabina danced beside Henry, taking every opportunity to touch his arm and point out something. Leah's lips twisted as she thought Henry mentioned a wife and family. That made no matter to Sabina. She was an opportunist. Nana would call her a gold digger. It must be natural for her to latch on to whatever man was around. The woman would throw her under the bus, or in this case the wagon, if it would benefit her somehow.

Then there was Margaret. The woman leaned heavily on the walking stick Henry had cut for her. She'd no qualms of letting Leah know she blamed her for everything, from the destruction of her house and livelihood to the disappearance of her feline. Margaret might not mean to harm her, but her loud protests would be enough to convict her.

Henry's back was straight, his head held high, as he moved easily through the woods. Compared to the other villagers, the man obviously ate well and was in excellent health. His robust appearance varied greatly from the villagers with their frail frames, sunken cheeks, and lackluster expressions. Why was Henry in such good health?

July was the starving month. She remembered that from history class. People butchered their livestock in the winter. All through the winter months, they ate well on the harvest and meat. Spring was the time of sowing. By July, often their supplies ran out and nothing was ready to harvest. People often resorted to eating grass and anything else vaguely edible.

It was summer here. The canopy of trees was full and thick, not like the new growth of spring. Even though it seemed chilly, she reminded herself that seventy degrees was sometimes as high as it got for a British summer in the twentieth century. Added to that, they were in a shadowy woods and five hundred years in the past. It made sense it could be summer. With that in mind, Leah's eyes rested on Henry. Of course, he'd be in good spirits if anticipating a generous reward for walking in trusting witches.

As preposterous as the thought seemed, she knew she was right. Her spirit guide had emphasized it would be someone she trusted. It was hard to betray someone who didn't trust you, simply because such actions were expected. Should she find out Henry's motives? Her pace slowed more as she contemplated her actions. If she got close enough to Henry, she might be able to scan his thoughts. So far, that little talent had turned out to be inconsistent, not working when she needed it and only working with people whose thoughts she pretty much knew already.

If she could get close enough, she'd read Henry's thoughts to decide what his true intentions were. The sun broke through the canopy, highlighting the trio in front of her. She stopped, looking at the three of them as they came to a standstill. The sunlight bounced off something shiny. Flashes of silver peeked through the greenery. Leah didn't need to be told it was a trap.

Slipping silently off the path, she searched for a climbable tree. Her best prospect's lowest limb loomed just out of reach. The women's screams echoed through the forest. She quickly pulled herself up into the tree. Climbing higher, she tried to ignore the shouts. The robe made it surprisingly easy to scamper up the tree, clinging close to her body instead of catching on limbs. The blue-green coloring disguised her among the leaves as well.

Crouched on a limb, she tried to slow her breathing. They might be able to find her just by listening for her panicky breathing. She reminded herself to inhale slowly through her nose. Her legs were starting to hurt from her crouched position. Definitely not a bird in another life. Her perch felt unsure, as if any type of movement might end with her falling to the ground. A rustling of leaves alarmed her. Turning her head slightly, she found herself almost within kissing distance of a brown snake that seemed equally surprised to see her.

Great, she was probably in its tree. Were snakes like dogs? If she didn't show fear, would it leave her alone? The sounds of masculine voices *and horses alerted her to men right below. The large draft horses carrying armored knights trampled the undergrowth, sending a variety of forest inhabitants scurrying for safety. Leah made the mistake of looking away from the snake to observe what was happening below.*

Henry, mounted on a horse, pointed in the direction they'd come. "She was right behind me. I swear it."

One knight pulled his horse to a stop and pushed up his visor. "Your loss, farmer. Our master especially wanted the one named Arabella who is now calling herself Leah. Women." He snorted. "The silly wench thought changing her name would fool us." He held out one armored hand to the man. "Your pay is little without her."

Henry turned his agitated horse in a circle and pointed to the trees. "Look up. She has to be up there."

Her betrayer kept pointing up, but the men in full armor had difficulty following his pointing finger. Any movement to look up caused their visors to shut. The metal collars limited their range of motion. One knight, frustrated with his inability to look into the trees, shouted, "Go get her, farmer."

Henry dismounted and with a thunderous countenance strode to a tree, muttering loudly enough for everyone to hear. "She's a witch. She comes and goes as she pleases. One moment she's here, the next she's gone."

Leah invoked the elements to watch over her as she tried to control her shivering. It felt like something was crawling on her skin. Henry looked at all the trees, probably looking for one with branches low enough for her to reach. He strolled to her tree with a triumphant smile.

Mother Earth, help me now," she whispered, rubbing her hands over her arms to discover they felt somewhat rubbery. A quick glance revealed the snake had draped itself over her shoulders. She realized it wasn't her skin that resembled a basketball covering, but the snake's. Her hands wrapped grasped the snake's body. The brownish reptile lay complacent against her, taking advantage of her body heat. She gently lifted the snake and held it in front of her. With a mental apology to the snake, she dropped it without a sound.

The six-foot snake landed on Henry. His screams indicated a fear of snakes, or of unexpected objects falling from trees. The knights laughed as he danced around, trying to free himself from the reptile. The snake wrapped itself around his neck, holding on after its most recent flight. "Do something!"

One knight unsheathed a sword and waved it over his head. "I can cut it from your neck." He demonstrated with a few sweeping arcs of his sword.

The knight looked a little wobbly. Leah was unsure if he was tired or drunk. Henry must have thought the same, because he yelped, "No sword!"

The two knights signaled to each other, put down their visors, and galloped off. Henry staggered to a stop and dropped to his knees. "This is how it ends." He fell forward, resting on his elbows. The snake felt close enough to the ground to slither from Henry's neck, making a slow turn through the grass to head back to its tree, which guaranteed Henry would not be climbing it any time soon.

Henry pushed up, threw a malice-filled look at the snake. The lower part of his tunic had darkened with moisture, demonstrating his real fear of reptiles. Nope, Henry wouldn't be climbing up the tree. Obviously, Mother Earth had sent her the snake. Thank the Goddess, it wasn't hurt.

Cursing, Henry swung into the saddle of his horse to follow the other riders. Would he come back and search for her again? Would he assume she'd just vanished since she'd before? Her thighs could only take so much of pretending to be a bird on a wire. The forest sounds of birds calling and animals rustling under the underbrush began to return, assuring her the men were gone.

Reaching to another limb for balance, she pulled herself upright, ignoring her protesting muscles. She'd give them another thirty minutes to get out of the area, but she needed to get moving while there was still daylight.

The brown snake moved slowly up the tree. Leah watched with both gratefulness and trepidation. Couldn't say she'd ever been fond of snakes, but then again, she'd never had any experience with them, either. This snake had saved her life. It really was a very special snake. As if reading her thoughts, the snake made its way to her branch. It slithered up to her and stopped. The lower half of its body twined around the branch, the other half, which included the head, rose to look in her direction as if trying to communicate.

Lowering carefully back down to her haunches, she reached out a hand to lightly touch the reptile's head. "Thank you, Brother Snake. I owe you."

A light of recognition shone in its beady eyes. Its tongue slid out, tasted the air, and withdrew into its mouth.

Leah kept her hand on the serpent's head deciding it wasn't that scary at all. "I'm sorry for throwing you. I understand now we're all pearls on a string."

An impression of flight, then a sudden ending of flight filled her mind. Her mouth dropped open. Could she read the snake's mind? Jerking her hand back, she considered the snake. Could it tell her which way to go? She doubted it.

Standing gingerly, she stepped carefully over the snake. Using the branches, she backed her way down the tree until she got to the last branch and had to jump. No clue, which way to go, she reached for the pendant Nana had given her. Fisting her fingers around it, she prayed for guidance. Gaia, your strength is strong in this world. Please guide me." The sun appeared to be on its descent. In that case, she'd head to the east, the direction of new beginnings.

CHAPTER TWELVE

*T*HE BIRDS CALLED *out to one another as she made her way through the undergrowth. Shoes would have been beneficial. Of course, back when she'd been in her house she hadn't had to worry about shoes. "Ouch," she yelped, and hopped. A nearby sapling held her up as she examined her foot. A good-size thorn had imbedded itself in her big toe. Luckily, there was enough base for her to pull it out. Blood trickled out of the wound. Not good. Even she knew walking on it in the dirt would cause an infection. Who knew what medieval germs might do to her? Possibly give her some disease they'd managed to eliminate through vaccinating generations of people.*

Some antibiotic cream would have come in handy. Better yet, a band-age would have been nice. Remembering hearing something about saliva being helpful in the healing process, Leah spat in her hand and rubbed the spit on her toe. All the spit did was rub off some dirt. She couldn't walk on a bleeding foot. Leah used the edge of her robe to apply pressure, which was challenging since she'd to keep her balance in a semi-crouched position on one foot. Mentally, she counted off the seconds. By the time she got to ten, she realized sitting down would make it easier. Letting go of her injured toe, she balanced on the heel of her hurt foot as she eased herself to the ground.

Holding her robe down, she made sure the fabric touched the ground protecting her skin. The last thing she needed was poison ivy on her butt. That would have been grand, as if things weren't already. Cross-legged, she was better able to examine her toe. Her thumb felt for the hole. Not finding it, she pulled her foot closer to her face. Nope, nothing, except a clean spot on her big toe, but that couldn't be right. It had to have been the other foot. Pulling up the opposing foot, she examined it, which was filthy. Employing her spit method, she cleaned the other toe, which looked fine.

Okay. Neither toe had a hole. She wiggled both toes. Both toes worked, and there was no pain. Had she stepped on a thorn? Had she imagined all of this? Was she starting to lose her mind? It might be a result of traveling through time rapidly. Leah placed her hands behind her for support, she rested as she considered the various scenarios. Right now, she could be in a padded room to keep her from hurting herself. None of this was real, not even the mild discomfort in her right palm. Pulling up her right hand, she looked at it. Pressed into it was a dirty, bloody thorn.

It hadn't pierced the skin. Apparently, it had been lying on the ground where she'd thrown it after extracting it from her toe. She held it up close to her. The blood was still wet on the thorn. The palm of her hand bore the impression of the thorn and a smear of blood. It had happened. She wasn't in a padded room somewhere. The only thing she'd done, other than clean it with her saliva, was use her robe to staunch the bleeding. It had to be the robe, didn't it?

Never a big one for pain, she forced herself to test her hypothesis. Jabbing the dirty thorn into her palm enough to pierce the skin, she watched it bleed before applying the robe to it. Concentrating, she felt the pain leave and the skin heal. Dropping the robe, she examined her unpierced palm. "Whoa, who knew?" Actually, she did. Nana was full of mysterious healings, and apparently magickal garments, too.

Still, this was the first time she'd experienced it. At home, when they'd wrapped her in bandages with the cream, she'd been so weary all she'd done was sleep. She'd believed she'd whip marks on her body because Stella, Nana, and Mother had assured her she did. She saw them too. Just a few minutes ago, she hadn't paid attention to when her toe stopped hurting, focused on leaving the woods before dark. This time, she knew. She'd felt the healing. She'd witnessed the magick. This changed everything.

Gingerly, she put her formerly injured foot down and felt no pain. That was good. Still, it was hard to get her mind around a magickal healing robe. Fingering the fabric, she continued eastward. The robe was attractive with all the blues and greens in it. Looking like leaves sometimes and flames when she looked it again. Occasionally, it flashed silver, but that color had somehow dulled when she'd crouched in the tree. You would think everyone would want robe so special that it clung to her when climbing or running to stay out of the way. No underbrush caught on it, either. It was almost as if it moved away.

Those thirteen women versed in the nature-based religions had each held her robe and put some version of themselves into it. They'd whispered incantations and invoked protection from the various goddesses. Since Nana's group was not pro-god, they only believed in the Divine Feminine, so they never bothered to call on any gods. Her father could have invoked the Lord of the Forest to look over her. He'd sent the snake.

Up to now, she'd been ready to distance herself from her family's faith to give herself a better chance to date Dylan. Wow, it made her wonder if this trip into the past had been more for the current Leah, than her past life as Arabella. Overall, she didn't really like Arabella much, but she tried to remember she was a product of her time. Emotions, motives, and *actions that didn't jive with her present-day interpretations weren't necessarily wrong for this time.*

A bunny darted in front of her. It sat and looked at her for a moment, showing no fear. This was odd, considering bunnies often ended up in stew pots in this century. Its casual attitude might have been more understandable in her neighborhood, where all the rabbits had to fear was a half-hearted chase by an overfed pooch. They usually outsmarted the dog by standing still, since dogs chased only things that moved.

The hare hopped forward about a foot, then turned to look at her. It stared at her with its gentle brown eyes. Leah took a step toward the creature. The bunny hopped a few more feet, then looked at her again. It acted as if it wanted her to follow. How weird was that? She took another step. The bunny glanced over its shoulder to make sure she still followed. After a while, it quit looking, confident Leah had finally gotten with the program.

The light in the woods grew dimmer as birds found their perches to roost for the night. Leah knew the nocturnal animals would be out soon. What ran around at night in the woods? True, she was a city girl, but she did take biology. Raccoons, possums, and owls tended to dominate the night, with the occasional shrew, mouse, and rat. A shudder ran through her at the thought of rats. Wait a minute? Didn't rabbits come out at dawn and dusk, too? This little fellow had come out early.

She considered the white-tailed bunny in front of her. It was an enchanted bunny, so that made sense. Enchanted? Really, those words were in her head. Better yet, she accepted them as if she were in a fairy tale. What if the harmless little bunny was leading her astray and taking her to some place evil?

Henry was a bunny, in a way. She'd trusted him, never thought he would hurt her. Yep, she remembered how that turned out. Barking sounded in the distance. Had the villagers returned with dogs to hunt for her? Another bark answered the first one. Then there seemed to be a chorus. Not dogs. She'd watched Dracula *enough to recognize the children of the night, wolves. Hurry bunny. Get us there. The rabbit increased its speed, which made sense, since rabbits were a wolf delicacy.*

They broke into a clearing where a neat little cottage sat surrounded by a wood fence. Glancing at the smoke curling out of the chimney, she wondered who lived there. A child brought up on Grimm's fairy tales would expect an evil witch, but she knew better. Nana had let her know most fairy tales scared kids into appropriate behavior. Children wandering off into the woods could end up as dinner for large predators. The thought had her swinging open the gate and hoping for the best. The bunny hopped in step with her, which didn't surprise her.

The door opened. A tall, bearded man stood in the door. Leah bit her lip, taking in the man, trying to decide if she could trust him. Everyone in this century had proved to be unreliable, always out for themselves, unlike in her century, where the intentions were the same, but people at least tried to hide them. His eyes were alert, intelligent. He allowed her to take his measure before smiling. "So, have you decided yet if you can trust me?"

How did he know? He'd sent the bunny. She looked around for the bunny, but it was gone. A man, a teen really, walked around the side of the cottage, attired in a tunic, drying his face. His brown hair was a bit unkempt and long. He lowered the towel and smiled when the bearded man praised him.

"Good job, Simon, leading my granddaughter home."

Granddaughter? She looked at the bearded man and tried to see the dapper man depicted in the pictures Nana had showed. His hair and beard were white, which time and living here would have affected. Her head swiveled to regard Simon, whose eyes appeared to have an interested gleam. Still, they were the same soft brown as the rabbit's.

Her grandfather? It felt weird calling him that. He flourished a walking stick and reached past her to rap Simon on the shoulder. "Take care to remember she is my granddaughter."

The teen colored, hung his head, and murmured, "Sorry, Master."

Master? This was becoming stranger and stranger. Was Simon a slave?

Her grandfather stood aside and motioned her in. "Come in, come in, I will answer all your questions. I bet your mother calls you Leah."

"How did you know?" This man she'd never met before could not only read her thoughts, but he knew about her.

He chuckled. "All in good time. Have a seat." Two chairs sat near the fireplace, where a large dog dozed.

She sat in one while she watched her newfound grandfather dip a cup into a bucket of water to fill a kettle. After several cups of water, he hooked the kettle on an iron arm that he swung over the fire. "We'll have tea in no time," he commented, as he turned to sit.

Leah cataloged all the changes in him since his last photograph. She'd had no clue he'd be so wizardly looking with his long beard and hair.

"I know you have questions. You may wonder why you can't read my thoughts. Well, I've walls in place as do most good ceremonial magicians."

She hadn't thought that far. She tried to open her mind to see if she could receive anything. A weak message came to her, but not in her grandfather's voice. Something about her being beautiful, special...she preened at those words, until they were followed by "sure she's not wearing anything under her robe." Her head swiveled as she pinned

Simon with a glare, obviously the source of the thoughts.

Grandfather stood, pointing his index finger at the door. "Out," he shouted in Simon's direction. "Stay out until you have control of your thoughts. I taught you better than that."

Simon scurried out of the house, his actions reminiscent of the rabbit. Grandfather shook his head. "He shows great promise, but still he's an adolescent male, and when faced with a beautiful girl his mind tends to run to the earthy side. Forgive him for my sake. There's much to like about him."

Leah nodded her head. It wasn't as if Simon had been the first boy to ever ogle her. She wasn't offended. The ability to read people's minds perplexed and intrigued her. Would she be able to know the answers for a test without studying for it? Would she understand people better? "Grandfather, you can read people's minds. Is it helpful?"

His teeth flashed in his beard. "The sad truth is most of what people think is not worth knowing. Humans must be the whiniest creatures alive. There's a lot of 'I'm tired,' 'I'm hungry,' 'this is too hard,' 'that's unfair.' When They're whining, they're hatching plots against one another for gain, sometimes revenge and, in some cases, love, but that's only what they call it. A person never hatches a scheme to snare love. It happens, one of the grandest occurrences in the universe."

Her plan to tap into her teachers' minds flamed out. She could do without knowing a teacher hated his job, had missed breakfast, or wore contacts that were bothering him. The last part about love had caught her attention. "If love is one of the grandest occurrences in the universe, why did you leave Nana?"

"Esmeralda." He said the name and placed a hand over his heart. "Is she still spitting fire?"

Leah had almost forgotten her grandmother's real name. She always called her Nana, her mother referred to her as Mother, while friends all called her Baba Esme. "Daily. I'm not too sure if she'll be thrilled if you're alive or will be ready to beat you with a stick. Can we go now and find out?"

Grandfather shook his head as he swung the kettle off the fire. Lifting the lid, he threw in a handful of leaves. "Ah, it's not that easy, little one. I came to this time when I divined one of my grandchildren would have need of me. The portals of time aren't always easy to find or to open. Twenty years ago, I found this one and knew it might be my only chance to help you."

If her grandfather had willingly gone into the past, why did she keep going back and forth? "It makes no sense to me. You wanted to be here and used your skills to find your way here. I don't want to be here, but I keep coming back. Why is that?"

Her grandfather stood to lift two mugs from the shelf. He poured steaming, fragrant tea into each cup and handed her one. "There's no real access to sugar, but I can offer you honey." He held out a small earthen pitcher to her.

She drizzled some into her tea, realizing Grandfather hadn't answered her question. She placed the cup to her lips and tasted the aromatic tea. It was quite delicious, even though she wasn't much of a tea lover. Everything wasn't bad in the past.

His eyebrows beetled down as he spoke. "I've given a great deal of thought and research to this. Because I'm here in this time, I witnessed the courtship and love of Arabella and Lionel and the corruption of that love for evil."

"Did you actually see it?" She imagined her grandfather in the bushes while Lionel offered his wildflower bouquet to Arabella.

"Ah, you'd make a Peeping Tom out of me." He sipped from his mug. He sighed and then gestured to a dark mirror leaning against the wall. "I used my scrying mirror to see them. I felt Arabella's soul, and I knew it was part of my future granddaughter. This was the reason I came. In a way, I spied on the two of them, but I needed knowledge to help you."

Leah wondered why he hadn't helped her when she was hiding in the trees from the peasants. Why hadn't he helped her when they'd lashed her? What about when she was hiding from Henry? Her gaze darted to the man sitting across from her. He'd already demonstrated he could read her thoughts.

"Ah, little one, I've helped you as much as I could. I cannot leave this place." He gestured to the room. "I cannot even step outside the fence. This time portal is my home until it blinks out of existence in three days. In that time, I will be transported back to my dear Esmeralda."

Her mind caught on the facts that he'd helped her and that he would transport back in three days. "When you go, I want to be with you."

"That's my plan." He leaned forward to pat her hand affectionately.

Leah considered him. He seemed nice and rather what you'd expect in a grandfather. Well, if your grandfather happened to be a ceremonial magician. "How did you help me?"

"Harumpft." He cleared his throat, clearly bristling at the implication that she doubted him. "As you know, I cannot leave this place, but I could see what was happening. Do you think the men and their dog turned away per chance? No, I put the fear of the tree folks in their heads. As for your lashing, it was a gentle one. Most people die from it. I held the wrist of the flogger, making it hard for him to put much force into his swing. He was a brute. It wasn't easy, let me tell you." He pointed to his head as an explanation of how he'd accomplished such a feat.

Leah thought she understood. "The snake I threw on Henry. That was you, too. Was the snake Simon?"

Her grandfather laughed. "Simon would not like to hear you liken him to a snake. No, that was Horace."

"Is he another apprentice?" How many did her grandfather have?

"No, Horace is a snake. I've become very familiar with the woodland creatures with my time here. I've named most of them. I'm not sure if I'm ready to socialize with regular folks." He pursed his lips and peered the fire.

Her grandfather had willingly given up so much for a granddaughter he'd never met because of something he'd seen in his scrying mirror. His faith and love had to be absolute. She wished she'd both.

Setting his cup down, he looked at her. "It will come. I imagine you want to hear the story about Lionel and Arabella."

CHAPTER THIRTEEN

L *EAH WANTED TO hear their story. In a way, it was her story, too. Often, souls re-enacted the same scenes from past lifetimes until they managed to get it right. Some reincarnation theories believed you met the same souls from previous lifetimes in other bodies, which explained why you might meet a total stranger and have an immediate dislike for them. On the other hand, you could meet a spouse or a lover from an earlier lifetime and feel an immediate pull.*

The door opened, allowing a rush of cool air and a sliver of darkness in, along with Simon. He sat near enough for Leah to notice his thoughts consisted of her being the granddaughter of the great wizard. He was trying. She'd give him that. Grandfather acknowledged him with a nod but continued speaking.

"Lionel's family was the only noble family in the area. There were some successful merchants, but no other nobles nearby. It wasn't surprising that Lionel played with the local children. As a boy and the third son, he was of little importance." Grandpa stopped long enough to stare into his cup with a frown, and he reached for the kettle to pour more tea into his mug.

Leah thought about her little brother, who was the third child and a boy. No way you could have ignored him. As if he would ever let you. "Why didn't they pay much attention to him?"

"In noble families, it is all about passing on the name. You need male children to do that."

Leah snorted her thoughts on the custom, but circled her hand for him to continue when Grandfather looked at her questioningly.

"The heir and the spare, they like to call the first two sons. The first one takes over the title and the estate. The second trains for the military. Reginald went to school to learn how to run the estate and make the important connections he needed with other first sons. Archibald, the second son, went to a different household to learn to be a knight. This ensured more connections for the family. The more connections you have, the better off you're. In a time of attack or need, you can call on your connections."

Simon spoke out, startling Leah because she'd forgotten he was there.

"Boys must learn a craft to survive. Farming is for the firstborn because the land goes to the firstborn. No land grants in my family."

Leah turned to look at the young man sitting cross-legged on the floor. "Did you decide you wanted to be a wizard and searched for my grandfather?"

Simon looked down as he answered, making his reply a little hard to hear. "The miller was my master. He found fault with my work and beat me."

Grandfather explained more. "He ran into the woods and became lost. He wandered for days, hungry and hurt. Simon was fearful to return to the miller, who would beat him more for deserting his post. I sent a wild creature out to bring him to me."

Simon made a rueful expression, mumbling something about a pack of wolves.

A smile flitted across Grandfather's face as he regarded the sullen boy. "The wolves were my last resort. I sent birds, a raccoon, even a bunny, but you ignored them all."

"Not true," Simon complained. "I tried to catch the hare for supper."

Grandfather shook his head. "That was two or three years ago. Simon has become a talented apprentice in the intervening time. Where was I in the story?"

"You were..." both Simon and Leah started together. Simon gestured for her to continue.

"The part about Lionel and how his family didn't pay too much attention to him," Leah prompted.

Stroking his beard for a moment, his eyes glittered with amusement. "I was trying to remember what things were like back in the twentieth century. Children were kings whose parents carted them around to numerous events for their benefit. Parents trumpeted their achievements, no matter how minor, as if they were gods who'd managed to create a new planet. Are things still about the same?"

"Worse in some ways," Leah admitted, wrinkling her nose as if she smelled something nasty.

"Here in this time, people do not fuss over their children. They try to avoid attachment because many die before five years of age. Often, the children don't get a name until they turn two."

Leah hated interrupting, but she'd to know. "Why don't they name the children?"

Simon volunteered the information with enthusiasm. "You're often named after someone in the family. If the child dies, the name is wasted."

"So for a while," Grandfather continued as if not interrupted, "most children roam free. For non-noble children, there might be chores to do to help maintain the household, but adult life comes fast. Boys often *apprentice as young as ten. While girls often marry as early as twelve. Lionel had more freedom than most with no chores to bind him and an indulgent mother. Both her other sons were sent away, and she wanted to hold on to this last son as long as she could. Since he was for the church, once he left, she might not see him again or very seldom. Her oldest would manage the estate. Her second born could visit between battles, but once the church has you, it's as if you have no family."*

Leah thought it sounded rather ominous, rather like going to prison. She said nothing because she did not want to interrupt the tale.

"Lionel knew all the children of the village. His kind manner made him a favorite of the girls, along with his handsome appearance. The boys tolerated him. To do otherwise would have resulted in repercussions to their families. He must have sensed this. He spent less and less time rough housing with the boys and more time with the girls, especially Arabella. Most everyone in the village knew they were special friends. Her family warned Arabella not to make too much of it, while hoping there might be a way to gain from an alliance."

Sucking in her lips, Leah knew there was a hidden message there. "I don't understand."

"Ahh," Grandfather breathed the word as he obviously stalled. "Girls are not considered valuable in this time. The best you can do with a girl child is to broker good marriage to increase your wealth or connections. Even though Arabella was a pretty child, they didn't expect Lionel to marry her. He was noble and intended for the church. His family held to the Catholic faith. Priests don't marry. Still, they also wondered about the possibility of a child. If Lionel had a child with Arabella, it would be a child of noble blood. His family would feel obligated to take care of it, especially his mother. This was risky, but they knew Lionel's mother well. She'd relish another child."

"What?" Leah may have raised her voice. "I don't get it. They wanted their daughter to be little more than a teen mom."

Simon watched the words fly between her and her grandfather and grinned. Was he smiling because Leah was so ignorant of the morals of this time? She decided against scanning his mind, afraid of what she might find.

Grandfather picked up the kettle and indicated her cup. She held it out as he poured and talked. "This was only an option. It never occurred. Still, there was deep affection between Arabella and Lionel. First love on Lionel's part, while Arabella's love grew in absentia."

"That makes no sense. How could she love him more when he was gone?" Leah wondered, since she often heard people tended to forget crushes once they left the scene.

"Keep in mind, she was young when Lionel left, not ready for mar-

riage, but she'd eventually have to marry. Her family encouraged several different suitors, good men with portions to ensure a decent life for the fair Arabella, but she chose none of them. She claimed none were as sweet, handsome, or as thoughtful as Lionel. Desperate families often resort to desperate measures. Arabella was developing a name as a difficult woman because she'd chosen none of her suitors. Still, she was the most beautiful woman in the area, which caused the single women of the village to dislike her. Ah, women. Are they still the same in your time, Leah?"

She was tempted to say worse, thinking of Cerberus, the three mean girls in her time, but she was unsure how bad the women in this time were. "What happened to Lionel?"

Simon leaned forward to comment. "They bundled him off to church, did they not?"

"They did," Grandfather acknowledged. "There was much weeping and gnashing of teeth from both Lionel and his mother. It was not a pretty scene, which only reassured his sire it was past time for Lionel to join the good brothers. The church, especially the Catholic one, has nothing good to say about women. In fact, they credit them with sin, temptation, and any other evil. Inside the cloistered walls, Lionel's heart was hardened against his former love."

"I saw it." Leah wanted to share the details of her dream or vision with someone who'd understand and would be better able to explain it to her. "Lionel sat with an abbot, I think. He poured water into a silver-lined bowl and did some sort of divination for Lionel. In it, he showed Arabella playing him false with some bearded man. I knew at the time this was a conjured image. Later, he offered Lionel wine in which he stirred in some powder."

"The Black Abbot is a bad one for sure. His heart is against all humankind, but he also uses the magickal arts to promote his own greed for power and wealth. He probably strangled puppies as a boy."

The thought made her shudder. "Isn't he a priest? I didn't think they believed in spells and magick."

"There has always been magick. There are even laws on the books about not using magic for nefarious purposes. It is still there for people who care to research. Ironically, in the last hundred and fifty years, people managed to forget this. All our current Christian holidays were originally rituals to welcome seasons, to encourage fertility, to show gratitude.

The Catholic Church printed out pamphlets showing lurid depictions of people tortured by witches and demons to turn people against everyday intentional magick. This encouraged people's natural fears. It also stamped out the earth magick people used to hunt and plant crops. Who would want to suffer a painful, ignoble death as a witch?" Grandfather's expression appeared unfocused.

Wiping his eyes with his hand, he said, "Religion has always been used to manipulate the populace for the benefit of one or two people. People swarm to do their bidding, expecting a heavenly reward or afraid of a hellish torment. Too many good people have died in the name of religion. Their only crime was they were in the way." He sighed deeply and folded his hands.

Leah wondered if that was the end of the tale. Was there more? She wanted to understand the part she played. Should she ask? She hated to bother her grandfather, who appeared to be off on another plane. Maybe he was witnessing the deaths of those who'd managed to get in the way of new dominant religions. It always amazed her how people never seemed to have a clue how religions came and went, often having the same claims as the previous ones. Still, this one involved her life and her ability to continue to live in the twenty-first century as opposed to dying in some medieval backwater village.

"I hear you, child." Grandfather pinned her with his intense stare. "I'm sorry for your suffering. In this time and the other, I've done what I could. I could not prevent all harm to you or Arabella. For that, I apologize."

His ominous words gave her goose bumps on her arms, and her stomach rolled. "Do I die here?"

"Arabella dies here, as she should because people do not live forever. Her death can be meaningful, as opposed to just another statistic, just another woman accused of being a witch. There are no creatures as evil as the witch catchers are. They defame, humiliate, torture, and kill in the name of religion." He turned to spit in the direction of the fire.

Okay. Arabella died in this time, which she understood. Her issue was that people kept confusing her for Arabella. Was Arabella running around currently, too? Did Leah somehow take her place? Was she supposed to make some bold statement to Lionel before she died? She understood less than she'd before. She'd the feeling she'd never get to go out with Dylan. It had nothing to do with him liking her, but more to do with being alive.

"Grandfather, I'm not sure what happens to me. I'm not sure if I take Arabella's place. Do we exist at the same time? Am I inside Arabella, looking out? If so, do I die with Arabella? I don't want to die." Her voice trembled as she spoke the words. She tried not to cry, but a few tears slipped out.

"Ah, my sweet, precious granddaughter," he said and stood. Grabbing her hand, he pulled her into his embrace. "I came here to rescue you."

He fingered the sleeve of her robe. "Look at this gown of yours. It crackles with protection magick so heavy it would sear a normal man." He pointed to the medallion. "I never thought to see that necklace off Esmeralda's neck. There are centuries of magic in that one charm. Do not underestimate the power in yourself. Then there's the most powerful magick of all." He tightened his embrace.

She hated to ask, certain she should know the answer. "What is this powerful magick?"

He loosened his embrace, stepped back, and gazed at her in surprise. "Really, Leah? The most powerful magick is love. Even though the abbot did his best to turn Lionel's love into hate, he still wants to love her. Remind him of that love."

"I don't know." Turning her back on her grandfather, she began to pace the small room, skirting the still-seated Simon. "I think this is too hard for me. Why can't someone else do it?"

"Trust me, Leah. I've tried everything I've known and have improvised a few other things I wasn't too sure of, but nothing changed. This is not my destiny. It's yours." His voice and manner were solemn, giving his words an air of finality.

It looked like there was no way to get out of this. It was like the time she'd transferred to a new school the day they were doing the presidential fitness challenge. It hadn't mattered that she'd just gotten over the flu. She'd still had to do it. Of course, this was ten times worse. "Can you promise I won't die?"

"No."

The one word settled on her like a weight, stopped her pacing, and pressed her to the ground. He wasn't supposed to say that. Didn't he have a clue what grandfathers were supposed to be like? Where were his words of cheer?

Grandfather walked to where she'd collapsed and held out his hand. It was obvious she could expect no coddling. She often thought of herself as an adult. It was time to start acting like one. She took his hand and allowed him to pull her up. He ushered her back to the chair and waited until she sat before resuming his seat.

"I've done the calculations, consulted the stars, and even used my scrying mirror without any definite results. There are three possibilities." He held up his index finger.

"You do whatever it is you're supposed to do and then return to me at this cottage. We blink back to modern time together."

That sounded good. She could do that. "And the others?"

He held up two fingers. "The second is you do whatever is needed, and you blink back into your time the way you have before. I follow through the portal."

"Okay. I'm good with that." Then there was the third possibility. It would probably be the one she liked the least. "What is the third?"

"Ah, yes, that one." Grandfather stalled by beetling his brows, flaring his nostrils, and finally he spoke. "You die here."

That one she liked the least. No doubt about it.

Shaking his head, he apologized. "I'm sorry to upset you. It is better to be prepared. This may be the mission of your existence, the reason you were born."

She'd hoped for something better, even the opportunity to fall in love, have a career, and possibly be a mother. Dying in the wrong century in a case of mistaken identity had never ever entered her mind. "I was hoping to do something noble, like cure cancer," she attempted to joke.

"I understand," he said. "If you're successful, many lives could be saved. These senseless killings will be stopped."

Leah was more concerned about one life, hers. Would it be petty to want to live if she could prevent others from dying? You might as well call her petty. "What is this thing I do to prevent others from dying?"

"I'm glad you asked." Her grandfather tried for a smile but failed. His expression took on a painful mien. "You have to convince Lionel he's been tricked, led astray with all these tales of witches killing babies, drinking the blood of sleeping people, and flying through the night."

"He actually believes that?" It was hard for Leah to accept. True, there were times she wished she could fly.

Her grandfather nodded, before continuing.

"There's one problem. Lionel is some type of addict. He looks horrible. I'd call him a meth head only I don't think it has happened yet. His pupils are tiny even in low light. He has bags under his eyes. His skin is sallow and just hangs on his skinny body. When he talks, it is sometimes hard to understand him, which just makes him angrier. Everyone knows you can't reason with an addict." Did her grandfather think she'd superhuman powers? The last noble thing she'd done was stand up for Jeremy, and that had been impulsive. If she'd thought it out, she'd never have done it.

"That does sound like an addict, which can be good and bad. Their minds tend to drift, which makes it hard for him to keep focused on killing witches. On the other hand, the abbot probably motivates him with additional fixes. The bad thing is reaching him in a coherent moment."

Did that make things better? Actually, no. She sucked in her lips, wondering what she should do. "The drug is mixed in wine. If he is not drinking wine, he should be okay." She knew better, but tried to find a tiny window of hope.

"Maybe." Grandpa said the word in a considering manner as he stroked his long beard. "You must convince him you still love him and that you waited for his return. Let him know he's mistaken about the witches. There's a small problem, though, which will make him doubt you."

This didn't sound good. Instinct told her not to ask, but it was better to be prepared than ambushed. "The problem is?"

"You're pregnant."

"I'm pregnant!" She patted the gown over her flat stomach. "I can assure you I'm not pregnant. I know what is required to create a baby. Trust me, it hasn't occurred. We move too much for it to happen. Technically, I haven't even been on an actual date."

"Not you. Arabella. When Lionel looks at you, he'll see Arabella, big with child. That is the reason she is still alive. The child is innocent of the mother's crimes, so Arabella cannot be killed until she delivers."

Great. This was worse than a soap opera. *"Is it Lionel's child?"*

"No." Her grandfather shook his head. "Arabella was raped, which is not too uncommon considering how pretty she is. You can tell him the truth. He might believe you. Rape is quite common, as is sexual abuse."

Every word her grandfather spoke made her mission even more impossible. *"Okay, here's what I have. My job is to convince Lionel of my enduring love while my belly is big with some other man's child. I also must convince him the religion he's pledged his life to is misguided and is killing innocent people. Is that about it?"*

"Keep in mind, many thousands are directing intention energy your way," her grandfather reminded.

Way to pile on the guilt. I will be letting down thousands if I don't sacrifice myself. *She used her sleeve to wipe the cold sweat off her forehead. "It will be a piece of cake," she said, knowing she'd never spoken a bigger lie in her life.*

CHAPTER FOURTEEN

*L*EAH SLEPT IN *her grandfather's bed that night, despite her protests. The sight of both her grandfather and Simon sleeping on the hard-packed dirt floor in front of the fire made her feel guilty for taking the only bed. Simon explained he usually slept on the floor, except when he chose to sleep outside, and then he slept on the ground. It wasn't too bad for Simon. He was young and used to it, but Grandpa was old, probably seventy.*

The pine needles managed to work their way through the thin mattress covering when they could and ended up sticking her. At least the mattress smelled good. It reminded her of the floor cleaner her mother used. Unfortunately, the rope bed with the pine-needle mattress was rather uncomfortable. Every time she moved, the ropes protested, as if they might break any moment. It was hard to get comfortable, not only with the bed, but knowing in the morning, she'd have to confront her death or near-death.

A roll had her facing the wall. If she didn't see the crude furniture, the open-hearth fire, the elderly man sleeping on the floor with his apprentice, then she could pretend she was home and be able to fall sleep. Her pillow, filled with dry grass, made a rustling sound when she moved. It wasn't uncomfortable, but the sound was disconcerting. It reminded her of the sound she might hear if a snake was slithering through the grass.

Forcing her eyes shut, she began to count. Sometimes it worked at home. Usually, by the time she got to two hundred, her numbers became confused as she drifted off. This time, no such luck. By thirty, she turned and looked at the semi-curled form of her grandfather. The man had committed almost a third of his life waiting for her in this primitive, dangerous place. She managed to start again and made it to sixty-four before Dylan's face crept into her thoughts. Oh, Dylan, we never even explored what was between us. *Did he wonder where she was? How many days of school had she really missed? Had her mother called the school and explained her daughter was out of the country, no, make that the country and century. She doubted it.*

Would it be small and petty of her to want to go to her junior prom as opposed to changing beliefs and righting wrongs in whatever century this was? If so, she was petty, not to mention scared, very scared. Each trip into the past had terrified her, but until grandfather had explained, she'd never realized she could die here. It was more like watching a scary movie that frightened you in the moment but became less and less frightening the further away from it you got. Only, this wasn't a movie with an automatic happy ending.

Were there ever happy endings? That would imply you were glad something ended. If a woman married her sweetheart, they called it true love. What was ending? The courtship? Many women would deplore that ending. She yawned, blinking her suddenly heavy eyes. Had Grandfather put something in the tea? Suddenly, she felt very, very sleepy.

Leah woke to sunlight streaming in the window and the sound of birds singing. For a moment, a brief second, she thought everything was right in the world. It was Sunday, and she could sleep late. Her father always cooked a hearty breakfast on the weekends, since the family could eat together. He'd wake her up when it was time.

"Leah," a male voice whispered close to her ear. It was familiar but not her father's. An elderly, bearded man with concerned eyes leaned over her. Who was he? It all came back at once, hitting her with the same impact as when the neighbor's over-friendly Great Dane had jumped on her. The dog had never had a grasp on how big he was.

She held her head straight, bit her bottom lip, and wondered if she could think herself home. Nana always preached to her the value of intention. A person could do anything if they just believed. Right now, she believed she wanted to be home. If she didn't turn her head to see the primitive cabin, she wouldn't be here. She could return to the world where her sheets smelled like fabric softener and she dreamed of dancing with Dylan at the junior prom. Technically, she'd have to ask him, since he was a year younger. Like that would ever happen. Her gaze moved around Grandfather to the drying herbs hanging from the beams to Simon squatting in front of the fire, stirring something in a cauldron. Simon turned, caught her attention and said, "Gruel is ready."

Gruel? Was that something people ate? It sounded like something from a Dickens novel. It didn't sound appetizing, either. No pancakes or link sausages for her, that's for sure. Her grandfather thanked Simon and turned to her.

"Rise and shine, Leah. Today will be the making of you. Not many could confront their destiny so early in life's journey. This can only mean a special life awaits you full of wonder and possibilities." His yellowed teeth appeared in a wide grin.

She mentally made note of the teeth, and the fact he still had any. It was miraculous. She'd noticed that Margaret had had a fair number of teeth gone, and she was younger than grandfather was. Her eyes narrowed suspiciously at her grandfather. Did he really believe half of what he said? On the other hand, was he trying to use some form of positive-thinking mumbo jumbo on her?

A slight singed smell permeated the air.

"Make haste," Simon urged as he swung the small cauldron up to the table.

He used a ladle to scoop out a light gray substance that had the consistency of soup into three carved, wooden bowls. Even though she was hungry, she doubted she could stomach it. "Um, what exactly is in it?"

Her grandfather opened a small box from which he took a pinch and sprinkled on his food. "It's better with salt, but since salt is hard to come by, we use it sparingly." Both Simon and Grandfather dug into their own bowls with vigor. In fact, they held up their bowls and drank the mixture.

Leah took a pinch of salt, hoping it would change the food into something edible.

Grandfather continued to eat, but he paused to notice Leah not eating. "Eat up, child. It is nothing harmful. Rather like cereal, it is a mixture of rye, millet, and sometimes oats. We're fortunate because Simon has proven himself very adept at relocating bags of grain at the miller's place. Some folks have to subsist on gruel made from tree bark."

The cooling bland cereal mixture sat in her mouth. It reminded her slightly of a breakfast cereal her mother had cooked for her when she was young, determined she'd have a hot breakfast before school. At the time, she'd assumed her mother was a bad cook. It had never occurred to her it was supposed to taste that way. She did remember not liking it, and her mother had let her return to cold cereal. Grandfather calmly mentioning that Simon had stolen the ingredients almost had her spewing her mouthful across the table. Instead, she made herself swallow.

The dog nudged her leg under the table reminding her that it would happily finish her breakfast. It was a thought, but she immediately dismissed it as rude.

Simon put his bowl down. His face bright with delight, he thumped his chest. "The look-away spell confuses my old master, who cannot fathom where the grain goes. Truth is, he steals much on his own. Too much and people begin to suspect."

Grandfather put down his spoon, cocked his head, and gave Leah a long look, before chuckling. "Did you think I conjured up groceries?"

"Truthfully, I never thought about it." She closed her eyes and swallowed another spoon of gruel. The substance would provide her with the nourishment she'd need to accomplish her mission. She figured the slightly burnt taste was her reward for lingering too long in bed. Simon served her grandfather cheerfully, but that had been for only two years or so.

"Grandfather, what did you do before Simon? How did you obtain

what you needed?" Obviously, he'd or he wouldn't be looking reasonably healthy today.

He nodded at his apprentice with an indulgent smile. "There have been more than a few lost travelers in the woods. Some didn't show the aptitude or willingness of young Simon. Most longed to return to the more populated towns. A few I graduated to working on their own."

At last, she finished her bowl of gruel. Simon, waiting for such a moment, dolloped more gruel into her bowl with a grin. Great, she'd have to eat that, too. Reaching for the salt, she wondered aloud, "Weren't you afraid of these former visitors leading the witch catchers back to your cottage?"

"Leah, Leah, did my sweet wife tell you so little of me?" He shook his head in disbelief.

"No, absolutely nothing. We could not speak your name. Even to make the mistake of mentioning it in passing would send Nana to her room, where she'd weep for days." He didn't need to know his wife had retired with a fifth of brandy.

"My poor Esmeralda, she didn't know. I could not tell her. One day I gazed into the mirror. I saw the portal and you and knew I had mere minutes to reach the portal before it blinked out of existence. Your grandmother had left to do a bit of shopping. I left her a note." His brow beetled, and his lips turned down.

"She never mentioned it. What did the note say?" If he'd left a note, then her grandmother should have understood.

His eyes rolled up in his head as he tried to remember. "It was something about having to do something. That's it."

Really? He considered that a note? "No wonder she's still mad after all these years. What type of note is that? You didn't tell her you loved her?"

"She knew I loved her. Didn't I marry her?" He folded his arms in an effort to look stern.

Men. Why didn't they get it? "She might have believed you loved her once, but leaving made her doubt it. Then there was the cryptic note about going to do something. That could mean anything. Maybe you were going to buy cigarettes."

"No, I only smoke a pipe. She should have known better," he corrected her with an eyebrow lift.

Leah searched her mind for what men of that age would have been going to do. "Could be, she thought you were going to play golf with your buds?"

"I never played golf, cricket, croquet, pool, or even poker," he admitted, almost with pride.

"Geesh, what did you do for fun?" Leah would be the first to admit

she did not know the habits of middle-aged men.

"Ah, yes, fun. Sometimes, I would meet other ceremonial magicians. We would engage in divination, trying to penetrate each other's mental barriers, astral projection, and aging spirits," Grandfather concluded *with a smile.*

Leah wasn't about to admit that none of it sounded like a good time to her. *"Why would you want to make ghosts older?"*

"Ghosts older," he repeated the words as if confused.

Simon comprehended faster. *"Aging spirits."*

"Oh, that," Grandfather said, then slapped the table as if it were the funniest thing he'd heard. *"The spirits I mean were whisky and brandy. Boniface decided to get into the home-brew business, but spirits taste their best with a little age on them. We often took a detour to his cellar and practiced aging a few casks."* His face took on a wistful expression that led Leah to believe they'd probably done more in that cellar than just aging the spirits. It sounded as if some sampling went on, too.

"All the same," she said, trying to explain a woman's outlook to a man, which just might be an impossible task, *"your vague note could have been misinterpreted to mean you were leaving with some bimbo to head to the Bahamas."*

"Esmeralda wouldn't believe that. She was the only woman for me. If she did believe such nonsense, I would have been very afraid. She's not a woman who forgives easy. I often teased her that her middle name was Payback."

Leah regarded her grandfather and his confused expression over the possibility his wife hadn't understood his note.

He threw up his hands, causing wind to whip through the cabin. *"Notes were not my strong point. Actions are."*

Leah admitted to being impressed. She'd never known anyone who could interact with the elements. All the same, a little breeze would not save her grandfather from the wrath of Nana.

"Oh." He drew out the word as if in sudden realization. *"I will have to woo Esmeralda all over again."*

Great, she'd forgotten her mind was an open book to the only ceremonial magician in their family. *"Grandfather, why can you do so much? You can read my mind. Control the elements. Change Simon into an animal.*

"Before, when I asked if Esmeralda ever mentioned me, I wanted to know if she commented on me being a great ceremonial magician. I was at that time. My life was rich with family, friends, and activities. I even had a job. I estimated risk for an insurance company. I was stupendous. Here, I've nothing to entertain my thoughts but my own magick and me. It has allowed me time to sharpen my skills, to perfect areas formerly lacking. All

those travelers and young wizards I interacted with have no memory of me or this place."

He spread his broad-tipped fingers on the table and studied them. "Which goes to show, Granddaughter, if you look hard enough, you can find some good in everything no matter what?" He lifted his brows at his own statement, asking a question.

What good would come out of this experience? It would depend on if she survived. "Well." She stalled, hoping the right answer would suddenly enter her mind. A quick survey of her experiences provided some insights. "I found out my family loves me very much. Even the women Nana sometimes quarrels with came to my aid." She held out the wide sleeve of her gown. "My protective garment came through the door with someone."

He nodded his head and gave her a significant look. She didn't need to be a mind reader to know it meant continue. Weren't you supposed to do all this debriefing stuff after the mission was finished? "My friend Stella and I were working on an essay on religious prejudice. I found out she is more predisposed to the Wiccan faith than I ever dreamed. I've hidden my beliefs because I never thought of them as mine. I guess I didn't believe in magick."

Simon jumped up. "Not believe in magick? Your grandfather is the most powerful wizard that has ever existed!" He threw his hands wide, as if to indicate the whole world.

"Thank you, Simon, but I prefer the term ceremonial magician." Grandfather twirled his two index fingers for her to resume her revelations.

Directing her words to both Simon and Grandfather, she said, "I do believe in magick now. I've experienced it. I've seen the results of it. I'm wearing it." She looked at both males and added, "I'm looking at it right now."

Simon whooped with delight. Evidently, no one had ever attributed magick to him in so public a statement.

"I also understand why people did what they did in the Burning Years. We allow others to manipulate our fears. When I return home, I refuse to be captive to my fears. Instead, I will be bold. I will do what I want and make the things I desire a reality." She finished with a hand flourish, excited about all she'd discovered and the new fearless life she'd have.

After running from torch-wielding peasants and dogs, hunted by drunken knights, betrayed by a so-called friend, and whipped by the resident dungeon master, high school didn't seem that frightening–even with Cerberus roaming the halls.

Grandfather steepled his fingers and grinned. "If my wooing of my wife goes well, we can chaperone you and Dylan at your junior prom. Esmeralda and I are quite the dancers."

Leah put her hands on her hips. "You'll have to stop reading my mind."

Assuming a solemn mien, he pushed up from the table, pointing a finger in Leah's face. "You will have to develop mental barriers. I may not be the only one able to read your thoughts. They're so loud they practically shout."

She never thought of others reading her thoughts. That wouldn't be good. What if the bad abbot was around? She didn't know if he would be, but she couldn't take any chances. What if she went back to ordinary times and there were a few who could read her mind? What if Dylan could? Obviously, it didn't matter if her math teacher called her obsessed. Everyone knew whom she liked, including Dylan.

"Can you teach me how to erect these barriers? I know it will be a quick course, but I think it will be useful." After all, she could use all the help she could get.

Simon moved closer to the table. "I could benefit from knowing how to erect such barriers."

Leah ended up snorting when all she really wanted to say was, Amen to that, Brother. *Simon, in time, might meet a pleasing witch. It would probably be best if she didn't hear Simon's immediate thoughts.*

Grandfather held both hands over his head, allowing them to skim just over his body down to his feet. "While your hands move, think of encasing your body in a white envelope of light."

Leah and Simon watched until they realized they should be doing likewise. They flapped their hands awkwardly through the air, resembling seagulls trying to find a place to roost.

"Not like that," he corrected, pointing to spots in the air. "You've left holes in your envelopes, easy openings for your enemies to breach. Keep moving your hands in a smooth fashion. Start over. When you do, recite after me:

Protect this body
Head to toe
Hand to hand
Foot to foot
Skin and bone
Head and heart"

Leah cast a doubting look. "Really? That's it? No long words, mysterious phrases and such? Not even a word or two of Romany?"

"Ah, I see you've been around Esmeralda too long. Nothing fancy. Anything else is all showmanship. Trust me, Leah. This will get the job done." He circled his hand to get them to start.

The spell reminded her of the protection spells they normally used at the beginning of a ritual. What made this one so different? She wondered as she chanted in unison with Simon.

The whiteness settled on her as if a blanket had been tossed from the ceiling. She picked up her feet, one at a time, allowing the protection to flow underneath. The shield felt heavy and thick, as if white cotton batting covered her body.

Simon asked the question she wanted to. "How does this protect our minds from being read?"

Holding up one finger, Grandfather explained, "First, we must protect the body before we can safeguard the mind. If a soldier ran you through with a lance, protecting your mind really wouldn't matter much. You two are ready. Here are some things to consider. Emotions are loud. Beware of the mind-sweepers who look for strong emotion. It can be love, anger, even fear. It is usually fear. The first thing you must do is not show fright."

Sure thing, all she'd to do was not look afraid. Leah looked from her grandfather to Simon, then back again. Neither cracked a smile, so it must not have been a joke. "How do you do this?"

"You do it all the time. Think of when you see those girls you call Cerberus, or a strange dog growls at you, or the teacher calls on you and you don't know the answer. What do you do?" His eyes peered intently into hers, as if he were confident of her answer.

Thinking back, she tried to remember what she did. With Cerberus, she never made the mistake of acting as if she cared. With the strange dog, she was casual, pretending she hadn't heard his growl. With the teacher, she tried to act confident. There had been times when she'd given the wrong answer, but because she'd acted confident, it had been accepted. "I tried to show no emotion."

Grandfather put his index fingers and thumbs together to form a triangle. "Our defense is triangular in nature. The base is," he wiggled his thumbs to demonstrate, "the lack of any outward show of emotions. There are people and entities, which would feed on your fear. Give them nothing."

Holding up one index finger, he said, "The second part is clearing your mind of all fear."

Just like that, she was supposed to clear her mind of all fear. Yeah, sure, and next she'd fly. She sucked her bottom lip in. Didn't fear keep people alive? While she'd never thought of herself as a fearful person, she'd lived most of her life avoiding things that frightened her, including anxiety about not being accepted at her new school and the alarm of moving again. There was always fear somewhere motivating her. Her head shook side to side as she considered his words.

Simon pointed at her, catching her grandfather's attention. "Yes,

Leah. Is there something you want to say?"

Not really. She never wanted attention in class, even if it was a class of two. "Well..." She hesitated, not sure how to make her point. "Fear keeps people alive." She motioned to the fire. "A person learns fire is hot, producing a natural fear of putting his hand in the fire."

Simon agreed with her, but she assumed he was just that type of person who would agree with whoever was speaking.

Grandfather graced her with a thoughtful stare. "The knowledge that fire is hot and that you shouldn't stick your hand in it is just that, knowledge. Knowing a bear could kill you is information. Fear muddles your thinking processes and slows your reactions. Sometimes, it can even kill you."

"Fear kills." She said the words slowly, thinking there may have been times when she'd wondered whether she'd live through a scary episode.

"Yes, often creating mental scenarios that are ten times worse than what could really happen. Sometimes you hear about people having a heart attack when a plane starts to plummet. The plane regains altitude, but the person died because, in his mind, he experienced the crash. The ability to control your fear is often the difference between surviving and not."

The elderly dog sitting by the fire began to growl intermittently. The hair stood up on the dog's shoulders and back.

"Esme hears someone," Simon announced.

The dog lurched to her feet on stiff, arthritic legs and swayed a bit. "You named the dog after Nana?"

Grandfather clapped his hands together for attention, Grandfather announced, "We need to work on our shielding. They're drawing closer. Leah, I would consider it a kindness if you didn't mention the dog's name. Women can be funny about these things. Remember, fear changes nothing. Fear doesn't stop a sword from coming toward you, but it will slow your escape. You must be always thinking of the next step. By thinking of moving forward, you're not trapped in fear."

Esme sniffed by the door and growled. The sound of horses milling about and men shouting to one another penetrated the thin walls. "Grandfather," Leah whimpered, trying to still the panic that wanted to creep into her voice.

"Do not worry about them. The whole area is enchanted. All they see is more forest." Clapping his hands together again, he spoke. "The third part of the triangle is mental fences. As we wrap our bodies in protective cocoons, we must guard our minds. Think of fences, brick walls, steel boxes, anything impenetrable that will lock out others. Your mind and thoughts are inside. You can also train yourself to go to safe thoughts to keep your mind busy if you think someone might be scanning your

thoughts." His attention strayed to the lone window, where the shadows of the horsed men cut out most of the sunlight.

"Safe memories. Should I be thinking of a time I was safe?" Leah wasn't sure how this helped.

"No, not exactly." He edged closer to the window to peer out. "Making brownies, swimming in the ocean, playing with the dog. These are memories that give no real information, or at least the kind they hope to get."

"Let's practice," he called from his stance at the window. "Set up your triangle. I will be Lionel, and I will try to read your mind."

Leah wasn't sure if Lionel had that capability, but she hesitated mentioning it. Instead, she worked on not showing any fear. Her grandfather waved his hands in a flourish and morphed into a thin, haggard man with dark eyes and a wicked-looking staff with some type of spiked device on the end. Terror definitely sought a return visit. Grabbing the emotion ruthlessly, she sat on it and wrestled it into her mental steel box. Quickly, in her mind, she padlocked the box. Simon showed no fear. The ability to change into anyone was another skill she never knew her grandfather possessed. It could have been very useful if he'd ever left the cottage.

"Simon, son of John, tell me where you hid the witch." He breathed the words in a sinister voice, shaking his strange stick threateningly.

The boy, to his credit, kept his face wiped clean of emotion. "Sir, I do not know of what you speak. This is a respectable woods with no mischief-causing witches within."

Leah wanted to applaud him. He hid his fear and thoughts well. The ominous figure turned on her so fast she stumbled back a step, but she reminded herself of the tenets of mental protection. She calculated angles in her head as she watched the man walk toward her.

"Do you think to fool me with your deceitful ways and wiles?" He loomed over her.

Still trying to keep the equation in her head, she managed to answer. "Oh, no, sir. I have no deceitful ways or wiles. I'm a simple girl. Pray, how may I be of service?" She made a little curtsey.

The figure transformed back into the now-familiar man. "Simon, good job, though thinking about how crooked the miller is might not be your best safe thought."

Turning to Leah, he smiled. "The geometry was an inspired thought. It would be enough to cause most mind-sweepers to doubt their own thoughts. That curtsey at the end was a bit too much. It would be the equivalent of giving Lionel the middle finger, and you don't want to do that."

"The middle finger. What does that mean?" Simon asked, but a firm nod from her grandfather ended the discussion.

The voices outside grew louder and more agitated. Taking a final peek out the window, he cast a measuring look in her direction. "Granddaughter, you're about as ready as you're going to be. Besides, we have less than two days to make it happen, if my calculations are correct. You must remember two things. Keep in mind to hold yourself proud. They will be more afraid of you than you're of them. By now, your legend has grown."

Leah protested, "I haven't done anything."

"By now," Simon added, "there will be tales of how you transformed into a fire-breathing monster and burned down entire towns."

Would it be to her advantage to encourage the tales? She decided she'd stay silent on the matter. It would be better for people to be unsure. "What is the second thing, Grandfather?"

"Love. There's the love of everyone holding you in his or her intentions. There's the love of Lionel and Arabella. I will always believe love is the ultimate magick." He stood near the door, but motioned the two of them closer.

Laying his hand on Leah's head, he urged Simon to do likewise. Even Esme stuck her cold nose in her hand. Grandfather's deep, resonant voice started. "I bless you in the name of the Lady and the Lord."

Simon's voice joined in, cracking a little. "Spirits, good and kind, go with Leah."

In unison, they spoke, "Elements Air, Fire, Water, and Earth assist Leah in her endeavors."

Her grandfather's voice thickened with emotion. "Woodland creatures, birds in flight, fish in the water, guide your sister home."

Esme barked, adding her own benediction to the blessing. It was time to go. She put her hand on the door.

Grandfather placed a hand on her shoulder. "I cannot go with you. How I wish I could, but Simon can go."

"I can?" His voice cracked on the question.

"Not as you, but as a stately escort. I think a pure-white falcon might do the trick." Waving his hands once more, he turned the open-mouthed Simon into a beautiful white bird. Leah lifted the falcon to her shoulder.

Esme gave three sharp barks.

Grandfather looked down at the dog. "I don't know, Esme, you really are too old for adventures."

The dog looked up at the falcon and barked again.

"Leah, Esme wants to go with you. As an old dog, this may be her last adventure, since she can't return with me. It's fitting she should go in style." He waved his hands once more, transforming the elderly dog into a large black panther with a jeweled collar.

The bird jumped around on her shoulder, squawking. Most people might think it was afraid of the panther, but Leah knew better. Simon was mad he didn't get to be the panther.

"Be at peace, Simon. You're the only one who can fly." Grandfather's words settled the bird some.

Leah turned to the door once more, steeling herself for her upcoming mission.

"One more thing." Grandfather darted to a dark corner and returned with a staff adorned with a rounded crystal sphere on top. He blew on the clear crystal, causing smoke to develop inside. It would seethe one way, then the other, forming images and shapes as it moved. "The ultimate parlor trick, it will, as you say in your time, freak them out." He laughed with delight.

Leah vowed to be brave as she used her staff to counterbalance herself. Simon didn't weigh too much, and the robe protected her from his talons. Her attitude would be like that of a mean girl. She'd show no fear and would expect everyone to do her bidding. Esme walked along beside her, soft-footed and menacing.

CHAPTER FIFTEEN

*D*ESPITE THE OPEN *door, none of the knights turned toward her. Peasants ran through the brush, calling out to the knights. The entire yard must be enchanted. As she strolled slowly toward the gate, she put her shoulders back and her chin up, trying to resemble some of the ancient queens she'd seen depicted on temple walls. This was the exam that she'd been preparing for all her life. She swung open the garden gate, attracting attention.*

The first knight removed his helmet and ogled her openly, until Esme growled, drawing his attention downward. "By St. Bartholomew's bones," he cursed, backing up his horse.

The other two knights turned. It was impossible to judge their expressions with their visors down, but their horses expressed their attitude clearly enough by side-stepping and pulling at the reins. It was time to take charge of the situation. It was like a mental order. She wouldn't be surprised if it had come from her grandfather.

Projecting her voice as she'd learned to do in choir, she told them, "You appear to be an adequate escort to take me to my beloved Lionel."

The three knights looked at each other as if confused by her words. "Do not give them time to think." She knew where that order came from. "Knights, where is my mount?" she demanded, stamping her staff to make her petulance more real. She didn't expect the lightning bolt shooting from the crystal. It was hard to tell who was more surprised, Simon flapping his wings wildly from his perch, the knights, or the peasants fleeing into the woods.

A white mare appeared in the clearing with a jeweled bridle and saddle. The white mare approached her and bowed down on its forelegs so she could mount. Thank goodness, for the trail rides in the park that Stella had insisted they do. She'd make a point of thanking her when she arrived home. Inclining her head, a mere inch, she said, "This mount is adequate," but her attitude said just only.

Her horse followed behind the knights with showy steps, while Esme stayed close by. Her staff proved problematic as she swung it around, trying to figure out how to ride with it, causing the knights to knee their horses to get out of her way. Eventually, she rested it against her thighs.

News of the slow-moving caravan must have reached people's ears. They peeked through doors and windows and climbed to rooftops to spy. Leah kept her head up. She was no fearful peasant. She was the Queen, the Beloved. She smiled, thinking how right the words felt. Who knew she'd her own inner mean girl to tap into? She certainly hadn't. When she got back, she might have to be nice to Cerberus. Nope, that was just crazy talk.

Hadn't she made this trip before? Hadn't she been half dazed by pain? Before she could mentally revisit those memories, a familiar voice spoke in her head. "Act as you want to be perceived. It was quite common for people to taunt those charged with witchcraft, rather like kicking someone when they were down."

A boy hid by a tree with a rock in his hand. Did he think he'd throw that at her or Esme? Simon lifted off from her shoulder and flew in the direction of the boy, who dropped his rock and fled. Simon circled the area and managed to scare out a few more people with rocks.

As they ran past, Leah looked at them, causing the women to scream and pull their aprons over their faces. What did these people believe that caused so much fear? It had to be something horrible to rationalize killing their neighbors and friends in horrific ways, all in the name of religion.

Miss Santiago had quoted some poem in class about a man in Nazi Germany. It was something about the man not saying anything when they took the Jews, because he wasn't one. Then the Nazis rounded up more groups, until when they finally came for him, there was no one left to stand up for him. Were the people so unaware that this was only another genocide operation? Their time would come. There would be no one to speak for them.

It was her time to stand up. They entered the courtyard of a long, block building. A burly man dressed in leather pants and vest approached her. A chill started up her spine–her torturer. He made a motion for her to dismount. "Do not dismount. You will be at a disadvantage." *This time she didn't need orders. She knew getting off the horse would have been bad. She certainly hoped her mount wasn't Horace the snake.*

People began to slide through the open gates to watch the proceedings. The torturer gestured back to her, making her wonder if he were a mute or a victim of torture who'd had his tongue cut out. You'd think, if so, he'd have been more merciful, but most bullies were misguided, torturing the weak, not necessarily the deserving.

The knights pretended not to notice his gesturing. She wasn't sure if they were mocking the man or unsure how to handle the situation. A young priest hurried out, spoke to the knights, who gestured in her direction, then spurred their mounts and left in a cloud of dust.

"Wait," he called after them, but they did not hear, or they pretended not to.

The priest looked from her to the man in leather, who shrugged his shoulders.

It was past time to move this along, and she knew that this meeting should take place outside so all could witness it. "Tell my beloved Lionel I await his pleasure." This caused some people in the crowd to titter. Most could remember the friendship between Arabella and Lionel. Some whispered she might have regarded herself well before, but now she was the bloody Queen of England.

The priest shuffled his feet and gestured to the open door behind him. "Come inside. Your beloved, I mean, Father Lionel waits."

"No." She only said that one word and regarded the priest as if he were joking. Her hands tightened around her staff, and she attempted to bring it upright. Simon lifted from her shoulder as if he didn't trust the staff in her hand. Esme took the opportunity to growl. The crowd grew uneasy, backing up.

Lionel ran out of the building with his black robe flapping behind him. "What farce is this, Arabella?" The thin priest stumbled to an immediate halt, the words stopping as he took in the princely outfitted steed and the jeweled collar on the panther. He walked slowly around the three, making Leah turn her mount to keep him in sight. She didn't trust the man, even if Arabella loved him now or had loved him in the past. Leah Carpenter knew a snake when she saw one. Placing her hand on her steed's neck, she muttered a mental apology just in case her steed was Horace.

"No farce." She smiled. "I came to see my beloved." The men and women jostled each other to see if someone else had entered the area.

Lionel put a cupped hand to his forehead and pretended to look in all directions. "The devil must be hiding. He can't stand to be inside the church walls. I'm surprised you haven't burst into flames."

"Hate to ruin your theory. I hear there's more evil inside the walls than there's outside. Who needs the devil when you have the good abbot who enslaves you with drugs and makes up tales using his magick divination bowl? The bowl is not exactly honest, either. Remember when he showed you a picture of me with another man?"

The crowd whispered as Lionel looked down at his hands. His head snapped up. "You must be a witch. No one was in that room except the abbot and me."

Inhaling slowly, she considered her reply. It was time to come out of the broom closet in a very big way. "I never said I wasn't a witch. I said what you saw was a lie. The abbot used magick for evil purposes. I was only twelve when I supposedly played you false."

Lionel held his hands over his ears, shouting, "Get behind me, devil."

If only she'd Arabella's memories. She turned to the crowd, "What was I doing when I was twelve? Did I take off with some bearded courtier?" She'd her fingers crossed, just in case she'd been a bit of a hussy. There was some chattering, but only one woman chose to come forth. "Your twelfth year was when your mother fell from the roof and broke her leg. She was mending the roof your father should have."

The woman earned jeers from the men, while the women hooted in agreement.

"I took care of my mother." She hoped that was the right answer.

"Not only that," the woman continued, "you repaired the roof and helped me with my brood when they fell sick. No longer did you think yourself better than others. You had no interest in marriage or boys. Some thought you were holding out for something better than the men in our village, but I knew the only man you cared for had left town." The woman looked pointedly at Lionel.

Nodding her head at the woman, she said, "Thank you." What was her name? It would have been nice to know the woman who'd chosen to champion Arabella.

"Agnes. My name is Agnes. I did not expect you to remember it since you moved away with your husband three winters ago."

Arabella was married. She'd left town. Maybe Arabella had found some happiness, but this man, this sick, sick man, was determined to snatch it away from her.

"Well," Lionel's voice took on a sneering quality, "it looks like the wages of sin pay well." He crossed his arms in front of him and rocked back on his heels as if he'd said something cleverer than a platitude repeated from countless pulpits.

"I'm not sure to what you refer." She wrestled the staff into an upright position over her burgeoning stomach. Where had that come from? Grandfather had warned her.

He looked pointedly at her stomach. At least she knew she was married, as opposed to being a rape victim, which was somewhat encouraging. Arabella had a chance at a decent life if she could just stay alive. Of course, declaring herself hadn't earned her any brownie points.

"Lionel, I wish for a moment you could hear yourself spouting these ridiculous platitudes. When you were a boy, you had a wonderful mind. You wanted to know the why behind things, and I loved you dearly. Now, you're a mindless cog in the church, striking fear into the people with your talk of demons and hell, squeezing them for tithes when they can barely feed their own families. You pretend to forgive their sins when yours are so much blacker."

Lionel darted forward, as if to pull her off the horse. Esme growled, while Simon dived at his head, forcing Lionel to cover it with his hands. "Witch, baby killer, blood drinker," he shouted from behind the shield of his bent arms.

She looked around at the crowd. Holding her staff, she waved it in a circular fashion, causing little spirals of dirt and leaves to lift off the ground. "Do you believe this?" A few shook their heads. Others nodded. Most managed to not move at all.

Looking at Lionel, she asked, "Do you believe this nonsense? After all, your church made it up, preached it from the pulpit, and printed the pamphlets. They had to use images since most people couldn't read."

One man volunteered in the crowd. "I saw one. The witch rode a broomstick across the sky." People crowded around him, asking about the drawings.

Simon returned to her shoulder, which allowed Lionel to lower his arms. "If you're so smart, Arabella, as you always imagined yourself, why would the church do such a thing? Be careful. If you lie, you might be struck down by lightning." He gave her a sly grin, declaring himself positive he'd outfoxed her.

She smiled, looked back at the crowd, swarming the pamphlet viewer. They needed to hear what she'd to say. It was as much for them as it was for Lionel. She shook her staff, wondering if she could get a lightning bolt out of it. Instead, fireworks burst into the sky, from Roman candles to pinwheels and bees buzzing across the courtyard. The crowd gasped, oohed and aahed, and eventually laughed at their initial fright.

"Very pretty," Lionel commented, lifting an eyebrow. "Is that your answer? I expected as much from you."

Leah would have liked lightning, but she'd to admit she'd the crowd's attention now. "I came back for you, Lionel, because I cared about what you were being turned into with the drugs, the lies, and the witch hunts."

Lionel started to speak, but she held her hand up. "I'm not finished. You asked me why the church started these witch hunts. Number one, they want to wipe out all competing religions. They want to get rid of all worship of other deities. They cannot control people or their money if They're not part of the same faith. They also cannot allow those who practice the old ways to live. They're wrong. I come from a place where many religions exist side by side. It isn't a perfect place, but people are free to practice their various faiths without fear of torture or death."

One woman yelled out, "I thought your husband's people were in the next village."

"Farther than that," was as much Leah was willing to commit to. She wondered why they only saw Arabella and not Leah. "More important," she projected her voice, "the witch hunts are to frighten you. First, they make up the evil blood drinkers that only the church can get rid of for a price. Convenient, when no such people exist. If you ever say anything against the church, they can call you a heretic, threaten to send your eternal soul to hell, and torture you in this world. Don't forget, they want

your money and your land, too."

The mob, swayed by the emotional images, began to gripe about the greedy church and bloodsucking priests stealing their immortal souls and their gold. The crowd seemed to change its tune. In fact, it might have been a great time to leave if Leah had had a clue which way to go. The sounds of a rowdy crowd were familiar enough to her. At least this time, they didn't have pitchforks or flaming torches.

A short, bald man slipped out the side door, carrying a cauldron. A sudden memory flash alerted her that she was in the presence of the black abbot, the clergyman who didn't care who he hurt or killed in his quest for money and power. Grandfather had described him as a bad one. The fireworks and a large cat with a jeweled collar were enough to impress the crowd. Who knew what this man might do?

No one else noticed him. He put down the cauldron, waved his hands over it, commanding it. Lionel was yelling something. The crowd jeered him, but no one noticed the black ooze taking form above the pot. It resembled some type of twisted creature with wings. He was shaping it for her, that she knew. Think ahead. Was there any firepower left in the staff? She certainly hoped so.

Mesmerized by the black, oily creature, Leah was afraid to look away. The second she looked away, it would attack. The sun must have slipped behind the clouds. The sky grew dark, taking a bright sunny day into dusk in a few seconds. The sounds of wings flapping behind her came nearer. It was an illusion to distract her into turning away. It wouldn't work. She'd be ready when the dark creature sprang at her.

The screams in the background vaguely registered, along with Simon's squeezing talons. The boy didn't do bird impersonations well. The abbot's smug smile crumpled before he screamed as a river of fire hit him and his creature, igniting them both. Looking upward, she saw the silhouette of a huge golden dragon. Simon danced up and down her arm in agitation, which meant the dragon had to be her grandfather. Why was he here? He might miss going back in time.

His voice spoke clearly in her head. "I had to, Granddaughter. I saw the black abbot was up to no good. Only a ceremonial magician can deal with that type of evil. Let's head back to the portal. I'll show you the way."

Holding the left rein tight, she turned the mare in a circle. Lionel stood near the smoking mess consisting of what was left of his mentor and his creation. Perhaps he hadn't learned anything. Then again, some of the people in the village might have. They might hesitate to start up another witch hunt again. Arabella would live after she'd her child.

Leah urged her mount after the golden dragon. The panther ran beside her while Simon flew overhead.

People cheered them as she rode. It was a little different from her earlier trip through town. Golden dragons had a way of reminding people that magick was afoot, even when they'd forgotten it.

She could see the cabin through the trees, shimmering, changing, and hard to see. The portal was open. She didn't have much time. The shadow of the dragon hovered over the portal, as opposed to landing. Grandfather was waiting for her. Digging her heels into her mount, she urged it faster, but her mount changed underneath her legs. Her white coat became brown and rough. Her beautiful, elegant head had huge horns. Her beautiful saddle disappeared, causing her to fall. Using the staff, she stopped her fall. She held herself up for a minute, watching the house in front of her blink in and out of existence. Her legs started running before she'd even formed a coherent thought. Her large pregnant belly slowed her down. Wrapping her arms around it, she sprinted for the gate. She made it inside the gate just as Grandfather changed to stand beside her. Outside the fence, Simon turned back into a teen, holding up the staff she'd dropped. Esme stood beside him, along with a beautiful, dark-haired woman who was obviously pregnant. Leah placed a hand on her flat stomach just as everything began to spin. There was a sense of movement and colors shifting that went on forever, only to end with them ejected as if out of a water slide.

Instead of being in a shallow pool, they found themselves in the back alley of a strip mall Laundromat that blew warm dryer-sheet-scented air on them.

Leah wondered if everyone who used the Laundromat always brought dryer sheets. *Dryer sheets?* That meant she was home. Her hand clutched her grandfather's hand. His expression remained shuttered. Leah hoped he made it through the portal okay since he was no longer young.

Not opening his eyes, he said, "Use your barriers, child. There are some things I'd rather not hear."

Good. Still alive. Barriers, she'd set them up. The area looked unfamiliar. Nudging her grandfather, she asked, "Do you know where we're?"

What if they'd showed up in the wrong country or century? They'd taken a right at that last portal when they should have taken a left. His eyes fluttered open. "Can you give me a minute? I want to appreciate things for the last twenty years I've been imagining. I don't want to rush it. Think my calculations may have been off by a day."

Leah stood still, holding her grandfather's hand and tried to pull him into a seated position. "I noticed. You may not want to hurry, but I do. I can't wait to shower off the smell of roasted human flesh. We need to hoof it home before the police pick us up."

"Okay," Grandfather agreed, as he struggled to stand. "I don't remember standing being this hard. Do you think I aged while traveling through time? Like a thousand years?"

"Not a thousand, but a good five hundred," she teased. She certainly felt years older than the girl who'd lived in fear of Cerberus. Once you met real evil face to face, mean girls were a poor second.

Pointing to the strip mall, he suggested, "We can go inside and use a phone and get a ride home?"

She couldn't see anyone letting them use their cell, but someone might. Wait, her grandfather had meant a public phone. Did they have those anymore? They rounded the Laundromat to see a bar that offered a blue-plate lunch special.

"The Red Rooster. Charlie's place." His pace quickened as he approached.

Instead of explaining that she wasn't allowed in the bar, she simply followed. The place was almost empty except for a woman contemplating a jukebox, while a bald man wiped down the bar. Grandfather stared at the man intently. "You're Charlie's son."

"Yep," the man agreed. "Who might you be? Already dressed up for Halloween?"

She watched her grandfather open and close his mouth without saying anything, upset that he wasn't recognized. Stepping up to the bar, she winked at the man. "Surely, you recognize Buell Hare, the man who disappeared off the face of the earth, say, about twenty years ago."

The man leaned forward his expression avid. "Yes, I remember that tale. My dad came up with some outlandish tale about you disappearing in time. Did you?"

"I'm not allowed to say," Grandfather said with a smile. "Can I use your phone?"

The bartender pulled a desk phone from under the bar and placed it on the slick counter. Leah reached for the phone. "Let me call. I know the number, and they were kinda expecting me back, so it won't be as big of a shock."

CHAPTER SIXTEEN

THE PHONE RANG once before a breathless voice answered. "Hello?"
Leah wasn't sure if it was her mother or her sister. They both sounded similar, especially with the slight edge of hysteria coloring the one word, both anxious to hear news but frightened, too. Thank the Goddess she'd made it back in one piece. Her family had suffered by not knowing what had happened in the past and being helpless to assist. It was better this way. No doubt, Nana would have opened a can of whoop-ass on the abbot. The thought made her giggle.

"I do not have time for prank phone calls," her mother practically shouted in her ear.

Oh yeah, she'd forgotten to say something. "Mom, it's me. I'm back."

"Leah, sweetheart, is that you?" Her voice trembled with uncertainty and a quiver of hope.

"Yes, of course." She tried to put all the love and affection in her voice she'd denied her mother the past couple of years. Suddenly, all her teen angst fell way. She'd always thought her parents never understood. Maybe they did understand. Who knew what shadows, and possibly dragons, their pasts held?

"Are you here?" Laughter followed her inquiry. "I'm just being silly now. No way could you call over the centuries." Her voice grew higher and lighter, losing the doubt.

"Mom, can Dad pick me up? I'm at a bar called the Red Rooster." Leah twisted around to see where her grandfather was. He stood in front of the old-time jukebox, peering into it.

"Never heard of most of these people," he grumbled. The bartender ignored him and continued polishing glasses.

The smell of stale smoke caused her to cough and miss her mother's reply. "What?"

"I said we will all come. Me, your father, Nana, and Ethan, since he's small. Nora won't like being left out, but I imagine she can wait." Her mother continued to babble.

"Wait, Mom. Are you listening?" Her mother chattered about making her favorite meal, chicken and dumplings. Knowing her mother, she'd eventually run down and get tired of talking.

"Maura, who is on the phone?" Her father's voice came over the line distantly, then more clearly. "Leah, is that you?"

She could hear the smile in his voice. "It's me. I was telling Mom she shouldn't bring everyone, since I brought someone home with me."

The bartender walked over to the jukebox and fed it a couple of quarters, to Grandfather's delight. He began punching buttons wildly, while her father warned her about the dangers of removing someone from another century.

The sound of Frankie Valli and The Four Seasons crooning *Big Girls Don't Cry* filled the empty bar, bouncing off the paneled walls and veneer tables. Grandpa jumped in on the chorus, "Big girls, they don't cry-yi-yi." The bartender snorted his opinion and turned away. The woman who'd been at the jukebox earlier reappeared tying on a white apron.

"Who is that singing?" Leah's father asked.

"Well," Leah hesitated with her explanation, not sure how to put it. "I bet it is someone you've been waiting a long time to meet."

Her father's words came slowly, almost in disbelief. "Is it? Could it be?"

"We could both benefit from a shower and dinner. Ask Nana where the Red Rooster is. Apparently, it used to be one of Grandfather's hangouts."

"Will do. We're leaving now."

"Don't break any speed limits," she teased. "We weren't going anywhere." The hum of the dial tone told her he'd hung up.

The server turned toward her grandfather, who warbled with gusto. The neon beer signs cast an unflattering glow on her heavily made-up face, emphasizing every wrinkle. Speaking in a smoker's contralto, she asked, "Buell, is that you under all that hair?"

Stopping his impromptu performance, he placed one soft-booted foot behind him and pivoted. "Beverly McClary, still working at the Rooster. Some things never change. Still as pretty as ever."

The woman laughed. "Now I know your eyesight is going." She brushed away the compliment as she gestured with her hand in the air. "What's with the costume? It's not time for trick-or-treating. Even if it was, I'd have to say you're a bit too old."

The bartender slid a soft drink in front of Leah, which she gulped gratefully. Normally, she'd have worried about money, but in the past week, little things such as money, school, and even hygiene had taken second place. As bad as the lingering aroma of cigarettes smelled in the small, dark bar, she knew she herself had to smell worse. A shower was the first thing on her list. Her robe was washable, she hoped.

She savored the cold sweetness against her tongue. On one hand, it had no great nutritional value. It certainly wasn't the same as drinking cool spring water or eating gruel. Although, eating would have been too generous a description for what they'd done with the gruel. That would imply it had had a chewable texture. At best, they'd consumed it.

Leah watched her grandfather talk to the waitress with obvious relish after twenty-plus years with no one to talk to, except for the travelers he'd willed to step in his direction. None of them would remember him as Buell Hare. The villagers would recall seeing only a magnificent golden dragon, or would they?

Draining the last of her drink, she refused the offer of a refill. No reason to fill up on a soda when she'd have real food in a few minutes. Had she done what she was supposed to do? It felt like she'd, and she felt a sense of completion. What had she done, really?

The fact that Arabella had already married and expected a baby made it seem like she hadn't really needed Leah's help. That was true, up to a point. Lionel might still have executed her as a witch after she'd had the baby. Grandfather had done a spectacular job of ridding the world of a singularly malevolent force, in turn preventing more torture and the deaths of suspected witches.

If her destiny hadn't been to go back in time, Grandfather wouldn't have been there. Bev, the waitress, teased her grandfather about looking like a cross between Santa Claus and an elderly Friar Tuck. Hard to imagine him as a fire-breathing dragon, but when it came to family, he protected his.

Was that it? Had she done anything? Had she changed Lionel's beliefs? No doubt, he'd have changed on his own without his regular drug supply and the abbot whispering evil lies into his drug-addled mind. The changes would start with Lionel. If not him, there was always Simon. Even if only a couple of the villagers changed their minds, it would be a start.

Most would go back to the old ways of thinking, because that was easier. The girl on the beautiful white mare, with the sleek panther and snow-white falcon, was a dream, a lie, a story told to confuse good Christians. As for the golden dragon, they would assure each other saying that dragons don't exist. They'd probably forget about the abbot, too. If they did remember his evil ways, they would question what happened.

As she slowly turned her empty glass around on the bar, spreading the condensation across the surface, a strange thought entered her head. Would history remember them? A quote Miss Santiago had attributed to Napoleon was that winners always wrote history. They could justify any horrific behavior or choose not to mention it. Were they the winners?

❖   ❖   ❖   ❖

THE DOOR OPENED, letting in the strong afternoon sun as her father, mother, and Nana pushed in at the same time. For a second, she was sure they'd get stuck in the door. Mother stumbled in first, blinking in the sudden dimness, but finally spotting Leah, she darted toward her.

"My baby girl," she cooed, wrapping her arms around her. Her mother pulled away slightly and wrinkled her nose. "Pew, what is that smell?"

"Trust me, you don't want to know." She rested her head on her mother's shoulder. The incongruity of having a family reunion at the local neighborhood dive was lost on her mother. Her father stood off to the side, waiting his turn, while Nana walked hesitantly into the center of the room, staring at the back of her grandfather, who slowly turned.

"Buell." Her voice was little more than a whisper but carried across the room.

He started toward her in a walk but jogged the last two steps and swept her up in an embrace that lifted her feet from the ground. Leah backhanded her eyes, suddenly tear-filled, and her mother did the same.

"My Esmeralda, my sweet girl. How I missed you." He gently lowered her feet to the floor, landing a kiss on her hair.

"I missed you, too," Nana confessed in a soft voice that Leah didn't recognize.

Her father drifted over to her and wrapped an arm around her. "I'm glad you're back, Trinka."

She leaned against her father, realizing this was as probably as emotional as he got. "Me, too. I even learned something."

"Oh, really?" her father replied, giving her shoulders a little squeeze. "Anything I might want to hear?"

Whenever something went wrong, instead of scolding her or placing blame, her father would ask her what she'd learned from the incident. The familiarity of the routine comforted her.

SIGHING, SHE RUBBED her hand over her face. "I appreciate my family more than I ever did. I also think I understand why the desire to have power over others is so incredibly dangerous. It should make you wonder about anyone in a powerful position or office."

The bartender snorted his agreement, while her father motioned for her to continue.

"People accept scary stories even when they're made up because someone, they believe to be smarter than They're relayed the information."

Her father's lips tugged upward into a smile. "Sweetheart, right now you know more than about eighty percent of the world. Anything else you care to elaborate on? Sounds to me like you had an eye-opening trip."

Eye-opening, yeah, she might call it that, or deadly, or transformative. "What can I say, Dad? It was something. Something I never want to repeat again." She laughed more out of relief than anything else.

"Thanks for the drink." She turned to go, wondering why neither of her parents had mentioned her sitting at a bar. Nana had her hand tucked into her husband's arm and her head held close to his, talking animatedly. She suspected they were exchanging sweet nothings. When she drew closer, she overheard their conversation.

"Goddess help me, Buell. There's no one I love more than you, but if you ever think of leaving me again, there's no place far enough that you'll be able to hide from my wrath."

Grandfather's voice held a bit of humor. "Ah, darling, there's no place I want to be but by your side."

Leah grinned as she climbed into the backseat of the car. Finally, she was getting to know her grandfather. Not only was he an incredible ceremonial magician, but it looked like he was a charmer, too. He'd the gift of charisma, which would be a beneficial gift to have.

Working her back into the cushioned seat, she sighed and closed her eyes. So much she'd missed about her century. Anything well cushioned was one of them.

Her mother twisted her body to peer into the backseat. "While you were gone, you had a visitor."

Who could that be? Especially since Stella knew she was gone.

Her mother's expression turned playful. "An attractive fellow named Dylan."

"Dylan? Dylan came by. Um, you didn't tell him I was out of the century, did you?" Odd things sometimes happened in her family, but crossing centuries might have been even more difficult.

Her mother's laughter filled the car. "Of course not. I mentioned you were too sick for visitors. I'm not sure if he believed me. He left a card and the cutest stuffed animal, a dragon."

Grandfather quipped, "The boy has taste. Dragons are so much better than silly teddy bears."

Dylan had come by and brought her a gift. That was a very good sign. Her certainty about what a perfect boyfriend he'd be began to shimmer in her mind, like the portal had before it had blinked out of existence. Then again, she almost hadn't made it back here. Why not see what he'd to say in his card before deciding on a happily ever after ending?

CHAPTER SEVENTEEN

NORA AND ETHAN ran out of the house before the car had even stopped. They danced around her, trying to push each other out of the way to hug her. Even Theodora, her cat, got in on the action by weaving through their legs, almost tripping her. Ethan was the first to step back, shaking his head. "Whoo wee, you stink."

She wrinkled her nose at her brother's comment, knowing it was true. Her charmed gown apparently did not keep her fresh smelling. Its abilities included keeping her alive and bringing her back, which it had done very well.

Both Nora and Ethan stared at the man exiting the car from the other door. Their expressions mirrored surprise and curiosity. Of course, neither had ever met their grandfather.

He turned to face his staring grandchildren. His eyes twinkled as he held his arms wide. "There are the rest of my grandchildren. Come here."

Ethan readily hurled himself into the man's waiting arms with an enthusiastic, "Grandpa!"

Nora hung back a bit, biting her lip, looking a trifle uncertain. Grandfather managed to smile at Nora over Ethan's head. "No worries. I'm real, not like the dreams you've had."

Nora's hand flew up to cover her gasp. "How did you know about my dreams?" Her feet moved her closer, even if she didn't seem to be aware of her actions.

"You told me yourself." Grandpa tapped his forehead. He winked at Leah and mentally reminded her of the importance of barriers. "You practically shouted that you've seen me in your dreams, which demonstrates your exceptional psychic abilities. I've been trying to communicate with the family."

Nora nodded vigorously. Ethan released Grandfather's waist, giving him a thorough scrutiny. "You stink, too, but not as bad as Leah."

Reaching his gnarled hand out, he mussed Ethan's hair. "The ability to speak one's thoughts without fear of condemnation is a magnificent blessing. I congratulate you, Ethan. My hygiene may have suffered from living alone too much. I will do my best to improve. I'm sure your grandmother will encourage me." Everyone laughed, as he'd intended.

He nodded in Leah's direction. "I will yield the shower to you since you're in the greatest need."

She'd have preferred to read Dylan's card first, but she could do that in the bathroom, since her family overwhelmingly agreed she smelled foul. At least in the bathroom, she hadn't had to worry about anyone reading over her shoulder.

Their noisy reunion attracted some gawkers among the neighbors. The widow, who lived closest to them, muttered to herself, loud enough for them to hear. "Dressed up for Halloween. They're all a bit odd. At least they keep their lawn cut."

Leah followed behind Nora and her grandfather, who were in deep discussion about her dreams. Ethan worked his hand into hers, surprising her a little. She squeezed his hand, hoping she managed to convey how glad she was to be back.

"I understand that." Nora's voice drifted back to her. "Still, there's this man who I'm sure is calling me from the past. Some nights when I close my eyes, he's there."

Ethan and Leah looked at each other.

Grandfather patted Nora's hand. "Sounds like we need to talk."

Ethan stood on his tiptoes to whisper in Leah's ear. "Looks like someone else is getting ready to have an adventure."

I hope not, she wanted to add, but chose to say nothing. Instead, she contemplated the smooth cap of hair covering Nora's head, a modern cut belonging to a practical woman, not someone who would enjoy the past. It wasn't as if she'd liked her experience, but then, she'd learned from it.

The aroma of chicken and dumplings wafted outside from the open kitchen door. Lifting her nose, she inhaled greedily. Better get the showering done. She could tuck into the food, but first she'd like to see the card and the dragon. As if sensing her thoughts, her mother handed over the card and small stuffed animal as soon as she cleared the doorway.

She flourished the dragon. "Look! It's golden."

Grandfather, understanding her reason in mentioning the color, grinned. "I don't even know the boy, but already I like him. Of course, he'll have to go through me before dating one of my granddaughters."

Her father cleared his throat, noisily, threw back his shoulders and puffed out his chest, she assumed to appear larger. "Buell, you'll have your turn after me."

Rolling her eyes, she headed to her room to grab some clean clothes before heading to the shower. If either of them was serious, she doubted she'd ever go out. Her father would quiz her date on the three basic laws of Newtonian physics and the Pythagorean Theorem. Her grandfather was a different story. It was hard to be sure what he would do, especially after he scanned her date's mind.

No wonder her mother had waited until college to seriously date. Her mother had mentioned something about her father disappearing shortly after she'd met Adam, her soon-to-be husband. No wonder he'd managed to date Mom. She suspected grandfather could be intimidating when he wanted to be.

She stood at the bathroom door and yelled, "Going in. Does anyone need to use the bathroom first?"

Ethan darted in front of her, giving a curious look to her armful of supplies. She waited, wondering why she'd said anything, but it was common courtesy when you had one bathroom. A few minutes' wait was a very small price to pay for running water and a flush toilet. The thought of a toothbrush with actual toothpaste excited her.

The sound of flushing accompanied Ethan opening the door. He glanced at the dragon again, but surprisingly said nothing, very unlike him. Was she getting a reprieve from his usual comments due to her recent absences? More likely, their parents had threatened to take away his dance video game. Most boys favored games containing mayhem, destruction, and death. The game manufacturers labeled the games with either patriotic or sexy names to fool indulgent parents.

After finishing her own real-life game in which she'd been the dreaded enemy, she found the idea of the single-player role-playing game repulsive. Music began to pulsate from the living room. Ethan was probably showing Grandfather his moves. The clatter of dishes in the kitchen signaled dinner loomed ever closer.

The bathroom door shut, she turned on the shower, giving it time to warm up. Using her index finger, she slid it under the flap of the barely sealed envelope. Still, it remained sealed, which proved no one had read it. Nana could have just rested it against her forehead, but she doubted she had.

The card featured a cartoon pair of animals with one tucked up in bed with an ice pack on its head. The card inscription read: Hope You're Back on Your Feet Soon. Underneath it, Dylan had carefully written in slanting letters, *I miss you. Geometry class has become even more boring, if that's possible. Can't wait to see you. Dylan.*

He couldn't wait to see her. Leah held the card to her chest and then read it again. She was tempted to read it once more, but that might cut into her hot-water time. She placed the card inside the vanity cabinet so an errant splash wouldn't smear the sentiment.

The warm water pelted her, both stinging and reviving her. A soapy loofah rid her body of all dirt and odor not belonging to the twenty-first century. Her body was soon red from the scrubbing and felt oddly vulnerable.

People tended to take showers naked, so that wasn't it. She was missing her magickal covering. Pulling the curtain back, she peeked at the robe wadded in the corner. It didn't appear too enchanted any longer, just dirty and wrinkled. Could it be she'd used up all the power? Maybe it had disappeared when she no longer needed it. Often, at the end of rituals, they grounded the energy, sending it back into the earth. Maybe in removing the robe, she'd grounded the magick. It made sense.

For the first time in her life, she shampooed her hair twice, as the directions stated, before using conditioner. Her mother's response to the directions was that they only said that so the manufacturer could make more money. Her mother was right, but she'd to get the smoke smell out of her hair.

She lifted her hair to the shower spray, thinking how light she felt. Her arms lifted so easily. Who knew magick had actual physical weight? If she dealt with it all the time, like Grandfather or Nana, she might become more accustomed to it. Now, it was gone, and she missed it. It seemed like the equivalent of snapping off a finger or a toe. Make that, three fingers and a toe.

A hammering at the door stooped her musing.

"Dinner's on"

Not too much had changed in the few days she'd been gone. Meals waited for no one in her family. Sliding clothes over her still-damp body proved difficult but not impossible. She wrapped her long hair in a towel turban. Looking at the cabinet, she debated taking her card. She plucked her card off the top of the toiletries. If she left it, someone might knock something over on to it.

A stop at her room allowed Leah to place the card and dragon on her dresser. Theodora, perched on her bed, thrashed her tail, expressing discontent that Leah didn't trust her. That was Leah's interpretation, though. She was unsure her pet wouldn't investigate her dresser. She opened a drawer and dropped the card and dragon inside.

Dinner was a noisy affair with everyone asking her questions about Arabella and Lionel. Grandfather regaled everyone with his impressions of various folks. Leah decided not to mention he'd never left his portal cabin until the last day. Before the meal was up, she found herself yawning.

"Off to bed with you, young lady," her mother urged.

After hugging everyone once more, she stumbled off to her room, excited at the idea of slipping between clean sheets. With her door ajar, she heard her mother speaking to her father as she combed the tangles out of her hair.

"Adam, I'm not sure if sending her right back to school is such a good idea. She may need a debriefing of sorts or at least time to recover."

Leah swung her door back open. "I'm going to school. I missed enough days already. It is what I want, and it will help me to get back to normal."

Her mother's face reflected surprise, while her father agreed with her. "Sounds like the right thing to do."

With another disaster averted, she was ready to sink into a deep, dreamless sleep, but she didn't. Instead, she visited the village she'd so recently left, but instead of being a person, she felt more like a hovering presence, rather cloud-like.

The village hummed with the sound of an anvil ringing, the bleating of goats, people chattering, and the thud of wagon wheels and horses' hooves.

A wagon came into view with a couple setting on the bench seat. The dark-haired woman rocked a small bundle. The man wore a floppy hat that shadowed half his face.

"I not thought to come back here," the woman commented.

Leah immediately recognized Arabella's voice. She tried to peer under the hat shadow to get a glance at her mysterious husband with no luck. Clouds, if that's what she was, were not that maneuverable. She drifted along with the wagon, listening to the conversation.

"The only decent thing is to thank Agnes for her interference and creative lies," the man commented.

She'd heard that voice before. It sounded different, though, deeper.

Arabella held the baby up to her shoulder, exposing a tiny white face and dark hair. "I would have been lost if Agnes had not come up with the story of my husband and such. It made a decent woman out of me."

The story about Arabella's marriage hadn't been true, then. She'd wondered why grandfather had said Arabella had been raped. This explained it somewhat, but who was the man with her?

"The baby is a mirror image of you," he commented, slowing the horses near a small cottage. Tying off the reins, he descended to help Arabella and child alight. The woman from the crowd appeared in the doorway.

She hurried out to peer at the baby. "Have you chosen a name yet?"

"Yes," Arabella answered. She glanced at the man, who removed his hat, revealing the clean lines of Simon's face. "We named her Leah, after a close friend."

Ah, now everything made sense. Simon removed something from the wagon as Agnes asked Arabella, "Have you heard the news of your old neighbor Lionel?"

"I haven't" Arabella answered while fussing over the baby. She held up the child, who was dressed in an elaborate gown.

"Not long after you left with the dragon and oversized cat, his heart failed him. Some say it was the devil taking his due. I suspect he died from

love of you."

"It was more likely the first," Arabella announced. "All the same, his death saddens me. He'd so much potential."

Simon rounded the wagon with a chicken in his arms.

"What is that?" Agnes called out.

Leah thought it was obvious, but it could have been a rhetorical question.

The woman grinned and held out her arms to accept the gift.

Simon gave her the chicken with an admonishment. "This is not a dinner chicken. It is a magickal chicken. You'll always have plenty of eggs and never starve. Never give her away. Never boast about her, or someone will steal her."

Agnes clutched the chicken tightly, causing it to cluck in protest. "I know how folks are around here. Things are good now. People tolerate one another. Before you know it, someone else will turn up threatening brimstone and damnation. Last thing I would do is talk about my magickal hen."

The three nodded in agreement, then looked up in the direction she hovered, almost as if they could feel her presence.

The dream ended as she lay in a state between sleep and total wakefulness, contemplating all she'd heard. It answered her questions. Life was better in the village, at least for a while, according to Agnes. There always seemed to be someone who wanted to rile people up. Sometimes they could do it by promising eternal damnation. Other times, as in now, they just threatened to take away whatever had value. The more things changed, the more they stayed the same.

Her alarm rang, startling her, since she didn't remember setting it. For a moment, she stayed under the covers, warm and safe, with the sound of Theodora's loud purring in her ear. If she didn't move, her mother wouldn't wake her. She already knew her mother's opinion on going to school today. Though she'd never been a morning person, the thought of Dylan had her vaulting out of bed.

She needed time to get ready to look her best to return to school. Opening her closet to find clean clothes, she thanked the school board members who'd voted for uniforms. Leah understood she might be the only girl who thought it was a wonderful thing. Her hair was clean, which was another plus. If only she could get in the bathroom before Ethan.

The sound of her brother singing killed that hope. Well, she could wash her face in the kitchen and apply her makeup in her room. If she'd to put up with a little brother who hogged the bathroom for acoustics, so be it. In another year, she'd be away at college.

Leah now found even the most mundane things about school thrilling.

She even gave Cerberus a big smile, causing Brianna to run into a locker. She reminded her of Sabina, obsessed about her appearance and the need for all boys to notice her. Sabina wasn't that bad, vain, self-absorbed, but she'd good traits, too. Maybe there was some good about Cerberus.

Leah accepted the homework her teachers gave her, although she was tempted to ask how long she'd been gone. That would have made her sound stupid. *Excuse me, but I've been away in another century, and I'm unsure if time progresses the same in both centuries.* Yep, that would probably get her a vacation at the residential facility that a tenth of the school regularly seemed to check into on a rotating basis. Leah believed that had more to do with the parents than the kids. Did the parents have good insurance? Were the parents tired of teenage moodiness and defiance? If so, the facility even had an admissions counselor, who looked a lot like a professional wrestler.

It was almost time for geometry. As much as she wanted to check her appearance, she bypassed the mirror stop to avoid detention. Hurrying to class, she fell in step with Dylan, who turned and stopped.

"You're back," he said, stating the obvious.

"I am," Leah answered in another understatement.

Dylan grinned. "I'm so happy you're okay." The math teacher stood by the door with his arms folded, looking less than impressed in the presence of young love.

"You're both late," he growled the words as a threat, causing the two of them to rush into class.

After geometry, Dylan walked her to English class, where they stood close in the hall, but not touching. Her heart beat as fast as when she'd been sure the oily creature was going to get her. Maybe not that fast, but close enough.

"I was wondering," Dylan started, and then stopped when the English teacher appeared in the door.

The teacher raised one eyebrow, then said, "Believe it or not, Dylan Torres, I, too, was young once. I'm going to write you a pass for your next class. Say what you need to say before I get back. Remember, this is the only pass you'll get from me."

Dylan looked astonished at the idea that Mrs. Barkin had been young once. He gauged her distance before blurting out his invitation. "Leah, would you go out with me this Friday?"

Her heart gave a little jump. Everything was turning out exactly the way she wanted. "I'd love to."

"You would?" Surprise colored his voice. "I mean, I'm glad you would. I know you heard about my father being a minister. I figured that might scare you off."

She heard the sharp heel taps of the teacher. "I'm not afraid."

The teacher appeared with a pass in her hand. "Mr. Torres, make haste to get to class."

Dylan took off in a slight run as Leah entered the classroom, only to have Stella wave at her. She weaved around the desks to sit next to her friend.

Stella hugged her with so much enthusiasm that it caught some of the other students' attention. "Thank goodness, you're back. I've been slaving away on our essay. The good news is I finished it. The bad news is Mrs. Barkin likes it so well she wants us to present it to the class."

Leah collapsed into her chair at the thought of a public presentation, quickly followed by the thought that plenty of people were willing to say stupid, hateful things. Why not try to make a difference for once? She and Stella might wake up a few students to help them realize they'd been guilty of participating in religious stereotyping.

Any female who could face down the abbot could deal with a high school English class. In a flash, Leah realized she could do anything as long as she believed she could.

THE END

REVELATION

PAGAN EYES, BOOK 2

BY
RAYNA NOIRE

CHAPTER ONE

*H*IS EYES SPARKLED *with humor as he held out his hand to her. "Climb up, darling. I've been waiting for you."*

Familiarity colored his voice as if he greeted an old friend. Nora knew she'd have remembered a dark-eyed hottie with curly hair and a wicked smile. Better yet, the bright green and yellow wagon he stood on was memorable, especially with its fanciful drawings on the side and the two draft horses in the traces. Was she remembering part of a movie or a story Nana told her? That was it. Nana was part Romany Gypsy.

Still, it didn't make sense if she was in the story and the unknown man spoke English. Part of her wanted to take his hand and step up into the wagon to take off with him. At times, he looked into her eyes, not only as if he knew her, but also liked what he saw, which made his invitation tempting, very tempting.

The man dropped his hand. "Oh, I see you're still not ready, my Nora."

"How do you know my name?"

The man jumped down from the wagon, startling her, invading her space. His face filled her vision. She had to admire his strong jawline, and the crinkles around his eyes when he smiled caused her heart to beat faster. Her lips turned up naturally in response.

"Nora, Nora, how could you have forgotten me? I have loved you through several lifetimes and searched for you in each of mine. My life was desolate until I found you in a dream."

She was dreaming. That made sense.

"Nora, Nora."

Why did he keep repeating her name? He said her name as if he knew it well, without a blink or a hesitation, not like those fraternity guys trying to hit on her who could never quite remember her name, calling her everything from Nadine to Noreen. One even called her Norad, which she promptly informed him stood for North American Aerospace Defense Command. As she recalled, her would-be Romeo stumbled away, muttering, "bitch" loud enough for her to hear.

Men never worked too hard to romance her. Her purpose in attending college was to get an education, enabling her to obtain a decent job. A good portion of the girls who came to school felt the need to cut loose by skipping class, drinking too much, and having sex with guys they didn't know or couldn't remember. Often those same girls flunked out in less than two years. As a scholarship student, she needed to keep her grades up.

Why didn't she know his name?

His voice became higher, sounding more like a woman's, and he shook her shoulder vigorously. Why would he do that? Ogden would do that, but not this mysterious man.

"Nora, get up right now, or you're going to be late to your clinical."

Tonya's voice broke into her sleep-drugged thoughts. Her eyelids fluttered opened to the morning sunlight streaming around her curtain, indicating the time. "Oh, I overslept. Thank you, Tonya."

Her clean uniform hung on the hanger in front of her closet where she left it. The ironed smock and pants gave her a little reassurance that she'd make it on time. Some of the students showed up in wrinkled uniforms, and from standing too close to them, she suspected a few were unwashed, too. How could a person make it this far in the physician assistant program and still not take it seriously? Nora took it seriously. Of course, she did. She took everything in earnest, probably the curse of being the firstborn.

Tonya kept a running commentary as she dressed. "It's not like you to be late. I even heard your alarm go off, so I came into the room. You had a big, stupid grin on your face. Was it a good dream?"

Thinking back to the man in her dream, she'd probably call it perplexing as opposed to good. Yet, she was happy she'd remembered. Part of her recognized him and was glad to see him. "I guess you could call it a good dream."

"Ah ha." Tonya grinned and shook a finger at her. "I bet you were not dreaming about Ogden then."

Grabbing a brush, she ran it through her short, dark hair. A shower would be better, but she'd given that up when she chose to continue to dream about the dark-eyed man instead of getting up on time. "How do you know I wasn't dreaming about Ogden?"

Snorting, her roommate shook her head. "Girl, now's not the time for it, but…"

Nora knew her outspoken roommate would say whatever was on her mind. Holding back wasn't her way. One of the things she enjoyed about the colorful Jamaican. "Go on."

"All right, I will." Placing her long-fingered hands on her ample hips, she started, "We've been friends for almost four years, right?"

Nora nodded, thinking back to the day they ended up together. Her assigned roommate had reported her when she'd lighted a candle in recognition of the Goddess. It hadn't been the lighted candle, even though it was against the rules. Nope, her roommate had told her the Goddess statue creeped her out. Called her a Satanist then reported her for open flames. She should have reported Crystal for smoking in the bathroom, but she hadn't. Instead, in a panicked moment, she'd pictured her career and scholarship vanishing.

Luckily, she'd argued religious freedom and kept her scholarship but had to move out of the dorm. Yeah, like, she'd had somewhere to go. Tonya, her anatomy lab partner, had asked why she'd missed class, and she'd explained the long story, not leaving anything out.

The usually jovial woman had grinned at the end of her story, instead of acting horrified as Nora had expected she would at the mention of the Goddess. "You and me, we belong together. My roommate found true love and is shacking up with her man. Could use help with the rent."

That had been that. Here they were, four years later. She knew good and well that Tonya would have her say. She earned the privilege by being the first, genuine friend Nora had had since Abby. "You know you saved me by inviting me to room with you."

"Don't you forget it. As your savior, I see how hard you work. Fun is not a part of your routine. Now, I know you are not a party-every-night girl, but you need to cut loose some time before you tie yourself to Ogden Thurston Graves the Third." Tonya pretended to shiver.

Sitting on her bed, Nora pulled on her socks and orthopedic white shoes. The shoes made her feel like a very unstylish sixty-year-old. "I know you don't like Ogden, but he's a brilliant resident. I am lucky to have him."

Tonya folded her arms. "Unlucky. The lucky-to-have-him nonsense sounds like something Ogden would say."

He did, but she'd never admit it to her roommate. "I need to hit the bathroom, then go." Suiting her actions to her words, she headed for the small bathroom they shared. One of Tonya's dates, after seeing the number of toiletries around the tub, had asked how many girls lived there.

Finished, she opened the bathroom door to find her friend waiting with a peanut butter sandwich. "Breakfast is the most important meal of the day."

Tonya had started out studying to be a nurse but switched to nutritionist in her second year. Often, Nora benefitted from her concerns about proper diet. "Thanks."

Tonya followed her to the apartment building hallway to yell after her, "If Ogden is such a prize, why aren't those other nursing students all over him? Remember, a single doctor is still a premium commodity."

Jogging down the stairs, Nora tried to ignore the words. It was no secret that her friend didn't like Ogden. When he'd started coming around, she'd pretended he was helping her with her studies. It hadn't made sense that a busy resident would want to help a college student, but Tonya had marginally accepted her excuse. She'd still narrowed her eyes, muttering about Ogden being a poor excuse for a man.

The bus arrived, tabling her thoughts for a moment. Her bus pass was in the same hand as her sandwich. The bus driver gave her an annoyed look but said nothing. She wouldn't be the first person to eat on the bus. At least she wouldn't leave her trash behind like the others. Spotting a pair of empty seats, she headed toward them, acknowledging a few of the other students on her way.

As she sank into the hard-plastic seat, her shoulders relaxed. For the next twenty minutes, she could veg out and eat her sandwich. She turned her wrist to make sure the bus was on schedule, but her bare wrist mocked her attempt. Great, she'd forgotten her watch, which would make things infinitely more difficult. She used the second hand on her watch to count pulse rate. Dr. Benjamin pointed out that often you didn't have a blood pressure cuff nearby in an emergency.

What else could she screw up this morning? Her breakfast disappeared in under two minutes with her rapid, angry bites taking out some of her aggravation on defenseless wheat bread. The sandwich left her thirsty and still hungry. No help for it. She should be grateful for what she had. That's how she felt about Ogden, even if other medical students or nurses weren't chasing him down. His prematurely balding head made him look older than his twenty-nine years, and she'd admit, he could be a bit stuffy talking about his Boston Brahman bloodline. Nora never said much about hers, not that he asked.

He'd told her once he decided on her because she showed the most intelligence among the students at the hospital. At the time, she'd thought that was high praise. It made her proud and happy. Later, she'd realized he never said how pretty she was, how sexy, or how he longed for her. Nope, not once. His interest was more in genetics. He'd quizzed her on any pre-existing medical conditions and if any diseases ran in her family. For a moment, she wondered if he'd drop her if diabetes or, worse yet, dementia had shown up. On one level, she knew he would.

Still, he was a solid man, who was going places. A good person she could depend on. Although, sometimes, Ogden was the one who did all the depending, asking her to do things like pick up his dry cleaning, drop a snack by the hospital, or buy his mother a birthday present. At least it made her feel needed. He did need her.

The familiar cityscape meant she was almost to the hospital. She glanced at the other bus riders, wondering what their lives were like. A few were students like her. Some were in whites, heading to the hospital, the same as her. Did any of the women expect a big romance in their lives? Some might. Maybe a few had one. Still, she didn't see that for herself, not after what had happened in high school.

She bit her bottom lip, trying to block the memory the best she could. Not remembering helped her to cope. Unlike her little sister, Leah, she'd chosen not to be secretive about her faith. If people could wear crosses and printed shirts proclaiming them hipsters for Christ, she was unsure why she couldn't wear a simple pentacle. She had for a short while, until she started to hear the rumors that she and her friends had kinky witchy sex.

Her fists closed, causing her nails to bite into her palms. Scenes from that horrific night flashed into her mind. The football players, her friend Abby screaming, the boys holding her down, mocking her with their boozy slurs as they penetrated her. The incident, as she preferred to call it, was all a horrible nightmare she worked to forget. She blamed herself.

She and Abby had made a pact to say nothing as they'd traveled together to the clinic for pregnancy and STD testing. Luckily, the tests had cleared them. The helpful nurse had lectured them on the dangers of STDs, and how even though a person could have an STD, you didn't always contract it. She'd warned against making the mistake about thinking the person was clean. Nora doubted those football players were clean by a long shot.

Ironically, the incident—as horrible as it had been—had made her consider nursing as a career choice. When she'd needed help, that one nurse had given her practical advice without judging her or Abby. She wanted to help other people when they needed help.

Technically, they both knew they should have reported the attack. Unfortunately, since the kinky witchy sex rumors had existed before the incident, she'd doubted anyone would have believed them. The attack had been premeditated, which made it somehow worse.

She'd never told anyone as she waited for some online tell-all, but it never came. Unable to stop them from ravishing her body, she'd cursed them, long and lavishly, using everything she'd ever read in spell books, threatening them if they ever breathed a word. She also knew she wasn't supposed to wish ill on people or it would come back on her threefold.

The depraved, sadistic males who'd jumped her and Abby were human garbage with fancy haircuts in expensive clothes. She could accept that, but still couldn't figure out why they'd picked her and Abby. It wasn't exactly like they were the school skanks. It could have been a crime of opportunity. Two distracted girls not paying attention to their environment while walking in an isolated dark stretch.

Her family had moved shortly after the incident. She was sure no one knew, but the timing of the move was suspicious. She never found out if anything bad had happened to the boys. They did lose every football game for the rest of the season, but she doubted that had been from a curse.

Worse, though, Abby had gone to a home for the mentally ill after having a breakdown. Nora was able to see her, but all her friend did was look off into the distance, retreating so far into herself, she shut out the world around her.

Nora's way of dealing was to give up on the idea of romance. Maybe the idea of love worked out for some people, such as her mother, but not for her. Those handsome, cocky males just wanted to do vicious, cruel acts to your body. The passionate romance scenes with the couple carried away with each other were not for her. In fact, she avoided those movies.

Ogden wasn't the type to inspire grand passion, and she preferred that. Not like her dream stranger, who made her heart beat fast and her hands sweat. Not a good sign, but luckily, he didn't exist.

"I'm hurt, my darling, that you would malign me so by saying I don't exist."

She cut her eyes to the empty seat beside her and the window next to her. There were no other places the voice could have come from, but her mind. Must be the sleeping pill she took last night. Perhaps she fell asleep on the way to the hospital. That was it.

The bus stopped. Students and a nurse stood to disembark. Nora joined them, anxious to get the day started and her mind off the past and the sexy male voice whispering inside her skull. According to her psychology classes, her personality could have fractured due to the incident. Such a coping mechanism would allow different aspects to take charge to protect her from future harm. There were a few flaws with the theory.

The elderly security guard called out a cheery hello.

"Morning, Herman," she responded.

The fact the hospital had guards at every door had surprised her at first, until she learned that the inner-city hospital was a favorite haunt for homeless folks or those sleeping off a drunk on the long vinyl couches in the lobby. Some less attentive, or perhaps more compassionate, guards allowed a few homeless in to pass the night, especially during the winter.

People crowded around the elevator. Nora headed for the stairs. The exercise would be good and would allow her time to think about the voice.

It couldn't be a coping mechanism. If so, why wait five years to show up? By this time, she was over it. The voice didn't represent some part of her or speak for her. No, it addressed her. Her workload, coupled with her schooling, could be the root. Tonya planting ideas in her head as to why Ogden wasn't right for her didn't help. No wonder this sexy stranger populated her dreams and thoughts. He was the exact opposite of Ogden.

By the third floor, she was rethinking her plan to climb to the fifth floor. No use, she needed to get to class on time. Her mind put up the image of Ogden next to her dream man, almost as if she were examining a textbook. The mystery man exuded charm and a lilting Irish accent, while Ogden held no claim to any type of charm but did have a haughty way of pronouncing certain words. He often informed her he was saying the words the correct way, implying everyone else wasn't. When the mystery man jumped down to stand beside her, she saw he was a couple of inches taller than her five-foot-seven, and his wide shoulders tapered down to a narrow waist and a flat stomach. Her only regret was she hadn't notice more in her dream.

Ogden loomed over her at six-foot-one. Despite his height, he lacked the muscle tone a person might expect from a tall man. He was already developing a potbelly, as well, not that she'd ever mention it aloud.

The fifth-floor door finally appeared. Nora pushed it open with a grateful gasp. A chattering group of students exited the elevator at the same time she entered the hallway. Some were juggling coffee and a doughnut. Envy jabbed her at their casual attitude and capricious spending. She knew good and well that coffee and a doughnut at the hospital would run almost five dollars. No telling how many peanut butter sandwiches she could eat compared to that one snack of empty calories. Still, she sighed a little. It would have been nice not to count every penny. Soon, she'd be making money and could buy doughnuts if she wished, not that Tonya would approve if they were still roommates.

Rushing to catch up with the others, she almost ran into Ogden. Her almost-fiancé glared down at her.

"There you are, Nora. I've waited"—he checked his watch—"almost eight minutes for you to show. I made a special trip to this floor to say hello. I am a busy man."

"Sorry." The apology popped out of her mouth before she even thought about it. What did she have to be sorry about? She'd spent the last thirty minutes of her life to get here. Her welcome was a morning scolding she could do without. "Hello. Now you can go back to your *important* stuff."

Ogden threw her a bewildered look before he walked away without comment.

In another man, his behavior might be insulting. Unfortunately, this was his normal behavior. A smirk crossed her face. He hadn't even recognized her sarcasm. Yep, his "important stuff" included telling the other residents why they were wrong in their diagnoses. Often, he acted as if he were the teaching doctor.

Another female student caught up with her as she walked to the briefing room. The redheaded woman grimaced before commenting, "Did God tell you that you weren't wearing your uniform right?"

Nora automatically gave the woman a slight smile while she mentally took inventory of the woman's uniform. Clean, ironed, a little tight. Still, that wasn't a big deal. Weight tended to fluctuate in college. It certainly didn't merit buying a new uniform, especially on a student's salary.

"Yours looks fine. He told me I was late."

Her companion rolled her eyes. "What is he, your father or husband? I'm unsure why the man has such an inflated opinion of himself. Word is he's annoyed most of the female students with unwanted comments."

Nora's eyebrows shot up. She'd never heard anything about this before. "Um, I didn't catch your name. Mine's Nora Carpenter."

"Katie Marshall." The woman nodded at a cute intern who returned her interest. "He's a cutie, but I heard he has a nurse on the third floor. You'd think as students that we get first chance at the doctors, but no. Even that officious boar you were talking to has a woman. Imagine that."

"Oh, really." Nora pretended some mild interest. "Didn't you just tell me he was flirting with all the female students?"

Tinkling laughter filled the air as Katie's face contorted in mirth. She stopped a moment for a breath, before answering. "I didn't say flirting. He feels free to make comments to all the females, from their uniforms or hair not being right to criticizing their chart notes. He's a chauvinist. Never says a word to the male students. He's probably afraid one of them would punch him out for his *help*."

The fact he never criticized the men said a great deal. Ogden must feel some natural superiority over all women. That didn't bode well for their future.

She entered the classroom and edged her way to the front to hear better and have a good view of the whiteboard, where Dr. Benjamin stood with a marker in her hand. Nora grabbed a front-row seat.

The female doctor spoke fast and did not tolerate slowpokes or whiners, a woman Nora could understand. The doctor began going over the various signs of diabetes before everyone had sat down. A pointed look landed on the students still consuming their doughnuts.

Nora took rapid notes in her notebook. Most of the information she already knew, but she still took notes. It wouldn't hurt to refresh her knowledge. Besides, Dr. Benjamin might mention something new.

One part of her mind dwelled on what Katie had said. The woman certainly was outspoken, but it didn't mean she'd lied. It gave her something to consider. Life with Ogden became less and less desirable with each day and each ridiculous demand and pouting behavior when she refused to do his piddly errands. Didn't he care that her life was busy? She didn't even have a car. How was she supposed to run all over town for him? Why was she dating him, anyhow?

"Ms. Carpenter, would you suspect diabetes in a patient losing weight rapidly?"

The doctor's voice jolted her out of her contemplation. "I would, but I would ask about other symptoms, including feeling thirst, bruising easily, and a continual sense of fatigue."

"Very good." The doctor gave her an approving look before moving on to another likely target.

Nora doubted she would be so approving if the woman knew she was analyzing her love life. "Love life" was certainly the wrong term. She doubted if there was any love between the two of them. They used each other for different purposes.

Ironically, Ogden probably thought she enjoyed the prestige of being his girlfriend. There was no honor connected with it. Embarrassment would better sum up her feelings. She hadn't mentioned to Katie that she was disparaging her man. Instead, she was curious to see what others thought, which was pretty much as she'd suspected. Still, it hit her in the face like a splash of cold water on a winter day. If she were honest with herself, she'd admit Ogden was her wall. He served as a barrier against other men's flirtatious banter. When she'd first started school, she'd frozen out the potential Romeos with her aloof manner. The tactic earned her the label of Ice Queen and made a few work that much harder, usually after they had three or four beers in them. A boyfriend was Tonya's solution, but her roommate never suspected she'd pick up a pretentious bore.

Ogden wasn't as much of a deterrent as she thought he'd be. Since he wasn't on campus, men tended to believe he was mythical or of no importance. Nor, despite his size, did the man intimidate. He also did not show any type of possessiveness toward her, unless it was when he wanted his errands run first.

By the end of the lecture, Nora decided that a future with Ogden might not be in her best interest. For now, she'd let things drift. It was easier that way.

CHAPTER TWO

NORA SLID INTO the staff lounge to grab a break. The day had gone faster than she'd expected while she'd taught a mother and her recently diagnosed daughter how to check the child's blood sugar. Children should not get diseases. It almost made her tear up watching the eight-year-old bite her lip as she bravely pricked her finger. The doctor would monitor the child's progress before recommending an insulin pump.

Nora's mind galloped ahead, imagining the young girl trying to eat a balanced diet while her friends gobbled fast food and sugary treats. It would be hard to resist. They had plenty of adults on the diabetic floor who couldn't resist overindulging in treats that could kill them, or at least put them in the hospital.

Discipline is what it took. She'd tried to explain this to the over-emotional mother that it would help if the mother cleaned up the entire family's diet, eliminating foods that might cause her daughter to secretly binge. Mom might do it for a few weeks, or maybe not at all, declaring that it wouldn't be fair to the rest of the family. People said they wanted to help a loved one, but seldom were willing to deprive themselves of a likable activity.

It frustrated her to see families reeking of smoke gathered around a lung-cancer patient. Alcoholics suffering from cancer of the liver rarely had to buy liquor, since it often was already in the house or friends brought it.

Her hands fisted. She could not make family members realize they played a significant part in their loved one's ability to heal. Her own family helped her to heal in their own way. Of course, they didn't ask her about her lack of dates. Her father believed academics came first and approved. Her mother made a few hints about boys her age at various gatherings they attended, but never pushed her. Nana never said anything but gave her the eye as if she knew. Her family believed Nana had *the sight*, which would explain her amulet.

Her hand went up to grasp the necklace she always wore. The amulet consisted of agate, galena, tiger-eye, chiastolite, and malachite. Each protection stone swung from a circle, which represented feminine power. She never took it off despite one of her clinical supervisors implying it was germ-ridden and inappropriate. Instead, she wore it tucked under her clothing. No worries about her wearing anything low-cut enough to expose the necklace or her cleavage.

If that wasn't enough, Nana also had given her an anklet composed of healing stones to wear. The delicate chain connected citrine, crystal, and ametrine. Crystal was a magnifier, while the other two were for depression. Often, when she'd returned from school those first weeks after the incident, the scent of sage lingered in her room. No doubt, her grandmother and mother were smudging her room, clearing it of negativity. The more she thought about it, the more she believed she hadn't conquered her fear and depression on her own.

Maybe Abby wouldn't have been in the mental health center if her family knew how to help her. It puzzled her, though, if Nana knew why hadn't insisted on calling the police and reporting the boys? Then again, Nana's ability probably allowed her to see nothing would happen to the popular boys, while Nora would suffer humiliation and harassment. Even if evidence stared the police in the face, they'd still doubt.

Sometimes, Nora wondered if there was an instinctive response for men to believe men and distrust women. Hard to say, but she did know she tended to distrust men. Often, she questioned the simplest actions by males, trying to decide if they meant her harm. Sure, there were decent men in her life, including her father, little brother, and a few of her instructors. The fact that she'd developed friendships with Brian and Damien, fellow students, was a plus, though them being gay may have been a factor.

What if her life were more normal?

Maybe it was. According to statistics presented in trauma medicine class, one out of four women suffered a sexual assault at the hands of someone they knew. Out of these assaults, only three percent ever resulted in jail time. The number of rapes rose with the use of rape drugs and inferences that the woman wanted it. How did the other women get past it? Did they have one true love who demonstrated how a relationship should work? No doubt, many would break up if they weren't able to deal with the situation.

The door opened, admitting a few residents. Nora looked at the two young men who'd entered. Neither was Ogden, solidifying her decision to leave. Caution warned her not to allow herself to be alone with multiple men.

One of the men glanced at her and smiled. His nameplate read T. Mangano. His curly hair reminded her of her mystery man.

"Don't leave on our account," Mangano said. He held out his hand. "My name is Terrence."

Nora gingerly took his hand, not wanting to touch him, and gave it a single firm pump, meeting social protocol. "No problem. My break is over anyhow."

Nora pulled the door shut behind her, but not before she heard the other man chide his friend. "Real smooth, Terrence, chased her off before you even got her name."

No reason to linger to hear his response, but part of her wanted to. Call it feminine curiosity. She thought she'd detected an actual desire to meet her. Tonya often reminded her that her aloofness pulled in men more than any outright flirting. What a shame, Tonya concluded, when she didn't want to attract them. No one could accuse her of being friendly to the residents. She treaded a thin line, between civility and abruptness.

Wasn't it enough she'd cut her hair, making it into a dark cap of curls? After the incident, she'd used a pair of scissors to shear off the locks that had provided a handhold for the football players. Her mother had cleaned up the ravaged hair and oddly never asked why Nora had done it, only sighed a little at the loss of her long hair.

Close to the end of her day, she glanced at the wall clock. A group of students headed toward the elevators. She'd joined them when she saw Ogden making his way down the hall. Without any conscious thought, she worked her way through the group to be the first to board the elevator. As the doors closed, she breathed a sigh of relief, thinking she'd avoided another errand. A smitten man would have raced down the stairs to meet the elevator, as a fellow student's beau did once. Ogden would not rush down the stairs to greet her. Good, because he'd meet her with a pout instead of a smile.

On the bus, she watched the familiar scenery flash by. Even though her eyes threatened to close, she had to stay alert or she'd miss her work stop. Her short-order-cook position allowed her both lunch and dinner, which was a measure in savings. As a cook, she didn't have to flirt with all the men who thought they were handsome or witty. Nora heard the servers' complaints about too-friendly patrons and blessed her skill to cook several meals at once.

After carrying her backpack into the restaurant, she changed into her cook whites. It seemed ridiculous to change from white clothes to white clothes, but she needed to keep her hospital clothes spotless. Once she became associated with a hospital or doctor's office, she'd have more variety in what she could wear. Until then, it was all whites, so the students were easy to pick out. Of course, the patients couldn't differentiate between actual staff and students and often asked her for assistance.

Dressed in her cook clothes, she was welcomed by the scent of frying onions and the first shift cook's enthusiastic greeting as she pushed open the swinging door.

"Thank God, you're here." Ernie motioned to her with a spatula. "Get your apron on."

Nora stopped to clock in at the time clock. She was ten minutes early for her shift. She perched the silly envelope hat on her head and wrapped the oversized apron around her slender body. "What's up?"

Ernie flipped a series of burgers before answering. "Legionnaires convention."

Nora reached for a long-handled spatula and started pushing the onions around. "Why didn't they head over to that girlie place with the wide-screen television?"

Ernie gave her an unreadable look before answering. "Their food is horrible, while Order Up is best known for quality."

Odd, that's not what she'd heard about the small restaurant. Its popularity stemmed from being open all night and being right next to a huge hotel. Eventually, the guests tired of paying twelve dollars for a burger and made the short trip. She didn't correct the man, especially if he took pride in his work.

Ernie grinned at her. "I was joking. I doubt their hearts could take the other place since their average age is eighty."

"Oh." Nora stored the information in the medical portion of her brain. Too much stimulation could kill an elderly man. Then again, Ernie could be messing with her. It wouldn't be the first time. He insisted one of their regulars had a crush on her. The middle-aged man he'd referred to had cold, light blue eyes and always wanted to talk to the chef about his meal.

The first couple of times she'd talked to him, there had been nothing wrong with her cooking, and she'd known it. The man's complaints had put her on the defensive, causing her to barrel through the swinging doors, much to his delight. One time he'd complimented the food while his eyes roamed over her body, making her cook whites feel filthy by the interaction. Why couldn't he have been satisfied with Bonnie, the waitress, who always wore her smock unzipped to the point of being R-rated? Evil had rolled off the man. She'd looked at the other people in the restaurant. None of them had seen him for what he was, only her. He'd known it, too, which was probably why he'd complained, knowing she could do nothing. It had made her feel helpless—not a feeling she liked.

Sometimes, the servers ran interference for her, saying she was too busy or could make him another meal if it wasn't to his liking. He never accepted a new meal. A pattern began to develop. He showed up only on the days she worked. How he knew, when she worked perplexed her, since her off days changed. It made her wonder if he watched her or waited somewhere close by for her to show up for work before entering the diner. The good news was he didn't show up every day, and he didn't always complain when he did.

Ernie knew the man made her uncomfortable. There was nothing she could do about it since he was a regular customer. He never raised his voice or used threatening language. Occasionally, he'd say something bizarre along with his usual complaints. Once he offered to bring in a sample of sauerkraut that he'd made. Her creepy feeling appeared to be just hers. The manager, Barb, had laughed at her fears and told her she was a pretty girl who could cook, which was what all men wanted.

Linda, an older waitress, stuck her head in the kitchen window. "Ernie, getting any closer on those burger plates?"

Nora arranged the bun and fixings on the plates as Ernie argued with Linda good-naturedly. A ding of the deep fryer sent her to the fries table as Ernie slid the burgers onto the plate.

"Hey, Nora, you are here. Well, I'll be. He was right," Linda commented, causing Nora to peer over her shoulder.

"Right about what?" She tore open another bag of fries and poured them into the fryer basket. Her hand lingered on the basket for a second as she debated about starting them.

"Your fan told me you were here, back in the kitchen. I told him your shift hadn't started yet. Goes to show how much attention I was paying when a customer knows more of what is going on than I do."

Linda's words caused the basket to slip out of her hand into the hot oil with a loud sputtering fall. Her body jerked back in reflex to avoid the heated oil. Great, not what she wanted to hear. Today appeared to be populated with troublesome males, from her dream man, Ogden's moodiness and demands, overfriendly interns, and her resident stalker.

Maybe she was paranoid. The man probably lived alone and thought of the people at the diner as his family. If so, she didn't want to know what family member she played.

The back door opened, catching her attention as the milk deliveryman backed into the area with his milk crates-laden hand truck. She abandoned her place at the fryer to hold the door open. The graying hair peeking out from the cap identified Otis.

Her first thought on meeting Otis two years ago had been that at his age he shouldn't be delivering milk. He had to be older than her grandparents were. The sweet-natured man had told her he was grateful someone would give an old man a job. Still, she felt obligated to help as much as she could to give the man a break. Originally, it was a battle. Otis was very old school and didn't believe females should lift heavy milk crates. Luckily, she'd managed to get him to change his mind.

She waved goodbye, and before she turned back to the prep counter, she saw Ernie make a waving motion with his hand, holding up four fingers.

Nora laughed before reaching into the freezer for fish fillets. Ernie had made up his own system for relaying information when he thought the kitchen might be too loud. His system relied on someone looking at him first to be effective. Nora never pointed out the flaw. Most of the time, the cooks worked alone, unless it was busy like today. She dropped the fish, jiggled the fries, and then began to put out a series of plates.

She glanced back to the exterior door. "Ernie, do they always keep the back door unlocked for deliveries?"

The man's eyebrows lowered. "How long you worked here?"

Nora had landed the job when she was sophomore. "About three years."

Ernie nodded in agreement. "You asking me something you already know." He rolled his eyes and snorted a little in disgust. "Cheese, four."

Nora placed the cheese slices on the burgers, wishing she hadn't mentioned the door, but lately it worried her. Ernie was right that the door had been unlocked for as long as she'd worked there. "I know, but it doesn't seem safe. What about late at night?"

The smell of hamburgers made her stomach growl. She'd be able to sneak a burger once they slowed down. It was amazing she hadn't gained weight at this job. Tonya joked that she'd have to slow down for weight to catch up to her.

Ernie slid the cheeseburgers on the buns and nodded in the direction of the fries at the same time the buzzer went off. Carrying the plates to the fries' area, she mounded shoestring potatoes on the plates. Generous servings kept the customers coming back. Tonya referred to it as maximizing heart attack risk.

As if remembering her question, Ernie replied, "I think they lock the door around ten, because no deliveries will come later than that."

It made sense. She'd worked the third shift only a few times, and she couldn't remember locking the door. That meant she'd worked alone with the door unlocked. Anyone could have come in and easily pulled her out of the building or into the walk-in freezer where her screams wouldn't be heard. A shiver vibrated through her, causing her hands to grasp the counter for support.

"Hey, are you worried about someone stealing our bacon?" Ernie laughed at his comment. "Heard about two guys taking a forklift and stealing six hundred pounds of bacon. They must have really liked bacon, right?"

"Right." She held her hands out. They appeared steady, which made it safe to carry the plates to the pass-through window. "Linda, four cheeseburger plates," she called out.

After setting the plates down, Nora pulled off Linda's order paper and placed it on the spike. Order Up held to old-school ways because they were cheap. Oddly, they seemed effective, too. No one stopped working if the computer went down. She scanned the room to see if Linda had heard her and caught him looking at her.

Their eyes met, and he smiled a genuine glad-to-see-you smile.

Nora spun away, refusing to acknowledge him. He'd told her once his name was Lloyd. Did she expect him to call him by his name as if they were friends? Her nametag identified her. She hoped Linda would make it to the window in a timely fashion to pick up her order. No way would she stand there calling her name while Lloyd tried to make friendly.

The rest of the shift was uneventful. Ernie stayed an extra hour and a half, which allowed Nora time to stand in the kitchen to wolf down a cheeseburger. The servers received one meal with their shift, while cooks received two. Ernie said it was because they didn't get tips. It was probably more based on not being able to monitor what a cook ate, so you might as well give them two meals. The only problem was Board of Health restrictions against eating in the kitchen. Cooks across the country managed to skirt this by not eating while health inspectors were there.

Brandon, the night cook, came in around seven to hang out and eat before his shift. The bald cook was a former Marine, sporting several patriotic tattoos. Nora imagined if someone made the mistake of sneaking in the back door when Brandon was working, he'd leave quickly once he saw the muscle-bound man.

Business had slowed enough that after she fixed him food, she left the kitchen to talk to him. Oddly, she felt at ease with the intimidating man. There was no aura of evil around him.

"Thanks for the omelet." Brandon delivered the praise after his first bite. "You have a nice light hand with the eggs. Know when to fold before it browns too much."

Her face flushed a little. People didn't normally compliment her cooking. They only griped when they thought it wasn't fast enough. "Thanks. It's just eggs, ya know."

He shoveled in another mouthful, chewed then swallowed before speaking. "Yeah, but you'd be surprised how the average person can't make a decent egg. Either they break the yolk or end up burning it."

Nora found herself smiling at his simple praise. In another man, she might have thought he was flirting with her, but this was Brandon. She felt she'd known him forever, as opposed to just the last three years. "I think you're just saying it to make me feel good."

He grinned. The simple gesture made him look younger. How old was he? Maybe in his thirties, hard to know with his shaved head.

He's not for you.

Blinking, Nora looked around to see if anyone else had entered the diner. Nope, it was still just her, Brandon, and Bonnie. That meant the voice had been in her head.

"Did I make you feel good?" Brandon asked with a wink. "If so, great, but the eggs really are good. What do you want me to make you for your meal?"

She started to ask for a BLT. Should she be wasting time eating when she was hearing voices in her head? "I'm real beat. I think I will go straight home and sleep."

"Tell you what," Brandon said, glancing in Bonnie's direction, "go make yourself a grilled cheese, write up a ticket, and take it home with you."

The restaurant had a cardinal rule about no food going home with employees. It had seemed ridiculous at first, when the workers already got a free meal, but one meal could easily morph into four.

"Okay," she mouthed, returning to the kitchen to make herself the sandwich she'd been thinking about earlier. It would be a secret just between her and Brandon. Before she went to sleep tonight, she'd eat it while she covered the chapter on infectious diseases. Hard to believe thousands of people died from the flu in the nineteenth century. She tucked the sandwich in her backpack.

Brandon came into the kitchen while she was tidying up. "Nora, stop cleaning. There will be nothing for me to do in the wee hours of the night."

She put the rag she'd used to wipe down the counter into the dishwasher tray for sterilization. "Okay. Are you good, then? I'll head out."

Brandon placed his arms behind him on the counter, causing his biceps to bunch up. The man had muscles, probably lifted in his spare time. "I'm good."

She turned away, thinking for the briefest second that the words were a double entendre. It almost felt like something had changed between the two of them. That couldn't be. She grabbed her bag and headed for the bus stop.

Brandon followed behind her. "I don't like you waiting for the bus in the dark."

Gesturing to the streetlight and the bench outside the diner window, she said, "You can see me from in here."

He crossed his arms. "That's what I intend to do, then."

Nora waved at Bonnie, who shot her a peculiar look and waved back. Had she entered an alternate universe where no one seemed to act normal?

Shouldering her bag, she walked to the stop. The headlights of the bus announced its arrival, along with a belch of diesel smoke and a mechanical grumble of gears. Turning slightly before she got on the bus, she noticed Brandon watching with his arms folded. He put one hand up when he saw her glance back. She waved in return.

Stepping on the bus, she ran her pass through before collapsing onto the nearest seat. Inside the diner, she could see Bonnie talking to Brandon. His eyes were on the bus and not on the server who often beefed up her tips with her flirtatious manner and revealing cleavage.

What part of "not for you" did you not understand?

The voice again.

Please, she couldn't break down so close to graduation. She'd get home, get some sleep, maybe, review the chapter in the morning. Yes, that's what she'd do, and everything would be better in the morning.

CHAPTER THREE

T ONYA CALLED OUT a greeting from the kitchen as Nora staggered into the apartment. Exhausted, Nora simply said, "I'm beat. Going to bed."

The smell of cinnamon and cayenne pepper lingered in the hallway. A curious combination. Normally, she'd investigate what new concoction her roommate had in development. Tonya's passion consisted of putting together nutritional and yummy foods to tempt the palate. This time it wasn't enough to keep Nora from bed.

A quick shower would strip most of the grease from her body and remove the smell of onions.

Later, in bed with her eyes closed, the image of the curly-haired charmer returned. Maybe she'd dream of him. It certainly would be better than her creepy diner fan. Her entire body stiffened at the unwelcome thought.

Dear sweet Goddess, do not let me dream of Mr. Icky.

Comforted by the short prayer, her body relaxed as she drifted into slumber.

Trees surrounded her, and the smell of campfire smoke drifted toward her. Nora gazed at the surrounding trees and the late afternoon sun. Evening approached, and she was wandering in unfamiliar woods? Why had she come? Couldn't exactly call her a nature girl and she avoided going places where she'd be alone and at risk. Walking through a forest alone at almost dark was foolhardy, serving as the beginning to several horror movies. It was right up there with the ones featuring the too-stupid-to-live females who investigated a noise they heard in the basement after the power went out and armed with nothing more than a flashlight, despite knowing a serial killer was on the loose in the area.

She always considered herself a cautious female, especially after the incident. What was she doing in the woods?

The nearby crack of a branch snapping sent her heart into her throat. The self-defense classes came to mind. A pat to her side revealed no purse to swing like a battle mace or keys to scour her attacker's face, which left her with nothing in the way of defensive tools.

A branch about as long as her arm lay near her feet. Picking it up, she gave it a few experimental swings. It would do since she didn't see anything else. Another twig snap and the rustle of dry leaves had her crouching into a defensive pose to minimize her height and widening her stance for good balance. Her fingers wrapped around the stick as she waited. More rustling, and then the culprit casually strolled into view...with her child. A delicate doe with a fawn stepped through the trees, checking every green plant for edibility. The acceptable ones merited a nibble, while a few others didn't. The fawn followed close to its mother's side. A glance in Nora's direction caused it to crowd up against its mother. She'd frightened it. The doe and fawn were so beautiful.

"Not as beautiful as you, my love," a voice whispered into her ear.

She whirled, slashing with her impromptu wooden weapon. The stick snapped against the man's shoulder, not even causing him to stagger.

The man from her previous dream grinned at her as he brushed off the wooden bits sticking to his embroidered vest. "Now, my sweet Nora, is that any way to greet your beloved?"

"You are not my beloved," she said, stomping her foot a little. Why did this man insist on flirting with her? She didn't flirt. Her eyes flickered down to her broken stick. "Why didn't my stick hurt you?"

The man pressed a hand to his heart and stumbled back a few steps. "It's hurting you're after, is it? We have yet to exchange any cross words." He squatted and picked up a piece of broken branch to examine.

Nora observed the man, but more important, she cataloged her reactions. The fear, which caused her to break out in a cold sweat and shift into a fight-or-flight mode, vanished. Her heart slowed down, but it was still beating a little fast. Certainty that she had nothing to fear from him filled her, odd since she'd been on guard against any man for the last four years. It had taken her four months before she'd relaxed her guard around Brandon, who seemed to be truly a decent person.

The man rose to his feet, brandishing the small portion of the stick. "Your stick was hollower than wood. Termites worked it good." He handed it to her.

In the fading light, Nora could see tiny holes riddled the branch. The thought of termites made her drop the branch quickly. The man laughed a low, pleasant laugh that somehow managed to warm her insides. Curious, it was hard to explain the sensation she'd never felt before. Maybe she had but had forgotten.

"Never fear the termites, Nora. They are the forest's gardener, helping things to grow. I am just getting ready to eat my supper and would be pleased to have you join me." He gestured to the drifting smoke.

An appetizing scent overrode the smoke aroma. Her stomach growled, embarrassing her and making her aware that she'd never eaten the sandwich in her backpack. "All right. You walk. I'll follow."

Maybe the man made her feel safe, but she hadn't lost all her sense. Better to have him in front of her. She watched as he gracefully slipped through the trees. No wonder she hadn't heard him sneak up on her. A part of her she'd suspected was dead, or at least dormant, appreciated the width of his shoulders, the straight back, and the very fine buttocks filling out his gabardine trousers. Interesting that she'd noticed. Even more, she could feel her body reacting.

Her fingers drifted to her neck to calculate her pulse. It kicked up some, not out of fear, though.

The man looked over his shoulder, and their eyes caught. Her fingers still on her throat caught the jump in her heartbeat.

"Are you coming, darling?" His voice, warm with promise, carried a hint of laughter.

Nora found herself smiling. How strange. She almost never smiled at men, because it could be considered an invitation. Odd that she'd ended up in a relationship with Ogden. Then again, "relationship" might be a misleading term. She ran errands for him while using their association as a shield to keep other men away. Their physical relationship was almost non-existent. Ogden was not a hand-holder or casual kisser. He never pushed her for sex, which made him the ideal pretend boyfriend. Nora felt the peculiar affiliation kept her safe from the wild emotional swings other women experienced when involved with men. She also believed it erected a barrier around her that other men dared not try to pass. Her interaction with various men had proved that wasn't always the case.

The man regarded her with patient and amused eyes. "Are you holding your head on? Was it about to tumble off your swan-like neck?"

He thought he was a funny one. "I was taking my pulse. It's when you—"

"I know what taking a pulse is. That's one of the reasons I need you here—to help with the sickness." He held her arm and helped her over a fallen log.

Illness she understood. "How can I help?" She considered his hand on her elbow. She had never been one to take assistance, even as a child. As the oldest, she felt the need to do everything on her own. She was a trailblazer of sorts. No one told her she had to, unless you counted her inner voice. No reason she couldn't have scampered across the log on her own, but she appreciated the gesture.

"What's your name? You keep calling me by my mine, but never mentioned yours."

"My sainted grandmother would have my head if she saw my poor manners." Holding on to her hand, he led her to two fallen logs bordering the fire. "Your chaise, my lady."

He sat on the other log and used a long-handled spoon to stir the pot suspended over the fire. "I am Clayton McFane. I supposed I expected you to recognize me since we have loved each other for several lifetimes. The first few were a little rocky, but once we got the sense of one another as soul mates, we came together quite well." A grin brightened his face as his eyes flickered up, demonstrating he was recalling times gone by.

Make that, times he thought had gone by. Nora wasn't all that sure she believed they'd known each other for lifetimes. Still, she'd witnessed both her sister and grandfather transported through time, as easily as if only going to the next city for shopping. Her nana swore she and Grandpa Buell were soul mates. There was also something reassuring about Clayton.

Placing her hands on the log, she leaned back and stretched her legs toward the fire. Her cartoon pajama pants looked wildly out of place in the woodland setting. You'd think she would have picked out something more appropriate to wear in her dream.

Clayton ladled the fragrant stew into a bowl.

"Clayton," she started, earning a smile for using his name. "How come you know me and where I was?"

"Oh, that." He straightened and walked toward her, carrying the bowl. "Granny McFane claims I have a touch of the fey about me. That's why I often know things that are going to happen." He presented the bowl to her, along with a spoon. "Eat."

Nora dug into the stew thick with potatoes, chunks of meat, and gravy. The taste resonated on her tongue with the right blend of spices. Tonya would have appreciated the dish. She closed her eyes and savored the flavor before swallowing.

"I'd count myself a happy man if I put that expression on your face instead of my rabbit stew," Clayton murmured the words close by, causing her eyelids to pop open.

Nora didn't know what to say to what was clearly flirtation. Instead, she ate more stew, even though the thought of rabbit made it harder to choke down the meat.

Clayton intertwined his fingers and gazed down at them as he spoke. "I've been warned that a person doesn't force fate's hand. I'd be agreeing with that, except, if fate didn't want you to be here, you wouldn't be."

The bit of cracked reasoning had her almost choking on a potato. A hearty back slap sent the errant vegetable airborne. Blinking, she looked into Clayton's concerned face. The firelight did nothing to negate the strong lines of his face or the lively blue eyes. Handsome he might be, but there was also sincerity, a sense of compassion that she often found lacking in twenty-first-century males. "How did you find me?"

His hand stroked his chin. "Well, I tell ya, it was no simple matter. I am growing older every day. I am nigh on to thirty-three."

Nora pretended to be horrified. "That old?"

Taking her pretense for real, he nodded his head gravely. "Yes, that old, and there's been no sign of my soul mate, despite my looking. I dreamt you were in America, but unfortunately the time I was unclear on. I left Ireland in search of you."

Nora stirred her delicious stew, debating if she could eat any more of it knowing it was composed of creatures, she was more used to seeing singing and dancing in children's movies. "That doesn't answer my question of how you find me."

He lifted his eyebrows. "I see you haven't changed much. Still demanding answers. I did some divination magick. Much to my horror, I found we were in two different centuries, both alone. This I found hard to accept. At night when my loneliness was at its peak, I searched for you across time, calling your name. Did you ever have a sense of me?"

"Well, at first I would say no, but lately yes. Your voice is in my head, making me wonder if I am losing my mind. I noticed it because it sounds like you and not my own internal musings. Why is that?"

Nora placed the forgotten bowl on the log. Clayton picked it up and stirred the stew before taking a bite that he obviously relished before finishing the rest in four rapid bites. He went back to the pot to dip up more food.

Noticing her attention on the bowl, he explained, "I have only one bowl. I know I should have bartered for another, but I wasn't too sure if I could bring you across. Even now you are here only on the strength of my will and need." He dug his spoon back into his bowl.

The idea that he could just snatch her out of time should have frightened her. Instead, it mesmerized her with possibilities. "Could I just pull Napoleon or Ben Franklin out of time if I chose?"

Clayton looked reflective as he chewed. "I'm no expert on these matters. I believe there needs to be a connection or a bond between two individuals to draw them to one another. We've had lifetimes to build the connections. You are the first person I ever brought through time. Unfortunately, you stayed only briefly before." He placed his bowl on the ground as he leaned slightly toward her, placing both hands on his knees.

"You brought me over before?" The memory of him jumping down from the wagon came to mind.

"I have. I believe you remember." He cocked his head, and his eyes twinkled as if he could read her thoughts. "My heart danced with joy, but then, you were gone that quick." He snapped his fingers to demonstrate.

How one man's will could carry her across time, even for a second, was a mystery. The idea of being out of control should have frightened her, but paradoxically it didn't. Clayton didn't frighten her.

"I have no say in this?" She placed her fisted hands on her hips and

threw him a glance that had the friendlier interns backing away.

"Ah, my Nora, the same fire as before." He shook his head at his words and then added, "I do not claim to understand the ins and outs of such matters. Your will enters into it, too. At first, you didn't stay long. I think I surprised you. Now, your stay has been much longer than before. It must mean you want to be here."

His confident smile and knowing look irritated Nora. She thought of a few put-downs that worked well on other men who tried to chat her up, but a log fell in the fire, sending up a flurry of sparks. The sudden motion stopped her automatic response and drew her attention to the sparks as they flared and disappeared.

Her gaze went back to Clayton, whose alert countenance was brighter than any spark. What if he was right? How could that be? She'd never had the opportunity to have a normal boyfriend as most teen girls did. It didn't mean she hadn't had a few crushes. Still, they paled in comparison to what she felt sitting there, a sense almost of belonging. It was hard to understand why this one man would have such an effect on her, especially after she'd given up on that part of her life. Still, it wasn't fair to this charming man to let him believe that there might be something between them.

She stood, unaware of how to explain what she needed to say, but it couldn't be explained sitting. Hands behind her back, she paced around the fire, one side of her body alternately heated by the closeness to the fire while the other side felt the nip of the falling temperatures. "Clayton, you seem like a nice man."

"Ah, here it comes." He raised his hand toward the sky. "Just like when you were a princess and I a lowly footman. You gave me the long speech about how different our stations were in life."

"I did?" Nora almost remembered, if she really tried, a haughty princess and a lowly footman in some dark corner of her memory.

"Do you remember now?" Clayton stood and watched her as she paced. "Do you remember how I responded?"

Memories of the offended footman sweeping up the haughty princess materialized in her mind. "You, you, you..." She was unsure how to say it. "You changed my mind."

"That I did. That was then. I understand things are different now, and you need healing more than a lusty embrace." He walked slowly toward her, stopped a foot from her, and held out his arms. "I am here for you."

A cry bubbled up in her throat as she took two running steps into his open arms. Clayton wrapped his arms around her and rocked her gently. "Go ahead, cry it out. You have the right."

The crying she'd denied herself for so many years suddenly erupted, flowing like lava. Nora wept until she could weep no more. Her sobs continued for minutes until they became less and less, morphing into occasional hiccupping.

The wood smoke irritated her eyes as she lifted her head from Clayton's shirt and vest. "I'm sorry. I don't know what got into me."

His embrace tightened as he rested his head on top of hers. "You needed the cry. I am willing to bet you do not allow yourself to cry or show any weakness often."

With an indelicate sniff, Nora wiped her nose with the back of her hand. "You'd be right. I can't remember the last time I cried. I suspect it was when my dog Brownie was killed when I was twelve."

Clayton gave her an extra squeeze before loosening the embrace.

Cold, she wanted to ask him why he let go, but realized he was fading away. "Clayton."

CHAPTER FOUR

NORA TOSSED AND turned in her sleep, aware on some level that she was searching for Clayton. No matter where she went in her dreams, she could not find him. Her alarm sounded, pulling her out of a troubled sleep, one of the few times she welcomed morning, even as early as it was. To continue to sleep and traverse the dream world in search of Clayton would only equal heartache. Might as well get up and study for her test. She stumbled out of bed and headed for the kitchen.

Carrying two slices of toast liberally coated with peanut butter, she sat down at the battered table and began to peruse the infectious diseases chapter as she consumed her breakfast.

Her fingers brushed the names carved into the table. She and Tonya had rescued the relic from the trash. Students moved out all the time, even tossing appliances away to avoid the trouble of carrying them home or perhaps hoping for a new style the upcoming year. Most of those students had parents who bought them everything they needed or wanted. Half the items tossed were usable, but still ended up in a dumpster. Finances forced Nora to be much less discriminating.

Between the diner and a food budget, including a steady diet of peanut butter and bread, she made the most of every penny she could. Good grades in high school had landed her a merit scholarship that paid most of her tuition. She seemed to live forever in hopes of getting a real job, eating non-diner food, and even getting a car.

Both she and Tonya had contemplated living together after school, since neither one had any plans otherwise, but suddenly those simple dreams were no longer enough.

Taking another bite of toast, she chewed contemplatively. What was wrong with her goals? They served her through four years of college and a lackluster relationship with Ogden.

Dusting the crumbs off her fingers, she turned another page in her textbook. Many of the students had switched to electronic books, alleviating the need to carry around twenty-pound monstrosities that caused her to bend under the weight, rather like a mountain climber. Still, the old paper textbooks crowded the shelves at the nearby thrift store. She'd even plucked a few from the dumpster. Half the students who dropped out had started in medical school.

Being financially independent used to be enough for her. Having a job where she helped others was her goal. It was all still good, but she wanted more. Why couldn't she have the feeling of belonging and comfort she'd felt in Clayton's arms? Why did everything have to be so damn practical? Wasn't she a witch? Wasn't magick part of the fabric of her life? It should have been.

Somehow, she'd suppressed part of her upbringing. Her determination in obtaining her nurse practitioner's degree demonstrated her belief that she could do anything if she imagined it and worked for it. While accepting that hard work paid off, she'd brushed aside the belief that one day she could fall madly, hopelessly in love. More important, she didn't believe anyone could feel that way about her.

No wonder she'd accepted her role as unpaid assistant in Ogden's life. Maybe playing the part of a human service animal was as good as she was going to get. Her stomach clenched and rolled at the thought, making her a little nauseated. Plenty of people fell in and out of love several times in their life. The residents of the surrounding apartments demonstrated that fairly well. Tonya stayed guarded in her affections, never allowing herself to fall headfirst, regarding the man as empty of actual value, rather like a dessert drink.

In the end, Tonya did partake, while Nora settled for a man who stirred none of her emotions.

Her fingers traveled the printed pages while she read the text aloud, hoping to imprint it on her memory. How could she study when her life spiraled out of control?

The sound of Tonya's alarm clock meant her roommate would be up soon. As much as Nora longed to talk to someone, she didn't dare. What could she say? Some dream man was making her doubt everything she thought was real, even though, unlike most people, she'd had real experience with the unusual in seeing her sister transported through time.

Only a few years ago, Leah had found herself in a past century, battling people who wanted to put her to death while she worked to correct a wrong assumption. Nana had called in all her coven friends, and Nora had gone home to do the protection magic that may have saved her little sister. She knew for sure her little sister had gone back in time—as had her grandfather.

That would mean she could, too.

How could she determine if her dreams were time travel or perhaps a form of astral projection, which allowed her spirit to travel by leaving her body? While she'd heard of people, especially monks, being able to do that, she'd never personally known anyone who could. Was there something she could do to determine the validity of the experience?

Should she ask Tonya to check in on her to see if her body still lay under the covers late at night? She'd hate to put her friend to all that trouble. It could be embarrassing, too.

Tonya walked into the room, yawning, and headed for the coffeepot. Some low-level grumbling reminded Nora she'd drunk the entire pot and forgotten to start a new one. Caffeine was probably the only dietary vice her roommate allowed herself.

"Sorry, roomie." She winced as she said the words. It was not a good time to have memory problems or hear voices. Was there ever a good time?

The smell of coffee drifted through the room. Tonya carried in two cups. Setting one beside Nora's textbook, she pulled out the other chair. "What's going on with you?"

Nora dropped the highlighter she'd been using to underline keywords, a trick to commit them to long-term memory. "What makes you think anything is wrong?"

Tonya took a sip of coffee and rolled her eyes appreciatively. "We've known each other for almost four years. I am willing to bet I know you better than your family."

Nora reached for her cup to delay answering. The first sip of the bitter brew had her wrinkling her nose. Even though she preferred sugar and plenty of it, Tonya called it the white death, which meant it seldom made it into the apartment, except for the few packets Nora smuggled home from the diner. She swallowed the dark liquid, appreciating the kick if not the flavor. Her stomach gurgled in response, since it was her fourth cup. Setting her cup down, she looked at Tonya, who appeared surprisingly alert for having just awakened.

"I've had trouble sleeping."

Tonya nodded. "That I noticed. Why?"

Biting her bottom lip, she considered how much to confess.

Tonya shook her head. "Out with it, girl. I can see you deciding how much to tell me."

"A person would think you were a mind reader." The fact her roommate could read her so well was disconcerting.

Tonya winked. "Nope, you're so OCD about everything that when you vary from your usual routines and start forgetting things, I know something is up."

Finishing her toast, Nora licked her fingers. "What did I do that made you think something was up?"

Her roommate laughed briefly. "What didn't you do? For almost five days, I haven't seen any lists anywhere with those black, finished slashes through the various items. One day, you forgot your watch."

Forgot her watch, she did remember that. It was as bad as most people forgetting their phone. Her hand slipped up to her neck and rubbed. The tension from the night before began to return. "I am a little worried myself. It seems like everything I planned for my life is wrong."

Tonya placed both palms on the table and leaned forward. "Medicine is your life. You're good at it. You don't want to do it anymore?"

Her roommate's words only added to her muddled state. "I didn't say that. I do want to be in the medical field in some form. It's just that the life I planned out for myself"—she threw her hands in the air over the futility of explaining something she didn't fully understand—"doesn't seem to fit anymore."

Tonya placed her index finger against her temple as she gave that some thought. "If you mean Ogden, I'd say he never fit. What are you going to do about him?"

Part of it was Ogden. Her roommate's casual reply helped her solidify part of her problem. "As for Ogden, I guess I am already doing it. I am making myself unavailable to run his little errands."

"About time." Tonya's accompanying snort relayed her feelings about the opportunistic Ogden. "That man saw you coming. He read you well. Must give him credit there. Most of the nurses would have told him what he could do with himself. I imagine more than a few did."

The picture Tonya painted was not a pretty one. Nora had hesitated to let her roommate know she was keeping company with the fussy doctor because she'd seen through him in a heartbeat. Unfortunately, the picture said more about her than she wanted to acknowledge. "You're right. I heard rumors, but I thought a man, any man, would keep other men at a distance."

Tonya knocked on the table in her mirth. "I am scaring away all the spirits who might carry news of your ignorance. Girl, men hit on women, especially young, hot women like yourself." She put her hand up to stop Nora's reply. "Go ahead and tell me you cut off your hair to be less attractive, how you wear your uniforms loose to disguise your curves. It's not working. Your Ice Queen act only draws the players closer. All you managed to do is discourage the decent, shy men. The users know your scent."

"Damn, those were the ones I was hoping to discourage." Nora scowled. Her roomie's words had a ring of truth that didn't please her at all. "Yesterday Ogden tried to flag me down when I left the hospital. Instead of acknowledging him, I got on the elevator with all the other students."

"Burned his butt good, but his type won't go away easily. Continue to make yourself unavailable. Men do this all the time. They quit coming around until you realize you haven't seen them for weeks when you see them out with some other woman." Tonya rocked back on the hind legs of the chair.

"I can do that without too much work," Nora admitted, slowly abandoning her plan to continue to see Ogden until she graduated. No doubt, Ogden used her, but she was just as guilty of using him. Strangely, seeing Ogden would feel too much like cheating on Clayton. This should have been the final sign she was losing it, fear of upsetting the boyfriend who existed only in her dreams.

A glance at her watch propelled her up. "I am late again. How did that happen?" She flew into the bathroom to brush her teeth, while Tonya trailed behind.

Tonya stood in the doorway of the bathroom, sharing her thoughts. "This is what I mean. You're never late. You're usually at the bus stop ten minutes before the bus. If I didn't know better, I'd think you were crushing on some guy."

Nora looked in the mirror as she brushed her teeth. Tonya's image hovered over her left shoulder. *Crushing on some guy? How ridiculous is that, especially, if I told her it was my imaginary friend?* Clayton's image formed behind her right shoulder. Her head whipped around so fast she dribbled toothpaste on her uniform. Her heart rate slowed when she realized only her friend stood behind her, wearing a concerned expression.

Nora tried to smile around the toothbrush. Spitting, she wiped her mouth on a hand towel and headed for the door. Tonya stepped out of the way at the last minute. Her friend followed her to her room, where Nora grabbed her packed backpack. Yesterday's soiled uniform lay on the floor with her abandoned pajamas. She picked up the pajamas and sniffed. Wood smoke.

"See that." Tonya gestured at the clothes. "You never leave your clothes on the floor. Now, you're sniffing them like a frat boy trying to find something clean to wear."

Her roommate's words registered as she considered the implications of her wood-smoke-scented jammies. She wanted to sniff them again to be sure, but she hadn't the time. "Don't do my laundry while I am gone."

Her unexpected pronouncement had Tonya balling her fists on her hips and opening her mouth in surprise. She sputtered before she got out, "When have I ever done your laundry?"

"Never." Nora shouldered her bag on and located her bus pass for the sprint to the stop.

Tonya followed to her to the door and yelled after her as she took the stairs two at a time, "What's wrong with you?"

Nora wondered that herself. Her roommate's shouting attracted the attention of other neighbors. Great, now everyone would wonder about her.

The man across the hall ran down the stairs in tandem with her to catch the bus. He assumed she and Tonya were lovers, since he shared his apartment with his guy pal.

"Problems in paradise?" he queried.

Nora just grimaced. It would be too hard to explain. Besides, the man would accuse her again of not having the courage to come out of the closet. The rumble of the bus turning the corner caused her to break into a jog with her neighbor following.

On the bus, she made her way to the back, where the homeless and sometimes crazies sat, such as women bundled up in several sweaters even when the temps were in the triple digits and men who had aluminum foil wrapped around their ball caps to prevent aliens from reading their thoughts. With her imaginary friend, she'd fit right in. Of course, her neighbor wouldn't follow, because the crazies freaked him out. It would give her time to think, as long as she acknowledged she'd buy some foil soon and cover up, too.

Wood smoke. How could that have happened? If her jammies smelled like onions, she'd blame that on the diner. The smell of onions and grease soaked into her pores, flavoring her skin and scenting her hair. A survey once proved that men were attracted to the smell of cooking food as opposed to the most expensive perfumes. Maybe that's what made her attractive to the opposite sex, as opposed to gorgeous eyes or a shapely torso. The siren call of frying meat probably netted her the creepy admirer at the diner. Still, it didn't answer the wood-smoke question.

If she'd had time, she'd have sniffed the pajamas to ascertain for sure whether the smell was there or imagined. Maybe she could get a whiff of rabbit stew, or better yet, a trace of Clayton would be nice. His arms around her had been warm and comforting, but his scent had reminded her of something spicy, though nothing current. She smiled at the thought.

"Whoever you're thinking about must be handsome, right?" a woman bundled in several sweaters inquired with a nudge of her elbow.

Nora turned to look at the woman rather than trying to ignore her. Her sweaters were all complementary shades and layered a way that seemed intentional. "Yes, yes, I am," she answered, not bothering to deny it. How had this woman ended up riding around in the bus endlessly? Although, Nora couldn't be sure the woman rode without a destination. "Are you on your way to work?"

"Goodness, no. I retired some years ago. Used to work in a meat warehouse. Almost thirty years working in a thirty-degree storage facility. Thought when I got out of there, I'd be warm finally. Didn't happen. The cold sank into my bones. Most people probably think I'm crazy always wearing sweaters."

Nora hurried to deny she'd ever had such thoughts.

The elderly woman gave her a broad smile. "Don't worry about it.

You are one of the few to ever sit beside me on purpose."

The woman's willingness to think the best of her made her feel about two inches tall. It also showed that if you took the time to really listen to people, instead of making assumptions, you'd find out a lot more. She'd have to remember that, since it would be helpful in her practice.

Her hospital came into view, causing Nora to pick up her pack. "See ya," she said, nodding in the woman's direction and standing to make her way to the door.

The woman waved and added, "Hold on to a man who makes you smile."

Nora turned to wave once her feet hit the pavement and found Allen, her neighbor, regarding her in confusion through the bus windows. Difficult to believe it took a woman he probably regarded as crazy to finally convince him that she wasn't a lesbian.

Perhaps she should listen to the woman and hang on to Clayton. She wished she knew how. The fact she no longer heard his voice worried her. Could she somehow be losing contact with him?

Not hardly, sweetheart. I chose not to talk to you since it appeared, I distressed you too much.

Her anxiety that she had lost contact with Clayton melted away with the sound of his soothing lilt. Her first reaction was to answer him with actual words, but she checked herself before she did. She thought the words: *You're back.*

I never left you, but often I can't talk to you. If I could have my way, I'd be with you every second of every day, but that would be selfish of me. Could be that's not what you want?

Nora entered the hospital, bemused by the sound of Clayton's voice. She answered the friendly guard's greeting as she drifted toward the elevator bank. The sound of a familiar voice broke through her absorption enough for her to make a break for the women's bathroom. *Great. Ogden.* It seemed the more she tried to ignore him, the more he seemed to appear. If he'd spotted her, then he'd wait right outside the door. If only, there was another way out.

The sound of lockers slamming reminded her that she was in the restroom adjacent to the female staff's locker room. One of the older nurses came up behind her.

"Who are you hiding from, sweetie?"

"Ogden Graves, Doctor." She bit her lips when she realized her mistake. The woman could march out there and tell Ogden she was inside.

Instead, the woman shook her head and guided Nora away from the door.

"Pompous ass. You do good to hide from him. He thinks women are on this earth to serve men. Heard he even has one nursing student dedicated to do his bidding. I'm not sure what he has on her to get her to run his errands. He's nothing to look at and is definitely a zero in the charm department." She gestured at the door to the locker room. "Go through there and use the other door. It opens up into the nurses' lounge. You can slip through there into the next hallway outside of the pediatric offices."

"Thanks. You're a lifesaver. I've never been in the nurses' lounge, being a student and all." She made a break for the door to escape before someone named her as Ogden's errand girl. People at the hospital didn't think for a moment that there was anything romantic between them. Instead, they believed he had some dirt on her to keep her running and fetching.

For a change, she didn't doubt her attractiveness, but wondered if Ogden played off their relationship to keep his options open. It sounded like him. With this exalted opinion of himself, he would assume he could do better. The fact he thought she was beneath him made her angry. Still, hadn't she accepted it all along. This wasn't anything new. Suddenly, the idea was repulsive. No more running and fetching for the grand and glorious Dr. Graves and she doubted anyone would replace her.

Her plan to fade out of Ogden's orbit was a cowardly one. Still, it wouldn't do any good to make a stand. He'd only ignore it. He'd blame it on hormones and assign her another errand.

Clayton's voice sounded inside her head, making her smile: *I would never let you go if you were mine.*

The resident from the other day came into view. She'd forgotten his name. All she remembered was he was friendly.

The man smiled at her, and his eyes lit up as they met hers. "That's what I like to see, a beautiful smile. Dare I hope that smile is for me?"

Scalawag.

Clayton's growled comment rattled her. She wasn't sure if she could handle a voice in her head and a conversation at the same time.

I will go.

A feeling of loss replaced his voice.

The young doctor still smiled at her. She wasn't sure what he'd asked her, but he expected an answer. She decided to go with something indefinite. "Possibly." Unaware of what she was being indefinite about, she watched the man grow even more animated.

"Great, great, I was hoping my excellent bedside manner would wear you down eventually." He fell in step with her.

"Um." Great, now look what she'd done. A quick glance at his name-tag identified him as T. Mangano. "Dr. Mangano, I think there's been a misunderstanding." Her stride lengthened as she saw the red light above the elevator bank, indicating a car on the way.

The man looked perplexed, and his smile lessened a bit. "It's Terrence. You really don't remember me."

She did, but not in the I-was-thinking-of-you-fondly way. It was better to admit she hadn't thought of him at all. "Um, no."

"I am so sorry I bothered you." He walked briskly away.

He might have been one of the nice ones Tonya had mentioned. Life was easier when she didn't interact with other people, though she wasn't sure she could get through life not interacting. Of course, it was also easier when she didn't have an additional voice in her head.

Hey, I heard that.

Nora stepped onto the elevator and worked her way to the back, making sure not to smile in reaction to Clayton's words. There was no reason to give someone else the wrong message.

CHAPTER FIVE

C LINICAL WAS FINALLY over and past lunchtime for most. Several students rushed for the elevator as the doors slid open. Nora moved back to allow others to enter. A woman jostled her arm and grinned at her before speaking.

"I saw what you did back there." She moved her eyebrows up and down rapidly, like a cartoon character.

"Um." Nora hesitated, trying to recall the female's name. It was something with a T. Tess, Trish, Tory. She tried out the names in her head. She threw an apologetic smile at the petite brunette.

The woman leaned closer and raised up on tiptoes enough to whisper in Nora's ear. "It's Tricia."

Of course, she would have gotten to that name eventually. "Yes, yes, I remember. You're the one who didn't like dissecting the cats in anatomy class."

Tricia grimaced about the same time the elevator doors slid open. They all shuffled forward into the lobby. "I will forever be remembered as Cat Girl. There's a story behind it, though. I lost my cat when I was a kid, and my loving, older brother told me it was picked up by cat bundlers who caught cats for medical research." She sighed a little and pointed to the outside doors.

Nora nodded and fell into step with her. Good chance they were both heading to the same place. *Yay.* "You heading to the university?"

"You know it, for the wonderful epidemic exam." The sneer in her voice allowed any eavesdroppers to be aware of her feelings about the upcoming test. "You drive?"

"I wish." Nora slid her hand into her pocket to retrieve her bus pass and glanced into the direction of the crowded bus stop. Sweet Goddess, how she hated balancing herself against the bus's motion while maintaining a death grip on the rubber strap that time of day. Plenty of jerks used it as an opportunity to cop a feel as they squeezed by. The first time she'd almost flashed back to that night so long ago. Now she settled for hissing, "Jerk," which usually made them chuckle. The last two times she'd taken advantage of her long feet by turning one slightly to trip the creeps.

"Would you like a ride?" Tricia offered. "You could quiz me about the test, since you're such a brainiac."

Nora started to protest the brainiac label but focused on another word instead. Ride. Tricia had offered her a ride. "Yes."

Would she rather sit in a seat and not be subject to pawing as she hung from a strap? That was a no-brainer. "I'd love a ride and would be willing to quiz you."

Tricia pointed to the right parking lot before she started walking. "I could use your help, but what I really want to know is how you got the sexy Dr. Mangano to follow you around."

True, he'd talked to her, but it wasn't something she'd wanted. "I'm not sure that I did anything." Her eyes traveled over the sea of parked cars. Instead of following the road, her companion created a crooked path by squeezing past expensive sedans. Obviously, they were in the physicians' parking lot. The pricey vehicles gave way to minivans and older vehicles, which meant they'd entered staff parking.

Tricia grumbled more to herself, but her words still carried. "Damn, I hate it when my mother is right. That's what she told me. The men always go after the ones who play hard to get."

Nora followed until they stopped at a battered-looking compact. Tricia unlocked it with a squeeze of her key fob. Her new friend opened the passenger door and swept the untidy piles of books and papers into the back seat.

"Sorry, I wasn't expecting company." Tricia grinned as she gave the last book a toss into the back.

Nora tried not to wince. She treated her books extremely well because she hoped to resell most of them. A few she might keep as reference, but constant medical advances made textbooks dated in a matter of months. "Don't worry about it. I'm glad for the ride. You have no idea how much I appreciate it."

Tricia started the car and pulled out into the slow-moving traffic before Nora began the questions. "What do you know about cholera?"

Tricia lowered her window, letting in a whiff of diesel-fuel-tainted air. "I know enough to know I don't want to get it. Seriously, it causes diarrhea, vomiting, and dehydration. People used to die from it awhile back."

Nora's muscles clinched as Tricia guided the small car across several lanes without signaling. It was better than the bus. Of course, on the bus she never paid attention to the driving because she was too busy either studying or, most often, collapsed in an exhausted heap. Inhaling, she tried to recover her train of thought. "How do people get cholera?"

The small car zoomed into a minuscule spot between two hulking SUVs, causing the driver of one to honk and swear.

Tricia answered the enraged driver with a flip of her finger, which resulted in more honking. "Hmm, is that the one that was spread by fleas on rats? No, wait. That was the bubonic plague. You got me. What is it?"

Nora's fingers lingered near her neck. Would it be rude to check her pulse? Probably. Besides, she knew it would be high. Her hand dropped back to her lap. "Cholera results from contaminated water and food. The bacteria are present in feces. People experiencing natural disasters, living in crowded, unsanitary conditions such as refugee camps are prone to contracting it as well. There have been cases of people getting it from seafood pulled from the Gulf of Mexico."

"Gives a whole new meaning to bad clams, huh?" Tricia giggled at her joke. "We haven't had much of a problem with it here in the United States, have we?"

Nora's eyes cut to Tricia as she drove without a care. The woman was right: She did need to study if her last question was any indication. "Well, actually, it was a problem until about 1870. People didn't really understand about sanitation and clean water. Their outhouses were often near water sources. If that wasn't bad enough, the domesticated animals crapped in the water, too. All they knew was the water made them sick. So, they stuck to a diet of ale and milk. The fermentation killed the bacteria in the water."

Tricia laughed as she turned into the university parking lot. "Those were the days. Ale for breakfast. Beer for lunch."

Nora stifled the desire to point out they probably had milk for breakfast. "Luckily, the germ theory caught on, which was amazing, since most people discounted Van Leeuwenhoek's microorganisms work. They chose to contribute illness to punishment for sins."

Tricia spotted another student pulling out and immediately punched the accelerator, cutting off a slow-moving pickup. She maneuvered the small car into the space before shifting into park and twisting off the ignition.

"That was lucky," Nora said, not knowing what else to say to her kamikaze-driver friend.

"Oh, no," Tricia said, opening the car door. "Not lucky. You must make your own luck, which is what I do. I saw you in the elevator. Everyone knows your smart, and I knew I wasn't ready for the test. I should at least recognize cholera, probably the bubonic plague, and influenza, right? Think smallpox, too."

Nora opened her car door, unsure how to reply to that remark. While the woman freely admitted her machinations to use Nora for information, she'd used Tricia for transportation, even if the ride had taken a few years off her life.

They walked toward the science building without talking while a few late students sprinted past them. The smell of cut grass rode the breeze as a grounds maintenance employee buzzed across the green expanse on his oversized lawn mower.

Make your own luck.

The words stuck in her mind. It sounded like something her nana might say. Working almost sixteen hours a day, she'd pushed herself through college. No luck, just plain hard work, but luck would have made it so much easier. Her father's voice echoed in her mind, reminding her that nothing was free. It didn't stop her from asking, "How do you make your own luck?"

Tricia's eyes sparkled before she replied, making her look a bit like Hollywood's stereotype of an elf or even a sprite. "You have opportunities. Lots of them." She abruptly threw her free arm out to gesture.

Nora jerked to a stop to avoid the arm. Opportunities, she understood that. "Okay, how will I find all these opportunities?"

"Looks to me like you've already found some on your own." Tricia smirked a little and waved at a male student passing them, several books clutched to his chest as he walked with a determined line to his lips. "Hi, Todd."

The student looked up. His eyes blinked a few times behind his thick glasses, before he located the source of the greeting. A smile tugged at his lips, making him almost attractive. "Hi, Tricia."

"Working hard, I see." Tricia angled her head toward the books. "It's no wonder you are setting the curve for the rest of us."

Nora watched a slight blush work its way up Todd's neck, but his smile grew along with it.

He tried to brush aside the obvious compliment. "Most of the professors no longer grade on the curve. They use a rubric."

"Really?" Tricia exclaimed with absolute enthusiasm that suggested the nervous Todd had imparted the true meaning of life.

Nora looked at her watch. She didn't have time to watch the byplay of medical students in their natural habitat. Dr. Lansky, the instructor, would lock the door against any late arrivals. Her actions were against school policy, but by the time a person got any results from a lodged complaint, he or she would already have flunked out of infectious diseases and would be almost a year behind in the program. Besides, who would want to take the class again from a hostile Dr. Lansky?

Nora elbowed her friend. "We're going to be late."

"Okay," Tricia said. "See ya later, Todd." She held up one hand to the student, who acknowledged her with a head bob since his arms were full.

Nora's long strides made her new friend work to keep pace with her. Aware of Tricia jogging to keep up, she murmured, "Sorry," but did not slow.

Tricia kept up her combination jog-walk and even talked. "Todd is an opportunity. He's a brainiac like you and helped me through chemistry. I'm not sure why nurses even have to take chemistry. It isn't like we're going to develop new drugs, only administer them."

"Don't you feel like you're using him?" The words slipped out of Nora's mouth before she could consider how insulting they might sound. Once out, she longed to retract them. The open double doors of the lecture hall loomed ahead. If she could just reach them, it would be a form of sanctuary. She doubted Tricia would ever want to talk to her again.

The tinkle of her companion's laugh surprised her into stopping. "You aren't mad at me?"

"No, of course not. How can I be mad at a person who actually says what she thinks?" She turned to wink at Nora, and they both continued walking. "All human interaction is give-and-take. I talked to Todd, and he's pleased. Other students see him talking to not one, but two beautiful women, and his value goes up in the eyes of both males and females."

It made sense. Instead of just taking from other people, as Nora had originally assumed, Tricia was bartering. It may have been an unspoken agreement. She wanted to ask more about creating luck, but Dr. Lansky's white-coated figured appeared near the open doors.

"Run." Nora yelped the word and suited her actions to it.

Both she and Tricia made it inside before the instructor slapped the doors shut and locked them. She turned and gave them both a measuring look, then walked to the podium.

Nora grinned at her companion, and then located an empty seat. Grumbling and some cursing slipped through the locked doors. Not all students took Dr. Lansky's reputation seriously. A few expected college to be like high school, where their parents or a kind counselor ran interference. Rules didn't apply to them. Not only did they soon discover the opposite, but also there were myriad expectations from various instructors.

The smack of a blue book caught her attention as it hit the desk surface. Most professors used the testing center for examinations. The students logged in on the network computers and took the usual multiple-choices exams. Not Dr. Lansky. She believed students were able to circumvent the testing center's safeguards and cheated.

Nora knew they did, from getting information from students who'd taken previous tests to sending other students to take their tests for them. Since fellow students manned the testing center, it was easy to persuade them to look the other way. Often, they never knew, since the test-taker might use someone else's login.

That would explain Dr. Lansky's diligence in monitoring her own exams. If that wasn't enough, the tests were in essay form. The woman believed those in the medical field should not only be able to put their thoughts down on paper, but it should be legible. Everyone knew doctors and nurses typed everything now. Still, it did spoil the plans of any would-be cheaters.

A glance at the board revealed their prompt, written in Dr. Lansky's perfect cursive of unusually straight lines. How she managed that baffled Nora. She pondered the prompt as she rolled the sharpened pencil between her fingers. Most students wrote in pen, but her confidence wasn't that high.

You enter a village in the late-eighteenth century. The residents are showing a lack of energy. Few are abed with diarrhea, while others complain of fever and show symptoms of a rash. What is it? How would you treat it?

Nora sneaked a glance at Tricia, whose mouth was open. Good, Nora wasn't the only one baffled. It could be several illnesses. It could be typhoid fever or cholera. It could also be influenza or even food poisoning. Exhaling a long breath, she watched Dr. Lansky slowly pace the aisles, having to squeeze past the students. Other students were writing as if they knew. Why didn't she?

Biting her bottom lip, Nora considered that most epidemics started with poor sanitation and crowded conditions. Epidemics usually started in cities. With that in mind, if a high standard of sanitation was implemented, and the sick individuals were quarantined, the illness might be controlled. There wouldn't be any antibiotics available, because penicillin hadn't been invented yet.

Nora gnawed on the pencil, trying to think of a way to relieve the people's symptoms with what they had in their time. Herbal tea, that's it. Nana tended to dose their family with tea, depending on their symptoms. Nausea or upset stomach merited peppermint tea, while fennel was useful for those with the runs. Unfortunately, Nana usually withheld it for a few hours, declaring the body was trying to rid itself of the toxin. Now, she knew what to do, but she didn't know what she was dealing with.

Go with what you know. She tried to reassure herself as she carefully printed all the illnesses that shared the symptoms and were common to that century. Her sanitation precautions, boiling all water and washing all clothing and linens in hot soapy water, might have been a hard sell in that period, but it was doable. One of her professors had mentioned that more people died during the Civil War from surgeons with dirty hands and dysentery than gunshot.

The other students left in spurts, interrupting her flow of thoughts as they clumped out of the room. With each group, Nora experienced a nervous twinge. What if she wasn't done in time? A few more students pushed past her seat. Tricia touched her shoulder and mouthed the word, "Bye." Nora nodded slightly, careful to avoid the appearance of cheating.

A quick look confirmed her fear that she was the last student in the room. Why did she make things so hard? Why didn't she breeze through like the others or even resort to an ink pen? Sighing, she realized she was who she was. A methodical worker and analytical thinker, which meant she never did anything quickly. Well, she could cook fast. However, she never did anything speedy that required actual thought.

Holding up the blue book, she carefully read each page, checking for missing or misspelled words. Finally, she forced herself to stand and walk to the front table, where all the blue books sat caged in a wire box. Dr. Lansky sat at the table, reading an exam with an uncapped red marker. Occasionally snorting with mirth, she circled a section and wrote a remark. Well, at least Nora knew it wasn't her exam.

Her grip tightened on her blue book as she drew closer.

Dr. Lansky looked up. "Nora Carpenter, I would be interested in your opinion of my prompt." The woman lifted her eyebrows a tiny bit.

"I found it to be a difficult prompt since many illnesses show the same symptoms. You also did not identify the location of the village, which in turn would give me a hint about the ethnic makeup of the population. Two important things I didn't know if good sanitation was in place at that time and if the illnesses would spread through contact, water, food, touch, and possibly the air. So, I was unsure how to treat and label the illness."

Whoa, what if Dr. Lansky hadn't really wanted her opinion? What if she'd just shot herself in the foot? After all, her test had yet to receive a grade. Would Dr. Lansky be willing to wipe out her pithy little speech?

Nora watched as her instructor capped the red pen and laid it aside. She pushed up from her seated position to stand facing Nora. "Were you frustrated that you didn't know immediately what was wrong with the residents of the mythical village?"

Nora had felt some frustration but had contributed it to fouling up her perfect 4.0 GPA. "I did feel a high level of frustration."

Dr. Lansky smiled, which to some would only have validated her reputation as being ruthless, but Nora didn't consider it a mean smile. There had been more to the question than a simple epidemic.

Nora asked, "Were you trying to show us how doctors in the eighteenth century were clueless about what they might be treating?"

The doctor nodded. "That's part of it, but even in this century, with all our special tests and equipment, medicine requires observation and experimentation. Physicians willing to go with the quick or popular answer can end up killing their patient. They'll explain it away in other ways, but it amounts to the same."

It was a sobering thought. As a physician assistant, she'd be making some of those calls on her own. It would pay to watch and listen very closely. "Part of good practice is listening to the patient?" Nora asked, already knowing the answer.

Dr. Lansky started to agree but stopped. "It is more than that. Sometimes it is getting the patient to talk. Other times, it's seeing through the words to understand what they aren't saying, and other times, it is asking the right questions. Unfortunately, we don't have any classes for those skills, but I believe you have them."

"Me?" Nora squeaked the word, much to her embarrassment. She pointed to herself, foolishly since no one else was in the room.

"Yes, you." Dr. Lansky punctuated her answer with an emphatic head bob. "You are my best student. Probably the best in the program. I would love to see you as a doctor as opposed to an assistant. With your level of ability right now, we could put you in the eighteenth century, and you'd save hundreds of lives, maybe even thousands."

Nora rested her hand against the table. Her legs felt a little weak. Could be shock. She'd never expected one of the toughest instructors in the program to heap praise on her.

"Thank you," she murmured the words as she held out her blue book.

The woman took the book and tucked it under the other ones. "Your exam will be my reward after getting through all the other tests. I had every diagnosis, from chicken pox to the plague, but not one student suggested that he or she didn't know what the illness was. It takes real character to admit when you don't know. Be glad you have that character."

Nora tried for a smile but was unsure if her lips tilted up appropriately. All she wanted to do was drop her mouth open in absolute amazement. Here was a woman who'd never cracked a smile the entire semester, and she was grinning at her as if Nora had done something great.

Covering her mouth, she coughed before she could say anything. Clearing her throat, she managed to croak out the words, "I appreciate your comments more than you can possibly know."

The other woman's brow furrowed briefly. "Maybe. I might have a clue. I was once a student like you, but at that time, they did not consider females as doctor candidates, medical or otherwise."

As wonderful as the conversation was, Nora felt awkward and longed to escape back to the life she knew. "I see you proved them wrong."

Dr. Lansky folded her arms and looked supremely pleased with herself. "I did, didn't I? Don't let me make you late to your next class."

Nora made eye contact before dashing out the door. Was she being rude? She yelled back into the lecture hall, "See ya."

As she half-jogged to reach the bus stop, her action replayed in her brain. Real stupid to say, "See ya" to one of the most-feared lecturers on staff.

The rumble of the bus along with a healthy belch of diesel fumes alerted her that her ride had arrived. Palming her pass, she hustled into line with the other passengers. It wouldn't do for her to be late to work. It wasn't as if she'd be fired, but the thought of inconveniencing her co-workers bothered her. Her lateness put her at the end of the line as the people in front of her grabbed the empty seats.

Damn. She wanted to rest before she started her shift. She scoured the area, hoping for an overlooked seat. There was one in the back, right between an earbud-plugged teen and a sleeping woman whose lips trembled with each snore. Not ideal, but it would allow her to gobble her mid-morning snack, which she had yet to consume. Her stomach gave a minor growl as if agreeing. Her feet were headed in that direction when she felt someone behind her. A glance over her right shoulder revealed a confused, elderly woman desperately searching for a seat. Nora sighed, moved aside, and pointed the seat out to the woman.

"Oh, thank you, dear," the woman said, as she made her unsteady way to the back of the bus.

Nora reached for the overhead strap. "No problem, ma'am."

Her stomach emitted another growl. Someone was bound to get off before the bus reached the diner, allowing her to sit and choke down her granola bar. It didn't make sense to eat before lunch but standing on her feet for six to eight straight hours took a tremendous amount of energy.

This small possibility lightened her mood. Why should she be gloomy? Dr. Lansky had told her she'd make a good doctor. She'd be willing to bet the good doctor seldom shared those words with many. More likely, she shared the opposite observation.

Her mind drifted into a stupor in which she was aware of the bus moving and its location, but little else.

So why aren't you going to be a doctor? You would be a good one.

Clayton's voice in her head caused her to stumble forward, but at least she still had hold of the strap to prevent falling. By this time, you'd think she'd be used to Clayton's voice. Well, at least she recognized it. Mental illness took many forms, she reminded herself. One out of four people had some type. The statistics, however, did nothing to reassure her.

I am not a mental illness. You are not crazy. It takes a great deal of work on my part to contact you. I would like it if you'd show a little more appreciation.

Sorry. Her face crinkled into an apologetic grin, making the man in a fast-food smock and seated just under her arm regard her strangely then look away.

Why aren't you studying to be a doctor?

Clayton's question echoed Dr. Lansky's remarks. Apparently, the man could read her thoughts. She tried to shape them so they made sense. *I never really considered being a doctor, ever. School is expensive. I got some scholarships. My parents scraped together a little bit of money to help. I saved that, though. I work at the diner to pay for my rent, food, and utilities. I'm going into my fifth year of schooling, too. Trust me. Scholarships dry up after four years no matter how good your grades are. I can't afford another two years to be a doctor.*

If she'd ever thought about medical school, it was more of a fantasy, rather like winning the lottery or becoming the queen of England. She had equal chances of either happening. For a very brief time, she'd played with the idea of being doctor. Ogden had brought it up, though not intentionally. As far as she could tell, she'd be ten times a better doctor than he was. She'd certainly have a better bedside manner.

I agree. Clayton's voice sounded in her head again.

Nora tried to keep her face from showing her aggravation. Did she not have a single private thought?

Nora, my girl, when will you accept what is? We are soul mates destined to be together throughout time. We are not meant to be separate. Together we are stronger than apart. Surely, you've heard the old story how the gods tore us apart in their jealousy.

She found her head nodding. Nana had told her the story with fervency, believing the gods had played the same trick on her, separating her from Grandfather Buell. Luckily, they'd managed to find each other again.

The image of her grandparents dancing together, looking lovingly into each other's eyes, almost made her tear up. Good Goddess, she didn't need that. Any more dramatics and she might end up on the curb before her stop. It did happen. It was more like a suspension, though. The offenders were back within a week.

With two loving grandparents who have managed to transcend the boundaries of time, why do you not believe? Why can you not accept we are soul mates?

Nora could almost see his handsome face and lifted eyebrows. Why couldn't she accept he was communicating through time when so much had happened in her family's life that should make her believe? It wasn't that she didn't believe people could pass through centuries, something like walking through a cosmic revolving door. Oddly, *that* she could believe. It was the part about having a soul mate. She'd never expected one. Maybe she'd felt undeserving after the incident.

Those animals would go missing if I were in your time.

Nora bit her lip. She never knew when Clayton was eavesdropping on her. There were things she'd rather he didn't know.

Do not blame me for that. Your thoughts came to me, so strongly it was as if you were screaming. How could I not hear? Remember, you didn't do anything wrong. As much as I hate to leave you now, I've arrived in a town with sickness so I cannot converse any longer.

His voice and presence disappeared from her head, leaving a little empty-inside feeling. She'd keep that information to herself. Plenty of people would make jokes about losing her marbles if they knew.

CHAPTER SIX

T HE DINER CAME into sight. Thank the Goddess. Her arm was stiff after twenty minutes of swinging from the bus strap. The seats she'd hoped would open up hadn't.

The crowded diner parking lot indicated there would no downtime for her. She sprinted across the pavement, trying to work the stiffness out of her arm by making circles with it. No sooner did she open the door than Ernie called out.

"Glad you're here. Get suited up. I could use the help."

Great. Not exactly what she wanted to hear, but it kept her mind occupied. The smell of frying hamburger and bacon made her mouth water. Was she drooling like a dog at the thought of food? The thought distracted her as she walked in the direction of the restroom and right into the path of a customer who stood up, bumping into her. A brush of chilling evil touched her. Her flesh cringed as she pulled away. Weird, rather like one of those cartoons when a character goes bad and a dark smoke starts spreading through the cartoon body until it is all black. The urge to wash her bare arm where she'd been touched overwhelmed her.

On the bus, in the elevator, even at the university, she brushed against people all the time without this reaction. Her eyes traveled up to meet those of her least-favorite customer.

"So good to see you, Nora." Mr. Creepy lingered on her name as if caressing it. Yuk. He'd probably intentionally stood so she'd blunder into him.

Nora bobbed her head. Anxious to escape, she continued to the bathroom, dodging a toddler who darted out from a booth.

Before the incident, she hadn't recognized evil. She'd assumed most people were pretty much the same, no worse or better than anyone else. Sure, a few were mean-spirited, while others were more kind, but that was the extent. Maybe that's what she'd wanted to believe. When she'd found herself helpless against evil, she'd decided her best bet was to play it safe, especially when she sensed evil nearby. But that man packed maliciousness in a huge, invisible suitcase, he carried everywhere. Why was she the only one who saw it?

Rushing into the tiny bathroom, she locked the door. The owner didn't like the staff to spend too much time in the non-gender bathroom since it kept out patrons. By the time she'd stripped her top off and turned on the hot water, the hammering began.

"Give me a minute," she yelled in the direction of the closed door, hoping the person would take a hint. Pumping a big glob of the antiseptic soap into her hand, she lathered her torso and arms with it. Wiping down with the wet rough paper towels left brown paper crumbs behind. She felt no cleaner. Maybe she should wipe her legs down, too.

The hammering started up again, along with a voice. "Hey, I have to go. That chili went through me like water."

Not what the other customers in the diner would want to hear.

Nora shrugged on her chef smock, not taking time to close the top two buttons before grabbing her backpack and opening the door to a red-faced woman. "Sorry," she mumbled as she squeezed around the woman.

You'd think a restaurant would have two restrooms big enough to accommodate more than one person at a time, a thought to preoccupy her until she swung open the kitchen door.

Ernie half-turned from his place at the grill. "It's about time—" He stopped talking, and his eyes dropped.

Nora looked down as well. Her smock gaped open, exposing her modest cleavage. Oh, my. Her fingers immediately buttoned the opening as her face reddened. Did he think she'd done that on purpose to catch his attention or something? Goddess, she hoped not. Not knowing what to do, she decided to go with pretending nothing had happened at all. "Wow, big crowd there. Still conventioneers?"

Ernie turned to flip the almost-done hamburgers and lifted the crisp bacon onto a paper towel to blot the grease. He answered without facing her and grumbled the words. "Some, but our regulars are here, along with your favorite, who refused to order until you arrived. Didn't want to take a chance on me fixing his food."

Nora mentally added what he didn't say: *Screw you, you nasty, foul, evil creature.*

Okay, maybe Ernie wasn't thinking that. It was just her. Perhaps she'd burn his food today. Of course, he'd insist on talking to her about it. Might even complain to the manager. Barb would act as if she cared while he complained but would laugh about it later. Herman, the owner, tended to react impulsively. He would fire Nora without a second thought. The same way he'd let Susan, a third-shift waitress, go when a customer had complained she was unfriendly. What he didn't say was Susan had slapped his hand when he tried to grope her. There was a good chance she would never know why she lost her position.

In Indiana, as well as several other states, employers could hire and fire at will. A person could hire whomever they wanted, no matter how unqualified they were. The owner could fire you if he didn't like your eye shadow if he didn't tell you. Legitimate complaints against firing could merit unemployment, which cost the company. It was best to give no reason for firing. No intelligent boss would admit he fired someone because she was old, smelly, ugly, or overweight, but many did. A few were dumb enough to admit it and ended up in the newspaper and in court for discrimination. She didn't know about Herman. He'd never struck her as smart or particularly interested in the diner. The diner ran well despite his interference, thanks to Barb.

It would be nice not be around Mr. Creepy. Thoughts of him caused her to open her paper cook hat too vigorously, tearing it. Ernie gave her another hat from the shelf over the grill without comment. As much as Mr. Creepy bothered her, there were bound to be men just like him elsewhere. Getting a job in a college town was no easy thing with the huge pool of available students to work. The diner always worked with her hours, which was more than most places would do. She'd just have to suck it up and deal with it.

Glancing at the order slips, she dropped some fries and chicken strips into the hot oil. Grabbing six plates, she placed them on the wooden prep bar to ready them for their eventual burgers and fries. People gladly paid a few bucks more for a simple fast-food meal served on a real plate with a dill spear on the side. Could be it wasn't the food that brought them, but the atmosphere. It was far from a trendy place, but there was a mellow aspect about the diner that no one was in a hurry. Lonely people could pretend the chatty server really was their friend, all for the price of a modest tip.

Nora supposed the diner was better than some restaurants. The fact they didn't serve alcohol eliminated most of the drunks. Staying open almost twenty-four hours brought in some interesting characters in the middle of the night, but by that time, she was asleep and dreaming.

The vividness of her dreams lately troubled her, as well as the possibility they might not entirely be dreams.

She put the open buns on the left side of the plate, allowing enough room to slide the fries in place. Placing the lettuce leaf carefully on top of the open bun top, she followed it with a tomato slice.

Why did the nocturnal meetings bother her? If she were honest with herself, she'd admit they were the most pleasant aspect of her life, wedging in between work, school, the hospital, and dodging Ogden. Clayton had been nothing but nice to her, she thought, as she placed a dill spear near the edge of a plate. An onion slice followed the tomato as the sandwich waited for the sizzling patty.

An alarm buzzed, alerting her that the fries needed attention. Flipping them into the metal container that allowed the oil to drip off, she wondered if Clayton was a figment of her imagination. She'd been having the dreams for years but had always had trouble remembering the details. Often, she'd awake with a sense of security that seemed to be woefully missing from her life.

Why were the dreams becoming so vivid now? Was she astral traveling in her sleep? Could you astral travel to other times? Whom would she ask? Her grandfather was her best bet, but he'd ask questions. She'd not put it past him to probe her mind—for her own good, he'd explain.

Ernie called out, "Get a move on with those fries or the order will get cold."

Using the scoop, she measured huge helpings of fries onto each plate. Another reason people came to the diner. Fries cost the restaurant almost nothing. It was surprising most restaurants were so stingy with them.

Her schooling required she take a variety of psychology classes to help understand her future patients. She often used the information she obtained in class on customers and even co-workers. She shoved another serving of fries on the plate, mounding it high. The customers enjoyed seeing a full plate. It made them think they got reward or a favor. The same plate served by a smiling server made the customer feel special. It was probably better than some paper-wrapped mystery food that a fast-food employee pushed across the counter.

Taking off her food-service gloves, she stacked the plates on her arms. No way could she carry the plates with the slippery gloves on. She approached the window with the food and called out, "Order up, Robin."

It was important to acknowledge the right server to prevent someone from snatching up specials meant for someone else. There was some rivalry among the waitresses to serve their customers first. Nora couldn't understand the backstabbing attitude, but she'd never belonged to the mean-girls club. Using what she learned in class, she could diagnose the women as having a fear of scarcity with a touch of paranoia. They might believe there were not enough good tippers to go around, while fearing the possible loss of their job.

Returning to the grill, she donned fresh gloves. Looking at the newest orders, she laid out seven frozen patties on the grill. "How much longer are you staying, Ernie?"

"How's the crowd?" He used the edge of the spatula to sweep the grease into the catcher.

"All the booths are full, but no one is waiting. I'd say it is slowing down." That was good, because she didn't want Ernie staying over his shift. Barb might expect other cooks to help in a rush, but that didn't mean they received any compensation for it. It was a common-courtesy deal.

The cook slid one burger away from the rest and gestured to it. "Want to spit on this one? We'll make sure it goes to your admirer."

The suggestion shocked Nora. A nervous giggle escaped as she shook her head. "Um, no. I can see myself villainized on social media in a heartbeat. I'll give it a mental spit and be good."

Ernie laughed and pushed the burger back into the company of the rest of the patties. "Just ignore him. If you stay behind the counter, there's no way he can touch you. Besides, there's plenty of cops who stop here, too. If you ever feel unsafe, call someone to come get you."

Nora smiled at the cook's attempt to give her fatherly advice. "Thanks, Ernie."

She didn't bother to tell him there was no one she could call. Neither she nor Tonya owned a car. No way would she call Ogden. Of course, with Ogden, half the time he'd tell her it was a bad time and he couldn't make it. As boyfriends went, he was majorly sucky.

Perhaps that was why she'd created Clayton. He was everything she wanted in a man but never expected to get. Like her father, she could depend on him. He'd never let her down. He was funny, charming, and not too hard on the eyes. It was odd that she'd envisioned him in a different century.

I'll have you know you did not make me up.

Clayton's indignant tone almost caused her to drop the plate in her hand. Sliding the plate on the metal window ledge, she said, "Order up."

She made the mistake of glancing toward her least-favorite customer. He looked up at the same time and waved. Inhaling deeply, she backed away from the window. She so didn't need this.

Need what?

Nora's head swung toward Ernie, who was untying his apron. True, she didn't want to talk to Clayton in front of the cook but carrying on a conversation in her head while she was alone wouldn't be much better.

Remember, you don't have to voice your thoughts, since I can hear them.

"Oh, joy," she grumbled more to herself than Clayton.

Ernie threw his greasy apron in the laundry but looked up at her words. "Whad ya say?"

Nora scrambled for an appropriate reply. "Could you give Mr. Creepy a shove out the door on the way out?"

"Love to, but I always go out the back door." He suited his actions to his words and headed for the door. "See ya."

"Yeah." Nora held up her hand in reply. She turned to the stove, where bacon sizzled and a few burgers steamed as they defrosted. Any normal person working so long around meat would have become a vegetarian, but not her. It could be a sign of something being not quite right about her. That and hearing voices in her head.

Will you stop debasing yourself, darling? I already explained we are soul mates, which means we function as one.

Nora flipped the bacon while trying to direct her thoughts. *What if I don't want to be part of your soul-mate oneness?*

I am truly hurt. If you felt that way, you should have made your decision seven lifetimes ago.

They'd known each other for seven lifetimes. How long had she lived? Maybe the better question was: How many lifetimes had she had?

Not sure how many lifetimes you've had, but I've had nine. Let me tell you, two were so bitter and bleak without you by my side I was determined to find you in this life. No matter where you were. Life was worth a handful of cold spit without you by my side.

Nora wrinkled her nose. *You almost had me tearing up until the spit remark.*

Well, it's true. Without you, my life consists of waiting for you to appear. When I tired of waiting, I tried searching across the centuries.

Scooping the burgers up with the spatula, she flipped them. She chased the diced onions one customer requested across the grill. That would explain her eyes watering. *Why don't I remember any of the lives we've spent together?*

A sudden silence from Clayton made her wonder if he had disappeared to attend to other duties, or maybe her imagination had run out of the ability to create dialogue for her imaginary friend. Then his warm voice returned, sounding a bit melancholy.

I wondered that myself. I wasn't born knowing you, but gradually there would be dreams of a dark-haired lass named Nora. Along with the dream came memories about who we had been in centuries past. At first, I told no one, thinking they were just dreams. Strange ones, but dreams. I met a conjuring woman who told my fortune for a few coins. She spoke of you by name and the love we shared. She convinced me I could find you. You know me. I felt you recognized me the first time you traveled through time. Do you not know me, lass?

A hard question she didn't know how to answer. She corralled the onions to place them on the waiting burger then topped it with cheese. She had a few regulars who had special orders. Another reason they came here as opposed to buying fast food. No matter how many other restaurants sang about having it your way, the customer seldom did. That cut into the assembly-line process.

She carried the finished plate to the window and simply rang the bell, since only one waitress was still on duty. Lorraine had stayed only until the shift fully changed over and the drawer counted.

Once she stepped back into the kitchen, she flipped her two remaining burgers and dumped the remaining fries into the drainer.

How did she feel about Clayton?

I felt safe with you when I hadn't felt safe in a long time. It felt like I belonged in your arms, and you would never hurt me.

Nora caught herself hugging her arms around herself as if surrounded by Clayton's embrace. The bread man could show up while she was embracing herself. She immediately dropped her arms.

You felt safe in my arms because I would protect you with my very life, and I have in the past.

A pang squeezed her heart, and her hand rested lightly on her chest. She knew without asking that Clayton had died more than once to protect her.

I believe you worked so hard at forgetting or at least burying the bad things in this life that you also stymied the memories of us from coming through. Only when you were asleep and your mind was at rest could I reach you before.

Nora plated up the last three orders and carried them to the window. Just her luck, she had the ideal boyfriend in the wrong century.

Would you be uncomfortable with a Wiccan girlfriend?

She'd never confessed to Ogden any of her beliefs. She knew how he'd react. He'd tell her it was something she needed to get rid of, rather like a pair of old shoes.

I am not sure what Wiccan means. If you are okay with me having a touch of the fey about me, then I am sure I am fine with a Wiccan, although I wouldn't be wanting a girlfriend.

What did he mean by not wanting a girlfriend? He was the one who'd called them soul mates. She was about to ask when the bread man swung open the back door. While he wasn't as chatty as the milk guy was, he did merit some attention. By the time she had signed the invoice, she realized Clayton had disappeared without another word. How strange.

CHAPTER SEVEN

T HE BREAD MAN slammed the door as he left. She wasn't sure why, but suddenly the idea that anyone could walk into the kitchen began to bug her. Tall metal shelving units with boxes of Styrofoam ware and napkins filled the wall behind her along with the walk-in fridge. There really wasn't any place to hide, unless someone was willing to stay in the fridge. The culprit would have had to slip in and conceal himself while no one was in the kitchen. The kitchen wasn't empty often, especially since cooks usually stayed around an additional twenty or thirty minutes, helping or shooting the breeze. Nora was probably one of the few who left almost immediately, due to the bus schedule.

The stainless-steel counters and wooden prep station didn't have any excess spaces a person could duck behind. The tall rack of buns pushed into the farthest corner of the room offered some possibility. Nora pulled the bread rack away from the wall and closer to the lights. Sure, it was awkward in the middle of the room, but she'd push it back before she left. Part of her mind thought she was being paranoid and ridiculed her for it, but another part wasn't so sure.

Taking a wet towel, she wiped down her workstation while she waited for an order. Accustomed to working alone, she used the time to recite medical information, keeping her voice low enough not to be heard in the diner. No one needed to hear her rattle off the names of bones or various muscle groups. Might cause them to wonder what she was cooking. Was it hamburger or something else? Other times she used the empty hours to contemplate her future home with a space for a little garden and flowers. The house didn't matter as much as wanting the stability a house represented.

Bonnie served as the second-shift waitress and seemed to enjoy her job, if her laughter was any indication. Her teased hair, heavily made-up eyes, and smock zipper pulled low enough to reveal her bountiful cleavage made her a stereotype. Still, Bonnie had regulars who enjoyed her calling them "hon" and "darling." Nora wasn't sure how old she was, but oddly enough, she felt the woman might be closer to her own age than she'd originally suspected. The hair and the liberal application of makeup aged the woman. It was almost as if she were disguising herself for work every night. The idea intrigued Nora, causing her to step through the swinging door that separated the kitchen from the diner, and watch Bonnie work. She might as well, since there were no orders coming her way.

A middle-aged couple had just finished their meal and were pushing themselves up out of the low booth. The man helped the woman up with a smile. Perhaps they were on a date. Not the classiest place in the world, but it served its purpose, especially if the guy wasn't that invested in his date. They walked to the cash register, conversing in low voices. The man turned toward the woman, listening to her while she spoke as if he cared about what she said. Curious to check out the couple more, she called out, "I'll get the cash register."

Using the gate that separated the service area from the booths, she passed Bonnie to reach the register.

The woman looked up from her conversation with a cop to give her a grateful smile. "Thanks, hon."

Nora squeezed past her in the narrow service alley, thinking if any of the servers gained weight, there'd be no way they could pass each other. Her glance flickered over the cop and Bonnie. The server leaned over the counter to pour the tired-looking man more coffee. His uniform stated he was a cop, but his posture, along with the frown lines in his face, announced he didn't enjoy being one. Ironically, the same uniform he probably disliked wearing had Bonnie fluttering over him like a bee that spotted a field of sunflowers. Bonnie was a big fan of uniforms, though not because of the authority, they represented, but rather it was an indication of a stable job.

Nora took the bill from the man and rang it up. The wide gold band on his finger caught her eye, confirming the two were married. The woman placed her hand on her husband's arm possessively, as if letting any other female, know he wasn't available.

Swallowing the urge to laugh at the woman's actions, Nora handed the change back. "Have a nice evening, you two."

The man's eyes twinkled. "How can it be anything but good when I'm married to the best woman in the world?"

His wife simpered and looked up at him adoringly.

Nora's breath caught in her throat. How sweet. Sometimes she forgot married people could be like that. Most of the married ones who came in either ate in a sullen silence, bickered throughout the meal, or tried to balance caring for all their young children while trying to feed themselves. Many of the younger couples spent more time looking at their cell phone screens than each other.

The bell rang as four men came into the diner, their paint-dotted white uniforms revealing their profession. Four orders coming up, she thought as she made her way to the kitchen. The bell rang again, announcing more customers. Her hand was spread flat on the kitchen door, ready to push it open, when she hesitated. An image of an unknown man lying in wait with a chef's knife in hand ready to plunge it into her back flooded her mind.

Her body felt frozen. Turning her head toward Bonnie took real effort. "I am going in the kitchen to make the orders you'll be giving me soon."

The server handed the four men menus but glanced up to give Nora a baffled stare. "Okay, you'll be getting those orders real soon, too."

Nothing for it, she'd have to go into the kitchen. No one had any use for a short-order cook who was afraid of the kitchen. It sounded like a joke, but unfortunately, she had no punch line. Pushing the door open, she found the same fluorescent-lighted kitchen as before with the strong odor of onions and grease. The sound of a door closing caused her heart to skip a beat. Her eyes flew to the back door that remained firmly shut. She took five fast steps to the door and locked it. The deliveries were over for the night, which meant there was no reason for it to be unlocked.

Taking the spatula, she scraped the old grease from the grill, prepping it for the next orders. The sound of a door closing again caught her attention. Nora realized with a sigh that it was the restroom door, which was directly across from the kitchen. Countless times over innumerable shifts, she'd heard that door open and close, but now she was as nervous as a long-tailed cat caught at a rocking-chair marathon. Paranoid, that's what she was.

Bonnie banged the bell, indicating orders. The thin slips of paper waved from their clips. Snatching them, Nora wondered why Bonnie couldn't call out the orders. The bell irritated her, making her feel like some trained animal. Go get the orders, prepare the food, put it in the window, and make sure to ring the stupid bell. Her level of irritability surprised her.

Placing three frozen patties on the grill, she tried to analyze her own behavior. Things had been hectic with her college career ending. Soon, she'd be out doing the things she'd spent so much time planning to do. Most people would have been excited and frightened, maybe a lot frightened. Those not quite ready to meet the real world packed the graduate programs. Despite the university's assurances that additional education was always beneficial, graduate students educated themselves out of getting a startup position. The lower the degree the less they were paid, which explained hospitals' preferences for hiring those with the lower ones. In a bizarre way, they made their fears of not finding a job a reality by over-educating themselves.

Squatting, she removed the bacon, eggs, and cheese from the under-the-counter fridge. Placing the six strips of bacon beside the burgers to sizzle, she returned to her contemplation. Sure, she was uncertain, but she wanted to get on with her life. She'd been in a holding pattern too long.

Her unease was probably more about Ogden than anything. Emotionally, she'd withdrawn from him but had failed to tell him they were finished. He'd find someone else to be his servant girl. The thought eased her guilt but simultaneously turned her stomach.

For the last two days, she'd cold-shouldered him. Had he called her? Sent her flowers? Show up at her apartment or work begging to know what was wrong? No, of course not. That would have required some work on his part.

Grabbing the seasoning container, she liberally shook the can. Working the spatula under the burgers, she flipped them with vigor, splashing grease on herself. No good getting worked up over Ogden. Count it as a lesson learned.

"Stupid horse's ass," she growled.

Why couldn't she have someone who loved her for who she was as opposed to what she could do for him? Her eyes narrowed at the burgers as if they were the cause of her problems. After testing the burgers with her spatula, she started the eggs. The men would expect their orders at the same time, even though the burgers took longer to cook. Timing was the hardest part of her job, especially when working alone. She held the egg up, ready to crack it open on the metal counter, when Clayton's voice returned.

I love you. I have for centuries. It doesn't matter what body you take, because your soul is the same, and that's what I love.

The egg slipped from her fingers to spatter on the floor. "Shit." She didn't have time to clean it up and get the food ready. Grabbing the salt container, she shook it over the oozing mess for easier cleaning later, a trick she'd learned from her Nana. The salt absorbed the liquid and made it sweepable, as opposed to requiring mopping. Once she got the food plated, she'd deal with it. Bending to get another egg, she mentally asked, *Are you going to say something else outrageous that will cause me to drop the eggs?*

Not getting an answer, she proceeded to crack the eggs into a greased skillet. Ernie always cooked the eggs on the grill, leaving them with a slight beefy tone. He called the griddle the great equalizer because all protein mingled on it. He jokingly referred to Nora as a segregationist since she used a skillet for the eggs.

Clayton's continued silence bothered her, unsure if he was miffed or just not talking. The fry buzzer rang as soon as she had the burgers plated. The toast popped up by the time the fries were on the plate. Damn, she was good. Well, at least when it came to timing food.

Placing the plates in the window, she hit the bell twice, drawing an irritated gaze from Bonnie. Slipping back into the kitchen, she knelt to clean up the egg. When she swept the salt-saturated mess into the dustpan,

Clayton spoke.

I could use your help here. There's an epidemic, and I could use another pair of hands.

This wasn't a conversation they'd had before, which puzzled her, but she could hear the strain in his voice.

Nora, I am sorry. That makes me sound no better than all those other people who used you. I do love you more than life itself. I've proved it over several lifetimes. Right now, this illness has me whipped. I don't know what to do.

He'd loved her over several lifetimes. What she wouldn't give to remember their lives together.

How can I help you? She asked him.

The anguish that had flavored his words, and the weary tone of his voice, indicated low energy. An image of Clayton formed with his shoulders drooping and his jaunty smile replaced by a grim, determined visage. His rolled-up sleeves and missing vest indicated a long day, probably one without a break or assistance. Clayton still managed a soft litany of encouraging words as he labored over a sick child whose fever-ravaged body tossed in delirium.

Did she really see Clayton somehow or did she imagine the scene?

His voice remained silent as she refilled the cook fridge for the next shift. Slamming the fridge door in frustration, she looked around for tasks to busy herself until her shift was complete. Buns, yeah, she'd grab a couple of bags to place above the grill. That done, she placed her hands on her hips and stared at the mute stainless-steel appliances and wire racks piled high with Styrofoam takeout boxes. Oddly enough, they didn't have too many takeout orders. People came to the diner because they wanted to sit. Besides, the diner didn't have a drive-through. By the time someone came in, placed an order, and waited for it, a person could have enjoyed a beverage and spent the time with a companion chatting. It explained the unopened tower of takeout trays in their plastic sleeves.

Nora tidied the boxes on the rack, thinking the cleaning was a waste of her time. Clayton needed her and the medical knowledge she had in her head. Her hands fisted as she considered how many elderly or young were dying even now in Clayton's century. The young and the elderly were often the first victims in an epidemic. The young often hadn't built up the immunity to fight off the diseases, while the elderly didn't have the strength to resist. Why was she here when she needed to be there?

Throwing her hands in the air, she spoke to the empty kitchen. "What use is it to study medicine when I can't use what I know?"

Bonnie's unnaturally bright red hair flashed into view as the server stuck her head in the pass-through window. "Something wrong back here?"

Great. Just what she needed, her co-worker doubting her stability. "Nope," Nora called and used her foot to jiggle the rack holding the trays until one stack slipped off, hitting the floor with a hollow-sounding plop. "It's these boxes. Not stacked right. One fell off and hit me in the face."

"Oh, is that all?" Bonnie's voice registered her disinterest as her head disappeared from the window.

Nora was good with Bonnie's lack of concern. The server probably experienced enough in the school of hard knocks that she didn't have any interest in worrying about other people. That was okay with Nora. Worried people poked into her business. Sure, everyone would be cool with the voices-in-her-head story. If the state hadn't closed its state-run mental hospital, she'd end up in a padded cell faster than she could say, "Bob's my uncle." Nope, it was best to keep the strange and bizarre info close.

Pushing the rack into place, she bent to pick up the stack she'd knocked free.

Now, if someone thought a person was loony tuney, they either had to criminalize their behavior so the penal system would lock them away or have wads of money to put them in a private facility. Since she fell into neither category, she was on her own, rather like the woman who sang arias while grocery shopping. The well-groomed woman had a nice voice, and she was no more disturbing than people muttering into their cell phones and better than the tired mothers threatening to rip off their child's arm and use it as a club.

Her voices...make that, Clayton's voice was mild compared to most people's idiosyncrasies. Her feet carried her to the pass-through window to check to see if their favorite alien abductee was in the house. He was. He kept a transistor radio plugged into his ear tuned to some news station that confused anyone trying to scan his mind. He cautioned the diner employees to do the same. Yep, she was the sane one here, but just in case, she'd call Grandpa Buell.

If anyone understood how to time travel, he did. Maybe he could explain her growing apprehension about the door, too. She'd have to explain about Clayton's voice in her head, which would almost feel like she was divulging a secret, hers and Clayton's. Still, she could depend on Grandpa to tell no one. He understood without words, which made it helpful. How much he knew might be an issue, too. Would he know she found herself growing fonder and fonder of this man trapped in the past or that she found Clayton's eyes and hair super sexy? That wouldn't do.

The door chimed, indicating someone had entered. Good, it would keep her busy. A quick peek showed it was Brandon. The wall clock revealed he was a good forty minutes early.

Seeing her, he waved. "Hey, Cookie," he said with a wide grin. "Think you can whip me up a three-egg omelet with cheese?"

His nickname for her came from his days in the service when they referred to the cook as Cookie. It seemed odd that a Marine would welcome Cookie as a nickname, but they'd also called the gunnery sergeant Gunnie. Maybe rough soldiers needed something playful in their lives.

Brandon sat at the counter with his muscular arms crossed and resting on the top. The man stayed in shape. As if noticing her perusal, he winked.

Flustered, Nora ducked out of the window view, but still answered, "Omelet coming up."

Cracking the eggs into the blender, she wondered about Brandon's behavior. Had he always been that flirtatious? Couldn't be. She'd have given him the cold shoulder the way she did all men who tried to flirt with her. What was different about him?

Maybe he'd ended a relationship and was on the rebound. The reticent cook never talked much about his personal life. The Marine tattoo on his biceps initially announced his military connection. Then again, it could be her. What if she was changing? Was it possible?

The sound of the blender whipping the egg mixture into a frothy mass filled the tiny kitchen. Ladling a tablespoon of oil into the skillet, she shook it to coat the pan. Turning off the blender, she removed it from the stainless-steel base and poured the eggs into the waiting skillet. A few shakes of the spice canister added the right amount of salt, pepper, and a few other spices she couldn't identify. It was part of the diner's secret, along with the blender. Sliding the skillet rapidly across the grill, she kept the eggs from sticking to the sides.

When had she signaled that she might be open to flirtation? Tonya had teased her that she'd give an iceberg a run for its money when it came to being frosty. The comment had pleased her, since it was the effect she wanted. It was hard to remember what she'd been like before the incident, since so much effort went into forgetting that time.

She'd never been the perky cheerleader type, but she did remember being friendly and helpful. The Wiccan Rede was: Do as you please but harm none. Nana translated it to mean to help others if possible. Nora felt obligated to do, because she often set the curve with her siblings. She did remember being happy and confident. It had been a good feeling. At the time, she'd felt safe in announcing her beliefs. Not in the in-your-face way many of the other teens did, constantly questioning your eternal destination. A tiny pentacle had graced her neck, but she might as well have had "Satan's Whore" tattooed on her forehead, considering the impression some of the boys had received.

Grabbing the skillet handle, she lifted the pan and gave it a good shake before placing the cheese on the omelet.

She'd done nothing wrong then. The nurse had told her the same thing almost six years ago, but she hadn't believed it. Instead, after reading countless accounts of sexual assaults, she'd realized none of the women had invited it. People would point fingers at victims, claiming they shouldn't have been at the party, the grocery, the park, or wherever the attack happened.

Nora had tried to analyze her own behavior, trying to discover the inciting factor. As a result, she'd sheared off her long hair that one of her attackers used to hold her down. Her clothes had become as conservative as any primitive religious sect's, with high necklines and dark colors. The only difference was she wore pants. Overall, she made no effort to be attractive. She froze out men who tried to get past her initial barriers.

There were always one or two who tried, convinced she was a challenge. A few others labeled her a dyke and felt a conversion was in order. Dissuading the last had been the whole reason behind Ogden, but he'd never served his purpose. He was just another man who used her. Goddess knew she'd had enough of that.

The toast popped up as she slid the omelet on the plate. She arranged the toast on the plate with a few slices of tomato, which she knew Brandon liked.

She'd settled for Ogden only because she'd never expected to have a real-live relationship. The love songs that portrayed a man who was so hopelessly smitten he'd do anything for the woman he loved? Nope, she'd never expected that.

Grabbing the plate, she backed into the hall door to deliver the plate herself. No other customers were there, which would allow her a few minutes to talk.

The same behavior in someone else she might have regarded as flirting, but she considered it more of an experiment. She centered the plate in front of Brandon with a smile. A ridiculous urge to whip off her paper hat and ruffle her fingers through her hair came over her. She quelled it, knowing she had a good thirty minutes left on her shift. Was this how normal women felt when around an available man?

It probably was. The part she'd frozen thawed a little. Clayton had told her she needed healing. Turned out, he was right. It was healing as well as forgiving—herself. Living the way, she had for the past years no longer seemed appealing. Closed off to everyone, including her family, to keep her hurt private was not the way she wanted to live. It'd happened. She'd survived, and now she wanted the life she'd been so busy denying herself.

Why couldn't she have a man who loved her? Her lips tipped up at the thought of sleeping in loving arms.

A nudge against her arm caught her attention. Brandon's eyes stared into hers, making her wonder if she'd done or mentioned something that had given away her most recent thoughts. Sliding off the stool, she shrugged her shoulders and teased. "I better go get the kitchen cleaned. The next cook is a real hard-ass."

Brandon's laughter rang out behind her. It was good she could make him laugh, but she didn't want to encourage him too much. It was never good for co-workers to date. Barb discouraged the waitresses from dating the customers, too. A rejected customer would abstain from visiting the diner but could also bad-mouth the place out of spite.

Another six months and she'd be out of here, and no one would request she make a cheeseburger with extra onions, again. All she needed to do was stay friends with Brandon.

Grabbing the rag soaked in bleach water, she rubbed it over all the surfaces, disinfecting them. Good thing the cooks wore white or their uniforms would have been dotted with faded spots. The smell made her crinkle her nose a little, and she wondered how Clayton disinfected in his time. Did they disinfect?

The door creaked open, catching her attention. She spun on her heel with the rag clutched to her chest. The fight-or-flight response had taken hold. Always a big proponent of flight, she still considered the weapons at hand: a skillet and a chef's knife, both formidable.

Brandon walked through the door with an easy gait. Her racing pulse slowed. She glanced up at the clock, aware her shift hadn't ended yet. Her upheld hand with the threatening cloth in it dropped to her side. Nothing too threatening here, which made her feel a tad ridiculous, but being on her guard had kept her safe all these years. She tossed the rag back in the improvised pickle tub bucket.

"Your shift doesn't start for another twenty minutes." She turned her back on him to go back to scraping the grill. While most of the patrons had nothing against grease, they preferred their artery-clogging fat to be fresh.

Brandon came up close behind her, causing the desire to flee to return.

"Go on out. I came back to fix you something before you leave. This way, you won't miss your bus." Brandon's arm reached past her head to grab a paper hat.

Nora ducked under his arm to put some distance between them. Obviously, she hadn't gotten over her aversion to men in her personal space. Why should he be in her space? She stared at his back, outlined by his tight white T-shirt. Brandon chose not to wear a chef smock. Ernie joked that if he worked out as much as Brandon did, he'd want to show it off, too, by wearing a tight T-shirt rather than a chef smock.

"Barb might come in and check," Nora said.

His head twisted enough for her to see the arch of one raised, disbelieving eyebrow. "I know she never comes out once she gets home anymore."

Technically, Barb was supposed to check in twice a night. In the beginning, she had, but once all the troublesome elements left or were helped out, she no longer bothered. Occasionally, she'd come back on the weekends with her husband and eat free.

Brandon continued to hold her gaze. "How about it?"

She was about to defer when she thought, Why not? It was hard to remember someone doing something nice for her without any expectations.

"Okay." She crumpled her paper hat and flung it into the trash. Whipping the apron over her head, she aimed it at the laundry bag.

As she opened the side door, Brandon caught it with his hand, holding it open, causing his bicep to bunch. His tattoo was at her eye level, filling her immediate view with the word "Marines." Blinking, she managed to tear her eyes away from the tattoo and up to his face.

His eyes laughed a little before he asked, "What do you want?"

Nora hesitated, biting her bottom lip. It felt like he was asking her more than if she wanted a burger or chicken fingers. It was probably her imagination. "Surprise me."

Except for two lone men at separate booths, both nursing cups of coffee with their plates pushed aside, the diner was empty as she took a seat at the counter. She recognized them, not by name, but as the type of men who stretched their time out at the diner because they had nothing at home. Bonnie would talk to them, making them feel important and wanted, even if only for the tip they'd leave.

Bonnie approached her with a smirk and her favorite diet cola. When she reached the counter, she slid the drink toward her and looked back in the direction of the kitchen. She flattened her hand on the bar to balance herself as she half-leaned across the counter, better to whisper into Nora's ear, "What's going on with you and our favorite Marine?"

"Nothing." She took a few pulls on her straw. Why would Bonnie assume something was up? She hadn't done anything to encourage the man. At least, she didn't think she had.

The man in question appeared in the window. "Order up for my favorite short-order cook."

Bonnie threw her a knowing look before she picked up the plate. "Oh, what's this? I've never seen it on the menu."

Brandon had his forearms braced against the window as he watched the reactions to his creation. "I consider it a gourmet grilled cheese. I used two different cheeses, plus bacon and sliced tomatoes."

Bonnie made a smacking sound with her lips as she put the plate in front of Nora. "Nothing?" The waitress mouthed the word in a mocking fashion, aware Brandon couldn't see or hear her.

What could Nora say? She hadn't done anything outside of her little experiment minutes earlier. "Thanks, Brandon. This looks good."

Bonnie walked away muttering, "Yum." Nora wasn't sure if she was talking about the sandwich or Brandon.

Taking a bite under the still-watching man's eyes, she chewed enthusiastically. "Hmm, that's good. It should be on the menu."

"No, it shouldn't." Brandon shook his head. "If it was on the menu, it wouldn't be special."

Oh, my. Nora wondered if her eyes got big. Talk about declaring his intent. She took another bite and continued to chew. When it doubt, eat. The sandwich was good, with the butter-crisped bread and the gooey cheese. The bacon added a salty bite, while the tomato complemented with a mild, juicy afternote. It was a delicious sandwich. Why this curious behavior now?

Clayton's voice returned. Hearing his familiar timber brought some reassurance considering his abrupt departure earlier. *I'm not liking this a bit. I am the one who is healing you, loving you, bringing you back to life. No need for that man jack to cast his eyes on you.*

The jealousy-flavored words sounded as if they were bitten out through clenched teeth. He thought he'd healed her. She wanted to object and explain she'd done any healing on her own, but she didn't. After the dreams she'd been having for years, though she seldom remembered them, she often awoke with a contented feeling. It could have been Clayton. Precious few other things could have caused her to wake with a smile.

That is right, darling. Remember that. You have loved me for lifetimes. Sure, and it has been difficult getting you to realize this almost every lifetime. I should be hurt that you've forgotten me so easily.

She didn't want to talk to Clayton under the watchful eyes of Bonnie, who kept smirking at her as she poured coffee for the lonely ones. It was odd that she'd forgotten, but Clayton had managed to get closer to her than anyone ever had. Would she have allowed that if she didn't recognize him?

No reason to work on convincing me, sweetheart. My jealousy of you working so close to a fine, strapping man overcame me.

How did he know about Brandon? Oh, yeah, it was all those walks he took around in her psyche. If she thought Brandon looked buff, then Clayton knew it.

This word "buff" makes no sense to me. All I know is you think about this Brandon more than I would like. I suspect he has his eye on you, too. Hard for me to imagine a man not being in love with you.

Nora fought rolling her eyes at his last remark, aware no one knew she was conversing in her head. It wouldn't have looked any less odd if she'd chosen to explain it. Placing a dollar by her plate, she made ready to leave. The growl of the diesel bus caused her to vault from her seat to catch her ride.

Running with her backpack dangling from her arm, she thanked the bus driver for his patience as she stepped in. It didn't matter that she'd been riding the same route for the last couple of years and left the diner at the same time. It never hurt.

CHAPTER EIGHT

THE BUS RIDE home was uneventful, if you considered having a voice in her head telling her how much he adored her as ordinary. Finally, Nora heaved a sigh and thought emphatically, "*Enough.*"

It must have sounded like yelling. Her eternal soul mate went silent and left. The resulting sensation was like stepping on a butterfly, leaving her with a feeling of guilt.

She half-watched the woman across from her count her money. Nora considered telling her a bus wasn't a good place to flash a wad of bills. The dollars were oversized and almost neon green bright. Play money. The woman had play money but treated it as if it were genuine. Some people might label her crazy, but money has only the value we give to it.

Love was like that, too. A woman in a nurse's smock rested her head against the seat with her eyes closed. The woman loved someone in her life. Could be a single parent trying to make a decent living to support a beloved child. The woman clutching her fake money was important to someone. At least, Nora hoped she was.

It wasn't as if Nora didn't have anyone. She had her family. She never doubted their love, but she still hoped for something more. Back before, she had been as frivolous as any teen, hoping to don a fancy dress to go to the prom with her favorite crush. On prom night, she'd taken a bag of chocolate-chip cookies and a book to visit Abby. She'd read to her friend of battling wizards, while her friend had wordlessly rocked back and forth.

Abby's parents had commended her for her devotion to her friend, which made her feel like a fraud. At the time, she'd felt she was the reason Abby was behind thick walls adorned with trailing ivy. Now, she could place blame where it belonged. Maybe they'd both been too innocent and trusting. Nothing bad truly had touched their lives before then. How could they have recognized evil when it wore familiar faces?

Evil in its many forms was to blame. Misogynistic males considered every woman was theirs for the taking. The police who were supposed to help often doubted victims, as if they were part of some huge conspiracy to make men look bad. Even other women were quick to accuse the female victims of enticing the man somehow. It made as much sense as pedophiles accusing their seven-year-old victims of leading them on.

The knowledge that she hadn't caused the rape to happen lifted a weight off her shoulders, allowing her to sit a little straighter. Next time she visited her parents, she'd make a side trip to tell Abby they'd done nothing wrong. It might help. Evil lived in the world, and sometimes it settled in people. That had been her first hard, face-to-face encounter with it. She doubted it would be her last.

For years she'd battled with guilt and remembering, even hating the concept of physical love, connecting it all together. Rubbing her hands over her arms briskly, she chased away the goose bumps that formed whenever she tried to remember. It was her body's form of an early-warning system. Clayton was the key. Even though she hid her pain and shame from everyone else, it was more difficult when a person meandered through her mind, examining various thoughts. Apparently, what he found did not stop his devotion.

Closing her eyes, she recalled the feel of his arms around her as she'd cried. Never had she permitted herself to simply let go of her rigid control. Instead, she'd been angry and wary certain that the male gender could not be trusted. Crying in Clayton's embrace had released the pain. His reassurance that she was not to blame had allowed her to consider the idea.

Logically, she accepted that victims of sexual assault were not to blame, even if they went to the party, drank too much, or trusted the male who wanted to see her home safely. She was willing to accept that other women didn't provoke their assault but denied herself the same acceptance. What chance had she had to fight off the guys who had planned their attack? None.

A couple of weeks ago, someone had sent her a newspaper article about one of her attackers being charged with the date rape of a woman he'd met speed dating. She suspected her Nana had been the anonymous sender, but she didn't know for sure.

The bus slowed, indicating her stop was next. Once on the street, she looked around, practicing her usual caution in watching for anyone half-hidden in the shadows. She stuck two fingers through her meager key ring, brandishing the ragged edge of her apartment key as a weapon to use to claw out the eyes of potential attackers.

True, she had allowed the self-blame to slip away, but she'd still exercise her hard-earned caution to avoid being a repeat victim.

Staying inside the circles of lights the streetlights threw, she walked to her apartment. Tonya, probably hearing her on the stairs, threw the door open wide. "Well, hello, Miss Carpenter."

From the way she sounded, coconut-flavored rum might have been on the menu tonight. "Good evening, Tonya. Everything okay?"

"Yesssssssh, why do you ask?" Her roommate clutched the door to hold herself upright. "You had a visitor while you were gone. Only a few hours after you left."

Nora squeezed in past her roommate. "Tonya, could you move? I don't want to catch your fingers in the door. Who was my visitor? Captain Morgan?" she asked, referring to the popular brand of rum.

"Ha, ha, aren't you the clever one?" Tonya took a few uncertain steps before plopping down on the couch and patting the seat beside her. "Come sit beside me and tell me what has put the smile on your face."

Nora perched on the edge of the couch, facing her buzzed roommate. "Who came by?"

"Ogden." She practically spat the word and then fell back into the couch cushions. "Lord have mercy. I knew he was a pompous jackass who considered himself better than God, but never had I ever spent so much time with the fool."

"What happened?" Ogden could be dry, snobby, and irritating, but she'd put up with it, feeling he served a purpose.

Tonya shook her head but moaned when the motion appeared to be too much for reeling senses. Instead, she propped her elbows on her knees to cradle her much-abused head. "You owe me big-time." Her hands and the position of her head muted the words.

An image of an angry Ogden raising his hand to her feisty roommate came to mind, immediately replaced by her roommate kneeing him, then threatening to do him more bodily harm with a dull knife. The man wouldn't have stood a chance. "He didn't hurt you, did he?"

Tonya's head lifted enough to pin Nora with a basilisk stare. "If you call being bored by his endless talk, then I was wounded savagely. How do you tolerate him?"

That was a good question. "Half the time I didn't even listen to him. Recently, I have been avoiding him altogether."

"Ah, yeah, that." Tonya rubbed a hand over her face as she struggled into a sitting position. "That's the problem. He decided to go out of his way and take time out of his busy schedule to check on you. He must have mentioned that at least ten times." She threw up her fingers several times, going past ten.

Nora decided not to mention her faulty counting skills in her present state. "So, what did you say to him? How did you get him to leave?"

"It wasn't easy, let me tell you. After he finally heaved-ho, I decided to reward myself with a drink or two."

"Or three or four." Nora couldn't help from commenting.

Tonya groaned slightly before falling back on the couch. "You know the man. He will drive any person to drink. Surprised you're not an alcoholic from keeping company with him."

"We didn't keep that much company. It was more like he'd give me my orders for the day, and I'd do them." It sounded bad when she said it.

She'd run errands for him for the privilege of being associated with the man. Ironically, no one had thought of the two of them as a pair, making the whole effort pointless.

"Yeah, well, that's what I tried to explain, that you were tired of the honor of playing Girl Friday for him."

Maybe Tonya had penetrated his thick hide of blue-blooded pride, whereas Nora could never nick it, not that she'd tried that much. "Did you convince him?"

"Not at first. It made no sense to him why you wouldn't want to continue doing his crap jobs." Tonya looked perplexed herself. She opened and closed her jaw a few times, popping it in the process.

"You'd think if he was so concerned, he'd shown up at the diner. Not that I want him to."

"Oh, yeah, that." Tonya scooched back into the cushion, trying to find a comfortable spot. She closed her eyes. Her mouth dropped open, and a snore emerged.

"Tonya, no sleeping until you tell me what he said." Nora pulled on her roommate's arm to get her attention.

The woman tried to shake her off before answering. "I told him you were letting the big buff Marine at the diner bang you. He went all red in the face. Said he'd see about that and stormed off." Tonya rolled onto her back and began snoring.

Nora couldn't believe her roomie could be so crude, but hey, Ogden could stretch anyone's patience. What had he meant when he'd said he'd see about that? Brandon's over-friendly manner suddenly made sense if Ogden had approached him and demanded to know if they were intimate.

Hard to know what Brandon's answer would have been. It should have been "absolutely not." If he'd been informed inadvertently, that someone, possibly her, had hitched their names together, would he have taken it, as she desired him?

Could her life get any more complicated?

"Really?" she demanded, but no one was awake to appreciate her ire.

Shaking out the afghan, she covered Tonya and slipped off her shoes.

Knowing Brandon as a man of few words, she figured he'd probably give a classic tough guy answer like, "None of your damn business," paired with a sly grin. Luckily, she had two days off before she had to return to the diner and deal with what Brandon might be thinking. It could have been he'd just been friendly tonight, but somehow, she doubted it.

Assured her roommate was sleeping soundly, she decided it was time to call Grandpa. Closing her bedroom door, she dialed the number. Maybe it was silly hiding herself away in her room to talk, but it was a private conversation, one she didn't want to share even with her closest friend. Only Grandpa would understand, and possibly her younger sister, Leah.

They were, after all, the only two time travelers she knew.

The phone rang four times, worrying Nora that her grandparents were already asleep. Maybe she should hang up before she woke them. The same time her finger hovered over the end button, her grandfather's voice sounded in her ear.

"Nora, sweetie, I've been waiting for your call."

His familiar voice relaxed her, bringing with it a sense of security and love. "How did you know?" Of course, he'd known she'd call the moment she'd thought about it. She probably had the only grandfather who could hear people's thoughts. Oh, he swore he didn't listen in, but he seemed to be tuned to the mention or thought of his name.

Nora looked at the phone curiously. Why did she bother with the device? But, then, she didn't have Grandpa Buell's ability.

"You had something to tell me about your young man."

Nora wondered whether he meant Ogden, although she'd never mentioned him, or Brandon, who was not her man, even though he may now think of himself as such. She hadn't said anything about him, either. The only thing she'd ever talked to Grandpa about was the dreams, which started as vague feelings of comfort and happiness. Sometimes the memory of a pair of kind eyes and a warm laugh were all that remained when she woke.

"Do you remember me talking to you about the dreams? As if someone, a guy, spoke to me as I slept?"

"Yes, I remember, child. That's who I was referring to when I called him your young man."

She could imagine her grandfather sitting with one leg crossed over the other, his white hair ruffled like Einstein's because he absent-mindedly ran his hands through it while thinking. It irritated Nana. She would try to smooth it down. He'd brush her hand way, declaring that people had to take him as they found him.

"Well, um, the dreams are coming more often. Every night. There are times when it seems so real, I am convinced I am there. The other night I sat with him, talking by a campfire. The next morning, my clothes smelled like wood smoke."

"Hmm, did he say anything unusual to you?"

"He told me he was my soul mate and that we had been soul mates in several lifetimes. He told me he couldn't find me in his lifetime. He searched for me using divination methods and found me in another century." Instead of being freaked out by what she was saying, it all made sense somehow.

"Tell me about this young man who has an interest in you. I need to check him out. The better question is, how do you feel about all this?" Curiosity and sternness mingled in his voice. As the patriarch, he wanted to vet the man who would invade his granddaughter's dreams.

Biting her bottom lip, she considered her words. No need to dance around the topic, since Grandpa probably knew anyhow. "His name is Clayton McFane, and he's a healer."

"Irish name. Good chance he has some fey ability."

"He claims he does. He must or how else can he contact me? He remembers our past lives together. When he tells me about them, I seem to remember parts. He told me because I have worked so hard to forget some things that I have forgotten him, too. He seems like such a kind, gentle man. When he speaks in my head, I almost feel like everything is right in the world. When he leaves my mind, I feel like something is missing." Her fingers strayed to her forehead. Where was Clayton now? Perhaps he was asleep.

"Ahh, I can tell by your voice you like this man. Did you say you hear his voice in your head? How often?"

She did like him, not that she had thought about it all that much. She tried not to. It would be just her luck to fall for someone in the past once she'd decided she could have a regular life that could include love and possibly a family. "I do like him. It's hard to explain, but I feel I can be myself with him. I don't have to hide anything, because he knows all my thoughts. He knows who I am and loves me anyway."

Grandpa snorted into the phone before speaking. "Who wouldn't love you? You're damn near perfect, beautiful, intelligent, kind, and a promising healer."

His fierceness at lauding her virtues made her laugh. "Grandpa, you are supposed to think those things because we're related."

"It doesn't mean they're not true." His voice sank into a gravelly grumble.

Nora laughed again. "I'll take any compliments I can get, but trust me, not all those around me see me the way you do."

"They're fools then, not worth your time. I am more curious about this Clayton. Tell me more about him."

"Ah, well, um…" She hesitated in answering, blushing a little to say the words. "He thinks his life has no meaning without me by his side. That's why he searched for me. He didn't want to live out his life alone."

Grandpa muttered a few indistinct words Nora wasn't sure he meant her to hear. "Tell me. Is he so ugly no woman would want him? Without charm or humor, forcing him to pay for company?"

"Grandpa!" She was shocked that her own relative hinted the man might purchase companionship. She'd seen the girls advertising for dates not too far from their apartment. There was a spa down the street from them that she knew didn't specialize in neck and shoulder massages as stenciled on their windows. The steady stream of unsavory men patronizing it made both Tonya and Nora cross the street when they had to walk by.

"Clayton is very handsome and charming. He has a lovely Irish lilt and an intuitive knowledge that helps him understand what is wrong with people. He reminds me of you, in some ways."

"Go pulling that last bit on me and I'm forced to like him, but it sounds to me as if you are half in love with him."

"Yes." A sob bubbled up in her throat as she pushed the word out. "What am I going to do?"

"What do you want to do?"

"Grandpa, that's why I called you. You're the time-travel expert. I want to be with him in his time, but on the other hand, I want to bring him here to mine. Tell me what has to happen so we can be together in one century."

His sigh carried over the phone and didn't bode well. "Sweetheart, I'm not sure I can help you. I discovered a portal somewhat by accident. I knew in that second, I would have to go through to be there for Leah, who hadn't been born yet. You might find a portal and end up in a time and place you don't want to be. If you do find a way to reach Clayton, you might not be able to come back to your time or family. Think about that."

"Oh. That's a troubling detail. All I know is Clayton needs my help, and I want to be there for him."

"I will look into this for you. Try to figure out where Clayton is and what year, even day, it is. The two of you seem to have a more powerful bond than I have ever heard of. I could not reach your grandmother when I was in the past. I did try several times. Tonight, when you go to sleep try to bring up an image of Clayton. Perhaps this will allow the two of you to connect, and you can ask him the needed questions."

"I will. I love you."

"I'm not really happy about the idea of giving up my granddaughter when I just returned to this time. All the same, I will not stand in the way of soul mates. The years were endless without my beloved Esmeralda by my side. Be safe. Call me when anything comes up, night or day. I love you, too."

"Okay, Grandpa." She thumbed off the phone and sat, looking at it. What if her association with Clayton meant breaking with her family? She'd always thought that as an adult she'd grow away from them, not that she disliked them. She spent less time with them with college, her job, and classes. She could count on one hand how many times she'd been home in the past year.

Still, that was not the same as never seeing them, which is what would happen if she could go to Clayton's time. It would be much nicer if he came to hers, which was selfish of her, considering the people he was helping.

"Really, Goddess, you have to present me with the perfect man and put him in the wrong century?"

No help for it. With no answer on the wind or in her head, she might as well get ready for bed. Brushing her teeth, she imagined what her conversation with Brandon would be when she returned to work. First, she'd have to inquire if Ogden had talked to him. If he hadn't, there would be no need to have the conversation. If he had, then she'd simply explain she already had a guy. No need to add he was in another century. Nope, that wouldn't make her sound very credible. Guys probably didn't care for mentally unbalanced females. It would, however, be one way to keep Brandon at a distance. Most probably feared an unbalanced woman might go psycho and pull a knife. Groaning, she discarded the thought of pretending to be crazy almost as soon as it occurred.

Running a brush through her hair, she considered growing it out. Maybe it was time to claim the right to wear her hair any way she wanted without fear of it being used to restrain her. She tiptoed into the living room to check on Tonya. The afghan lay in a heap on the floor, indicating Tonya must have retired to her own bed.

It was time for her to sleep, as well. Did she want to dream of Clayton? She'd thought she had a desire to be with him, near him, hear his voice, but now she fought uncertainty. Would being with the charming Irishman mean giving up all she knew? She didn't know. All she really knew was that she was tired, and sleep sounded excellent.

CHAPTER NINE

NORA STRETCHED OUT on her bumpy mattress, twisting one way, then another, the metal frame protruding through the thin padding poking her in the back or side whenever she rolled. The idea behind the futon had been that it could be a couch when not used as a bed. It had failed as a couch, too. After graduation and landing a job, her first big purchase would be a mattress that didn't torture her all night.

Exhaustion wrapped around her, making her joints ache and her eyes gritty. Still, sleep eluded her. Better put, she didn't dare sleep. What if she ended up in another century? Grandfather hadn't been as much help as she'd hoped in that department. He'd seemed to think she had to decide, suggesting if she made a decision to stay with Clayton, then somehow, she'd end up with him.

Wow, didn't she even get to go out for coffee a few times with the man before committing to his century? She wanted to see Clayton and explore this feeling between them. Life without Laundromats and cell phones didn't hold too much appeal.

Rotating her body diagonally, she located a spot without a bar. Closing her eyes, she imagined a white light cocooning her, a veil of protection. She remembered Nana teaching her the visualization when she'd been afraid of the neighbor's dog. The chained dog had often lunged and snarled at her when she walked by, and she'd feared it would break free and have her for breakfast. The protection spell had helped relieve her anxiety, and eventually the neighbor moved.

Exhaustion pinned her arms and legs to the bed, and she slipped into the corridor between awareness and sleep. She felt the final tumble into sleep almost as if she were in a boat and pushing off from shore. Her lips tipped up at the image, thinking how pleased her English professor, Dr. Hadley, would have been. He despaired of getting anything creative out of medical students.

She drifted in a fog of sorts. Nana called it lucid dreaming when awareness allowed you to take control in your dreams. People chased by animals or monsters could turn and tell them to stop chasing them. People dreaming of their own death could resurrect their lifeless body.

The white mist swirled about her, obscuring everything as she walked, but voices still penetrated. Soft, muted voices, as if she were listening through a wall. Nothing sounded familiar, but she did notice they altered as she walked. What was the place she was in? It wasn't frightening, but she had never been there before. Maybe the mist was the white light of protection she had wrapped around herself.

Clayton's voice came through clearly. "I need some help here."

Nora burst into a jog, moving toward the voice coming from in front of her. Breaking through a heavy cloud, she entered a clearing where a fire burned. Behind it, a large building had the doors flung open. The smell of vomit and decay rode the air. Her nose crinkled at the stink. A rough-looking Clayton appeared in the doorway with beard-shadowed face and stained clothing. His eyes showed his relief.

"Thank goodness, you heard my call."

Her eyes took in the high-noon sun as she approached the weary healer. Hours were different as you traveled through time.

"What's happening?" She could see rows of pallets holding moaning occupants inside the building. One woman, garbed in a long dress and apron, went from person to person, offering sips of water from the same ladle.

Clayton reached Nora in two long-legged steps and grasped her hands tightly. "I knew you would come."

Her eyebrows arched on their own, since she'd had no intention of coming, not that she was willing to confess that. The fire flared and sputtered behind her, drawing her attention. "Are you burning something or sterilizing?"

"Both. I have some general utensils in a pot near the edge. I am burning all the clothing and bedding to prevent contamination." He let go of her hands and stepped closer to the pot.

Nora clamped down on her bottom lip, unsure if she should point out that, the people were sharing the same water dipper, which went back into the water, mingling germs. The last person to drink would have a germ-laced cocktail and would probably be the first to succumb.

The helpful nurse eased a child into a seated position to help him drink.

Pointing to the child, Nora asked, "How healthy is that child?"

Rubbing his hand over his face, Clayton's expression remained tired. "Ahh." He shook his head before continuing. "Little Jimmy should be well by now. He shows signs of getting better, but then he takes another downturn. I know the boy. He was a healthy ten-year-old until his little sister contracted the illness."

She nodded as she listened. "It's probably because he is getting a fresh exposure to the illness every day."

Sweat formed on her upper lip and brow from the heat. Here she stood in pajama pants and T-shirt, and perspiration dampened her clothes. How much worse was it for those inside? "All the germs are circulating in the air inside the building. The sickness stays inside, re-infecting those who could get well. If that isn't enough"—she indicated the ladle-wielding matron—"on her errand of mercy, she is gathering the germs of all and serving them up in a dipper of water."

Clayton's eyes grew larger as she watched the woman. "Margaret, could you bring me the bucket and the dipper?"

The woman looked up in surprise and nodded. She carried the bucket over and set it near Clayton, giving Nora a curious stare in the process.

Feeling the woman's scrutiny, she fingered her soft pajama pants. "What am I wearing?"

Did others see her? Maybe only Clayton saw her, but the woman did appear to be staring at her.

Clayton tipped out the water and allowed it to drain into the dry ground. He carried the bucket to the kettle of boiling water and dipped it in. He turned back to Nora and allowed his eyes to roam over from her head to her feet and back again. Only, on the second review, his eyes seemed to get stuck at breast level. Oh, great, she wasn't wearing a bra. Plucking her shirt away from her breasts, she managed to break the man's sudden absorption.

Shaking his head, he managed a sheepish grin. "Your costume is a top and pants decorated with a smiling cat." He stepped closer to rub fabric between his fingers. "It is soft."

His actions caused her to sweat a little more. It had to be the fire, until he whispered into her ear, "I believe you aren't wearing any undergarments."

She gave him a hard shove that only made him laugh. Clayton, while speaking the truth, was only teasing her. If any other man had said that to her, it would have seemed a threat, a prelude to a possible rape. Clayton, while speaking the truth, was only teasing her.

"Nora, my dear, what do we do about the drinking water?" He kept his distance; perhaps aware he might have overstepped his bounds.

She recognized what he was doing with the change in subject. Men across time were similar in some ways. Ah, yes, the water, she had an easy answer for that. "I think the safest thing to do would be to use disposable cups."

"Disposable cups?" He cocked his head and hoisted an eyebrow, perhaps challenging her statement.

"You know, paper cups. You use them and throw them away." She mimicked drinking and then throwing the cup away. Still, he looked puzzled, as if this was all a joke. The invention of paper cups probably hadn't happened yet. The dirt street only contained a few raw lumber

buildings. No railroad track in sight, which indicated everything had to come by wagon. Paper cups probably did not rank up there with nails and bridles. Sucking in her lips, she considered the problem. "Well, uh, I guess that's not an option. Each person could have a cup only for personal use. Clean water could be dipped into that."

Clayton pushed back the lock of wayward hair dipping toward his eyes with an impatient push of his fingers. "That we can do. What other words of wisdom do you have from the future for me?"

Words of wisdom from the future. Was the man mocking her? He didn't look like it. No smart-aleck smirk, no crossed arms, just a bone-weary man trying to do the job of a dozen people. "What are the symptoms? Have you had any fatalities?"

His eyes rolled up as he thought. "Well, before I got here, Granny Wagner passed, along with the Timmons' youngest. Most of the folks display weakness, fever, vomiting, general aches and pains, some coughing, stuffy noses, and runs. What do you think it is?"

The symptoms were rather flu-like and could indicate almost anything from the flu to typhoid. Lack of modern sanitation methods was the culprit with typhoid spreading, which was true with cholera, too. Cholera was a problem throughout the time until last century, her century. "Do you know if the water the population uses is possibly contaminated with fecal matter from humans or livestock?"

His brow furrowed as he considered the possibility. "This is a fairly dry area. Most people use deep wells. People use a few streams for livestock. Could be they might draw from the stream the livestock use." His hand scrubbed over his beard a few times before he continued speaking.

"Most folks know enough to get water from the springs. Imagine a lad told to fetch water might dip his bucket in whatever body of water was closest."

Nora found herself nodding in agreement. "Cholera is only one possibility. Has there been any news of outbreaks near here?"

She glanced around the dusty town, looking for any sign of life. A few women stood outside a building and stared in her direction, even shading their eyes to get a better look. Better chance they were looking at Clayton, still gorgeous despite the stubble and the mixed scent of sweat, sickness, and the musky masculine note. They weren't close enough to smell him, but she doubted they'd mind. Angling her head at the women, she commented, "Do you think my Hello Kitty pajamas are causing outrage among the populace?"

Clayton gave her another casual once-over, starting at her feet, but his eyes snagged again right at the cat's eyes on her shirt. He jerked his head up. "You'll be needing to change. Rose might have something you can wear. I'll not have the men, even if they be sick, looking at my betrothed in such scandalous attire."

Placing both hands on her hips, which only seemed to tighten her shirt, she protested his remark. "Hey, I'm decent. All covered up, only my feet and arms showing."

"Too much for this century," Clayton grumbled as he headed to the building that housed the sick. "Rose."

It might have been helpful to know time-wise where she was. "What century is it?"

Not stopping his stride, he threw the words over his shoulder, "The nineteenth, of course."

Jogging after him, she stepped on a stone, causing her to curse and hop about on one foot. Clayton stopped, turned, and dropped to one knee, taking her abused foot in his hand. Nora balanced herself by placing her hand on his shoulder.

His thumb rubbed over her bruised instep, causing a twinge of residual pain, but the simple touch sent a flicker of electricity through her like the time she'd touched a frayed lamp cord. The man had chemistry to spare and then some.

"Aye, another reason to wear shoes. A lass doesn't show her feet off to anyone, except her intended. Seeing that it is me doing the seeing, there is no scandal in it."

He glanced up and speared her with a look from his heavily lashed eyes. Her knees weakened at the desire she read there. If a man could brand her with a simple glance, then she stood well marked.

Her fingers tightened on his shoulders to keep herself upright. Difficult, considering the man still held her foot. Pulling it back a little, she signaled him to release his hold. Her foot touched the ground, and she shifted her weight to get her balance. Even though she was hesitant to release his shoulder, there was no way he could kneel all day at her feet.

A pair of birds trilled overhead, interrupting the moment. There was an epidemic to investigate and stop.

Clayton stood, brushed off his knee, and gave her a slow, promising smile. Then, as if remembering what he was about, he turned again toward the building, calling out to the mysterious Rose. "I need a favor."

Watching the ground carefully for other painful rocks, Nora scampered after Clayton, touching his elbow. "Um, I have a question about what you just said."

He grinned at her, and then turned his head toward a woman coming his way. Nora took in the shapely woman, who had red curls and wore a colorful dress half-hidden by an oversized apron. As she came closer, Nora realized the woman sported makeup, a lot of it.

When she was about a foot away from Clayton, her lips tipped up in obvious appreciation. "What can I do for my favorite Irishman?"

The woman's words grated and Nora's spine stiffened with dislike at how the woman talked to her intended. She'd been about to complain about all his references to her being his betrothed and soul mate, but never mind.

A cloud of rose-scented perfume floated around the beauteous Rose. Nora coughed, choking on the strong scent, drawing attention to herself.

The woman appeared surprised. Hadn't she seen Nora standing a foot away from Clayton? At one time, Nora's goal had been to be ignored. Who knew she succeeded so well?

Clayton grinned in her direction and took a step closer to her, which pleased her very much. Might as well let Miss Heavily Made-Up Rose know where things stood.

"Nora, my darling, came to my aid without a stitch of clothing to her name."

Whom he was calling my darling? It had better well be her. The surge of possessiveness—or was it jealousy?—had never shown up before. Then again, she'd never ever had anything someone else wanted.

The look Rose shot her did nothing to relieve her jealousy. The woman gave her a snarky look similar to a few she'd encountered from the nurses at the hospital. "I see." She managed to wrap the two words with a heavy layer of contempt.

"Yes, I was wondering if you might have a dress, or even shoes, to lend our visiting healer. I'd count it as a favor, if you did." Clayton's hopeful expression cinched the deal.

Rose managed to inflict one more disdainful look at Nora's attire before answering. "I'd do anything for you, darling." Using her red-taloned hand, she gave Clayton's chest a pat. "Remember your offer. I'll collect on the favor."

Nora's hands fisted. Rose would not collect on the favor if she could help it. Pictures of the redhead entwined around Clayton had her wanting to punch the woman, or at least give her a satisfying push.

Unaware of Nora's desire to do serious damage to her smooth face, Rose said, "Follow me. I am sure I can find you something more appropriate to wear." The redhead turned and walked away with hips swinging, aware that people would be watching.

Nora moved directly behind her, blocking the effect of the show. If she ever tried to walk in that manner, she'd probably knock her hip out of joint. Her roommate, Tonya, would laugh herself to death first.

An embellished sign hung from the porch Rose mounted. Nora picked out the words between the fancy lettering and decorative flourishes. It certainly was fancier than the impromptu hospital. She read the words aloud, "Heart of the Rose Gentleman Parlor and Saloon."

Rose opened the front door and half-turned to see if she was following.

"What is a gentleman parlor?" Nora asked.

A black-haired woman with a general air of weariness and attired only in a scarlet poppy robe walked toward them. "Well, where did you find this one? She must be green if she has no clue that 'gentleman parlor' is a genteel way of saying whorehouse."

Aha, now she understood the overuse of makeup and the amazing hip swing. It was advertising.

Rose's eyebrows lifted as she considered the woman lounging against the bar. "Lydia, I have a job for you. Get the Irish's healer doxy dressed." She paused, as if considering her words. "Suited for ministering to the sick."

The women exchanged a look, which said more than their words. Lydia grabbed Nora's arm and tugged her along.

"I can walk." Nora jerked her arm out of the woman's grasp.

Lydia grumbled to herself, more than to Nora. "You speak English. With your chopped hair, tanned skin, and clothing, I figured you for an Indian or a half-breed, not a resident of the town of Dalton."

They passed a series of doors as Nora examined her skin. It wasn't all that dark, though it was darker than Rose's or Lydia's. "I am American, same as you. As for my hair, I chose to cut it. These are my sleeping clothes. I arrived unexpectedly without other clothing."

Lydia threw a knowing look over her shoulder. "Uh-huh, I can see how that might happen with a handsome, charming Irishman."

Nora started to protest the assumption, but what could she say? That she and Clayton were betrothed, or that she was from a different time, or maybe that the two of them had been a couple for the last seven hundred years or so? Each statement sounded worse than the last.

Lydia threw a door open and gestured for Nora to enter. Inside were clothes hanging on hooks and spilling out of boxes, shoes scattered around the floor. A rickety-looking dresser with half-closed drawers revealed stockings and corsets. "Looks like Imogene did a number on the wardrobe. A settler passing through asked her to be his wife. She must have ripped the place apart to find something matronly to wear."

Satin dresses that dripped with lace tempted Nora. Her fingers smoothed over a red dress bedecked with black trim, cheap perfume and body odor still clinging to the fabric. She never dressed alluring. Never had any reason to, just the opposite to play down her curves. All the same, she was still amazed at how much attention she received from men. Tonya blamed it on how she still had a pretty face and how men liked to unwrap packages.

Lydia turned with what looked like a long swatch of brown burlap. "This will do." She handed the fabric to Nora. Nora shook it out. It did resemble a dress somewhat, an ugly one. Bringing it up to her nose, she sniffed it. At least it didn't smell bad.

"Wait," the woman said before Nora could leave the room. "Dress won't do much good to dampen masculine interest if we don't tie those down." Her out-flung hand was at chest level. Her point was a valid one. She pulled out a corset and a chemise.

Nora eyed the corset and its many laces with disapproval. She wasn't a fan of a sports bra, and this looked like one for her entire body. Oh, well, if it was a dream, it shouldn't hurt. Still, shouldn't she get to wear what she chose in a dream? Brandishing the burlap dress, she shook it. "I don't like this dress. Why can't I wear something pretty?"

Shoving the drawer shut, Lydia turned and put both hands on her hips. "Lord have mercy, you are green. A claimed woman, that's what you are."

Nora was about to protest the designation, but the woman continued speaking, enlightening her. "It does not matter if you are married, hand-fasted, promised, or even just sparking. Once a man claims you, he does not want any man looking at ya. The best way to discourage that is ugly clothing. Get dressed and let me see how it fits." Lydia shoved a pair of cotton socks at her already full hands.

Nora looked pointedly at Lydia, who turned her back to allow her some privacy.

The woman grumbled, "I have no clue how you are going to survive here in the West."

Pulling a chemise, more like a short slip, over her head, she muttered through the muslin material. "You and me both."

The corset baffled her with its many laces and hooks.

Lydia removed it from her hands and began loosening the ties. "It is best to never unlace it because it will take forever to do up." She held out the widened undergarment. "Pull it over yer head. Then, I will lace you up. I cannot believe your mother never had you in a corset. Were you raised by heathens?"

Nora started to answer, "Pagans," but the tight squeeze of the laces cut off her breath. Working her hand under the corset, she managed to loosen it. "What do I wear underneath?"

She didn't expect any panties or thongs, but she expected something. Hadn't she read that they wore bloomers or something?

Lydia guided the dress over Nora's head. "Oh, you mean the drawers with the slit in them."

There was a slit in them? That was news to her. Although it made sense when the women had to deal with long skirts and corsets, the idea of walking around with a hole in her underwear was a bit unsettling.

"None here. As working girls, all that extra material just gets in the way." Lydia smoothed the material over Nora's back and buttoned up the dress. *"It looks like it will fit you fine. That will make Rose mad."*

There was a faint design in the material, and it didn't look as horrible on as she'd expected.

"Take a peek in the mirror while I hunt for giant shoes for your big feet."

Nora winced at the summation of her feet. She pulled up the hem of her dress to gaze at the body parts in question.

Before she knew it, Rose was guiding her back to Clayton with a less-than-pleased attitude. Maybe she did look good.

Clayton looked up from where he squatted beside a pallet, holding the hand of an elderly woman. "Who is this vision of loveliness that Rose is escorting?"

A blush crept into Nora's cheeks. The corset gave her an hourglass figure that threw both her hips and breasts into prominence. It wasn't something she'd wear all the time, but she was glad to look good for Clayton, especially when standing next to the showy Rose. A giggle bubbled up in her throat, making her sound like a teenager. Maybe it was to be expected, since she'd bypassed those teenage years without a boyfriend. She was starting rather late, but at least she was starting the romantic dance when only a few days before she'd never thought she would.

Rose gave her a little push as if she were a wayward child or a wandering cow. "Here she is. You can thank me later over at the parlor."

Call her green, but even she'd figured out what was going on at the parlor and what type of thanks Rose might want. The woman on the pallet blushed at Rose's bold words.

Clayton shook his head. "I'll be thanking you right here, Rose. A lovely job you've done with my intended. I had no doubts, because you had such a beauty to work with."

An angry flush mottled Rose's cheeks and exposed neck. Nora could tell the woman was not pleased to hear Clayton make his intentions clear.

Clayton looked back at the flushed woman. "Will you be volunteering with us anymore this day?"

Rose pivoted on her heel and walk swiftly away without answering or any extraneous hip movements.

The woman on the pallet whistled. "Thank ye. I am feeling better already what with seeing that tart handed her comeuppance. The woman stayed to make sure none of her regular customers died and to secure the attentions of your man. Good thing you showed up when you did."

"Good thing," Nora agreed, lifting an eyebrow at the man in question.

Placing his hand on his heart, he swore with his Irish accent growing thicker. "I am loyal to you throughout time."

There were many ways she could have replied to his declaration, but not in front of the dear, sweet, old lady. "Clayton, I was wondering if I might help your patient out of the building. Maybe to sit under a tree. With her doing so well, I'd hate for her to stay in such a germ-infested area."

Before Clayton could answer, the woman pushed herself up. "Name is Mary. Some call me Granny. Either would do. Come, help me out to that tree, and you can tell me all about your courtship."

Crouching, she helped Mary up and outside to sit underneath a spreading oak tree. "Tell me, Mary, do you live near a stream or use water from a stream?"

"Good heavens, no. My late husband, Jonah, drilled a deep well that has never run dry," the woman announced with a smile.

Helping the woman to sit with her back against the tree trunk, Nora considered discarding cholera as the possible cause for the illness. The woman held her hand and urged her to sit, a bit against her will, since she was eager to return and help Clayton. Wasn't she in control of her dream? Resting her back against the tree, she realized Mary had the same spunkiness as her own grandmother.

"Tell me about your beau. Most people do not have any use for the Irish, but I can tell your man is different. Was it love at first sight?"

That would depend on when she'd first met him. Apparently, she hadn't fallen for him immediately the first time or the second. "The first time I saw him, this year," she clarified to separate this time from all the previous lifetimes they'd shared, "I was surprised because I didn't expect someone like him, and yet I felt as if I knew him."

Mary cackled with glee and slapped Nora's leg, demonstrating her much-improved health. A bird trilled with the woman as if it were laughing too.

CHAPTER TEN

THE BIRDCALL MORPHED into an alarm waking Nora. A hammering began on the door. "Shut that stupid alarm off." The door popped open under persistent knocking, and Tonya stumbled into the room, grabbing on to the open door for balance.

Nora pushed herself up, her ribs hurting, to see her roommate looking at her in horror. She fingered the offending area only to discover a cover equivalent to the compression bandages used on burn victims.

Tonya swayed a bit while using the door as an anchor. Releasing her grip, she stumbled a few steps and fell onto the bed. Grabbing the long skirt, she held it up, rubbing the material through her fingers. "It's real."

Nora looked at the dress in bewilderment. It was what she'd worn in her dream. Was this part of her dream? Touching Tonya, she asked, "Are you part of my dream?"

Tonya pinched her hand.

"Ouch!" She jerked her abused hand away from sharp fingernails. "Why did you do that?"

Tonya sighed. "Do you miss the obvious? I had to see if you were dreaming."

Nora eased herself close enough to twist a good chunk of caramel-colored skin on Tonya's arm.

"Hey, that hurts. What was that all about?" Tonya complained and scooted out of pinching range.

"I'm sorry. I was just checking to see if you were dreaming."

"If I was dreaming, my head wouldn't hurt so much. What I can't figure out is what you are wearing. You aren't into some of those kinky role-playing games, are you? If you are, then who are you playing with?" Tonya pushed up the hem of Nora's dress to expose the rough work boots Lydia had finally located for her. "Those are some butt-ugly boots."

Nora tugged her skirt away from her friend's fingers. "Help me get out of these clothes. There is no way I can do it on my own." She turned to present her back.

Once the tiny buttons came loose, the top of the dress sagged, and her roommate's voice carried a tone of amazement. "I'll be damned. Is this one of those *Gone with the Wind* corsets?"

"I just want it gone. It is squeezing me." Nora wiggled her shoulders and tried to draw in a deep breath. "I can't even breathe in this contraption."

Tonya slid off the bed. "Stand up, this thing seems to go on forever. Who put it on you?"

The eased laces allowed her to breathe a little deeper. She swallowed the reminder not to unlace the corset all the way to make it easier to lace up again later. No way was it going back on. It felt as if it had left permanent grooves in her skin. "Oh, Lydia put it on me. If I'd had any clue what it would feel like, I would have axed the idea."

Tonya grunted and pulled at a tangled section. "Would you object if I got a knife and cut this off you?"

Nora followed her to the kitchen, where Tonya located a knife and carefully sawed away at the laces. The offending corset dropped to the floor, allowing Nora to breathe again. She stepped out of the corset and slid the dress from her body, leaving her in a chemise, petticoats, and work boots.

"You look like something from those steampunk illustrations. Tell me about your playmate, Lydia. Personally, I didn't think you swung that way, but on meeting Ogden, I could understand if you didn't go for men." Tonya opened the fridge to search for something edible.

Placing both hands on her hips, Nora talked to Tonya's back. "I do, too, like men. I even have a charming Irishman to call my own."

Tonya straightened too fast, hitting her head on the fridge. "Woman, you are killing me." Resting against the counter, she retrieved a bag of peas from the freezer and held it against her head. "What crazy shit have you got mixed up in?"

Picking up the corset, Nora held it out for a friend's inspection. "Look at it carefully. This is no fancy lingerie. It's the real thing. Over a hundred years old, maybe more. A saloon girl in the tiny town of Dalton gave it to me to wear. Showing up in my Hello Kitty pajamas was not acceptable."

Tonya put up one hand. "Stop, let me at least sit down." Holding the frozen peas in place, she pulled a chair out from the table. She eased down as not to jar her head. "Go ahead."

Nora pulled out another chair and bent to unlace her heavy boots, talking from her upside-down position. "I met my soul mate, but he isn't in this century. He's a sexy Irishman with eyes I can lose myself in. Strong arms to hold me tight. He has this great curly hair that is always falling into his eyes."

"Okay. Enough. You convinced me you're still hetero. When do you have time to meet this sexy beast of a man with school, clinical, work, and the ever-obnoxious Ogden?" Tonya lowered the peas and placed them on the table.

Boots off, Nora peeled off her socks before sitting up to face her friend. It would be hard to explain, but she needed to try. "I meet him while I'm asleep. He came looking for me across the centuries because we have been soul mates forever."

Tonya blinked a couple of times and then pushed out of the chair. "I think I need caffeine to understand what you're saying."

Nora stood up, too, wiggling her bare toes against the floor. Who would want to wear such heavy footwear? "Tonya, I know you believe in reincarnation. With that being the case, why can't you accept that I've met my soul mate from several past lives?"

Her friend stood with a can of coffee in one hand and the measuring cup in the other. "I believe in reincarnation in theory, just like some people believe in heaven, and those religion nut jobs who think they are going to get their own planet and those other religions that say there is going to be an Armageddon. It is only a theory. No one has seen any of this stuff. We might like to believe it, but we have no proof it is real."

"Look at me. I'm your proof. Remember the other morning when I woke smelling like wood smoke?" Nora held her arms out, not knowing how she could explain time travel or past lives when she didn't understand them herself.

"What's that smell?" Tonya's nose crinkled as if offended. She began to search the room while Nora sniffed herself.

"I will admit to some body odor. I'll take a shower. It was really hot in Dalton." She shrugged her shoulders apologetically.

Her friend's lips formed a mulish line. "That isn't it. It's a familiar aroma from my childhood."

"Does it smell like the sea? Fish? Coconut? Shrimp on the barbie?" Nora questioned, watching her friend pick up a discarded sock and sniff it.

Tonya threw her a long-suffering glare. "I am from Jamaica, not Outback Steakhouse." She picked up the ugly boots and turned them over. "Bingo. Horse shit. Now I believe you."

"Why do you believe me now? I've come back in period clothes, down to some torture-device underwear, but horse manure convinces you?" She threw her hands in the air in frustration but was secretly glad that someone outside of her grandfather did believe her.

Tonya laughed at her frustration. "I will tell you. First, this is a mixture of manure. Old, new, different horses. Trust me, when you had to clean out the stables every day, you got good at recognizing the smells. We are in the middle of the city. I can't even think where you would go that had horses. Even if there was somewhere within a thirty-mile range, I doubt they'd let you come in at the dead of night dressed in period costume to stomp around their fields or stables. Now that makes sense. More sense than someone loving you over centuries does. Do you think you just might be lonely?"

Why could her friend accept involuntary time travel, but not the fact someone had loved her for centuries? "Of course, I'm lonely. I have been lonely all my life. I didn't realize what was missing until I met Clayton. He's my other half."

Tonya placed her hand on Nora's forehead as if feeling for a fever. "Girlfriend, you are starting to sound like one of those teen novels. Did you forget we are grown-ass women? We don't need no man to make things work."

Nora rolled her eyes, trying to keep her temper in check. She had so few friends she could not afford to offend any. "That may be true, but it doesn't stop me from wanting to be part of a couple or having someone to love. Clayton is that man. If you met him, then you'd know. You'd see it."

Wagging a finger, her friend exclaimed, "Don't be calling me closed-minded. I see it in your face. Show me this great love of your life, and I'll make up my mind."

Her blood pressure shot up with her anger. Why couldn't she get her friend to believe her? "I will get him here. I will introduce him to you. You'll see." She stomped off to the shower, as well as one can stomp barefoot and in a period petticoat.

Turning on the shower, she realized she had traveled back to his time. But how could she bring her man to the twenty-first century when didn't know how she'd done it? Life certainly would be easier if they could be together in the same time. They could scrape together something that resembled a normal dating relationship. Shedding her chemise and petticoats, she stepped into the shower. Had she even helped when she'd returned to Clayton's time?

Squeezing the shampoo, she managed a healthy dollop for her time-ravaged hair. No doubt, it smelled as bad too. Hair lathered up and suds running into her eyes, she stepped under the warm stream of water while Clayton spoke.

You were a mighty help, darling.

Her automatic response was to try to cover her breasts and lady parts with her hands. Unfortunately, she was short one hand. A chuckle reverberated in her head.

I am not able to see anything. More's the pity.

Nora wondered if he was telling the truth as she rinsed the shampoo out of her hair. It was good having him with her. It would give them a chance to discuss the epidemic. Bending, she picked up the conditioner and flipped up the lid with her thumb.

You doubt my honesty? I am hurt. Use your mind. There's no reason you can't read me as easily as I read you.

The thought intrigued her but somehow seemed wrong. Leah had explained when she'd slipped into the past that she'd had the ability to read minds, but that ability had slipped away with Leah's return. Just as well, since Nora didn't really want to know what some people were thinking.

I know your thoughts, lass, because we are one. I thought if you knew my own heart was set on only you, perhaps that might relieve you.

Maybe. I guess in a way I am reaching your mind already since we are conversing.

She picked up the body pouf and wondered if he really couldn't see her. The bath gel scent filled the shower with the heady aroma of blackberries.

Clayton, can you tell me what I am doing now?

I cannot see you. Your mind speaks of bathing in blackberries. This I don't understand. Milk baths, yes. Blackberries, no. Does it not stain your skin?

Nora laughed, imagining a tub of berries. *My soap only smells like blackberries. Tell me about the people of Dalton. Are they improving?*

Dalton's crisis has passed. Rains came. Felt like they washed away all the germs, fears, and horrible heat. You were right about sharing the water. Once we used different cups, the sick became better faster. I cautioned people about using the streams. In fact, I left Dalton more than a week ago.

Nora stopped in mid-motion of drying herself. *I was just there last night.*

No, my love, it was more than a week ago.

How could that be? Time wasn't linear. Einstein had expressed the idea that time was stacked on top of each other rather like an unrolled ribbon. The time continuum must not line up day by day. *To me, it was last night.*

Trust me, darling, it was a week. A long, lonely week without you.

Nora's lips tipped up, imagining Clayton's eyes twinkling as he spoke the words. He did miss her. That she knew to be true. It made sense, because she missed him every minute, they were apart.

This does my heart good.

Wrapping the towel around her body, she picked up her toothbrush. *That last part I didn't mean for you to hear.*

Perhaps you did. Could be you wanted to give my old heart some ease. I thank you for it. Oh, wait, someone is calling me. I'll be back when I can.

Just like that, he winked out right after she brushed her molars, but before she got to her bicuspids. She sighed, wondering if they'd ever shared a space for more than a day. Did she astral project? The fact she came home in different clothes meant she'd had a physical body. It shot down the idea of astral projection, because only your soul or essence traveled with none being the wiser.

Someone had to know more about this than she did. Toweling her hair dry, she made plans to visit the metaphysical bookstore near the university. College towns were fertile ground for eclectic stores that stretched the boundaries of accepted thought. Both she and Tonya had visited to buy herbs and charm candles. Most of their business probably came for spell supplies and Tarot readings. An older man helped the owner by photographing auras and did past-life readings. She wasn't sure how he was related to the owner, but he was usually there, manning the cash register or the aura camera.

Tonya had persuaded her one day to have her aura photographed. That had been a mistake. She kept her secrets close, but the camera had exposed them. The white-haired gentleman had explained their photos separately. Tonya's showed strength with the orange and flashes of turquoise. However, Nora's photo had disappointed her. There had been a white cloud over the green and yellow colors, making them hard to see. The cloud represented a barrier or block masking, making it difficult for some of her natural abilities to shine. While she hadn't liked the photographer's interpretation, she couldn't have said it was untrue. He'd be the perfect person to talk to about past lives and slipping in and out of centuries.

Her phone rang before she could leave the apartment. The temptation was to let it ring. No good would come from her answering it. It could be Ogden, ready to forgive her attitude if she'd just run a few errands for him. More likely, it was Barb wanting her to come in and work. The swing-shift cook who was supposed to replace each cook two times a week wasn't working out that well. Bonnie called him a crybaby because he complained about not having a normal life with a swing schedule. She thumbed her phone and held it to her ear only to hear Barb's voice.

"Oh, good, I was hoping to reach you."

Nora hadn't said a word. Maybe if she didn't respond, her boss might think she had the wrong number. The apartment was quiet. Maybe she'd think it was a dropped call. Besides, she was tired. Who knew how much sleep she'd managed to grab last night? It sure didn't feel like much. She dug her knuckle into her gritty left eye.

Tonya yelled from kitchen, "Was that your phone or mine?"

Busted. No way, Barb couldn't hear that. She cleared her throat. "Oh, hello, Barb."

Her boss chose not to mention her earlier silence, but instead started her plea. "I need you to come in for second shift."

Nora's responsible part mentally agreed to work. After all, she could use the money. The other part, the one that had stayed up most of the night talking to dance-hall girls and a handsome healer, emphatically vetoed the idea. "Well, Barb, this is my first day off in an eight day stretch."

Saying no was not something she did well, which explained all the endless errands she'd performed for Ogden. Sometimes it seemed easier to agree than to explain why she logically couldn't do something. Today, she wasn't going into work, no way, no how.

"I know, I know. I wouldn't ask, but Doug called and asked me if he could be off."

Nora snorted her response, realizing too late that one should not snort at her boss.

"Hear me out. His little girl is sick. She's only two. It's touch-and-go. He needs to be by her side." Barb finished the words in the rush.

It all sounded over-the-top. Since they'd hired Doug, the man was off more than he worked, but if his little girl was sick, wouldn't she feel terrible if she refused to work? Still, she was willing to bet it was a far-fetched tale to get out of work. Bonnie would know the truth. The woman should work for the FBI. All it took was one look at her amazing cleavage and men would babble secrets they'd held for years.

Biting her bottom lip, Nora knew what she was going to do. "Okay, I'll be in at two. Maybe a little after. I have some errands to run. Is Ernie good with that?"

Barb's voice suddenly became cheerier. "Yes, yes, Ernie is great with that. You'll have to work only six hours since Brandon agreed to come in earlier. Bye."

Of course, Ernie would get orders as to what he'd do. He was already there. Barb had had to sweet-talk her. Apparently, she'd already called Brandon. But it would have been unreasonable to expect a cook to work back-to-back shifts. Maybe her boss had made up the story about Doug's daughter. Working would cut into her bookstore time.

"Tonya, I am heading out to Spiritual Dimensions. Do you want to come?"

It would be nice to have someone with her because the store's neighborhood was on the rough side, which explained the bars on the windows. The shop owners trusted in cold hard steel as opposed to amulets and charms. Nana had always warned her it was stupid not to use all your options. Bars represented another form of protection.

Her roommate held on to the bedroom door. "You go on. I need to rest. Captain Morgan is having a knock-down fight with the coffee. I think I am going to eat something to settle my stomach." She placed a hand over her stomach as if she expected something to jump out of it.

The definite greenish undertone of her skin kept Nora from mentioning how she felt about Tonya's helpful comment about Brandon. Her roommate was feeling bad enough. No reason for Nora to add to her misery.

"See ya in a couple of hours." She pulled the door closed with as little noise as possible.

CHAPTER ELEVEN

THE BUS WAS less crowded than usual, but then again, she was heading to a section of town most people avoided. The good news was Spiritual Dimensions had a bus stop close to the shop. She pulled her amulet out from under her shirt to make sure it was on prominent display. There was usually a variety of aimless males roaming Division Street where the small shop sat. The cleaner, better-groomed males might be heading for the temporary office, which provided a variety of day labor positions. Nora never worried about them. It was the others, the ones who grabbed their groins while making kissy sounds in her direction, who scared her.

She was supposed to find that attractive? Perhaps it was only to frighten. Last time, Tonya had come with her. When one male had had the nerve to approach them, her friend had turned around so fast Nora almost got whiplash from avoiding her outstretched arm as she threw some magickal sand in the man's face, accompanied by a few unfamiliar words.

The man had run away, yelling about witches and spells. Tonya had reminded her that many ignorant people feared witches.

With that in mind, Nora hoped her exposed amulet of protection would serve as her own shield.

The streets looked relatively clear, probably due to the locals sleeping off the night before. Her stop was coming up. An elderly woman pushed up out of her seat to stand beside Nora to wait for the doors to open. Catching sight of her necklace, the woman fixed her gaze on it as if caught in some hypnotic trance. The woman stumbled back a couple of feet, as if Nora could zap her with an evil look.

Well, the necklace still worked with the uninformed. Normally, she might have tried to explain that it had sentimental value, but not today. Too much to get done before she headed in for her extra shift. She did not feel up to dealing with prejudiced people who believed all the nonsense the church made up centuries ago about witches killing babies and drinking their blood. Thousands died as a result, some actual witches, though most only had the misfortune to cross someone in power. The church made it easy to wipe out the competition. The same ignorance made the skittish woman on the bus act as if Nora were some sort of demon.

Whenever she thought about the Burning Times and the thousands who had died, she became almost as incensed as Nana did.

A stubbly faced man shambled in her direction with one hand clutching his baggy pants but still exposing most of his dollar-sign boxers. Great. He'd either hit her up for a dollar or pretend to stumble to cop a feel.

Her fingers fisted around the amulet Nana had given her before she left for college. She mentally projected a thought—*don't come any closer*—surprised when he stumbled to a stop.

Casting one last look at the stunned man who stared straight in front of him as if he'd hit a brick wall, she began to jog to the shop. Why press matters? Who knew how long he'd remain that way? Her fingers ran across the cool metal and polished stones of the amulet. At one time, she'd believed in charms, amulets, and protection spells. Nothing, including the pentacle she wore then, had saved her from the attack. She was never sure why. Had the magick not been strong enough? Had her belief not been enough to power the charms? Maybe the combined evil of the players had overwhelmed any protection. She would never know.

After that, magick had become something her family did. Even though she'd witnessed it bringing Grandpa and Leah back from the past, it hadn't really seemed to touch her. Nora did, however, still celebrate the sabbats with Tonya, which knitted the two of them closer together. Last time they'd been at the bookstore, Tonya had wanted red charm candles for love spells.

A woman left the shop and nodded in Nora's direction. Her lips tried for a smile but she was too caught up in memories of the past visit. Had Tonya found a man after her love spells? Nora had sat with her and chanted, not expecting any results from the spells for herself. After all, she never expected love. The dreams had grown stronger after that, though. Before, she'd had a sense of dreaming, but that was all. After the spell, she'd remembered Clayton's eyes, if nothing else. They were always so welcoming.

An elderly man met her at the door with a smile. "She's here, Martha."

A woman with gray-streaked hair came through the curtains separating the store from the reading rooms. She looked relieved as she hurried toward Nora and reached for her hands. "Praise the Goddess, you've arrived. We have much to discuss." Still holding Nora's hands, she attempted to guide her to the back.

Nora stood her ground. She'd come to see the man to find out about her past lives. It was odd this woman was expecting her. Her eyes flickered to the hands still grasping hers.

"Don't worry, sweetie. We'll close the shop. Owen, lock the door. That way, we can both sit in on the reading."

The soothing recorded sounds of a rushing stream and birdcalls failed to counteract the effect of the woman's words. A quick glance around the store showed no one in the book aisles or hovering near the candle and oil counter. Could Martha and Owen really have meant her? Her first impression was that they couldn't have, but the nagging sense of unease during the past week had made her nervous, too. "I think you have mistaken me for someone else."

Martha tightened the blue-veined hands grasping Nora's. "I wish I were, child. The good news is we reached you before the evil did."

Before the evil did. That sounds ominous.

Nora inhaled briefly. Were all the Carpenter women doomed to have close encounters with evil? Why couldn't she live an ordinary life? Of course, who was to say her life wasn't ordinary? Not everyone confessed online everything that ever happened in his or her lives, despite the general impression.

Owen turned over the closed sign and switched off the neon lightning that read TAROT READINGS. He turned the lock and attempted to smile, but it didn't reach his eyes. The three of them turned to the backroom without a word.

The benevolence of Martha and Owen was evident in their faces and manners. If Nora had been anywhere else, she might have wondered about the intentions of an old couple herding her to the back of their store. Ironically, some non-pagans would have believed the two were up to nefarious purposes, from drinking her blood to harvesting her organs.

Martha pushed aside the curtain to reveal a small room crowded with a folding table decorated with a purple triquetra altar cloth featuring three interlocking ovals. Most people called the symbol the Celtic knot, and a few mistakenly tried to associate its origin with Christianity. Nora recognized it as the triple goddess emblem of the maiden, mother, and crone.

A pack of dog-eared Tarot cards sat on the table beside a dark scrying mirror. Three metal folding chairs sat scattered around the room, as if the previous occupants had left in a rush after getting bad news. Good chance she'd receive the same. Would she run from the store, too?

Not before the bus came. She knew that much. The store's neighborhood held enough real menace to keep her within the stone walls.

Owen offered her a chair with a gentlemanly flare that reminded her of Grandfather Buell. Martha placed a fat white candle in the center of the table for protection. The woman nodded at Owen, who began to walk the circle, scattering salt. It must be serious if they were resorting to salt.

At her family rituals, Nana usually created a protective circle with only mental energy. If her mother was feeling seasonal, flower petals or even seeds could serve as a barrier. Salt was for the serious stuff. It kept out entities and spirits that might prevent the ritual or possibly do the participants harm. Surely the store was protected, as stocked full of charms as it was. No doubt, the couple did a smudging ceremony each day before opening for business. Nana believed in smudging the house once a month to cleanse it of any negative energy. Her grandmother clutching the smoking stick of sage and waving it over Nora's crib was one of her earliest memories. The acrid aroma symbolized safety to her. Her nostrils flared as she tried to differentiate the lingering scent. The spicy smell was a familiar one, but not sage.

It was sandalwood. That made sense, since it promoted visions and spirituality and opened the third eye. Maybe Martha had used it earlier after seeing something that alarmed her.

Owen finished creating a tight circle around the table, leaving a thick trail of salt. Nora glanced at the worn deck of cards, expecting the woman to pick them up. Instead, she lighted the white candle and withdrew a box from under the table. Polished stones of different minerals and a few ragged, cut ones crowded the box. She identified the smooth black stone decorated with patches of white as snowflake obsidian. The brownish gold jasper and smoky quartz were both protection stones. Maybe they all were.

Martha pushed the box in her direction. "Take four."

Nora picked out a blue-colored stone, a yellow triangular one, a square one that looked almost like a crystal ice cube, and a smooth gray one that almost looked metallic.

The woman nodded in the direction of the stones lying on the table. "Hold them in your hands. I want you to concentrate on all that matters most to you in the world."

Placing two rocks in each hand, Nora fisted her hands. The triangular one's edges bit into her skin. All that matters to her? That should be easy. She expected to think of her family and career, maybe even Tonya. The image of a smiling Clayton came to mind and refused to budge to make room for any others. When had this one man become so important in her life? She hadn't really known him that long. Maybe a month at the most.

Seven lifetimes, my darling. Have you forgotten already?

Clayton's voice startled her. She hadn't been expecting it. She never knew what time of day it was in his century. Should he be sleeping? Maybe she only remembered his voice. Did anyone else hear him? A quick glance at Martha caught the woman with fingers crossed and head bowed, trying to reach the plane where she could foresee.

Owen looked amused and whispered, "How wonderful it must be to carry your sweetheart with you."

Nora started to protest that it was damn spooky, but then she reconsidered. "It is rather nice."

Martha's head jerked up, making Nora wonder if they would be scolded for whispering while she meditated. The woman's voice was deep and somber. "Give me the first stone."

Nora placed the ice-cube-shaped rock in Martha's palm while holding on to the other three.

The woman turned the stone around, intently looking at it as if she'd not seen it only minutes before. "Much magick and travel are attached to your family. You are not the first to travel into the past."

Nora's breath hitched. You'd think living in a talented Wiccan family she'd be used to those who could foresee, but it always surprised her. Martha was the genuine article, not that Nora had doubted her before. She just preferred that nothing bad would happen. With her own time-traveling romance, a co-worker who thought she wanted his body, an angry Ogden, and only a few months until graduation, she didn't need anything else happening.

Martha put the cube rock down and motioned for the next one. She accepted the blue one and held it up to the light. A slight, raspy chuckle escaped the woman's lips.

"Oh, my, he's a handsome one with his dark eyes and wavy hair. Irish in his current lifetime, a charmer for sure. Yes, you've been soul mates, but I have never heard of people connecting over centuries." She put the rock down and looked at the man. "Have you, Owen?"

The man looked thoughtful. He spoke to Nora, who still had one hand clenched around the remaining two rocks. "Once. It was a powerful love forged over many lifetimes. I believe you two have such a bond."

A powerful love forged over many lifetimes. Wow. All she really wanted was a man who would love her as she was. Apparently, she'd found a man who had done that repeatedly. The pull he had on her wasn't something new at all.

Owen angled his head in the direction of Martha's outstretched hand. Nora fingered the gray shiny rock then dropped it on the table. Her actions surprised her. Why hadn't she given it to the woman? It was rather rude of her. Either her hand or the rock had taken charge of its location.

Martha placed her fingers on the rock to pick it up then jerked her hand back with a high-pitched yelp. Owen lunged up and leaned over the table to pat the aged woman's hand. "Are you okay, dear?"

Inhaling deeply, the woman motioned for Owen to sit. "Sit, do not break the circle." She touched the rock with the side of her hand. "So much evil I cannot bear to hold it." Martha settled a pain-filled look on Nora.

Nora felt horrible that somehow, she'd hurt the woman. "Is the evil in me?"

It had never occurred to her that she might carry evil in her. She'd certainly never forgiven those who'd harmed her. Often, she became inpatient with others. A few times, she *had* wanted to hurt people. The

Wiccan Rede forbade hurting others. Of course, she'd never lain a hand on anyone, but she'd wanted to.

Martha continued to bat the stone around with the corner of her hand and winced each time the stone touched her skin. "Oh, no, it's not you, but someone you encounter on a regular basis. So much evil that even slight contact with this person has coated you with the stench of malice."

An unpleasant foreboding snaked up her spine. "Is it someone I know?" She mentally reviewed everyone she knew, trying to decide if any of them were capable of pure evil. Tonya would say Ogden was, but he'd never tried to deceive her into thinking he was something he wasn't, or had he?

"Perhaps. It is hard to say without a better reading." The woman placed her palm over the stone then let out a bloodcurdling scream.

Nora grabbed Martha's hand and pulled it away from the stone. A surge went through her, almost like an electrical current. For a second, she could see darkness and the intent to harm her. Letting go of Martha's hand, Nora sat abruptly. How could she be carrying all that residual evil around with her?

Martha sat back in her chair with her eyes closed, breathing heavily.

Good Goddess, Nora hoped she hadn't caused the woman to have a heart attack. Owen grasped the edge of the table with whitened fingers, trembling a little.

"Is she okay?" Nora asked, wanting reassurance that she hadn't harmed the kindly woman, but feeling Owen might need it more.

Owen shook his head. "I hope so. Never saw a reading as bad as yours. Heavy magick at work." He pointed to the amulet around her neck. "I bet you didn't buy that at a street festival."

Her fingers drifted up to grasp the necklace, which seemed to be warm and throbbed as if alive. "No, my nana gave it to me for protection."

Owen glanced at Martha whose eyes opened. She sat up straight and assumed a somber expression as if nothing had happened. "Your nana must be powerful, because the magick has kept you safe."

Thinking back on that one terror-filled night when the whole course of her life had changed, Nora almost said that it hadn't always kept her safe, but Nana hadn't yet bestowed this charm upon her.

As if reading her thoughts, Owen's weathered hand covered her empty hand. "I am sorry for the pain, but that one night changed you and set you on the path you needed to be. Not all evil is purely evil. Sometimes it teaches us something we need to learn or teaches others. It wouldn't be as wonderful as we think to have no pain in our lives."

Sucking her lips in, she wanted to argue his theory. She'd enjoy a life free of pain just fine. Of course, she wouldn't know it was free of pain if she'd never experienced it, just like she wouldn't appreciate companionship if she hadn't ever been without it. The man had a point. No way would she rejoice over the evil in her life, but she could see that she'd used it in a positive fashion. Poor Abby had turned it in on herself.

Martha's voice interrupted her thoughts. "May I see the last crystal?"

Nora slowly opened the cramped hand she'd clenched tightly through Martha's screams. The stone appeared tiny in her hand, but a few of the sharp edges bit into her skin. Droplets of blood decorated the yellow mineral. She moved to wipe the blood on her shirt.

Martha held up her hand to halt her. "Stop. It is as it should be. Leave the blood."

She placed the blood-stained stone in the woman's hand, expecting her to scream in pain. Instead, her fingers wrapped around it and held it for a few seconds. "Good news. Your sweetheart will come to you as evil that stalks you."

It would be wonderful if Clayton could come here. There was so much she wanted to show him. Maybe prove to Tonya that she wasn't just making him up. The specter of evil she could do without, though. "How can this happen when he is in another century?"

Martha allowed the stone to fall to the table. It rolled toward the silver one but veered away, almost seeming to be repelled. Even the stones recognized evil.

The woman sighed. "I can tell you only what I see. What I see is only one interpretation of events."

That didn't sound good. "You mean Clayton might not rescue me? I will be on my own against the big evil?"

The woman signaled to Owen. He stood and circled the table with a broom, sweeping up the salt in the circular passes.

Martha placed her hands on the table, making sure not to touch the gray rock. "Well, I'd like to tell you that you won't be on your own, but I don't know."

"That sucks." Nora crossed her arms, not happy about leaving this place and going out to where something lurked.

Owen finished with the salt and took his seat quietly. "You can avoid danger. Anything that seems iffy, don't bother with it."

Despite the merits of Owen's plan, about sixty percent of what she did was iffy, from visiting the shop to riding the bus to working at the diner late at night with its unlocked back door. She didn't care if Barb did gripe the way she did when she found out about her locking the door. The door was staying locked. "Is this negative force close by?"

Martha pressed her hand over her heart. "It is very close. I can't say when, because the Fates don't work that way. If you listen, they will give you warning, and then you have to decide what to do with it."

Nora stood. This was the same type of cryptic talk her Nana always spouted. She needed hard facts: Stay home on Saturday between one and four to avoid a painful death.

In addition, why now, when it looked as though she could make something out of her life?

Even the thought of walking out the door and catching the bus made her knees shake. Resting her hands on the table, she tried to catch her balance. Didn't she come from a tough family? Hadn't her younger sister faced down her fears in both centuries? How could Nora do any less?

"Owen, we're driving this young lady home," Martha announced in a tone that also told them she did not expect any discussion on the matter.

The man jingled the car keys, anticipating the order.

"Wait, you don't want to take me home. It is a long way from here. Besides, it would cut into your business time." Nora secretly was glad of the offer but did not want to take advantage of the couple. While there had been customers when she'd come before, no one lingered outside the doors waiting for it to reopen. "Stop fussing," Martha ordered. "We are taking you home. Besides, most of our business is online. Our real business is looking after humanity. What was your name?"

"Nora." She wondered why the woman who'd seemed to know all the hidden facets of her life hadn't already known.

Owen chuckled behind her. "Nora, granddaughter of Buell Hare. No way could we ever let you come to harm. Most people fear Esmeralda's wrath, but I know enough to keep from running afoul of Buell as well."

What was the man talking about? He'd gotten her grandparents' names right, though. "My grandparents are sweet, loving, elderly folks, not unlike you."

"Maybe so," Owen admitted with a grin. "You didn't know them when they were your age."

Martha pushed the back door open to a tiny parking lot that housed a worn-looking compact car. Nora briefly hoped the car could make it to her side of town.

Owen noticed her scrutiny of the car. "Don't worry about old Galahad there. He runs fine. I didn't know you were a Hare granddaughter until you got a determined look on your face that reminded me so much of Esmeralda. I thought I was the one time traveling. As far as I know, you have the only time-traveling family on the continent."

The man pushed the fob to release the door locks and hurried around to the passenger side to open the doors for Martha and her.

Safely ensconced in the car with her seat belt on, she gave her address to Owen.

Martha talked while Owen made his way out to the main street. "It makes sense why I would have such a strong reading with you. Your nana was always my dear friend. I suspect the amulet you're wearing was originally a gift from me to her. We are all tied together."

Nora considered her words. The Pagan community was often small and close-knit. It wasn't as unusual as it had first seemed that she might bump into someone who knew her grandparents.

The car slid through the neighborhood at a sedate pace, never stopping, even for stop signs. Obviously, the man didn't worry about the police. Through the tinted windows, she noticed two women dressed in crop tops, short skirts, and flamboyant blond wigs standing at the edge of the street, deep in conversation until the car came closer. Almost like windup toys, the two stopped talking and yanked up their tops as the car cruised by. Yep, the police had a little more to worry about here than someone slowly going through a stop sign.

It was like watching another world, one she wasn't a part of or familiar with. Two men in the shadows of the building exchanged money for something so small that the palm of the one man's hand covered it. The man quickly pocketed the money, spun away from his customer, and looked directly at Nora. She slumped in her seat, hoping he couldn't see her. A glance at his intense dark eyes warned her that the man could be very dangerous. If she'd walked to the bus, she might have passed him. Would she have witnessed the drug deal? Would he have felt obligated to kill her? Perhaps he was the evil lying in wait for her.

The car kept moving, gradually picking up speed as it moved out of the neighborhood, leaving the unknown menace behind. It would have been nice if the evil in Nora's life had been that stranger. She would be safe now. However, all future shop business would have to be the online sort.

Owen made a few rapid turns without warning as gunshots sounded behind them. Not a good neighborhood, that was for sure. It would have been easy for anyone to get in the way of a wayward bullet. Making herself as small as she could by sinking back in the upholstery, she noticed Martha did the same.

The buildings grew less ramshackle, still a little shabby but inhabitable, as they continued. There were planters of hardy geraniums and petunias on the stoops and children's abandoned toys on tiny patches of green. Small houses standing shoulder to shoulder gave away to small businesses, restaurants, and a tiny Mexican grocery. Young people strolled in groups, sometimes in pairs, and a few alone. Their shirts bore band names or goofy slogans identifying them as college students, as did their laughter and smiles. While this section of town might not be affluent, it did have a wealth of ambition and hope in the students who swelled the population to twice its normal size. Those same students kept pizza parlors, Laundromats, and liquor stores in the black. Nora briefly wondered what would happen to the city if the college pulled out. The thought was abandoned as soon as she conceived it.

The city could take care of itself. Her job was to locate evil and avoid it. Wasn't that every woman's instinct? Threats took different forms. Early on, she'd learned to pick up tacks, needles, and other sharp objects to save her feet. In school, she'd managed not to garner the attention of the mean girls by being too vocal or pretty. On the street, she knew not to make eye contact with the disgusting men whose eyes devoured her as if they owned her body. Knowing all that, she never truly escaped the tendrils of malevolence.

Martha half-turned to look at her. "I hope you don't have to go any-where today. We can do a protection spell as we leave."

The thought initially comforted her as she thought of watching movies and eating whatever healthy concoction Tonya whipped up. Then she remembered work. No way, she could not go in. No need to mention it to the old couple after all they'd done. It would only make them worry. She'd managed to take care of herself for years. No reason to believe anything would happen today. She crossed her fingers, realizing it would do no good, but hey, it couldn't hurt.

CHAPTER TWELVE

MARTHA AND OWEN insisted on walking her upstairs to her apartment. They would not leave until they saw her safely locked inside. She swung the door open only to realize the apartment was empty. Like rooms seen in furniture stores, the apartment had the appearance of a home but without any texture. The lack of sound was her first indication. A human in residence created a disturbance in the air. As a fellow human, she found this disturbance usually preferable, especially now. She needed someone to talk to about her latest issue.

Smiling at the older couple, she gestured to the living room. "Home, sweet home."

Martha took a slow appraisal of the room. "Where's your roommate?"

The question startled her, because she was sure she'd never mentioned Tonya. "Um, I don't know. I expected her to be here since she wasn't feeling well." It would have been a disservice to mention her friend was hung-over. Tonya seldom overindulged. Ogden would drive a Baptist to drink.

Owen began to prowl through the small apartment, opening closets, which was a big mistake. He swung open the hall closet only to have skis and ski poles assault him, remnants of her roommate's flirtation with cross-country skiing that hadn't lasted more than a week. Nora rushed forward to disentangle the man from the sporting equipment.

"What are you looking for?" Exasperation colored her voice.

"Prowler." Owen uprighted a ski and pushed it back into the closet.

It probably wouldn't be a good time to point out that an elderly man didn't stand a chance if the prowler had a gun.

The man managed a slight grin. "I know, you're thinking what help could an old man be. I know a few things that could stop a man in his tracks, as does Martha. Then there's you, too. Three is always better than one."

Nora bent to gather up the ski boots and waterproof gloves that had tumbled to the floor. Rising, she nodded to Owen. "Good point. Feel free to look in the other rooms, but be warned, most of the closets are a bit stuffed."

Martha examined objects in the living room, picking them up and putting them down. Seeing Nora, she lifted her eyebrows. "Good news."

"Oh." Maybe the woman would tell her they'd somehow bypassed the threat. A few steps brought her closer to Martha, who was examining a glass whale Nora had purchased at a yard sale.

She placed the whale back on the shelf. Throwing out both arms, Martha slowly turned. "Lots of good energy. I see two young women living clean, promoting positive energy, and honoring the Gods and Goddesses. No imprint of evil here."

Inhaling deeply, Nora waited. She could pretty much bet there would be a "but" tacked on to the thought. The woman looked thoughtful and pointed to a spot on the couch.

"Recently, there has been someone in your apartment. I think he or she sat there. There's deadness about this individual. No love or vitality." She cocked her head, twisted her lips slightly. "I would almost say soulless, but he or she is more of an individual who has never really learned how to live."

"Ogden. You described him perfectly. You didn't sense any evil about him?" She'd wondered earlier, if he'd been the menace, but rejected the idea as soon as it occurred. Placing two fingers on her temple, Martha looked at the couch. "This Ogden is basically selfish. He does not mean you intentional harm, but…"

That was a relief. Her gaze danced over everything in the room, trying to see the décor as a stranger would. Tonya insisted on tacking up a four-foot-square poster that portrayed hoodoo symbols in concentric circles. She often wondered why she never had any dates after they'd been in the apartment. Most of her dates were probably worried about her collecting hair strands and nail parings to make a doll in their image. Failure to bring flowers might result in a sharp pin jabbed through the doll.

Nora knew Tonya wasn't like that, but non-pagan folks held close stereotypes they'd collected in darkened movie theatres as the true way of things.

Their secondhand furniture sported bold geometric-print cushions that Tonya had stitched up. An old battered flat-topped trunk served as their coffee table. A handful of live plants added greenery and vitality to the small room. There were only a few items that were hers. The brass candelabra Nana claimed belonged to Nora's great-grandmother and a small brass wolf figurine. Martha drifted over to the candelabra and stroked it lightly.

"Much history here. Your entire family tree is impressed into this one object. Esme left a definite imprint." She chuckled to herself. "Your grandmother was a wild woman. All the women wanted to be her, but all the men just wanted her, even if they were afraid of her."

It was an uncomfortable way of thinking of her nana, but Nora could still see traces of the same woman in her feisty, opinionated manner. What was it she'd wanted to ask Martha? Oh, she remembered. "Um, you say Ogden was basically harmless, but you hesitated and never finished your sentence."

Martha's hand fell from the candelabra she was examining. "Yes, this I did, because I did not want to alarm you anymore than needed."

Great. Nora blew out her breath. It was going to be like pulling off a bandage. "Tell me. Knowledge is power. Don't you watch the commercials?"

Owen walked into the room, stood behind Martha, and placed his hands on her slender shoulders. "Tell her," he urged.

"The man himself is shallow, a tool," Martha began.

The description surprised a laugh out of Nora. Many people called Ogden a tool. Others had much worse names for him.

The woman ignored the laugh and continued. "It will be easy for those with a stronger will to manipulate him and use him against you. Be on your guard."

Well, that didn't seem to be too scary. Her plan was to continue to avoid Ogden. Maybe that meant she'd inadvertently miss any evil directed her way. "I can do that."

Martha pulled a bottle out of her handbag. "Good. Before we go, I want to anoint your windows and doors."

She and Tonya had already done that, but a little extra help was always welcome. She followed the couple room to room while they touched the windowsills with their fingers, murmuring a protection prayer at each opening. After bidding them good-bye and closing the door, Nora could hear them murmuring prayers on the other side. To think she'd wondered why her neighbors kept a wide berth of her and Tonya.

The sound of her visitors' footsteps on the stairs as they left reinforced her aloneness. Nora twisted on the portable radio they kept in the kitchen. She had to adjust the dial a millimeter at a time as if searching for signals from other planets to find her favorite station. Her reward for her effort was a tinny sound often interrupted by static. She had paid only a dollar for it at the local thrift store. It was probably older than she was. The high-pitched whine it made as it failed to grab the station signal grated on her already frayed nerves.

Clicking off the radio, she picked up the remote and aimed it at their flat-screen television. It was the only actual theft-worthy item in their abode. Tonya had won it in a bingo game down the street. She'd had to ask for help to move it and had paraded down the street with her cargo and helpers. Since the box identified it as a television, they'd expected it to disappear within days. Ironically, it hadn't. Maybe the rumors portraying the two of them as a witchy pair had paid off.

The first image on the television screen was a frightened woman pressing an alarm while a burglar ransacked her home. It was only commercial, but Nora didn't need to see that. A barrage of gunfire came with the channel change to a Western. Normally, she liked Westerns. The idea of people carving out new lives for themselves on the frontier appealed to her. However, what Hollywood depicted as real had very little to do with what had happened.

She changed the channel again. This time to an infomercial with scantily clad women who insisted the featured product had improved their love lives. This infomercial usually came on later at night. She glanced at the time in the corner of the television. It was 12:58.

Her shift started at two. She'd have to catch the 1:15 bus. She needed to change into her cook whites. Forget about eating anything. She could get food at the diner.

She poked at her stomach to judge whether it was getting any softer after her numerous meals there. Maybe. Put that on the list of things she didn't need to think about.

Grabbing her clothes, she headed to the bathroom. Why did she have to go to work, when Doug seemed to take off whenever he felt like it? For Pete's sake, it had been her day off. Splashing water on her face, she continued her mental rant. Anger felt better than fear.

Her hairbrush kept snagging on a snarl at the back of her neck. Twisting around, she saw hair tangled in her necklace. That's what she got for not trimming her hair. A quick snip would free the chain. Her hands were on the haircutting scissors she kept in the bathroom, but she hesitated. Didn't she want to grow her hair out as a symbolic gesture that her past no longer dictated her choices? The rape had been the reason she'd cut off her hair. Putting down the scissors, she decided to work the chain free. Unclasping it, she tugged the eye with the smaller clasp through her hair.

Gently pulling the tendrils from the chain, she managed to free the necklace without sacrificing any hair. A quick glance at her watch had her swearing under her breath. That operation had taken longer than it should have. Pulling on her white top, she decided to forgo brushing her teeth. As it was, she'd have to run to the bus stop. Grabbing the small backpack that often served as a purse, she headed out the door.

Taking the steps two at a time, she made the landing in record time. The bus was on time for a change. She could hear its throaty roar and smell its heavy, gagging diesel fumes. The lumbering vehicle shuddered to a stop in front the Plexiglas bus shelter. Several people crowded around the bus entrance, working their way onto the bus as Nora broke into a full-out run.

Two teen boys cheered her on, or more appropriately jeered her on. "Run, Forrest, run."

No time to glare at them. Her only mode of transportation was getting ready to depart. Someone on the bus pointed to her. The bus driver reopened the doors he had closed.

"Just made it, Little Missy," he commented as she staggered onto the bus.

Normally, she'd tell him her name wasn't Little Missy. Instead, she flashed her bus pass and collapsed into the nearest seat. That unexpected run had emphasized her need to work out on a more consistent basis and eat less burgers, starting tomorrow. The familiar scenery flew by as she bemoaned the fact, she'd missed Tonya. Digging through her backpack, she located her phone to text her friend.

Got weird news at the shop. Will tell u later. Let no strangers into the apartment, not even Ogden.

Her hair was probably a mess after her impromptu dash. Running her fingers through, she tried to comb it into some semblance of a hairstyle as opposed to her impersonation of a homeless person. Her fingers slid down the back of her neck, feeling the lengthening strands. Something was wrong. Her thumb rubbed across her neck. It was bare. Her right hand slapped against her upper chest, searching for the amulet. Where was it?

An image of her necklace on the bathroom sink came to mind. She'd left it in her rush to catch the bus. Her fingers lingered at her neck. She could have used the reassurance it provided. She could text Tonya, but it wasn't exactly like someone would break into their apartment and steal it. It would be there when she got home. She tried to calm herself. Come nine o' clock, she'd be home.

The diner came into view. She stood up, eager to get her shift over with. The bus door had barely opened when she shot out of it like a sprinter from the starter block, gasping by the time she reached the door of the diner and swung it open. Bonnie gave her a disgusted look as she leaned against the inside wall. Moving closer, the waitress leaned across the counter to address Nora privately, meaning only half of the patrons could hear her.

"You're getting as bad as alien-phobic Barney. You'll have to start wearing a ball cap lined with aluminum foil. Were the giant mosquitoes going to grab you and carry you away?"

Two nearby men, hunkered over pie and coffee, laughed at Bonnie's comments. Nora worked on slowing her breathing and settled for fixing the server with a stare that promised retribution. No way could she explain what was going on. It didn't make sense even to her.

A quick visual inspection showed a handful of usual customers and a family dressed in matching shirts, which identified them as tourists. They must have been going to the nearby theme park. A few looked up at her entrance, but most looked away, except for Bonnie, who raised an eyebrow. Refusing to answer her inquiry, Nora headed toward the kitchen.

The smell of onions and the jump in temperature hit her as she pushed open the door. OSHA had come through once and required a fan for the cook's comfort. Barb had mounted the fan with strict instructions not to turn it on. The fan tended to cool the food and made too much noise for the cook to hear the orders. Various cooks would plug the fan in just to cool off for a few seconds between rushes. Ernie had the fan going and didn't hear her enter. He jumped about a foot when she reached for a paper cook hat.

"Whoa! Don't sneak up on me like that!"

Nora made a mental note not to use the fan. She couldn't take a chance on not being aware.

"The fan makes such a racket you didn't hear me." She had to yell the words to be heard over the fan and the sizzling meat.

"Hey, what are you doing here? Isn't it your day off? As a young single gal, aren't you supposed to be out enjoying yourself?"

"I wish." Nora felt that the media image of college students engaging in numerous hookups did her no favors. Knotting her oversized apron in the front, she added, "Doug called in."

Ernie snorted. "Yeah, that's right. Barb did say something to me earlier. I guess it went in one ear and out the other. Thing is, he's off more than he works. Well, I hope he decides to come to work when it's my day off. The missus is not a fan of me working seven days a week."

Nora wasn't a fan of working seven days a week, either. Her joints ached from lack of sleep. Had it been only last night that she was helping Clayton with an epidemic? It felt like forever ago. Lack of sleep was making her irritable on top of already being paranoid.

The fry beeper went off, sending her into action. Pulling the wire basket out of the hot oil, she hooked it off to the bar and bounced it twice to shake off the residual grease before dumping it into the fry station. Ernie had five plates set out, which meant she needed to get five servings out of the fries. Ernie was good at his job, so she had no doubt there would be enough potatoes to go around. Too bad Ernie wasn't the relief cook. If he were, then she'd be at home enjoying her day off. She'd probably be sleeping right now. The thought of a nap was a glorious one. Who knew that at the grand age of twenty-three she'd be yearning for a nap rather like a senior citizen?

Ernie hummed under his breath as he placed burgers onto the open buns. Scooping up the fries, she deposited a stack on each plate. She watched as he capped the burgers. Picking up the plates, three on her first trip and two on her second, she delivered them to the window. Seeing that Bonnie's back was turned, she pummeled the bell with relish, startling the waitress and drawing attention as she announced, "Order up."

Yeah, it was petty of her. Stupid, too, since she'd have to spend the next six hours with an irate co-worker.

Bonnie mainly flirted with the customers, but the woman majored in spiteful. Good thing Nora was the cook. She hated to imagine the vindictive things the woman might do to the food if their situations had been reversed. Yep, she could expect a night of window silence. No bells, no calls, she'd have to keep checking for order slips to keep Bonnie from lambasting her for being slow on the food.

Nora watched Ernie leave with a wave, letting the back-door slam behind him. Nora stared at the door for a few seconds, wishing she'd been the one who'd left. She darted toward it, securing the lock. A quick glance over her shoulder assured her there was no Barb on the premises. Sometimes the manager was up in her office, behind the two-way mirror counting money or watching the employees. Today would have been a day she made certain to slip out early to avoid listening to both her and Brandon griping about working extra hours for the invisible Doug.

Brandon. Good Goddess, she had to deal with him, too. Well, she could pretend nothing had happened, which might have been the case. The man had been very friendly the last time they'd worked together. She did not look forward to trying to explain to him the weirdness that constituted her life.

Gathering the prep pans, she stacked them in the dishwasher tray. She'd have a couple of hours to think of some reasonable explanation for Tonya's claim that she was hooking up with him.

A knock on the door reminded her that she'd locked the back door. Red-faced, she opened it for the bread guy, while pretending surprise. "Was the door locked? Goodness, I wonder if Ernie tripped the lock when he went out." She crossed her fingers, hoping Ernie would forgive her for throwing him under the bus.

The bread man grunted and backed into the narrow kitchen with his tall load of bun trays. He moved a couple of trays from the old rack and pushed it out the door with him. The man never said anything, didn't even look at her. Nora made sure to lock the door again. Not everyone was a talker, but he was plain creepy. Thinking about the man made her shiver. He wasn't the usual delivery guy, which meant he couldn't be the evil she needed to avoid. It had to be someone she met on a regular basis.

Something made her turn quickly and look at the window. A scrap of paper fluttered in the breeze from when the outside door had closed. How long had that been there? So, began Bonnie's revenge. Snatching the paper, she found it was for a fish sandwich platter. Didn't get that too much. Opening the freezer, she grabbed the box of fish fillets and carried them to the stainless-steel counter. She made a mental note to replace the box as she dropped the fry basket into the oil. The walleye would taste a little bit like fries, but so far, no one had complained.

Bonnie's voice, reminiscent of nails on a chalkboard, carried through the window. "Did you break out the fishing pole to go find me a walleye platter?"

The order could not have been there for more than a minute, and she knew it. Nora decided to be the better person and say nothing. Well, she wasn't exactly being the better person. She just didn't have anything pithy to say. She could hear Bonnie slinging dishes around in the front and hoped the diners enjoyed the show.

Most of her shift went the same way. Her eyes stayed trained on the window, ready for the appearance of the elusive scrap of paper for her to pounce on. In the end, she rang the bell every time she had to deliver an order. There was no reason for a customer to suffer due to the help's bad attitude. A quick glance at the clock reminded her when her shift was minutes away from ending. Bonnie's attitude kept her mind off the back door and things that went bump in the night. In less than an hour, she'd be home with her feet up on the trunk, telling Tonya about everything that had happened today, including Bonnie's six-hour-long hissy fit.

A metallic jingle announced another customer. Bonnie greeted him with a hearty, "Hello, handsome."

That's how she greeted all the men who showed up without female company, which made her a popular server.

A familiar masculine voice answered her. "Hello, yourself."

Brandon was here. It was his agreed-upon time to help cover the missing Doug's shift, but Nora wasn't ready. Too busy anticipating Bonnie's sneak orders, she'd never developed a story to explain everything in a way that would almost sound normal. The bell jingled again.

"I wasn't done talking to you, soldier boy," a belligerent voice called out.

A drunk? As if, she needed that, too. Let Brandon handle him. He was the only one with muscle to boot the guy out. Maybe she should call the police. Her hand hovered over the black wall phone, ready to press nine, when the man spoke again.

"I'm not giving up Nora. Had a good thing going with—" The voice choked off.

Ogden? Damn, she was going to have to deal with this side of him. He had to be drunk. Why else would he act like this? Nothing was on the grill, so she was free to go out there and attempt to make her personal life a little less public.

Not sure what she would say, she hit the swinging door at half-jog, only to find Brandon with a chokehold on Ogden's Oxford shirt. Despite Ogden's height, Brandon still managed to get the man up on his tiptoes.

Ogden's eyes bulged as he gasped something about suing everyone.

Brandon growled his reply. "I don't care if you're a medical doctor. I'll tell you what you aren't—smart. Nora's done with you. She wants someone without ice water in his veins." He shook Ogden for emphasis before letting go of his shirt.

Ogden smoothed the creases, muttering something about lawsuits. Several of the patrons were quick to volunteer to serve as witnesses that Brandon was the one who was assaulted first.

Ogden backed toward the door. He cast an angry look at Nora.

Nora knew it was time to make the break clean. "We're through, Ogden. I found my soul mate. You better hurry. The police are on their way."

Ogden darted out the diner door to the delight of the patrons. A few called out physically impossible suggestions.

Brandon pivoted, taking Nora's hand. "I wouldn't call us soul mates, but I wouldn't mind researching the subject with you." He gave her his most charming smile, causing one of the female customers to "aw" in response.

She snatched back her hand. Could anything else go wrong tonight? "I didn't mean you."

One man yelped, "Ooh, that stung. Damned if you do, damned if you don't." His three companions laughed at his remark.

Nora had had enough. She was going home and none too soon. She headed for the kitchen but threw over her shoulder, "Clayton's my soul mate."

"Who's Clayton?" Brandon asked.

She pushed open the kitchen door to grab her stuff. Brandon was on his own as far as cleaning. A brief survey revealed there really wasn't that much to clean, anyhow. The loud rumble of the fan drew her attention upward. She hadn't turned it on. If no one had been back there, then how did it get on? A hand and odd-smelling cloth muffled her mouth before she could even consider screaming. A needle plunged into her arm. Things grew blurry. The evil had found her.

CHAPTER THIRTEEN

A DRIPPING SOUND was off to her right. Nora kept her eyes tightly shut, buying herself time. A musty smell permeated the air, along with the smell of sauerkraut. Was she in the basement of a German restaurant? Kidnapped to cook sauerbraten against her will? She knew better. The whimsical musing helped her to not freak out.

Rolling on the lumpy mattress, she tested her muscles. Rope tied both her ankles and wrists. It felt like regular rope, not that what kind it was mattered too much. The important thing was she couldn't use her limbs. What if he were sitting there watching her? The thought creeped her out. Opening her senses as her grandfather had taught her, she swept the room. No human, but there seemed to be rodents. Ick. Not rats. She didn't think she could bear the thought of rats chewing on her fingers. True, she realized she was supposed to honor all life-forms. Honoring worked much better when she didn't meet some of the creatures up close and personal.

Slowly, she opened her eyes to a dim textile weave. Blindfolded. Damn, was there anything he hadn't done?

A sense of light penetrated the fabric. He must have left a light on. Why?

She had to be smart, calm, and logical. Apparently, she'd screwed up, even when there had been so many warnings on different levels. Foolishly, she'd overcome her instinctual reaction by rationalizing why the warnings hadn't merited serious consideration. Early on, she'd felt evil roll off the man. Instead of doing everything she could to avoid him, she'd simply counted him as one of the diner's offbeat regulars.

People have instincts for a reason her mother was fond of pointing out. Locking the diner's back door had done little good when she'd been taken through it. He had to have been inside. Hiding in the bathroom?

Now it was time to use the intelligence she prided herself for. An unconscious person, especially a blindfolded one, wouldn't need a light. The light might be for him or a camera.

Right now, he could be in another room, watching her on a monitor. Her reprieve would last if he thought she was out. Stilling her movements, she tried to act as if she were still under the drug's influence. Luckily, at the hospital she'd witnessed enough people under anesthesia, who could not even blink, let alone move, to mimic them.

Holding herself rigid, she took inventory of her body. Clothes were all on. Thank the Goddess. Her shoes were missing. Some chafing on her wrists and ankles from the rope appeared to be the extent of her injuries. Her stomach growled, letting her know its empty state. She couldn't remember when she'd last eaten. Her bladder urged her to get up and relieve its fullness. Not that she needed one more thing to worry about.

If only she had help. Did anyone know she was taken? Brandon and Bonnie might have assumed she'd left in a huff, slamming out the back door instead of the front to avoid them. Nora bit her lip. She'd have thought the same unless there was a tip-off. Was her backpack still there? Had whoever taken her known enough to pick it up? Did Tonya miss her yet?

She had told her they would talk when Nora returned home. She and her roommate were the opposite of social butterflies. They spent most of their evenings together at home, like an old married couple. Surely, Tonya would be worried by now. Still, what could she do?

Tonya might call the diner. Brandon might say Nora had left in a huff. The police would say she was over twenty-one and could do what she wanted. Her roommate might hint at foul play. The police would take her report but consider he missing as the result of too much partying and assume that she was sleeping it off somewhere. No doubt, Tonya would call her family, who would hop into the car and immediately drive up. If anyone could whip the police into action, Nana could. Still, how would they know where to look?

There was nothing to identify her location. She might not even still be in the city. If she'd had her backpack, her phone would be in it. The police could use the GPS unit in it to track her. A small spark of hope flared. Then the memory of a television show in which the kidnapper had taped the woman's cell phone to her dog's collar and left it alongside the road stomped out the spark. Whoever had her could have searched her bag and dropped her phone far from her actual location.

If only, there was some way to reach her family. At one time, her grandfather, or even her sister Leah, had read people's minds on close contact. Maybe they could help her. All she needed to do was get a message to them. Squeezing her eyes shut, she concentrated on her grandfather's face. Nothing.

Nora, where are you? What is happening?

Clayton's voice calmed her a little. Maybe he could help. But how, being stuck in another century? As far as she knew, he could talk to her only because of their soul mate bond.

Clayton, I need help. Someone has kidnapped me. I don't know why. I was warned evil was looking for me. I am tied up and blindfolded.

Oh, my sweet darling, I will kill the monster that would do such a thing.

He growled the last few words, demonstrating his anger. Unfortunately, there was no way Clayton could touch the malicious creature.

How did I come to you? The few times I crossed over into your time I don't remember doing anything special. Maybe I could cross over now.

The thought excited her. She'd had the way to escape all along.

Hurry now, sweetheart, come to me. Clayton's voice conveyed urgency.

Squeezing her eyes shut, she concentrated on his handsome face, willing herself to be beside her soul mate.

I am coming, Clayton.

Her voice sounded loud. She must have said the words aloud. Now, Mr. Creepy might come investigate. Everything felt the same, though. She was still horizontal on an uncomfortable cot mattress in a damp basement as opposed to being in the past with her sweetheart.

Clayton, it didn't work. Why didn't it work?

The urge to cry tempted her. It wouldn't help anything.

What had been different before? She had always been asleep when she'd slipped back into the past. She thought of Clayton often during the day but did not pop out of her time. What was the difference?

Time travel was theoretically impossible. Grandpa Buell had slipped through a time portal, which many people readily concurred, could exist. Leah had commented that she'd felt pulled back in time by a previous life. Maybe that was why she could go back, but Nora's previous lives were associated with Clayton.

His voice returned as if hearing his name. *I've given it some thought. The times you came to me, I needed you sorely. Perhaps my need was so intense you felt it.*

The thought had some merit. She heard a door rattling to her right, followed by a feminine voice. "Hello, hello? Is there somebody there? I'm Ellie. I am locked up in this room. I don't know how long I've been here."

Nora held herself perfectly still. Was this a test? Was she being filmed? Her mind rushed through the probabilities of someone else being the victim of the kidnapper. "Ellie, I'm Nora." Her voice was low and raspy, reflecting her dry throat.

"I'm here," a surprisingly young voice answered. "I heard him bring you down last night. He ordered me not to talk to you, but he's gone now. I heard the door slam when he left. I think he has a job when he's not kidnapping women. You're the cook he talked about grabbing."

He'd talked about grabbing her. No wonder she'd had premonitions. "Are we—does he have a camera set up monitoring us?" Nora could picture a small camera mounted in the corner of the room. Ellie could be wrong. The man could thunder down the steps at any moment, realizing she'd awakened.

The woman made a derisive noise. "No, I doubt the man would be smart enough to operate one. Then again, he was sneaky enough to pick me off the street. I never saw a camera, though."

Picked her off the street? She sounded so young.

Ellie spoke, her voice resigned and weary. "I was holding up a sign to sell fireworks along 38, a real busy road. I thought the female owner was the creep because she kept insisting, I wear a bikini top and short-shorts. My mom was totally against it. I wouldn't do it until Kayla, my boss, offered me an extra twenty. My mom was already at work, so I figured I'd get back and change before she knew."

"Fireworks," Nora said, thinking aloud. "It must have been before the Fourth of July."

"Yes, that's right," Ellie agreed. "What month is it now?"

She didn't want to tell the young girl that months of her life had trickled away while she'd remained trapped in this dungeon. "Ellie, how old are you?"

"Sixteen. No, wait. I had a birthday while I've been locked up. I am seventeen now and missing my senior year at school." The girl's sigh carried more information than her words.

A sixteen-year-old girl being picked up by some perv wasn't right. Her only perceived crime was being female.

Clayton's voice nudged her away from imagining the various violations committed against women. *I think if I concentrate hard enough, I can come to you.*

That would be wonderful. Not only could he rescue her, but they could free Ellie, too. *Please try. There's another woman here who needs your help, too.*

Time and the laws of a normal universe will not keep me from your side. The sound of his familiar lilt reassured her.

Then he was gone. She felt his absence. Where would he go to find the help he needed?

Ellie asked her something.

"What did you say?"

"I asked where you were when he grabbed you."

Nora tried to work herself into a sitting position. Lying prone on the mattress made her feel too much like a sacrifice. She managed to wiggle her feet over the edge while trying to swing her body into an upright position. Her bare feet slapped the floor, sending a tremor up her legs and reminding her of her urgent need to pee. Sitting up made her feel a little better. She imagined she looked like one of those stone pharaoh statues with her tied hands and feet keeping her in a rigid posture. "He grabbed me at work. I am so mad at myself for letting it happen."

"I know what you mean." Ellie snorted. It was hard to tell if it was a cough or a sign of disgust. "My mom kept telling me I was sheltered because I went to Catholic school. I thought I had street cred. What a joke. He pulled up in white panel van. Ya know, the one the crime shows always have the killers using. That should have been a hint. He wanted me to look at some fireworks he'd bought that didn't work right. I told him it wasn't my job. He should go into the store to complain. He kept asking me just to look at them. I thought if I humored him, he'd go away. No sooner than I peered into the van, he pushed me and stuck a needle in my side. Something hit my head, too. I may have screamed. I can't remember. I just remember waking up here, like you."

"Oh." Nora didn't know what else to say. It didn't look good, considering Ellie had been there awhile. Since Ellie was a minor, the police had probably pulled out all the stops to search for her. Her mother had probably gone public, making tearful pleas on television. "Wait a minute. I think I saw an Amber Alert for you on television. I remember a photo of a blond girl standing by a horse."

"That's my Kimber. I compete with her in junior steeplechase. Well, I did. At least Mom used a good photo and not my horrible school picture. I never even got my senior pictures taken. I had an appointment the week after. Had it all planned out. The photographer was coming to my dad's place so Kimber could be in the photos." Ellie's words choked off as she began to weep.

"Ellie, Ellie, listen there are two of us now, two smart women against one male criminal. Surely, we can make that work in our favor. Tell me about the first day. What happened?" If Nora knew what to prepare herself for, she'd be ready.

The crying tapered off. Ellie inhaled deeply, loudly gulped before starting. "I don't know how long I was out. I remember waking up tied up and wearing an adult diaper. You've probably got one on, too."

Nora shifted on the cot, hearing a telltale crinkle and feeling bulkiness in her pants. Ooh, she didn't even want to think about him putting it on her. "Yes, go on."

"I think he does that because he's gone more than he's here. I'm not even sure if this is his regular home. He might go home to a wife and kids, which somehow makes it worse."

Ellie was getting off track. "Tell me about the first day," Nora urged.

"By the time I saw him, I was starving, thirsty, and had to go to the bathroom. I refused to use the diaper, but I wish I had now."

"Why?" Nora knew she wouldn't like the answer.

Ellie cleared her throat. "He walked me to the bathroom with my hands still tied. He pulled my shorts down, watched me pee, and then raped me. In the tiny bathroom, where there was no place to escape, and my hands were tied."

Nora could hear the shame in her voice. "Ellie, stop blaming yourself."

"Maybe if I hadn't listened to my boss and worn the bikini top, I'd be at St. Ignatius instead of here." The clatter of things falling and a few hard kicks at the door echoed off concrete walls.

"Stop thinking like that. They want you to believe that so they don't have to be accountable for their actions. I see guys all the time running with their shirts off. Good-looking, fit men, but they don't have women throwing them into panel vans. As women, we blame ourselves for men violating us. Trust me. I know." She blew out a breath after her long speech.

Ellie voice sounded hesitant. "Has this happened to you before? That must really suck."

Nora thought back to Owen's words about how bad things can change the course of your life. It certainly had hers. Now, it was time to use that information to help someone else. "I wasn't kidnapped. My friend Abby and I were leaving school late at night. We'd been working on the school newspaper. We drove together. It was winter, which meant early night-fall."

If her hands hadn't been bound, she probably would have dropped her head into them. She'd never told anyone, except for Clayton, and she never really told him, either. He'd just picked it up while tiptoeing through her mind. Nora shifted on the cot suddenly feeling as if someone sat down beside her. "Abby and I were talking. I remember being happy, laughing. Abby was telling me about this guy she liked flirting with her. Then, suddenly all these football players surrounded us. They were still wearing their practice jerseys. At first, I had no clue what they wanted. One of them grinned and said, 'I hear witchy sex is really hot.'"

"What does that mean? I know I am sheltered, but I've never heard of witchy sex."

Nora cleared her throat again. "Abby and I are both witches. The other students knew it. For the most part, they were cool with it, or so I thought. I'm not sure what the football players' reasoning was, but we were there for the taking, or so they thought."

"As a witch, couldn't you cast a spell and freeze them in place?" There was a curious lift in her voice.

"Common misconception. Being a witch sometimes involves spells or incantations, but it is more about the person finding her path as opposed to people flying through the air. It isn't like in the movies. If I dislike someone, a huge wind doesn't blow him away. If that were the case, then no witches would have burned at the stake. My confidence in my various protective amulets led me to act in an unsafe manner, though."

"What could you have done? You were at school. You were supposed to be safe there."

That's what she'd thought, too. She'd thought being a witch was enough to keep her safe, despite all the harm witches had suffered in the past at the hands of misguided individuals. "Neither one of us was paying attention to our surroundings. We had a guard at school. We could have asked him to walk out with us. I had my keys in my purse. I could have had them wrapped around my fingers to use as a weapon. Looking back, I see there was a lot we could have done."

"How many were there?"

Nora pondered the question for a minute. They'd seemed to be everywhere. Grabbing her, holding Abby, and dragging them to the darkest part of the lot where a trio of tall pines had thrown shadows, blocking out the security lights. "I don't know. I remember one held a hand over my mouth and my wrists tight. There was one at each leg holding me down and another one raping me. That would be four on me alone. I am not sure about Abby. Did someone hold her and force her to watch or were there more? I only remember now that they switched off without ever releasing my arms or legs, as if they had done it before." Nora bit down hard on her bottom lip. They had done it before. Of course, they had. They'd kept on doing it.

"That's horrible. Did you call the police?" Ellie's tone carried the unspoken message that, of course, a woman would call the police.

In retrospect, Nora's decision not to call the police seemed cowardly. "No, when they were done, they threatened us. Told us they'd tell everyone we enticed them. Apparently, they'd been planning it. They'd already told several people we'd been coming on to them. What chance did we have against popular players? Two lone witches, you already know some of the stereotypes. I helped Abby to the car and drove her home. She asked me to tell no one. Her parents were out for an anniversary dinner. I put her in the shower, where she just stood there not talking or moving. I stepped into the shower with my clothes on, scrubbed her and shampooed her hair. I tried to scour away every mark those monsters put on her. I dressed her and put her to bed. I took her clothes with me and threw them in a neighbor's trashcan. That was the last time Abby ever spoke about the incident."

"Oh," Ellie said softly. "You never saw your friend again?"

"I saw her several times in the facility her parents placed her in, but she never talked again. I know she blamed herself, as I blamed myself. Something snapped in Abby. I'm not sure if it can ever be fixed. I tried to explain what happened to her parents. At first, they were anxious to file a report. Her father was vocal about filing charges until I mentioned the names of the boys I recognized. One's father was a powerful trial attorney."

Nora coughed trying to clear her throat. "I remember his face when I said the name. He whispered something like, 'Not him, everyone would think he was trying to stir things up again.'"

"What did he mean?" Ellie's sounded as tired as she felt.

"At the time, I thought it was peculiar, especially after he was ready to call the police. Then I remembered Abby telling me her father had spent time in prison for embezzlement. Apparently, the football player's father was the guy who put him there."

"Was he guilty?"

Odd, but she never considered the question too deeply. Abby hadn't thought he was and that was good enough for her. "I don't know. Maybe not, if he was so afraid of the lawyer. Their sudden desire to hush things up convinced me no good would come of filing a report."

Ellie sighed audibly. "Then you never said anything to your family."

"Never told my family but being who they were they probably knew. Claimed to be sick for the rest of the week to avoid going to school. The next week we moved." It still amazed her that somehow her family had known. They'd said nothing. Even Leah and Ethan hadn't complained about the sudden move or the need for it.

"How could it be either one of your faults? Those animals planned it. Not much you could have done against all those muscular guys." Ellie gave the door a hard kick and yelped. "Mr. Creepy doesn't let you wear shoes. Too much of a chance of running."

"That was my point for you, Ellie. It didn't matter if you wore a bikini top or not. Abby and I had coats on. That didn't slow the guys down. This creep planned it. Why else would he be driving around with a syringe full of tranquilizer? If it hadn't been you, he might have found another girl by herself." Using her bound hands, Nora managed to raise them to scratch at her face, knocking off her blindfold in the process.

A couple of blinks helped her eyes adjust to the yellow pool of light a fluorescent bulb threw out. Definitely a basement. It looked more like a cellar with its dirt floor. There were stacks of some wood frames with bricks on them against one wall. Rocking on the cot, she tried to stand. Her first attempt ended with her face planted in the dirt. "Oomph."

"What are you doing?

Kneeling, Nora leaned against the cot, trying to get her butt back on it. "Trying to stand." Seated back on the cot, she scooted down the folding bed. The hopping hadn't worked too well. If she could get next to the wall, it might catch her. Turning, she made sure her shoulder touched the wall.

"Ouch, that hurt." Her legs proved to be a little shaky, maybe the result of the drug or lack of circulation. "Ellie, do you know what type of drug he used on you?"

Nora took one small hop that reminded her of her need to pee. Hopping was not advisable. Penguin walk it would be. Rocking side to side, she slowly made her way around the room. Who would have known that what she'd learned at summer camp would have some benefit?

Spider webs clung to the corners, while dust particles danced in the yellow light. Cleaning was not the man's strong point. Walking like Penguin from the old Batman movie, she made her way closer to the frames. A strong whiff of fermenting cabbage demonstrated her mind wasn't playing jokes on her. It really was sauerkraut. The trays of sauerkraut were stacked in front of a plywood wall. Hobbling closer, she almost jumped when Ellie's voice sounded near.

"I'm not sure what he used. He joked about it being an animal tranquilizer and that he used too much on me."

Nora was close to the wall. Lifting her secured hands, she tapped on the plywood. "Are you in there?"

"Yes. You're up and around. I cried and prayed for days that someone would rescue me. No one did."

Working her way to the door, Nora leaned against it to be closer to the girl. "Don't give up hope. We'll get out of here. I think he used ketamine on us. It's called Special K. Possibly Telazol. Still, we both went out fast. Real fast."

She could feel Ellie's presence on the other side of the door, sensing it more than physically feeling. Her essence grew cooler as if the life were ebbing out of her.

"I want to believe, Nora, but I've been here so long. I watched him build the cage I'm in now. Even then, he was planning on taking you. In a couple of months, you'll watch him build another one. The fact I've seen his face means I'm never leaving. I think there is another girl upstairs, but I'm not sure. I thought I heard steps once, even singing."

A glance back at her abandoned blindfold chilled Nora. She refused to believe Clayton and her family would not try to rescue her. In the meantime, she had to gather what information she could to help herself and Ellie. Sitting around waiting for people to rescue you didn't work too well.

"Ellie, we need to gather information. I have a friend I can tell what we found out. It might help him find us. We are in the basement with a dirt floor, meaning the house is very old. It might be considered abandoned. Could have the windows boarded up or the door padlocked. We know the man makes sauerkraut. He also possibly has access to veterinarian drugs. You've seen him."

Ellie interrupted her. "How will you tell your friend?"

Um, that was a hard one to explain. "We have a telepathic connection. He knows I've been kidnapped. He's trying to get help now."

Ellie considered her statement for a second. "Is he a witch, too?"

That was a good question. One her mother would have asked if she'd ever had a chance to meet the man. "I'm not sure, but we're very close, have been for years."

Ellie voice sounded a little exasperated, which was a nice change from hopeless. "How can you be close and not…"

The sound of tires on gravel stopped her questioning. Ellie hissed as if he could hear from the outside. "He's back. Get back to your cot. He won't be pleased that you've been moving around."

The rasping of a lock sounded. Padlock, not a regular door lock. The sound of chains falling confirmed this. The exterior door groaned a protest as he opened it.

Great Goddess, help me now. Nora shuffle-walked as fast as she could, creating a cloud of dust in the process. She was about a foot from the cot when she tripped, falling onto the mattress. Now, all she had to do was flip over and get her legs up. Nothing could be done about the blindfold.

A masculine voice joyfully called out, "Honey, I'm home."

She squeezed her eyes shut. The familiar voice touched her, chilled her. People thought the evil you didn't know was bad. Those people had never really known anyone thoroughly evil. Unfortunately, she had.

The basement door swung open.

CHAPTER FOURTEEN

THE FOOTSTEPS REVERBERATED as her captor worked his way down the stairs. His pace was slow, as if he deliberately prolonged her agony, but maybe the man was simply tired, too. Exhaustion might work in her favor. He might be too tired to torture her or Ellie or carry out whatever his plans were. It took all her concentration to keep her breath even as if she were sleeping. Why hadn't she used the time to come up with a plan as opposed to waddling all over the place like a penguin?

Wait, the footsteps had stopped, on the stairs at least. The dirt floor wouldn't make any sound. The swish of stiff fabric rubbing together came closer.

Keep eyes shut lightly, not squeezed shut, body relaxed, not tense, and perfectly still. She reminded herself of what the surgery patients looked like when they were fully under the anesthesia. Maybe she could fool him and buy herself a little bit more time. She didn't know for what, since no foolproof escape techniques took form. All she knew was she refused to be a victim. Realizing her captor probably expected to take her against her will, like Ellie, she gritted her teeth.

A tsking sound erupted from the man beside her. "You almost had me fooled, Nora. Until your jaw jutted out and your nostrils flared with anger. Even though I saw signs you'd been busy in the paths in the dirt and your discarded blindfold." He tsked again.

Did it serve any purpose to keep her eyes closed? It was better to be prepared. If she drew her legs up, she could still manage a good push or kick. Her eyes flickered open, confirming what she already knew. It was the jerk from the diner, the one who always wanted to talk to her about his meal. Bonnie fussing over him had never been enough. He'd always wanted Nora's attention.

His dark eyes glistened with delight as he observed her bound state. His smell was rank, fetid, as if someone or something had died inside of him.

His hand came closer, allowing her to see the dirt under his fingernails. Nasty. She'd never noticed him being so filthy at the diner. Her eyes drifted down to his pants, which appeared to be new and stiff, though the knees were dirty, as if he'd been kneeling in dirt.

The man wasn't dressed as a laborer. His appearance made her think of an accountant or some middle manager who would always find fault with his underlings' performance. His physique was on the soft side, not a man who earned his pay with his muscles.

Her eyes drifted back to his knees. The dirt meant something. *Think.*

He laughed. He pointed at her with one index finger. "I see where your eyes are. I chose you for your cooking abilities. My previous cook is no more." He attempted to look sorrowful, but he failed when he turned his eyes to the floor, especially when he'd spoken with laughter in his tone.

My previous cook is no more.

She seriously doubted anyone would voluntarily cook for him. Maybe the man had a profile on some dating site. Unfortunately, there might be one or two women desperate enough to cook for him. Not too many, though, she assumed, since he always seemed to be at the diner.

Distraction was her plan. The police would be on their way if she were in a crime drama. "Far as I can tell, you ate at the diner five days out of seven." Her voice came out raspy but controlled. Good.

"Your throat is dry. I'll have to fix that. Gotta take care of my investment. Took me awhile to find a cook I liked. Yours wasn't the only diner I visited." He grinned, showing all his teeth, even a gray incisor.

That tooth was dead, Nora noted. Lifeless, like his soul. The man was without even intrinsic values. No use appealing to his compassion or logic. He had neither.

Where was everyone? Shouldn't Tonya have raised a search party by now? Where was Clayton? Something touched her. It was more like a feeling that she wasn't alone. There weren't any voices in her head, besides her own screaming in panic.

Prolong the conversation. "Um, how did you pick me?"

He squatted and placed a grimy hand on her hair, stroking as if she were a cat. Ellie whimpered in the distance.

Nora kept her eyes locked with his, watching him as if he were a deadly cobra that would strike the instant, she broke visual contact. Her breaths were shallow as she tried not to suck in the awful odor. Part of her mind worked on the smell, trying to pinpoint it. Another part pleaded with any spirits, any entities to assist her.

Lord and Lady, forgive me for not honoring you properly. It wasn't that I didn't believe. It was more like not understanding properly.

"Nora," the man crooned, inching even closer. "You may call me Lloyd. Lloyd and Nora." He chanted the names in a singsong fashion. "We were meant to be together. That's what I thought the first time you came out of the kitchen when I complained about your cooking."

"There was nothing wrong with the burger. You admitted it when I came out. Why me?" What had she done to make him choose her over anyone else? Not that she would have wanted anyone to replace her.

Her eyes drifted to his bushy, unkempt eyebrows. She couldn't keep looking into his eyes. Nana had often commented that she could see evil or feel it roll off a person. How she did used to puzzle Nora. Seeing evil wasn't particularly hard when looking into Lloyd's bloodshot eyes. His pupils were small, which shouldn't be too surprising in the dim light, but they were narrower, rather like a snake's. How could she have not noticed that before?

All the times he'd insisted on seeing her she'd usually looked beside his head as opposed to into his face. His accusations that she hadn't cooked something right had made her angry enough that she'd deliberately looked away from the man. Barb would have been all over her if she'd glared at a customer. Chances were, she wouldn't have been here if she'd told Lloyd what he could do to himself. Of course, she'd have been out of a job, too. Unemployed would have been infinitely preferable to her current state.

Lloyd kept stroking her hair as he spoke, his grimy fingers sometimes touching her cheek. "I'm a meat and potatoes kind of guy. I chose the smaller diners. No way I could snatch someone out of a bustling kitchen." He chuckled as if he'd found her question amusing.

Nora had turned down jobs at bigger establishments because they wouldn't give her enough hours. Order Up was the only one to provide free meals and guarantee her enough hours to pay her rent. It had seemed like the only logical choice at the time. Part of her mind turned over various scenarios. If the police didn't find her, would her face end up on flyers? Nana would insist on doing memorial ceremonies, maybe even monthly.

Lloyd continued to talk. It was fortunate he enjoyed explaining his twisted rationale. Nora was willing to bet few people listened to him any other time.

"I found most places tend to hire men as cooks. I had no use for some cranky old man who chain-smoked as he cooked. Didn't want that muscle-bound guy who works the shift after you. Nope, I wanted a woman. Hard to find one in the small diners. I found another woman, but she looked to me the type to win in a knife fight. She overcooked the eggs, too."

Her history professor used to say no good deed goes unpunished. Nora used to think it was a dark way of looking at things. Apparently, giving too much attention to her cooking hadn't paid off.

What could she ask him next?

"I decided on you because you could cook the way I like my food. You were always polite, even though it almost killed you sometimes. It made me think you'd be an easy one to train. The fact you've already trotted all over the room and ripped off your blindfold shows I've underestimated you."

Her breathing stopped for a second as she held her breath. He was on to her, but what captive didn't try to escape? If he remained confident in his superiority, he'd slip up. It was time for her critical thinking skills to kick in. A memory nudged at her. Her parents had allowed her to join a scout troop.

At first, they'd been reluctant, fearing the troop might support traditional religious views, but their first activity had found approval. Her first scout excursion had been her last, though. Their troop had planned to help clean up the shore of the local river. Images of her young self proudly wearing her uniform, skipping along the shore with another girl, brought back the joy she'd had at the start of the trip. Truthfully, Amber and she had done very little trash pickup. Instead, they'd played hide-and-seek in the small caves that riddled the shore. One of the parent chaperones had complained it wasn't a great place to be after discovering the homeless took refuge in the caves. The leader must have decided that was a good enough reason to gather up the girls, while Amber had screamed.

Nora had gone to locate her new friend, only to find her pointing at a shallow grotto from which a stench had emanated, wrapping its horrendous scent tendrils around them. Somehow, Nora had known enough not to look in the cave. Later, she'd heard her parents whispering about the dead body Amber had found.

Her body went rigid on its own. Dead body. He *smelled* like a dead body. He'd mentioned the former cook was "no more." Ellie had said she'd thought there might have been someone upstairs. Sweet Goddess, would she ever see the light of day again?

Lloyd quit stroking her head. "What's wrong?" He looked at her quizzically, as if confused why there might be something wrong with being captive. "Oh, oh, I got it." He pulled a large knife out of his pocket. A reddish-brown substance covered most of the blade. "I know what you want."

Nora recognized immediately that it was dried blood, even without the familiar coppery scent. Most likely, the blood belonged to the former cook. She wondered what the cook had done to merit death. Burn the eggs?

Shrinking away from him was the best she could do as he lowered the knife. Kick. She needed to kick with her legs. Partially drawing them up, she was almost ready when he threw his body weight onto her, pinning her legs against the mattress.

"What's wrong with you?" He grunted as he kept her legs firmly held in place. "I was trying to cut the rope off so you could go to the bathroom and cook me dinner."

Cut the rope off her feet. "Nothing. I will need the rope off my hands to cook. What ingredients have you brought me?"

Lloyd sawed away at her ankle restraints while she considered what she needed to do. A meal rich in starch, bread, and sugar would make him sluggish. It might also give her the tools she needed to make her escape. Did the man have any spices? Remnants of the ropes fell to the floor. A sensation of pins and needles started in her feet. Lloyd pulled her into a sitting position then helped her up.

The last thing Nora wanted was to lean on her possible murderer, but even with the ropes off, her stiff legs were uncooperative. She was able to shuffle but bending her knees to ascend the stairs hurt. Swallowing her pain, she limped up the stairs with Lloyd's help. Her chances of escape would improve greatly if she were above ground. Her thoughts drifted back to Ellie as she gained the first floor. She couldn't leave Ellie behind even if she had the opportunity to escape. The girl had to go with her.

Lloyd shepherded her down a narrow hallway. Empty squares on the wall indicated pictures had once hung there. The peeling floral wallpaper and the dusty floor confirmed Nora's initial suspicion that the structure was derelict.

A rank sewage odor came from an open doorway. It looked like they'd arrived. Nora remembered Ellie's description of what had happened in the bathroom. Instead of entering, she held her hands out. "I need my hands free."

Lloyd shook his head. "I'll help you with your pants."

Nora stared him down. No way were things going to go down as he planned. "If you make the mistake of helping me and think to help yourself, then there will not be food."

His head came up fast, and he fixed a bewildered look on her. "No food? None? You won't cook?"

The man looked uncertain. A former soldier had mentioned in her psych class that it was hard to deal with terrorists because they were always willing to die for their cause. A person who had no fear of death could not be threatened. War used the threat of death to coerce people into doing things. She decided to make her point clearer.

"None." If her hands had been free, she'd have crossed her arms. She leaned against the wall, hoping she appeared stronger than she felt. With any luck, her leaning would look like nonchalance.

The knife reappeared in Lloyd's hand. The blade came closer to Nora's face, allowing her to see the serrated edge. "What if I threaten to kill you? You'd cook for me then."

Her eyes followed the knife as he waved it in front of her face.

Show no fear. Bluff.

She wasn't sure if it was her thought or possibly Clayton's. It still sounded like good advice.

"Go ahead and kill me. You'd just have to start the hunt for a cook again. In the meantime, I guess you'd be cooking your own dinner." Despite her bonds, she managed to shrug her shoulders, pretending she could care less if he plunged the knife in her heart. Her loose cook whites covered her quivering legs.

Lloyd stared at her for a few more seconds, cursed, and then lowered the knife to the rope at her wrists. "I'd thought you would be easy to boss around. If I knew you'd be this difficult, I would have kept looking."

Her bonds off, she darted into the bathroom and slammed the door shut before Lloyd could squeeze in. With the door shut, one foot and shoulder wedged against it to keep it closed, she felt for the lock, found the knob and twisted, not that it would do that much good. A butter knife could spring the locks on the interior doors except for Ellie's, which was padlocked. Lloyd already had a knife.

The absolute darkness made the smell worse. Her fingers flipped the light switch, but nothing happened. "What's wrong with the light?" she grumbled, mainly to herself.

"Burnt out two months ago," Lloyd said. "No reason to replace it since I always leave the door open."

Not something Nora wanted to contemplate. Moving her right foot slowly forward, she found the toilet. Squatting in the general direction of the commode, she hurriedly peed. Lloyd could come through the door at any time. She pulled up her adult diaper, glad of it. She was unwilling to touch anything in the filthy place to blindly search for toilet paper. A shiver passed through her before she yanked the door open. Might as well discover what she had at her disposal in the kitchen.

A smart cook could disable a threat with the food she served. Lloyd would not provide her with any handy poisons, but if she had the right herbs, she could make him very uncomfortable. A man retching his guts up tended to make mistakes.

Lloyd stood right outside the door, startling Nora for a second. Did he have a clue what she was thinking?

He grabbed her arm, dragging her behind him into a cluttered kitchen. A rickety fridge, which appeared fifty years out of date, had a red cooler sitting in front of it. An equally ancient stove served as a base for a camp stove with a flexible hose attached it to a propane tank. *Propane.* There was potential. Make that, potential for killing the three of them if she wasn't careful.

"Where's the food and pans?" She mentally cataloged everything in the cluttered room, sorting it all into two divisions: things that might help her to escape and things that wouldn't. Newspapers, dirty dishes, a scrapbook, and a pair of scissors covered a rectangular Formica table. The scrapbook and papers indicated Lloyd was keeping track of his crimes. That demonstrated a certain amount of pride and egotism, which meant she might be able to flatter him. Most people didn't have an inflated sense of self-worth, which was why they downplayed flattery and tended to be suspicious of people who were in actual awe of them.

Lloyd pointed with the knife toward a drawer underneath the oven. "In there."

Turning to keep him in view, she squatted to reach the drawer. She wouldn't put it past him to stab her in the back. Logically, that would put him out of a meal, but she doubted logic played a part in his thought processes. If it had, he wouldn't be grabbing women off the streets or out of diners.

Her fingers wrapped around a heavy cast iron skillet. One whack with the skillet should knock her captor out cold, maybe giving her enough time to rescue Ellie. She eased the heavy skillet out of the drawer and turned slightly, using her body to block her weapon, and straightened slowly. Her only window of opportunity was to catch him unaware.

Normalcy was the key as if she cooked for her kidnapper every day. "So, I notice you're using propane when you have electricity."

"Electricity has been shut off to this house for years. I got the lights on a gas generator. Running the stove and fridge would take too much fuel. No heat or air, either, not that there was all that much when I lived here as a kid."

A clue. *He used to live in this abandoned house, away from everyone else. Good chance the title is in his name.* She felt as if she'd shouted the words in her mind, but there was no hint Clayton had heard them. What did she expect him to do? Best he could do was to write a letter in his time addressed to Adam and Maura Carpenter. What were the chances it would find its way across the centuries into the right hands in a prompt fashion?

Not knowing how to answer Lloyd's previous statement, she ignored it. Instead, she asked about dinner, hoping to get him to drop his guard. "What did you say you brought for me to cook?" Her head pivoted with her question while both hands kept a firm grip on the skillet.

"I didn't say." The man met her glance with eyes filled with silent laughter, probably due to the pistol in his hand pointed straight at her back.

Damn. Pistol beats a skillet every time. Where had that come from? She hadn't noticed it earlier.

Lloyd answered her silent question. "It's obvious to me that you are much smarter than the others. They could be controlled by their fears and some force. Never even had to display the Sig to get them to do what I wanted. You're a different matter. More difficult, more cunning. You'll be more of a challenge to break, but I will break you." His lips tilted up to match the laughter in his eyes.

Think again. I am the sharper knife in this drawer.

No way would she give him the satisfaction of seeing her distress.

Nora turned back to the stove, staring at the skillet with food stuck to it. "Is there any way to clean this? It's disgusting."

His voice caused her to jump, since it was closer than she'd expected. "Water in the sink. It's cold from the well, but I guess you could scrub on the pan."

Lloyd was only a foot behind her. He must have moved closer while she'd tried to concoct an escape plan. The gun barrel rubbed against her neck.

"Nora, Nora, what you need is a man to take charge of you. I am the man to do it."

His fetid breath brushed the back of her neck. The thought of his dirt-encrusted fingers on her body caused vomit to creep up her throat. A gulp sent it back. If there were no escape for her, then she'd prefer to die now. If she could get him to shoot the propane tank, they'd all go up in a fiery death. It wasn't the ending she'd pictured for herself, but she'd not be his sex slave.

Should she elbow him first or lead with the skillet? There was a chance he might shoot her no matter what, which would be preferable to dying in a fire. If she failed, then another captured woman would take her place. Apparently, Ellie had failed in the cooking capacity. "I could start on dinner as soon as you give me the supplies." Her goal was to have her voice sound normal, as if she were discussing the possibility of rain.

The pistol barrel dropped away from her neck as he took a step back. She heard paper rustling as he pushed a grocery bag toward her with his foot. The man wasn't taking any chances. What had she done to indicate she'd be a challenge? Too bad, she couldn't go back and rethink that strategy. A bag of potatoes crowded the bag, along with a tube of hamburger, onions, and burger buns. She'd be making his favorite diner meal, with some modifications.

The ingredients didn't yield much hope as far to escape, though a heavy meal of fried potatoes and burger should render him lethargic. The potato bag smacked the scarred counter as she dropped it, sending up a small cloud of dust. The place was filthy.

Currently, she had to appease Lloyd if only for the fact he was holding a gun on her. He'd want a diner-quality meal prepared on a camp stove, a test she never would have asked for. At one time, she'd thought having the love of her life in another century was trial enough. Speaking of that, where was Clayton?

I'm here. I tried to come to you, but all I managed to do was float around the room like a ghost.

That explained the feeling she'd had in the basement.

I'm not sure why I can't cross over. Nora, darling, this frustrates me more than I can tell. Stall. As much as it pains me to say it, play to his vanity. Insist you want to make a meal worthy of him. Ask for spices.

Spices. She'd already thought of that but hadn't asked for them. Still, she had to try. "Do you have any condiments? Cayenne pepper, ginger, garlic?" She tried to remember which spices would cause the runs in high doses. Listing unusual spices might make him suspicious, though. "And salt. Do you have any cooking oil? I'll need it to fry the potatoes."

Lloyd shoved some items around behind her. He slammed a box of table salt, followed by one of black pepper. "That's all I got. Don't see why you need all those other spices."

Well, that wouldn't do her much good. She unpacked the rest of the items from the bag. *Oh, I need those spices to cause stomach cramps and keep you in the bathroom for most of the night.* Nora chose not to share her thoughts. "I want to make dinner special for you." Luckily, she wasn't facing him, which allowed her grimace to go unnoticed. "I want to make you a dinner you deserve." Did she ever.

Lloyd grunted in response. "Sounds good. Not tonight. I'll try to pick those up tomorrow. Anything else you need to get started on the food tonight?"

She glanced at the supplies assembled on the counter. Her eyes lingered on the onions, nature's laxative. Of course, combined with red meat, bread, and potatoes, she might end up making the man regular. Geesh. Why couldn't she wear a poison ring like a Borgia? A flick of poison, while it wouldn't be enough to kill him, it would be enough to have him writhing in pain while she and Ellie escaped.

"I need a cutting board, plate, paper towels, spatula, and a knife." She listed the requests in a practical tone, unsure of how he might react.

"Knife? You think I am stupid enough to give you a sharp knife?" Lloyd half-growled the words as if to make a point.

It would be easy to answer his rhetorical question, but a bullet would be her most likely reward. Instead, she opened the potato bag. Nora pulled out a couple of potatoes and placed them in the skillet. She added a few onions, too. Turning, she brandished the skillet in front of Lloyd, who still held the gun on her. "I suppose we can try cooking the potatoes like this. Guaranteed to be burnt on one side and raw on the other. The other option is cutting them into home fries, which will reduce your wait."

His eyes flickered over the skillet, before he withdrew the blood-stained hunting knife from his pocket and offered it hilt first. "Remember, I'll have my gun on you every minute. Bullets are faster than a knife."

He held out the knife for several seconds, drawing her eyes like a magnet. No doubt, the blood on the knife was from the last failed cook. No way could she bring herself to even touch it. The knife could serve as evidence connecting Lloyd to the missing woman. "Um, do you have anything smaller? I might cut myself peeling the potatoes."

Lloyd pocketed the knife before stooping to blindly root through a cabinet as he kept his eyes and gun trained on Nora. He pulled a rusty steak knife out and offered it.

Nora's hand closed over the blade. Her thumb rested on the blade, feeling its dull edge. Peeling anything with this knife would be difficult. Best she'd go with just slicing the potatoes. "What about the cutting board?"

Lloyd slapped the table with his free hand. The noise startled her, making her jump, much to her captor's amusement. "I don't have any damn cutting board. Where do you think you are, the diner?" He chuckled at his own perceived wit.

The scarred counter probably held enough germs to wipe out an army, which wasn't exactly a bad thing, though heat tended to kill most germs. Even if Lloyd did contract some bug from ingesting the various microbes in the house, it wouldn't be fast acting.

The dull knife made cutting the potatoes difficult. The knowledge that a lunatic with a gun stood less than a yard away made it worse.

Act calm.

The words felt like something she might say, but they weren't hers. Nor were they Clayton's.

Help is on the way.

That had to be wishful thinking. She wanted to believe someone would rush in to save her.

A small pile of potato slices formed on one side of the counter. Soon, she'd switch to onions, which would make her eyes water. Too bad, she couldn't get Lloyd to chop, but she could keep him busy.

"How do you turn this stove on? I need the cooking oil if you want your potatoes to be crispy as opposed to sticking to the skillet and crumbled."

She had her hand on the last potato and her eyes lowered as she watched Lloyd root about the kitchen through her lashes. He swore as he pawed through the cabinets. She thought about rushing him when he was halfway into the cabinet, but the man could easily shoot through the cheap cabinets. What she needed was some way to disable him.

Knife was dull. No available spices for stomach cramps, and any viral infections would work too slowly. Lloyd pulled out a dusty tin of oil that appeared ancient.

He held the oil aloft. "I found some. Might be a little old, but oil never goes bad."

"Good." She pushed the word out, stopping herself from explaining that oil does go rancid. That's why she kept hers in the fridge.

He placed the dusty can beside the potatoes. A quick glance confirmed that the can itself would probably bring a few bucks from itinerant antique and junk dealers. A plan formed in her mind. "I need the stove on, too."

A quick twist loosened the lid. A whiff of the heavy, foul aroma indicated it had gone bad. Still good for her purposes, she decided, as she began to pour a generous quantity into the skillet.

Lloyd watched her as he fiddled with the propane tank. He awkwardly clutched the gun, as he pushed the lighter mechanism on the camp stove. A huge flame appeared along with the rotten-egg smell of propone. Lloyd almost fell backward as the flame leaped up, but he caught his balance then adjusted the flame.

Talk about missed opportunity, Nora grumbled to herself. Still, she had a plan.

The cast iron skillet smoked a little as it heated, demonstrating she must have splashed some liquid on the exterior of the pan. She sliced onions into the skillet. Even Lloyd would be suspicious if all she did was heat the oil. Silently, she beseeched the elements for help.

Fire, assist me in my endeavor. Air, carry my pleas for help to those who can understand your language. Earth, give me strength to do what I must do.

A simple sideways step brought her into a half-turned position. Lloyd's hand still gripped the pistol, but his interest was on the newspaper. He flipped the pages. "I'll be able to paste your missing story soon."

There will be no article for your scrapbook. Instead, she replied, "Paper doesn't get too excited about college kids. They are always disappearing. Usually turns out they went home, went to another college to visit friends, or even took off with their current squeeze."

She threw a potato slice in the grease and watched it sizzle slightly. Not hot enough. The combined fumes of the propane and rancid oil made it hard to breathe. Did Lloyd notice the smell? If so, she needed to distract him to keep him from investigating. It wouldn't do for him to discover she was heating oil as opposed to frying potatoes.

She slid to stand in front of the stove, blocking his view of the skillet and the bubbling oil. Hot pads would be nice, but she didn't dare ask for any. Her damp hands rubbed down her loose white top. If it had been bigger, she might have been able to use it as a hot pad, but she wanted the pan away from her body when she tossed the hot oil on Lloyd. Her best bet was to go for his face. How much would the oil incapacitate him? On television, the people usually fell to the floor, screaming in pain, leaving the good people plenty of time to escape. Nora knew better than to take what she saw on television as accurate.

The camp stove made a slight hiss while the oil bubbled. Her captor hummed the theme song of a television show she couldn't name. Underneath it all, she thought she heard something, maybe a stick breaking or bush rustling.

A quick glance at Lloyd revealed no alarm over the possibility of someone snooping closer to his house. Maybe she'd imagined the noise.

Hold on, Nora, we're coming.

The voice again. Not Clayton's. It was her grandfather. She was sure of it. How could she not recognize her own grandfather? Could be the kidnapping and drugging had slowed her down.

The sound of a dog barking close by jerked Lloyd out of his perusal of the newspaper. He sprang out of the chair and rushed to the boarded-up window.

On his tiptoes, he tried to peer out between the slats. "I think someone is out there. It is hard to tell with the falling light. It could be just kids and a dog. After all, I've used this house for over two years, and no one ever bothered to come looking."

Nora knew the time had come to act.

CHAPTER FIFTEEN

*G*ODDESS, GIVE ME *strength.*

    She glanced at Lloyd's back, willing him to turn. It would do her little good to hit him in the back. He held the gun loosely in his hand as he peered out the window.

"Can't see anyone. Must be a stray dog." Lloyd started to turn. "When are those hamburgers going to be ready?"

Grabbing hold of the hot skillet handle with both hands, she bit her lip as her hands burned and tightened against the blistering heat. Hot oil splattered her hands as she tried to hold the skillet level.

"Right about now." She launched the hot oil in Lloyd's direction. The oil spattered him as if in slow motion, covering his face, shirt, and arms. Burn blisters formed immediately. The gun dropped from his hand, and he fell to the floor with anguished screams.

She lobbed the skillet at him. It bounced off him, causing him to yelp. "Bitch, you'll pay."

The man wasn't as incapacitated as she would have liked, so she didn't have much time to release Ellie and get out of there. She scooped up the gun with one hand, tucking it in her waistband. There had to be something she could use to release the girl. As she ran for the stairs, she scoured the area, begging any good spirits to assist her. It was highly doubtful any existed in such a horrible place. An old, weathered hammer caught her eye.

She might be able to pry the door open or at least break off the knob. "Ellie, I'm coming. Try to break the door down from your side."

The sound of a body hitting the door assured her Ellie was trying to help. In her rush, Nora missed a step and rolled down the remaining ones. Dizzy, she stood up, shook her head to clear it, and then went to grab the hammer.

The door looked more formidable up close. The small hammer didn't appear capable of tearing the door from its hinges. How one man managed to get the door down the stairs was short of amazing, unless he'd had help. Not something, she wanted to consider.

The first blow with the hammer reverberated all the way up her arm. Steel, it was a steel door. No way would she be able to take that down.

Running would be her best bet. She'd bring back help. "Ellie, I am going to have to get help."

"Don't leave me. I'll die here." The pleas dissolved into weeping.

Hammer in hand, Nora looked between the door and the steps. She couldn't leave Ellie. What if Lloyd killed the girl while Nora tried to find her way back to civilization? He would burn the whole place down to hide the evidence. The thought of Ellie trapped inside like a caged animal caused her to examine the box-like cell.

The hammer hit the plywood vigorously, knocking a small hole in the board. A big-enough hole would allow Ellie to crawl out.

Crouching at the end of a square of plywood, she found a place where the two boards came together. It was a tiny space, but enough room to edge the claw end of the hammer into the crack. She pulled back with all her weight. A three-foot section splintered off, sending her wind milling backward before crashing against the sauerkraut wooden trays with a thud spilling fermenting cabbage on her and the floor.

Ellie's voice urged her back up. "I think I can see some light. Hurry, please. There's another panel inside. You can break it."

Nora pushed the sauerkraut off her face. The salty liquid on her hands exacerbated the pain from the burns. *Goddess, help me now.*

Hammer in hand, she crawled to the small opening she'd made and felt for the interior wall. The low-hanging plywood made it hard to get much force behind her hammer pounds, but on the first hit, the board crumpled, which caused Ellie to squeal from the other side.

Together, they knocked and pulled at the drywall to create a space big enough for Ellie to crawl through. Excited at the idea of escaping, both women worked feverishly, throwing drywall pieces to the side. The only noise that filled the small area was their labored breathing and the soft falls of drywall chunks. *Almost done. They would escape.*

A knife tip touched her throat, stilling Nora's actions. A slight twist of the knife left a long slash on her neck. Blood flowed down her neck as Lloyd hauled her up by the waistband of her pants. The medical professional in her automatically diagnosed the cut as a surface wound that wouldn't kill her. The blood would probably congeal in a couple of minutes. No doubt, the man intended to make her pay.

Grabbing for the gun, she was horrified to discover it was no longer in her waistband. She must have lost it in her tumble down the stairs. Lloyd tried to haul her upright but stumbled, dropping her. Nora rolled to get out of reach, resorting to techniques she'd learned in her self-defense class.

No needle full of animal tranquilizer would take her down this time. Her movement brought her up under the stairs. No gun in any obvious location. It must have fallen under something. She needed a weapon—anything.

Lloyd regained his balance and headed her way, half his face blistered with third-degree burns and one eye swollen shut. A grim, determined set to his lips promised retribution, but his footsteps were unsteady, showing some signs of trauma.

A weapon, any weapon, might be enough to bring him down. Like a hammer. It was next to the wall. Somehow, she had to get close enough to pick it up without signaling her intentions. She sidled closer to the wall, keeping eye contact. The last thing she needed was for Neil to look down. "Not as fast as you used to be, old man."

Lloyd growled in response but kept walking toward her. "I underestimated you. I won't do that again. Obviously, you have more brains than that silly fireworks slut."

Nora moved her body to the right, though she planned to go left, sure Lloyd would go right to attempt to grab her. A quick glance to her left revealed a filthy blonde in a bikini top and shorts, kneeling by the hole she'd so recently crawled out from. Ellie held the hammer in both hands.

Time to think of another weapon. Better yet, it was time to move Lloyd closer to Ellie who had the hammer. Most likely, Ellie would crumple when confronted with her attacker. At least, that is what most pop psychology believed.

What would be a good weapon? The gun would make a great weapon, but no sign of that. Sauerkraut. The memory of the salty juice stinging her burnt hands inspired her to work her way toward the kraut, moving herself and involuntarily Lloyd away from the squatting Ellie.

"You can run, but you're not going anywhere. Go ahead and wear yourself down. It will only make it easier for me."

Nora contemplated everything she'd like to say, but she needed to get to the sauerkraut. The open crate beckoned her. She did her best to ignore the pain as she submerged her hands into kraut, grabbing huge handfuls to fling.

Lloyd walked closer, chuckling to himself. "Is this your big escape plan? To put your hands in sauerkraut? I'll admit I make good kraut, but it won't be your salvation."

In the split second before she flung her string missiles, she considered the man in front of her. People would consider him ordinary, nothing special, too bland to be considered attractive, a trifle wimpy and on the soft side. Most would dismiss him as harmless. Despite her initial impression that he was evil, she'd refused to listen to her instincts. Well, she knew better now.

Ellie straightened from her squatting position. She sidled across the room, never taking her eyes off Lloyd. Nora cut her eyes toward the steps, signaling her to get help. Lloyd, catching the eye movement, started to turn. The first sauerkraut launch splattered harmlessly against his shirt.

"Really? You're throwing sauerkraut? Just when I thought you might be smarter than the average woman, you do something that confirms you're not."

The second handful slapped him in the face. "Stupid woman, that hurts." He swiped away dripping strands. Nora pelted him with two more handfuls.

Ellie held her hammer over her head like a Norse Goddess and sprinted for Lloyd, slamming the tool into his skull. The man dropped to his knees. Ellie pounded about his head and shoulders, driving him to the floor. She screamed as she struck the steel head against his vulnerable body. "This is for ruining my life! Stealing my belief in the basic goodness of people! Causing my mother endless worry! Raping me again and again!"

Nora seized the hammer from her hand. "Ellie, you can't kill him." She tried to herd the hysterical girl up the stairs.

The girl shook off her shepherding arm. "I can kill him. I need to."

She made a grab for the bloody hammer that Nora held out of reach. The slender girl clawed at Nora in her frenzied state, opening the burn blisters on her hands. Only a firm belief in harming none kept the hammer clutched in her hand.

"Ellie, he has to stay alive so he can be punished. Besides, he knows where the bodies are."

Ellie's hands dropped to her sides. "Bodies." She said the word as if it were a foreign language she didn't comprehend.

The sound of breaking wood sounding from the rooms above cut short Nora's explanation about possible other abductees. Ellie grabbed her arm, tears welling in her eyes. "What now?"

A strong masculine voice shouted, and footsteps ran across the room. "Police!"

A familiar female voice cut through the sound of running feet and shouts of "Clear!" coming from the various rooms. "I know my granddaughter is here."

"Ma'am, you have to wait outside," a man answered.

Ellie whispered as if afraid of being overhead. "Is that your grandmother?"

Before Nora could answer, Nana's voice sounded closer to the basement door. "Get out of my way, officer, before I turn you into a toad. I can do it, too."

A police officer blocked the doorway. Nana peered around him and yelled, "That's my granddaughter and fellow victim, Ellie!" She poked the policeman. "You might discover she's a missing person you failed to find."

Sometimes her grandmother could be opinionated enough to find herself inside a jail cell. The woman continued to try to get around the officer blocking her. "Ma'am, this is a crime scene. You'll contaminate it."

Nana pointed into a corner of the basement. "Look, my husband and Clayton are already downstairs."

Nora turned slowly, not expecting to see Clayton. Not really expecting her grandfather, either. Clayton jogged across the basement, sidestepping the unconscious kidnapper.

He held his arms wide. "Nora, my darling, I came for ya."

The policeman jogged down the stairs. "How did you two get in? I told you to wait outside."

Her grandfather made a bow in the officer's direction. "I've mastered teleportation. We couldn't wait. I thought we would give the girls a hand, but it looks like they managed on their own." He nodded in the direction of the prone man. "That man smells evil."

Ellie, perhaps feeling more normal now that the danger had passed, quipped, "That's sauerkraut."

Clayton herded Nora and Ellie toward the stairs, Nana and Grandfather following. Nora stopped near the confused officer. "Don't let him die without finding out where he buried the other women."

Ellie repeated the words in the sudden silence. "Other women?"

They stepped outside into a heavily wooded area. Nora twisted to look back at the house. The windows were boarded up, except for one that allowed a triangle of light to spill out. The paint was peeling on the neglected building showing plain weathered wood. Those who passed by the house would consider it abandoned. Then again, she doubted many came so far out from the main road.

A policewoman met them, speaking into her shoulder-mounted walk-ie-talkie. The uniformed woman used her flashlight to guide them through the dark woods to where a small fleet of police cars, an ambulance, and even a SWAT van waited. A K-9 officer kept a short leash on a large dog. Had he and the dog tracked them, and if so, how? Nora was sure she'd arrived in a van, even if she didn't remember the details.

It was almost full dark, especially with the sheltering trees. The vehi-cles' headlights illuminated the scene, giving it a surreal feeling as groups of officers huddled together. The crisp air with a hint of winter in it was a welcome change from the foul-smelling house.

Nora gave the girl beside her a quick glance. Ellie had arrived in the summer and was leaving in the cool fall weather. A male paramedic shook out a blanket to place around Ellie, but the girl shied away from him. Intercepting the man, Nora took the blanket and wrapped it around the shivering girl. It would be a long time before Ellie would be able to look at an unfamiliar man without fear.

Clayton stayed behind Nora as she headed for the rest of her family huddled behind the police line where two officers kept watch over the small group. The officers directed suspicious stares at Clayton and her grandparents. Nana's complaints carried in the still air.

"If the stubborn police would have believed me when I told them that Clayton had astral-projected to the area, we would have been here so much sooner. Ignorant fools."

Her outspoken grandmother's grumbling brought an upward twitch to Nora's lips. *At least some things stayed the same in her very topsy-turvy world.*

She startled when Clayton placed a hand on her lower back, a very solid, real-feeling hand.

How had he gotten here? Would he stay or blink back in time once she no longer needed him? Turning, she grabbed Clayton's hand, intertwined her fingers with his, and squeezed hard. "I can't believe you're here. In case you're wondering, I need you all the time—as in forever."

Clayton used their clasped hands to pull her closer. "At last, you've finally figured out we were meant to be together."

She half-whispered, "Yes," but knew he heard.

Tonya waited with Nora's parents and siblings, Ethan and Leah. Clayton let go of her long enough for everyone to hug her. It felt good to be alive and so well loved.

Ellie stood at the edge of the group wrapped in the blanket. Maura, Nora's mother, handed her a cell phone. "I am not sure how cell service is out here, but if we all work together, I think we can give it a little boost."

The small group circled Ellie. She held the phone up to her ear, and her countenance wavered between uncertain and outright fear, until someone picked up on the other end.

"Mom, it's me. I'm alive."

The tears flowed down the young woman's face as she assured her mother, she'd see her soon. As she sobbed harder, Maura took the phone and spoke into it.

"Hello, I'm Maura. My daughter Nora was a kidnap victim, too… Yes, I know you want to be here. I know how you feel. If it hadn't been for the determination of my daughter's"—she glanced at Clayton—"boyfriend, I doubt we would have found the two of them. The man searched day and night with no more than a few leads after she vanished from her workplace."

That answered a few of Nora's questions.

Leaving the warm embrace of Clayton's arms, she walked over to Ellie and hugged her, rocking her slightly. Remembering the trauma, she'd felt after her own rape, she made sure to tell Ellie what she wished someone had told her all those years ago. "It's okay. It's over. It's in the past. It's not your fault. There are evil people in the world who do evil things. You were simply in the path of one evil person, that's all."

Ellie quit sobbing enough to look up with reddened eyes. "People will know. People will judge me. I'm dirty."

The words were familiar. The same as what she'd thought herself. Tightening her embrace, she reassured Ellie. "No reason for people to know. Your name won't be in the paper."

"It has to be. It's news."

"It is. I agree. I am okay with reading Nora Carpenter and another woman were rescued." She pushed the dirty blond hair out of Ellie's eyes.

Ellie looked up in disbelief. "You can do that, how?"

How indeed? It had never amazed her for a moment to see her family standing outside the house. That's who they were. No matter what, they supported one another. Strange to think she hadn't told them about her rape. They wouldn't have judged her. Somehow, they had known and never mentioned it, just doing what they knew would help her. Their sudden move, her grandmother's insistence on giving her cleansing potions and protections spells, her mother taking her to the Y for self-defense classes, all indicated some knowledge. She'd chosen not to tell because she'd blamed herself. At the time, she'd thought she'd somehow brought shame on the Wiccan community. She'd rationalized that her behavior and Abby's, as proud Wiccans, had invited the violence.

Now, she realized that the two of them had only been females in the wrong place at the wrong time. It was important that Ellie realized this about herself, too. Together, they'd shared a struggle against unthinkable evil that most people wouldn't understand. Leaning toward the other girl, Nora touched her head to Ellie's. It was then that she vowed to always be there for Ellie.

"You've met my family. They are a force to be reckoned with. News media don't reveal the identities of rape victims. You'll be okay. You might want to finish out the school year at home, or at least until you feel like returning to school."

Using her hand to wipe her nose, the girl nodded. "Yeah, that sounds good right now." She looked around at the circle of people surrounding her. "Your family is pretty cool."

A man followed by another man carrying a large video camera on his shoulder attempted to film her and Ellie. It only took a glance in the direction of the cameraman, and he fell, dropping the camera. The sound of the camera hitting the ground and shattering into several parts, along with the reporter's cursing, assured Nora that there would be no live interviews tonight.

Three probable culprits—Nana, her grandfather and Clayton—all sported identical grins. No wonder the man had fallen so hard.

The cameraman stood, brushing the dirt from his clothes. His glance swept the ground suspiciously. "There's nothing there. Not a tree root or a rock. It felt like my feet were pulled out from under me."

Nora patted her friend's shoulder. "See? I told you it would all work out."

A burst of pride swelled up inside her. It was an emotion she hadn't experienced in a while. She'd always considered her family decent people. Somehow, being pagan in a non-pagan world made them more special and precious. They were the salmon swimming upstream in a world of religious conformity.

Leaves crackled under Tonya's feet as she headed their way. She angled her head in Clayton's direction. "So that's your honey? I can see why you might trip through time to find him."

Ellie looked up inquiringly, but Tonya didn't notice the girl's look of astonishment as she continued, "Even in those old-timey clothes, he's still sexy. Never have I witnessed a man who loves a woman as much as he does you. Your grandfather searched until he found a portal and was able to connect with him. Clayton came through to get to our time. Even knowing he could never go back, he never hesitated."

Nora met Clayton's eyes. "Of course, he didn't hesitate. That's the way it is with soul mates. You just know."

Tonya directed a small push at Nora's shoulder. "Listen to you, sounding so sure of yourself. A couple of days ago, you weren't."

Her roommate was right. Amazing how looming death made all the pieces fall into place. "A few days ago, I was worried about graduating. That pales in comparison when you consider dying and your method of death. I'm thankful, very thankful, to be alive and to have another opportunity to love my soul mate over there." She winked at Clayton, drawing a laugh from him.

The reporter edged closer, asking the waiting officers for information. Most ignored him, while a few offered, "No comment."

The diligent reporter had turned in the direction of the small family group when a large barn owl took aim at his head, causing him to drop to the ground again.

A few officers took delicious delight in the reporter being the one harassed as opposed to the other way around.

Her grandmother's distinctive voice carried over the noise of the man hitting the ground and the laughter. "Buell, I did not cause that owl to dive at that annoying news fellow. That was natural. Don't underestimate nature."

Nora watched her grandparents good-naturedly bicker. She knew as well as her grandfather did that the owl was Nana's creature. Owls were her token animal. It could have carried a banner reading, "This owl attacked you courtesy of Esmeralda Hare."

Noise near the front of the house caused Ellie to huddle closer to Nora. She wrapped one arm around the girl, pulling her closer. Together, they watched two SWAT officers wrestle a handcuffed Lloyd down the porch stairs. Despite the large, armed men on either side of him, he kept up a constant stream of profanity, debasing the female gender. His head jerked to where Nora and Ellie stood. He managed to stop long enough to direct a glare so malevolent at the two that it seemed to glow in the evening air.

Clayton moved in front of Nora and Ellie, blocking Lloyd's view of them with his strong body. "Be glad," he growled, "that the police are taking you away. If I had my way, you would pay a thousand times over for the evil you did. You'd not live long enough to see the inside of a cell."

Nora could see only the masculine back blocking out all the evilness pouring off her kidnapper. She felt safer, warmer, with Clayton protecting her from harm. His voice became deeper as he made his final pronouncement. "I may not be able to touch you. Rest assured, though, consequences will occur in this lifetime and in all your future lifetimes."

Lloyd's cursing shut off as the police car door slammed on his tirade. The waiting personnel turned toward the huddled group while a few drifted off to the house to photograph and map out the crime scene.

A female medic motioned to Nora. "Ma'am, we need the two of you to go to the hospital and be checked out."

Ellie snuggled closer to Nora. Sensing her fear, Nora offered an alternative suggestion. "Couldn't we just drive to the hospital in a car? I think there has been enough trauma in Ellie's life. Her mother could meet us there."

The medic's eyes roamed over the two of them. "Not really standard procedure. I could get in trouble if you don't arrive via ambulance." The woman glanced back at the other medics waiting beside the ambulance, clearly torn about what to do.

Nora's mother, Maura, worked her way to the front of the group. She touched the medic's arm. "I'm a registered nurse with the trauma unit at St. George's. I can monitor their condition as we drive to the hospital. I must agree with my daughter. Anything else might be too much at this point."

The medic ran a hand through her short, bleached locks. "Well, um, this is highly unusual." Her gaze went back to the other medic and driver who had drifted over to chat with the remaining officers.

One of the officers said, "Barton, let them go in their own cars. We'll give them a police escort to the hospital. Probably better all the way around."

The medic gave a short nod. She pivoted and walked back to the ambulance. Nora watched the stiffness in the woman's shoulders; sorry for her annoyance, but if it helped Ellie even a little, then they could deal with breaking protocol.

The officer who'd sent the unhappy medic on her way turned to face the group. "I guess we'll all head out to St. George's. I'll lead the way. You can follow me. We'll debrief you once we get there. Grieg"—he pointed to the other officer—"will follow you."

Nana grumbled under her breath about procedures.

The shadow of a large owl blocked the moon as it cruised over their heads. "Esme," Nora's grandfather hissed, "behave. We have to get these girls to the hospital. Later, you can rant. Why you never saw the inside of a holding cell baffles me."

"Who says I haven't? You don't know everything, Buell."

Her grandmother kissed Nora on the forehead, and her weathered hand rested on Ellie's cheek. "Be at peace, child. The worst is over."

Ellie's stiff body relaxed in Nora's arms. Nora kept one arm hooked around her waist just to keep her upright. Her mother joined her, wrapping an arm around Ellie's other side. The two of them half-walked and partially dragged her to the sedan.

Her father directed car assignments. "Leah, Tonya, Ethan, go with the Nana and Grandpa. Clayton, you ride shotgun with me."

The cars crept down the dirt road in a ragtag line until they hit the paved road, where their escorts turned on the sirens and lights, clearing the way but never going above fifty. They probably doubted her grandparents could keep up.

The lights and buildings flashed by Nora's window. It was almost like another world, one she'd left not so long ago.

It must be even odder for Ellie, who had lost months of her life. Nora's arm stayed wrapped around her new friend. The now-sleeping girl's head rested against her shoulder. Nana had a knack for putting people at ease.

The sleeping girl resurrected memories of Abby. There had to be something Nora could do for Abby. Her family didn't know the truth. All they knew was one day she'd had a psychotic break and hadn't spoken again. It was time for Abby to break out of her self-imposed shell. Nora possessed the hammer to help break through her calcified exterior.

The hospital passed in a whirl of stainless-steel counters, white-coated individuals, and an antiseptic odor as they were hustled through emergency as priority patients with an entourage that included uniformed officers. People probably thought they were criminals of some sort. A weary-looking blond woman sprang up at their entrance.

Her gait and direction sent her on a collision course for Ellie. A policeman stepped in front of her, blocking her. Her head popped around the officer's body.

"That's my baby, Ellie." Her voice carried as they were rushed through swinging doors. "That's my baby. I must see her. I thought she was dead."

The last door thumped into place. Ellie stayed glued to Nora's side, whispering. "I can't see her. What do I say? I'm not the girl who left for work so many weeks ago. As the door shut, she whispered to herself, "Might as well be dead."

Nora gave the whispering female a squeeze. "I heard that. I know how you feel, but believe it or not, you can get past this, too. Make up a story if you want. I used to worry about all the people in my high school knowing. Ironically, only months later I cut ties with all of them. That's how little they mattered in my life."

Ellie shivered, wrapping her blanket tighter. "Easy for you to say. You're strong. You have a family that cares about you."

Nora inhaled deeply. How could she make Ellie understand? Putting both her hands-on Ellie's shoulders, she turned her, putting them eye to eye. "First, I don't ever want to hear you say you're not strong. You survived. That makes you very strong. People who love you will always love you. This doesn't affect how they perceive you. Be careful that you do not allow your self-perception to be altered."

Ellie's teeth worried her bottom lip. "I know you're right. Still, I feel so dirty."

Wrapping her arms around her, Nora hugged her hard. "That will pass, too. Trust me."

A nurse attempted to separate them to direct Ellie into a room for an examination. Ellie's grip on Nora tightened. No way should Ellie experience a medical exam with strangers probing her body and discussing her as if she weren't in the room. It was another reason why many rape victims hesitated to report the crime.

Nora looked at the nurse's name badge. "Nurse Cooper, I think you can understand that Ellie has been through a great deal. The examination, while required, is not only uncomfortable, but also emotionally trying. I want to be in the room with her."

The nurse nodded, flashed an understanding smile and handed her a cloth gown. "See if you can get your friend into this."

Nora accepted the gown with one arm still wrapped around Ellie. Nora turned to ask her mother to inform Ellie's mom to get clothes for her, but all her family was gone, including Clayton. Her gaze swiveled around the small room, expecting them to appear. The nurse, noticing her distress, answered her unspoken question.

"They aren't allowed back here until after you've been processed."

Ellie mumbled, "Processed—whatever that means." She shrugged her thin shoulders.

Of course, Nora knew that. She'd worked in hospitals enough to know that. They were outside the door somewhere, milling around with all the other anxious loved ones. "I should have remembered. I guess I expected—no, never mind."

She searched her mind for Clayton, finding nothing but her own thoughts. Did that mean with him here in this century with her they could no longer share thoughts? They'd have to communicate the way other people do with all their garbled messages and things not said. "I can't believe it."

Ellie nodded in agreement. "Your grandmother wasn't one to give up easily. I thought my mother was loud, but your grandmother was telling him how it was and waving her cane. They might have even called security if it wasn't for your grandfather."

Strange, Nora hadn't noticed any of that. Ellie's abuse and thoughts of Abby consumed her. She'd often wondered what she'd end up doing with her degree, and now she knew. Her purpose was to help rape victims.

Shaking out the gown, she held it out to Ellie. "You need to put this on. They'll take your clothes for evidence. I'm sure you don't ever want to see them again anyway."

Ellie took the gown and turned to undress, talking all the while. "You got that right. I doubt I'll ever wear a pair of shorts or bikini top again."

Nora wanted to tell her she would, but she hadn't herself. She'd avoided all clothes that were even vaguely feminine, convinced that the smallest ruffle or display of skin would turn men into beasts. The nurse picked up the discarded clothing with latex gloved hands and bagged it for evidence.

A female doctor handled the examination, putting Ellie at ease. The doctor also solidified Nora's desire to work at a rape-crisis center or even in an emergency room. Brutalized women did not do well with men examining them, even one with medical intentions.

Ellie held on to Nora's hand all through the exam. The doctor didn't talk too much. The few comments she made were about how brave and clever they'd been to escape the maniac. Nora was about ready to explain that the police had rescued them after following Clayton's tip, but she didn't.

A mental replay of a burned Lloyd hopping down the steps unrolled, along with the fight that had followed, rubbing salt into his burns via the sauerkraut, and the hammer to the head. The man had been down and out. The two of them could have run out of the house. They'd have been in the middle of who knows where, but she had confidence they'd have found a way to civilization. Together, they'd conquered their fears enough to fight back. *Concentrate on the solution, not the problem*, was her grandfather's advice. It had worked for them.

CHAPTER SIXTEEN

ELLIE'S FATHER STOOD in the lobby, looking both lost and weary. His clothes were rumpled, his hair mussed, not a bit like the debonair charmer Nora had expected from his daughter's description. The only way she knew it was him was the way his face lit up when Ellie walked through the ER doors dressed in blue scrubs the nurse had found for her.

Nora touched her friend's hand, passing her the scrap of paper on which she'd scribbled her phone number. Her intention was to stay in touch, but she wouldn't be surprised if Ellie chose not to. After all, Nora represented a very bad experience in her life. She would want to forget everything associated with that time. If that were the case, Nora would understand.

The hospital had allowed only the mothers in after the initial examination, while a parade of relatives crowded the already busy waiting area. Nana probably had already worn out her welcome with her previous behavior. Nora's family stood as she exited with her mother. She watched as Ellie ran to her father's arms. Tears rolled down the man's face, not the actions of a man who abandoned his daughter along with his former wife.

Her own family stood with expectant faces, reminding her of when Leah and Granddad had returned from the past only a few years ago. Speaking of the past, where was Clayton?

As if hearing his name, he came around the corner. Spotting her, he broke into a jog to get to her, where he wrapped his arms around her and swung her around.

The admitting nurse stood and shook a finger in their direction. "None of that." The twinkle in her eye revealed her true feelings, despite her words. Laughing, Clayton put her down. Turning to the nurse, he placed one hand over his heart.

"Forgive me, ma'am. The sight of my beloved overwhelmed me. To spare you from the joy of our reunion, we'll depart."

The nine of them crowded out the door, practically emptying the waiting room. A brief parking lot consultation had them all heading to the pancake house for something to eat. Nora attempted to demur explaining she must look and smell horrible, but her family pushed aside her worries.

Her brother Ethan wrinkled up his nose as if sniffing. "Not too bad,

I've smelled plenty worse."

A quick spray of perfume, a comb through her short hair and the hood-ie sweatshirt Leah handed her made her ready to eat breakfast closer to midnight.

Over pumpkin pancakes and sausage, Tonya revealed how she'd discovered Nora was missing. "It was probably eleven when I realized you weren't home. It didn't seem right. I called the diner. Brandon answered the phone and told me you'd stomped off in a tizzy. I explained to him that you had no way to get home but the bus, and the buses stopped running at ten."

Clayton speared the last bite of his pancake and gestured with the syrup-laden morsel. "This Brandon is no friend of yours. He doesn't care enough to make sure you get on the bus safely."

Nora felt obligated to protest but reconsidered. Brandon had made sure other nights. Mentioning how thoughtful Brandon could be might only rile Clayton. Ogden, on the other hand, was a jerk who wouldn't have made the effort to make sure she was safe. Still, if Brandon and Ogden had noticed her absence earlier, the police search could have started much sooner. Clayton had jumped centuries without a second thought.

"Did Brandon say anything after that?" Nora asked.

Tonya shook her head. "I did get a call back from a waitress."

Nora gestured for her to continue. "What did she say?"

The server hovered nearby, refilling coffee cups. After she stepped away from the table, Tonya continued, "She walked in when Brandon and Ogden were arguing, attracting the attention of most of the people in the diner. Bonnie was leaning on the counter watching, too, and saw this creepy guy get up to go to the restroom. She remembered because she didn't want to meet up in the narrow hallway between the kitchen entrance and the restrooms. She waited for him to come out, but he never did."

"Did no one else notice?" It seemed like it should have been such a no-brainer.

Grandfather felt the need to comment. "People seldom notice what is right in front of them."

Nana and her father agreed. Tonya looked at the three, grumbling about unobservant people. "The waitress who worked the next shift, I forgot her name, mentioned it to both Brandon and Bonnie. The man left his money on the table for the food, which meant Bonnie didn't care too much, how he left. They did find your backpack still in the kitchen with your bus pass, wallet, house keys, and phone. They knew then you hadn't left on your own."

Clayton wrapped his arm around Nora, pulling her closer under the disapproving eyes of both her father and grandfather. Her father cleared his throat, but her sweetie left his arm where it was and asked, "What took so long to locate this evil man?"

Her mother joined the conversation. "The police called him a person of interest. They didn't know he took Nora. No one knew his name or where he lived. Even if he had given out any information, it could all have been false, considering he'd planned ahead of time to take Nora."

The memory of the elderly couple warning her and taking her home came to mind. "Oh, oh, there was a couple who runs the metaphysical book shop in the south end, the one with past-life readings and aura photographs."

Nana's brow wrinkled for a moment before she announced, "Martha and Owen Carlisle."

"That's right." Nora had forgotten their names but remembered they knew her grandmother. "I was going to have some past-life readings done so I could better understand how Clayton and I were connected."

Clayton's lips touched her hair, causing her brother to exclaim, "Please, some of us are still eating."

Instead of Ethan's behavior offending him, Clayton laughed. "Become accustomed to it."

Her brother grinned but continued eating to the point of reaching for Leah's sausage. She slapped his hand, but then placed the link on her brother's plate.

"Anyhow," Nora said, trying to gather her thoughts. "They wanted to tell me something bad was headed my way. They drove me home because they didn't want me to take the bus. The two sweet dears acted like they worked for a secret government agency as they drove through the streets as if we were being followed."

Grandfather quipped between sips of coffee, "They were probably being followed, not you."

That seemed odd, but she chose not to reply to it. "All they wanted was for me to be safe. Martha kept saying something about how she had to protect the granddaughter of Esmeralda Hare."

Nana slammed her cane on the floor for emphasis. "Damn right. Now, why didn't they protect you?"

"They tried. Owen checked the apartment. The couple even did a protection spell on every window and door. Of course, I left and went to work. It was my day off, too. The new guy they hired never works. He's always calling in. Come to think of it, it's odd Lloyd was there that night at all. He usually wasn't when I don't work." Nora took a sip of water, turning the idea over in her head.

Leah looked up from eating. "Who's Lloyd?"

"The kidnapper." Nora picked up a bacon strip and chewed on it. It was rubbery and fatty. Obviously, the cook did not understand the concept of crisp bacon. "Doug, as a cook, is useless. It didn't seem like the man wanted to work. He'd been around for weeks occasionally working but usually not. The fact he wasn't fired bears witness to how hard it is to get someone to work swing shift."

Her father directed his gaze at her. "Explain. I can see the wheels turning. Share your thoughts."

"Well, I hate to accuse an innocent man. No one can figure out why Doug even works at the diner. He is always coming up with excuses why he can't. Once or twice might be believable, but not all the time. I had to work that night because he called in with an excuse. From what my co-workers said, Lloyd came in only on the days I worked, apparently the better to harass me. Everyone noticed it, too. I'd call that night a coincidence, except Lloyd had had a syringe full of ketamine, what had to have been chloroform, and his van parked outside of the diner's back door. Sounds premeditated to me."

A white business card rested on her father's plate as he punched out the number on his phone. "Detective, remember you said I should give you a call if we thought of something."

Clayton whispered in her ear. "Your family is the vengeful type. Makes a person pay for hurting one of their own. Whatever happened to your attackers?"

Nora looked down at her plate. "I try not to think about them. A friend told me they lost every game that season, but that hardly seems enough. I guess the few who were counting on scholarships lost them."

His hand tightened on hers as he half-whispered, "Tell me their names, I'll hunt them down. No one hurts you without retribution. I don't care if was in the past."

Before she could answer, Nana rapped his legs with her cane. "I like your spirit. As for the boys, none of them came to a good end. One is in prison due to a sexual-battery charge."

Nora snorted, not surprised. She wanted to ask whom but was unsure if she could even attach the names to faces anymore.

Holding up one finger as if remembering, Nana continued, "Another one was murdered, not sure who did the killing or the why behind it. I have my suspicions, though."

Clayton squeezed Nora's hand before murmuring, "Sounds like I'm not the only person seeking revenge."

Leah interrupted. "I remember that case. They ruled it was self-defense, even though the circumstances were suspicious."

Nora nodded at her grandmother to continue. If anyone knew, Nana would. She had more contacts than the FBI with both living and dead informants.

The waitress hovered as she poured coffee, her eyes growing large. Unashamed of her eavesdropping, she added, "Are you talking about the cursed football players? Saw a special on television the other night, one of those news magazine things."

Grandfather raised both eyebrows as he inquired, "What did the program say?"

Putting the coffeepot down, the waitress raised both hands to gesture as she talked. "Local football team starters were bound for big college scholarships. Rumor was they were bullies. Beat up the nerdy boys and assaulted their share of girls, too. The only problem was people tended not to believe the girls because the football players were golden boys with rich parents."

Seeing everyone's attention was on her, the server smiled and continued. She looked behind her to see if anyone was watching from the kitchen before, she leaned forward to convey the rest of her story. "One of the former students from the school called the football team cursed. At some point, they assaulted the wrong person, or people. Everything went wrong from them. Losing games, they should have won. One died in a motorcycle accident. Another one, driving drunk, is now paralyzed. You were talking about the others. None of them came out okay. That's why people say they were cursed."

The waitress reached for her coffeepot and gave an emphatic nod. "I figure they got what was coming to them. You can't do that much evil and not expect some consequences."

Her father slapped the table. "Amen to that, sister."

His unexpected reaction caused the family to erupt into laughter, except for Nora. Had she caused all the misfortune that had happened to her attackers? Did that make her an evil person?

Clayton's half-hearted laughter stilled as he noticed her silence. Placing his head next to her bent head, he whispered, "Never blame yourself. Evil sows its own consequences. We both know the fates will have their way."

Her teeth worried her bottom lip. She'd like to believe Clayton. It would certainly resolve some of her guilt. "You don't understand. I cursed them."

His fingers untangled from hers. Did he find her repugnant now? Using both hands, Clayton framed her face and gently pulled it up for her to look into his caring eyes. "Let me ask you this, Nora, my love. Did you fight your attackers?"

Why was he asking her that? He had to know she'd fought. "Yes. I did." She forced the words out through gritted teeth. This is why she'd chosen not to go to the police. She was afraid of questions like this. "I kicked, screamed, and bit, but there were so many of them. They laughed at my efforts."

Tears blurred her vision. As she blinked to hold them back, Clayton's thumbs wiped away those that escaped. "Now, sweet darling, I do not want to make you cry. All I wanted for you to see was that your curses were only a way of fighting back. As for them harming those monsters, I imagine many have cursed them long and hard. Together, all the curses and strong emotions may have hastened their consequences, which is as it should be."

Nana raised her cane over the table to nudge at Clayton's shoulder. "Are you making my granddaughter cry? Keep in mind, we are not the forgiving sort. Very vengeful. Break Nora's heart and it will do you no good to hide in the past, because I will find you."

Sometimes family could make you want to drop into the floor, no matter how well meaning.

Clayton gave Nora a kiss on the cheek. "Nora is my soul mate, and she has been the last seven lifetimes. Destiny has made it so."

Her Irish charmer faced down her daunting Nana. Her grandfather folded his hands, and his countenance took on a somber expression. "Been riding on destiny all these centuries? Well, it ends here. You have to prove yourself worthy of my granddaughter."

Her family had gone all nineteenth century on her. Clayton didn't seem too disturbed. He stroked his chin before asking, "What would you have me to do to prove myself?"

Her father was the first to answer. "How would you provide for my daughter?"

Great Goddess, she wanted to hide her face. There was no way Clayton could provide for her. He'd come from another time and had no skills to work in this century. That didn't matter to her, though. If all he did was love her that would be enough. Eventually, he could learn new skills, maybe even go into medicine.

Clayton removed his arm and placed both hands on the table. When he spoke, his voice no longer held a trace of laughter. "I've known about Nora longer than she realized. I was waiting for her in the wrong century. Some people assumed that the Irish are shiftless, given to drinking and fighting. I'm not. In fact, I've been blessed by my fey grandmother with the gift of knowing. Sometimes, it is what card to play in a poker game. Other times what stock to invest in. These skills allowed me to acquire wealth that I squirreled away in different places from hiding it in the ground to having a trust made up for a Nora Carpenter not yet born. It is not as unheard of as you might think. People set up trusts all the time for children not born. I also buried a box of gold in your backyard."

Her mother gave him a dubious look. "How did you know where to bury it? How do you know someone hasn't dug it up?"

They were probably the same questions Nora would have asked if she'd had a chance. It would be interesting to hear his answers.

Clayton's familiar smile reappeared. "The plot of land your house sits on has stayed in the same family. My family actually I bought the property, I buried my treasure, and asked my cousin to watch over it. Not the same house, but pretty much in the same location."

Nora's mouth dropped open. Who was this wheeler-dealer from times gone by? Where had her gentle healer gone?

Clayton reached for her hand and entangled their fingers. "Did you truly think I managed on the occasional chicken or firewood a grateful family gave me?"

His question caught her unawares, because she'd thought just that. "Well, yes, I did. I would have loved you as a simple traveling healer. I did love you."

He brought her hand up to his lips for a kiss. "Do you not love me anymore, then?"

Aware of all the interested stares and listening ears, she decided to demur. Why announce her feelings in front of everyone? "We haven't even had a real date yet." Thinking of an older word he'd understand, she added, "You haven't courted me."

Still holding her hand, his eyes twinkled as he gazed into hers. "If it's a courtship you're wanting, I promise you a grand one. But I hope not to use up all my gold wooing you, especially when you had a crisis clinic in mind."

"How did you know?" Here she'd thought he couldn't read her mind in present time. Apparently, he wasn't as heavy-handed about it when they were both in the same time.

Clayton winked, causing Nana to hoot. "Reminds me of you, Buell, back when you were young and handsome."

Her family laughed at Nana's remark, except for Grandfather. He looked affronted. Holding a hand to his chest, he asked, "I'm still handsome, right?"

Every one of them rushed to assure him he was the most handsome ceremonial magician they knew, which catered to his vanity. He settled back into his seat with a contented expression.

Nora's mother elbowed her father. "I am going to enjoy watching this courtship."

Tonya chimed in from the other end of the table. "I know I am, especially from the girl who was not going to have anything to do with men."

Clayton quickly corrected. "She is still not going to have anything to do with men, just me."

They all chuckled, as intended. Nora looked around at her family, including Clayton and Tonya. The things she'd worried about amazed her when only family truly mattered. Well, and love, of course, and her health.

Her grandfather's face registered a measure of chagrin as he sat ramrod straight. "I am the only ceremonial magician you know."

Then there was humor, too. She could live well on love and laughter. Very well.

Epilogue

I T WAS HARD to believe it had been a year since she and Ellie had first met. An electronic buzz alerted her that Ellie had arrived. "She's here."

Clayton, checking off supplies on his clipboard, stopped and looked up with a grin. "I'll stay here and allow the two of you your reunion.

"You're the best." She kissed her handsome husband's cheek before dashing down the hallway like a giddy six-year-old instead of behaving like a sedate director of a sexual-trauma clinic and rehab center.

Security at the clinic was tight. Not just anyone made it past the lobby doors. Traumatized women didn't need people trooping around making a difficult situation worse.

A confident, smiling Ellie waited, along with her father, in the cozy lobby crowded with overstuffed furniture and live plants. A large aquarium full of colorful fish took up most of the area next to the reception desk. She turned to the worried-looking man. "See? Nora's here, I'm fine. Come back in a couple of hours."

Ellie's father looked unsure, but then started for the door. His hand rested on the door as he turned to look at Nora. "Keep her safe."

Ellie rolled her eyes. "He's like that all the time. I swear, my mother is worse. No way I'm going away to college, either."

Nora hugged the still-talking woman. "I will," she assured her father as he exited. Addressing her friend, she added, "Of course, they worry about you. They feel responsible even if they aren't. They're acting out of guilt. You seem to be dealing with everything fairly well."

"I'm okay." She grimaced a little. "I didn't really want to go away to college. I prefer to stay home, but I don't want my parents to know that. It would probably make them even more overprotective."

Nora nodded, totally understanding. "I'm glad you came. Your continual contribution to our rape recovery group is a big help, especially today."

"Why today?" Ellie's eyebrows lifted with curiosity.

Nora motioned to the left corridor and turned in that direction as she spoke. "Remember my friend, Abby?"

"Yes." Ellie lengthened the word as Nora pushed open a door.

A young woman reading a book looked up at their entrance and smiled. "I see you brought me company."

"Ellie, I'd like you to meet my best friend, Abby."

The suddenly silent Ellie looked from Nora to Abby, then back again. Thrusting out her hand to the seated Abby, she said, "I'm thrilled to meet you. Better yet, talk to you."

Abby took the outstretched hand. "Me, too. It's been awhile since I could communicate with my visitors. Thanks to my parents' devotion and Nora's concentrated efforts, I found my way home." She sighed deeply and released Ellie's hand. "For a long time, I was wandering around in some mental fog. This one"—she gestured to Nora—"she's been saving the world and conducting an across-the-centuries romance while I slept."

Nora tucked a hank of Abby's hair behind her ear. "That I did. I was waiting for your assistance with the women's center. I'll need your help, too, Ellie."

Abby stood up, swaying slightly as if she wasn't used to standing. "I'm here now. I believe this calls for a group hug." The three of them wrapped their arms around each other, laughing, and crying, too. That continued the healing for all of them.

Love, acceptance, and finding your purpose comprised the best medicine of all.

THE END

DECLARATION

PAGAN EYES, BOOK 3

BY
RAYNA NOIRE

CHAPTER ONE

E THAN HID IN a dark doorway, panting, while he considered his options. No way Caulb and his felons in training would give up once they figured out, he outsmarted them. Shouts echoing in the cavernous hallway alerted him. Danger was closer than he'd thought. *Great.* Weren't schools supposed to be crawling with staff members looking out for the welfare of the students? Yeah, right. Too bad, he'd left his cell phone in Leah's car. Not that it would have done him much good since the school used a dampener to keep students from texting in class.

If high schools were a theme park, then tenth grade was the roller coaster. It started uneventfully. The most stressful part had been fending off all the teachers, who wanted to redirect him to the middle school, assuming, since he was shorter than a good portion of the girls, he wasn't old enough for high school.

The voices veered off to the left, down the science corridor. A window of opportunity opened. Ethan shot up the hallway to the gym, where the wrestling team practiced earlier. His father had nagged him to try out for the wrestling team. Even the coach asked him to give it a go, because they needed someone in his weight class. Most of his matches would forfeit due to not having anyone in his class or he'd end up wrestling a girl, the coach said. *No thanks.* He already had enough things to be teased about.

The dimly lit hallway stretched as if it were endless. Maybe this was a dream and he'd wake up soon. Caulb's voice filtered down the hallway. His bass timber was menacing enough without the eerie quality of it bouncing off the metal lockers and taking on an almost mechanical sound. Caulb was a deadly droid, on the mission of annihilating anyone who didn't conform to his standards. Unfortunately, no tip sheet existed to specify what his standards were. All Ethan knew was, he didn't meet them.

The gym doors came into view. *Sanctuary.* He swung the door open with a gasp, unsure what he was going to say. All he had to do was stick close to the coach. Maybe he could say he needed to use the phone to call home. His eyes darted around the empty gym. Where was everyone? An image of the wrestlers in their spandex suits came to mind. They were dressed in their team apparel when he'd seen them earlier, which meant they were probably at an away meet, and why no one was in the gym. The lights illuminated the wooden floor and abandoned mats.

He took a few steps into the gym, stopped, and turned slowly, seeing no sign of following bullies, or an almost friend who stabbed him in the back. His lips pulled down into a frown, remembering the different expectations he'd had for the night, much different. The choir teacher, Mr. Zimmer, asked him and Brendon to practice for Saturday's choral competition. The man was almost giddy at the prospect of the two of them taking gold. Washington Heights' reputation didn't involve any of the arts. The saying about the school of hard knocks must have originated with Washington Heights. There might be an adult inside. His hand was on the locker room door when he heard Caulb.

"Look, the little faggot is heading for the boys locker room. No surprise."

Ethan's blood froze in his veins, paralyzing him. No telling what would happen to him with Caulb and his crew. Mr. Zimmer had left in a rush when he received a call from his very pregnant wife. A janitor should be around, but none in sight, and no telling when he would get there if he screamed for help. Ethan couldn't even count on the non-existent janitor's help. With his luck, he'd probably be the father of one of the four boys approaching him.

Caulb taunted, while flexing his oversized arms. His arms belonged on an Olympic weightlifter on steroids. The football team would have benefitted from his brawn, but he, unfortunately, would have to pass a few subjects to qualify.

"Look at the little queer. Too scared to move. Probably pissed his pants."

His small group of bullies in training laughed hysterically. Of course, they laughed. Their only goal was to keep Caulb from turning on them. Brendon trailed them, looking apologetic and lost. Well, at least his almost friend wasn't going to end up beaten to a pulp.

Caulb fisted his hand and pounded it into his opposing hand as he came closer. As a threatening gesture, it worked. The only thing Ethan had going for him was his intelligence.

"Time's up, gay wad. Don't even know what a dick is for."

In a moment of calculated bravado, he used the gossip he'd overheard about the bully's mother. "That's not what your momma said last night."

The other boys snickered, as Caulb turned red. He ran straight at Ethan with death in his eyes. It wasn't hard to guess whose death it was going to be either. Ethan waited until the last minute, dropped, and rolled away from the charging bully. Gaining his feet, he rushed out the door, listening to Caulb curse after punching his fist into the steel locker room door. An outraged bellow sped his flight toward the exterior door. The sound of running in all directions indicating his posse was scattering for safety. It was hard to say whom the enraged bully would turn on.

All he needed to do was outpace the rest of them, like outrunning a lion on the savanna. The slowest antelope would be the one caught. It wouldn't be him today. Part of Ethan hoped it wouldn't be Brendon. Hitting the door bar, he burst out of the school at full speed. The setting sun gilded everything with golden light.

The glowing sight stopped him in his tracks. His nightmare scenario should be composed of deep darkness with flashes of red. Instead, everything outside the school was normal. The grunts of the football team practicing reached his ears, along with the sound of a reedy soprano singing about returning to the Goddess. He recognized that voice. Leah, his sister, sat in her vintage compact car singing along with the music. Of course, she was supposed to pick him up. *Rescue.*

He startled when one of the exterior doors opened, it only took him five strides to reach the car and pull the door open.

"Go, go now. *Burn rubber.*" He slumped down in his seat as if his personal bogeyman might start peppering the car with machine gun fire.

Leah, not understanding his need for speed, after checking her rear-view mirror, pulled leisurely away from the curb. Instead of flooring it, she felt the need to question his actions.

"What's your problem? Why did you feel the need to come tearing out of the building as if it was on fire?"

Ethan inched up enough to check the mirror himself. Yep, they stood in the street watching the car leave. Thank the Goddess none of them possessed a license, although that small legality wouldn't have stopped them if they had a car to drive. *What if they followed him home?*

"Leah, let's not go straight home." Ethan tried to think of something that might appear reasonable to his suspicious older sister. "We could stop for ice cream."

She braked for the red light and gave him an odd look. Oh great, he had forgotten about her lactose intolerance.

He tried again. "I have a library book that's overdue. We need to go to the library."

Leah continued to make all the appropriate turns toward home. A quick glance assured him Caulb and his gang was not following on foot or using a 'borrowed' vehicle. Thank the Lord and Lady for that.

His sister's hand landed on his arm and squeezed hard. "Tell me, what's going on? You were happy when I dropped you off earlier. You had on so much cologne I practically choked. You were excited about seeing your new friend." Her voice emphasized the word friend in a playful fashion.

Being read so easily was embarrassing. Leah and Nana were the two people he was closest to in his family. Nora was ten years older than him, which always made her seem grown up and distant in his eyes. His grandpa had disappeared into the past for the first ten years of his life. His mother loved him, but her entry into nursing school had made her too busy to spend much time with him.

As the only boy, she probably expected him to spend more time with his dad, the man who seemed continually disappointed in him. He never said it, but Ethan could tell. The best they managed was watching television shows filled with explosions, car chases, and barely dressed women. It was hard to swallow his urge to ask if something else was on. That would only cause his father to give him a baffled look. Only Leah never expected anything from him.

Leah might call him an annoying little brother, but he was still her little brother. He remembered when he was ten and came home with a black eye. Leah hunted down the culprit and had a talk. 'Just a talk' was as much as she'd confessed after the fact.

Then there was Nana, his grandmother, the resident clairvoyant you had no secrets from, but she usually kept them to herself. Could be that Leah could give him some advice on how to handle the situation. He couldn't exactly bring it up with his father. It would be just another way he failed as the only son.

"Yeah, that friend, I thought I had. Stabbed me in the back. A regular Brutus. For Pete's sake, Brendon enjoys the opera. How long does he think it will be before Caulb comes after him too? He's only a tool."

Leah snorted her response as she cruised through the intersection. "Hmm, not exactly what you expected when I dropped you off."

Talk about an understatement. When Brendon showed up the second week of school, something inside Ethan shifted, bringing his life into focus. Suddenly, all the uncertainties about what he wanted fell away. Mr. Zimmer paired the two of them together for a duet. Brendon's rich baritone blended well with Ethan's tenor. Rather like the two of them blended.

"I thought Brendon and I were developing a friendship. We had so much in common." His mind shifted back to the moment he saw the grinning face of his nemesis before the lights went out in the hallway outside the soundproof practice room, courtesy of Brendon. At the time, he couldn't believe his recently made friend would resort to such a stunt until Caulb entered. Brendon had directed the thug to his location without hesitation.

His only alternative was to not be where he was. Silently, he climbed on top of the upright piano and slid down the other side, making his way out of the room, while Caulb and his buddies slammed around in the corner where he had been moments earlier.

Leah turned the car into their neighborhood. "So, your friend, Brendon did what to stab you in the back?"

What did he do? Besides turning him over to the one person who was intent on cracking his skull, open like an egg. His simple action, not only allowed Caulb the opportunity to pulverize him, but it also made him doubt everything he thought he knew. How could he explain the life he thought he had, did not exist?

"I thought he was my friend. I thought he liked me. I thought we were close and clicked on a deeper level, but obviously, I was wrong. I must have been wrong. Why would he team up with that redneck Caulb to run me down like a hen in the chicken yard?"

Leah's nostrils flared, as her hands tighten on the steering wheel. "Someone needs to do something about Caulb and his bully friends. Doesn't your school have a no bullying policy?"

Ethan normally didn't have a problem with bullies since he was a likable person. In grade school, he entertained his classmates with his clever wit and a few simple magic tricks. Middle school was more of the same, especially since he hung with so many of the popular girls. The male students wanted to be his friend to get closer to the girls. One of the reasons he had so many female friends was because he understood them. They often shared similar interests.

"Bully policy, Ha!" He snorted his disdain. "They plastered a few posters in the hall. The captain of the academic bowl ended up, slammed against one of those posters. Not exactly the result the administration expected."

Leah flicked on the blinker as she turned into the driveway. "I don't like this. Something needs to be done. I think you need to tell Mom and Dad. They could go talk to your principal."

The image of Caulb slamming him to the ground to extract retribution from whatever punishment the school deemed appropriate made him shudder. Most likely, they'd do nothing. Throw up their hands and declare it was a case of one student's word against the other. All he'd have is an even bigger target on his back. "No! Please don't tell them."

He must have shouted the words. Leah's head whipped around so fast she almost hit the garage until he yelped at her to watch out. The car jerked as she slammed on the brakes. They both sighed in relief as the car shuddered to a stop mere inches from the aluminum door.

Spearing one hand through her long hair, Leah half mumbled to herself. "Glad no one parked in the driveway today."

The lack of cars meant he'd forgo all the questions about his day. His grandfather would ask him what three new things he learned that day. Sometimes, it was hard to think of three things to tell him. Sometimes, it made him wonder if he was even learning anything at school. What was the use of attending? Every day presented an opportunity to have an oversized menace pursue him as if he was a mouse in a maze. Maybe he was part of some bizarre social experiment.

His sister shifted the car into park and removed the keys. She had her hand on the door when a look crossed her face as if she saw something wonderful. "I've got it. A different school for you. That's it."

The idea appealed to him. It would be nice to go somewhere free of Caulb. His spirits perked up a bit. He straightened up, thinking what it would be like to go to school without fear, to not have to choose his path through the school to avoid isolated hallways and dark corners. Nana managed to confuse the issue at registration, so he didn't have physical education, but that wouldn't last long. The curriculum required all students to have PE to be well-rounded individuals. "That would be amazing."

Leah turned in her seat toward him, her face animated. "Just think, no bullies. Maybe you could find a school where you could pursue an area of interest. What do you think you'd like to do?"

The spark of possibility grew in his chest, sending out streamers of energy to the rest of his body. He would have a chance to pursue something he wanted to do, instead of trying to follow everyone else's plan for his life. It was hard; forcing his square peg personality into the round hole life allotted him. What would he like to do?

An opportunity to choose, it almost overwhelmed him. "There's the theatre, art, choir. I like science, especially environmental science. English lit."

A snort of laughter interrupted his recital. Leah gave his shoulder a slight shove. "You, English, I wasn't even sure you knew how to read."

Grinning, he shoved her back. "Ha-ha, you should be a comedian. I've been reading a great deal lately. You don't know everything about me."

Leah's smile flickered, and then went out. "I know more than you might think."

Damn, he kept forgetting about his sister's ability to read people. Her skill had shown itself when she tumbled back in time. She confided it was unreliable at best in the present, showing her people's thoughts, she would rather not know, while keeping mum on others. The family assumed her skill would last as long as she needed it, but Leah had never mentioned, if it had left totally, which made him wonder.

At school, he'd been very careful to keep his doubts and questions private. At times, he wondered what was wrong with him, since he was unlike the other boys, consumed with sports and violence. He instead enjoyed helping Nana grow seeds and nurture plants.

By the age of ten, other boys were starting to notice the prettiest girls. He already knew the girls because they were his friends. He admired their beautiful, shiny long hair. His goal wasn't to touch their hair, but have his hair look as gorgeous. What was wrong with wanting to be clean and well groomed, even if it didn't rank up there with being tall and muscular? A school change could land him in a place where he'd meet others with similar interests.

It was possible. Once a year, his family journeyed across the state to attend a Pagan Pride Day gathering. His father insisted the festival couldn't be in their state since he might lose his job if his employer found out. During the day, Nana set up her fortune telling shop and mother assisted her. He was free to roam the grounds, taking in energy raising workshops, drumming with the drum circle, and participating in the rituals. He had stumbled across one group that consisted of young men. Their smooth, beardless faces and open expressions convinced him, they were near his age.

The five were sitting cross-legged on a patchwork quilt, passing around food. They invited him to come join them. Unsure, he sat hesitant-ly. While he usually got along with most people, he learned to avoid groups of males without the softening influences of nearby females. Males, in general, had weird bonding rituals that consisted of insulting each other, bumping bellies, punching, and hitting. He was never quite sure where the bonding ended and harassment began.

An air of ease and acceptance had shown in their faces. One boy had indicated an empty spot beside him, gesturing with a loaf of bread. Ethan had gazed at the empty spot, wanting to belong, if only for a day. Reinventing himself constantly was hard, or keeping his mouth shut on controversial topics to belong. He followed his family's lead of keeping their beliefs close. Well, make that all except Nana, who didn't care what people thought. Most were either frightened or too fascinated by her to cross the outspoken woman.

A boy with slipping glasses looked up at him, as he pushed the heavy frames back up his nose. A thought took form in Ethan's head.

Be at peace, none will harm you here.

He knew without being told the thought was not his own. Who knew there were so many telepaths? He nodded once at the telepath, before sliding into the empty space. That had been the start of the perfect afternoon.

The five boys included David, Kev, Orin, Sean, and Forrest. Orin was the boy with the glasses. He didn't speak much. Apparently, he didn't have to. A few were Wiccan followers, another Druid, still another Shamanic in his faith. Orin smiled at him.

I am Kemetic. I worship the ancient Egyptian deities. People also refer to me as being non-verbal as if I were incapable of hearing or understand-ing.

Ethan nodded his head to indicate his acknowledgement, but then he decided to try to form a thought in his head.

Orin, he started the thought as if it might go astray and enter the minds of the other four. *I know what it's like to be treated as if either you're not there or incapable of understanding.*

That's how the afternoon started, as he conversed audibly with the other four throughout the day, learning they were from nearby towns. Sean and Forrest were a couple. After hearing that information, his eyes dropped to where their fingers entwined on the blanket. A yearning washed over him, so fierce, he closed his eyes. How wonderful it must be to belong to someone. To have one person know him with all his idiosyncrasies and eclectic tastes and still like him because of it, as opposed to disliking him, must be wonderful.

I always thought it would be. Orin touched his nose indicating the thought was his.

It wasn't as if anyone else was sending him thoughts. He believed not only Leah, but his Nana and Grandfather could all read minds. They had an uncanny way of knowing things, but not once did their thoughts ever enter his mind the way Orin's did. Why was that?

Orin, why do you not speak?

Orin cocked one eyebrow playfully and smiled before replying. *At first, I had no reason to speak. My parents were so overjoyed to have a child they met my every wish before I could utter a cry. After a while, I grew used to not speaking. Then I discovered I could choose whom I wanted to communicate with by touching their minds.*

How did Orin manage to escape the school without bullies? They always seemed to seek out the different.

Answering his thought, Orin jumped to his feet, towering over Ethan. He flexed his arm to display a sizable bicep. He resumed his seat a little closer.

Not so weak, not so small, either. My parents homeschooled me until I was ten. I took karate too. My father was downsized, which meant my mother had to work. My first day in school was fifth grade. Because I was 'special', Orin paused to make air quotes. *My teachers watched me like a hawk to make sure I wasn't ridiculed.*

Would it have been better to be protected as opposed to scratch out an existence in the public system as he had? *No one bullied you?*

His new friend removed his glasses and used them to gesture. *I didn't say that. In fact, the teachers' protectiveness made me more of a challenge. Two boys cornered me in the restroom the first day.*

Images of a bloody, younger boy on the tile floor made Ethan shiver. It may have been in the past, but no less horrible. Orin gave him a slight shove.

No, no, that's not how it went. Remember, I took karate lessons. I also wore some heavy hobnailed boots to school. Only ten and I already wore a size twelve. The bullies staggered out of the bathroom. One had a busted lip, the other a bloody nose. Never bothered me again. They started calling me the silent ninja.

Laughter had bubbled in Ethan's chest, eventually breaking free. Thinking of having the tables turned on the tormenters was great. "Good for you," he said the words aloud, touching Orin's large hand. An electrical jolt met his fingertips.

What happened? He watched his friend, who looked equally stunned.

Orin reached for his hand and covered it with his. Warmth grew between their hands. Ethan's gaze stayed on their entwined hands on the patchwork quilt, trying to see the aura around them. The energy pulsated wildly. *This is where my life changes for the better.*

Leah's voice had cut into his moment. "Ethan, it's time to go. The car is already packed up."

Orin's thoughts had shouted. *You're leaving. Where do you live?*

Ohio. Ethan hated the distance the word represented. He kept his hand under Orin's, unwilling to end their connection.

Leah stood nearby and pretended to look elsewhere.

Orin's thoughts came fast, almost too fast for Ethan to answer.

When will I see you again? How can we stay in touch? Do you have an email? A phone number?

The only computer in the house belonged to his father, who occasionally allowed him to use it for homework. Because it was a work issued laptop, he forbade him to use it for social networking or looking up Pagan sites. Apparently, his company IT person tracked the usage. They might not care too much about looking up the natural resources of Guam, but did when it came to occult sites.

I don't have an actual phone of my own. I have an email address, but I can only check it when I go to the library. It's lunarknight. I know it's a little silly. My sister made it for me when I was ten. It's on..."

Orin's thought broke into his recitation. *Who is that angry looking middle-aged man staring at us? He's not your lover, is he?*

Ethan looked around to see whom Orin was talking about. His father's arms were crossed, and his lips drawn into a firm line, and his father's face grew increasingly redder. *Oh, that's my father. Lover, Ha-ha. Never even had a boyfriend.*

Before he could even finish his thought, his father grabbed his shoulder, jerking his and Orin's hands apart. "Ethan, we're leaving now."

He stumbled upright, looking back at his newfound friend, trying to memorize his features. His father kept a firm grip on his arm as he dragged him toward the car.

Orin's thoughts trailed away the closer they came to the parking lot. *Don't forget me, Ethan. I won't forget you.*

CHAPTER TWO

THE CAR DOOR slammed, shaking Ethan out of his reverie. The feel of Orin's voice took shape in his mind, warming him, making him feel not quite so alone. Hard to believe it was six months ago. Sometimes their meeting felt like only yesterday and other times, forever. His logical side pointed out he'd never see him again.

The chances of casually bumping into him were, at best, non-existent. This reasoning had propelled him toward Brendon with his ambiguous advances and endearing smile. Half the time, he wasn't sure if the traitor was hitting on him or not. Turns out, he wasn't.

Slamming car doors caused him to peer out the back window. His mother and grandmother were unloading groceries. With a sigh, he opened his door to assist them. His mother flashed him a weary smile, making him glad he chose to help. He rescinded that thought with her first question.

"How did practice go? Making any inroads with Brendon?"

How was he supposed to answer that? *I survived to be bullied another day.* "Okay, not exactly what I expected."

His mother was halfway up the path to the door. Her lack of response indicated she hadn't heard. Knowing her, she'd ask again.

Nana clutched a cane in one hand, but instead of using it, she latched onto his arm. Ethan often thought the cane was an accessory and less a necessity. Her recovery from the stroke she'd suffered was nothing short of miraculous, once her husband had returned from the past. She'd put it down to the amazing properties of love. At the rate his life was progressing, there would be no such properties in his life.

Her soft withered hand clutched his arm tighter as she leaned closer. In a soft whisper, a low sotto voice as if the neighbors stood on their steps waiting to hear what she might say, she told him, "Be patient. Your time is coming. I suspect it will be glorious."

Glorious, his heart leaped in response to the word. It was about time for something good to happen. Nana's divination skills were renown across the nation. For her paying customers, she only gave them the good news. As for the family, she felt compelled to tell them the good and bad, so they could prepare. Were there no more details, besides glorious?

Nana continued as if hearing his inquiry. "You'll go through a dark time, very dark." She shivered as if thinking about it scared her. "At times, you'll want to die, or at least expect to die. There's also a possibility you will die, if you do not make the right choices."

"Nana!" Ethan stopped walking and peered at his elderly relative.

She shook her head, refusing to deny the disconcerting words. "Do you think I want to tell you these things? No, I don't. Our family is a special one. We are marked by time itself."

"Special sucks," Ethan, mumbled more to himself.

Nana's arched eyebrow meant she heard him. Her sharp nails bit into his bare arm, getting his attention. Her dark eyes waited until she knew he was listening. "Ethan Demetrius Carpenter, don't you ever say that again. It's an honor to have so many challenges presented to our family. The Universe recognizes our strength and sets obstacles for us to surmount."

His free hand lifted to his temple to check to see if his eyes were rolling upward. Good, they weren't. Normal people feared Esmeralda Hare, his grandmother, because they were afraid of what she could do. Living with her most of his life, he was aware of what she would do. That was enough for him to school his face into a respectful demeanor, even while listening to the 'hardship is good for you' lecture.

The lecture occurred on a weekly basis, sometimes twice a week. Non-pagans thought witches conjured whatever they desired. Put hexes on people they didn't like, and flew on broomsticks. His family moved a lot to escape persecution, and worked hard for what they wanted. Often, they still didn't get it, but Nana would point out, they got what they needed.

Still, all these obstacles and possible death stuff weren't doing it for him. "Don't some people die trying to surmount obstacles?"

Planting her cane on the pavement, she tugged on his arm indicating her desire to go forward. "Yes, some do, but that is only their current life. They have many more to pass through."

"I'd kinda like to stay in this current life. I'm only fifteen. Can't say I'm done living yet. Haven't really done anything yet. Can I get out of this obstacle thing?"

Nana looked horrified. Her head swiveled right and left. Holding a finger to her lips, she shushed him. "Lower your voice. You don't want the fates to hear. They design your destiny and can cut it short if they will. What will happen has to happen. I only want you prepared."

Ethan helped his grandmother up the two steps leading to the modest front porch. Most people would call it a stoop. His mother had tried to enhance it with a concrete planter filled with petunias. The plants were long and straggly with the cooler fall temperatures threatening to snuff the life out of them. His eyes stayed on the flowers for a few seconds, while he wondered how different he was from them. Unlike the flowers, he had to protect himself from imminent death as opposed to simple seasonal change.

"What can I do to protect myself?"

His mother held open the screen door to allow them both inside. As they squeezed in past his mother, Nana chose to answer.

"I am not sure what to do to protect you from dying. I'll ask your grandfather. He's better about such matters."

His mother's sharp gasp alerted them, she had overheard. Nana looked up briefly at her daughter, shook her head, and walked away muttering, "Not sure how a daughter of mine has no ability to see into the future."

Ethan watched her hobble away, putting a little more emphasis on the hobble than usual. The woman literally threw him under the bus. He slowly turned to face his mother, who had her hands fisted on her hips and her eyes so wide, they might pop out of their sockets. He remembered reading about some man's whose did. It was rather rare, but his mother might be the second person to perform such a feat.

"Ethan Demetrius," she started, but stopped when he held up his hand.

"That's the second time since I've been home that someone has used my full name. Why did you name me Demetrius? I know Ethan is for an uncle that died." He hoped his mother would not see through his attempt to change the subject.

Her face relaxed, as did her fisted hands. "Help me get the rest of the groceries and I'll explain it to you."

The two of them managed to secure the remaining canvas bags. A small dark bag decorated with a pentacle emitted a fragrant aroma. "I see you made a stop at Witches R Us."

He made his ongoing joke as they walked inside. A small natural foods store close by also stocked herbs, candles, and essential oils for both medicine and potions. The store had a more ordinary name, something to do with earth.

His mother glanced at the bag. "Oh, that, Nana decided we needed to stop. Said something about the dimensions shifting. Major change was about to happen."

Ethan opened the cabinet door with two fingers while juggling the bags. He wanted to snort something about always being the last to know, but didn't. He didn't want to remind his mother. Instead, he continued distracting her. "You never told me about Demetrius."

"Oh, that's odd." She placed her bags on the kitchen table. "I thought I did. Sometimes, I do that. I think of something and think everyone knows what I'm thinking. Half the time with this family, they do."

His mother was so right. Psychic eavesdroppers surrounded him, but Orin had been the only one who could mentally communicate with him, making no sense. Most people thought telepathy didn't exist.

Theo, Leah's cat, began to wind around his legs as he unpacked groceries. Unlike most felines, she was not standoffish at all. It made it hard to put things away though. As he knelt to put away the canned goods in the bottom cabinet, he scratched Theo's furry head, earning the start of a full-throated purr.

"Demetrius is an old Greek name. You'll find it everywhere in history, from kings, to a lover in Shakespeare's play, Midsummer Night's Dream. I didn't name you for any of them, though. I named you after Demetrius in the Bible."

Ethan's head came up so fast at the mention of the Bible he bumped it on the cabinet opening. "Ouch!" He fell to the floor, rubbing his head.

His mother knelt beside him and ran her fingers through his hair checking for bumps. He was sure she'd find one.

"No blood, but a possible lump later. Let me get you a bag of frozen veggies." She rooted through the freezer, returning with a bag of corn to put on his abused scalp.

Sitting on the floor, clutching a bag of frozen vegetables to his head, he urged his mother to continue. "Try not to mention the Bible again, but what Demetrius did you name me after? The shock of hearing that word come out of your mouth, so casually, caused my accident."

His mother laughed as he intended. Cradling the produce in one arm, she opened the fridge and continued her explanation.

"I doubt you know much about the Bible. Demetrius showed up twice, once as a disciple. We didn't name you after him."

Ethan managed a smile, knowing his mother was staring at him. "I figured as much."

She placed the veggies in the keeper drawer as she spoke. "Oh no, there was another Demetrius mentioned. It was a very popular name at the time, almost as popular as..."

"Demetrius," he reminded her. While he did want his mother to venture as far from danger to himself as possible, he still wanted to know the story behind his middle name.

"Oh yes, that." She gave a small trill of laughter. "Demetrius is mentioned as being a silversmith who incited a riot against the Christians. He was a worshipper of the Goddess Diana. The Christians were big on tearing down all the Goddess' temples to erect churches. Demetrius wasn't cool with it. He was one of the few people willing to stand against a wave of aggressive conformation determined to wipe out all female deities. That makes him a folk hero of sorts."

He bore a hero's name. It made him feel a little different, proud even. A bag of corn on the head, however, did not make him look heroic. Standing up, he carried the corn to the freezer. He pushed his shoulders back and straightened his spine to reach his full height of five foot six inches. Even his sister, Nora, was taller than he was.

His mother's voice continued, detailing the story as she usually did. "Of course, we don't know if there ever was a silversmith named Demetrius. Considering that most of the Bible is full of folk tales and myths rewritten with different names to support the new religion. Demetrius could have been a fictional character just to add conflict. He represented an obstacle for the new converts to overcome.

At least she didn't say surmount, that was a plus. His shoulders dropped a little. Named after someone who might have never existed didn't do much for him. In the end, it worked as a distraction. Now, he could go to his room and consider how he should act when he saw Brendon again.

His mother's voice halted his escape. "Not so fast, Ethy."

Argh. She had even used his childhood name, how he referred to himself when he couldn't quite pronounce Ethan. His mother and sisters thought it was so cute they begin using it. It took years of retraining to get them to use his real name. He lived in fear they'd accidentally use it in public.

He stopped with one foot in the hall and his head turned toward the basement door. His bedroom waited at the end of the basement stairs, a half-finished refuge of two by fours and drywall. Heaving a sigh, he turned to face his mother.

She pulled out a chair from the kitchen table. Pointing to it, she ordered, "Sit."

Talk about not catching a break. He dropped into the chair, slumping slightly and splaying his legs out. The scenario would consist of his mother fussing over him and telling him to be cautious, and to watch his actions because it was all about perceptions. People tended to take the negative view of everything as opposed to the more realistic one.

Nana might lecture about great growth coming from trials, but his mother's discussions focused on perceptions. He was tired of other people's assessments of the Pagan lifestyle. Most assumed they sacrificed children, caused accidents, and danced naked under a full moon. They didn't know Jack, except for the moon part.

The scrape of the chair legs against the linoleum floor indicated his mother sitting. She rested her head in a propped-up hand and stared. It wasn't an angry, condemning stare. Instead, it was full of love. He could almost see the love spilling out of her in waves.

"Ethan, you realize you'll always be my son. I will always love you. It doesn't matter to me if you're gay."

What? He blinked a few times. He pinched his leg to make sure he wasn't asleep. No, it hurt which meant he wasn't asleep. "Wait, Mom, I never said I was gay. What makes you think that?"

His mother rolled her eyes and sighed. "Okay, maybe I jumped the gun there. Didn't let you come out on your own, but I figured this was what all the drama was about, right?"

She was right, mostly. Ethan bit his lip. This wasn't how he wanted to announce it. He had never really thought of a way. In time, he thought he'd find a romantic partner. They'd start spending time together, and everyone would figure it out on their own without any uncomfortable scenes. After all, no one ever has a big scene to announce heterosexuality.

"Half-way, I'm getting some grief at school about not being masculine enough. Then Nana tells me some cryptic prediction about a glorious outcome, but first I must remove obstacles and walk through the valley of death, or something. It didn't make much sense." He slowly shook his head, realizing half the things Nana said never made sense on the surface.

Clarity usually came after you'd experienced them, which was usually a tad too late. Sometimes, her predictions were akin to reading Nostradamus' writings. They could mean anything, depending on who was interpreting.

His mother sat across from Ethan, looking concerned, but not disturbed. It didn't matter to her if he was gay. He never thought it would matter due to her participation in the Pagan Community. There were groups within the network exclusively for Pagan males who were also gay. Most people would assume it was some sort of hookup club. Some men probably did date, but a gay Wiccan or gay Druid needed an entirely different type of support as opposed to just being gay or just Wiccan.

His mother opened her mouth, then closed it, then gave him an apologetic look before mumbling, "I know what you mean. Mother utters these pronouncements with such certainty; I'm unwilling to ask her what she means. It always seems as if I should know."

It amazed him to hear his mother's words. He'd always assumed she understood Nana's cryptic messages. They always sounded like lines from a poorly translated horror movie. *Beware the one-legged man who swims at night. Take cover from the giant turtle that flies at high noon.* It was hard to know if a person should be peering into bodies of water for a one-legged man, or if the message was symbolic. If so, what would it symbolize? He probably should ask his grandfather.

"Is grandfather home?" he asked, half-rising from his chair.

His mother stood quickly, grabbing his arm, possibly sensing his exit. "Not so quick, we aren't done talking."

Ethan shrugged his shoulders as he sat. "What is there to say? You're cool with me being gay, and Nana gives out weird predictions that no one understands." He hoped he struck the right level of casualness to calm his mother. Her eyes narrowed. That couldn't be a good sign.

She folded her hands and leveled her sternest gaze on him. It was the 'I'll know if you are lying to me' one. As a small child, he always believed his mother could see right through him like glass. He had told enough fibs to test this theory. She always knew. Perhaps she had magical abilities, maternal instincts, or he could just be a bad liar. It was probably a combination of the three.

"Tell me about the bullying. Does it happen online? Have you reported it to the school officials?" She reached for her purse and dumped it out. Finding her cell phone, she turned it on and began to search for a number.

Sweet Goddess, it was exactly what he'd feared. She'd call the school. Gripe at the principal. Tell him he wasn't doing his job. He'd pull the bullies out of class and threaten them with expulsion. Why that would bother them, he had no clue. It wasn't as if any of them were shining stars at school. Still, they'd want retribution. He had to stop her.

Jumping up, he grabbed for her phone. "No."

His mother started and jumped, as his leap for the phone sent both him and the phone crashing to the floor. *Oomph*. What else could he do to himself?

His mother knelt beside him. "Are you okay?"

She seemed to be making a habit of that today. His abrupt landing rattled his teeth, making his head ache a bit more, but other than that, he was fine. Better than the phone though. The medium blue phone had split into two pieces. Maybe his mother wouldn't notice.

Her eyes followed his gaze. "My phone!" Her shriek of dismay filled the kitchen. His cheek rested against the linoleum as he watched his mother try to reconnect the parts without any success. He certainly hadn't meant to break her phone.

"Nora sent me a text earlier about her and Clayton's hand fasting. After a quickie courthouse wedding, she's finally going to have a traditional ceremony. She asked me to look for a certain type of ribbon for her. I think that text was the ribbon photo." Her mother stared at the phone as if wishing it whole again.

"I didn't hear it chime." Twisting to sit, he realized from his unexpected close inspection that the kitchen floor wasn't as clean as he assumed. The phone was broken, losing the ribbon text. What else could go wrong today?

His mother placed the broken parts on the table. "Maybe your father can fix it." Her expression looked doubtful.

Pushing to his feet, he wondered how to discourage his mother from talking to school officials and taking his life from moderately hazardous to downright scary. As much as he hated to do it, he'd have to face the situation. "Is Dad cool with me being gay?" He dropped back into his seat as if it was an everyday question, rather like 'can I borrow twenty bucks for the movies?'

His mother's absorption with her broken phone changed into the demeanor of a cornered animal. She did not want to talk about it. Well, he didn't either. The alternative was his mother stirring things up at an already dysfunctional school. Their school mascot was a rebel running with a rifle. It could easily be mistaken for a redneck. Often opposing teams referred to it as just that. Instead of being offended, it usually pleased the students. One of the cheerleaders would usually yell a cheery reply such as, "This redneck is going to crush you." Ah, and to think his mother wanted to wade into that morass, quoting new laws and anti-bullying guidelines. So far, no one at the school knew his family was Pagan. His goal was to keep it that away.

"Well, your father…" his mother started. She wrung her hands and looked miserable. A person would think she'd lost her last friend.

He hated seeing her like this. "Stop, don't say anything else."

"I have to." Her lips shut in an unyielding line.

If they were English, he'd make some comment about his mother keeping a stiff upper lip or soldiering on. Fifteen years taught him when his mother decided to do something, she was doing it, no matter if it pained her.

"I think you know," she tried to start again, gulping audibly. "Your father loves you, but he was brought up very strictly. They were not even allowed to play on Sundays."

He'd heard the stories from his father. Currently his father's father was little more than an aging hippie who made his own beer. Far away from the fire and brimstone preacher, he used to be. He even joked about his former 'stick up his butt' attitude. "What of it?"

She cleared her throat again. It had to be something bad if it took that much throat clearing. "Well, he was raised that way. It rather took root in some ways. He tends to think of some things as just not being right."

He always found it odd that his serious father had wooed a witch, but he did. Even though he married her, he still held onto his rigidness as if it was a life jacket. The man tolerated his family's unusual practices. *Wait a minute. He* got what his mother was trying to say.

"Oh, I get it. He thinks I'm bad because I am attracted to males." He suspected as much. His behavior at the Pagan Pride Festival spoke volumes.

His mother's mouth took on a pinched expression while the lines in her forehead deepened. "Not bad, exactly. Just, not right, not normal, I guess. Whatever that means."

He sighed since he knew exactly what it meant. "All those times he signed me up for various sports teams, he wanted me to be some super athlete. Why? Dad was no athlete. He's not even that tall. Why do I have to be everything he wasn't in school?"

He shot both hands through his hair, inadvertently hitting his bump.

Inhaling deeply, he stifled a whimper. Wouldn't that be exactly what a gay son would do? A straight son could take a knife to the thigh and not wince. He didn't believe it for a second, but other people did. Stereotypes always seemed to carry more weight than reality.

His mother rubbed the bridge of her nose and muttered behind her hand. "He didn't want an athlete as much as he didn't want a gay son." She sighed, placing her hands on the table. "It's easy to judge your father harshly, but let me try to present his side. He didn't really grow up until college. He was the quintessential short nerdy kid with glasses and no athletic skills, except for one."

His father was athletic? His shock showed. "What skill?" He expected a solitary sport like archery or bowling.

His mother raised one eyebrow, stalling, messing with him.

"Archery? Bowling? Lacrosse?" he guessed. He would have said chess if it could have been classified as a sport. A sport of the mind, maybe.

"Lacrosse? What type of school do you think he attended? A prep school?" She shook her head as if her words didn't already negate his guesses. "He could run fast. It was the only way to stay away from the bullies. Apparently, the slowest target got the swirly, got trapped in his locker, or was on the losing side of a wedgie."

The thought of his father sprinting everywhere made him realize they were more alike than he originally thought. The larger, heavier bullies would not be able to keep up. He had probably hidden a lot, too. "Well, at least we have that in common."

His mother cradled his hand in hers. "He didn't want you to have that in common. He wanted you to be the tough kid no one would hassle. It was especially important when he realized you weren't going to get Grandfather Buell's height. Boys tend to pick on smaller boys."

"Some girls do too." He remembered the angry British girl who had given him a bloody nose and a black eye. It may have started over an argument about fairies, but ended when he had called her a ginger beer. It didn't matter that he only repeated what she said, unaware of the meaning or the repercussions of his words.

Her fingers tightened on his, perhaps remembering the incident. "He wanted things to be easier for you. As Pagans, we've been victims of discrimination. Even dancing in a circle in the yard to welcome spring caused one landlord to cancel our rental agreement. He told us he was going to sell the house, but he never did."

"That's against the law." Anger at the unknown property owner rushed through his veins. He never knew why they moved so much, but he did recognize that no one ever seemed eager to go.

His mother snorted her response. "It's only illegal if you can prove it. The landlord could say he had a buyer for the house, and it fell through, which forced him to rent the house after we moved out."

His mother released his hand only to tick off the reasons. Holding up her index finger, she declared, "Being a Pagan, or better yet, not a Christian, would make you an easy target most places." Her middle finger joined the index finger. "Then there's the disadvantage of being smaller than the other boys. The good news is you're attractive and friends with the girls. The bad news is the bigger boys don't like those traits."

Ethan crossed his arms and ankles. "I noticed that."

His mother brandished three fingers under his nose. "Not good at sports. A boy who isn't good at sports or obsessed with sports sticks out like a two-headed calf. It's better to just to be average."

She waved the fingers slowly. "Three things against you. Three targets on your back. It is enough to make your time in school into an extremely long prison term. Your father noticed the signs probably before anyone else. He tried to suppress them by forcing you into masculine activities. You probably hated them." His mother waited for a response.

"Majorly. Although, I did like sailing."

"Figures, that's one of those 'on the line' sports that usually the wealthy engage in, somehow making it less manly because your average Joe can't do it. Your father wanted you to escape the bullying and abuse he went through. He wanted you to have a better life than he did."

The way his mother presented it, didn't sound too bad. He always felt his father disapproved of everything he did and who he was. Maybe all he wanted was for him to have an easier time. Then again, his mother could be making it up so he wouldn't feel bad. It wouldn't be the first time she had tried to smooth things between him and his father.

Chapter Three

A LL HE WANTED was time to consider everything that had happened today. It wouldn't hurt to recover from the physical and emotional injuries. His father looked up from his newspaper as Ethan headed for his room.

"Hey, sport," his father called out.

Instead of answering, he lifted a hand in response. Even his nickname felt like an attempt to make him into something he wasn't. He might as well call him 'straight' or 'hetero', but they lacked the playfulness that 'sport' embodied. Plenty of athletes were coming out gay. Most haters tried to ignore the news conferences as anomalies, complaining that the outed athlete was never very good anyhow.

For his father to condemn him for being gay wouldn't make any sense, especially since they were Pagan, Wiccan to be exact. Goddess knew there were plenty of gay Wiccans, along with bi, transgender, and even polyamorous unions. Three people in a relationship with everyone getting along was difficult for him to imagine. Sighing deeply, he threw himself down on his bed. "I'll probably die alone."

Ethan pushed aside his decorative pillows to stretch out. His bare window allowed the night to spill into the room. In turn, the fluorescent stars in his room glowed a greenish-white light, reminding him of all those fake alien autopsies on the Internet. Movies depicted aliens that often looked more like Olympic athletes than ordinary people did. The shimmery green people with big heads and almond shaped eyes worked for him.

A random planet interrupted the ceiling stars. His lips tipped up remembering his great idea to decorate the ceiling. It was only a few years ago when they decided to buy the house. The neighborhood had proved itself uneventful, which meant no one tried to run them out. It wasn't as if they were bad neighbors. No ritual bonfires or any outside ceremonies to keep peace with the neighbors was always Nana's complaint. His grandmother wasn't the type to keep a cap on her views.

They never advertised their faith, unlike the neighbor who put a statue of Mary in a half-buried bathtub. Most advertised no faith whatsoever. Occasionally, the Mormons, the Jehovah Witnesses, or a local church would come knocking on the doors, trying to convert people. It was odd they never knocked on their door, but he suspected Nana had something to do with that.

When they decided to stay in this neighborhood, the family bought the house and started remodeling. An extra bathroom in the basement was the first thing. Second was to work on his room. His mother insisted on enlarging the bedroom window, so he could escape in case of a fire.

The ceiling was the third, after a larger window to meet building codes. A couple of sheets of drywall went up. After that, the project derailed while his father worked long hours. Still, he had a ceiling instead of a mass of pipes. To celebrate having his own ceiling, he bought a box of stars online.

When the box arrived with an illustration of a smiling young boy looking up in awe at his father applying the stars, he'd had doubts. Was he being childish? The box jolted his father into action. He downloaded diagrams of the night sky at different times of the year to guide them in placing the stars in the proper order. The only problem was he didn't want the stars as they occurred in the sky. What was the point of having his own room if he couldn't decide for himself?

Instead, he spelled out his name. A few random planets showed up here and there with a handful of stars to keep them company. His refusal to do things the right way caused his mother to intervene. His father, frustrated at his failure to arrange the stars logically, took the ladder and left. It didn't matter. He didn't need the ladder or the diagrams.

The dresser had served as his base as he balanced himself, pressing the plastic stars on the ceiling. Many times, he had fallen asleep, staring at his star-made name, with the sense of peace the sight gave him.

He stared up at the stars waiting for the peace to come. Just to add to his lack of peace, one star chose to fall, hitting him in the eye. The adhesive had probably dried. Maybe the magic was gone too. The peace definitely was. The sounds of the television drifted through the vent. The theme music told him his father was watching his favorite police drama. Normally, they watched it together. Part of him wanted to go sit on the couch beside his father and have everything return to how it used to be.

He held out the dropped star in the diminishing light. It appeared to have lost its glow. Yeah, he knew the feeling. What now? The room grew dimmer with the setting sun. A light would help, but he preferred the dark. It fit his mood.

The half-moons of his nails were hardly visible as he waved his hand through the air. What he wouldn't give to put a major hurting on Caulb and his crew. The Wiccan Rede, which was a type of commandments for Wiccans, stated to do no harm. There were exceptions of course, such as self-defense.

Harm was relative, according to Grandpa Buell. A person who performed a work spell to find a job might risk taking a job away from another applicant. A lack of clarity resulted in some Wiccans deciding the only alternative would be to do nothing.

Grandfather tended to temper his magick with practical thinking. Harm only happened when you meant it to happen. If a person you didn't like fell down the steps and broke his leg, and you did nothing to cause the accident on a spiritual or physical basis, then you were free of blame. Often Karma took things in hand. Other times, the elements and those who had gone on before meddled too.

A snort escaped him as he wondered how long before Karma caught up with Caulb. An image of Caulb stomping sand castles as a toddler came to mind. No doubt, he had progressed to breaking Lego towers and crushing blockhouses in kindergarten. His name probably served as a type of alarm, warning children to scatter.

As far as he could tell, no one really liked him in school. The girls tended to look through him. Despite his massive muscles, he was no prize. A crooked nose, showing signs of being broken more than once, dominated his face. His eyes were small, almost hidden by his heavy lids. His expression always appeared to be that of a sly, mean-spirited rat. Those were probably his good features, too. His hair was short enough to display his pink scalp through the blonde fuzz. The right hairstyle would have taken attention away from the nose and softened his face, not that he'd ever give the bully any grooming tips.

Poverty and puberty conspired against Caulb too. Puberty showed itself in his zit-marked face, while poverty sat in his mouth. Not only were his teeth crooked, a couple were broken and a few might be dead. At least that is what Harry Chou said, who sat by him in English. Whenever he opened his mouth, the smell of death and decay escaped.

Ethan always thought it was going to be his death whenever he saw the bully. Still, he couldn't understand why Caulb hated him, or felt the need to stomp him out. As hard as it was to put himself in Caulb's shoes, he tried.

While he wished he could be taller, he accepted he probably would not pass his father's five foot nine. His parents were both reasonably attractive people and had the courtesy to pass on their well-formed features. A good haircut, braces, and dermatology visits remedied any other issues.

His ability to be quick on the comeback kept most malicious bullies at bay. They didn't want to be embarrassed in front of his posse of girls. His appeal with the females, besides reasonable looks and charm, was he listened to them. Living in a houseful of women made him more aware of the nuances of feminine communication. They often relayed messages without the exact words, or sometimes with no words at all. All Caulb knew was the females preferred Ethan. The Neanderthal could respond with violence or name-calling. With his limited intelligence, he figured gay was the worse slur.

Being a moronic thug was at the top of Caulb's list. He resorted to the only thing he knew how to do, to terrorize him by showing up in isolated locations. A hulking brute of a friend would be nice to have his back. His thoughts went back to Orin.

Unlike Caulb, Orin was kind. There wasn't a trace of malice in the young man. Their minds had touched briefly. In a moment, he knew Orin was an old soul who learned to accept the stupidity of humankind. He didn't necessarily feel a great need to interact with them, which explained his refusal to speak.

Ethan ran a hand over his face, wishing it were Orin's hand. Would Orin find his face attractive? Did Orin ever laugh, since he didn't talk? Next time he saw him, he swore he'd make him laugh. Wasn't sure how he'd do it though. Ethan didn't know how they'd ever meet again, but there had to be a next time. It wouldn't be fair to meet someone you were so in harmony with and never see them again. Was this to be his life, just a mangled mess of chance encounters never resulting in anything?

His muscles tensed at the thought. Forget relaxing and trying to forget the problems of the day. His breath came out in a gusty sigh. No way could he go back to school tomorrow. However, not going would be paramount to letting Caulb and his cling-ons win. Still, showing up at school would be the stupider of his two options.

What about Brendon? How could he look at him, let alone sing with him in competition? Was there any way to get out of it? Mr. Zimmer was counting on the two of them. Secretly, this coming Saturday meant almost as much to him as it did to Mr. Zimmer, his time to shine.

Never being much of an athlete, he never garnered any attention. No one was handing out awards for decent academics, good grooming, or witty comebacks. A gold medal in the choir competition might earn him a brief two-second mention during the daily announcements. With his luck that would be the day, the chosen student would whisper the announcements. It had happened before.

Even if no one heard, it would matter to him. A medal would represent the completion of a goal. A panel of unknown judges would decide for one brief moment in time that Ethan Carpenter was superior to all the rest. He'd never really excelled at anything before.

Was he going to let Caulb take that away from him? The gritty sound of his molars grinding together demonstrated his body was ready for the challenge before his mind and spirit agreed. It was a challenge. One he had to meet. It would be great if a psychic message or prediction of good times in the future arrived. Yeah, that would be sweet.

His stomach growled as he tried to meditate, hoping to contact his spirit guide. Lately, all he'd been doing, besides dwelling on the menace Caulb presented, was thinking about Brendon. From the few shy smiles and ambiguous remarks, he had created a romance of watching old black and white movies together and strolling around the lake as the sun set, painting the water with vivid strokes.

Clearing the failed romance from his mind, the seashore from Nana's guided imagery scenario replaced it. Johnny, his spirit animal, was probably behind the large clump of boulders. The shaggy black wolf was easier for him to relate to than a human guide. The animal never mentioned its name. Ethan felt odd about the guide not having a name.

Johnny was the name of an old movie actor, Johnny Weissmuller. The wolf reminded him of the actor since they both were alpha males, powerful and quiet. The wolf didn't seem to mind the name. Of course, they never carried on conversations.

The wolf's head poked out from the clump of rocks. Spotting Ethan, he trotted toward him with a welcoming mien. The animal took his place beside Ethan as they strolled the deserted beach. His hand rested against the large wolf's shoulder. Johnny allowed the action, enabling them to communicate. By touching the wolf, pictures formed in his mind.

Sometimes they were answers to his unspoken questions. Other times the images prompted him to take actions. When he was tired and weary, like he was today, the scenes provided comfort.

A peaceful valley unfolded with birds singing and majestic mountains in the background.

"Thank you." He whispered the words, not wanting to interrupt the warm, enveloping comfort that wrapped around him. "It feels like everything will work out."

A masculine voice spoke near his ear. "That's because it will."

Ethan's head swiveled in surprise to face a familiar face. The eyes were higher and larger than his were and the chin sported a carefully styled goatee, but he recognized the face. Ethan peered at it every morning in the mirror. What was going on? Wasn't he supposed to be in charge of his meditation?

His other self arched an eyebrow and grinned. "You still are. Just not the current you. Your struggles still pierce my heart, even though it has been years. Your mind was open, and I thought I'd slip in to give you a view of your future."

His eyes devoured the man beside him. Taller, more filled out than he was, muscles in the right places, but no 'roid freak like Caulb. Still had great hair, it was lighter and thinner. He visually measured the difference in their heights. Nope, he wouldn't reach six feet. Oh well.

"The fact that you're here means I live a full life. I survive high school."

The smile slipped on his older self's face. "Well, that depends on your choices. I was worried you might make the wrong ones, so I felt the need to encourage you."

How great was this! Having his future self, guide him on the right path. He had several questions, including how to get in touch with Orin. Which question should he start with first? "Should I...?"

"Ethan," his mother's voice called, startling him at its nearness. The rattling of the door handle meant she was right outside. His older self melted away to be replaced with the darkness of his room.

"Ethan, honey. You never ate anything. I brought you a sandwich because I thought you might be hungry." The door swung open, allowing light to spill into his room and silhouetting his mother.

His stomach growled, emphasizing its empty state. His mother flicked on the light and stared at the room as if she hadn't seen it before. Shaking her head, she carried the plate to his bedside table. Her brow furrowed and her mouth took on a pinched look, signaling her displeasure.

Ethan cringed, if only mentally, knowing his mother might remark about the dark or want to continue their earlier awkward conversation. Instead, her eyes stayed on the walls, or rather where the drywall should be. Muttering to herself about half-finished rooms, she turned to leave. She stood at the door, backlight making it impossible for him to note her expression. "It's not right, you having an unfinished room. It feels like you are stuck in one place, unable to move on. I must insist your father get your room finished. It's hindering you."

The door closed as he stared in open mouth amazement. Lack of dry-wall was causing him to be stuck. *Interesting.* On the surface, it appeared improbable, but his mother could sense things. She was also good at moving things around in a room to promote better harmony and positive energy flow, not a showy talent. Grandfather Buell could make things appear and disappear, or even go invisible himself when he felt like it. Although, he was never invisible. He only compelled people to look away from where he was. It would be a useful trick for him to learn.

Ethan picked up the sandwich, peeking under the bread to discover ham and Swiss cheese, his favorite. He took a bite and peered around the room. The two by four boards and one bare sheet of drywall stared back at him, the same view since his father's work schedule had dominated his time. For a short while, his father had enthused about fixing up his room, but then lost energy due to extra work. A fellow employee's worsening health, had forced him to work from home. He'd heard his father grumble that working from home was just another term for not working. That was about as harsh a criticism as he'd ever heard from him. The time never felt right to remind him about his room, which is why he said nothing. Everyone else had appeared to forget too. He chewed slowly, thinking about something he'd heard on the radio.

Some woman had called in to a home interior show to ask about making her basement into a mother-in-law suite. The designer was against it, stating you put things in the basement that you want to forget, such as discarded clothes, broken items, and holiday decorations. Psychologically, by putting them in the basement you forgot about them.

Did his family want to forget about him? Better yet, his father? The house was decent sized with four bedrooms and the framed-up room in the basement, which served as his bedroom. Once his parents bought it after renting for three years, they put in a downstairs bathroom. Truthfully, it was his. The only time other family members used it was in an emergency.

A forgotten person wouldn't rate his own bathroom. Still, he turned the idea over in his head. His parents, unlike some, didn't interfere in his life. No hovering over him, asking trivial questions about his day or homework, no impromptu visits with his teachers, or wanting to get to know his friends. He used to think that was a good thing. Now, he wondered.

His parents might explain it as a sign of trust. With his grandparents, he accepted that they already knew everything and had no reason to ask questions. As Wiccans, they honored the fact that everyone had to walk their own path. You could not dictate another's direction. The corner of his mouth listed in a wry smile. *Yeah, right, explain that to his father.*

The man had tried though. About a year ago, his father had somewhat accepted that his only son had no athletic inclinations after a severe beat down in a hockey game. Ethan touched his nose, reflecting on the incident. At least, it hadn't been broken in the fight. Otherwise, he might resemble Caulb.

He understood hockey, in theory and even proved to be an amazing skater. Still the sport was an excuse to fight on the ice, wearing heavy padding. He wondered at the time if the attack was an initiation of sorts, or the players didn't accept him. He was suspicious, since most of the players who got jabs in were on his team. His mother, who almost never made demands, insisted he quit the team.

That ended his athletic pursuits. *Thank the Goddess.* Even the simple expression he grew up with grated on his nerves. His family emphasized the divine feminine as opposed to any real emphasis on a male deity. Not too surprising, since most people worshipped male deities who insisted on absolute conformity and left no room for individuality.

Well, to be honest, the women in his family called on the various

Goddesses in their worship. His father mainly hung out, doing nothing. It could be his father didn't know what to do. His fire and brimstone minister father and Bible-thumping mother emphasized all the various religious rules to escape eternal damnation, until one day the two of them parted ways from the straight and narrow, and each other.

Grandmother Eunice, whom he seldom saw anymore, had taken off with a visiting evangelist. They were living in Canada. His father's dad, Grandpa Ted, still came around. Disillusioned with religion, he became an atheist, attended aging rock star concerts, and grew his hair long. He'd even started brewing his own beer.

His conservative father grumbled about his father's transformation. His mother would laugh, pat his hand, and remind him each had to follow his or her own path. Was his father angry with his parents divorcing? Maybe he felt tricked, spending his early life adhering to a god and rules that both his parents had discarded so quickly.

Whatever it was, it hadn't caused his father to experience a spiritual catharsis. If it did, he certainly kept quiet about it. Nana and his mother tended to stay with the Dianic group, worshipping the Divine Feminine, while Nora and her husband took a more balanced approach, honoring both the Lord and Lady. Leah had started hanging with earth-based religious groups at the university. Grandpa Buell hung with a men's group he belonged to before he had slipped through time. The group may be more into sampling brandy and spinning tall tales regarding their pasts as opposed to anything spiritual.

As for him, he searched his nightstand drawer for matches. Standing, he clutched the box of matches in one hand and approached his makeshift altar. A purple-fringed cloth with a pentacle design covered the small wooden table. On it sat a porcelain statue of Apollo, a few sprigs of rosemary, and a small votive candle in a holder. He knelt in front of the altar and lit the candle.

"Thank you, Apollo, for providing a safe passage home."

He could be lying on the locker room floor bleeding out, instead of being safe at home. He touched the white figurine with the side of his finger. It was hard to believe he never knew there were deities favorable to the homosexual lifestyle. He'd heard plenty from several sources about gays getting a ticket on the hell-bound express from the Christian God.

His epiphany had occurred under the same tree where he met Orin. The guys at the Pagan Pride Festival informed him that several of the Greek Gods were gay. Not too strange that his school mythology unit skipped that part. The school had no problem making him sit through an awkward positive relationships class. The female instructor talked too fast and looked as uncomfortable as the students acted, while she emphasized abstinence. The talk was only about attraction to the opposite gender, never the same.

Because no one ever talked about it, he assumed all the deities were straight. Yet, it puzzled him that so many Pagans were gay. The discovery of Apollo and his love for Hyacinth made something inside of him shift. He soon discovered there were many more deities who often took lovers of the same gender.

Eros, Hermes, and Hercules assisted in the matters of gay romance, probably due to their own tendencies in that matter. It certainly wasn't part of the mythology taught in school. It did explain some of those ancient illustrations. Forrest, one of the boys from the Pagan Pride Day, explained the reason behind the sanitation of the Greek Gods as a bit of an 'out of sight, out of mind' philosophy. Christianized emperors might not be able to wipe out the memory of the pantheon, but they could change the tales to suit their own morals.

It was hard to believe something was wrong, evil, or a ticket to damnation, if the Gods did those things. Plenty of Goddesses took female lovers, including Artemis. The ancient deities often changed, depending on what prevailing religion ruled the day.

Getting actual information was difficult. Many people worked diligently to wipe out any reference or deny it, similar to the scholars who insisted the holocaust never happened. All he knew was that he was grateful to have a deity he could worship, an entity to understand his struggles.

He watched the candle flame as it danced, taking in oxygen and growing stronger. Staring at the colors in the flame, a feeling of strength filled him. He had no clue how he would overcome his current problems. Only seconds before a future Ethan had visited, looking capable and content, reminding him his right decisions would lead him to this life he desired.

Exhaling a sigh of relief, his shoulders relaxed, dropping back to their normal position. Everything would work out okay. After all, his future self had told him that in so many words. Well, he may have said *if he made the right choices* they'd work out. *Damn it*. How was he supposed to know what the right choices were?

If only his mother hadn't come down to his room. Ethan's future self had been close to telling him what he needed to do. Grandfather warned him the art of divination could be cryptic. You only received tiny peeks, never the whole picture, leaving a puzzle with several missing pieces. As far as he could tell, he only had one piece.

The thought caused him to drop back on his hands, sliding into a prone position on the floor looking up at his ceiling. The good news was one version of his life had turned out happy. Then again, he blinked, as another thought invaded his consciousness. The whole thing might be a dream.

CHAPTER FOUR

MORNING CAME BEFORE he was ready for it. Chairs scraping the floor overhead, along with footsteps served to announce the new day. Nothing miraculous like sudden death, or reappearing in another time occurred during the night. Knowing his parents, they'd expect him to get up and go to school.

His father would give him some pep talk about Carpenters always facing their fears. Of course, he imagined most of his father's fears didn't involve an enraged bully who'd slammed his fist into a steel door because of him. Ethan didn't stick around to see the damage, but the door no doubt triumphed. That meant an extra target painted with fluorescent paint on his back. *Great.*

The thought caused him to pull the covers over his head. His family was involved in their usual chaotic rush. He could tell from the voices. A quick peek at the alarm clock showed it was already seven. A slam of the front door indicated his sister left for the commute to her part-time job at the coffee shop.

Ethan found it ironic that a person allergic to mornings as much as Leah was would have to get up early for work, not that she did it without complaining. Far from it. A high-pitched honk indicated his mother's ride had arrived. She carpooled with another nearby nurse. Two down and only three more to go before he had the house to himself.

Of course, he'd have to concoct an excuse of sorts to keep the attendance person from calling his house. Maybe he could call and pretend to be his mother. Mr. Zimmer appeared to love his clear tenor voice. There was no reason he couldn't disguise it to sound like his mother.

The garage door rattled open, indicating his father was on his way. It didn't surprise him too much that his father hadn't noticed his absence. He always seemed to walk around in a preoccupied fog, thinking about things left undone at work. At least, that is what he assumed his father thought. Leah or his mother not checking on him was more of a surprise.

His grandmother might not leave for another couple of hours. Her clients were not early risers. That meant he'd have to stay in bed, not making a sound, or getting up to use the bathroom. For two elderly people, his grandparents had hearing like hawks, or maybe they just sensed things.

Pulling the covers back over his head, he contemplated what might happen at school if he went. Brendon would be there, making him feel ashamed that he'd ever imagined the soft-eyed baritone had ever liked him as a fellow singer, or as a romantic interest. The blood rushed to his face as he relived how Brendon had played him for his own security. It sucked. Sure, it made sense Brendon wanted to avoid Caulb and his lackeys. Who wouldn't, but it still sucked.

No clever retorts came to him. The best he could do was ignore Brendon whenever they encountered each other. Mr. Zimmer wouldn't understand why they couldn't perform together. It wasn't as if he'd explain the incident to the earnest choir director. The man wanted the gold medal more than Ethan did, and he wanted it bad.

Footsteps vibrated on the basement steps. He curled up, trying to resemble a pile of mussed blankets and pillows as opposed to an actual human trying to avoid death from the hands of Caulb, or a slower demise from humiliation. Neither one would be good. At best, it was Nana doing laundry.

Inhaling, he held his breath. Nana's housekeeping skills were minimal at best. She considered herself the psychic guardian of the family, as well as the liaison to the next world. Sometimes, she even referred to herself as a hedge witch, but never—ever—did the term *housework* cross her lips. The best she did was grocery shop and cook occasionally. A trio of knocks sounded before the door swung open.

Grandfather cleared his throat in his usual trademark fashion. It was often his way to indicate he was about to announce something important. "Brought you some cinnamon toast and hot chocolate."

His favorite childhood breakfast—actually, it still was. He pulled down the covers to face his grandfather. His elderly relative flashed an understanding smile before settling on the bed.

"How'd you know I was home?" He'd been exceptionally quiet. "I didn't sing, talk, or make any type of noise."

Grandfather made a harrumphing sound. "The silence pretty much did it for us. It's never been that quiet in the morning around here."

The comment sounded like a slam to him. Since his mouth was full of cinnamon toast, he opted for chewing. He sipped the hot chocolate, tasting the milk and cocoa. It was the real stuff instead of the instant mix. Someone was coddling him.

"You make the cocoa?" He hoped the question would stall the inevitable questioning about why he hadn't gone to school.

His grandfather shook his head. "Nope, your Nana did. She thought it would make you feel better about that bully who is hounding you and the other fellow who gave you the brush-off."

"Leah!" He grumbled his sister's name in disgust. *Couldn't tell her anything.* Forget the special bond he thought they had.

"Stop right there." Grandfather held out his hand as if directing traffic and his expression took on an intimidating air. It was easy to see why some people might have the good sense to fear him. He'd only known his grandfather the last five years of his life. All that time, he was always joking and playful.

Chastised, Ethan mumbled, "Sorry." Not sure how to regain his grandfather's favor.

His grandfather's eyes narrowed. "It's not me you should be apologizing to, but your sister, Leah. By all the Elements, did you think no one in this family could sense your turmoil? It literally keeps me up at nights, with your thoughts screaming out that you hoped Brendon would like you. I'm not sure who is more disappointed about things not working out with Brendon. Me or you?"

Ethan found himself chuckling at his grandfather's outraged expression as he'd intended. "Why do you want Brendon to like me?"

His grandfather reached back to rub his neck, before speaking. "You have such loud thoughts. The stronger the emotion the more it screams. If things worked out between the two of you, I'd have more of a chance to sleep."

Ethan finished the toast in a couple of bites, and then polished off the hot chocolate. "Would it have been better if I had thought about his soft brown eyes?"

Grandfather's mouth pursed as if he tasted something sour. "I see I'm going to have to teach you to shield your thoughts."

Shielding thoughts would be useful. It might not be particularly useful at school, but would provide some privacy at home. "I'd like that. Could we start today?"

"You'd like that, no doubt, picturing yourself spending the day working on the magickal arts, instead of world history." He shook his head slowly, which Ethan recognized as a bad omen. "You will go to school, and in the promptest fashion."

What was wrong with his family? Did they want him to die a painful death? Ethan swung his legs over the side of the bed to stand. "I am not sure what is wrong with you people. Do you want me to be a bloody residue in the school hallway?"

His grandfather pushed up off the bed. At six foot, he towered over his grandson. His crossed arms and full mustache added to his attitude of no nonsense. "Ethan, I know today will not be an easy day for you. If we could let you stay home, hide under the covers, and murmur platitudes about the unfairness of life until you felt the urge to return to school, we would."

It sounded rather good to Ethan. Besides, he was tired. Running for your life tended to wear a person out. He could use a mental health day. Plenty of kids took them. A few of the girls took spa days with their mothers, since the weekend appointments were so hard to get. One look at his grandfather's unsmiling face indicated no mental health or spa day today.

No one had a spa day in his family. About the closest thing may have been Nana when she talked about escaping something by wading through a peat bog. His family had a long history of fleeing danger. Peat bogs weren't the same as a Dead Sea salt scrub. He waited for his grandfather to say more, but he didn't.

"I guess that means you expect me to go to school today." Even as he said the words, he felt himself growing smaller as his anxiety ballooned. Too bad, he could not physically shrink like Alice in Wonderland. With his luck, Caulb would spot him and put him in his pocket.

"No expect about it." His face held the same stern expression that probably sent his medieval apprentices scurrying in terror, afraid they might end up as a toad or something worse. Of course, no one following the ancient ways resorted to hexing or black magic. They were too aware of how it came back three times on a person.

No one needed a Karmic hammer nailing him or her to the ground. Most of the time he wanted something bad to happen to Caulb, or just have him vanish off the face of the earth. Still, he'd never resorted to any hexes.

"Yes, sir." He used his best manners, hoping to look like he was compliant.

His grandfather snorted and turned toward the door. "You don't fool me. I know you're cursing me in your mind." He threw the words over his shoulders.

Not exactly cursing, but he may have grumbled a bit.

His grandfather turned in the open doorway and managed a slight smile. "I think you might find things aren't as bad as you imagine."

Yeah, and Caulb was the tooth fairy. He snorted his disbelief as he went to pick out his clothes. At least the school had abandoned the uniform policy that'd existed when Leah attended. A trio of upscale mothers, who couldn't display that their daughters were richer than anyone else was in the school in the standard uniform, took it to court. They didn't win the first time, or the second, but they did the third, probably due to the school not wanting to fight any more.

The side benefit allowed him the freedom to dress any way he pleased. It pleased him to be different. Last week, he wore dark jeans with combat boots and a ruffled tuxedo shirt he located in the thrift shop. His father was none too happy about that outfit, but the girls at school were crazy about it. His lips twisted as he looked at his varied wardrobe. It could be part of his problem too. He didn't fade in the way Leah urged him to do.

Instead of making it hard for the bullies to find him, he dressed like a neon sign. A good example was the lime green shirt he pulled from his closet. He examined the shirt and decided against it. Did he have anything in his closet that didn't demand attention?

His grandfather returned to hurry him up. A dark hoodie with an ugly mascot on it hung from his relative's hand. *Great. Well, not* great, but it would do. "Thanks."

He grabbed a pair of distressed jeans. He'd resemble most students, the ones who couldn't put an outfit together. He sighed deeply as he walked past his grandfather on his way to the bathroom.

His grandfather called after him. "Remember. Adversity builds character."

Character. Everyone always talked about it. What did it mean really? He never once heard a guy or a girl comment on someone's great character. Sexy hair, tight ass, even a perfect smile, but not one character reference. Sure, teens were shallow, he should know, since he was one. Did he even care about character?

He lingered in the bathroom parting his hair one way, then another. Given enough time, his Nana would leave to go to her shop. He wasn't sure what grandfather would do. Maybe if he hung out everyone would leave.

A familiar rapping sounded on the bathroom door. "I know you're done in there. Let's go. Get a move on, and I might even tell you the secret behind my charisma."

That's all he needed to hear. Dropping the comb, he turned to open the door. Everyone loved his grandfather. Even complete strangers hung onto his every word, a glory to behold. Good thing the man never took advantage of people. Most would have done whatever he asked them to do. He swung the door open only to run smack into his grandfather.

"Oomph." He grunted and placed his hands on Ethan's shoulders. It wasn't clear who was steadying whom.

Great. He almost knocked over the same man who gave up running water to wait for Leah's appearance in the Dark Ages. "Sorry."

"No problem, Ethan. Let's head out. I might be able to do a quick look away spell, but I think your attire will do it for you."

"Unfortunately, you're right." He never thought of himself as an attention ho, but apparently, he was one. Always quick with the funny remark or entertaining trivia. It's what people tended to expect from him. They also depended on him to be upbeat. He was the one who cheered up the girl who'd just sobbed her eyes out in the restroom because her boyfriend broke up with her via text in the previous class.

Not once did he think of himself as highly visible, but he was, which put a completely new spin on why Caulb felt the need to wipe him out of existence. He followed his grandfather, pondering his most recent insight.

Nana met them at the top of the stairs. "Buell, I knew you'd get the boy up. You have the charm of the Irish."

His grandparents exchanged smiles. Grandfather cradled Nana's chin with his hand. How the two of them were so in love awed Ethan. He hardly knew anyone who had parents still married, never mind grandparents. Theirs was a special bond, perhaps made stronger for the time apart. Unlike most people, they both knew what it was like to live apart.

The two of them moved away from the open door. He was hoping for a protection spell, since the two of them were rather renowned for their skills. It would be the equivalent to going to school in a military tank. A tank would be good. A fortress would be better, but he'd settle for the tank.

"So, about the protection spell?" he prompted, figuring a full-blown ritual could last about a half an hour. That would keep him out of biology. Normally, he liked science, but Mr. Fletcher made it painful. The teacher expected the worse out of the students, and treated them likewise. There were no experiments because an accident might happen, no group projects because someone might slack off. Sometimes, Ethan was the slacker. Other times, he really contributed.

Yep, he could use a day away from Mr. Fletcher's nasally voice and endless worksheets. It made him feel like he was back in third grade. Inquiry was not encouraged in his class. Instead, rote memorization ruled. Memorization was not his strong point, unless it pertained to dancing. That was body memory more than rote memory. Like riding a bike, you just rode it as opposed to telling yourself how to ride it.

Nana slapped him on the shoulder, hard. "You won't need any protective charms today, kiddo."

It surprised him someone as petite and delicate as his grandmother could hit so hard. Equally shocking, she didn't think he needed any protection. Didn't she care? He knew better than to question her judgment. When it came to her divination skills, the woman could out diva anyone.

Reaching into her pocket, she pulled out a small purple bag decorated with gold stars and smelling slightly of cinnabar. The slight rattle indicated her runes were inside. The small smooth stones had symbols carved into them. She usually arranged them in a cross formation with the character side turned over.

Ethan's gaze rested on the small pouch. It wasn't often Nana brought the runes out. The cards were her preferred divination method. When she did, it was always a serious matter. Unlike most in the profession, Nana allowed the grandkids to watch as she told outcomes, but only if they were quiet. Her reasoning was they could learn from doing.

Not all her clients shared her attitude. More than a few insisted the grandchildren not be in the room. Probably afraid something best left hidden might surface. Nana stood her ground, often calling him her assistant. He'd make a big production of smoothing the rune cloth on the table, even mixing up the runes for the draw. One fortuneteller at the yearly psychic fair went so far as to scold Nana for allowing him to assist. Her complaint was the energy fields wouldn't align with his juvenile thoughts and immaturity in the mix.

Nana winked at him. "I bet you're thinking about that charlatan back in our carnival days who thought to tell me how to divine for my clients." Her eyes crinkled, indicating laughter barely suppressed.

Grandfather didn't hold back. His boisterous laugh lifted Ethan's mood some. It was hard to be down around grandfather. "Good Goddess, Esme, I never saw you so vexed in my life. I expected fire to shoot out of your eyes."

Her eye crinkles smoothed out some, as her expression turned somber. "Well, you didn't see me when I got that slip of a note you wrote before you disappeared into the past."

Grandfather's jovial mood vanished. He knew good and well it would take more than a simple apology for spending twenty plus years in the past. It took time, apparently more than what had passed since his return. Ethan had no doubt his grandparents would work it out. Odds were more in their favor than his were.

Nana patted his arm with her free hand and rattled the rune bag with the other hand. "Not as bad as you think."

What would it be like to have a conventional family that didn't meddle in his business? "You already consulted the runes… for me?" Forget about stalling for a reading.

His grandmother nodded as his grandfather gestured to the door. Time to go and they were determined to see him get to school. He didn't need to hear the old analogy about getting back on the horse that bucked him off to conquer his fears. Didn't mean he wanted to do it, though.

No help for it. He'd to go to school. Scooping his backpack off the floor, he turned to ask Nana about her absolute certainty that he wasn't calmly going to his own funeral. "Um, what question did you ask?"

Normally, a person who asks for a reading thinks of a question and does not share it. It keeps things more personal that way. Often people, who do not want to share information, ask for a runes reading. Nana shot him a confident smile. "Should Ethan stay away from school today?"

Yes or no questions were usually rare in the asking. Nana discouraged it because often the runes would choose to give no answer. Why she would choose to do what she had warned others not to was peculiar. Then again, rules never seemed to apply to his outspoken relative.

He followed his grandfather out the front door thinking about the question. It should have cheered him up. In a way, it did, but something seemed to be wrong. The crisp air held a tint of fall, and he regretted not wearing a jacket, but he wouldn't be outside long. The sunlight angling through the changing leaves indicated an average autumn day. Why did it feel anything but ordinary?

The realization came with the click of the seat belt. "Nana, you just asked about today?" He'd make it through this day. What would happen the next day?

His grandmother, climbing into the front seat of the car, didn't even bother to turn around to answer. "Daily readings are best. Things get confused when you try to look too far ahead."

✧   ✧   ✧   ✧

A KID RIDING a bike caused grandfather to swerve to avoid hitting him. Ethan stared out the window at the boy looking little more than twelve. Why wasn't he at school? His failure to pay attention to what was happening around him could have easily ended his life. Turning against the seatbelt restraint, he tried to follow the path of the boy.

The boy's carelessness symbolized his own assumption that his life would go on as it had without any real effort on his part. He wanted to see the boy's face. The clothes, the bike, all of it seemed very familiar. The bicyclist grew smaller as he stared out the car window. As if feeling his gaze, the boy turned briefly.

Even though it was only a brief glance, Ethan realized he looked into his own face, his younger self. The boy rode feverishly away. Apparently, he was less thrilled to be looking at his future self. His head swiveled to see if his grandparents noticed anything unusual. Instead, Nana pointed to an elderly woman walking an overfed poodle.

"There's that hussy from Elm Street walking her fat dog all the way over here hoping to bump into you." A low growl emanated from the front seat as if his elderly relative might jump from the car and chase the woman and her dog back to Elm.

Grandfather laughed and patted her shoulder. "No worries, Esme. You are the only woman for me. That woman just asked me for directions, that's all."

Obviously, neither one of them had noticed anything about the boy who pedaled by. Maybe they didn't see. Sometimes visions worked like that. Could be that his grandfather hadn't even swerved to avoid the bicyclist. It may have appeared to be a dog to him.

Were there any messages besides being more aware of what was happening around him? His lack of bruises indicated he stayed alert enough to escape Caulb. What else could he do? His high school filled his view as his grandfather turned the car into the parking lot. Time to face the music. His nose wrinkled at the idea of talking to Mr. Zimmer about not participating in the competition.

The car door swung open, surprising Ethan. Nana gestured for him to get out. "Buell and I are going to sign you in. The story we're going with is you had an appointment."

He scrambled out of the car, anxious to get ahead of the disaster he knew would happen. In no way his colorful grandparents could enter the high school office and chat up the staff without someone noticing them. Nana proudly had a bit of a reputation as a gypsy fortuneteller. It depended on whom you talked to if it was good or bad. Most thought she was an elderly con artist. A few whispered she was a witch. While he was grateful Nana had eliminated the need for him to take gym, he didn't want them entering the school. Jogging ahead of the two, he called back. "No need for you to go in. I can sign myself in."

Nana looked ready to disagree, but Grandfather squeezed her hand, stilling her protest. Using two fingers, Grandfather saluted him.

"Be strong, Ethan. Leah will be by to pick you up at the usual time."

He saluted him back, wondering for a moment if his relative ever served in the military. Not willing to bet on how long Nana could be dissuaded, he headed toward the office.

Once inside the building, a bell rang, spilling students into the hall. He weaved through the students to make it to the office and signed in under the gaze of a disinterested student aide. English would be his next class on his schedule, which he happened to like this year. His sister might not think he read anything, but she didn't know everything about him. With any luck, it would be an ordinary day. A remnant of a conversation he had with his father came to mind as he strode to class. His father did not believe in luck, but accepted magick readily enough. He often declared we make our own luck. The troublesome factor was he never explained how to do it.

CHAPTER FIVE

B ROOKE, ONE OF the trio of blonde-haired women outfitted in cheerleader uniforms, waved at Ethan as he turned the corner.

"Hey, Ethan, I heard you weren't here today."

His lips tilted up, taking in the perky threesome. Unlike most of the males in school, he didn't want to hook up with them. He also didn't despise them because they were beautiful and cheerleaders as did the rest of the school's female population. Brooke, Kennedy, and England were friends who shared similar interests in fashion, dance moves, and movies.

He used both hands to gesture to himself. "You heard wrong. Here I am in the flesh." To demonstrate everything was the same as normal, he flashed his trademark smile, which always received a positive reaction. Well, at least from the females it did, and most of the adults too.

Truthfully, it was hard to distinguish between the three girls on games days when they all had matching ponytails with big ribbons and the same uniform. Kennedy recently switched to some intense turquoise contacts. He wasn't very sure if she needed contacts, or if it was just a fashion statement. England was taller than the other two. For the most part, the trio was mellow, until you called one of them by the other's name. Then they all acted as if they had been insulted or something. A mystery when they worked so hard to be the same.

Kennedy eyed him up and down. After giving him such a thorough once over, he began to wonder if his fly was open or a major zit had taken up residence on his face. Finally, she shook her head. "That stupid Dorrie," she stated.

England interrupted her, "It's Donnie."

"Whatever." She shrugged off the correction to continue. "He's telling everyone that Caulb beat you down good, and you wouldn't even show your face at school. Looks like he's a liar." Kennedy grimaced as if she had bitten into something rotten. "I don't know why I even listen to him."

Brooke laughed at her friend. "You should know better. Trust me. I wouldn't believe anything he told me. He's such a loser."

Ethan mentally winced. He often overlooked the trio's mean girl tendencies, until they showed them. Luckily, it was never on him. Leah would no doubt hate them. His sister had come to some type of epiphany about her own mean girl trio after her adventure in the past.

A few lilting notes alerted Brooke to an incoming message. She studied her sparkly purple phone for a minute and then gasped. "Look at this." Each girl peered at the text until the cell phone ended up in his hands. It was a status update from Brendon's account.

> Won't be back at school due to parent's immediate transfer. Wanted to let you know Ethan Carpenter put a major hurting on the school's favorite bully. Check out Caulb's right hand when he returns to school. Carpenter's too shy to brag about it. Peace out.

Ethan stared at the screen. Well, at least it gave him a way out of performing with traitor Brendon. The message puzzled him, though. Brendon witnessed his running like a scared rabbit. Why would he say he faced off with Caulb, unless it was his way of apologizing? Obviously, Brendon was never showing up at school again. The transfer excuse was just that.

The poor kid would probably end up being homeschooled, or attending one of those on-line schools. He'd be afraid to go to the mall or the movies because someone might recognize him. The information would leak back to Caulb, who would hunt him down. It wouldn't surprise him if Brendon hadn't already changed his hair color to be safe. Might even pick up some vanity contacts like Kennedy, or even start sporting glasses.

Yep, he understood how Brendon felt. Overall, he hadn't really done that much. The only thing he did was cooperate with the thug. His only sin against the bully, if you could call it that, was witnessing the one moment Ethan outsmarted Caulb. Of course, his status update didn't help much. Although, the more he thought of it, maybe he did help Brendon, since Caulb's attention would be focused on him, instead of hunting down the missing Brendon. That sucked. His eyes narrowed as he considered if that was Brendon's intention.

One of the football players, whose name he didn't know, slapped him on the back, causing him to almost drop Brooke's phone. "Way to go Carpenter. Didn't know you had it in you."

Brooke reached for her phone. Kennedy stepped closer and felt his bicep through his shirt. "I guess you outsmarted him as opposed to knocking him out, huh?"

Great. Anything he said would get him in bigger trouble. He wasn't sure if he had been at the top of Caulb's hit list before, but he was now. He could deny it, but people believe what they want, which was why he kept his romantic preferences quiet, knowing that certain people would find him suddenly repulsive. It wouldn't be as if he changed at all, but in some of his friends' eyes, he would have. Others wouldn't care. Right now, he wasn't exactly sure who would stick beside him.

Ethan shrugged his shoulders and gave them what he thought was an apologetic grin. Something the hero in a 1950's movie would do. The warning bell sounded, saving him from replying. They all scattered to their different classes. This wasn't the end of his troubles.

His English teacher clicked on the LCD projector and dimmed the lights to start her lecture on Edgar Allan Poe. Unlike most teachers, who glossed over important literary figures because they were in the textbook, Ms. Gleason did a more thorough job, showing the authors were people, not unlike themselves, with hard decisions and often made bad choices. Normally, he loved her literary exposes, as she called them.

Not today, however. He had to concentrate on all that might happen, which was too bad, because he liked Poe. Technically, the incident happened on school grounds. If the administration heard about the fight, he'd be in trouble, even though he'd done nothing wrong. Nope, whenever there was a fight the school punished both people. The puncher and the punchee. It didn't seem right, but that's the way it was.

If he were suspended, he'd be the first person in his family to do so. The alternative would be for him to voluntarily report that Caulb had systematically bullied him. *Yeah, that would work.* There was no way the school could keep him safe. Harassment happened in the restrooms, which led to special doctor's notes, allowing the student to use the restroom during class. Half of them probably used the staff restroom just to be safe.

He peered around the dimly lit classroom trying to identify who was here today. Ms. Gleason's voice continued her narrative.

"Edgar Allan Poe experienced censure from many of his fellow citizens for his inability to hold his alcohol."

A few kids giggled. One nameless boy commented, "I can hold mine."

Caulb didn't have any classes with him, for which he was eternally grateful, but some of Caulb's friends did. In the corner, one of the bully's sidekicks glared daggers at him. Instead of looking away, the way he usually did, he stared back. Beetling his brows together, he hoped he looked menacing. Surprisingly, the boy dropped his gaze.

The classroom door opened, spilling in light from the corridor. The light immediately dimmed when the large, bulky figure of the principal filled the door. Ms. Gleason stopped her narrative. An annoyed look passed over her face briefly, before she cleared it.

"Can I help you?" she asked politely, but the tightness of her unsmiling mouth indicated she wished otherwise.

In the short time Ethan had been at the school, he'd noticed the teachers saved a special brand of contempt for their leader. It was apparent in the way they pronounced his title, lengthening it as if they couldn't quite push it out without gagging. A few teachers even engaged in an eye roll if they were talking to other teachers. When rounding a corner unannounced, he'd heard a couple teachers gossiping about the man. Principal Lowenson was a very rare and unpopular creature, an administrator who'd never taught.

He married that undesirable trait with a lack of insight, as if he didn't know the teachers despised him. The man bragged about being an offensive lineman at the last school assembly. Never said anything about being a superior student, or a gifted musician, which made Ethan suspect his method of administrating was he rammed through his decisions against other staffers' misgivings, pretending they were the opposing team.

The hall lights silhouetted Principal Lowenson's torso, making him appear ominous. Ethan could well imagine that he'd been a fearsome sight with the football uniform padding. England joked, he could easily model for a troll, or any creature that relied on brute strength and limited intuition.

So far, he'd done his best to avoid the man. He pitied the student who caused the ogre to leave his office cave. Lowenson's head swiveled, peering at the students. The brightness of the hallway probably left him with limited vision as he peered into the dark room. Only Ms. Gleason, who stood by the illuminated screen, was visible. Still, it seemed as if the man was staring in Ethan's direction. A sense of foreboding grabbed Ethan, similar to Leah scaring him by lurking in the doorway, and jumping out unexpectedly. Why his sister thought it was funny baffled him. Luckily, she grew out of that habit by age twelve.

Besides, what would the man want with him? He doubted if he knew his name. There were over three thousand students in the school. He hadn't done anything bad enough for his name to be noteworthy. Then a horrible thought occurred. The hairs on the back of his neck stood up.

He tried to recall the moment he'd left his grandparents today. They were both out of the car as if they intended to walk in with him. How embarrassing that would be. Might as well dress him in a cartoon character sweatshirt and hold his hand to make his humiliation complete. His explanation that he could sign himself in was legit. His impromptu sprint took advantage of Nana's bad leg. No way, she could keep up, so he had assumed they turned around and went home.

No memory of them getting into the car existed. Why would they talk to the principal? Nana read the runes and was a big component of not forcing fate. She believed your destiny would unfold as it willed. Actions to change it would possibly speed up whatever you were trying to avoid, and at best delay it, but it did not change it.

The heavy sweetness of a girl's perfume next to him filled his lungs. Was he experiencing things more intensely because his life was about to end? He reminded himself of Nana's reading. Nothing bad would happen today. The analytical part of his brain asserted itself, pointing out a fine line difference. She merely mentioned it would be safe to attend school. A quick glance to his left revealed his classmate spritzing perfume. It ruined his theory of experiencing life more vividly.

Principal Lowenson cleared his throat, as if he were about to make an announcement of great import. "I need to see, um...." He hesitated and patted down his shirt and pants' pockets. He withdrew a scrap of paper, peered at it, and then held it at a distance trying to focus. Whispering erupted as his fellow students speculated on who was in trouble. Several probable names came up.

Still holding out the paper, the principal sounded out the name as if he'd never heard it before in his life. "Elf-fan Carpenter."

A few students giggled at the mangling of his first name. It wasn't hard like some of the other students' names like Elijachwon or Karrillia, whose names sounded nothing like their spelling.

Great. Somehow, he knew it would be him. He rose to stand, desperate to get this over with. It didn't seem like it could be worse, but he'd underestimated the principal.

"Get your backpack; you're not coming back to class."

If the kids were whispering before, they slipped into regular voice now, allowing him to hear their comments amid Ms. Gleason's inability to shush them.

"Do you think he's getting kicked out of school for beating up Caulb?"

Ethan cringed when he heard the words. The speaker, he easily identified as Dane South, whose name lent itself to future professions such as actor, war correspondent, or even athlete. With Dane's love of spreading gossip, Ethan could picture him as a Hollywood reporter sharing tidbits about the stars' lives with his celebrity-obsessed audience.

Jennifer McKellen answered his query with her usual, no nonsense attitude. "Are you kidding? The drug dealers are back at school, even after the drug dogs hit on their lockers. Supposed to be waiting on a court date. Nothing will happen to you. Caulb, either, for that matter."

Ethan slipped out the door, mulling over her comment. He'd missed that news. Principal Lowenson marched ahead, not even looking back to see if he followed. Each class door beckoned to him as a source of sanctuary. Both Leah and Nora's ability to disappear into the past was preferable to walking into what was going to be an unpleasant interview. What if Caulb was in the office?

Ethan's eyes darted to the outside doors, then back to the principal. His running ability had saved him on several occasions. As a big muscular male turning to fat, his principal's ability to sprint was subpar at best. For one second, he stopped and considered. Running would shape his future to be little better than Brendon's. Most of the school, he liked, except for the impromptu challenges to his continued existence.

His eyes went to the doors again. Leah thought he could get in one of those magnet schools with a theatre and music program. Many cities had moved to a new school system picking out various schools to specialize in different disciplines. The buildings were often the oldest buildings in the system, usually located in unsavory neighborhoods. Some were math and science magnets, appealing to future engineers. A few were accelerated college prep schools, offering AP courses and classical studies. Then there was the arts academy. Admittance would demand a good recommendation from his present school. A behavior issue label wouldn't do it. Principal Lowenson kept walking, leaving him behind. Ethan took a few jogging steps to catch up. Maybe the man could move faster than he originally thought.

The office loomed ahead as menacing as any dark alley filled with unknown dangers. Last time he'd been there to sign in it hadn't looked so frightening. The same bored student aide leaned against the counter. She looked up briefly, but no interest or recognition flared in her eyes.

A twisting hallway revealed several small offices with signs identifying as belonging to nurse, counselor, and curriculum alignment developer. The last title made him smile as he imagined someone arranging textbooks to stand in a straight row. His smile vanished when he saw the principal's office.

Lowenson strode through the open door without greeting anyone that meant there was no Caulb inside. Of course, it could mean the man felt no need to show any courtesy to students. Ethan's feet slowed on their own. Standing in the doorway, his eyes surveyed the room. No Caulb or anyone else, unless you counted the irritated man who showed his aggravation by his expression.

Leah joked about the former principal being frightened of Nana. It'd be nice to have him back, instead of this large, silent hulk. His initial glance, upon entering the room, catalogued the décor. You could tell a great deal about people by how they chose to decorate, or sometimes by the lack of decoration. Counselors and idealistic teachers papered the room with motivational posters with bright colors and catchy affirmations. Teachers, who didn't care, didn't put anything up on the walls. There might be a plant, barely hanging onto life on the back windowsill, which summed up their outlook toward teaching and life in general.

A classic glory days motif served as a decoration theme. A parent might mistake the pictures on the wall for the current football team. It wasn't. The dated hairstyles, along with the emblem on the uniforms, gave it away. Instead of framed diplomas as most people might have expected. There was a cheap certificate about being a most valuable player. The certificate looked familiar, since Ethan had similar awards. They meant nothing, since he sucked at every sport he tried.

The trophies in the display case intrigued him, but not enough to make him check them out. He wondered if they were as suspect as the certificate. There were glory days, and there were *alleged* glory days. No doubt, the man had played ball, but not as well as he pretended. In a way, it was sad how he glorified his football years. It made Ethan wonder how pitiful the rest of the principal's life had been, given the fact a few years in shoulder pads and spandex pants was the pinnacle of his existence.

A loud wheezing sound came from the principal's oversized rolling desk chair as he sat. Lowenson cocked one eyebrow at Ethan as if daring him to comment. To be safe, Ethan sucked his lips in to prevent a nervous giggle. The principal's large head dissolved into his equally large neck, making his resemblance to Caulb unmistakable. Maybe the thug could be his natural child, the result of some forgotten tryst under the stadium bleachers. Wouldn't that be wonderful?

Don't think about it, he mentally chided himself. Already anxious, that would only make it worse. True, the principal and Caulb had the same build, but that was true of at least a third of the male population. It didn't mean anything. Large men weren't necessarily bullies. Tristan, a fellow student in history class, could give both men a run for their money sizewise. All he cared about was fantasy novels and role-playing games. He never showed the least desire to bully anyone.

Think good thoughts, positive ones. Grandfather always reminded him whatever we thought about we attracted. If Ethan were honest, he'd admit a good part of his thoughts did center on Caulb. Maybe he had dwelt too much on the bully and his possible actions.

Principal Lowenson directed an intimidating stare his way. It made him drop into a nearby chair to avoid it. Ethan squirmed, still unaware of why he was in the office. Sure, he had suspicions, but he wasn't a hundred percent certain. Nana would caution him to confess to nothing. A person would think his aged relative was a hardened criminal with her suspicion of all authority.

The principal cleared his throat before speaking. "Mr. Carpenter, do you know why I brought you here?"

Manners were always good when in a bad situation. They usually bought time and favor. "No, sir." He crossed his fingers, which were below the principal's desk and view.

The man's lips twisted to one side, expressing a degree of disbelief with his grimace. "That's odd, considering your father came to see me today."

His father! To think, he had worried about his grandparents or his mother showing up to make his life worse. Lately, even Leah had been getting a bit confrontational with more of a chance of his sister showing up than his father. Adam Carpenter's motto had to be 'Fly under the Radar,' along with 'Do Your Job, and Keep Your Head Down'. He never did anything to attract attention, which was difficult with Nana as his mother-in-law. Rather than guilt by association, it was more like attention by Nana.

His stomach dropped. What had caused his father to make a surprise stop today? Trying to tap into the positive thought factor, he lobbed a distraction. "He stopped by to be the parent sponsor of the chess team?"

Principal Lowenson's bushy eyebrows furrowed down further, giving him a hairy V over his slightly bulging eyes. "We don't have a chess team."

He had known that. They also didn't have a robotics club, an academic team or Gay and Straight Student Alliance, either. Nope, all they had were sports and the few musical options that Mr. Zimmer had managed to eek out. "I know that, sir. I thought that maybe my father wanted to start one. He was one of the top contenders in college chess."

The belligerent expression on the principal's face disappeared only to have one of mild confusion replace it. "People actually compete in chess?"

He uttered the words the same way Ethan might have questioned competitions involving beheading chickens. He said nothing. Deciding it was rhetorical. The bewilderment passed as quickly as it came, along with the return of the menacing look. Ethan knew his 'look' was to intimidate the student. It had to be, since he felt threatened.

"Your father came," he practically growled the words, pausing for dramatic effect, "because he said you were being bullied."

Whoa, it was what he thought. Hadn't he explained how talking to school officials would make it worse or had he only thought it? Once again, Ethan chose to remain silent, since there didn't seem to be a correct response.

Principal Lowenson placed his beefy forearms on the desk and leaned toward Ethan, closing the space between them. "I don't like parents coming to my school and telling me their child is being bullied."

"Guess what, I don't like being bullied, either." *Oops, did he say that?* The stunned expression on the principal's face confirmed he probably had.

"Carpenter!"

His name came out with the crispness and energy he'd expect from a drill sergeant. He almost felt the desire to jump up and come to attention.

"I don't appreciate smart aleck answers."

Ethan's eyes focused on the principal's right hand, the one that was balling into a fist. He wouldn't hit him. It would be in the papers. He'd lose his job. Apparently, however, that didn't stop some school officials from doing stupid things. His answer wasn't disrespectful, just honest. There may have been a better way to say it. His gaze traveled around the room looking for a possible escape route if needed.

The principal must have considered his silence answer enough because he continued. "I tried to talk to Caulb Anderson, the boy your father named, for verification, but he appears to be absent today."

Really? He couldn't believe it. He'd ask the bully if he had been terrorizing any students. He would deny it. The principal would be happy with that and let it drop. No chance of that now.

While the teachers may not consider their principal smart, he must have some intelligence or at least a well-placed relative on the school board to get where he was. His father had probably come in making implied threats about newspapers, anti-bullying laws, and such. Lowenson had no way of knowing his father would never act on them. Then again, he had never expected his father to show up at school either.

"Anything you want to add to that Carpenter?"

It might sound like a question to most people, but it wasn't. No, it signaled the end of their discussion. It would go into his file with the fact his father had visited. A handwritten notation would denote the problem no longer existed. Unfortunately, he'd probably inform Caulb, which would incite the already perpetually angry male even more, if possible.

"No, sir." He knew there was no reason to dig the hole even deeper.

The man behind his desk grunted his assertion while writing out a pass. "Go back to class. I don't want to see you in my office again."

"Yes, sir." He didn't want to be in his office again either. He took the proffered pass and turned to leave.

"Carpenter."

The sound of his name stopped him at the door.

"Make sure you tell your father the matter has been handled."

He heard the unspoken message that accompanied the words. *Great*, now the principal was bullying him. Needed to ask Leah how to transfer to one of the magnet schools, immediately.

The bell sounded as he walked to class, sending his classmates into the hall. He looked for a friendly face, any type of reassurance, maybe a smile, eye contact. Instead, he received a beady-eyed stare from Donnie, Caulb's premier hanger-on.

As far as size went, the slight student might even be shorter than Ethan. On one level, being a bully's lackey probably assured his survival. He watched as the various students bumped into Donnie. One sizable football player knocked him into a locker. The day sucked for him, without his belligerent leader to clear the way.

It looked like most students knew Donnie was toothless and no threat without the hulking, angry Caulb by his side. The young male made a determined effort to pass through the hall, like a salmon swimming upstream, even though there was some order to the chaos of passing period. Those on the right side were going down the hall, while those on the left went up. Most of the students could drive and used the rules of the road for getting to their next class.

Ethan happened to be in the right lane and allowed the momentum of the crowd to carry him as Donnie grew closer and closer. He reminded him of a confused driver who had turned into traffic the wrong way onto a one-way street. Ethan's eyes stayed on him as if they were magnetically drawn.

Between the broad backs and heads, often blocking his view, he glimpsed Donnie. At one point, he noticed he was talking. The noise level in the hallway wiped out any chance of hearing what he said. His lips moved, repeating the same words over and over.

The science lab appeared to his right, his next class, and Ethan elbowed his way out of the pack. Students milled around the room chattering loudly, since the teacher was out of the room. Ethan went to his assigned seat and sunk down in it gratefully. He tried to recall what Donnie was saying. His grandfather was a big believer that lip-reading could come in handy.

The man now looked at the world very differently after spending time in another century. Everything gave you the information you needed to survive. You could smell an enemy. Even feel them from how their position in the dark woods blocked the breeze. Reading lips also gave you the information.

The mental image of Donnie speaking occupied his thoughts. The first word looked like "He's" even though it was pushed out through gritted teeth. "Coming" was the next word. Donnie may have realized he couldn't hear in the chaotic hallway and held up four fingers. Then he pointed at Ethan on the last word. "*He's coming for you,*" he whispered the phrase.

That should be no surprise. He expected as much, but his heart still dropped into his stomach. This must be how animals on the verge of extinction must feel. Maybe they didn't know, so it wasn't as troubling. Not knowing would have been preferable.

CHAPTER SIX

S IMON SLID INTO the seat next to him. "Hey, pard, I have an idea for the science fair." Without waiting for a response, Simon ruffled through an accordion style binder pulling out several different papers. After scanning them, he shook his head and pushed them back in.

Most of his friends considered Ethan lucky, since Mr. Palatino had paired him with the one boy in the class of Japanese descent. Their reasoning was Asian kids were crazy smart, especially in math and science. Brooke pointed out Simon would do most of the lab work himself, being a perfectionist. Ethan's first response was to point out they were all feeding into ethnic stereotypes. However, Simon demonstrated the first day they worked together that he was the template for that stereotype.

Ethan half-watched his partner paw through his stuffed binder. His immediate concerns dealt with the possible shortness of future life. Caulb may not intend to kill him, but people die every day from head injuries.

His mind wandered and an image of the two smiling brothers flashed into his memory. It was last winter and the Torres brothers were going somewhere together. He couldn't remember if they'd gone to a movie, out to eat, or even to a job. All he remembered was they always went everywhere together, which wasn't that unusual.

He couldn't quite remember the name of the older brother, Rod or something like it. *Rodrigo* that was it. He was off at community college, but Pablo was still in high school. Leah knew them more than Ethan did, but he'd seen them around. Leah introduced them when they bumped into the two at the strip mall the summer before. Rodrigo had come to pick up his little brother. Apparently, the younger brother bussed tables at the Mexican restaurant in the mall.

Ethan remembered thinking it was ironic that a Mexican was working at a Mexican restaurant, but it wasn't really. He applied for the job, and they hired him. Maybe the owners knew Pablo would work harder than the usual slacker teens, the same ones who usually gave Pablo hostile looks full of pent-up hostility, and begrudgingly did as little work as possible, after finishing their texts or gossiping with another employee. No, Pablo was the exact opposite of the typical teen fast food worker.

On the day they met, he remembered the bigger brother wrapping an arm around his little brother as he came out of the restaurant. He acted as if he were genuinely happy to see him. At the time, he wondered what it must be like to have a brother. In a family dominated by women, he missed brotherly camaraderie. Sure, he watched television with his father, but that wasn't the same.

Remembering the friendship between the two made the accident, so much harder to swallow. As rumor had it, the two of them had come back late from somewhere. They were in the deserted mall parking lot and arguing about whose turn it was to pay for gas. The two of them stepped out of the car and continued to argue on that frigid winter's evening. Rodrigo claimed Pablo slipped and hit his head on the concrete parking lot marker.

Some of the kids at school whispered, they had been drinking. He didn't know if it was true or not. It wasn't in the papers, so he doubted it. The same kids declared the two brothers were fighting, and Rodrigo, being the bigger of the two, easily knocked his younger brother to the ground. On his way down, Pablo's head bounced off the concrete parking lot marker, killing him instantly.

His brother was inconsolable. He blamed himself, of course. That's all it took. One little slip on an icy road and you were dead. The finality of that stuck in his head. Maybe the brothers argued some. That wasn't unreasonable. Heated words could have been exchanged, but he doubted punches happened over gas. If it had, imagine how much worse it must be on Rodrigo.

The message he took from the incident was the human body was a delicate organism, and a random accident could end existence. Caulb's fist wouldn't be so random.

Simon snorted with glee and waved a paper over his head. "I found it. This will make our science fair project a guaranteed winner. We'll go to Regionals."

The paper clutched in Simon's hand bore a series of complex formulas that made Ethan's head hurt just thinking about it. Math wasn't his strong suit. He'd have to ask, and clearly, Simon fully expected him to. "So, what's this great idea?"

"Idea?" Simon used his index finger to push up his slipping glasses. "It's more like a vision, a dream. It was Einstein's really. Many others, too."

At the mention of Einstein, Ethan immediately knew he didn't want to participate in the project. Why couldn't they just grow something like tomato plants and entertain the plants with different music to see which one grew best? Sure, it'd been done to death, but it seemed to be a crowd favorite. "What idea did Einstein have?"

Simon's face lit up, just waiting for the right question to explain the intricacies of science to him. *Yay, him.* Well, at least someone was happy today.

"I am so glad you asked. Einstein came up with several theories, many he saw proven, but this one never was." Simon gestured with the paper wielding hand. "He believed people could time travel. Are you not astounded?"

Ethan bit his bottom lip to keep from confessing he wasn't amazed. With his time traveling family and his new brother-in-law who happened to step through a time portal from a previous century, time travel wasn't a mystery. "Um, yeah. What did you have in mind? A tiny time machine to transport mice through the centuries?"

Simon stopped gesturing with the paper, considering the comment. "That would be great, but I'm just at the theoretical point. I thought we could demonstrate with diagrams or animations how it could work. Supposedly, the space lab is orbiting faster than the earth, which puts it into the future. Mere seconds, but it's still in the future. Imagine. What you could do if you could travel to the future?"

The idea tantalized him, but not for the usual reasons. He had no noble desires to learn cures for various diseases. Right now, the only life he wanted to save was his own. After that, he might be able to concentrate on helping others.

What if Simon somehow figured out how to travel through time? Like Brooke said, the boy was crazy smart and gifted. "So, how does this time travel work? Are there time portals you can find, and walk through?"

Simon placed the paper on the table and smoothed it out. "Time portals." He snorted briefly. It may have been a laugh, but it was hard to tell. "You've watched too much television."

It would be easy to have Clayton come and talk to his partner about walking through the portal as indisputable proof. Still, who would believe Clayton? As a family, they agreed no one would speak of it. Declaring his brother-in-law as a recent immigrant excused his strange ways. "How does it work?"

"I'm glad you asked." Simon grinned, shifting into his lecture mode. Taking the paper, he'd previously smoothed, he shook it out and allowed it to stack in gentle ripples on the desk with a little downward assistance from his hand.

"Einstein believed time was folded." His free hand gestured to the paper as if it was a prize in a game show and he was the show's display model. The announcer would say 'And here we have Einstein's folded time theory.'

"What difference does this make?" He knew all the responses Simon wanted. In a way, the two of them were a regular science act.

Simon bobbed his head enthusiastically. "It makes a huge difference.

If time were linear as most think, we could never travel through it. We would be stuck in the here and now. If time is indeed folded, with the right angle, speed, and happenstance we can go to different times or technically different dimensions."

Even though he knew it happened in his family, no one could definitively explain it. "If people have traveled through time, why don't we hear of it?"

"Those who talk about it end up in a padded room. Others choose to say nothing, so they won't be locked up. Makes sense, right?" Simon leaned forward waiting for his reply.

He had no clue how right he was. Then again, it was Simon. He'd figure out the mysteries of the universe if given enough time.

"Um, yeah." Ethan hesitated to agree, since people might think he was whack. What else did he really need to make his life more complicated? He never mentioned his family's beliefs. While some wouldn't care, a few of the students would think he participated in animal sacrifices and would force him to watch endless hours of PETA videos on YouTube to deprogram him. A few would want to watch the *alleged* sacrifices. Those were the ones who truly creeped him out. That was only one part of his life.

"Simon, what has got you so interested in time travel?"

"Well." Simon hesitated and looked around the room in a furtive manner as if concerned anyone was listening. "You know my family practices Shintoism. Some people say we worship our ancestors, but it is more than that."

His classmates never mentioned Simon's religion, if that is what it was. Could be all Japanese were participants in Shintoism. The concept interested him, so he nodded, instead of speaking, hoping Simon would explain.

Simon sidled closer and lowered his voice. "We believe everything has a spiritual essence, which is called *Kami*. The trees have it; people have it, and the spirits have it. Those who have gone on have it. Often people will ask the ancestors for advice and get it. This makes me wonder if people don't so much leave this world, but shift to another dimension. In this new plane, they can still interact with those left behind.

Ethan shifted his weight between feet as he considered Simon's words. "I don't know. Maybe you can talk to those who died, but what does that have to do with time travel?"

The fact the teacher hadn't shown yet piqued his curiosity, some, but it didn't seem to bother anyone else. Teachers delayed class start time by gossiping in the hallway with their fellow employees. They were as reluctant to teach the boring curriculum, as the students were to absorb it.

Appearing distracted, Simon opened his accordion binder and ran his finger over the tabs as he talked, refusing to make eye contact. "I saw my grandparents."

He was talking about ghosts. Well, that was something entirely different from time travel. He wasn't sure if the whole-time travel argument was a way to introduce the subject of things that went bump in the night. If so, did Ethan have *medium* tattooed on his forehead? His family may have played their Wiccan beliefs close to their chest, except for Nana, who was more flamboyant than most drag queens.

"Um, really?" He tried to remember if Simon's grandparents had died recently. He didn't remember Simon saying anything about it. "Wait. Don't your grandparents live with you? Aren't they still alive?"

His friend nodded vigorously. "Yes, yes, exactly. I saw them young. Maybe just after being married. I was walking through the house one morning, and I turned the corner and spotted them."

Talk about weird. "What were they doing?"

Simon looked up enough to make eye contact. His somber countenance solidified the fact his friend was telling the truth. Besides, Simon wasn't given to pranks or teasing. "They were sitting at the kitchen table holding hands. Not sure what they were talking about, but they looked so serious and young."

What would he do if that had happened to him? For a second, he tried to imagine his grandparents at a younger age. His mind dressed them as young hippies. He knew for sure, there had never been anything ordinary about Nana.

A student standing near the door gestured that someone was coming. Most of the students moved to their assigned seats. A couple going at it hot and heavy in the corner ignored the warning. Since he and Simon were already in their places, they didn't have to move. He eyed the couple in the corner and wondered if he should nudge them with his foot or something. He decided against it since he was much more interested in Simon's story. "Do you think they saw you?"

His friend opened his mouth, only to close it without answering. His face took on a thoughtful expression as his eyes rolled upward. He could hear the booming fake heartiness of Principal Lowenson's voice indicating he was on the way to their room, which was unusual, especially since they didn't have a teacher.

Ethan glanced at the door, then back at his friend. Simon still looked mildly perplexed. He could imagine his friend's mind working like one of those old mainframe computers with the reels spinning and lights going on and off as it executed each command. Tamping down his urgency, he fought the urge to tell his friend to hurry up with an answer.

Simon was a linear thinker. Any type of interruption and he'd need to start from the beginning again. The classroom door swung open just as he started to answer.

"I think they did see me. For a second, they stopped talking and both looked at me, as if they could really see me."

"Really? The question is did you enter their time or were they in yours?" He figured his friend had stumbled into their time, which meant the future crossed into their time if only for a moment. It also explained how future Ethan had paid a visit, sort of. He felt like his older self had made an intentional visit.

The students busied themselves as the principal entered the room with an older woman. Most of his classmates had enough sense to open the biology book or a notebook as if working. The principal's voice bounced off the hard-topped lab tables and steel fixtures.

"You see, Mrs. Appleby, the students are hard at work. Sure, was good of you to come at such short—"

The woman yelped and pointed to a corner, causing everyone to turn. The fondling couple must have sensed something was wrong when the room stilled. While both their faces mirrored shocked expressions, they were still prone on the floor. Ethan craned his head to look around Simon. Yeah, that's what he thought he saw. Devlin still had his hand up under his girlfriend's skirt. The principal and most of the room stared at where his arm ended at the edge of her cheerleader flounce. *Skirt* seemed too generous of a word for that article of clothing.

He fought a smile over how much his inner thoughts sounded more like his grandfather's than a typical male teen. The principal spotted him, took a step in his direction and growled.

"Something funny?"

Damn, he was sure he hadn't smirked. "Oh no, sir, science is a very serious business." He looked down at the table before the man could try to pull him into confrontation. After all, he wasn't the one rolling around on the floor in front of twenty-two captivated pairs of eyes. Captivated may have been overstating it. Devlin and Bree tended to go with their most basic tendencies whenever they were within a yard of one another.

Kennedy told him once the history teacher no longer turned off the lights to watch movies due to Bree and Devlin's efforts to make their own sex tape at school. Apparently, Bree's mother was so incensed she made sure they were both in separate history classes after that. Bree never mentioned to her mother that she had science with her sweetie, too.

Someone giggled, causing Lowenson to abandon his one-sided stare down to locate the culprit. *Thank goodness for gigglers.* The woman was still pointing at the couple, but at least Devlin had enough sense to retract his hand. Red-faced Bree stood up and tried to move to her seat as if nothing out of the ordinary happened, but then from her point of view, this was all normal.

The principal snapped his fingers as if the girl was a dog coming to heel. He pointed to the door. Then he motioned to Devlin and directed him with an abrupt gesture to the exit. He strolled past the open-mouthed woman. At the last second, he turned and fixed the class with an icy stare. "I am not in the mood to find out any of you misbehaved for Mrs. um, ah...."

The woman took a step in the principal's direction while offering a verbal lifeline. "It's Appleby. Miss Appleby."

The principal's neck flushed at her assertion, probably more disgruntled at his need for assistance than thankful for her providing it. He gave an abrupt nod and headed out the door to deal with Devlin and Bree.

Ethan doubted they'd get much of a punishment. Principal Lowenson would warn them about the difficulty of finishing school with a child, while most likely winking at Devlin while delivering the lecture. It would be better than the inference he had received that he was somehow to blame for any bullying happening. It would be the same as telling the Thanksgiving turkey that his actions caused him to end up stuffed on an oversized platter. Most turkeys would prefer to be elsewhere other than on the platter. Same with him, except it wasn't a platter; he worried about, but more about keeping himself intact and alive.

Miss Appleby assigned them to read chapter four and do the questions at the end of the chapter. There was a little grumbling as folders and books opened. Swiveling his head, he took an informal survey of who was working. A few students were working on math. No big surprise there, homework was a major component of the final math grade. The fruity scent of lip-gloss alerted him a nearby student was in the process of refreshing her make up. Four others were texting, while two slept.

Tessa typed feverishly away on her laptop on the novel she was writing, amazing him how teachers never suspected she wasn't doing classwork. The truth was they probably didn't care, as long as she didn't disturb anyone, or the lesson presentation. Ethan assumed she turned in her work. A sideways glance revealed his partner carefully printing answers to the chapter questions. *Of course.*

"Simon," he hissed the words so as not to attract the sub's attention. Simon stopped writing to look up.

"Yes?" His eyebrows arched above his heavy framed glasses.

The boy couldn't have picked out better glasses if he wanted to be a walking stereotype. Oddly, it worked for Simon, who didn't care about fashion, but only practicality. The glasses added to his geek image. "You do realize when Mr. Koppel returns, everyone will tell him there was no homework."

Simon nodded in agreement, but turned the textbook page to see the next question. "True, but Mr. Koppel could believe it's a scam student often perpetuate when teachers are absent. He could collect work and count it as a grade or extra credit. Why not be safe? The worse that could happen is learning something. Isn't that what school is all about?"

Once again, Simon had bested him. Theoretically, school was about learning. Of course, he always wanted to know what lessons he was learning. Ripping a sheet of paper from his notebook, Ethan wrote his name and date. His eyes drifted over the question about equilibrium within an organism.

He knew an organism tried to remain the same. Sometimes this happened by expelling a foreign substance or allowing water to pass through its membranes. How could he express that in an answer? The school was like a large organism in a way. A strong click of his mechanical pencil indicated his readiness.

Nana used to say that writing was like opening a vein and bleeding all over. It had discouraged him from writing at first. Luckily, he had an empathetic English teacher who explained it meant we put a part of ourselves into writing. That he could accept.

Our school is a large organism of sorts. The doors serve as the membranes, allowing the students to enter and exit at will. New freshmen are often treated like invaders. Some manage to fool the guards posted near the membrane doors by mimicking the behavior and dress of the upperclassmen. Often, older versions of the new students transport the newcomer to the right clique. Those who managed to get through the membrane/doors, but still appear odd or not fitting in, must provide a service.

The student has to prove useful to exist within the organism. This can be by being a class clown, a brain who helps other students with homework, or having a unique, but useful talent such as computer hacking. This is usually truer of the male students. The male students easily accept attractive female students.

This acceptance creates disunity in the organism with the female students trying to eject the new female students via rumors or cyber bullying. Often the ejected student enrolls in a parochial school, which is an entirely different type of organism. The school community works hard to maintain their equilibrium.

Simon peeked over his shoulder to read his answer. "Do you think Koppel will be okay with your answer?"

That might be a problem. He considered his short, slight science teacher with glasses as heavy as Simon. "He'll get it. He might even appreciate some creative thinking on my part."

"It's your funeral. I'm going with the textbook stuff." Simon snorted, before returning to his work.

The sub walked over to their desk with rapid steps and rapped a ruler on their lab table. "Boys, boys, silence."

Ethan stared at the clearly anxious woman. What did she expect him to do? If he said anything then he wouldn't be silent. Simon mirrored his actions. For a few seconds they engaged in an uncomfortable staring contest until someone on the other side of the room giggled.

The woman pivoted in her orthopedic shoes to investigate the laugher. It kept him from lying if she asked what their names were. Another trip to the principal's office was something he'd like to avoid. With his luck, Simon would not only give their right names, but spell it correctly for her too.

Thank the Goddess, the scenario never took form. The digital clock on the wall indicating he still had twenty-one minutes of mind-numbing boredom until lunch. A shrill siren and a blinking light indicated a fire drill. At least, he thought it was a drill.

Miss Appleby ran to the door and threw it open only to see students streaming past. "Oh! Where are we supposed to go?"

Tessa saved her document, closed her computer, and tucked it under her arm before standing to explain the emergency procedure to the clearly startled woman. The girl might not talk much, but she did manage to radiate confidence. He watched the heavyset girl calmly indicate which way they should travel by gesturing with her free hand. A familiar emblem on a chain swung free as Tessa turned to motion the class to stand up.

Surprisingly, none of the dramatic girls screamed about dying a fiery death. Instead, they exited the room without a sound, probably due more to Tessa than the sub, who was clearly wringing her hands. Simon and he were the last to leave.

Tessa's necklace intrigued him with its assorted crystals, stars, and tiny medallions. He'd never gotten close enough to examine it without looking odd. He worked his way through the shuffling students, noticing a scent of something burning. Maybe the school was on fire. Oddly, the thought didn't overly concern him. He felt everyone would get out safely.

"There he is!"

A voice he recognized too well destroyed his certainty that everything would work out fine. Caulb and one of his henchmen stood at the end of the abandoned hallway. A blue cast reaching to his nemesis' elbow attracted his attention for a second. Wow, he must have really messed up his arm. Sirens screamed in the distance.

Time to get out. He started for the exit where all the other students had crowded through onto the football field. The door slammed shut. The grinning face of another henchman peered through it. That explains where the missing henchmen went. *Crap.* What happened to concerned administration patrolling the halls to make sure everyone got out?

Caulb stalked toward him thumping his cast into his hand as opposed to his fist. It wouldn't be good to use it for wailing on him if his bone was broken. Ethan kept the thought to himself, realizing the bully wouldn't listen to a word he said, even if it was for his benefit.

Ethan stood frozen to the spot. The smoke smell dissipated, indicating it had been a ruse to get everyone out of the building and isolate him. Unfortunately, he had played into Caulb's hands by being slow to exit the room.

In a few moments, the firefighters would be running through the building. He just had to stay alive that long. It didn't make sense. Nana said he would be safe. He tried to keep his focus on Caulb, while mentally checking out escape routes.

Caulb's lips turned up in an evil grin. He almost drooled. It looked like Ethan had waited too late to make a break for it. His sidekick would herd him into Caulb's fists. He wasn't going without a fight though.

His nemesis's eyes grew wide with shock, the same time Ethan felt a hand on his shoulder.

CHAPTER SEVEN

E THAN'S HEART SKIPPED a beat as he wondered whose hand landed. It could be the principal's, which would make sense. It would mean both he and Caulb would be suspended. Something he was trying to avoid. His nemesis's eyes bulged, followed by a dropping of his jaw. The principal wouldn't cause such a reaction. Caulb's lackey stood frozen in a darting pose. It was hard to determine if he was circling around to prevent Ethan from escaping Caulb or if he was leaving while he could.

"We need to talk."

The voice sounded familiar. He tried to place it. Anxiety over whom he would find behind him kept him from turning.

Caulb managed to shake out of his stupor long enough to stammer. "There's two of you. No freaking way." He pivoted and headed the other way, spurring his little toady to run with him.

Oh yeah, now he remembered the voice. It was the future him. The firefighters crashed through the doors at the other end of the hall, distracting him for a moment. "Great, now they'll pin the fire on me."

"No, they won't." His future self spoke as he twirled him around. It was peculiar looking at an older version of himself. The eyes were different, more almond shaped and darker. *Odd.* Had he opted for cosmetic surgery and colored lenses? He was shocked to see next to him was a muscle-bound monstrosity. No wonder Caulb ran.

The silver man had no face. However, a visor reminiscent of a science fiction movie blinked colors as if it were thinking or gearing up to shoot a death ray at him. Running looked like an option, one he'd used before. Future-Self tightened his grip and shoved him in the direction of the chemistry lab.

"Not there, that's the first place they'll look." He stumbled in the direction of the lab, even though he was sure he resisted going. Future-Self was a great deal stronger than he looked or maybe he had some high level magick he could use to control others. *Sweet*, he could use some of that.

As if hearing his thoughts, Future-Self frowned in his direction. "No, you couldn't. Anyone who wants to have power over other people is definitely not a candidate for that type of magick." The large silver creature bounded into the room, acting more like a friendly dog than a menace. He slid next to Future-Self, dwarfing the man with his metallic bulk.

The running footsteps and doors crashing open indicated the close location of the firefighters as they searched for the source of the fire. Would he give a little wave when they entered the chemistry lab and say, "Oh, don't mind me? My future self just dropped in for a visit with his silver pal."

The silver creature touched him, stilling his words. Would the creature hurt him? Could Future-Self stop him even if he wanted to? The coppery taste of blood filled his mouth. In his anxiety, his upper teeth had clamped down hard on his bottom lip.

"Be at peace. Are all people of your time, so fearful?" Future-Self asked as he completed the circle holding onto him and silver robot dude. To a stranger it might look like they were playing Ring around the Rosey. Was everyone fearful? That was a good question. It depended on whom you were talking to, but he figured most people did fear something. Their fears just differed. His father worried about losing his job due to rumors about his Pagan associations. His own fear was Caulb and non-acceptance if he officially outed himself. Then there was the issue that identifying as gay might not work out. Maybe he couldn't make a go of it with the gay community.

Before he could explain his fears, his body began to vibrate and hum. *Earthquake? Bomb*? He tried to focus on any stationary object in the room to see if it were shaking. The clock didn't appear to be moving, but it did shimmer in and out of focus. The firefighters' voices in the hall became distorted, getting louder, and then softer, almost inaudible. The room grew darker, until he could no longer see it. The floor melted away, sending him falling into the dark.

The only thing he knew for sure was his arms were still gripped by Future-Self and Robo-man. As quickly as it grew dark, white light surrounded him, blinding him. Instead of falling, he was spinning in a fast circle reminiscent of the twirling rides at the Viking World theme park, the ones Leah begged him not to spin because they made her feel sick. It made him a little nauseous too, but he spun the rides anyhow. That's what brothers did.

The spinning slowly stopped until he almost felt like he was floating. They drifted to a stop. Images and colors began to form around him. They were in a valley with a thick cushy grass, spattered with groups of purple and yellow flowers. Nearby pine trees perfumed the air while a pair of courting cardinals flew past them. There were mountains in the distance. The sun rested almost on the tip of one. He blinked.

Wasn't the sun by the mountain on his right? Now, it looked like it was by the mountain on his left. He swung his head rapidly side to side.

There were two suns. That couldn't be right, but it might explain the hot, dry air.

"Where am I?"

Future-Self smiled at him. "You're home, my home, my city, Terra Nova."

Both Future-Self and Robo-guy had dropped their grips on his arms. The robot made a sighing sound. In a crisp British accent, the droid commented, "It's certainly good to be back in a civilized place."

The upper-class Brit accent startled Ethan, almost as much as the insistence on calling the valley a city. A deer wandered out between trees and began to graze. Even though they stood conversing barely a yard from the doe, she paid no attention to them. "Why isn't she afraid of us?" He gestured toward the deer, certain his gesture would send her fleeing. Instead, she looked up briefly, regarded him with large, gentle eyes before returning to grazing.

The man he thought of as future Ethan motioned to himself. "I don't mean any disrespect, seeing you're my ancestor and all, but I'd liked to be called by my actual name, Martel."

Ethan nodded his head as he softly uttered the name. "Martel." Then he remembered Martel mentioning the word ancestor. "You called me your ancestor as if I lived hundreds of years in the past." The thought made him laugh.

The metal man cocked his head. "It is true. You may call me Davin. I am the companion, not a monster as your earlier apprehensions might indicate."

Wow. He looked around for somewhere to sit before he fell from the shock of it all. Leafy trees threw shade into the thick carpet of grass. Patches of wild flowers added color. A couple of large boulders huddled together amid the temperate paradise. Ethan made his way over to them. Each step was difficult and slow as if moving through water. Finally, he reached the stone grouping.

Davin followed him, keeping up a running monologue. "As the ancestor, you have demonstrated great sensing skills, immediately locating the entrance to the city despite it being hidden."

He had no clue what Davin was talking about. It was hard to be frightened of anyone who sounded like him. "Are you from England?"

The lights chased back and forth across Davin's visor. Martel finally caught up with them. "That's not a question he can answer since he has no concept of his creation or where he came from. *He simply is.* I chose his accent as well as everything else about him." A blush accompanied this statement.

Okay, he was sitting on a boulder somewhere with two suns. Discussing, with a version of himself, how to design your own companion. *Yeah, right*. He pinched himself just to be sure he wasn't still asleep. It hurt.

Martel drew closer, looked pointedly at the red spot on his arm. "You hurt yourself. Why? Is this the custom of your time?"

Why did he ever think this man was an older version of himself? Had he implied he was? Had he only said he was from the future? Resting back on his hands, Ethan stared up at the blue sky and fluffy clouds as he considered the question. Did the people of his time go around hurting themselves?

They didn't. His answer was ready as his eyes continued to survey the sky. There were the two suns again same as before, reminding him, even if the landscape looked somewhat familiar, he was still far from home.

Davin answered for him when he continued to stare at the sky, trying to reconcile to himself that he was far from home and his time.

"I have researched your time. Did not your people use chemical substances that often messed with their senses, causing harm to themselves and others?"

Chemical substances, what was he talking about. Oh yeah. *Drugs*. "Yeah, some people get messed up on drugs. They end up screwing up their lives or someone else's."

Martel nodded in agreement. "Your time is a troubled time with so much hatred and bullying. People feel the right to harass each other for their differences, instead of embracing what makes them unique."

The image of Caulb thumping his cast threateningly in his hand filled his head. "Yeah, I gotta agree. Currently, we aren't big on diversity. I heard there are some places that are, but they don't seem to be anywhere close to my house."

Memories of the Pagan Pride festival flickered to life, and the ease he felt came with a longing for Orin. Where was he? What happened to him? Would he see him again? There was a tightening in his chest, which could be either despair or hope. It was hard to tell. If Martel knew his future, perhaps he could tell what happened. "How do you know so much about me?"

The face so like his, except for the dark elongated eyes, simply grinned. "Come to the city and I will try to explain."

A beeping and whirling sound came from behind the rocks and one rock shifted, revealing a staircase. Martel moved ahead, gesturing for Ethan to follow. "Davin will close the door."

Inside the subway-like tunnel, sounds floated up, including a mingling of people talking, music, and laughter. The sounds grew louder as they walked lower and the light grew brighter. The trio emerged into a large open area that went on forever. Smooth streets glistened as if made of marble. Trees flourished their branches, reaching up. His eyes followed the branches expecting to see a cave-like roof or even industrial beams, instead he saw blue sky complete with birds soaring back and forth.

Martel gestured to the sky. "Yes, we are underground. The whole purpose of building underground was to preserve the natural environment. Even underground people need to see the sky and feel the grass under their feet."

Okay, he could buy it, but he didn't understand why everyone was underground like moles. An air vehicle passed them, hovering above the ground, silently gliding by. The occupants turned to stare at him, the focus of their attention as they blinked their elongated eyes while pointing in his direction.

"Why underground?"

Pulling on one ear, Martel appeared to be deep in thought. "Even though I pulled you from your time to ensure my own survival, I am still not allowed to reveal the details of the future. I can explain some details and then later wipe your mind free of it the way I did to your friends back at your school."

Mind wipe didn't sound like something he wanted. Would he forget who he was or those who were important to him? "Not my friends. I don't want a mind wipe, if possible. Can you just generalize, so it won't be like you told me anything that would change the outcome of the future?"

An appetizing smell wafted from nearby buildings, causing his stomach to rumble. *Lasagna*, he'd recognize that smell anywhere. Thank the Goddess Italian restaurants still existed. His stomach growled again, adding its own commentary.

"You're hungry? You should have said something." Martel gestured to a building with a red and white striped awning. A family was walking under the canopy. They caught sight of him and stopped. Then, as one, they put their hands together and bowed. Unsure of what to do, he put his hands together in a prayer-like fashion and bowed back. The gesture seemed to please the family who smiled almost on cue, bowed again, and began to walk backwards.

Strange behavior, that's for sure. "What was that about? They acted like I was the queen or something."

"The Queen, the queen." Uncertainty sounded in the British accented voice as the lights blinked off and on Davin's visor.

Martel shook his head. "He searched for the term, but since there is no type of royalty in our world, he won't find the answer he's looking for. In a way you are like the queen because you are one of the founders of our little world."

Founder. He was a founder. That would imply he had children. That was unexpected, but Martel did resemble him in some ways. "Am I a father in my future?"

Placing a hand over his mouth, somehow Martel managed to make his already large eyes look even larger. "I may have said too much. A mind wipe may be inevitable."

They turned and walked under the awning, following the enticing aroma. This threat of a mind wipe thing was getting old. The darkened interior, tables with checkered tablecloths and candles glowing stuck in Chianti wine bottles, reminded him of his own neighborhood restaurants. People were at various tables. A couple of females close by were holding hands and whispering in one another's ears. At the next table, he noticed two elderly males getting up to leave. One helped the other one up by wrapping an arm around the frailer one. They were both dressed in plain tunics, and leggings bearing no type of decoration. Everyone he'd seen wore the same functional clothing with no patterns or designs.

It appeared that same sex couples were neither unusual nor controversial. A waiter led them to a table. They passed what Ethan considered a traditional couple with a small baby between the two of them. Then he passed a table with two males and one female who all seemed to be actively flirting with one another. He'd heard of it, but never witnessed it.

"Ah, looks like a poly bond wooing is taking place." Martel cooed the words as if pleased. "Our population is limited. People cannot always expect to find a perfect companion or even a companion. That's why some of us must create our own or end up being alone."

Well, that explained Davin, but surely, he could have made him more human-like. They passed another two men sitting together. Martel waved to them, but murmured behind his upheld hand. "That Cigna insisted on a lifelike model. He's not fooling anyone."

Davin snorted his opinion. Ethan turned back to gaze at the older man and the ramrod straight younger male. Ah yes, he must be a droid too. Everything was so different here. Still, it seemed calm, even restful. They finally arrived at the table, where the waiter flourished menus. He bowed slightly in Ethan's direction. Ethan bowed back, unsure what the protocol was for being a founder.

He opened the menu and found beautiful glowing pictures of mouthwatering entrees, complete with aromas. It all looked good. He pointed to the lasagna. "I want that, please."

Martel pointed out his selection to the waiter. The man pulled out a device that resembled a pepper grinder and dispensed a pill onto each of their plates.

The waiter kissed his fingers. "Bon appetite," he said before walking away.

Martel picked up the pill with his spoon and carefully placed it in his mouth. A look of sheer bliss passed over his face, and then he swallowed. "Their Eggplant Parmesan is to die for. So generous with the portions, I'm stuffed."

"All you had was one little pill." He knew one capsule was not going to fill him. Nana used to joke he must have a hollow leg. Fingering the pill, he popped it into his mouth, not expecting anything but the sensation of a simple pill going down his throat.

Flavors danced on his tongue, sautéed onions, sweet garlic, robust plum tomatoes, chewy noodles, and the rich hearty taste of ground beef. It was all there, along with some unidentified spices. He swallowed, almost reluctantly, and found himself full. He patted his stomach that pushed against his pants. His eyes met Martel's. "How?"

"It's kitchen magick. The chef is one of the best in the city. The capsules provide the appropriate nutrients to counter our dwindling food supply. Those who remembered eating still wanted to have the same experience, which explains the popularity of sensation restaurants. You experience the meal."

Magick in everyday use, how freaky. "So, people use magick everyday here?"

Davin's visor lights blinked off and on, as he followed the conversation. He appeared to be interested, although he said nothing.

"Oh yes, without magick we couldn't create the world we have now. Isn't it wonderful?" Martel flung his hand out to indicate the restaurant and probably the smooth roads outside, complete with flying cars and trees that reached to a fake sky. It was different from his world, but all the people seemed to be content. That was a huge change.

"Um, what about…" He hesitated now, not really knowing how to put it. "Um… the people, who are against magick and all."

Martel tapped his index and middle finger against his nose. "I can't remember their names. I think they were called the unbelievers."

"No, I think that is what they called us, the Pagans." Ethan gestured for Martel to continue.

"Well, to my parents and grandparents, they were the unbelievers. The planet you now live on had much of its natural resources diminished. The population was rampant and the seas fished out. Crops wouldn't grow despite all the special chemicals put in the genetically engineered seeds. It really was the end. Scientists predicted the sun would go supernova, which would finish off an already dying planet."

It was a dismal picture, but Ethan knew it could happen. Even Mr. Stobel, his science teacher, commented how we were on our way to wiping out most species existing on the planet. "What happened?" How did he become a founder?

"Rocket ships were built to function more like intergalactic cruise ships. Advertisements went out begging people to take a chance on a new earth. Scientists had located several inhabitable planets, including this one."

There were plenty of movies about the end of the world and only the very wealthy or the important people were able to get a seat on such a ship. "So, you're telling me my descendants were rich enough or important enough to get a seat on these ships?

Davin broke into the conversation. "This part is in my memory banks." He nodded in Martel's direction. "I appreciate the upgrade. All the rich people, those who considered themselves better than others, even a few titled scientists, got on those ships, but they never made it out of the atmosphere without crashing."

It was hard to imagine people eagerly boarding the ships for a new life only to die a fiery death. "What happened?"

Martel shook his head. "The usual human nature. Failure to follow the rules, believing the rules did not apply to them. I think you know the story. The ships were too heavy to generate the necessary velocity to overcome Earth's gravity. Often people tried to smuggle in their possessions, even carrying things like gold bars and jewelry, knowing there was a strict weight limit. One individual even tried to hide servants in the cargo hold. In the end, all three ships crashed."

Greed was the short answer. Greed and the belief they could circumvent the rules. They probably had bypassed the rules most of the time, but the last broken rule had finally caught up with them. The waiter hovered near the tables with small menus. Martel spotted the man.

"Ah, dessert." He clapped his hands in delight. "You are in for a real treat. Chef Limone's specialty is the lavender sorbet."

He didn't see how a pill could simulate something cold and creamy, but he'd try it. Nodding, he watched the waiter move away instead of flourishing his ever-present food pill dispenser.

Martel paid no attention to the disappearing waiter and continued with his story. "After the three crashes, ministers began saying it was God's punishment for trying to leave Earth, trying to escape the coming retribution. Some called it the rapture. One billionaire chose not to believe it and built his own flying fortress. He didn't bother to make pleas for travelers. Instead, he believed those who needed to go would come to the ship."

"Ah, a regular 'If You Build It, They Will Come' sorta thing." Ethan remembered seeing a movie with that exact line.

"They did, too." Davin added. "Five hundred came. Every one of them had polytheistic beliefs. You see, they did not fear God's vengeance. They feared the sun's going super nova. Legend goes that the ship ran on pure magick for the last two months before it finally landed on this planet."

Martel smiled at Davin with pride. He held up one finger. "You understand why we are so careful with this planet and our food supply. We know what happens when you take things for granted."

The waiter returned with a tray on which set two glass sundae dishes filled with rounded scoops of lavender sorbet. It was honest to goodness food.

His mouth watered as the waiter placed his in front of him.

Davin sighed. "There are times when I wish I could consume food. This is one of them."

Picking up his spoon, Ethan dipped it into the frozen confection. It smelled sweet with the light hint of lavender wafting off in chilly waves. He allowed it to melt on his tongue, saturating his taste buds while indulging in the trickle down his throat. It was so good. He hurriedly scooped up the rest of it, realizing if he ate too fast it would be gone, and yet he couldn't stop himself.

"That was amazing." He licked the bowl of the spoon, unwilling to leave any of it. "Why don't you eat like this all the time?"

Winking, Martel picked up his spoon and licked it too. "If we had it all the time it would no longer be special. Besides, we must control the food supply as to not end up as old earth did. I believe someone in your family came up with our food plan."

He tried to think of anyone in his family that was associated with food. Then he remembered Tonya, Nora's college roommate. It appeared as if families existed in different forms than he was used to. "It may have been Tonya's children."

"Could be," Martel readily agreed. He pressed his thumb onto the check, the waiter presented.

Ethan looked at the check with the glowing thumbprint. "Don't you use money or plastic?"

Davin was quick to supply a definition. "Currency. A symbolic item with a designated value traded for goods or services."

Martel nodded, indicating he understood.

The three of them headed toward the exit. Ethan found himself bowing in return to four more groupings of people, all dress similarly. Apparently, they hadn't seen him when he entered earlier. News of his arrival must have spread throughout the restaurant.

They made it all the way out to the sidewalk before Martel was able to answer. "Greed caused most of the problems in the old world. The founders decided to do away with money. Everyone gets so many credits to spend on whatever they please. You can save it, spend it, or share it. Every year, everyone gets a new supply of credits."

"Wow." Finally, someone figured out a way to curb greed. "Your world is sounding better and better. I think I would just like to stay here."

"You can't! If you do stay, our world will never be. I was only trying to save you to make sure our world happened in the first place."

CHAPTER EIGHT

E THAN SLOWLY SHOOK his head in disbelief. Sure, he'd heard the theories about changing one thing in the past totally rewriting the present and the future. Sure, his disappearing would mean one less person for Caulb to terrorize. Sure, his family would miss him, but they'd understand, since so many of them seemed to be winking in and out of the present anyway. Maybe they wouldn't even remember.

He hadn't made any mention of time shifting. His grandparents hadn't even noticed the younger him when he pedaled by them today. No, they were too busy arguing about some woman and her dog. If he never came back, they might think he ran away. Worse yet, he had been kidnapped. Maybe, he met with foul play. They'd suspect Caulb, since he'd already mentioned him.

His lips tilted up at the thought of his nemesis questioned by the police. Having his friends cast suspicious glances at him. Yeah, it wouldn't be such a bad deal. Caulb had a sly way of weaseling out of things. Most people understood Caulb was a bully, but they could never pin anything on him. Yulia, the soft-spoken Russian girl who had only attended their school briefly, for example. Apparently unaware of the true nature of Caulb, she made the mistake of being nice to him, even befriending him online. Her reward was a series of pictures, suggestions, and threats that horrified her. Her adopted parents did complain to both the school and the police.

Yulia confided to Ethan that the words and images disappeared. Messages that were more acceptable replaced them, the kind you get from an Eagle Scout or someone who was squeaky clean and always looking on the bright side. The police even asked for Caulb's online ID, since they took cyber bullying very seriously. He provided it. Apparently, he had two accounts, one he used to harass people and another as a cover.

Not surprising, Yulia left, too, just like Brendon. He hated thinking Caulb had been her first exposure to America. Knowing what he knew, Caulb would shape a tale to frame Ethan. He could infer his absence was due to starting the fire. If Ethan reported him, he'd probably say Ethan threatened him. Of course, no one who knew either of them would think such a thing. Then again, it would be an easy way to tie up loose ends.

Martel continued to look seriously upset. How could one person matters, that much? For Goddess sake, he was a teen. So far, he showed no signs of having a glorious future. What could he do that would matter that much? "I think you might have me confused with someone else? I'm only a short teen from a Midwest town with a bully problem and unclear sense of identity. Definitely, not hero or founder material."

Davin answered, somehow managing to show a perplexed state with his crisp, accented voice. "I say, this isn't going well at all. I did warn you this could be an outcome."

How long had they thought about grabbing him from his lifetime? Although he had to admit, the timing was good. His hands automatically went up to his face. He was rather used to his present appearance and hoped to keep it. Martel had his cheekbones, his chin, even his smile, but not his eyes. Outside of his eyes, he'd probably pass on the street with no one looking twice at him. The words popped out of his mouth, not even giving him a chance to answer his earlier question.

"Why are your eyes different? Everyone's eyes are different here."

The elongated eyes, he referred to blinked a couple times. "When we arrived, roughly five hundred years ago, the early ones decided it would be beneficial to live underground. Some of them were still afraid of what would happen if the new suns would stop one day. They felt they would be protected in the natural caverns."

It was hard to imagine living in a cave, huge caves, but their worlds did not resemble caves in any way. He looked at the pristine city with an occasional tree or flowering bush to break up the clean lines. The blue sky might be an illusion, but it looked real to him. Martel continued to talk as he looked around.

"It was dark. Hard to see in those times. Often people wore lights on their heads like miners. Eventually, with each generation the eyes got larger, more almond shaped and the pupils bigger to take in more light."

That was it. His eyes were almost all pupil. No wonder they were so dark. "You have light now. Why don't your eyes become smaller?"

An eyebrow lift accompanied his reply. "Change doesn't happen that fast, especially evolutionary change. The light you see is not real, it is an illusion like the blue sky, but our mind accepts it."

If that were so, why wasn't he stumbling around? Something caught the toe of his boot sending him flying. His flight ended against a slightly moist surface. That wasn't right. His spread fingers touched the bumpy surface. It wasn't surprising he fell. "The walk beneath my feet was smooth and dry. What happened?" he asked from his prone position.

Martel offered a hand while Davin's visor glowed in the dim light as he summarized. "The illusion only lasts as long as you believe in it. Your ability to separate reality from engineered reality is extraordinary. None of the citizens have this ability."

Taking the offered hand, Ethan regained his feet and looked around the dim cavern. It certainly bore no appearance to the light, attractive city he first encountered. Lights at meter intervals shed meager light, leaving the passage dim. No wonder the large eyes had developed.

There were modest buildings lining the street, but none of them had any of their former glory. Why didn't they live on the surface? He heard their reasons about preserving nature and fear of the sun blinking out on them. The people of this world decided not to take any chances with the sun or food supply. Suddenly an underground world developed. Subsiding on food pills didn't seem as attractive.

"Are you telling me almost everyone else sees the beautiful city I saw when I came in, all the time?" The thought was incomprehensible. It would be the same as eating dirt and thinking you had the richest chocolate.

"Yes," Martel's answer was abrupt as if he was the one upset by this. "People see what they expect to see. It is the same in your time. Your media tells you that very thin women are beautiful. The ones who look as if they'd been to a death camp and their bones are showing. Suddenly, everyone thinks they see a gorgeous female."

Okay, he understood his point, but it really wasn't the same. "I know what you are trying to say, but that is more a cultural norm or fashion bias. In the same world, among different nationalities, the curvy woman or even the heavy woman is attractive. Everyone here thinks the sky is blue." He pointed upward to the ceiling covered with dripping stalactites. Another thought occurred to him. "Have they ever been outside?"

Martel's silence was answer enough. This world wasn't as perfect as Ethan originally thought. The people seemed happy, probably because they didn't know any better. A documentary he had watched on happiness showed desperately poor people in inaccessible areas as very happy. The narrator pointed out they had no connection with the rest of the world. They were clueless that people in other places wiped their faces on towels that cost more money than they would ever make in a lifetime.

The documentary shifted to well-fed Americans living in houses with roofs and four walls to keep the elements out, complaining about how bad their lives were. Of course, they compared themselves to billionaire rock stars. Here, apparently, everyone was the same and accepted it.

"How come you go outside?" Something wasn't right here. His voice grew louder with his aggravation. "Better yet, how come you were in my time?"

Davin inserted his large bulk in front of Martel. "There is no reason to talk to The Guardian in such a manner."

The droid was obviously protecting Martel. Did he think he was going to hurt him? Was he being a bully? Guardian? The word was an odd one, usually applying to someone who wasn't your parent, but still looked after you.

"Davin, please, he won't hurt me."

Once the sizable droid moved, Ethan realized the expression on Martel's face must mirror his own, a mixture of confusion and anxiety.

"Ethan, it is hard to know what to tell you. Revealing anything about your future could change your timeline. Still, it is difficult to hide things from you. Mere minutes after you entered our world, you perceived it was an illusion, while the entire time I've been a guardian, no one else has." He flung out one hand indicating the cave walls.

This was hard to believe. Plenty of politicians and televangelists fooled people on his world. Was this so different? "Why? Is it magick? Can't anyone else do it? Surely, there were more than a handful of magick users on that ship?"

"There were," Martel agreed with a rather somber nod. "They were people with short human lifespans."

Ethan didn't like the sound of that, being one of those with a short human lifespan. "What happened?"

Martel walked silently, looking down at the ground. Davin kept pace beside him, watching with a cocked head and his upper torso angled protectively toward the Guardian. It was as if neither needed to see where they were going.

"Leaving Earth was difficult."

Martel's voice sounded loud after they'd walked for a while in silence. Ethan noticed there were no sounds of a bustling city either. Was that an illusion too? "Didn't they want to go? Did they come to board the ship voluntarily?"

Shoving his hands into his pockets, Martel sighed. "It was their only option. Those whose minds, not soaked in sentiment or clouded by propaganda saw how the Earth would turn into a charcoal briquette. Still, it meant leaving what they knew. Often leaving family behind who refused to accompany them. The trip was long. Plenty of time to regret their choice, or at least, question it."

Whoa, he had a hard time with long car trips. He couldn't imagine being in a rocket ship for months.

"Toward the end, some people became weak and unreasonable in their fears." Martel continued.

Ethan regarded the grayish brown walls wondering what the citizens saw when they looked at the surroundings. Did they see a meadow that stretched forever? Maybe there were avenues of skyscrapers? "Some of them freaked out?"

Davin repeated the words. "Freaked out. It means?"

Wow. It was hard to explain an expression to someone who had never heard it before. "Um, become unreasonable in their fears," he used Martel's example. He decided to tack on, "They do things that make no sense that can hurt themselves and others."

Davin's visor lit up in a solid line of blue lights. "I comprehend."

He'd try to remember that blue meant taking in new information or at least understanding the information." What happened when they landed?"

They arrived at a small door in the wall. Martel touched a wristband unit, pushing a series of buttons. The door opened. Inside, shafts of light touched a half dozen spots on the floor. Ethan wondered if this was another illusion he hadn't quite figured out, until he saw skylights built deep into the ceiling. They seem to tunnel up forever, yet they let in streams of sunlight, which flooded the room.

Noticing Ethan's fascination with the windows, Martel pointed to one of them. "The former guardian had these put in by his companions to remind him what was real."

In a world of illusion, it's hard to track what's real and what isn't. The room was crowded with furniture and books. Ethan walked over to the bookcase and pulled out a book. It felt real in his hands. The dusty cover revealed pages with heavy type. Placing it close to his face, he inhaled the smell of paper and mustiness that accompanied old books. Cases crammed with books. "How did you get all of this here?" Martel carefully removed the tome from his hand and placed it back on the shelf as if afraid he might hurt it. "The books came on the ship. The original guardian was the man who financed the enterprise. He included all he thought a new world needed. Including a library, works of art, even comfortable chairs and tables for reading. It worked well on the ship since there was little to do, but that might have been when the problems started."

Ethan edged his way around the tables covered with books and charts, working his way around familiar statues to another bookcase filled with books on herb lore, working with crystals, and lunar magic. It made him wonder if there were two moons in addition to the two suns. "What problems?" There were bound to be problems on a crowded ship hurtling away from their home.

Picking up a tiny figurine, his host considered it before replacing it on the table. "The homesickness. The books made it worse, since they came from Earth, spoke of things there. It would make the space travelers long for home, or think of it fondly. Nader, the original founder, thought it would be best to make a clean break from earth history, one reason we went underground. The other reason was safety."

"Safety? All I've seen above ground is a pair of birds and a doe, not exactly scary animals." Going underground was not the 21st century answer to safety. Arming oneself to the teeth was. Well, he saw how well that worked out.

"Oh, those." His host shrugged. "Manufactured illusions. What would be the chance of having the same wildlife on a planet hundreds of light years away?"

Put that way, Ethan felt silly in assuming they were real. "None, I guess."

Davin's head turned and white lights lit up. "Actually, it could happen. It would be a one in seven billion and two chance of occurring."

"Good job, Davin." Martel nodded at the droid as if encouraging him. "As for safety, there were many things to worry about. Mainly, they worried about other ships landing on this same planet. What if it were a ship filled with Caulbs determined to take over? The refugees from Earth could be the invaders to this planet, and the native population might try to wipe us out. Underground was the best bet. Strangely, it was calming to those who had been on the ship so long. Wide open spaces tended to frighten them."

Hard to believe, but he could understand it being familiar. "The caves are large?"

"They go on for miles. We are only at the beginning. The farther in you go, the more it becomes like a city with rooms carved into the walls. It is more like an abandoned city or a ghost town. Maybe we should have worried who abandoned it, but it was so convenient for those seeking a place to belong. It was supposed to be our base camp, but eventually, after the creation of the generator, there was no need to move or even build."

Ethan watched as his host relaxed in a wing chair covered in a fabric consisted of multi-colored books. Davin took the matching chair and crossed his silver legs, reminding him of an English gentleman settling into a club chair and awaiting tea.

"The generator. Does it power the lights I saw along the walls?" He wondered what they used for power. They were probably past using fossil fuels, since they learned their lesson from Earth.

"Among other things." Martel picked up a book and began to flip through the pages, failing to elaborate on his answer.

Maybe feeling the need to complete the thought, Davin's head swiveled, so his visor faced Ethan's face. "The generator creates the illusions of the world the people have enjoyed on Terra Nova. Without it, they would be refugees simply living in a cave. A large cave, but still a cave."

He could accept that everyone was living in a cave. The fact they were living a false life was more troubling. "You are doing this all with magick?"

Martel continued to look at the book pages. "More or less. Part of it depends on what the people want to believe, rather like a curse. They want this world. I can tell by your voice you find it offensive." He looked up to meet Ethan's eyes, directing a calm blank stare his way.

How did he do that? Show no emotion. "It's not real." Ethan's hands pointed to the crowded book laden room. "You took their history away, their legacy."

Holding his finger in the book to mark his place, he shut it to answer Ethan's charge. "The original guardian took away the history of being oppressors, murderers, and thieves. They have no memory of doing anything for a buck or betraying those who depended on them. As far as they know, their ancestors, the founders, were good people who did kind things. You are a founder."

Not that again. "What would happen if I ceased to exist?"

Martel put his book down, losing his place, and stood. "Then I would cease to exist. Five thousand and two souls would perish because an overwrought teen in the twenty-first century refused to do his part."

His future relative did guilt trip better than anyone he knew. Ethan might be the end of humans. That was harsh. "How do you know they wouldn't survive without the illusions?"

Davin interrupted. "I've said as much myself."

"Some might, but there is no guarantee. Most aren't ready for the transition." He shook his head at the very idea.

"Still," Ethan waved his hand in the air for emphasis. "Magick done without positive intentions is never good."

"You think my intentions aren't good." Martel seemed to grow larger as his face flushed red.

Great. Now he made his time shifting host mad. "I didn't say that." He looked around hoping there might be some sign he was only in a dream. An exit sign over a door would be great right about now.

"Did I not save you from facing major hurt from Caulb?" He placed his hands on his hips and glared down at Ethan.

"Um, yes, you did. I'm grateful. Thank you." His upper teeth worried his bottom lip. Leah always warned him about speaking before he thought. He tried to most times, but zipping to a new planet and time tended to make him forget those basic rules.

This wasn't going well. He wasn't sure where he had made the wrong turn. A quick glance at Martel's unsmiling countenance indicated he'd worn out his welcome. If he left now, Caulb might leave him alone after seeing the sizable Davin. "I guess Davin scared Caulb." The thought of returning no longer frightened him. No doubt, the bully would keep his distance.

The flush began to fade on Martel's neck, returning it to a flesh color. Make that a pale skin color from living underground. He glanced at Ethan, cleared his throat, and talked as he paced in the tight confines.

"He might have avoided you if he associated you with Davin, but since

I had to wipe his mind..." Martel's voice trailed off.

"You did what?" Ethan balled both hands into his fists. Talk about a day not working out. Something about a mind wipe did drift back, but so many other things had filled his mind since then. "Do you realize he'll be even more eager to capture me now, rather like a dog after a bunny? Each time he doesn't get me will egg him on more. It builds the anticipation."

Davin sat still, his head swiveling to follow Martel's pacing. "The logical thing would be to give up his pursuit."

Yeah, right. He wished that were the case. Even tried being friendly, per grandfather's suggestion, but Caulb thought he was mocking him and only became angrier when Ethan acknowledged him in the hallway. The sudden lack of footsteps caught his attention. Martel had stopped pacing and stared at him. This didn't seem like a good sign either.

"Ethan, you can't go back until you learn what you need to know to survive. The entire universe rests on it." His dark eyes bored into him.

Disgruntled by the turn of events he muttered to himself. "I thought it was just this city, now the universe."

"More or less. Not sure, what else is on this planet. Good chance it's a small universe too." His lips tilted up in an apologetic smile, realizing he had overstated his case. "So, what do you say, Founder Ethan?"

Geesh, not that founder thing again. It made him feel like a Pilgrim or something. He had to decide. Stay here and learn what he needed to survive, or go back and live a very short life, with no guarantee Martel and Davin would even return him.

CHAPTER NINE

E THAN SHRUGGED HIS shoulders, neither agreeing nor disagreeing, but it seemed to be enough. Martel gave an abrupt nod, stepped over to a table littered with open books and papers. Shoving the majority of clutter aside, he managed to unearth a worn book with faded print on the spine.

Mouthing the words, Ethan read the title. Book of Shadows 2138. Was he in 2138? The book looked rather used. "Is this 2138?"

Martel waved his hand for them to follow him. His host didn't answer, maybe he hadn't heard. They meandered down narrow winding passages behind the great cavern. The citizens probably didn't know about this labyrinth of tunnels.

Two large metal doors were at the end of the hallway. On arriving, Martel hammered on the door, in a definite pattern. The doors swooshed open to bubbling and electronic sounds spilling out. Martel entered, allowing Ethan and Davin to trail him.

Inside a huge glass sphere, liquid rippled, hissed, and occasionally shimmered from an intense blue to a light peach. Tubes radiated from the sphere leading off into the walls, ceiling, and even the floor. Built in stations around the room were staffed by smaller droids, like Davin. A few didn't bear any resemblance to humans. Some looked like garbage cans on wheels. Not surprisingly, the latter was picking up broken glass and burnt paper. He looked around the bustling well-lit area. This was the heart of the place, where everything happened.

Martel strode to an empty table, placed the book on the surface, and pulled up a stool to sit. "Shafer, report."

A bluish droid turned and snapped a salute. "Section Delta operating at full capacity."

The guardian nodded and marked something in the book. "Diccus, your section."

"Well." The small droid looked about as if looking for assistance. "There has been an attempt to escape to the outside world by a handful of boys. It is as if they know it is there."

Martel grumbled and turned a few pages, not replying to the droid.

Even though it seemed obvious, Ethan felt the need to ask, "Does no one know this whole city is an illusion?"

All the droids stopped to look at him. If they were capable of whispering, he'd be surprised if they didn't start asking one another who he was.

"Of course, they do, all of them," Martel growled the words, showing he didn't like the direction Ethan was taking.

Ethan turned slowly, taking in the whole room. "This is where the illusion starts, a regular magick factory." He remembered a theme park calling itself that once, but he had no clue how real illusions could be. This was much more than dancing cartoon characters.

The sound of the pages fluttering indicated Martel was looking for something. "Stupid boys. Why didn't they heed the look away spell I had in place?" He sat at a table paging through an oversized book.

Look away spell? He should have tried that with Caulb or at least had a charm. He could try it when he returned home. Davin hurried over to Martel, placing a consoling hand on his shoulder. "The look away spell works best on minds easily swayed. Maybe these are curious boys. A potential guardian in the bunch."

A speculative gleam flashed in Martel's eyes. "Your suggestion has merit. Still, it was boys, not a boy, who tried to get out."

Davin continued, not easily dissuaded. "The city is large. Too much for one guardian. You never have time to relax. We never spend any time together simply talking, playing games, or reading. You are always fixing holes in the illusion."

"I don't know." Martel rested his head on the book. The open text muffled his words somewhat. "More than one might compromise the security. That's why I never had a human friend. I couldn't risk it. All those years alone, before I created you. I'm not sure I would wish it on any citizen."

"Think, Master, the boys would be together, a unit. They're already friends. Obviously intelligent. It would be a perfect answer." The droid's head bobbed as if acknowledging his own suggestion.

"It has merit." The mumbled words grew louder as he pushed himself into an upright position.

Ethan watched the entire scene in disbelief. Why couldn't they see what was so obvious to him? "Why can't they go outside? How long has it been since you left Earth, a couple hundred years?"

Davin corrected his estimation. "It's been two thousand, twelve years, and seven Earth months."

The correction didn't upset him or even slow him down much. "Okay, it's been a long time. It's obvious no one from Earth is coming. I'm not saying you must live on the surface, but why be so secretive about things. Allow people to explore your planet."

"Easy for you to say." Martel pushed up from the table and continued to check in with each droid. Checking off as he went until he came to the last droid. "Maia is dying. She is slipping away."

Martel's took a step toward the small robot. "What?" Anger rode his one word, but the droid showed no response to it.

Maybe he wasn't supposed to react to it. Davin certainly did, taking two large steps to place him by Martel's side. "Maybe your sister has contracted a sickness?"

Gesturing to a ceiling lined with a type of folded fabric, he commented. "How does this happen when every molecule of air is pushed through the filters to keep out any harmful microbes?"

The small droid, not realizing it was a rhetorical question, pushed a button on the panel in front of him. A young woman's image flickered to life on the view screen. She moved about a small room talking to herself. "What use is there in living when nothing I do is productive? Everything I need already exists with no effort from me. I serve no purpose. Even my brother has some purpose, although he is secretive about it. I have none. I wish to live no more."

The droid appeared to be unaware of the distress the image on the screen was causing. Martel shot his hands through his hair while lamenting. "She's only two hundred."

Pointing to some lines, flashing on the screen, the droid explained. "Her vital signs are dropping, almost as if she is willing her body to stop."

Ethan slid closer to the station, watching the steady beat of her heart become slower and slower. "She's using her power of intention to stop her heart."

Martel looked at Ethan expectantly, as if he could produce a miracle. Great, how could a kid from the past effect a cure for someone in the future. When he was little, it seemed like everyone had a job, except him, especially when the family went to the psychic fair. His father would set up the tent, while his mother and sisters decorated it. His grandmother usually waited under a tree, clearing her head. One day, she noticed his restlessness and directed him to get her four special stones.

The image of Nana grew clearer in his mind in her colorful skirts and heavily embroidered purple blouse as she rested against the tree with her hands folded in her lap, her bracelets silent for once. She opened one eye. "You still here? I thought I told you to get me four special rocks. Not just any rocks, but magickal rocks. Look well for them."

Suddenly having a sense of purpose, he searched the ground for the helpful stones. Some sites were harder because the area was clean of stones, probably due to other grandmothers demanding useful rocks. As he grew older, he wondered how much help the stones were, other than helping him to feel connected and important. That's what Maia needed.

CHAPTER TEN

T HE VEHICLE FLEW silently about two feet above the ground. Ethan tried to look over the side to understand how it propelled itself. Was it on electrified wheels or electric rails? Martel's pale face and clenched fists indicated he wouldn't be a good person to ask. Inching forward, Ethan stood to look over the side of the open car. The ground rushed by in a blur as they moved forward. A firm hand pushed him back into a seat.

Davin's no-nonsense voice reprimanded him. "Do not attempt to leave the vehicle until it has landed and powered down."

Of course, he wasn't trying to leave. He just wanted to know how it worked. Wouldn't it be sweet to have something similar back home? People would call him a genius. Maybe he'd end up being a millionaire. Then again, the mind sweep thing would wipe out all he saw. If that were the case, how could he learn anything beneficial for his future? It didn't make any sense.

He observed the tight lips of the Guardian, which showed he cared about the fate of his sister, even though he was so determined to follow the rules. Where did Maia live? How far did the caves stretch? He wasn't sure he understood this world at all. From what he could see, magickal intentions powered the illusion, aided by technology.

The residents received what they needed from the simple fact they believed they would. Their intentions fueled their own rewards. Nana explained how her regular customers were easy to read, even without the use of the Tarot cards. Their wants centered on their families and homes. Naturally, their intentions followed these desires. All they really wanted was Nana's reassurance that all would be well. Most of the time, she could give them that, but occasionally changed things up.

What changed in Maia's world? The idea of her being two hundred years old was hard to reconcile. What if he lived a safe life without any demands? There would be no need to outsmart thugs like Caulb. Uncertainty wouldn't be an issue. No real expectation or hope, either. Still, there were couples and families here. Martel's remark about the small population explained the need for droids as companions, and not everyone could expect to meet a perfect partner.

True, he was no expert on romance, but creating someone who had to like you was rather like cheating. The few brushes he had with attraction ended badly. Well, except for Orin. Rushed away by an irritated father wasn't exactly an impression to inspire love. Orin had to think he was a child as opposed to a possible romantic option. It shouldn't matter. He'd never seen him again.

The vehicle began to slow as it neared colored doors in the cavern's walls. Martel stood as the vehicle shuttered to a stop and a door opened, turning into a short walkway. Davin immediately followed, keeping up low-voice chatter. Ethan followed the two, wondering what the droid had to say, considering Martel programmed him. Back at the power hub, Davin had shown no emotions regarding Maia's decline. He reacted as if she was a machine that needed replacing. Of course, that could be exactly what he thought.

Instead of knocking, as he expected, Martel pushed through the door with Davin as his towering shadow. Ethan hung back. He'd never seen an actual dead person before. Wouldn't they need some privacy or something? The sound of voices reached him with one the higher pitch of a female. It sounded like they had arrived just in time.

"Where is this off-worlder you brought me?" Maia demanded.

A woman came to the door, looking slightly more animated than she had in the video the three of them had watched. "Welcome." She smiled, giving him a thorough once over.

He nodded, unsure what to do. He turned slowly, realizing he was more like an exhibit at the zoo. It reminded him of some story he read where people from Earth discovered a new planet and ended up caged as an attraction. The stares, whispers, and bowing started to wear on him. Still, he chose to humor Maia. "Am I as you expected?"

Her large eyes blinked slowly. "Not really. Come in." She backed up to allow him enough space to enter. "There really hasn't been much talk about off-worlders, but I expected you to be much larger, rather like Davin."

Even here, being short wasn't good. "I'm considered small by Earth standards. Most males are larger. I'm young, so there is a chance I might grow." He didn't believe his hopeful pronouncement of future height, considering how tall his parents were, but he still had a tall grandfather. Was being tall a recessive gene?

Maia nodded. She reached forward and touched his eyes, causing him to stumble backwards in surprise. Personal boundaries obviously weren't a big part of this society.

A slight laugh erupted from Maia, causing Martel to smile. "I scared you. I am sorry, Off-Worlder. Do you have a name?"

Remembering his manners, he held out his hand. "Ethan Carpenter."

Both Martel and Maia stared at his outstretched hand curiously. About the time, he was ready to withdraw his hand; Maia straightened her fingers and touched the tips of his gently. "Ah," her whispered exclamation hung in the air.

Davin's visor lit up. "A most curious custom. The meaning behind it is?"

The droid had already demonstrated his need to accumulate as much information as possible. Ethan decided against mentioning they hadn't done it exactly right. "It is a show of goodwill and friendship. In the early times, clans were always warring against one another. To show they meant no harm, they shook hands. They usually used their right hand, since most people were right-handed, to demonstrate they didn't have a weapon in their hand."

Thank goodness, his father had explained the custom to him or he wouldn't have been able to explain it to these three. The handshake was falling out of favor in his world due to germs and the general isolationism technology introduced. It wasn't uncommon for students to text each other at lunch as opposed to walking over to the table where their friend sat.

Maia looked at where their fingers met. She slid her palm across his and gripped his in a surprisingly firm grasp. He didn't expect females of the future to be so strong, especially when they were over two hundred. The age thing had to be different here. Maybe they counted by months. If so, Maia would only be about seventeen, which worked as far as her appearance.

Her large dark eyes studied him as if aware of his thoughts. Still clutching his right hand, she reached forward and placed her left hand on his chest with a slight slap. "If I were left-handed, which I am, I could have killed you. Where would your goodwill get you then?"

Martel laughed as if it was a hilarious joke. Outside of his sisters, and the mean Brit girl who punched him in the nose when he was ten, females did not challenge him. Instead, they accepted him as a treasured friend into their circle, since he didn't compete with them. He also flattered them outrageously on the smallest things, from new nail polish color to shoes. Early on, he realized this worked for making strong friendship bonds with females. They depended on him to offer something upbeat to kick-start their day. He generally complied. By now, it was more than a habit, a part of who he was.

His left hand covered hers. "If I were to expire by such a beautiful hand, then I would count myself content." His chest swelled with pride thinking how easy the words came to him. Ah, he sounded poetic, Shakespearian.

Maia's laughter, along with Martel's, punctured his smugness. Apparently, his comment wasn't nearly as smooth as it sounded to him.

Davin moved closer, angling his head, and gesturing to their clasped hands on his chest. "Your remark makes no sense. Why would you be happy to die? Are the people on your planet suicidal?"

Ethan shot a look at Davin that pleaded for him to say nothing, despite the fact he'd stolen a line directly from Romeo and Juliet. The droid either could not interpret the glance or did not see it because he continued to talk. "It sounds as if you are happy to die. Is this a trick to play with her mind, telling her you'd die happily?"

Great. Did he ever want a robot friend? No, he couldn't remember ever thinking that. Obviously, they did not read social cues very well. His left hand dropped from his chest, as Maia let go of his right hand and took a step back. It could be she considered him dangerous or disturbed.

"Well," he started, wondering how to answer all the questions without looking too stupid. As founder, people would expect more than empty flattery and running from bullies. His top teeth worried his bottom lips as he waited for some type of inspiration.

Nothing. It wasn't as if he had become someone new by jumping to this new planet. The comment about dying at her hand was his best stuff. "People on my planet aren't suicidal."

He considered those who did find their lives too difficult and chose to end it. Then there were those who flirted with death by engaging in risky behaviors. "Most of them aren't. A few might be because they might have a terminal disease or feel like their life is pointless."

Maia's eyelids fluttered a few times as if she was attempting not to cry. Why did he have to say that? Martel leveled a glance at him that asked the same question. He rushed on to correct himself. "Truth is their lives were very important. It could be a situation or a hormonal imbalance that didn't allow them to see it. As a Wiccan, I believe everyone is part of the plan. He or she serves a purpose and deserves respect."

Maia's eyelids stopped fluttering, as she mouthed the word, "*Wiccan.*"

Davin seized on the statement. His visor blinked rapidly before he asked. "Can your kind be designed with a purpose in mind, rather like the cleaning droids or the transport vehicle," his shiny long fingered hand rested against his chest, "or myself?"

Ethan wondered briefly, what Davin's real purpose was. If he was some type of droid, why design a casing similar to a body builder on 'roids. Why bother giving him a stereotypical robot head? Back in the restaurant, Martel sneered at the man who chose a droid who had a human likeness except for his stiffness and absolute perfect features.

"We all have a purpose. Often, it takes someone a lifetime to discover it. Sadly, a few die never knowing what their purpose was." He wasn't sure what his was. The fact he somehow influenced the people who founded the planet astounded him, and he wasn't even sure how that was going to work out, being gay and all.

Maia looked intrigued by the idea, but Martel was the one who asked. "When do you know what you are supposed to know? Why don't you know immediately? It would make your life simpler."

Ethan rubbed his neck trying to smooth out the tension settling in there and he stalled. Martel's questions sounded like the ones he used on Nana. With any luck, he could reuse her answers.

He cut his eyes to Maia before speaking; knowing he might reveal information her brother might not want to share. "Would you willingly embrace the life you have now if someone informed you what your job would be when you were twelve?"

The guardian's eyes widened, then he released a husky laugh. "No, I would have run into the forbidden places and hid."

Maia regarded her brother with some surprise. "The forbidden places are where the monsters hide. The ones that gobble up the young ones."

"About that," Martel turned to look at his sister. "There is a good chance there are no monsters."

"What?" Maia looked confused and stumbled back. Her brother steadied her and led her to a seat.

What was this? It looked like Martel might take his advice, but he had never mentioned monsters. Hard to know where he was going with this.

Davin and Ethan loitered near the brother and sister in order to overhear their conversation. Ethan struck a casual pose leaning against the wall, looking out the window at a manufactured scene of a sun setting behind the mountains. The reds and purples of the sunset filled the room, painting the four of them with color.

Living in a cavern might start out as cool, but it would get depressing after a while. Rather like living in the half-finished basement. The only difference was he had no cool special effects to convince him he was in a fashionable neighborhood or a beautiful valley. The fact he no longer had to look at exposed pipes was the highlight of his room.

Martel's low voice drew him out of comparing his room to the cavern. The brother held his sister's hand as he spoke. Seeing the two in silhouette the resemblance was obvious. "Maia, I have been studying the history of when the founders landed and what happened at that time."

"History," she wrinkled her nose as she spoke, almost as if she didn't understand the word.

"It is written down, the records of all that went before." Martel held out his hands indicating an expanse, holding both hands about a meter apart.

His sister shook her head, denying his words. "What does this written down mean?"

Ethan's jaw dropped. Did he hear right? It was wrong that The Guardian manufactured a trouble-free life for the citizens, but it never occurred to him that the right to learn disappeared too. How peculiar was that? Wouldn't it be beneficial to have an educated population? His Nana had already complained that people knew less and less than in her time. Of course, she was talking more about Pagan history, than history in general.

Martel's eyes met his, begging for help from his place beside his sister on the armless sofa.

Well, he did know about history, stories, and writing things down. Even if people chose not to record history as it actually happened, but as they might want it to be read, making them into heroes or at least better people than their actions proved them to be.

"Well, um," Ethan started, unsure where he was going with his explanation. He took a seat beside Martel on the backless, armless unit. Putting his two hands together, he opened them as if a book. "We kept information in books, sometimes in audio and video files. It allowed people to know what people did hundreds of years ago. Sometimes, it helped people not to make the same mistakes. Not always though."

He kept silent on his thoughts about persecution of people being different. Nodding in Maia's direction, he asked, "How do you find out things?"

She shrugged her shoulders, a gesture that had changed little over the centuries. "What is there to know when each day is the same as the next?"

"What about the weather, traffic, school closings?" His voice grew softer with each word, realizing these things meant nothing in her world. What weather? They lived in a cavern. Traffic was slight, not exactly resulting in any traffic jams. Then there was school.

As if monitoring his thoughts, she cocked her head inquisitively. "What's school?"

Here Maia was living most students' dreams never having to wake early to ride the bus, no homework, and no bullies to avoid. Of course, she didn't seem pleased about it either. "School is a place you go to learn. It takes anywhere from twelve up to sixteen years for most."

Maia listened intently, only blinking her eyes once. "Why?"

Why, indeed. He often asked himself the same question after an especially long day of busy work, group projects, and a session of ducking the bully. How did you explain a concept to someone who had never heard of it?

"School teaches us things like books do and prepares us for college and jobs." Ethan crossed his fingers, hoping she wouldn't ask about college. So far, he hadn't sold school and doubted he could do any better on college. The scent of fresh cut grass wafted through the room. Distracted, he turned his head, looking for its source.

A small off-white cube sat on a nearby table puffing out the scent. Cocking an eyebrow, he watched as it labored to push out another scent.

The block flashed blue for an instant before the smell of sun-dried sheets followed the color change. Odd they'd even have that aroma in the first place.

Maia leaned forward to touch his arm. "Tell me about jobs, does everyone have one?"

Employment statistics were never something he kept track of, but he assumed most people did work. Those who didn't have a job wanted one. "Yes, most everyone has one. It gives people a reason to get up in the morning. It also gives them money to buy food, pay rent, and get whatever they need."

Holding up one finger, Maia stalled his explanation of life, as he understood it on his planet.

"Do you mean there is no food dispenser in your quarters?" She gestured to a device on the counter that resembled a gumball machine, filled with different colored pellets.

Ethan didn't have the heart to tell her it resembled the goat food dispenser at the petting zoo. He'd have a hard time not chewing his food. "No, there is preparation involved. Nana or my mother buys our food. They bring it home and cook it, and then we eat it, followed by clean up time."

Martel clicked his tongue as if surprised. Ethan knew Martel must have witnessed people eating during his observations of Earth.

"It sounds complicated," Maia exclaimed, smoothing her tunic across her legs.

No wonder everyone dressed alike. Since they all received the same clothing. Like one of those mail-in offers where they promise to customize an outfit, but in the end, everyone has the exact same outfit except for color. He considered her remark for a few seconds.

"It probably is compared to your process. Still, I enjoy helping prepare meals. It is a time to chat with my family. The meal is all about the family coming together and talking."

Maia looked across the table at Martel. "I usually eat alone."

Martel was quick to add, "I do too."

Davin hoped to deflect her accusing look by saying to Martel, "Oh no, you take every meal with me."

"You don't eat," Martel, pointed out, while casting an apologetic look at his sibling.

Davin plowed on. "I may not eat what you eat. This is true. I am there. We converse, which means you do not eat alone. Earlier today, you had lunch with the off-worlder."

Ethan grimaced. He was really getting tired of that term.

Maia stood up abruptly. Pointing to her brother, then at Davin, then Ethan, she managed to choke out the words. "All of you were together, at lunch, but not once did you think of me? Maybe I might want to do something, too."

Ethan recognized that tone of voice, since he'd heard it enough living with four women. His sisters used it most often. Loosely translated it meant the offender did something horrendous, unaware he or she had committed such a heinous act at the time. The bad part about it was what was done was done. Still, his sisters usually allowed him to apologize and make extravagant promises never to forget about them in the future. It usually worked, until he did something similar again.

Martel's eyebrows shot up in surprise, demonstrating that he too was truly confused about the bad thing he had done. His sister, who had nothing to entertain herself, didn't even know about his arrival. True, he never thought of lunch with him as a big event, but in a world where nothing changed, it probably was.

Maybe he should say something to defuse the tension. He shot both hands through his hair, stalling. His specialty was compliments about shoes, hair, or dance moves. Family dynamics wasn't on his list of specialties. To avoid looking at the panicked expression on Martel's face, he wiggled his legs, just enough to angle his body toward the view screen showing the pretend landscape. Twilight came with lengthening shadows and the deep indigo blue of the sky. A few stars twinkled.

What time was it on the surface? Was it evening? The hiss of the scent machine expelled wood smoke along with toasted marshmallows. It made his stomach growl. He'd bet no one in the city had ever sat around a campfire and toasted marshmallows on a stick. In fact, his eyes rolled up as he tried to remember any time he had. He'd only done it twice.

Once when he was with the scout group, he'd joined with he was nine. His mother had insisted he drop out of the group, since the leader had the boys constantly handle his personal guns and practice target shooting. His mother didn't believe in the use of guns for anything. Her motto was *gun violence begets more gun violence*. After she convinced him to drop out, despite some resistance from his father, she built a bonfire in the backyard after he'd commented he'd only miss the bonfires.

The sound of conversing voices made him aware of Maia and Martel working out their problems without his intervention. *Thank the Goddess*, since he was sure he wouldn't be much more help.

"Martel," Maia's voice still held a bit of a tearful choke, "You could have asked me. No one ever thinks of me. Here, alone since our parents left and Triona took a mate, there is no one. I have nothing."

Ethan turned his head slightly to look around the living quarters without being obvious. It *was* rather Spartan. Couldn't exactly call it homey. It wasn't that big either. No artwork on the walls, no family portraits, nothing broke the blandness of the light gray walls or even identified her own personal tastes.

Maybe the ability to be unique disappeared with their history. How did a person develop his or her own style, tastes, and opinions? Most of the time you took what came your way as a child, until you discovered there was something different. Often you wanted the different thing even though you might not like it or want it in the end. The acrid taste of dark black coffee came to mind. He remembered sipping his father's coffee when he was barely three with longing to have what the adults appeared to enjoy so much. Once he had the bitter lukewarm coffee in his mouth, he had spat it out. His family laughed so hard at that. He took another sip and did it again. The second spewing of the coffee received an entirely different reaction. He decided then he did not like coffee. Maia had never had the chance to make those types of decisions.

Martel's eyebrows beetled down, and his shoulders hunched forward in a defensive position. "Everything is provided for you." He held up one finger. "You have a place to live." He put up another finger. "You have food to eat." By the third finger, Maia had crossed her arms, and her lips firmed into a single line. Her brother continued, unaware of what her stance signified. "You are safe."

"Safe from what?" Her voice rang aloud, bouncing off the hard-stone surfaces.

"Um," Martel stumbled, looking unsure.

His sister stood and paced. She took three long steps, stopped, turned, and then paced three steps in the opposite direction. After doing this twice, she stopped, pivoted on her heel to face Martel. She gestured with one hand at her brother. "You just told me there were no monsters in the hidden passages."

"Yes, I did," he agreed, nodding his head.

Ethan recognized the trap apparently before Davin did, telling her, "You are safe from sickness. It causes your type to malfunction and sometimes stop working."

"Sickness," she said the word as if trying it out for the first time.

Could it be she'd never been sick? No one in the city had ever suffered a cold or a stomachache? This must be a doctor and pharmaceutical company's nightmare. It didn't stop people from dying, or falling into a depression though. Their physical bodies might be protected, but not so much their minds.

She turned slowly, staring at each of them. Ethan wasn't sure if she wanted more information on sickness or what, so he added, "Sickness is bad. It's terrible." He knew he was babbling, but he needed her to understand she didn't ever want to be sick. "It causes pain and suffering. Sometimes your head hurts, other times it is your stomach. Often you feel like you can't get out of bed in the morning. You have no energy to do anything."

He thought he'd explained it pretty well without going into any medical details. Maia's hand fluttered to her head, then her stomach. A look of comprehension crossed her face.

"I know this sickness." She nodded her head.

Martel waved his hands as if trying to stop his sister's speech. "You can't know this sickness. The filters remove all harmful microbes out of the air. Disinfectant enters the home and public areas via the scent machines. There are no germs."

Instead of paying attention to her brother's inadvertent revelations, she looked at Ethan. "When I open my eyes in the morning, I have no desire to get out of bed. No energy to face a day full of nothingness and no company. The idea of living one day the same as the next makes my head hurt." She touched her forehead with her fingers.

Some commercial used to be on television about depression. Ethan tried to remember the details. Some type of windup doll that slowly wound down as a narrator listed her symptoms. Since the doll stopped, there had to be a lack of energy.

Maia's hand dropped to her stomach. "Most of the time I don't feel like eating. Often I skip the prescribed meal pellets."

Her brother's eyes grew big, while Ethan nodded, understanding the need to not want to subsist on meal tablets. Still, that's all she knew. As she listed her various symptoms, he realized how much she sounded like the narrator of the commercial. She did know sickness.

"What's wrong with my sister?" Martel asked, as he stood and took a large step to reach his sister. He wrapped his arms around her.

Her thinness was more noticeable in Martel's arms. They both looked at him as if he had a miracle cure. Did he need to remind them again that he was only fifteen? People didn't expect fifteen-year olds on his planet to do much of anything, except go to school. Well, that wasn't totally correct. In some countries, he'd be working a fulltime job, helping to support the family.

"Ahh," he stalled again, hoping for a brilliant, but easy solution. "She needs a pet." Hadn't he read somewhere that lonely people's health improved with a pet? The person could bond with the pet, giving them a reason to live. The pet, of course, depended on the person, and maybe that article was just about the elderly.

Both brother and sister spoke in unison. "Pet?"

It was hard to believe they didn't have pets, but up to this point, he hadn't seen any. No dogs would be satisfied with a few food pellets per day. A cat would probably cause their germ filters to clog up with hairballs. Forget about guinea pigs and hamsters with their cedar shavings.

How did he explain pets? "Well, ya' know dogs." He put his hand down around his knee to demonstrate how big a dog might be. "And cats." He used his fingers to motion for whiskers near his mouth. They stared at him uncomprehendingly, including Davin, although it was hard to be sure, since the robot had no visible emotions.

Martel blinked twice, and then smiled at Ethan. "You have such a creature in your house. It gives orders for food and care."

Obviously, he meant Theodora, his sister's cat. He never thought of the cat as giving orders, but when the cat meowed, the family jumped into action. It also meant Martel watched him a lot more than he had let on previously. It creeped Ethan out some, like being on a reality television show, and no one had bothered to inform him he was.

"Yeah," he agreed. "That would be my sister Leah's cat. "Do you have no pets? No animals?"

Davin answered, instead of Martel. "There are no such creatures on Terra Nova. What benefits would there be to such creatures?"

There had always been animals in his life in the world he knew, from the birds at the birdfeeder to the squirrels in the trees, even Harvey, the black snake who had a burrow under the driveway. He had never thought of animals in a how did they benefit him way. He struggled to put together some answer. It would be like asking what benefits humans provided for each other. He wouldn't want the wildlife to answer that question. The reply might be disconcerting.

He had to think about what he knew, from his sister with her cat, to his neighbors who walked their dogs daily. "They provide companionship, loyalty, exercise, even a sense of balance to people's lives. They have a creature to look after, and often the pet looks after them, saving their lives in times of crisis.

Maia pressed her palms together and looked up at her brother pleadingly. "I want a pet."

"No pets. We have no animals here for pets." Martel dropped his arms from around his sister and resumed a stern expression.

Ethan imagined it was his guardian look as opposed to his concerned brother look. "When I arrived, I saw birds and a deer. Not that either would make a good pet, being a wild creature, but you do have animals."

Maia watched the two of them avidly, her head turning to face the speaker.

"No animals. I created those from videos of Earth. It pleased me to see them. Everything you saw was an illusion. It covers a small area." He used his hands to indicate a box. "The image is anchored to the portals of the city.

There was an entire planet above no one had explored. "Have you never explored the surface? There could be animals, even food and water sources above. Maybe even people or humanoids in other settlements."

"Other people, animals, food," Maia repeated the words slowly, with a growing suspicion showing in her eyes and voice. "Tell me more about this surface." Suspicion and anger flavored her words.

Martel shot him a distressed look. Ethan shrugged his shoulders. "I'd say she's showing a great deal more energy than before."

The Guardian's extra-large eyes emphasized their roll, indicating what he thought of his comment. He turned to his sister, motioning for her to sit. He sat beside her and interlaced his fingers with her before he spoke. "Sister, there are a few things you need to know. You might be able to help me, too."

CHAPTER ELEVEN

THE FOUR OF them returned to Martel's apartment. The conversation went better than Ethan expected when Martel lead his sister into a room she'd never seen before. She could have thrown endless questions at him and then complained he was slow to answer. No, Maia sat quietly and took it all in, while Martel explained what his predecessor had told him.

Since it was the second time, he heard the story, Ethan began to analyze the words using the methods his father taught him. What parts of it appeared suspect, were there other reasons and possible benefits than the ones stated, and why was this not the best interpretation for all. He wondered about the secret man who built and supplied the spaceship. Did he stay on Earth to become a charred relic?

He could have left on his own spaceship. As for theirs being the only one that had broken free of Earth's gravity, how would they know? It wasn't exactly as if they were keeping in contact with home. Martel commented that since it wasn't a sanctioned lift-off, there had been a communication silence.

What if the Earth, as he knew it, hadn't vanished? It could be the sun had never gone super nova. It wouldn't be the first *end of the world* scenario predicted over the centuries. Religious cults whipped people into a frenzy until they committed suicide rather than face the outcome.

What would a person or group have to gain by creating a false story? Maia stood and walked close enough to bump into him. She threw him an apologetic smile as she headed for a crowded bookshelf. Staring first at the multitude of books, and then fingering their spines, she pulled one out and flipped through it.

The most rational thing would be to store the books on computer memory. It certainly would save space. Martel mentioned he did have thousands of books stored digitally. Apparently, the original planner had made contingency plans in case technology failed. However, technology appeared to be in full stride here.

Davin hovered near Maia looking over her shoulder, rather like an anxious librarian. "That volume is in the original Greek, as it was written. There may be a translation of *The Odyssey* that you can read."

Maia's brow knitted as she asked, "Read? I'm not sure what you mean."

Ethan's eyebrows, once again, shot up in surprise. He knew the citizens had no reason to attend school, since The Guardian, along with his mechanized work fleet, provided everything. It was a hard concept to accept that an adult lacked basic reading skills.

Davin, never one to understand emotional cues, continued to plow forward with his explanation. "The book you hold in your hand is full of symbols, which have meaning. These meanings are a way to convey information. Some of the books tell of things that have happened decades, even centuries ago."

Make it a millennium or two at least, my metal friend. Of course, in some ways, even Davin was in the dark about his origin. Martel thought it wouldn't benefit him to know too much. Would it upset him to realize he was a machine as opposed to a living, intelligent being? From what he saw so far, the machine knew more than the people did. Still, Martel felt like he was protecting Davin.

Maybe the original founder used similar reasoning. It made sense, reminding him of the time his family had moved suddenly with no real preparation. His father came in and announced they would move the next day. And they did. They loaded items from the cabinets into clothesbaskets, heavy-duty garbage bags, and assorted liquor boxes they had gathered from the nearby store.

Later, he realized the move was because of an attack on Nora. He wouldn't have understood that at seven. No wonder no one explained. Maybe the founder had the same idea by treating them like children. How, in a spaceship packed with intelligent, talented people, did one become the leader?

The man or woman who paid for everything could have boarded the ship. This person could have easily assumed leadership since he or she knew the ship and their end destination. It was hard to believe everyone on the ship naturally went along with everything, though.

Equally hard to believe was a mishmash of Wiccans, Druids, Shamans, and a half dozen other spiritual beliefs quietly agreeing to go underground. Some, because of their relationship with the sky, would insist on doing the opposite. The only way to convince them to do otherwise would be to trick them with rumors of other spaceships, aliens, and monsters. Why would someone do this?

Maia cradled the large open book in her hands. She spoke loud enough for her brother and everyone else in the room to hear. "Does my brother know how to read?"

Davin's visor flickered. Throwing rapid flashes of color onto Maia's upturned face. He was in processing or thinking mode. "Of course, Martel knows how to read."

Slamming the book shut with enough energy to send the old book smell spiraling out from the tome, she asked, "Then why have I never learned to read?"

An excellent question. It would help Ethan to know the answer. So far, he was less than happy with the image of an Earth in peril and some unknown savior stepping in at the last minute. It sounded to him like someone had a god complex who managed to strip away options from people until they were dependent on him with no original thoughts allowed.

Martel's attention was on the tablet in his hand as he scrolled down the view screen. "No need for you to read. Nothing for you to read. After all, you have everything you need." He never looked up as he murmured his reply.

Placing the old book carefully on a nearby table, Maia balled her fists on her hips and stared at her inattentive brother.

Obviously, he didn't feel her stare. Instead, he jabbed at the screen a few times while murmuring to himself. "The problem is with the droids, and they seldom problem solve."

Ethan was tempted to point out if he wanted them to think on their own, he could have made it so, but he didn't. There was a good chance the original founders created all of this, including the droids and robots, which operated everything. Truth was The Guardian was little more than a glorified plant operator, who kept everything running. What would happen if something truly broke down? Especially with a population who was used to doing nothing on their own.

Even their so-called businesses were little more than hobbies with their supplies coming from The Guardian's production system at no cost. It was a façade of Earth, without any of the decisions or hardship. It should be a perfect world. Maia demonstrated that it wasn't.

He was curious how this lifestyle had affected the residents. "How long do people live here?"

Martel finally looked up from the tablet. His eyebrows shot up. "What do you mean?"

His sister moved closer as if interested in his reply. Ethan thought what he meant was obvious. "You took over from the other Guardian. How old was he when he died, passed, left, was no more?" He tried to remember all the euphemisms people used for death.

Maia rubbed a knuckle against her furrowed forehead. "What other Guardian? What is died?"

Frustration firmed up Martel's lips, as he glanced at Ethan, probably mentally cursing him for stirring up another issue. "Maybe four hundred years. It is hard to say since we do not talk about our age or celebrate it as your time does."

Four hundred was ancient. Maia looked like she was barely twenty so maybe she was about that in earth years. If that were true, it meant the last Guardian had died at forty. It also could be true that living underground with no worries meant they lived on indefinitely. "How do you keep track of how old you are? Who dies? Who is born?"

Hearing the word die again, Maia piped in. "Yes, yes, how do you keep track of those who die?"

Sighing deeply, Martel shoved his hands into his tunic and began to pace in the cramped quarters. "We don't keep track of those who die. We have no ceremonies, no memorials. They cease to be. We do not talk about them and eventually they disappear from the collective memory."

To wipe out the memory of those who had lived as if they were words on a computer monitor and all a person had to do was backspace. Those who moved on could teach others. The memory of their love and support could help their offspring. It made no sense to him. "Why do you not remember the dead?"

Maia touched her brother's shoulder and said softly, "I remember our parents."

He covered his sister's hand with his own. "Of course, you do. It hasn't been that long, but eventually you'll forget. That's one of the reasons for the essence in your quarters."

The small machine that puffed out a variety of essence, from cut grass to burnt marshmallows, had a purpose, he thought, to preserving Earth-based memories. Apparently, it introduced a drug in the air to help people forget.

"Why?" Maia's question mirrored his. She tightened her grip on Martel's arm and shook it, demanding an answer.

"The first founders decided the concept of death was too disturbing for those who just undertook a trying voyage to reach the stars. Those left behind were incinerated by the blast of the sun going supernova. Those memories would be unwelcomed and traumatic thoughts. Somehow, the early ones found a way to mask certain areas in the brain while retaining memories of basic functions, such as walking and eating. The memories aren't gone, but as long as the population lives in the enhanced environment they will not remember."

Maia's hand on her brother's arm dropped. She stumbled away from him to collapse on a chintz cover couch that had to be centuries old. Maybe the founders created it to have something reminiscent of home. She buried her face in her hands.

Ethan expected tears, but heard nothing, outside of a few deep gasps. Women on this planet may have reacted differently than females of his century. Maia looked up suddenly, her eyes blazing with anger. Well, maybe not so different.

"Where are my memories? I want my memories." She stood on the last word, her posture rigid, as she stabbed the air with her index finger. "What right do you have to steal my memories?"

Davin swiveled his head, trying to follow the conversation, but for once remained blessedly silent.

Rubbing his hands over his face, Martel stalled. Ethan recognized the tactic. He had used it a few times himself.

"Um, it is the way of The Guardian. It is what is best for you. I spared you pain." He held out his open palms in front of him, begging for some type of understanding.

Maia shook her head back and forth, refusing to give it to him. "No right, you had no right to my pain. It was mine. It would be better than drifting through this fog of nothingness. It has to be better than this." Her hands fisted by her side as her chin took on a belligerent angle.

Ethan could have told Martel he was now in the no-win zone. The man opened his mouth as if to speak, but then closed it. Instead, he maneuvered around the furniture to reach his sister. Placing an arm around her shoulder, he eased them both down to the couch.

Interlacing his fingers with his sister's, he spoke in a resigned tone. "I was only following orders from the former Guardian, who followed those before him and so on. I thought this was the perfect way of life. What else could a person want? It never occurred to me people would want those things that cause pain. The fear, anger, and pain, troubled Ethan. I thought we'd be better without it. Obviously, one of the first Guardians thought so too."

Now Martel was bringing him into the argument. Sometimes, Ethan had dreamt of a world free of prejudice, fear, and financial problems. On the surface, this new world excited him. The people were on vacation forever. A vacation is only good when it is a rarity. People get used to it, and they no longer value the experience. That was it. He had to make Martel understand.

"Wait now, before you describe my century as everything that is bad, allow me to explain a few things. Life is like a roller coaster." He noticed the uncomprehending stares of the two siblings. He moved his hand up and down, demonstrating the highs and lows.

Continuing, he explained, "It was a ride in my time. A fun ride, and yet some people hesitated to ride it. They feared the fun, in a way. On the ride it goes very slow up the hill, *chug, chug, and chug.*" He used his hand to demonstrate shaking in an upward direction.

The two of them mimicked his actions.

"Yes, that's right. It's a bit like life, my life. I get up, go to school, and try to do the right thing, occasionally avoid bullies. This is all uphill stuff." He straightened his hand and stopped it.

He made eye contact with both Maia and Martel before he started again. "At the top, for a moment, you can see everything. It is a glorious experience. Sometimes it is reaching a goal, other times it's falling in love."

Maia's mouth opened to form a perfect O. He wondered if she would ask a question, but she motioned for him to continue.

"This is a wonderful time, knowing you could do anything. Then there is the rush going down at incredible speeds. Some people laugh, others scream, a few close their eyes because they can't stand to see things rush by." He plummeted his hand suddenly.

The other two followed with their hands. Martel pointed out, "You are at the bottom again and you must start over."

Nodding in agreement, Ethan smiled. Just maybe they were getting it. "This is true. There is anticipation again, the effort to get to the top once more. Then the triumph of reaching the top again." He moved his hands several times in a roller coaster movement.

Martel shook his head. "But you're in the valley again, the low painful part."

Ethan bit his bottom lip, realizing he wasn't explaining this as well as he would like. "True, I'm in the valley several times, but it's short. Mainly, it's all about the climb and resting at the top. Would you want your life to be more like this?" He moved his hand in a straight line held down at his waist.

"In this life, there are no valleys, no peaks, no euphoric highs, or soul numbing lows, no anticipation, nothing." Both siblings' faces mirrored confusion, demonstrating they were unaware their existence was the straight line.

Davin spoke, breaking the sudden silence. "I would like to see a roller coaster, or better yet, ride on one."

Ethan almost assured him he could before remembering a seven-foot silver manlike droid might cause some attention in his century.

"That's it." Maia yelled. Her bright eyes mirrored her excitement. "You described it." She moved her hand in a flat line. "This is my life. I want the highs and lows. I want drama."

If she only knew what she was asking for, but then again drama wasn't always bad. His mind drifted back to Orin. Everything had seemed so easy the afternoon they shared under the oak tree. Conversation flowed around them. Ethan remembered passing around a loaf of French bread where each participant tore off a chunk before passing. He'd passed it to Orin and their fingers touched.

When Orin spoke to him in his mind, he was startled to hear a voice different from his own. It was rather like entering your room and finding a stranger inside. The more they silently conversed the more he knew he'd found a kindred spirit.

On the outside, they were nothing alike. Orin was the type of large male he normally avoided. While Ethan was chatty, upbeat, and fashionable, his newfound friend was non-verbal and brilliant when it came to math and science, one of the reasons his parents had decided to homeschool him, and his tendency not to talk much.

Orrin made it clear he could talk. Nothing was wrong with his vocal cords. He had just chosen to exercise the option not to speak. Silence took incredible willpower, similar to Tibetan monks and their training. Unfortunately, Ethan often spoke when he should have kept his mouth shut. Leah had pointed this out to him on several occasions.

Maia bumped up against him, startling him. "Uh, what?" He bit his bottom lip before he voiced unhappiness at his separation from recollections of Orin.

The woman smiled up at him, her eyes bright. "Tell me how to get this roller coaster life." She moved her right hand up and down rapidly, more in a down dog motion than the undulations of a coaster.

Her sudden upward mood swing from her formal despondency demonstrated the difference a purpose could make in life. "I think you've already started."

Martel laughed at his comment, and then shook his head. "I am glad to see Maia excited, but I am unsure of the changes." His head swiveled toward Davin, who appeared to be unaware of the undercurrents in the room. He slowly paged through a book he had previously announced was in Greek.

Ethan regarded his new friend, one he'd once considered a future version of himself, someone wiser and more knowledgeable. How ironic they expected him to give them the answers on how to make their lives and planet better. Wasn't it obvious he wasn't doing all that great with his own life?

CHAPTER TWELVE

D AVIN LOOKED UP from contemplating a text and turned in Ethan's direction. "What should we do first, Founder?"

There was that word Founder again. It made him feel he should be six-foot-tall, sixty with gray hair, a firm chin, and a thousand-mile stare. What now? Good question, not exactly one he was up to answering quite yet. Instead, he put his hands in his pockets and allowed his glance to travel around the crowded room. Bulging bookcases looked ready to break apart at any moment, spilling their contents onto the bare floor.

This hidden room needed to be open, allowing people to know their own heritage. Most of the library was stored on computer chips. Of course, knowing how to read would be helpful, but it seemed doable. He was willing to bet that once Maia could read, she'd be an excellent teacher.

Although all good in theory, an overall plan would be better to present to the people. Nothing worse than having people clamoring for answers the leaders didn't have. He pivoted to face the others. "I think we need to go outside. Research what is really here."

Maia gasped. Her eyelids opened wider, giving her a startled and excited look. It was hard to decide which it was. It could be the thought of a world outside the cavern was both stimulating and frightening.

Martel held up a hand as if directing traffic. "I'm not sure that is wise. What if something happened to me? How would the people manage on their own?" He shook his head slowly.

Holding up his index finger, a thought crystallized in Ethan's head, he'd swear wasn't there before. "We need to evaluate what natural resources you have. If there are dangers, then we need to know what they are. You can't protect yourself against a menace you don't know about. Does Davin have any defensive capabilities?"

While Ethan had learned how to run and hide as a survival tactic, he wasn't sure if Martel and Maia had similar skills. Running might not work, especially if the landscape was barren as opposed to the rolling meadow the illusion generated. A person would be little more than a moving target. With the ability of predators to track any fleeing prey, it was the same as having a target painted on your back.

Davin answered before Martel could. "I have enhanced vision and hearing. I am five times stronger than any human." He held out one arm straight. "I have also been fitted with micro missiles and have the ability to shoot a laser from my fingertips. I've only used these in target practice."

"Very impressive," Ethan answered and could have sworn the droid's chest puffed out with pride. He couldn't help thinking a laser shot just above Caulb's head might do a lot to reform the bully's menacing ways. Of course, he wouldn't remember it, since Martel would eventually erase his memory. Would the people here remember him when he was gone?

Martel moved about the room shifting books, bending low to peer into cabinets. His behavior perplexed Ethan for a second, but Maia understood more quickly. "Brother, what are you looking for?"

Kneeling on the floor, his upper torso submerged inside a large cabinet, he replied with a muffled cry that sounded triumphant. "I found it!" He slowly crawled backwards, holding up a large sack. It was hard to discern much about the clear sack packed with smaller similar sacks. He brandished the bag as if everyone should recognize his find.

Ethan realized they expected vast stores of knowledge from him as a founder. He wanted to argue, at barely fifteen and not exactly a stellar student, there was little he did know. "What is it?" It looked like giant baggies to him, maybe heavy-duty ones.

Walking closer, Martel shoved the large bag at him, forcing him to grab it. The surface wasn't as slick as he thought it would be and it weighed almost nothing. Still, he could see several bags crammed into the bigger bag. He hefted the bags and lifted an eyebrow.

Martel cracked a smile. "They're specimen bags to collect what we find above and bring it back here to analyze. I think they may have been from the original party. After a while, the early Guardian just lost interest in exploring." He shrugged as if it was just one of those things. Martel behaved rather like, 'I thought I'd start exploring my planet to survive, but I was too busy with other stuff.'

An Earth-like would offer many opportunities to the settlers, even the possibility of spreading out beyond the city. Perhaps they had wanted to discourage this and created a technology and society that made its citizens dependent on The Guardians for even the food they ate. It would depend on what they found outside that would determine if The Guardians were protective parents or just lazy ones.

Maia held up a closed hand and pointed an index finger as she counted. "We have Davin for defensive purposes."

Ethan kept silent, knowing that one well-aimed missile could take the chatty droid out.

Holding up another finger, she continued, "We have specimen bags. We'll need food capsules and water." Her last two fingers followed the first two.

When they first arrived on the planet, Ethan remembered thinking he was on Earth. Apparently, they had a similar atmosphere. Did Martel manufacture it? Was it an illusion like the cardinals and the deer? "Can we breathe the air outside?"

Martel nodded before adding. "You were able to breathe on your way in. This planet was one of the few capable of supporting human life that the spaceship could make it to within a reasonable time. Although from some of the tales I've heard, most occupants didn't find the trip length reasonable. They were more than willing to step aboard the ship to avoid a gruesome death, but six months into the flight the majority were complaining about the food pellets and the monotony."

At least that explained where the technology for the capsules came from. It was probably a short-term plan, since the ship could only carry so many supplies. It would be hard to estimate how long they would be in space, which meant they needed a food source capable of lasting indefinitely. Being able to manufacture the capsules had worked well.

Would it be cold outside? He didn't remember frigid temperatures when he arrived, but Martel showed no concern as he packed a messenger-like bag full of water tubes, capsules, and specimen bags. Davin handed a similar bag to Maia, and then shouldered a much larger backpack himself. It made sense to allow the droid, who was five times stronger, to carry the specimens on their return trip.

Surprisingly, Maia asked no questions about the outside world, even though she had lived her entire life never knowing it existed. Instead, she bounced on the balls of her feet, eager to get going. Who hasn't wondered if their world was all, there was? Most children were convinced they were in the wrong family since their parents appeared to be clueless about the wants and needs of their own offspring. A few secretly imagined they had parents that were either royalty or special in some way. Enough switched at birth stories in the tabloids convinced frustrated children and teens it was a possibility.

Falling into line with the others, he followed them out, allowing the door to swoosh shut behind them. Instead of turning right toward the city, Martel turned left. After hiking a quarter mile or so without seeing another soul, the ground beneath their feet sloped upward.

Maia swung back to grin at him and announced unnecessarily. "We're going up."

They were heading upward. Into what? He reflected on his family and how being born into a Wiccan family probably made it easier to accept his new location and sexual preference. His nose wrinkled up considering what would have happened to him if he'd been born into a strict Fundamentalist family like Leah's boyfriend, Dylan. He'd end up at a special camp to be brainwashed into behavior that was more appropriate, and cured of his sinful nature.

The air changed. It smelled different, fresher, and it was cooler. Maybe they should have brought jackets. Not that he had brought one in the first place. Maia's hair swung side to side as she practically skipped along. Did she even own a jacket? Probably not in her climate-controlled world. By introducing them to the concept of sweating and shivering, along with the temperature changes, would he be doing the citizens a disservice?

The tunnel became darker the closer they came to the surface. It made sense to discourage adventuresome boys from reaching the outside. A deep growling preceded the appearance of a fearsome creature in front of them. Maia yipped in fright and stumbled back into him, almost causing him to lose his balance. His knee dropped a little, but he was able to straighten it while holding onto the frightened female.

Martel and Davin acted nonchalant, almost as if the creature didn't exist as they hiked past it in the dim light. Their attitude confirmed his suspicion that their monster was a manufactured illusion to keep the curious away from the exits.

"It's not real," he whispered to Maia. "Look at your brother and Davin. They didn't even stop since they've been past it so many times."

The words stiffened Maia's spine as she stood on her own, grumbling. "They go wherever they please without a thought about me. Maybe I'd like to see something different than the same old walls, same old city. Oh no, they never ask me along." Her step picked up as she continued her monologue.

Anger should keep her going for a while. What was out there? What if there were other creatures or sentient beings? Most likely they wouldn't be welcoming, since they would be an unknown threat until proven otherwise. With that in mind, he pushed past Maia, excusing himself in the process.

Reaching Martel, he tapped him on the shoulder to gain his attention. "It's best to let Davin take the lead."

"I plan to," Martel agreed. They walked in unison through a darkness that became gray as they moved forward. Davin's visor added some illumination to their path. Gesturing ahead toward Davin, he said, "We're coming out at the exit. It was the closest to my quarters. We'll see the planet as it is, since I didn't bother with any illusions here."

"Good," Ethan agreed, but something about this half-thought out plan was bothering him. Davin could be a formidable weapon, if he didn't draw attention to himself and continued to stride down the middle of the path. There might be nothing here, no intelligent life, but he doubted it. The same forces that created life on Earth could be at work here.

Davin slowed, allowing the others to catch up. Once Maia reached the small landing, Martel manipulated a small keypad, creating a standard door size opening in the stone wall. Filtered light flooded in, indicating it was day.

All eyes were on Martel as he motioned for Davin to proceed. "Let's go and see what wonders await us."

Davin moved forward cautiously, his head swiveling all the way around, which was a little weird. Ethan could almost accept the droid, as Martel's friend and companion until he did something like that, reminding him of the vast differences between man and android.

The sunlight caused Ethan to blink. After being in the dim light for so long, it was blinding. Still, it was great being out in the open, feeling the sun on his face. Stretching his arms over his head, he felt like he was waking up from a long dream, except for the presence of a large silver droid, and Martel and Maia, whose heads swiveled almost as much as Davin's. Their human anatomy stopped them at a mere 180 degrees with each head turn.

The scenery was different here. No soft rolling mountains in the distance, or thick fields of green grass dotted with flowers. No pine trees, courting birds, or shy deer stepping out into the clearing to graze. A semi-arid landscape greeted them with stretches of dry, dusty land, and huge boulders rested in random clusters as if tossed by a playful giant. Tufts of hardy grass brightened the unrelenting brown with splotches of green. Small, wizened trees squatted in the shadow of the boulders, showing a few leaves. It wasn't the most pleasant place he'd ever seen, but it was still somewhat earth-like.

The two suns hung high in the blue sky, sending their combined heat. His earlier thought of a jacket was ridiculous. Maia shielded her eyes with one hand, and used her free hand to point in the direction of the suns.

"Martel, how come I only had one sun in my view screen?" At least she understood the pretend window in her quarters was not some portal to the outside world. However, if she thought that, why wouldn't she want to visit the beautiful landscape?

Her brother pulled some type of dark goggles out of his bag, passing them to Maia and Ethan before answering. "All the view screen images are from Earth. Since no one has bothered to explore the planet. I think the whole purpose of the view screen windows was to comfort those who were homesick for a planet that no longer existed." He pulled on the dark goggles, effectively ending the conversation.

Ethan examined the clumsy thick goggles in his hands, not stylish by a long shot. He would have thought in all the intervening years they could have come up with something better. Maia and Martel both sported the goggles, which made them look somewhat like Davin without the silver skin. Of course, with their oversized eyes and living underground, they needed the extra protection the goggles provided. Reluctantly, he donned his, aware no photo ops loomed in his immediate future.

Once on, he blinked twice, surprised by how much the eyewear enhanced his vision. It bathed everything in a pale green light, making it look more alien than it already did. The three of them stood out in the open examining geographic features, collecting stones, leaves, and dirt.

Davin moved forward as if unaware that the group had stopped. The troubling aspect of their exploration that had nagged at him came back in full force. *Ambush*. He'd seen enough sci-fi movies to realize danger wasn't always ahead, sometimes it was behind you. Nudging Martel, who happened to be close, he pointed to Davin's back, disappearing behind some boulders.

Acknowledging his unspoken question, he answered, "Oh, he's doing a perimeter search. He'll go about a quarter mile circumference and report back."

A dozen possible things that could go wrong, including monsters that resembled Bigfoot, crossed his mind. Maybe a cloud of toxic, but intelligent gas might cause their demise. In that case, Davin would be no help. Here he was conjuring up all the scenarios stolen from dated sci-fi television shows.

The fact they were in caverns meant there had to be water somewhere at some time to carve out the subterranean pathway. No telling how old they were, there might have been water here hundreds, or thousands of years ago. The outlook didn't do much to cheer him.

More rocks, more parched terrain, and the spotting of a peculiar creature that resembled a cross between a bobcat and a rabbit. It would have been comical animal if it weren't so large. Its size made it dangerous, but oddly, it appeared to be afraid of them and hopped furiously in the other direction. The three of them shook off their fright quickly, trying to pretend the strange critter hadn't scared them.

Davin stood staring after it, his visor blinking wildly. "I have no data on such a creature. Guardian, what is it?"

Using his hand to shade his eyes, Martel looked in the direction the animal disappeared. "I don't know. There are no records."

Maia, who had kept her observation to herself for the most part, chose to break her silence. "Why is it no one has ventured out before?"

Her brother's lips took on a mulish aspect, similar to the one all brothers make when questioned by a younger sister, especially, when they had no real answer. "It wasn't safe. I already told you that."

"Hmm." She took a few steps forward and slowly turned in a circle with her hands out from her body. "I see what you mean. It isn't safe to feel the rays of two suns on my face." Her rapturous expression on her upturned face indicated her remarks were sarcastic.

Maybe there was no disease or sickness here. Perhaps people just stopped living because they were tired of existing. Nana firmly believed purpose motivated people. Other times, even revenge could keep a person going. Without anything to look forward to, people slowly wound down, which explained people dying after losing a spouse or after taking retirement.

That the people on Terra Nova had lived as long as they did was amazing. However long that was. True, some of them appeared to have families and relationships to give shape to their lives. Still, how could you enjoy the calmness of life underground when you didn't know anything else?

At first, even though the people were literally living in a cave, he'd considered it perfect. That was before he consumed his food in a capsule form and learned nothing below was real, from the interior to the view screens that served as windows.

A scent tickled his memory. Maia stood on a small boulder making a production of herself by inhaling. "Smell the air. That's what freedom smells like."

Not quite. It smelled like something from his distant past, but he doubted if he would label it freedom. Martel frowned. He tried to reach for his sister, who, standing on the stone, towered over him by a foot or more. "Come down from there. It isn't safe."

Jerking away from her brother's reaching hand Maia almost lost her balance, but caught it before tumbling off the rock. Her nervous laughter shimmered over the landscape, filling the barren area. "You say that, but you come outside enough."

Part of the joy of his life was new experiences and surviving the bad ones. Apparently, they had neither here. Martel suffered too much stress trying to keep the city afloat, while everyone else suffered none. As the Guardian, he struggled to provide for the people, while they went on their way with no real occupations, although a few played at being a merchant.

An acrid, slightly familiar smell rode the air, causing him to wrinkle his nose, taking in the scent. A memory of his failed scouting experience resurfaced along with the memory of his father creating his own backyard bonfire. A smile tugged at his lips, remembering his engineer father pretending to be all outdoorsy. The man almost caught himself on fire trying to start the bonfire. When the green wood failed to catch, he squirted lighter fluid on it.

Wood smoke, that's what it was.

Maia pointed in the direction of a thin strip of smoke coming from behind a nearby hill. "What's that?"

Her soft voice sounded unusually loud. Martel must have thought so too, as he hushed his sister, motioning for Davin to return. "Lower your voice. I think our adventure is about to get interesting."

CHAPTER THIRTEEN

U SING HIS HAND to shield his eyes, Ethan stared in the direction of the smoke. Things getting interesting might be an understatement. A quick glance over his shoulder didn't yield any sign of the portal to the underground city. Even though the rocks were supposed to look natural, the L formation indicating the entry was nowhere in sight.

Davin moved closer as the three of them huddled together. His visor flickered, but the droid was blessedly quiet. If this were a science fiction movie, the alien would appear right about now and kill a couple of them. Why were they crouching in plain sight? Davin motioned to a tumble of nearby rocks as he arrived.

The four of them moved silently, almost in slow motion. Martel's light complexion appeared even more bloodless, if that was possible. Maia's eyes shifted between fear and excitement. Her mouth pulled into a rounded O, reminiscent of someone enjoying a firework show. It appeared the possibility of blood and mayhem had merit.

As far as he could tell, the women here didn't have a wide array of emotions. The few he saw had rather bland expressions that hovered between melancholy and joy. Females back in his world enjoyed their drama. His sisters would deny it though. Truth told he enjoyed it, too. It kept the blood pumping. Why shouldn't his descendants like a jump in their heart rate as well?

Martel's hand clutched his chest as if he expected the overworked heart to propel itself from his chest. Obviously, this little adventure upped his stress level. Davin dropped to his knees and crawled toward Martel, his visor lights flickering rapidly. "How can I assist you?"

Drawing a ragged breath, the white-faced guardian shook his head. "I wish I knew. I wasn't ready for this. I knew there might be a possibility of someone else living here. Still, none of the other guardians ever recorded any life forms."

The smoke rose in small puffs as if mocking them. It might be nothing. A natural phenomenon, such as a hot spring might produce steam, which could be mistaken for smoke. He was ready to share the information when he remembered the aroma. Steam never smelled like wood smoke.

Directing his question to Davin, he said, "How far are we from the entrance?"

"A little more than a quarter of a mile."

The news had Martel sighing, wringing his hands, and wilting against the rocks. Ethan could empathize. Running in the hot, dry air might be somewhat challenging, especially since the gravity appeared to be heavier. Walking was like shuffling through the sand, as if the ground didn't want to give his feet up, or at least let them get too far away.

Running the distance would be difficult. He might be able to since escaping bullies did have the advantage of building his stamina. Although his getaways depended on short bursts of speeds and the ability to hide or blend into crowds. Neither would suit his current predicament.

Maia peered over the rocks until a sharp tug on her tunic, via her brother, pulled her butt back onto the hard surface. Not very appreciative, she snarled at her brother, "Why'd you do that?"

Martel shot Ethan an exasperated glance as if asking for help with what to do with his outraged sibling. Knowing he'd be no help in that department, Ethan shrugged his shoulders. It would be quite a disappointment to learn the founder was ineffective against his own sisters, especially if they united against him.

Half listening to the siblings fuss at one another, he worked his way to one side of the smooth boulder to gaze into the distance. The most probable cause of the smoke was that some intelligent life form had created a fire. The bickering continued assuring him siblings managed to stay the same throughout the years.

Martel's voice became louder as he tried to influence his sister. "I am The Guardian. Therefore, you must do what I say."

A dismissive sniff undermined his pronouncement. Davin angled his head as if watching the action.

Ethan slid down the boulder to crouch at the foot while watching the family drama unfolding in front of him. Maia stood with folded arms, showing major attitude for someone who barely had the will to live earlier in the day. Amazing how a little information and fresh air changed everything.

Martel motioned they should proceed in the opposite direction by gesturing. "Let's head back."

Davin immediately complied, moving directly behind his master. If Ethan had the advantage of mechanical limbs, he'd have beaten the droid, but he was a close second, make that third in line. A backward glance showed Maia hadn't moved and was growing smaller as they marched away.

The merciless suns would toast her if some alien monster bird didn't swoop down and get her instead. Ethan hesitated, half-turned to look at Maia, then back to the retreating forms of Martel and Davin as they moved away. "Wait." Davin and Martel kept moving as if they hadn't heard him, too intent on their march to safety. The smartest action would be to follow his host, but he couldn't leave Maia. It would be the same as leaving a puppy on a busy highway. His request echoed off the stones.

A yip, grunt, and garbled yelling floated through the air. The response didn't come from Martel. Instead, it came from the same direction as the smoke. Maia's folded arms dropped to her sides, as her eyes bugged, and she peered behind her at the approaching threat.

Great. Whatever it was, had found them. Ethan dashed the few feet separating him from Maia. He grabbed her arm, pulling her down behind the rocks. Their sudden drop to the ground stirred up the loose soil, sending up clay colored puffs. The dust filled his nose and lungs, tickling his throat, causing him to choke. Shoving his fingers under his nose didn't work as well on coughing as it did for sneezing. A harsh barking cough erupted from his dry throat, despite his attempts to quell it.

The hard rock surface appeared to magnify the sound as opposed to absorbing it. Whatever was out there would know their location. It was hard to believe twenty-four hours ago that he thought Caulb was his worst threat. Crouched behind a couple of boulders on a strange planet, something much more dangerous than Caulb searched for them. His mind flip-flopped between his options, all two of them. *Run or don't run.* Running meant whatever was on the other side of the rocks might take them down as they fled. Not running meant they'd die sooner. Using hand motions, he tried to signal that they'd need to make a run for it. The woman bobbed her head as if she understood. Her gasp alerted him something was up, combined with her eyes looking up over his shoulder.

Oh great, he'd waited too late to make his move. Stiffening his spine, he readied himself to look into the eyes of his killers. The smell surrounded him first, almost gagging him. It reminded him how Bigfoot smelled, reminiscent of a gym locker room. Maia peered around him, obviously interested in the unfolding adventure.

Ethan turned slowly, unsure if a knife or a spear might be the response to a quick movement. Sweat beaded his brow. If his death was imminent, he only hoped he wouldn't end up wetting himself. Worse things could happen, but he wasn't too sure what those were, if you left out death and disembowelment.

Three swarthy men surrounded them. What they lacked in height they made up for in bulk. Attired in loincloths, it was easy to see the ripple and play of their muscles. Their hair was long and hung halfway down their backs. One had a scruffy beard and appeared to be the leader by the way he shook his wooden stick with a loop on the end.

It reminded him of a device the dogcatcher used to catch feral animals by looping the wire over the animal's head, and then tightening it.

Crossing his fingers behind his back, he hoped he didn't play the role of the dog today, although the three males appeared to have no interest in Ethan. Their eyes touched on him, dismissed him as no threat, and moved onto Maia.

Three sets of eyes pinned the woman down as if she were a butterfly specimen on display in a collection. Instead of cowering, she stood, holding her head up, proving she was unafraid. This show of strength caused an outburst of jabbering incomprehensible to Ethan. Each man pointed to Maia, then back to himself. The leader disagreed, loudly thumping his stick.

Pivoting on one bare foot, the older male snagged Maia's wrist, drawing her against his bare torso. "Mein, Mine!" His shout made the others back away.

Ethan understood, as did the other males, whose expressions mirrored identical disappointment at having so fine a prize snatched away. Maia didn't struggle in the leader's grasp, nor did she melt into him. Her back remained erect keeping as much of her body away from her captor's as possible.

Using his stick to gesture, the leader barked a directive. "Home. Hogar."

Ethan watched as they turned and headed back the way they came. Their language appeared to be a mishmash of different languages. Every third or fourth word appeared to be English, giving him some sort of a clue about the meaning.

The group moved off with no move to kill him or even include him for that matter. Maia wiggled free of her captor's grip and ran back to Ethan. Wrapping her arms around his meager form, she cast a defiant look at her captor.

Two running steps brought him directly up to Ethan. Staring into his eyes, the man questioned. "Lovuh?"

Ethan wasn't sure what language it was, but realized the wrong answer would shorten his own personal timeline. Using his fist to gesture to himself, he said, "Brother."

Mr. Muscle Bound and Mr. Angry considered the word. Motioning to his two henchmen, he ordered, "Bring brother."

Two sets of hands grabbed him, pulling him between them as if he were a wishbone. Maia's grip loosened on him as the leader pulled her back to his side, draping one muscular arm around her waist, dragging her along.

"I am sorry, Ethan. This is my fault." Maia's words trailed back behind her as she stumbled to keep up.

"No, no it's not. I could have run," he apologized as he considered what might happen to him. Martel should be here, not him. Maia wasn't even his sister. If he died here somewhere in the future, his family wouldn't remember him since it would be as if he'd never existed. Then again, maybe that only applied to disappearing into the past. Instead, his family might speculate on why he had run away without even leaving a note.

There was a good chance the school fire would be pinned on him. The rumor would be he vanished to avoid getting caught. He'd put good money on Caulb starting the rumor. It was probably already circulating. Sighing deeply, he reflected on why there seemed to be so little he could control in his own life as he stumbled between his two stinky prehistoric captors.

The rag tag group climbed endless dusty hills as the suns started their slow descent, sending shifting shadows in front of them. If their suns set in the west too, then they were moving east. If he could keep track of the direction they were heading, it would be useful when they escaped. For orientation purposes, he'd refer to it as east and west even if it wasn't.

Listening carefully, he managed to attach names to the males. At least, he thought they were names. They could be insults, since males often enjoyed labeling each other with nicknames.

One of his captors asked, "Gayle, done day."

The leader answered with a grunt, then added. "Jorb, silencio."

His other captor laughed at the man's reprimand.

"Silencio, Tally!" Gayle barked the order, causing the laughing man to cut off his chuckling.

It was hard to tell if the three were a family group or a hunting party. They did form a united band. Whatever Gayle said, they did. There would be no playing one against the other. There had to be a time when they could slip away.

Escape. The word gave him more hope than he was currently feeling. *We shape our world with our thoughts.* His grandfather reminded him of this more than once when he felt overwhelmed. His future depended on escaping and taking Maia with him. To do this, he'd have to learn as much as he could about these taciturn hunters. He assumed they were hunters, primitive ones by their clothing.

They stopped once by a tiny rivulet of water coursing down the face of a rocky outcropping. Imitating the men, he placed his cheek flat with the rock and licked up as much tepid water as he could. It tasted wonderful on his parched tongue.

Anytime now, he expected to spot a cave with a cavewoman squatting beside a campfire. A scarcity of women would make Maia a prize. Then again, it could be the women were equally squatty, muscular, and as hairy as the males.

It was almost dark when they stumbled to the apex of the last hill. Ethan stood between his captors as they chattered excitedly. Their leader gestured with one arm to the sparkling, glowing city surrounded by a high wall. "Your new home," he said in flawless English, proving not only did he know it, but could speak it too. The city appeared lit from within. The white domed buildings and bricked walkways looked nothing like the caves he expected.

The sight of their city appeared to change them. The men stood up taller and shed their bent primate posture. Their eyes glistened with intelligence and humor. The leader nodded, and they proceeded down the hill. His captors dropped his arms, perhaps unworried about his fleeing.

Ethan wanted to question why they had brought them back to the city as if they were captives. Why not talk to them normally and invite them for a visit, ask if they would drop by and all that? Maia beat him to the punch. Elbowing the man hard, she shed his hold.

"Why didn't you talk to me before, if you could, instead of all that grunting nonsense?" She shot him a disgruntled look that baffled men through the centuries. No excuse would satisfy, but still the man tried.

He reached for Maia, who danced out of reach. Her lighter body allowed her to shift quickly on her feet, dodging the man's lunges. Too bad, she hadn't used that skill earlier. Oddly, she didn't seem upset or frightened.

Gayle, unable to retrieve Maia easily, decided to go with an explanation. "We were on a spirit quest. Trying to get a sense of our ancestors. Speaking in their language."

Ethan wanted to object that early hunters did not speak French, German, Spanish or any of the other languages they were using, but he chose to keep silent. Freed of the restraints of two large bulky men holding him down and limiting his peripheral vision, he observed his surroundings.

The buildings had smooth lines and the occasional arched window or rounded corner. The majority were white with a spattering of pastel buildings. Patches of greenery caught his eye. While they were not the smooth, thick lawns of his hometown, small shrubs and flowering plants in large, colorful pots lined the walkways and building entrances.

His assumption about them being cave dwellers embarrassed him now. Good thing he never said it aloud. It reminded him of Nana harping about witches on television. She'd griped about the stereotypical portrayal of a woman, usually dressed in black, mumbling a few spell words until something major happened. Of course, she added, the portrayal was no better than the average person thinking they could become a witch in three easy steps.

A few strolling people called out greetings to the returning three. Two of the greeters jogged up to the group. The heavy gravity slowed things down. No doubt, they'd be fast on Earth with the lighter gravity. Maybe that was why none of the buildings reached over a story. Then again, maybe they didn't need the buildings to be higher.

The two new males appeared younger due to their size and smooth faces. Unlike the older males, they hadn't learned to hide their emotions. Excitement glistened in their eyes as they rapidly exchanged words with the older men. It seemed to be yet another language. One Ethan couldn't understand. Perhaps it was slang.

Whatever it was, the males must be referring to Maia. One of the younger males reached forward to touch her long pale hair only to get his hand slapped by Maia for his efforts. The other males laughed, while the leader moved to stand in front of Maia, blocking curious fingers and eyes. The larger man, with his legs spread and his arms folded, made a formidable barrier. Obviously, he'd already decided, since he'd stumbled across the exotic beauty, he was keeping her.

Martel's sister never showed any terror, except the few moments before they had met their captors. Her calmness impressed him. She dealt with her captors like how the dance team girls dealt with their athletic boyfriends. A quiet confidence radiated from the dance girls proclaiming they were the smarter of the two, accompanied by an indulgence for their often brutish beaus.

Her certainty that the cavern dwellers were superior might be tested, especially considering the residents of this city didn't have everything provided for them. They were probably aware of what was real in their world and what wasn't.

Gayle stared down the young males who kept trying to get a look at Maia. "Yonder, Jola, prepare for our arrival."

The two young males saluted, pivoted, and slowly jogged away. Ethan watched them, wondering if they were younger brothers. They didn't show any real fear of Gayle. The salute might be a playful gesture. Overall, none of them had been aggressive or rough, just firm.

Another building came into view. People, waving and cheering, lined the walkways. As they drew closer, he could see the people were wearing a variety of heavily embroidered clothing. Nana would so approve. Speaking of Nana, he also saw grinning, wrinkled faces along the way.

There was much chatter about Maia, but not so much about him, a trifle insulting. It made him feel unwanted. The group surrounding Maia moved into a building.

"Are you one of us?" a voice asked near his elbow.

A small female looked up at him with curious brown eyes. Her smooth brown hair fell to her shoulders. Outside of being slightly muscular, which would be called buff back on Earth, she could be from Earth. *That was it.* He didn't attract much notice because he looked like them, just less muscles.

How should he answer her question? "Do you mean am I from the city?"

Her nose wrinkled up at his answer. "No, not exactly. I think I would have seen you. People would talk about one so puny." She reached to pinch his bicep for emphasis.

"Hey," he complained. Even on this planet, his physique lacked the muscles to attract favorable notice. Maybe he needed to hit the weights and bulk up some. Of course, if he stayed here it would happen on its own. Staying wasn't an option though. Too bad, he hadn't come up with any revelations on how to travel back without the helpful Martel.

The girl giggled. "No, I meant are you from the mother planet, Earth. I do not think you are one of the others."

One of the others. What did she mean? "I am from Earth. Who are the others?"

The girl pointed in the direction Maia went with her crowd. "She's one of the others. In the beginning, we all came together in a ship." Using her open hand to point to herself, she shook her head. "I don't mean me, but the old ones, the first ones on the planet."

"Okay." Ethan bobbed his head, encouraging her to continue. He wanted to hear this story, especially since he was willing to bet it was different than the one Martel told.

Grinning, perhaps glad for a receptive audience, she continued. "There were two brothers on the ship. Many said they built the ship and outfitted it. The voyage was long. Many became angry at leaving Earth behind."

The upset, people part of the story was the same, but he hadn't heard about the brothers.

The girl motioned for him to continue walking as she talked. "When they landed, the people divided into two factions. One faction was fearful and hid. The other, my people, decided to work the land."

This explained a lot. "How has working the land worked out?" The fact they had a beautiful, thriving city should be answer enough.

The girl slid in beside him, never once looking up. "Oh, we have good years and bad years. The scientists explain that the planet has a wobble in its rotation, which messes with the seasons. Some years, lots of rain, good crops, while the next year might be one of extreme storms or even drought, like now."

That explained the arid climate. He wondered how they dealt during the lean years. Before questioning the expertise of the child, the words slipped out on their own accord. "How do you prepare for the hard years?"

The small female reached for his hand. "I like you because you don't treat me like I don't know anything."

Ethan looked down at their interlaced hands wondering if this is what it would be like to have a younger sibling. "Sounds to me like you know a lot."

"I do. My name's Twilin. What's yours?" She smiled up at him with a gap-toothed grin.

"Ethan." He smiled back at her, which seemed to delight her. He was wondering if she'd return to the subject of the lean years. He might be able to gather enough information to free Martel from his guardian duties. "Um, the lean years, what do you do?"

Twilin's high-pitched giggle floated around them. "Oh yeah, in the beginning, they tried to store food stuffs for the next year, but often animals ate it. People tried making better containers. Finally, someone remembered or found the information in a book about building greenhouses. Someone else started domesticating the small *trammars* that always ate our grain and we ate them instead."

"Trammar? He tried to imagine what type of creature it might be. He hoped the people were not eating rats.

Twilin used two fingers on each hand and put them beside her face to indicate tusks while she pawed at the ground with one foot. "Trammar."

It must be some type of boar or cow. It was sure to be an unfamiliar animal. "Oh, thank you. I think I understand. Were the men who found us looking for *trammars*?"

"Of course not." She squeezed his hand. "They were on a spiritual mission. Couldn't you tell that they were only wearing the clothing of the ancestors and speaking the old language?"

Ethan fought the desire to point out the gibberish they were speaking didn't belong to any language. "How come you speak English?"

Her lips twisted to one side. "Is that what it's called? I always heard it called the language of commerce. We kept the language because the oracles told us the others spoke it. This way we could communicate, but the others hid from us. How can we honor the oracle's command when the others will not cooperate?"

Good question. He often found it hard to do the right thing when so many were determined to do just the opposite. Wasn't that what they discussed that day under the shade tree with Orin? He had to get back, if only to meet again his silent friend with the beautiful mind.

This small one might hold the answers. "What did the oracle command?"

Twilin sighed and rolled her eyes. "It's the same every year. You'd think the oracles would come up with something new." Her free hand covered her mouth. She cut her eyes before whispering. "Don't tell anyone I said that. It would be sacrilegious."

Ethan agreed, while tamping down his impatience. "What does the oracle say?"

"Yes, that," Twilin started. She lowered her voice to a dramatic, somber tone. "You must find the others and unite with them. Together you will be the answer to each other's dilemma and you will prosper. Apart, you'll both die out."

It made sense. Apparently, the ground dwellers mastered the art of growing food and living on the land, a skill the others were sadly lacking. The real question was what would the others bring? New genes, but what else?

Twilin led him into a long hall where people talked over one another while crowding around a laden table. All sorts of savory scents emanated from it as he tried to relate the various dishes to something similar, he might have eaten at home.

"Twilin, bring your guest over here." An older woman pointed to some free chairs.

He was a guest. That certainly put a different light on things. Maybe he wouldn't need to escape. All he would need to do is ask for a safe escort for Maia and him back to the entrance. Where was she? Her blonde head was easy to pick out among so many dark ones.

Sitting in a place of honor at the head of the table, Maia's bright countenance denoted she enjoyed all the attention. No wonder, considering she spent most of her days alone. Various people were offering her food and drink. A look of confusion passed over her face as she put the plate down. A woman nearby gestured to the food, then to her mouth.

Giving the woman a weak smile, Maia gingerly brought what looked like a drumstick up to her mouth. She sniffed it first, before biting. Ethan watched her chew, wondering if this was the first real food that she'd ever consumed. A blissful expression bloomed on her face indicating not only was the food tasty, but she enjoyed it too.

Hungry, Ethan took the proffered seat, ready to dig into the plate of goodies Twilin passed to him. It smelt appetizing even though the colors were odd. The blue blob reminded him of mashed potatoes and it tasted like a root vegetable. It could be potatoes if the tuber came from Earth. The planet's soil and gravity could have turned the humble vegetable blue. Color didn't affect the taste though. He could be back on food pills by morning, so he savored each bite. The thought caused him to glance in Maia's direction. Her utensil laden with food stopped mere inches from her mouth as if something had caught her attention. Something impressive, by the look of astonishment on her face. Ethan wasn't sure he wanted to know, but felt obligated to look.

He turned in his seat to see what had riveted her attention. A man stood there dressed in an embroidered tunic that hung over his tan leggings, stopping about a foot short of his soft boots. The outfit was a type of gypsy bohemian, like what many of the other men wore. It still didn't explain Maia's expression. Maybe he was missing something. He gave the man in question another look. Hadn't he just met this man a few short moments ago?

He was a little taller than most of the surrounding men, which really wasn't saying that much. His hair was the same shaggy style favored by many of the residents. Obviously, a hairdresser was not one of the lucky few to snag a ride on the escape pod from the mother planet. A few of the older men crowded around him slapped him on the back and called him "Gayle."

Couldn't be. He watched as the man shrugged off the compliments and hands as he made a direct path to Maia. A few of the local girls smiled at him trying to get his attention, but his eyes were on Maia, who looked at him adoringly. This was worse than watching one of those rom-com movies Leah favored. Maia's expression did not bode well for Ethan.

CHAPTER FOURTEEN

E THAN'S APPETITE FLED as he witnessed Maia's reaction to Gayle. She all but melted at the sight of her cleaned up captor. Sure, he cleaned up well. In the land of height-challenged people, he stood out. Maia was practically a super model with long pale hair and a slender body. Ironically, her differences didn't repulse the surface dweller, just the opposite. Was it only Earth where your differences made you an outcast?

The place beside Maia opened as one older woman stood and offered her chair with a smile. The woman who had saved the seat for Gayle while he changed could be his mother. Most of the adults made approving sounds at the young romance unfolding before their eyes. He noticed the younger residents looked sullen or bored. Twilin at his left was one of the bored ones. Yawning loudly, she covered her mouth with one hand and pointed to the couple with her bent elbow.

"Oh good, Gayle finally decided on a mate. That will have more than a few crying into their pillows tonight."

Ethan pondered her words. Well, at least they still had pillows. "Gayle is popular with the girls?"

Twilin buffed her fingers on her tunic and managed an uninterested mien. "Please, girls have swarmed around Gayle ever since he passed every man in height. Superior genes, ya' know. He's my brother."

It explained why she knew so much. Females hoped to garner his interest because of his height. It seemed so unfair. An accident of the chromosomal kind made him a babe magnet, while rendering the rest of the male population inferior. It looked like things weren't that different from Earth in that regard.

Maia appeared to have forgotten the oath she took earlier that day not to reveal any information. She looked up at Gayle while explaining the intricacies of living underground. "My brother is The Guardian. He controls the entire city from filtering the air to supplying daily food supplies."

This information caused much chatter and exclamations. One man raised his voice over the commotion. "How can one man do all of this? It's impossible."

Ethan held his breath, unsure how much she'd reveal. Even he knew you didn't tell all your secrets, especially when you were unsure of the other side's intentions. He could have underestimated Maia's age. She was acting more like a pre-teen than someone who was closer to two hundred. Her hands were over her heart as she continued to stare up at Gayle. She answered the inquiry, never breaking eye contact with her new heartthrob.

"Oh no, my brother is assisted by many robots." Maia allowed Gayle to feed her tidbits off her plate as if she were a tame deer, appearing to ignore the chatter surrounding her.

"Did you hear that? Robots?"

Another man complained, "We've had no technology since we chose to follow the wrong brother."

Twilin nudged him. "What's a robot?" She turned her face expectantly up to his.

How did he explain something she'd never experienced? Obviously, they had no science fiction movies he could use as references. Lanterns on the wall and candles on the table provided illumination. Electricity didn't exist, so forget television.

"Well, a robot is a machine of sorts, not organic. People make the robots. They're a type of servant." His explanation failed to describe the total complexity of what all a robot was.

Twilin nodded. Her lips pursed as she considered the concept. She laid one finger aside her face. Suddenly, a broad grin bloomed across her face. "Could a robot clean my room?"

"Well, I think it could, but you don't want a robot to do things for you." There was a chance they could learn the technology, but then they would become as helpless and unaware of their world as the cavern dwellers.

"Why not?" Twilin stood, balled her hands on her hips, and stared him down.

Ethan recognized the look. She dared him to answer, but he had plenty of practice with two sisters. "You would forget how to do things on your own."

An eye roll and a snort greeted his prediction. Maybe only a few days ago, he would have reacted the same. Truly, he'd have exclaimed about not needing to know how to clean a room, cook, or even study. Martel's people took that attitude to an extreme. It was hard to know what shocked him more, the fact they believed everything on their view screen, or that they couldn't read.

"Twilin," he tried to inject some wisdom into his words. Somehow, grandfather did it without even trying. "I know you think it would be easier not having to do simple tasks around here. I would have thought the same at your age. Those tasks are how you learn to do things, bigger, more adult things."

The young ground dweller cocked her head to one side and regarded him with disbelief. Yeah, he'd probably do the same. It sounded like the crap adults were always saying.

How could he make her understand? He wasn't sure. "Do you read?" The sudden thought that these people might have the same lack of education occurred to him.

"What?" She barked the word, while motioning to herself. "Do you think I'm a baby? Of course, I can read. Why do you ask?"

Ethan sucked in air, allowing it to *whoosh* out in a relieved sigh. "Thank the Goddess." If half the people in this world could read, then they could help the others. Just because Maia was enraptured with the ground dwellers, did not mean everyone else would be. It might be a real test of how open they were to diversity.

Feeling Twilin's eyes on him, he flashed a brief smile. "It's good to read. Very helpful."

She arched one eyebrow in response. "Yes," she started to say more, but shouting near the front of the house interrupted them.

The chattering stopped as everyone stood and stared in the direction of the door. One man, garbed in a solid color ensemble that was uniform-like, announced, "High Counsel, Sir. Intruders have crossed the border."

People shoved one another, knocking chairs out of the way to push through the one arched entry to see the speaker. A few stood on tiptoes to see over the others. One enterprising youngster scrambled onto the table to see better, sending a platter of food to the floor with the act. A large lizard creature rushed out from under the table and gulped the scattered vittles. Ethan jerked his feet up in a hurry even though it must be a pet. No one would allow a dangerous reptile in the house. Would they?

News reports about people attacked by their pet tiger or rescued from the embrace of their boa constrictor came to mind. His eyes stayed on the large creature that slowly weaved its way through chairs and table legs in search of more food. A few people brushed up against it, but none seemed shocked when they looked down to see what touched them.

Gayle's voice cut through all the shouted inquiries. "You said there was a silver man?"

"Yes, High Council. A man like us held a light aloft. The silver one wore a glowing shield on his face where his eyes should be. Should we try to surround them and bring them in?"

The title registered. Apparently, Gayle was either *the* high council or part of it. It sounded as if Martel mounted a mission to rescue them. If Davin spotted them first, he could turn his firepower on the ground dwellers. It would not be a good meeting between the two.

"Wait." He jumped up toppling his chair. "Don't do anything. Let Maia and I go meet them. Davin could kill all of you if you surprised him."

Maia paused while chewing on a flaky delicacy to add, "Listen to him. He's telling the truth. It's my brother and his companion. They are looking for us. Let me explain to him what happened."

Gayle shouldered his way through the densely packed crowd to reach Maia's side. Sliding into the empty chair beside her, he took her free hand and held it up to his face. "I will accompany you to meet your brother. It is only natural he would worry about you. Please be aware that you aren't going back. Your place is by my side. Maybe we could just send your other brother to inform him."

Ethan expected Maia to object to such an autocratic statement, or at least ask about the other brother. Her desire to help Martel with Terra Nova may have dwindled, when faced with the twin temptations of chewy food and a ripped male. Maia put down her pastry to put her other hand up to Gayle's face. Ethan couldn't see her expression, but he could imagine her going all doe-eyed. Why did females get all soft when men went alpha, despite saying how much they detested such behavior?

The two of them must have stared at each other for five minutes or more. The crowd of people grew quiet and turned to stare. A few of the older women "awed." One commented while nudging her husband with her elbow, "Doesn't it remind you of us?"

The man grunted out his reply. "No," earning a sharper nudge.

Looking down at the ground, Ethan tried to locate the lizard-pet. It would be good to know where it was. No sign of it. Wait, a tail was sliding into the other room. A snout appeared to his left. *Oh great*, there were two of them.

Gayle ended the staring contest, by releasing Maia's hand and standing. "Well, my sweet. I think it is best we go meet your brother."

Snagging another sticky treat from a plate, Maia agreed. "Sounds good. I can't wait for Martel to taste all this delicious food."

Nodding at the tart in her hand, Gayle asked, "Is that for your brother?"

"Oh, no." Maia took a bite of the treat to prove her point. "I might get hungry on the way." Her response garnered a few laughs and a large smile from one woman.

Gayle nodded in Ethan's direction. "Ready to go?"

Ethan glanced at the floor trying to locate his reptilian friends. "Sure." No lizards in sight. He moved toward the door only to have a large black lizard, bigger than all the rest, rush toward him. Surprised by the creature's speed, he jumped back, but not fast enough to avoid it crashing into him. The collision propelled him back into a group of nearby people.

One man laughed in his ear, adding, "It looks like Boomus likes you."

Boomus looked up at him with an opened mouth, exposing several sharp pointed teeth. In a bizarre way, it did resemble a smile. The creature even thumped his tail creating a booming sound, which might explain his name. Several hands pushed him upright as he regarded the besotted creature.

Knowing everyone was watching him, he reached out one cautious hand to pat the lizard. Boomus wagged his tail even harder when petted, hitting several people with his muscular appendage. A few complained as they stumbled out of range.

Gayle stood near the door with one arm wrapped companionably around Maia. "Let's go. Don't have all night for you to play with your new friend."

This remark caused another outbreak of laughter, making Ethan blush. He removed his hand from the lizard, stepping over its large torso to reach the door. The two guards on duty turned to follow until an abrupt gesture from Gayle stopped them.

Ethan silently concurred the less people the better. He only hoped Martel, or at least Davin, would recognize them in the dark. They strolled into the night with Gayle's arm looped around Maia. She leaned against him, murmuring something too low for Ethan to understand. He had a feeling he was on a double date. However, his date had stood him up. A rustling noise caused him to turn.

All he could see in the dark night was the buildings' silhouette. Lighted window squares spilled out light onto the surrounding countryside. It didn't explain the noise he heard. Neither Gayle nor Maia appeared to have heard it. *Great.* Here he was on another planet with the possibility of ambush.

Still, he knew the cavern dwellers and the ground dwellers and he had nothing to fear from either of them. The monsters The Guardian had warned about proved to be non-existent. The ground dwellers worried about droughts and some re-occurring illness, he'd heard discussed around the dining table. *Trammars* seemed to be their main nuisance, and they had successfully domesticated that animal. Nothing to fear. It wasn't exactly as if Caulb was hiding in the shadows.

A hiss, a skittering across the dry leaves alerted him, before a solid body knocked his feet out from under him. Two crescent moons shed their light down on him reminiscent of the two suns during the day. Was there two of everything? A puff of hot fetid breath on his face reminded him of his predicament. Two glittery eyes regarded him intently. Was this the end? He felt two scaly feet, complete with claws, scramble for purchase on his chest.

Maia's voice rang out over his own internal monologue. "What happened?"

Gayle's shadow loomed over him and brushed aside the certain death that was currently resting, panting on his chest. "Looks like Boomus has taken to you. You may have ruined him for other households."

Peering into the darkness, he made out the basic shape of the overfed lizard. It was dark enough that his humiliation didn't show. He coughed to clear his throat. No reason for anyone to know how terrified he really was. "Yay Boomus, I'm a lucky guy."

Boomus must have taken his words for praise and swished his long tail smacking it into Ethan's ankles. "Ouch!"

"Boomus has the type of loyalty that takes a strong man to endure. I am betting you're that man." Gayle nodded and reached out a hand to help Ethan up.

"Um, thanks." Grabbing the hand, he peered into the night to locate the lizard.

A voice rang out from the direction of the bobbing light. "Maia, Ethan is that you?"

"Brother," Maia called before Ethan could answer. "It's us. Don't let Davin shoot us. We are with friends."

Directing a look at his lizard companion, who rubbed against him, he wasn't sure if he'd classify him as a friend.

"I second that," Ethan projected his voice, hoping Martel heard.

Davin's emotionless voice responded instead, "I resent the inference that I would shoot wildly in the dark, not knowing my target. I can see your infrared heat signatures. One of you is very short and cold-blooded."

Ethan sighed. "That would be Boomus."

They walked closer to each other. Martel held up a type of flashlight while Davin provided his own light. Maia sprinted forward to greet her brother. "Stop Maia, wait." Gayle lunged forward only to grasp a handful of air.

Cavern dwellers might not be as easy to handle as Gayle first imagined. That's what happens when you encounter someone totally out of your realm. Sometimes you're repelled, other times attracted, but often there's a huge learning curve.

Martel greeted his sister's spontaneous hug with a tight one of his own. "I was so frightened, Maia. You are the last of my family. I had no clue what happened to you after those savages took you and Ethan."

Gayle slipped up noiselessly to the embracing siblings. Davin noticed his presence, probably from his heat signature. "Identify."

"One of the savages," he growled the words, causing Maia to extract herself from her brother's arms to wrap one around the disgruntled man's waist.

Laying her head against his shoulder, she attempted to console him. "Don't take it too hard. He didn't know who you were then. No way would he know you are my mate."

"What?" Martel's loud voice caused Davin to react defensively, hurtling himself in front of his companion and powering up his laser array.

The prospect of a peaceful resolution died a swift demise. He had to stop it somehow. Jumping in front of Gayle, Ethan held his arms wide trying to make up for height. "Stop! You are the answer to each other's problems.

CHAPTER FIFTEEN

E THAN SQUEEZED HIS eyes shut, expecting to feel the burn of a laser. Since he had never felt a laser before, he was unsure if they burned hot or cold. In the end, he'd still be dead. His held breath building up in his chest reminded him he was still alive. He opened his eyes to find both Martel and Gayle staring at him.

How could he protect Gayle if he didn't stay behind him? Davin's lasers were no longer red, indicating he'd deactivated them. A deep sigh escaped him. Still alive, he might make it to his sixteenth birthday, Of course, back on Earth it may have already passed.

He felt both pairs of eyes trained on him. He turned enough to locate Maia, who regarded him curiously too from about a meter away. His sudden movement propelled Boomus to move. The critter came hurtling toward him.

Davin powered up with a warning. "Danger!"

"No, not Boomus!" Ethan found himself standing in the direct path of the over-friendly lizard. It had come to this. His Grandfather would be proud that he died protecting another living creature. Was it too late to rethink his decision? It wasn't exactly how he wanted to go out.

The lizard must have recognized his eminent demise on some level and hunkered down to the ground, even burrowing in the dirt, sending up puffs of the iron rich soil. The small cloud of dust caused them all to cough as they inhaled the metallic-flavored dirt. Ethan thumped his chest with a fist, trying to clear it.

Gayle's voice, slightly garbled, rasped out. "Stop it, Boomus."

The dusty lizard stopped his frantic digging and looked up at them. His overlarge eyes blinked as if questioning them. The peculiar behavior of the bipeds must have puzzled Boomus, but he did stop.

Davin turned his head to look at Martel, who explained, "No danger. It's a pet, I think."

"Pet," the droid, repeated the word.

Gayle eyed Davin with avid curiosity, only half-listening.

"An animal," Maia spoke slowly as if thinking aloud. She gestured in the direction of Boomus, who had moved enough to lean against Ethan's leg. "Ethan thought I could benefit from a pet like this creature here."

Ethan replied, "Yes, but where I live most pets are cats and dogs. My sister has a cat named Theo." The thought of Leah's cat reminded him of just how far away he was. At best, Theo was a difficult pet. She did exactly as she pleased, often ignoring their requests to do otherwise. The only thing he could say about the feline was it adored his sister. Even Theo made him long for home with a strong pull that made his eyes water. Right now, he wouldn't mind if Theo jumped in his lap and hit his face with her fluffy tail.

Gayle tore his eyes away from Davin long enough to explain the lizard. "Boomus' kind eats the pests that destroy our food stuffs. Luckily, they don't eat the same food we do. By domesticating them, we have a constant surveillance around our homes and grounds. Some do show a preference for a certain human, as Boomus has for Ethan."

The lizard rubbed his head against Ethan, almost knocking him over. The animal was solid. He certainly hoped it did not consider itself a type of lapdog.

"We can talk about this at my home over a meal. It is dark and is often the time the *tygons* come out. During the day, they lay low, waiting until it is dark to take advantage of their night vision. Their sharp claws can be fatal. Unfortunately, we can't outrun them. Let's go." He motioned toward the glowing city.

No one needed to be told twice to get a move on as they moved quickly back to safety. Martel crossed over to walk next to his sister, who stubbornly stuck by Gayle's side. They weren't holding onto each other, but they were close enough their hands and hips occasionally brushed. Their attitude announced louder than words their refusal to part.

Maia whispered, perhaps afraid the *tygons* might hear, "Do you think these beasts might be the monsters the former Guardians mentioned?"

There was a long hesitation before Martel spoke. He appeared to be formulating an answer.

Originally, Ethan thought the *tygons* might resemble a warthog, but now they took on mythic proportions, growing into huge creatures that could rip apart a dozen people in a blink of an eye. Casting anxious glances over his shoulder, he walked faster.

"They could be, but I am not sure. Apparently, Gayle's people are able to live on the same land as the *tygon* and suffer no consequences." Martel said the words with awe. It must be surprising to discover people living, even thriving in a world so full of hazards, especially considering their underground world eliminated both hazards and challenges.

Gayle snorted his response, drawing attention. "We take precautions." He pointed to the wall that surrounded the city. "This keeps out unwanted visitors."

Guards framed the gate they had left through earlier. One of the guards swung open the metal gate. It groaned with the motion. The guards saluted Gayle while staring at Davin. Gayle snapped off a salute, while adding, "Might want to lubricate the gate."

Ethan imagined Davin stared back, if you could consider the lights on his visor staring. Once inside the city their pace slowed. Lanterns hanging from posts illuminated their path, along with the two moons hanging in the sky.

The two men continued talking over Maia's head, whose bottom lip announced her petulance at their actions. Gayle directed his comment to Maia's brother. "Martel, is it okay if I refer to you by that name?"

"Yes, go on. You were telling me about the challenges of living on the surface." Martel encouraged the man, while Davin moved closer to take in the new information. The droid hoarded information the way Ethan collected clothes.

"Most of the real problems were conquered before I was even born. As you can tell, we keep out the trouble by using barriers or deterrents, like Boomus. At first, people were starving because we hadn't figured out the weather cycle. Lush harvests, due to the heavy rains one year, then drought the next. We're currently in a drought cycle."

"I noticed," Martel, agreed. "What causes this, or the better question, how is it dealt with?"

Ethan was curious about his answer, although there had been discussions about it earlier at the table. Faces peered out the windows, but unlike the earlier welcome, people stayed inside. The presence of Davin added an unknown element.

"Some of our early scientists explained there was a wobble in the planet's rotation. The angle of the axis creates the season, but the wobble changes the intensity. Records show the weather changes about every other year. At first, we tried to store food from the good years. We still do, but we have developed other ways to improve our food production."

"Tell me more," Martel requested as they turned onto the path to Gayle's house. People drifted away from the house, often only holding a hand up. By the time they reached the door, it was empty except for the older woman, Ethan had identified as Gayle's mother and Twilin, who grinned at their return.

Twilin ran forward to greet them, passing Gayle, to hug Ethan. He looked down at the surface dweller. How sweet. She'd missed him. Her actions tugged at his heart, reminding him of his own sisters who would be looking for him, wondering about his disappearance. It was time for him to return to Earth. Whatever problems he had with Caulb, he'd handle on his home planet.

The men were still talking as they sat down at the cleared feast table. Only a few crumbs and a small bone remained on the wooden surface. The aroma of roasted meat and spices still hung in the air. Night sounds drifted through the window, including a grunting, snuffling noise and some high-pitched whistling. Gayle ignored the sounds and continued talking earnestly.

"The oracle tells us we must find the others." He pointed to Martel and Maia. "You are the others. You will help us with a disease that comes every seven years and kills a good amount of our people and livestock. Currently, we are in the sixth year of the cycle." Gayle's eyes flickered to Maia.

Ethan wondered how old she was. Time, as he knew it, probably wasn't the same here. It was hard to believe people would live over a hundred years and yet fail to grow old. Back on earth, knowing the secret behind Maia's youthful appearances would net him thousands. Of course, if she was only twenty in his timetable, all it would earn him was ridicule.

Davin interrupted the silence. "How do you explain your survival?"

Gayle's mother brought in a platter of food and set it in front of Martel. "Our best scientists tell us we are evolving, learning to live on the planet. The strongest, with the abilities to adapt, live on, while the others die out." She sighed sadly before adding, "Including my mate and two of my children."

Ethan wasn't sure how Martel and his droids could help. The cavern dwellers were unaware there was a surface. "Is there a portent or a sign when this sickness is coming?"

Both Gayle and Martel turned to stare at him. He wondered if they were shocked, he could concoct such a pertinent question. It surprised him. Back home, he was superficial. Not only did he keep his appearance polished, but also, he made sure to notice every detail about his friends and then use it to flatter them.

Twilin kneeled on her chair making herself about the same height as the others. "The moons turn red before the sickness blows in."

Her brother wrinkled his nose. "That's an old shepherd's tale."

His mother carried in a pitcher just in time to hear the last bit of conversation. "What's an old shepherd's tale?"

"We're talking about the sickness. Ethan asked how we knew it was coming, and Twilin started talking about red moons."

Gayle's mother pulled out a chair and sat. "It may be an old shepherd's tale, but sometimes there is a lot of truth to those tales. We've forgotten more than we really knew over the years too. I've lived through six sicknesses, and I have seen the moon turn red. There's a smell in the air also. I think the illness might be airborne."

Martel was the first to respond. "If this is so, the easiest route is to move the people below the surface when this time comes."

Such a move would cause an upheaval in The Guardian's world. How would he explain the sudden influx of people who looked like them, but weren't? More important than their physical bodies, they would bring new ideas below ground. The people around him began to discuss how such a move could happen and who would care for the town while they were underground.

Davin's head swiveled back and forth, as he took in the information. A series of lights flashed across his visor. Holding up a metal index finger, he announced. "Might I interject?"

Martel nodded in the droid's direction. "Go ahead, Davin."

"I have a plan. First, your buildings need air tight coverings to prevent whatever it is from entering your homes. Once secured, you go underground. We can construct simple droids to carry on your hothouse agriculture. Anything grown outside will probably be tainted by the disease, so it is best not to use it."

Maia touched Gayle's shoulder, drawing a frown from her brother. Seeing it, she made sure to leave her hand where it was as she spoke. "What if it isn't windborne?"

The beginnings of smiles melted away from everyone's face. Ethan wanted to return to that moment of hope. "We have to try. We filter the air below, so there are no harmful microbes."

Gayle's mother drew signs in the condensation on the water jug. "I remember my mother speaking of a time when there was magick. People used it to influence their environment."

The yearning in her voice demonstrated her missing the absence of something she never really had. Still, was Ethan any different? Often, he yearned for total acceptance of who he was, not who he pretended to be. Sure, his family loved and accepted him, but he wanted something more. He felt it briefly that day under the oak tree. Why shouldn't someone feel the same about magick?

"You yearn for magick, but you already have so much more than most," Martel explained with a tired smile.

"How is that?" Twilin asked the question before her mother could.

Gayle looked interested and leaned forward. Ethan hadn't noticed any amulets or altars to any deities. All he'd heard was talk of an oracle.

"Your ability to grow crops and domesticate animals is a type of magick. It's one unfamiliar to my people. How you care for one another is the best kind of magick. I can teach you how to appreciate the elements more, but you already have a decent start. Most people experience or even utilize magick in their everyday life without even realizing it." Martel made eye contact with each of them as he spoke. When he finished, he picked up a piece of fruit and bit into it, allowing the juices to slide down his chin.

Holding the fruit aloft, Martel swallowed. "Even this fruit you don't think too much about is magick."

Ethan realized the speech wasn't for him, or was it. It made sense, almost, but he needed confirmation. "I think I understand, but I need clarification. My Nana tells me I am going to have a safe day, and I believe it. Is that the magick part?"

Instead of replying, Martel wiggled his eyebrows as he chewed. "The belief, the imagining, is the magick part. I spend much of my day imagining what my people need, but the result isn't just the droids, the technology, or me. It's that they believe too."

That launched an entirely different discussion, at least in Ethan's mind. Were the bullies, his troubles, partially because he expected them to be? Were acceptance and love unavailable because he didn't expect them to happen, or felt he wasn't worthy somehow? Only minutes before he was dissing himself for not having a serious thought in his head. That wasn't true. It was humbling to discover his worst enemy wasn't the bully, but how he thought about himself.

Conversation whirled around him as they discussed preventive plans to avoid the sickness. Davin had a plan on how to build respirators for those left behind, or as a precaution since they couldn't get it down to the exact minute when the moons might turn.

Ethan considered his life as they talked. His early years were easier. He remembered being popular and liking everyone back. Initially, he put it down to being attractive and friendly. Those things may have influenced others, but it was his attitude. He expected to get along with other people. Some kids require more modification to get along with, but it was possible. The result was a reasonably happy life.

Middle school changed everything. His identification issues may have been more troublesome since he didn't shoot up in height as other males did. His voice not changing was another trick nature played on him. The interests, he once shared changed, not his so much, but others around him.

The way he dealt with it was to draw back, not allowing too much of the real Ethan to show. He was afraid he wasn't good enough. A short kid with no athletic skills, if you discount dancing, was his physical side. No one really knew who he was.

His family had the best chance of knowing him, but he doubted even they knew everything. Sometimes, he worried about disappointing his father. When his father married into his mother's Wiccan clan, he was probably clueless what he was getting into. When Grandpa Carpenter morphed into an aging hippie after his wife ran off with the visiting evangelist, it must have messed with his Dad's internal compass. For years, Ethan tried to be his father's true north.

No way, he could do it. His father had never asked him to, either. It was all a matter of perception. What did his grandfather say? *Perception often deceives.*

Martel had rescued him, not from a bully named Caulb, but a bully named Ethan, who refused to accept himself as he truly was. The real rescue had occurred when he realized he was the creator of his life, not a reactor to his life.

CHAPTER SIXTEEN

E THAN FELT LIKE he'd been gone for months instead of a week. Martel decided it would be best to go back before the fire alarm had occurred in Ethan's own time. At least he would know what was going to happen. Having the jump on Caulb would certainly be different. Images of outsmarting the bully and his cronies tantalized him. The first thing he'd do was to make sure he got out of the building in time to escape his pre-determined beat down.

Martel and Davin managed to land them in an empty custodial closet. Ethan cracked the door to peer out, finding no one close by. Now would be a good time to head back to class, but what excuse could he use for his late entrance?

"Go," Martel hissed, and pushed on his shoulder, shoving him out the door. He stumbled out, almost losing his balance, but he caught himself before he kissed the floor. Straightening up, he turned his head to check to see if anyone saw him. Feminine chatter alerted him company was on its way.

He brushed down his clothes, aware he'd been wearing the same outfit the last few days. Maia did some type of waterless cleaning that rid the material of the obvious grime, but it still didn't feel clean. The science door was partially open, allowing the sub's voice to carry into the hall.

"Ethan Carpenter, Ethan Carpenter."

Obviously, she was still taking attendance. He slid into the room and took the closest desk. "Here," he called. A few students snickered, spotting his late arrival.

The sub didn't bother looking up from the roster. "Declan Danes."

Ethan stood and moved to his normal seat. His lab partner greeted him with a grin. "Thought you were absent. I heard you were hiding out from the wrath of Caulb."

Oh yeah, dropped back into his real life where an angry bully wanted to make him his personal punching bag. Striking a cocky pose, he leaned against the lab table, posturing for the surrounding students. The sub was mispronouncing an exchange student's name. Enrique refused to answer to a mangled name, even though surrounding students kept pointing to him.

"I'm not afraid of Caulb. Doesn't matter what lengths he'll use. I heard he even plans to set a fire today. Not sure what exactly the point behind that is. I guess we'll all find out eventually."

The news caused a spattering of whispering as the gossip flew around the room. No way would he report Caulb. Most of the student body, talking about his conversation, would do the job without earning the reputation as a narc. Of course, there might not be a fire and then he would look foolish. Doubt cropped up at the same time the fire alarm went off.

"Let's go." Ethan motioned to the door leading the way out of the room, with the sub urging the remaining students to vacate by clapping her hands like a trained seal. The students didn't need any encouragement to escape class. They all poured out of the rooms mixing into the halls and surging toward the outside door.

As one of the first out of the class, Ethan half jogged to the exit, weaving around slower moving students. His hands hit the push bar on the door, causing it to swing out with force just in case one of Caulb's cronies was on the other side. The teens spilled out onto the football field with the odor of burnt paper drifting out the door behind them. A few students held their hands over their ears as they hustled past the strident alarm. Outside, safely away from the building, the students began to chatter, despite barked orders from their teachers not to. The lack of flames coming from the school failed to frighten the students into obedience.

The flashing lights and scream of the fire engine's sirens caused the students to jostle for a better view. Ethan worked his way to the edge of the crowd to spot the firefighters in action. From his spot, he could see the ladder truck. A lone student stood by the door, staring directly at Ethan with a look that managed to combine both loathing and bewilderment. Ah, one of Caulb's crew probably couldn't figure out how he got the jump on him. What was his name, anyhow? Brad, Brent, Blaine, something with a *B*. He usually referred to Caulb's cronies as Thing 1 and Thing 2. Well, he only mentally referred, as to say it aloud could endanger his health.

Could the *B*-name boy somehow remember the earlier past? The boy's open mouth gave the impression he expected Ethan to be wandering around in the building for some reason. Last time around, Caulb had managed to cut him out from the other students while exiting the building. Life was easier if you knew how it would turn out.

Unfortunately, the ten minutes he already knew about was over. The students milled around on the field gossiping about Caulb starting the fire and his reasons behind it. Some speculated he was out to burn the school to the ground due to failing again. Others suggested he bore a grudge against the principal and was out to kill him. The rumors swirled around him. At first, a sense of justice swept over him.

About time, Caulb paid for some of the misery he put others through. Arson or premeditated murder carried heavier penalties than bullying. The laughter rang out as various students speculated on how long Caulb would go to prison.

Kennedy spotted him in the crowd. "Hey, Ethan, over here." The smiling blonde waved at him, motioning him over to her side. A quick glance over his shoulder revealed the sub counting heads to try to keep track of the students. The students kept shifting and moving. No doubt, she probably counted twenty different students every time. Only three original students remained from his class, including him.

A car with a loud muffler peeled out of the school parking lot. Apparently, some of the students were using the chaos to leave. It made him feel a little less guilty as he pushed his way to Kennedy.

"Hey, what's happening?" He choked out the words as he pushed up to his friend. Ethan eyed some of the males pressing up against the attractive female. "Give her some room. It's not like you don't have an entire football field." The students surprisingly backed away at his command, which was a new twist. Before, people had disregarded him, or perceived him to have no real power or no status. Maybe he had come back from the future as a real hard ass. The thought made him laugh.

"What's so funny, Ethan?" Kennedy nudged him, wanting an explanation for his laughter.

Unfortunately, he didn't have a good answer. "Looks like we get a free period."

"Yeah," Kennedy agreed. She held her palm out. "At least it's not raining. It would have ruined my makeup." Her lips drew up in a duck face. It was practically the cheerleader's trademark expression.

Ethan knew what to say. "You look gorgeous today, and I bet you'd look just as marvelous without the frosting." Kennedy simpered and batted her eyelashes.

For a moment, he could hear the conversations around him. He could see the people milling in the field as if he were hovering above the entire group. He could even pick out himself and Kennedy. The scene rolled out with his reply and Kennedy's response. A sense of unease washed over him. He was watching his life from a distance.

The daily routine he had acted out suddenly felt false and forced. Did any of the people he called friends know the real him? Of course, now that he was back, he wasn't sure who the real Ethan was. While on Terra Nova, watching Maia slowly drift away because she had no life, he vowed to live a more authentic life. Now, here he was, stuck back in his old life, doing the same actions as before.

Back in Terra Nova, people had expected him to have answers because he was one of the founders. Both Gayle and Martel looked to him for ways to blend their two societies together. His suggestions to allow those who wanted to become surface dwellers that chance. This would increase the food output, allowing those below to enjoy actual food.

There were even plans to manufacture robots to maintain crops during the sickness cycle. Ethan wasn't sure that the microbes wouldn't taint the non-greenhouse crops. Still, that wasn't his problem. It was up to the people of Terra Nova to figure out their own future. The same was true of him.

The principal appeared on the field with a bullhorn. The siren function sounded several times before the noise level dropped. "The building has been cleared by the fire department. It is safe to return to your current class. We will dismiss by the bell. Could Caulb Dorrance report to the office?"

The chatter resumed as students pushed toward the open school doors. Two teachers monitoring the doors spoke in low voices to each other.

"I expect that is the last straw for Caulb."

"Good riddance, he's been here two years too long in my opinion."

The other snorted her agreement.

A school without Caulb would be a better place for all, not just for Ethan. No doubt, the bully's alleged friends would give him up in a hurry, just to distance themselves. As for him, he wasn't so sure he wanted to stay here. To be real, a new school would be preferable. It would be hard to wipe out an image he had tried so hard to cement only a few months earlier.

A few of his friends called his name as he shuffled through the hall. A raised hand acknowledged them as he worked his way back to the science lab. As far as they knew, he hadn't ever left the premises and traveled a gazillion miles away and who knows how many centuries into the future. His family didn't know, either. No one knew.

Back in the classroom, the sub insisted on calling everyone's name again, not allowing anyone to leave despite the buzzer sounding, just to prove everyone had returned. His classmates groaned, while trying to get around the diminutive woman who was checking names off the roster mounted clipboard.

A few students muttered loudly, "*Lame.*" "*Stupid*" and one slacker male grumbled, calling the teacher "*a Nazi.*" Ethan watched the flustered woman's face redden as she went through the names, allowing the students to depart once she had checked their names. This was a difficult job, and she was persevering to do it right. A couple of days ago, he probably would have called her behavior lame too, but that was before. He now had a clue how hard life could be without a purpose.

"Shut up, Terrence," Ethan made sure to use the offending student's real name. It didn't sound half as cool as his nickname, Ter. "No one believes you're anxious to get to your next class."

The remaining students giggled, and Terrence gave him an evil look.

He started to say something back, but another student hissed, "*Remember Caulb.*" That was all it took to stop the remark.

That's not what he wanted. He certainly didn't want students to be afraid of him. All he wanted was to give the sub a break. Caulb going to jail wouldn't help Ethan become more authentic, instead of living as one of the stereotypes that existed within the school walls. Maybe that's why he had become so flip and shallow. Athlete or scholar didn't suit him. His father and Nana would put a kink in any plans to become a slacker.

Nope, there weren't too many roles left. Leah could explain to him how to get into the magnet school. If he confessed to his impromptu traveling and knitting together two completely different communities, they would have to see this school wasn't right for him. The warning buzzer reminded him at best he had sixty seconds to make it to history.

A burst of speed helped him to reach the door before it closed. Mr. Patterson instructed the students to open their books to chapter ten without looking up from his computer.

The flutter of pages surrounded him. Ethan didn't need to look down to realize he didn't have a history book, notebook, or even a pencil. He couldn't quite remember if he left those items in the past or the future. Jillian, the girl who sat beside him, motioned that he should slide his desk next to hers to share the text.

Remaining in his desk, he half stood and shoved it the remaining foot and a half to reach Jillian. He noticed a few other students were without books too, but had found someone with one. "Thanks." He smiled at the brown-haired girl who grinned back, revealing her braces.

It surprised him that he even knew her name. They weren't friends. The soft-spoken Jillian would be someone his friends would ridicule with her discount brand clothes and unfashionable hairstyle. Brooke would joke that Jillian's mother put a bowl on her head to cut her hair.

Mr. Patterson droned on about various wars while Ethan took a hard look at himself and his so-called friends. They were fun for the most part until they started ridiculing another student, which made him uncomfortable. Apparently, none of them ever heard of the *Rule of Three*. Whatever good or evil you produced came back to you threefold.

Did being with them when they chose to take apart others make him just as guilty? His only thought was at least they weren't picking on him. Being reasonably socially perceptive, he had picked out who would benefit him as friends. Middle school taught him most people would tolerate you if you flattered them. Mentally, whenever he thought he might be toadying up or brown-nosing someone, he referred to it as being positive. *Yeah, right.*

Jillian turned the page following along with the lesson. She threw him an apologetic smile since he had to remove his fingers from the page to allow her to turn it. Dropping his hand from the book, he shrugged. It was probably obvious he wasn't following along. Still, she didn't seem upset about it, only determined to do her part. Maybe he didn't want to learn, but she did, and wasn't the least bit apologetic about it either.

He could learn a lot from Jillian. She wasn't busy trying to be someone she wasn't. As for his posse, if he confessed, he was gay that would be cool because every stylish girl had a best gay friend. They served as this year's accessory. Being a Wiccan would not be as cool, although a few would think it was, especially if their parents were straight up church people. Nothing pleased most teens more than rebelling against Mom and Dad.

His lips tilted up a little bit, realizing he'd have to become narrow-minded and judgmental in his views to rebel. Speaking his mind is the one thing that would rattle his friends. They never really knew his opinions on anything and most probably thought they did. He acted more like a mirror reflecting their opinions and views. They mistakenly thought they were his.

Kennedy might know he liked boot cut jeans, especially paired with Italian leather half boots with stacked heels. England knew he enjoyed three-part harmony often associated with acapella groups, but still very few things out of thousands of choices he'd made. None of them knew he had a crush on a gentle giant who refused to speak, not that he'd ever tell them. They wouldn't understand. They lived in the land of the superficial. Nonverbal people were not tragic players in the drama called life. His friends would just call Orin a freak.

Mr. Patterson stopped his lecture when the principal strolled into the room. He pointed at Ethan, and then looked at Patterson, who gave a slight nod.

Oh great. Hadn't he already lived this part of his life? What could he be in trouble for now? His last visit happened because his father had the nerve to show up at school to discuss bullying and the school as an unsafe environment for students. Both things were true, but telling the principal would do no good.

He stood up and followed the principal down the hall. He kept up with the man's purposefully long strides. Several of the various staff members looked at him curiously, even with a little speculation as Principal Lowenson marched down the interoffice hallway. A shaggy explosion of curls appeared in his peripheral vision. The counselor was in for a change.

Stepping into the office, he signaled to the woman whose name he didn't know. "Could you come to the office with me? I think I will need an advocate." The panic tinged Ethan's voice, causing her to jump from her seat.

"Of course."

The Principal kept striding ahead, not even looking back to see if he was following. The open office door revealed a figure sitting in it. His suspicions were confirmed when Caulb turned to smirk at him.

The bully wasn't even the least bit scared of being caught trying to set fire to the school. Oh, he knew that wasn't Caulb's intention, but the principal didn't. The counselor slipped in behind Ethan, not speaking to draw attention.

Lowenson stayed standing to use his height and sizable presence. He grasped his hands behind his back, which he knew pulled back his shoulders and pushed out his chest. Ethan had seen several his cheerleader friends do the same thing. Only on him, it didn't slim his burgeoning beer belly. "Well, Caulb tells me you started the fire."

Seriously? When did a school bully become a reliable source? "Oh really? That's not what I heard. I was in the science lab when the fire started. Our class was also one of the first ones out too."

Caulb snorted his disbelief, while the principal narrowed his eyes. "Can you prove it?"

He couldn't believe this. When did he get to be so untrustworthy? Taking a deep breath, he closed his eyes briefly. His palms sweated as he tried to order his thoughts. *Spirit Guide help me. I am too angry to make sense of anything. Maybe I was better off at Terra Nova.*

Images came to mind of the sub checking people off the roster. She'd remember him, especially since he stood up for her. Then there was his lab partner, and Kennedy, who he went over to talk to, plus Caulb's friend, but he wasn't sure he could trust him.

Holding up his closed hand, he counted off his witnesses by putting up a finger for each one. "The sub made a careful check of all who were present outside and inside."

The principal shook his head. "Subs are unreliable."

Holding up another finger, he said. "What about my lab partner, Arturo, and the other students in the class?"

Caulb snorted. "Oh really, all your friends you mean."

Ethan was ready to argue the point about them being his friends too. The principal stroked his chin as if considering something, but he wasn't sure if he was thinking about his statement or Caulb's response. What else could he say?

"I spent most of the time outside with Kennedy Jamison. She would verify where I was."

Caulb was quick to reply with an eye roll. "Another friend, a cheerleader friend too. Not exactly known for their—"

"Stop right there." The counselor's irate voice cut the bully's speech short. He looked startled that anyone else was in the room. Ethan had to admit to being surprised even though he had asked her to accompany him.

She hadn't said a word until then while he'd felt caught in some grudge match with the principal and Caulb tag teaming him.

The counselor continued, unaware that everyone would have showed the same surprise if one of the chairs had sprouted lips and spoke. "I am tired of these stereotypes. Cheerleaders can be both smart and athletic. Neither negates the other."

Caulb's mouth dropped half-open, probably still in surprise over someone telling him what to do, even if it was an adult.

Ethan imagined the bully probably did what he wanted at home.

The principal cut his eyes to the counselor. He seemed a little unsure of the mousy woman who was ready to battle it out over stereotypes. "Um, good point. Miss, um, Dela."

"It's Ms., and the name is Delaney. Ms. Delaney. I've been here eight years."

Ethan knew a slap down when he heard one, since the principal was a very recent addition. The man apparently didn't detect it. He continued to stare at the wall with a wrinkled brow, mumbling to himself. "Jamison, Jamison, where have I heard that name?"

Ms. Delaney was quick to inform him. "School board. Kennedy's father is the president. Probably wouldn't like to hear his daughter referred to as an empty-headed cheerleader, or a liar."

The principal choked, but managed to pretend it was a cough. "Nasty cold. No reason to detain Ethan any longer."

Caulb, seeing his opportunity to escape blame almost leave the room, yelled. "I know he did it. I saw him set the fire myself."

"Seriously." Ethan balled his fist on his hips. "How could I have set the fire in the teacher's lounge and be outside in time to talk to Kennedy?" He couldn't believe the nerve of him trying to pin something on him that he knew he did.

Caulb's eyebrows shot up. The slightly confused look vanished from the principal's face replaced by a grim countenance that had to be like a Berserker's right before he lopped off someone's head. In this case, he figured it would be his, but he couldn't figure out why.

Ms. Delaney nudged his elbow. "Ethan, is there something you want to talk about? Some personal problems, maybe?"

What an odd thing to ask? Sure, he had personal problems and the biggest one was snickering. What was so funny?

The sun came out from the clouds sending a ray right through the windows, practically blinding him. For a moment, he tried to figure out what part of the puzzle he was missing. The soft-spoken counselor bit her bottom lip and looked as if she'd rather be anywhere else but here. He knew that feeling. Then there was Caulb grinning. It didn't make sense.

Theoretically, he should be smarter than the bully who failed most of his classes. Not only that, he had the advantage of traveling through time and knew all about the fire and Caulb's plan. He knew. Caulb knew.

A sideways glance revealed the principal giving him a stare down, probably the same one he used on the football field to intimidate the other players. It may have worked on a few. It certainly worked on him. Hey, what happened to his big goal to stand up for himself? Where was his courage?

Ethan pushed his shoulders back, ready to stand his ground, when the final piece fell into place. Caulb had never confessed to the fire. Like him never confessing to any of his previous crimes, but people still had suspicions. Unlike real life, you couldn't suspend or expel a kid for what you thought he might have done, even if there was circumstantial evidence. Eyewitnesses were dubious, especially if they were students or substitute teachers.

He had identified the location of the fire. Since Martel sent him back minutes before the actual incident happened, nothing had changed about the fire. Caught in the crosshairs, there was no way he should know so much. If he were just another student fleeing the building he wouldn't know, the drill wasn't routine. Oh, sure, he'd be curious like the rest of the students milling about the football field, but he wouldn't know.

"Caulb told me." The words came in a rush. No, Caulb didn't tell him, but a convincing lie or fabrication, as grandfather liked to call them, contained a good portion of the truth. "He told me he did it to set me up because of his arm. Oh yeah, he tried to beat the crap out of me because he's jealous that I get to talk to Kennedy every day when she can't even stand to be close to him."

The bully's face reddened as he shot out of his chair. "That's not true." He lunged forward and grabbed Ethan's shirt, jerking him up in his beefy fist, forcing Ethan up on his toes to prevent choking.

Ms. Delaney screamed, and then assumed her officious voice. "Violence is not the answer."

"It's my answer," Caulb growled the words as he drew back for a solid punch.

Not versed on close quarters fighting, Ethan dithered between a drop and allowing his shirt to rip or delivering a swift kick to the nuts. A shimmering noise, like what he heard before Martel and Davin appeared, sounded in the hallway, drawing attention and giving Ethan the opportunity for a good solid kick.

Caulb grunted and dropped to the floor.

"Oh, my goodness," the counselor gasped the words, putting her hands to her face.

Ethan watched the pain arc across the bully's face, realizing he no longer feared him. It didn't mean Caulb would never try to take a punch at him again, but he now knew he intended to fight back. Bullies tended to avoid fighters. It probably wasn't as much fun.

A large shadow dropped over the both of them. "Both of you are suspended. Indefinitely," he said the words with a hint of smugness. Ethan, Caulb, and the fire had introduced a situation that needed insight and expertise, but as an inexperienced administrator, he had neither.

Stepping over to his phone, he murmured a directive to his secretary. No doubt, he'd be heading home soon.

The counselor, whose name he forgot, stood near the principal trying to get his attention. "Fighting is only a two-day suspension. No one can be suspended indefinitely."

Ethan knew that, but decided not to mention it. Caulb stopped holding his nuts and stopped moaning. His baleful gaze promised retribution. Ethan glanced over his shoulder to confirm the adults were busy. Using his toe, he nudged Caulb's ribcage. "Not so mighty now, are you?" He pulled back his foot as if to give a mighty kick. The bully winced, pulling up his legs to protect himself.

With no reason not to kick him since he was already suspended, Ethan's foot stayed suspended in the air for a few moments as he considered his actions. Luckily, his dance skills gave him good balance. He dropped his foot back to the floor, watching the bully lower his arm. Caulb looked up at him in surprise. "That's right. I chose not to kick you. If I had, I would be the bully now."

The shocked expression morphed into a sneer. "That's your mistake because I will destroy you."

Caulb pushed up on his elbows. No doubt, he'd make another go at him. Ethan's show of defiance had done nothing to smooth things between them. He may have made it worse. The bully moved into a crouched position. Ethan took a few cautionary steps back.

The gym teacher rushed into the room, his whistle swinging from side to side, indicating he had run most of the way. The young teacher scanned the scene and grabbed Ethan's arm. A hard jerk removed him from the office and out of Caulb's path.

The two of them stumbled into an office piled with huge notebooks with papers sticking out of them. Bookcases were crammed with similar binders and a few open ones crowded an antiquated desk. The closed blinds allowed in filtered light, leaving most of the room in shadow. It had a musty, unused smell rather like an attic or a basement.

"Why did you grab me?" Ethan regarded the young teacher who looked barely older than most of the students. A sketchy beard, whistle, and a school ID hanging on a lanyard around his neck identified him as a staff member.

The slender man grinned. "You looked like the easier one. Even though the principal asked me to break up a fight, there's no reason for me to get hurt."

He made sense. The gym teacher looked more suited for playing tennis or golf than wrestling enraged bullies to the ground. "Yeah, I can see that."

Even the adults had similar situations they had to struggle with every day. Dusting a place off against the desk, he leaned on it. "What is this place?" He gestured to the books, not caring, but feeling the need to make conversation.

"Oh." The teacher turned slowly, picking up a dusty binder and opened it. "It looks like it's a record archive. This binder is from 1967. You'd certainly think they could do a better job than this, but the newer records are probably on the central computer drive."

Rubbing his neck, he wondered where he might be in the pile. True, he hadn't been at the school that long and the dust looked rather permanent. "I hope my records aren't in here. I wanted to transfer to a performing arts magnet school."

Using his index finger, he wrote his name in the dust on the desk. The man leaned over and read it.

"Tell me, Ethan, why performing arts? Besides getting away from a semi-truck sized bully."

Was that concern in the man's voice? Maybe it was simple curiosity. He glanced up to find the man's eyes on him. He shrugged, not sure what to say. *Sweet Goddess*, the man worked at the school he despised.

"Well, um," he stuttered to a stop, realizing he didn't even know the man's name.

"Gauge, Brad Gauge." He nodded his head for Ethan to continue.

"Well, ah, Mr. Gauge. I will be the first to admit I wouldn't mind leaving Caulb behind, but it is more than that. I've been drifting along for so long. Doing what people told me to do without considering what I wanted to do. As a male, singing and dancing are not good skills to have, but that's what I like. It's what I want to do. The only skill I'm developing here is running. I think I need someone to recommend me to the magnet school, more than one teacher maybe. I have no hopes for the principal giving me a good recommendation after my father riled him up." He looked down at his feet noticing their footprints on the dusty tile.

"Hmm." The man stroked his meager beard. "I imagine you can get a few teachers to write up a recommendation letter."

Even though Leah had mentioned it in passing, he'd never seriously thought about it before. A woman cursing in the hallway signaled Caulb's mother had arrived. His grandparents wouldn't be too far behind.

"It was that stupid gay wad's fault." Caulb's voice carried into the room. Ethan didn't need to explain who the gay wad was.

He was tired of being the problem, even when he wasn't, a convenient scapegoat and punching bag. Ironically, the school banished the dress code in an effort for students to be free to be individuals, as one parent expressed it. She was also the one behind the general push to break the code, and yet all the students dressed almost uniform in their jeans and shirts.

Occasionally, a fellow might go out on a limb and wear a tie or a girl a dress. The one boy who tried to wear a kilt was suspended after three guys jumped him in the locker room. His kilt was too provocative, but none of the mini-skirted cheerleaders were ever suspended. Talk about distractions, he'd even caught Mr. Robertson, the Chemistry teacher, checking out England's rear in her tight uniform skirt.

Remembering the thread of the conversation, he tried to bring up possible teachers. "I think Mr. Zimmerman would write one. My English teacher is a possibility." He wasn't very sure of anyone else.

Mr. Gauge used his hand to indicate himself. "I'd be glad too. I've encountered a few Caulbs in my time."

"You?" Ethan pretended to be surprised. Acting was another one of his passions. Often, he felt he was acting about seventy-five percent of his life. "No way!"

Mr. Gauge could have wrestled with self-confidence, acceptance and even bullies while in high school.

"Yeah, me, they used to call me Fatty Braddy, which was one of the nicer names. I didn't start dropping weight until my senior year of high school. In college, I decided to major in health and physical fitness. My goal is to reach out to students who find solace in junk food from the cruelties their fellow students perpetuate. There are alternatives." He stopped speaking to give Ethan a measuring look.

"I have never seen you in any of my physical fitness classes. Why is that?"

Oh yeah, that. There was no way he could explain his grandmother had confused the registration personnel when they tried to put him in gym. "Must be a scheduling mistake. Besides, I'm not really good at sports and all that."

Gauge's hand returned to stroking his almost beard. "I try not to make the class about sports, but more about learning how to develop your own fitness goals. There is no dodge ball or rope climbing. We do engage in some sports in a non-competitive manner such as golf, tennis, bowling, even gymnastics."

"Gymnastics?" His voice squeaked a little on the question, heralding the voice change he hoped wouldn't destroy his singing ambitions. "I always wanted to try the pommel horse and the rings."

"You'd probably be good at it too. You certainly have the build for it. As a dancer, you're used to exercising a certain amount of control over your body. The PE instructor over at the performing arts magnet school is a friend of mine. Nick is a former Olympic finalist. He could get you up on the rings."

They had gym at the magnet school too. He wanted to protest the injustice of it all, but it sounded like fun. "Sweet."

The jingle of Nana's bell charms and the tap of Grandfather's cane heralded their arrival. He remembered Leah's revelation that her principal was frightened of Nana. A slam of the inner office door affirmed that maybe his principal wanted to avoid his grandparents too.

"Um, Gauge, I mean Mr. Gauge. I'd love to have that recommendation. I'll see what I can do about the other two also. My ride's here." He slid off his perch, stirring up a small cloud of dust in the process.

"Want me to explain what happened and all?"

Ethan smiled. The helpful teacher had no clue what happened. "No, it's better if I do. Nana tends to get a bit worked up over insults to her family."

"Where's your cowardly leader?" Nana's voice carried over Ethan and the gym teacher's combined low laugh.

Heading for the door, he waved. "That's my cue." Spotting his grandparents, he headed in their direction in hopes of moving them away from of the administration offices.

"Hey, Nana and Grandpa. Ready to roll?" He pasted a smile on his face as if heading out for ice cream.

Grandpa's bushy eyebrows shot up. Nana stopped her character assassination in mid-word. "There's my favorite grandson."

Somehow, it never bothered him when she said it, even knowing he was the only grandson. It still counted. "Let's go." He tucked his arm into hers and urged them down the east hallway. It was the direction to go, if he was going to beg for recommendations.

Normally, suspended students were hustled out the nearest door to prevent interaction with other students. Stuck in the middle of such a harmless elderly couple, how could anyone object? He waved at the office staff. The attendance clerk hurried to the counter to share her opinion. "I think it is wrong to suspend you. Everyone knows that worthless bully is at fault."

"I appreciate your support," he searched for her nametag, "Mrs. Morris."

Once they had taken a dozen steps from the office, he decided to explain before they drew too close to a classroom and were overheard. "We really aren't supposed to be in this corridor, but I need to ask two of my teachers to write recommendations for the performing arts school. They may not have an opening, but I'm not coming back here."

Grandfather patted him on the shoulder. "You shouldn't come back here. Too much unrest is in the air. Negativity abounds."

Their steps echoed down the strangely empty hallway. It reminded him of when Caulb had caught him in the hall. Only now, it would never happen. The closed doors looked similar in the long hallway. He had to read the small nameplates beside each door. "Here it is. I'll talk to my English teacher, then we'll hit choir."

Both teachers promised glowing letters, but still there might not be room for him, or his suspension would possibly hurt his chances. No school wanted a troublesome student. The three of them walked slowly to the car to accommodate his grandparents. Sometimes, he forgot how old they were, and they couldn't move as fast as he did. Their cheerful, energetic attitudes often overshadowed their physical limitations.

Outside the sun was shining, and a bird trilled in a nearby tree. A deep heaviness fell off him as he walked out. It was strange that, in addition to shedding his fear of Caulb, leaving the school allowed another layer to sloth off.

"Grandpa, you're right about the school. Knowing I'm not coming back makes me feel so much better. I'm not sure about getting into the magnet school, though." Uneasiness began to fill the open spot the fear had recently vacated.

Nana laughed. "No worries. I'll take care of that."

That could mean almost anything. "You're not going to work any confusion on the admissions staff, are you?

He wasn't totally against it, but he wanted to earn the right to be there too. There would probably be an audition. Mentally, he went through what routines he knew. It had to be something none of the other students already used. He wasn't too sure, how well he would stand up against them. Originality would be another benefit.

He spotted his grandparents' yellow cruiser. The car suited them both. Grandfather took a couple quick steps to reach the passenger door, opening it for Nana. Nana giggled and batted her eyes at her husband.

Ethan always found his grandparents genuine fondness for each other endearing. Their separation, caused by grandfather's jump into the past, made them act like newlyweds, elderly newlyweds with an adult child, but still very much in love.

He slid into the back seat and buckled his seat belt. "I was thinking about doing the Gene Kelly routine from *Singing in the Rain*."

"Which one?" Grandpa asked as he twisted the key in the ignition.

"You know the one. He kisses the girl goodbye, and he's all happy and stuff. He's alone. It allows me to sing and dance, but not so strenuous that I am gasping for air."

"Sounds good to me," Nana agreed. "I always had a thing for a man who could dance. That's how your grandfather swept me off my feet."

They both laughed fondly, and Ethan joined in.

A couple of right turns signaled they were almost home. Ethan mentally tried to recall the exact movements of the dance. A review of the movie DVD would help. His grandfather asked him something he didn't quite hear. "Pardon?"

"I said when are you going to tell us about your time traveling adventures to the future?"

"Great Goddess, haven't you heard of privacy? Maybe a man might want to keep a few things to himself." In a house with more than its share of clairvoyants, keeping anything private was a challenge.

His grandfather chuckled, as Ethan expected. He liked the sound of him referring to himself as a man. Possibly, saving another world had to count for something. Then there was facing down his personal nemesis. He couldn't forget that. There wasn't much to do, unless it was living his own dreams. "Nana, how exactly are you going to get my foot in the door of the magnet school?"

Resting her arm on the seat, she half-turned and smiled. "You will have your excellent letters and your magnificent talent, but one of my twenty-year regulars is married to the president of that particular school board. Endless times, she's told me how if I ever need anything, she could help me with, just to ask. Well, it's time to ask."

"Do you think she'll actually do it?"

Her eyes narrowed, and her brows moved down into a menacing V, which made him sorry he'd even mentioned it.

His grandfather's voice pierced the moment. "No one ever crosses Esmeralda Hare."

Ethan was surprised. His grandmother was a loving, caring woman, but the words *sweet* or *gentle* were never a part of her description. Memory like an elephant, wickedly clever, creatively inventive all suited her, along with dramatic, passionate, and a tendency to safeguard those she loved.

"No one does it twice, you mean," Ethan couldn't help adding. Instead of taking offense, Nana leaned toward him to pat his face.

"You're learning, grandson."

The car turned into the driveway before he could even explain about his impromptu trip to the future.

CHAPTER SEVENTEEN

DINNER THAT NIGHT was a big affair in the Florida room since the kitchen table wouldn't hold everyone. Dad dug out the folding banquet table, along with the wobbly folding chairs that went with it. Apparently, somehow his family knew they were welcoming back a time traveler. Nora and her husband, Clayton, arrived with the grand dog, Emory. Leah invited her boyfriend, Dylan. The family crowded around the table passing cornbread while his mother ladled out bowls of chili.

"It's hard to explain what it was like on Terra Nova. At first, I thought it was wonderful. There didn't seem to be conflict of any kind, no obvious prejudice or bullying. It is a simulated world underground, made to look like they were in a city with blue skies and smooth stone buildings. Often the homes had a fake front and were alcoves in the cavern walls." Ethan did his best to make the city come alive for his sister, but realized his memories were already fading.

Nora rested her chin in her hand. "Tell me how big the houses were." His mother scooted a steaming bowl of chili in front of her.

He only went into one house, if he discounted Martel's jumble of rooms. "Maia's house was one room with a view screen that functioned as a window. It would change to suggest it was evening."

His sisters marveled that they survived on pills as opposed to cooking. His mother handed him a bowl with a smile, remarking that such a system would cut down on cleanup time. "Maybe so, but I noticed that most of the people stopped living because their lives were purposeless. The Guardian developed such a complicated system of sanitizing the air and providing nutritional supplement there was nothing left for the people to do. They didn't even have school or real jobs. A few had hobby jobs, but The Guardian provided their food and wares. They'd even stopped reproducing and their small population was dwindling."

"Thank the Goddess they managed to pair up with the surface dwellers who seemed to be a more robust version of their race." He dug into the spicy concoction, glad he could play a part in bringing them together.

"Conflict, challenge, goals, call it what you want." Grandpa brandished his soupspoon as he talked from the far end of the table. "It is what made our pioneers such strong stock. The immigrants are like those early adventurers willing to put down roots in a new land and all that it entails."

Nora's husband grunted his agreement through a full mouth, causing most of his family to laugh, since he had come from another century.

"Yeah," Nora agreed. "Clayton has it hard. Central heat, showers, cars, and cable."

Swallowing, the man was able to speak for himself. "It's a hardship; I am willing to undergo to be near my beloved."

This caused more laughter as they passed the ice tea pitcher around. A quick glance around the table assured him his family was all there. When did they all develop into couples? Even his prickly sister, Nora, found a soul mate. It wasn't that unusual, and it hadn't come easy for any of them. Still, it pointed out his singleness.

Moving to another school would only make it worse. Sure, some of his friends were on the plastic side, but still they were friends. Starting Monday, if he was accepted, he'd be at ground zero again, making new friends.

A plate of rhubarb pie appeared at his elbow. "Nana made your favorite pie. Seemed like an appropriate dish for our space cowboy." His father teased while staring at him with a twinge of concern. "What's up?"

What could he say? He didn't know how to explain it, but everything kept changing. Had he been gone only a week? A few times, he thought he wouldn't live to sit around the table and eat with his family. "I guess I am just tired. Didn't really sleep much."

The dinner wound down after that with Nora and Clayton returning home. Dylan and Leah went outside to say goodbye, while the rest of his family cleaned up.

Though he'd only been gone, a short time, he felt strange, as if he wasn't sure what his place was anymore. Normally, both he and Leah would help clean up. Some of the flatware and napkins still rested on the table. Circling the table, he picked them up.

His mother noticed what he was doing and rushed over to take the utensils from him. "Go get showered. I imagine you're almost asleep on your feet.

Loosening his fingers, he gave up the spoons he gathered. "Okay, thanks." He left the overwarm, fragrant Florida room for the cooler basement.

Bath and bed, but then what should he do? A one-eighty-degree turn left him not knowing what to do next.

✧   ✧   ✧   ✧

HE WOKE ON Thursday with a bad case of the butterflies. The recommendations reached the magnet school, along with a tendered invitation from the president of the board to audition. The last forty-eight hours were spent twirling, singing, re-watching the movie, and practicing with the umbrella. His father even put the sprinkler on to simulate rain.

A trio of knocks sounded at his bedroom door. "I made you pancakes for breakfast."

Nana must have walked down the stairs sideways with her cane to tap at his door. He didn't feel like eating, but guilt gnawed at him thinking of her effort to make today special. His Nana wasn't the cook in their family. When she made something, it was a labor of love.

"That's great. I'll be right up." He spoke through the door, giving his outfit one last tweak. The trousers lay across the chair. His buttoned-down shirt and tie were the closest he could get to the suit Gene Kelly wore, considering he didn't own a suit and both his grandfather and father's clothes wouldn't fit. A trench coat was a serendipitous find at the local thrift store. His grandfather contributed a fedora and his black umbrella.

The CD he'd burned of the audition music he placed near the fedora. He was ready for breakfast, at least. His footsteps sounded loud as he ran up the stairs, but they usually did. Concrete walls tend to magnify sounds.

Nana pushed a plate of pancakes toward him that probably could feed three lumberjacks. "Whoa, there's only one of me."

"Yes, I know. I may have gone overboard. You know I don't cook much. I guess I am not that good at judging portions. Eat as much as you can." She pulled out the chair across from him the better to watch him eat.

His grandfather walked into the room. "Esmeralda, did you make me anything to eat?"

"You're not auditioning, are you?" She arched an eyebrow at her husband. "You have no need for magickal hot cakes."

Magickal, well he could use that. He took a couple syrup-drenched bites and chewed. His stomach rolled a bit, letting him know it wasn't open to overloading.

His grandfather found another plate of pancakes in the microwave. "Ah ha, look what I found. It must be magick." He laughed at his own joke and carried his plate to the table.

Ethan cut his pancakes, moved them around the plate to give the illusion he ate more than he did. After a couple minutes, Nana grabbed his plate.

"Enough, you aren't eating. Go brush your teeth and get dressed. We'll drop you off."

He pushed out from the table, focusing on the part of the sentence where they dropped him off. Everyone in his family wanted to come to the audition, but he begged them not to. Besides, they had seen the routine numerous times, and he didn't need anyone watching him. The director and whoever else might be there would be enough.

In the bathroom, he practiced different smiles. A few times during the number, he needed to smile, rather goofy, deep in love, expression. He wasn't sure he could do that, but he'd try it.

On the way out to the car, his grandfather shook the keys at him. "Do you want to drive? You'll be sixteen in a week."

A few months ago, he wanted to drive in the worst way, but that was before his life decided to make a seismic shift, reordering his priorities. "No, maybe on the way back. I need to mentally rehearse."

A few raindrops splattered on the sidewalk. Great, even the weather was cooperating. A kid on a bike with his hoodie pulled up pedaled past them. It could be him from the past, but he refused to look. Somehow, the kid on the bicycle denoted time shifts. No way, he wanted to jump to the future when he was on the brink of having the life he wanted.

He reminded his grandfather to turn, so he didn't accidentally take him to his old high school. The gleaming new school came into view with a large banner announcing they were putting on *The Wiz* and tryouts were next week.

The car moved slowly to the front of the building. "I think this is it. I can get out here. Come back in about an hour. I'll be waiting."

His grandfather stopped and shifted the car into park. "You know the Hare men have always been wonderful showmen."

It probably would serve no purpose to point out he was half Carpenter. No doubt, his father's side didn't lean toward the theatrical.

"Ethan, I read your cards. This day will be significant in a good way." Her eyes were bright with knowledge, which usually indicated there was something she wasn't telling him.

He waved to them, placed the umbrella on his arm, and tried for a jaunty walk as he dodged raindrops. The smart thing would be to use the umbrella, but not yet. It was for the show.

A girl with multi-colored hair pointed him in the direction of the auditorium. Students lounged in the hall. One girl was dressed all in black, complete with a long skirt trailing the floor. The bearded man beside her had on a tuxedo shirt, jeans, and cowboy boots. He totally rocked it.

Ethan wondered if they were students or staff. His eyes roamed the decorated hallway. Colorful mosaics decorated the walls, while 3-D mobiles hung from the ceiling. Skylights allowed the muted sunlight to cast large white blocks on the floor making it look as if it were a trail. "Follow the illuminated road," he murmured to himself.

A guy in a black jacket with his thumbs in his tight jean pockets asked, "Are you talking to me?"

Great. First day here and already caught talking to himself. "Um, well, no, I was looking for the auditorium."

"You found it." The male's voice changed growing more animated.

"How did you like my impression of DeNiro from **Taxi Driver**? Did I sound like him?"

Oh, that's what he was doing. "You nailed it. Are you auditioning?" It never occurred to him, he might have to beat out someone for the spot. He didn't really want to, and there did seem to be many students milling around. The sound of laughter and chatter drew closer.

"Nope. I have a slot in the performing arts program, but a new person is going to audition today. The program director asked a bunch of us to come to watch. Performers need a live audience's energy to feed off." He stopped talking and angled his head to give Ethan a thorough look. "You're him, aren't you?"

He felt the stare, but quit listening after the words live audience. "Um, what?"

"The guy who's auditioning is you."

It sounded more like a statement than a question, but either way it demanded a response. "Yeah, it's me." *Yay me. Live Audience.*

"I'll take you to the director them." He reached for the door, but stopped to shout over his shoulder. "The show is about to begin. Go get the others."

Was it too late to walk out? The image of Caulb muttering under his breath as Ethan lay on the floor was enough to keep his feet moving. *I can do this. My family is a live audience, and they watched several times. They can be a critical audience, too. Grandfather insisted on showing him the appropriate way to soft shoe. He had this.*

They stopped in front of a middle-aged man with a shaved head. "Mr. Largent, I found your newbie in the hall."

"In the hall, you say," the man drawled, indicating he was not a Midwesterner by birth. "A truly amazing place for him to be. Go round up the other students."

He looked down at his clipboard before addressing Ethan. "Mr. Carpenter, do you have music for me?"

"I do." He handed him the CD. "It is a four-minute segment featuring both singing and dancing. It is from Singing in the Rain. It's the part where Gene Kelly tells his girlfriend good night."

The man looked intrigued. "An unusual choice for someone your age. Would you like to run through it before we get the whole crew in here?"

"Yes, please." *Great Goddess, do not let my voice crack.* Mr. Largent walked away to plug the CD in the player resting on the piano. Climbing up on the semi-circular stage, he began to block out his moves, where he wanted to be at each spot in the song.

"Ready," Mr. Largent called out more as a warning than a question as he depressed the key. A trio of notes indicated the beginning of the sequence. He darted back to his spot, cocked his fedora, and grabbed his furled umbrella.

He started with a few soft slides, a twirl, and hands out. *It was time to walk and sing.* He opened his mouth and the words came out as rehearsed. He could hear some of the students hushing the others as they strolled inside the auditorium and slid into their seats. A few stood at the back, not taking seats. *Umbrella open, spin, smile. The male in the back was tall. Looked like a giant. Close the umbrella, plant it on the floor, sing, then place it on shoulder and walk away whistling.* He walked near the steps whistling. The big guy had walked forward into the beam of a skylight.

The music ended, which was just as well because he was staring right at the tall guy, who was looking hard at him. It was Orin, but how could that be? He lived in another state.

Ethan, is that you? I can't believe my eyes.

It was him. Was he standing on the stage with his mouth open in shock? Mr. Largent clapped his hands.

"Nice warm up, Mr. Carpenter. Now, I want you to pretend you just saw the love of your life. Your heart is beating extra fast. Everything is right in the world. Do you think you can do that?"

Boy could he. He merely nodded and went back to his first position. Thank the Goddess he'd rehearsed the number so much he could do it in his sleep. Oh yeah, he could do the smitten smile. His soft shoe was spot on; his voice didn't crack, he smiled and twirled on cue, and managed to whistle as he walked off stage.

The wild clapping and whistles caused his heart to leap with joy. This was it. This was what he was born to do.

Ethan you were magnificent.

He recognized Orin's deep voice. Of course, it was the only voice he'd heard in his head besides his own. Could the day get any better?

"C'mon out, Mr. Carpenter, and take a bow."

Ethan jogged out onto the stage and made a standard Broadway bow. He had practiced that too. The students cheered and clapped some more. *He could get used to this.*

Mr. Largent climbed up on stage with him and grabbed his hand holding it up. "Welcome your new classmate, Ethan Carpenter."

Apparently, his day could get better.

CHAPTER EIGHTEEN

H E COULDN'T BELIEVE Orin was here. After his bow, he thanked the director and jumped off the stage. Several students pushed toward him.

"Great job!" The actor he first met pushed through the crowd to slap him on the back. "I knew you had it in you when I saw the trench coat and fedora."

He craned to see around him, but all he could see were more unknown faces beaming in his directions and offering congratulations. "Um, thanks." Rocking up on his tiptoes did no good. It seemed like most of the world was taller than his five foot six.

I'm here, Ethan. I can feel you looking for me. I can see you. Orin's voice sounded in his head, bringing warmth and joy.

If only he could politely shove his way through the chattering students. Different faces pushed in front of him offering advice and praise for his performance. The variety of students impressed him from the dreadlocks, tattoos, the Boy Scout uniformed girl, to the dress-wearing dude. No one felt the need to conform here. He had found a home.

A bully and a brush with the future had pushed him in the right direction. A sharp clap of hands softened the chattering until the students completely stopped, to look up at the stage where the director stood.

"That concludes the audition part of our day. Return to your original classes."

There was some grumbling as the students headed for the various doors. Ethan watched them leave. Orin stood against the back wall, staring at him. At last, he walked toward Orin as he pushed away from the wall.

"Mr. Laughton, that means you too."

Orrin stopped in mid-stride, gazing up at the stage.

Laughton. He had never known Orin's last name. He watched as Orin put a hand up and turned toward the doors.

Goodbye, Ethan. I will see you soon.

The director came up behind him. "That one doesn't talk, but I am told he's an artistic genius. Everyone here is a genius in his or her own way. Okay, go to the office, fill out the admissions forms, and we can get started."

That was all it took. "Okay, will do." He pivoted to leave, but remembering his grandfather's umbrella, he turned back to retrieve it from the stage.

Musing to himself more than talking to Ethan, the director commented, "Laughton actually looked like he was going to speak."

Grabbing the umbrella, he managed to recall the image when their eyes met. His were soft with recognition. It was the good kind of familiarity, instead of avoiding someone's eyes out of fear, guilt, or plain awkwardness. Yeah, it almost felt like he could say something. Not sure what, his name maybe, hard to say, but some day Orin would talk to him. Call it a feeling, intuition, precognition, or just simply knowing.

Not bothering to reply to a remark probably not meant for him to hear, he left the auditorium through a side door. The halls were empty now. Sounds drifted out from various classrooms as he strolled toward the office. The sound of a piano and singers running the scale greeted him, causing him to remember the room location. Good chance he'd be in there next week.

A few more steps and he heard shouts and possibly a fight. Seriously, he thought he had left the bullies behind. A quick peek into the room revealed two students gripping wooden swords while other students milled around them, shouting Shakespearian curses. An acting class, of course. They were probably working on a scene from *Romeo and Juliet*.

His initial fear faded away. He had nothing to fear here. Caulb filled his mind for a brief second until he dismissed the image. No reason the two of them would ever cross paths again. The thought put a little more bounce in his step. Life was grand. At least it was now.

At the office, an admissions counselor named Barry walked him through his schedule. "You do need the same credits here that you'd need at your other high school, but the classes dovetail more with your major. Yours is?"

Whoa. He had a major. Well, he knew this was mainly a performing arts school. "Musical theatre." His uncertainty made his voice squeak, but the counselor typed in the words as if it was a perfectly normal major.

"All right. You will have to take English, but there will be more focus on plays as opposed to writing endless essays about what you did on your various breaks."

Ethan removed his hat and fanned himself with it. "Well, that's a relief." It was getting hot in the room. It could be nerves or the belted trench coat he was wearing inside, combine that with dancing his heart out and meeting the love of his life again. Yep, he was burning up. He answered the counselor's questions while removing his coat.

"Ethan, you could start tomorrow if you want. You don't have to wait until Monday." The counselor handed him his printed schedule with a lifted eyebrow.

Tomorrow. He could start tomorrow, which meant he could see Orin too. "Um, do the visual art people mix with the performing art people?"

Barry pulled on his ear. Maybe it was a tic or maybe he was stalling since the new student had asked him a totally unrelated question.

"I have a friend in visual arts. That's why I asked." That might make his question sound less weird.

"Ah, a girl. I see." The man winked.

No reason to correct him, especially if it gave him the information he needed, yet a part of him felt not pointing out his friend was male. It made him a little less authentic. He wasn't ashamed of who he was or ashamed of Orin, either. "No, my friend is a male."

His comment made him feel better, but appeared to have no effect on Barry. For the most part, people probably didn't give a damn. Nana always said most people were too involved in their own lives to give a hoot about yours. Apparently, she was right. As if his canny grandmother was ever wrong.

"Well," Barry's eyes rolled upward as if trying to remember. "You might have general classes together. Both visual and performing arts take place in the same building, although technically it's classified as two different schools."

The thought of sitting next to Orin in history or trig would almost make the classes bearable.

"That is if you're in the same grade." Barry continued to explain.

Since Orin was older, they wouldn't be in the same classes. His face must have reflected his feelings because Barry hurried to explain.

"You'll have many opportunities to meet at lunch, before and after school in the commons, extracurricular activities, even electives."

True. Once he figured out Orin's schedule, they'd find times to meet, not unlike Kennedy and her boyfriend who seem to meet if only to touch hands in the hall. Somehow, that kept them going until they met again. At least, that's how she'd explained it. He wasn't sure if her boyfriend felt the same. It was probably mostly prestige for him. Never hurt to be with one of the hottest girls in the school.

Tucking his schedule into his welcome folder, he headed out to the steps to wait for his ride. Was he assuming too much? Just because their minds had touched one day, make that their souls. He knew Orin on a more intimate level than even his family. In that knowing, he had recognized his soul. Was it because they were both Pagan? It was hard to know. His experience with romantic love was zero.

The trench coat hung over his arm while he clutched the umbrella in his left hand and fedora in the right. He stood on the cement stairs, scanning the area for a bright yellow cruiser. His thoughts drifted back to

Orin. Strange, how he had never felt intimidated by Orin because of his large stature. The difference was Ethan had encountered Orin's essence before he had stood up.

Unlike him, Orin attempted to make himself seem smaller by slumping. On the other hand, Ethan stood straight, hoping to use every inch of height he possessed. He had even gone so far as to buy boots with stacked heels since it made him feel almost normal height. He couldn't wait for his family to meet Orin. No doubt, Nora and Leah would like him even if he didn't speak. His father would be thrilled he had a male friend until he figured out, they wouldn't be tossing the football around.

A car came into view with the windows down and the soundtrack from *Wicked* blaring. How did he ever expect to escape notice, when these people were his roots? He could hear his grandfather's baritone belting out the lyrics.

Nana waved at him as if he hadn't seen or heard them arrive. As he opened the car door, she asked, "Anything special happen?"

Throwing the coat and hat in first, he scooted in after them. "Yeah, I got in."

Grandfather turned down the music. "Of course, you got in. You're talented. They'd be more the fool not to take you."

His initial reaction was to explain how hard he had worked for the part. Still, when they drove him here, they already knew he had the part. That was part of living with clairvoyants. Sure, they didn't know everything and most of the time they shared nothing. His grandfather declared it was important to experience everything, even if you knew how it was going to turn out. Sometimes, you took the other path if you had foreknowledge.

"Anything else?" Nana called from the front seat in a wheedling tone.

They knew about Orin. Of course, they did. Might as well give it up. "I saw someone I met at the Pagan Pride Festival."

He watched as his grandparents turned to look at each other with smug knowledge. At least, they seemed to be all right with it. Thank the Goddess for his family. Otherwise, he'd be making videos to put on the Internet about how much his life sucked.

Oddly, he thought his life had sucked for a while. Meeting Martel was what he needed to change his perception. He picked up his folder and flipped it open to see if he needed to get anything for school tomorrow. "Where did you go while I auditioned?"

Grandfather looked into the rearview mirror to catch his eyes. "I went on a date with the prettiest gal in town."

Nana giggled. "We saw a wonderful musical act and went for ice cream."

A sticky sweet smell of ice cream filled the car. He inhaled deeply.

"Ah, I see," he used a pseudo ominous voice. "One chose a pumpkin pie while the other went with chocolate chip mint."

The three of them laughed as he used some of the same skills Nana used in her readings. Thirty percent was observation. Other forty percent was receiving information, and the other thirty percent was knitting it together and coming up with an interpretation. It wasn't too hard for him since he was acquainted with ice cream aromas.

"Wait, what musical act? I wasn't gone that long." A suspicion needled him, but he had asked them not to come.

Nana turned to look at him. "Don't go getting all gloomy on us. You were marvelous. Sure, you told us not to come, but you might as well tell an eagle not to fly. Besides, we only changed our minds after you got out of the car. It didn't hurt you because you didn't know we were there anyway."

She had a point, but he seriously doubted they had abruptly changed their minds.

"You were marvelous," she added. "We're old. What if we never lived to see you on stage?"

He held up his hands in surrender. "Please stop. Not the *We Only Have a Few Years Left* speech. No doubt you'll outlive me."

"Hush, don't say such a thing." Nana made a quick sign with her hand. It was quick, not easy to read, but probably warding off the evil eye.

If people knew they were witches or just plain run of the mill Wiccans, they'd try to ward them off. Most people made the sign of the cross unaware the cross began as the symbol for the Sun God. Being Kemetic, Orin probably used it.

The rest of the day was anticlimactic with purchasing a series of colored highlighters for his play class. After informing his family of his success and gobbling down dinner, he spent the rest of the night deciding what to wear on his first day of school.

His father inquired about the length of the suspension only to find out there was no suspension. When the principal heard about him moving to another school, he felt the problem had resolved itself, and there was no reason to suspend him. It could also be possible that the counselor had managed to get through to the over aged bully. More likely, it was Kennedy since he had texted her everything that happened.

School board presidents had a way with making principals listen. This was probably mostly true, since the principal was little more than a sub waiting for a board confirmation.

✧   ✧   ✧   ✧

UNLIKE ORDINARY SCHOOL mornings, where he forced himself through a cobweb of sleep that threatened to pull him back into slumber, his eyelids snapped open. *Today is important.* He lay there for a moment, trying to remember why.

It came over him like an epiphany. Somehow, he'd earned the grand life he'd always wanted. Well, maybe not always dreamed of, since he was clueless it was out there. He stumbled into the bathroom. Splashing cold water on his face, he tried to remember how he used to think of his life less than a month ago.

Looking into the mirror, he'd seen this same face so many times. A less troubled version smiled back at him today, since he wasn't planning on dodging bullies or wearing any masks. He tried parting his hair on a different side to be symbolic of his new life, but the hair kept flopping over. Oh well, everything didn't have to change.

The clothes he'd laid out the night before, he realized they were more flamboyant than what he would have worn to his old school. The skinny jeans with the stacked heel boots weren't too different from the norm, but topped with a poet shirt and a black embroidered vest, he wasn't sure he felt more like a pirate, a gypsy, or someone coming out of his own personal fashion closet. The analogy made him laugh.

Leah was walking out the door when she saw him. She wolf whistled as she closed the door behind her. Both his parents had left for work already. Nana stood by the stove making tea. Her back was half-turned to him when she spoke.

"Flying the rainbow flag today, are you?"

"Nana!" He was surprised his own grandmother would make such a remark, but there was no malice in her tone.

She carried her tea to the table and sat down. "What? I figured by now you'd realize I say what I mean. I wondered how long you'd stay in that little case you had made for yourself."

"What are you talking about?" She made him sound like a mummy or something. Grabbing a cereal box, he shook it. Still, some left. Instead of getting up to get a new bowl, he used Leah's abandoned bowl. He shook the cereal in the bowl and covered it with milk. His mouth was full when Nana answered.

"You had this image of what you thought everyone wanted you to be. I am not sure exactly what it was, but it wasn't you. Sometimes, you would leak through the cracks. Those were always the best times. I am not sure when you started building it. Often I think it may have started when you were ten and that girl punched you in the nose for liking fairies." Raising the teacup to her lips, she took a sip.

Ah yes, the angry Brit girl. She had made an impression on his nose and eyes. "No, I don't think I was hit for liking fairies. It was more of me likening *her* to a fairy. Of course, I didn't know what a *ginger beer* meant and why a person didn't want to be one." Using his spoon to chase around the floating flakes, he waited.

"Yes, that was it."

Ethan kept his eyes on his bowl, not revealing his shock that his opinionated grandmother would stand corrected. Did he start to change then? He certainly learned not all people were open-minded. Some folks tended to express their narrow-minded views with their fists.

"Well, anyhow, you made this mold of who you thought you should be. I'm not sure who you were trying to please." Her nose crinkled as if she tasted something distasteful.

"Did you forget my father?" *Great*. He didn't need to have that discussion before he went to school. Although, it was always somewhere close to the surface. How he had disappointed his father by not being a manly heir. The fact he hadn't reached the average height for an American male demonstrated his body was conspiring too.

His grandmother spooned another teaspoon of sugar into her cup and stirred. "Of course, I haven't forgotten Adam. Why do you think who you like would matter to him?"

A snort escaped him. Nana was clairvoyant. How could she miss so much in front of her face? "He's spent most of his life encouraging me to play sports, watch sports and cop shows. How much more stereotypical can you get? He probably died a hundred deaths when I saved up my money from grass cutting to buy a dance video game."

"Ethan." Her hand covered his on the table. "I forget sometimes how young you are. You tend to look with your eyes instead of using all your senses. Have you really paid attention to your father, or just perceived him as how you thought he was?"

On some level, this was probably a deep, meaningful conversation, but he wasn't getting it. "What do you mean?" Noticing the bowl was empty, he pushed it aside with his free hand.

"Not everyone is like you, finding it easy to talk to anyone. You are like your grandfather in that way. Your father has difficulty talking to people, even his own family. Your mother might be the only person he can really be himself around. He spent all this time trying to talk sports or encourage you in sports because he thought it was what you wanted. Usually you dutifully joined any sports league to gain your father's approval. Ironically, he was trying to bond with you over sports. That is a joke, since your father was never an athlete. You blame him for not accepting who you are, when you wouldn't even show him who you are."

Nana folded her arms as if to signal the end of her speech. His grandfather's whistling came closer. Part of his brain tried to identify the tune, while the rest turned over the information. His father had tried to bond with him over accepted male touchstones; sports, and violent television shows. It made sense now. His father had enough knowledge to know what sport was in season and who was ahead, which was about the same as him. No wonder their conversations never went very far.

"Still, I know you want me to feel like everyone is accepting of me, if I'm different and all." He stumbled to a halt. Was there anything more different from a Wiccan family in the Bible belt?

His grandfather entered the room without calling a greeting and busied himself near the stove. The whistling stopped, meaning he was listening.

"Not everyone. There will always be people who don't accept you, no matter what you do. People have turned themselves inside out trying to get those types to accept them. Some have even committed suicide. Truth is they will never accept you no matter what because they can't accept themselves." His normally spirited grandmother heaved a long sigh after her insight.

His grandfather patted her shoulder with one hand. "It's hard to tolerate their cruel ways. Their young souls lack experience."

"Okay," Ethan readily agreed. "There are people like Caulb. It's okay if they never like me." Personally, he'd like to keep those people at a distance.

Bringing the teapot to the table, his grandfather freshened up Nana's cup. "Fear is what makes most people act badly. Sometimes they're afraid people won't accept them. Religion keeps some people scared, telling them if they don't hate the right people, they won't make it to heaven. We fear what we don't know, which explains most of racism. Think about how people treated the gypsies. They still do, if you get right down to it. There are all these stories, from gypsies stealing children to being little more than skanks. Of course, we know these are untrue, but those who don't know any gypsies, believe."

There was some truth there. Until he had made friends with Arturo, he thought all Asians were serious. The cuckoo clock in the living room announced the half past with a single chirp. "I need to be getting to school. I don't want to be late."

Nana placed both hands on the table, pushed up halfway, but sat back down instead. "I know you want to get to school on time. First, you need to spit it out. The question you have about your father."

It was hard not to roll his eyes. Most of Nana's clients paid good money for this type of insight. His teeth dug into his bottom lip. He might as well spit it out or be late to school on his very first day.

"You say Dad is cool with who I am, but just has a hard time relating to people. I'll accept he loves me because I'm his child and fathers love their kids. When we were at the Pagan Pride Festival, I found a group of young men under a tree. It was the first place I could just be me. We were chilling and eating. Then Dad storms up and insists I have to go, all in a panic. Are you going to tell me he wasn't freaked out that I was hanging with gay guys?" His father practically foamed at the mouth trying to get him to leave.

Grandfather laughed. It was an odd reaction until he explained. "Oh that, that was more about my dear outspoken Esmeralda than you, Ethan. There were rumors of a news crew on the grounds. Someone had made a big fuss about Pagans in the local park. They wanted the news to investigate to see if they were performing live sacrifices or something."

"I wondered why Adam hurried me out of there." Nana slapped the table. "I would have explained to those news people how it was. We have just as much freedom of religion to practice our faith as the cross wearers."

Ethan watched as his grandfather grinned, patting his wife's hand. This gave him something new to consider. His father on the anxiety branch most of the time, never declaring himself. He was half-afraid his engineering firm would fire him if his Pagan leanings were uncovered. It didn't seem fair. You couldn't fight it unless a company admitted they fired you for your religious beliefs. Few companies were that stupid.

"It makes sense now. Thanks, you two. I'm ready to head to school." It was amazing how the pieces of his life kept falling in place. It was as if he'd been in a dark room and someone had just switched on the light.

His new phone lying on the living room couch vibrated. He scooped it up along with his jacket. Obviously, he had a message, but he'd check it in the car. His unexpected trip into the future netted him his father's old cell phone. It didn't serve any purpose to point out to his family that a phone wouldn't work across the centuries, especially because he was glad to have one.

In the backseat of the car, he watched as the kid on the bike rode by again. This time, he stopped and looked at him. The boy waved his hands as if to get him to pay attention, but Ethan tried not to look. He wanted to stay here this time. No time traveling into the future or back into the past. Right now, was where he wanted to be. As they drove past the boy, he turned and looked out the back window.

Who stared back at him wasn't young Ethan. A bloody, bruised face instead mouthed the words, "Beware."

Flopping back into the seat, he refused to acknowledge the warning. Why ruin a perfectly good day? The face looked like his face right now, not a future face or a young one from the past. Inside the hoodie was the collar of his poet shirt. The one he was wearing right now.

A sense of foreboding came over him. Was he never going to be safe anywhere? He could stay at home and be homeschooled like Brendon, but he didn't want to live like that. He had to face his fears head on.

His shoulders drooped a little. The sun went behind the clouds taking with it some of the anticipation of meeting Orin. What if this was some grand joke? Maybe Orin didn't like him at all. Could be their souls had never touched. He was as bad as any middle school girl who developed a crush on a boy because of his perfect smile or great hair and scribbled his name on everything from folders to skin as if such an act would make him like her. Usually, it just embarrassed the object of her affection. Was he guilty of doing the same?

Uncomfortable with the idea that Orin didn't feel the same way he did, he picked up his phone for distraction. A text message from Kennedy was the perfect distraction he needed.

Caulb was expelled. He swore he'd get you. His mother kicked him out of the house, too. Now's he's a thug on the loose with time on his hands and a car. Take care.

His heart jumped into his throat. Well, that didn't help. He may have taken one step forward, understanding his father, but two big steps back, doubting Orin's attraction and knowing Caulb was gunning for him. *Yay me.* The phone buzzed again indicating another incoming message. With his current luck, Kennedy would report that Caulb would be joining him at his new school. The number was unfamiliar, but the text was all in caps.

YOU CAN RUN MUNCHKIN FAGGOT. PAYBACK IS COMING TODAY.

The words reached out and grabbed him, as effectively as Caulb's oversized hand. Would he ever be free of him? They were involved in some cosmic dance that never ended. *New dance partner needed, please.* If Caulb had his number, did he know where he lived? Better yet, did he know where he was?

His grandparents discussed the upcoming psychic fair with some interest since they both were participating. Would Caulb harass them? The day that started out bright had grown oddly dark.

The car stopped in front of his school. Several other students were arriving. Due to being a magnet school, there was no bus service.

"You'll be driving yourself to school in a couple of weeks," his grandfather commented with an eyebrow waggle.

It would be more than a few weeks according to the permit guidelines, but it didn't bear mentioning. "Yeah, can't wait." The sinking feeling plummeted to his stomach.

Instead of walking into the building, he stood on the sidewalk watching his grandparents drive away. What to do now? Technically, he should walk into the building and go to class. What if Caulb had a gun and hunted him down at school? It wouldn't be just him that was dead. His hand went for his shirt opening feeling for the small hammer amulet that represented Thor. *I call on Thor to protect me and give me the strength I need to face the upcoming ordeal with Caulb.*

A quiet sense of reassurance filled him. Everything would work out okay.

I am here.

Ethan blinked twice. While he understood that the Gods and Goddesses represented characteristics of a higher force within the unified force of all, he had certainly never expected one to answer him. It was good to know they were listening to his prayers.

It's me. Orin.

He turned slowly to see him leaning against the building wall with a slight smile. His long duster suggested a cowboy theme, but he figured artists deserved to be just as creative in their dress as performers.

Orrin pushed away from the wall and walked toward him. *Forgive me for overhearing your prayer, but I've been waiting for you.*

He was waiting for him. That was a good sign. It might not have been all on his part.

Orin casually allowed his hand to bump against his. *Sometimes I thought it was all me. How could someone as handsome and articulate as you feel anything for a silent giant like myself?*

He did care. His heart sped up as they strolled into the school and down the hall. Their direction was unclear, but he didn't want the moment to end. *How can you not know you're beautiful, inside and out?*

The buzzer sounded, ending their soundless conversation. He fumbled for his schedule to see where he should go. Orin peered over his shoulder and pointed in the direction of his class. *Thanks.*

Orin touched his shoulder. The small touch was the same as cradling his heart. *You need to tell me why you need Thor's help. Could be I am Thor's messenger.*

He touched the hand on his shoulder, appreciating his strength and the fact he could depend on Orin. He knew it without having even experienced it in this lifetime. *I will.*

A girl replaced Orin by his side as he rushed to *Introduction to Musical Theatre*. "That's amazing what I just witnessed. Apparently, you can communicate with tall, silent, and handsome. No one else can."

He didn't know how to answer her, but being real was his motto. "We know each other from before."

"Oh." Her mouth puckered up as if she didn't quite accept his answer. They both turned into the same classroom. "Hey, we both have the same class. How weird is that? I'm Jenny."

"I'm Ethan. Anything I should know about this class?" It would serve him well to make friends on his first day. Jenny was curious and outspoken, not unlike his Nana.

She slid into a seat behind a long table and pointed to the empty seat beside her. "It's fabulous. Most of the time, I don't even think I am in school, but rather in some extended play practice."

His phone chimed about the same time he sat down.

Jenny gave him a quick look. "Turn it off. Before you get caught. Dr. Loren is cool about most things, but she takes cell phones." She nodded at the small woman with the ramrod posture entering the room. "And keeps them."

The glowing number showed it was another unwelcome missive from Caulb, but he didn't have time to react to his intimidation tactics. This weekend he'd get his number changed. The day moved fast until it came to lunchtime, then came to a screeching halt as he wandered into the cafeteria with a handful of other kids.

Did Orin have the same lunch? Jenny explained that since the population was so small there were only two lunch periods. Their school didn't get the same funding as other schools, so they did without the lunchroom staff and managed with vending machines. Jenny explained it was an open campus too, but there weren't many places to go eat.

He walked in with Jenny and some other students. She introduced him to the wonders of the sandwich vending machines when he saw Orin. His new friend looked up as if he felt his stare. Orin sauntered over to meet him, his duster flapping behind him.

Jenny noticed Orin's approach, and she bent to grab her soda before speaking. "Have fun, Ethan. Remember class starts at one-twenty." She waved and moved away to greet some other friends at a nearby table.

Ethan stared up at Orin, wondering what the tall rugged male saw in him.

Could be I like boy scouts. There's a diner a block away from here. Pagan owner, I can talk to her. Orin angled his head in the direction he wanted to go.

They walked out the doors, attracting a few glances. The nip of the wind not only reminded him he hadn't brought his jacket, but winter was on the way. He chafed his arms and tried to control his shivering. A body warmed duster settled around his shoulders.

My fault. I should have considered you didn't have a jacket on. I don't like the commons because of the noise level. I spend a good part of my world in silence. I like it that way.

Ethan shot his arms through the duster's sleeves rolling them up a couple times, so he could see his hands. *I probably look like the fool in your coat.* It sounded like it was dragging the ground.

Orin rubbed his face with his hand as if he were hiding his smile behind his fingers. *Adorable, delicious, I'm not sure which one describes you best.*

Ethan's face warmed under the compliments. Of course, he was human and appreciated a compliment as well as the next person, but when it came from someone he cared about and admittedly fantasized about, it was even better.

The buildings around the school were old, but still managed to hang on to their beauty with turn of the century arched windows and scrolling along the walls. A few buildings sported new paint adding a splash of color to the scene. A neon sign of a bubbling cauldron over a section of ground level windows had to be the diner. The owner wasn't one for subtlety.

They were only a few steps from the diner when a car squealed to a stop beside them. There were no stop signs or stoplights. No obvious reason for a driver to slam on his brakes, so along with this knowledge, a sense of unease arrived with it. The slamming car door drew his attention to the rust dusted sedan as Caulb jumped out.

Ethan swallowed hard. He should have read the message. It may not have stopped anything, but then again Orin *would* be safe.

Another door slammed, and Caulb's favorite toady jumped out, his eyes on Orin. "Caulb, he has a friend. You didn't say nuthin' about a fair fight."

Ethan was ready to run, but he couldn't leave his friend. *Orin, run.*

His friend didn't answer, and he didn't hear running feet. Caulb could have the same effect on Orin as he did on him, a hypnotic one, aware that danger existed in the unpredictable Caulb, but unable to look away from his evil stare.

The bully ran at him, and he tried to jump to one side, but ended up tripping on the duster. He stumbled to his knees, causing Caulb to fall right into Orin's punch that sent him flying backwards.

Rolling to his back, Caulb managed to kick up to his feet, which was rather impressive. He yelled at his cringing sidekick, "I could use some help here. Get the piece."

Did he mean gun? He hoped he heard wrong. What had he ever done to make Caulb want to kill him? He stood up and peeled off the coat, ready to face his fears and Caulb. Still, he preferred not to die, considering he had just mapped out his life and met his soul mate. *Orin. Go into the diner. I think he has a gun. This is my problem.*

The little toady ran around the car with a gun in unsteady hands. He might miss him and end up shooting Caulb instead. A shove propelled him to the ground again, but he wasn't even close to Caulb. He looked down at his white shirt for a bullet hole and blood. Nothing.

In front of him, Orin had Caulb's arm twisted behind his back and his other arm was across his throat, causing a sputtering plea to emerge.

"Don't kill me. Please don't kill me."

A bell jingled indicating the diner door opening. Ethan glanced back.

A woman with a sawed-off shotgun and a determined expression appeared deadly. Didn't he see her in one of those apocalyptic movies? "Best drop that piece you little piss ant. Mine's bigger, and my aim's better. I don't mind going back to prison."

Toady must have seen the same movie. He not only dropped the gun, he jumped in the car and sped away causing Caulb to yell. "That's my car!"

Sirens filled the air as two black and whites squad cars squealed to a stop in front of the diner. One cop jumped out of the car, eyed the scenario, and approached the diner owner. "What's going on here, Lila?"

Lila lowered her gun and pointed to Caulb. "This one comes speeding down the street, jumps out with his buddy, ready to beat up my steady customer, Orin here and his friend."

The police officer nodded his understanding and motioned for the other officer. "Bill, cuff him and read him his rights."

Bill stared at the restrained Caulb for a second as if trying to remember. "So, we meet again." Grabbing the arm Orin had pinned, he snapped on one cuff, then the other. A nudge had the bully heading in the direction of the squad car. Orin stretched to his full height and held out his hand to Ethan.

Ethan grasped his outstretched hand. *I feel like a fool. All I did was fall around the place. I was more like a bowling pin than a hero.*

The police officer clicked his tongue and angled his head toward Orin. "That boy is a fool to take on a guy that size."

Lila pointed to the gun on the ground. "He considered that to be the great equalizer."

Orin helped Ethan to his feet and wrapped him in an embrace. *This is the first time it was ever good to be the giant freak. For once in my life, I got to be the hero, instead of the silent freak. You did that for me. I can't explain how great that makes me feel.*

Ethan stood inside Orin's embrace, resting his cheek on his chest. It didn't matter who looked.

"Eth-than." The voice was rusty and rough, as if his voice hadn't been used in a long time.

It couldn't be. He tipped his head back to stare into Orin's face.

Orin's eyes met his. *Yes, it is me. After meeting you that first time, I secretly practiced talking. I decided if I ever met you again. I wanted to tell you how I felt, even though, I didn't totally understand it myself. We connected. I knew then with just a glance, a thought, that you were the one. My soul mate.*

"How do you feel?" Ethan wanted to hear the words, although his actions were clear enough.

"I think I might love," he paused slightly before pushing out the last word, "you."

Lila, who was standing nearby, smiled. "This calls for pie." She waved them into the diner. The officer followed, asking about statements.

The diner owner placed one hand on her hip and flashed a grin at the uniformed man. "Sebastian, I think you could use some pie and coffee too. It will give you time to write up everyone's statement."

As they walked through the door, Orin took the opportunity to entangle his fingers with Ethan's. They both slid on the same side of the vinyl booth facing the officer.

It felt like the sun came out once again, brighter than before. Gathering up his courage didn't seem as difficult with Orin by his side. "Tell me what will happen to Caulb?"

Lila leaned over the counter and topped off his coffee. "I'm anxious to know too. Make sure you get his little piss ant friend along with him."

Sebastian thanked Lila as he continued, "As long as you come down to the station and swear out charges, I imagine your attacker will merit some time behind bars. He isn't new to the system, obviously since Bill knew him."

"I will do that," Ethan declared, feeling courageous for a change.

Lila shoved another piece of pie toward Orin. "I think it was really brave how the two of you tried to save each other."

Orin blushed and shrugged. Ethan protested. "I didn't do anything, but stumble around."

"Not true," Orin forced the words out.

Lila nodded vigorously. "Lots of men brag about how they would take a bullet for a friend or even a spouse. In the end, they won't. Instead, they'll leave the way the little piss ant did. You were willing to take a bullet for Orin." Her voice choked as she reached for a napkin to wipe her teary eyes.

Ethan felt somewhat teary himself. His fingers snagged the paper napkin on the table just in case. It never hurts to be ready. A sense of quiet satisfaction settled on him as he watched his companion devour his slice of Dutch apple pie. Feeling his stare, Orin stopped chewing to look at him with a tender expression.

I know. I never expected to feel like this. Couldn't understand how something so wonderful could happen to me, but it did.

The officer, unaware of the silent conversation, shoved the incident form in front of Ethan.

"Go ahead and glance over it. I think I got it all. Let me know if I missed anything."

Ethan read over the slanting print. Hard to believe the most intense moments of his life constituted only two paragraphs. His name badge identified the man as Wells. Sebastian must be his first name, or a pet name Lila bestowed on him. A glance at the two adults made him wonder if there might be something between them.

Wells handed him a copy of the report. The paper fluttered in his hand as the door swung open. A disheveled man entered with the breeze. "Hey, Lila, what's the police car out there for? Did they finally find that still you have out back?" The man laughed at his own joke until he saw Sebastian, who made a point of standing up, which dried up his amusement.

Lila wrinkled her nose at the man's humor and walked over to wait on him, while Sebastian retook his seat.

The officer capped his pen and gathered his clipboard. He remembered the text. "Wait, would written threats be good in building a case? Caulb sent me some threatening texts."

He pulled out his phone and powered it up. "Had to turn it off for school. I didn't even get to read the last text. He thumbed to the text.

Today is a good day to die. LOL

He passed the phone to the officer, who looked at the text and let loose with a long whistle. "This just keeps getting better and better. Can I take your phone for official transcription?"

A mental summary of the various messages from his friends that Caulb was out to get him filled his mind. "Yes, you can. You'll also find many messages from other students warning me that Caulb was out to get me. My father even tried to reason with the principal who just laughed off his concerns."

"Too often that happens. People sometimes forget that age doesn't stop anyone from being dangerous or deadly."

A quick glance at the clock showed they were already late. "We're late to school. I guess we don't need a note from the police explaining why?"

Ethan grinned engagingly, not expecting a note. He was happy to be alive and in love.

"Nope, but I'll give you a ride to school and explain what happened. I assume you're both from the arts school?"

Ethan wanted to protest since they were obviously gay, which resulted in being stereotyped as artist types, but he remembered it was the only school around. "Yes."

"Thanks, Lila," the officer called out as he waited for the boys. He pulled out his wallet to pay, but Lila shoved the twenty back at him.

"Keep doing your job and you can cage a free meal here anytime." She gave a wink and laughed.

On the drive to school, the officer half-turned and asked. "What caused that thug to be so bent on wiping you out of existence?"

Ethan had this. "I thought it was because I was different, but that wasn't it at all. It turns out I was very tight with the girl who he had a crush on, and she wouldn't give him the time of day. Kennedy even had a boyfriend, but that never seemed to discourage Caulb. He must have thought I was poisoning her against him. Being so much smaller than Caulb made me an easy target too. At least, I could run."

"Someone caught up to him by that cast on his arm," the officer commented as he swung the school door open.

"Um, that was me. Quick reflexes and a not so forgiving door." He had never laid a finger on Caulb, but karma managed what he couldn't. Officer Sebastian explained the latest incident as the principal signed passes.

He could hear the officer still talking. "Life's ironic."

Yes, it was. He bumped knuckles with Orin as they separated to go to their different classes. It was good, too.

THE END

AFFIRMATION

PAGAN EYES, BOOK 4

BY
RAYNA NOIRE

CHAPTER ONE

T HE PROFESSOR'S VOICE bounced off the cement block walls and lab tables giving his words a brittle quality. Stella twisted around to see if any of the other students noticed, but most weren't even taking notes. Those with laptops open were either shopping or updating statuses. A chime caused her to glance at her phone. Instead of seeing a message from her co-worker, Mitch, about dying from boredom, the text was from Cameron. Her heart leapt a little when she saw his name.

Need to see you right away. Ditch class.

Besides being the resident bad boy, he was her bad boy. The thought made her smile. It lasted only a few seconds as she considered his behavior. Lately, Cam had been no treat, always demanding she do things for him, never considering she might have a life too.

Part of her wanted to jump out of her seat to see what the dark-eyed junior needed. Another part counseled her to stay. The only reason she'd made it to college was due to a merit scholarship. If she didn't keep her grades up, she'd lose the scholarship. Leaving class, especially during Dr. Engelhard's exam review, could be academic suicide.

Still, Cameron wanted her. He needed her. Quite a difference from her father, who dropped out of her life the same time he divorced her mother. His parting sally as she and her mom stood on the front lawn was, "You ruined my life." Its intended target could have been either of them, although, a search for her shot records for college uncovered her parents' marriage certificate, proving they married shortly before her birth. Other parents divorced. At least half the kids on campus came from divorced parents, but few had battled as bitterly or as publicly as hers had.

Picking up her pencil, she forced herself to concentrate on the notes on the board. Her attention wandered. Lately, it went down pathways she'd rather forget like her parents red-faced, screaming at one another, somehow unaware she was even in the house. Not only did she discover her mother got pregnant which forced her father into marriage, but she also learned her dad was no prize in the bedroom, all things she could have lived without knowing.

Her phone chimed again. Cameron. The man might be hot, but not patient. Sighing deeply, she slumped in her chair. No way around it, Cam would keep texting her until she showed.

Mitch leaned over to whisper, "I'll make you a copy of my notes. I'll bring them to you at the computer lab."

"Thanks."

Her reply, unfortunately, attracted the prof's attention. He stopped writing to stare right at her and spoke. "Some of us think this review is for my own benefit."

The few students who were paying attention giggled nervously.

Stella picked up her pencil and pretended to write until the prof turned back to the board, giving her a chance to escape. She gathered her notebook and phone and shoved them both in her bag. Mitch gave her a wave as she turned for the door.

The lanky male with the bad haircut had traits she wished Cam possessed. A few of the girls joked about a blind man cutting Mitch's hair. At the time, she'd said nothing, but she should have stood up for him. Mitch trained her for her computer lab job and never lost patience with her no matter how many times she had to ask him the same questions. Now, he was taking notes for her too.

The sunlight hit her as she pushed the heavy exterior door open. Her feet stumbled to a stop, her pupils adjusting to the bright light. A student behind her shoved past, jostling her a little. Voices made her step out of the way before someone else rammed her.

Wasn't that Cam near the weeping magnolia tree talking to Carlotta? The exotic Puerto Rican had most of the males on campus running into walls. The beauty not only had plenty of curves, but her accent attracted too. Stella's mother always said men loved anything new and different. At the time, she thought her mother meant cars.

Seriously, she left class for him and here he was flirting with Senorita Skank. Well, screw him. Maybe she'd just return to class and hope the prof hadn't noticed her exit. Not likely. The best she'd do was go to her room and study. Of course, she'd have to walk past Cam, unless she wanted to make a half-mile detour. No problem, she'd pretend she didn't even see them.

Don't act upset. Shouldering her backpack, she speed-walked in the direction of the couple. *Almost past,* the pain that grabbed her heart when she first saw the two of them squeezed a little tighter. Once she was in her room, she'd locate her Wiccan books. For Cameron, she'd dropped everything from her interest in Art Club to observing her Wiccan faith. Her mother had warned that men take everything but leave you with nothing. Her mother's newest obsession was the church, which seemed to demand everything too.

Cam's deep voice called after her, "Stella, wait."

His voice as warm and smooth as caramel had won her over initially. That and the fact that he didn't give up easy since he asked her out six times before she'd agreed. It baffled her that he wanted to go out with her. Rumors had him practically dating everyone in her dorm, but never more than once.

Realistically, he should have moved on after their first date. Maybe this was her wake-up call. Cam's hand latched onto her arm, pulling her to a stop. "What's wrong with you? You act like you didn't hear me."

The impromptu sprint ruffled his hair, making him look even sexier with his well-shaped brows arched over his brown eyes. Stella often wondered if he'd had his eyebrows shaped, but never felt like she knew him well enough to ask, despite sleeping together. He'd probably lie about it anyhow.

"Looked like you were busy. I didn't want to interrupt." Her shoulders went up in a shrug, hoping it looked like she didn't care too much.

His brows lowered as he grinned, displaying for a moment that wicked smile that devastated feminine hearts, especially hers. Stella's ire began to melt away under the full wattage of his smile.

"You think." He shook his head as if what he was about to say was ridiculous. "I was flirting with her?"

Stella sucked in her lips wondering if she'd been hasty in her assumptions. After all, she hadn't heard what they said, even if their bodies turned toward one another, blocking out the outside world, indicated an intimate meeting. "The two of you had your heads close together. People might mistake it for flirting."

Good, she didn't say it looked like flirting. No reason for him to think she was needy and insecure, even if she was.

His laugh garnered attention from passing students she could have done without. "Please, Stella." He wrapped one arm around her shoulders and pulled her into his side before continuing. "How could you imagine such a thing when I only have eyes for you?"

The words soothed her some, but part of her pointed out that his eyes checked out the passing women too. The reassurance helped a little, but it didn't restore the euphoria from their first date. Romcom movies oversold her on the wonders of love. The rush disappeared, leaving behind irritation at the demands of a relationship. Right now, she should be taking notes for a crucial exam. People assumed she was naturally smart, but she wasn't. Studying, making flash cards and endless notes earned her the scholarship. Thank goodness, Mitch was copying notes for her, which was the behavior she'd expect from a boyfriend, but didn't get from Cameron.

The man had some type of sexual magic he did with his eyes and lips that short-circuited her rational thought process until she forgot why she was upset with him. Not happening. No way, she'd fall under the spell of his bedroom eyes now. She directed her gaze over his shoulder to where she could see dozens of students strolling the commons. Some hurried, most carried books, and a few ambled prolonging their time together in the stage of initial attraction. She remembered it well.

Before Cameron, she'd gone out in high school a little, but not much. Truthfully, she was afraid of being too attached to someone. Her goal centered on bypassing love and the accompanying devastation that happened when it ended. Her heart and a desire for companionship interfered. Cam wore her down on a night when her inability to reach Leah left her feeling unusually lonely and friendless.

Cam asked her out the first time they'd met in the campus bookstore. She'd refused, thinking he wasn't serious. Another girl at her dorm went with him instead, proving her original assumption right. Despite her full schedule and a work-study job in the computer department, she wasn't so busy she didn't notice that almost every hot girl in her dorm claimed to have gone out with Cam.

They'd usually gush about his cut body and fabulous hair, not that they ever spoke to her. She overheard them. College courses demanded more of her time than high school ever did, leaving her little time to socialize. Her mingling skills, while never stellar, grew stale with her determination to keep up her grades.

The weight of Cam's arm pulled her from her impromptu reverie. Not totally over her irritation over the romantic tryst she'd witnessed caused her to jerk away, but he tightened his hold, pulling her back to his side. A burst of chatter as students passed by quelled her initial protest. Currently, she wasn't feeling all that loving toward Cam. She could do without his arm wrapped around her, even though his gesture didn't signify much since many students walk arm in arm or with an arm wrapped around the other. Cut off from their familiar family support, the younger students often clung to each other, joking about their actions. The addition of alcohol blurred personal boundaries even more.

Cam's lips brushed her ear. "No need for jealousy since you're mine now."

The half-growled words sounded more like a threat than a romantic promise, especially when accompanied by a tight grip. No, she didn't feel the love. She wiggled her shoulders to loosen his hold without success. Not his usual behavior, which ran toward texted meeting places as opposed to arriving together. His public show of affection should make her happy, but instead it made her suspicious. It reminded her of the magazine article about cheating stating that the offender pours on affection hoping to cover his tracks.

"What was so important that I had to leave class?"

His arm dropped from her shoulders as he grinned. "Oh that, I have a great idea. I know as a female you always are looking for romantic ways to show your love."

Stella chose not to point out that, in truth, she was hoping he'd find romantic ways to demonstrate his love. Even her roommate Cece's stoner boyfriend planned a romantic treasure hunt with the treasure being him stretched out nude beside a picnic basket in a wooded glen. She wasn't hoping for a naked picnic, but anything to demonstrate her specialness would be nice.

"Ohhh," she stretched out the word not knowing how to reply. A couple of girls passed by and gave Cam a thorough once over while giggling. Her presence didn't seem to deter them one bit. It reminded her of how lucky she was to have him as a boyfriend when so many other females wanted him.

A bird high up in the tree began to sing. It sounded so carefree and joyous that she envied it. The tiny, feathered creature had a simple life and didn't have to try to understand its mate's cryptic suggestions. It could be singing because the sun was shining or because it just felt like it.

Cam tucked a lock of her hair behind her ear as the wind pulled at her long hair, whipping it around her face. He'd used the same gesture on their initial date. At the time, she considered it incredibly tender. Then, her hair blowing in her eyes somehow shielded her from the effect of his seductive glance. Strange, she needed some sort of a barrier between her and the man she should love. Would she recognize love if it ever happened? Her parents certainly didn't demonstrate it, especially during the last couple of years before the divorce. Even before things got bad, they seemed more like amicable roommates than people in love.

No wonder Cam's persistent pursuit eventually won over her. The fact that one of the hottest guys on campus picked her may have influenced her, although she'd like to think she wasn't that shallow. Cam's preference made her feel important. Her gaze lifted to over his shoulder, avoiding "the look" as the other girls classified it. Only last week, Elena, a fellow student, joked that when Cam turned "the look" on a girl, she'd rip her clothes off without him lifting a finger. Apparently, she hadn't heard about Stella dating the notorious owner of such a compelling glance.

No telling what Stella said or if she even replied when she heard it. Maybe she'd just stumbled away in a stupor. The offhanded remark alerted her that their relationship was unknown. Part of her assumed all his sleeping around was in the past. All she wanted was to keep things the way they were, even if she did have doubts.

Then there was the old Stella. The girl she'd been before her parents' marriage very public implosion. Before that, her worst issue involved her mother snooping in her room and confronting her on Wiccan reading material. Old Stella had no trouble asserting herself. That woman was much more opinionated. Oh, she'd drop the man like he was an STD. *Ooh, she could have done without the metaphor.* Too bad, she couldn't be the old Stella anymore. She wanted to, but just didn't know how to get back there.

Cam smoothed his hand over her long straight fall of blonde hair while using his deepest voice, making her feel like a skittish dog. "Aren't you going to ask what you can do to prove your love?"

The waggle of his eyebrows made the request seem playful, but it wasn't. Oh yeah, she knew the routine. Made it sound like a question, but it served more as an edict. The words felt like an anvil dropped on her foot.

Her teeth clamped down on her bottom lip almost willing her not to ask, but she had to. "I'm sure you have a suggestion."

His eyes had lighted up before he planted a quick kiss on her hair. A light touch to her elbow got her moving in the direction of the library building. "Stella, you're working at the computer center still?"

"Yes." Of course, she was. Since it was her only source of money, why wouldn't she? She didn't have the luxury of having rich parents as Cam did. Her steps slowed since she didn't see the use of heading for a building, she had no plans to visit today.

"Good. That's what I hoped, but we don't talk much."

He got that right. They ate together, went places, watch television shows he liked and had sex about as often as they could, but talking was the one thing they didn't do. To be more exact, Cam didn't contribute much. Sometimes she might be over at his place folding laundry or fixing dinner while chattering about something she'd learned that day. After a few more attempts at sharing, she realized he didn't pay attention. Shouldn't be too surprising. Most people didn't enjoy learning the way she did.

"Yeah." She knew she wasn't contributing much, rather like asking a blind man for directions. On second thought, a blind man would be more help. Didn't they have to count their steps and everything?

Two smiling co-eds, with shampoo commercial worthy hair and shirts that dipped low to display their twin assets, waved. They spoke in breathy unison, reminding her of the ads for the gentleman clubs. "Hi, Cam."

While he didn't reply, he gave a slow salute that acknowledged their greeting. Seriously? She elbowed him, earning a grunt for her effort. Most girls would wear a camisole or tank top under those shirts. Talk about desperate. *Who were they? Did he sleep with them too? Were they hoping for a return visit?* The thoughts flew through her head, making her uncomfortable. Asking would reveal her insecurities. Instead, she consoled herself with the thought that they were too obvious and fake to attract him. So far, however, her small interaction with the male species demonstrated they often preferred obvious and fake.

They walked in silence for a few steps, allowing the overly friendly girls to pass out of hearing range. "How does me working at the computer center have anything to do with proving my love?"

Instead of answering her question, he bestowed one of his sexy as hell smiles on her. The man must practice in the mirror to do it so effortlessly.

"You're able to get into the personnel files and stuff?" His right brow arched with his inquiry.

"Yeah, but I don't think you want the address of the hot new psych prof that all the girls have been hounding me for." The prof was a cutie, but she didn't dare give out that kind of information on anyone. No doubt, it'd come back to her even if the females in question didn't blab. An inappropriate information release could change her work-study position from the computer lab to landscaping. She'd landed a primo job. The director gave her more responsibility than students who had been there longer because he trusted her, which meant more to her than the badly needed raise.

Cam's brow knitted as his eyes flicked upward. "You mean that short dude who always wears a fedora?"

"Yes."

Cam probably compared him to his own height and found the man lacking. Whatever the instructor lacked in height, he made up for in charisma and wit. At first, she felt rather special knowing she could look up the prof's phone number at any time, not that she'd do anything with it.

"What does he have that'd interest women?" The smug tone of voice indicated the man wasn't any competition in Cam's mind.

Good question and an even harder one to explain to your boyfriend. She settled for a word. "Panache, he has panache."

A snort was his initial reply. "Panache. If you must go looking for a foreign word that I don't know the meaning of, then it means nothing. It must be some fluke brought on by the climate, hormones, or pumping some chemical into the classroom."

It amused her a little that Cam refused to accept there were other attractive men on campus. He didn't own sex appeal. "Panache means having verve, style—"

He interrupted before she had time to finish her statement. "I didn't ask what it meant."

Cam hated it when someone gave him directions. He preferred to live in a world of ignorance while her world consisted of gathering information. Talk about opposites.

His fingers entangling with hers surprised her. A new romantic side might be emerging. Her gradual unease that had been growing about their relationship died a fast death with mere handholding. Technically, she considered it more a declaration than the 'bro' arm around her shoulder.

The path wound around the library building and down to a small pond. A narrow dock with wooden Adirondack chairs beckoned students to rest between classes. Watching the ducks glide across the water help eased academic stress. The ducks' plump bodies hinted at their scavenger nature. Good chance they never turn down a chip or a cookie. As their direction veered toward the pond, her irritation eased at missing class. For once, the possibility of a grand gesture loomed in front of her.

Back in high school, some people would do everything from putting up billboards to making videos that made their way online to ask out a girl or even express their interest in a girl. Stella envied the girls and thought it incredibly romantic. Her best friend, Leah, remarked that it was both manipulative and egocentric. It would be hard for a girl to turn down such a public gesture without seeming a jerk. Any guy who chose to share his feelings in such a public venue loved the attention too.

Leah could have been right. It didn't stop Stella from wanting to be the girl who got the unexpected balloon bouquet in class. Even if it was from a boy, she didn't consider date material. It still signaled her desirability. A few males did pursue her with subtle gestures, including walking her to classes, chatting her up, and showing up at places she frequented. It was hard to remember when it stopped. Could have been her junior year when everything else fell apart.

The ducks quacked a noisy welcome the closer they came to the water. Too bad their enthusiasm resulted from whatever tidbit they could solicit. Quacking equaled a natural plea for attention. *Look at me, over here, not my cousin, but me, here, quack, quack.* Ducks resembled humans in that regard.

A small scattering of young weeping willows hugged the banks. The slender bowed branches were not enough to hide a brass quartet that might begin to play once they came into view. Nor was there a splash of color against the browning grass to indicate a picnic. Could be Cam was the creative type and had penned a poem he wanted to recite privately. A sideways glance at her lover didn't reveal any anxiety or even excitement about the upcoming grand gesture.

A park bench boasting a broken slat and hundreds of students' messages either scratched or written squatted by the path. A swoop of his free hand indicated they should stop at the bench. *Seriously, the pond was close, and it would sound so much more romantic in the retelling.*

Cam dropped her hand and sat on the part of the bench that didn't have the broken seat. Great, now she'd have to balance on the edge of the seat or fall off. It wasn't a desirable setting. Ten minutes ago, she didn't even know a romantic gesture was a possibility. Moving her feet about a foot part, she managed to balance herself on a two-inch wood slat. If she lost her balance, she'd fall off the bench or slip back into the hole created by the broken slap. It would probably snag her new jeans too.

Her hands smoothed down the thighs of her jeans. Stella couldn't afford to ruin the jeans since it had taken forever to save up for them. It had been an extravagance, but she felt the jeans were worth it. The polite thing would have been to let her sit on the unbroken part of the bench. Of course, not sitting on the bench at all would have been better. *Concentrate on the moment. Don't ruin it by picking it apart.*

What details could she remember when she pulled it out to reexamine it as an older woman retelling the story for her grandchildren or anyone else who might listen? The sky was blue, which wasn't that unusual. The sun was shining until a fast-moving cloud blotted it out making everything a little dimmer.

"Stella, I need you to do me a favor."

Cam's baritone melted her stiff, upright posture, but the words were wrong. Was she wrong about the grand gesture? Could be she wanted it so badly that she'd created indicators that weren't there. An audible sigh escaped her lips. Favors were never good. Usually, they consisted of copying her homework. Some favors were harder such as her mother's request to have nothing to do with her father after the divorce became final. She'd only agreed because she was living with her mother. Ironically, she didn't have to break it because her father had no interest in seeing her. He didn't even bother to show up at her graduation.

"Um, what is it?" She did not intend to promise until she heard it. The acrid smell of duck poop irritated her nose. A rather fitting detail for a romantic gesture gone south.

His hand reached for hers resting on her thigh. Maybe the romantic gesture wasn't totally gone. He might ask her to love him forever or something else like that. If so, she didn't want that type of long-term commitment. After all, Cam was her only real relationship and their connection status was a bit vague.

He held onto her hand but angled his body to look into her eyes. "What's wrong with you? Why are you sitting so weird?"

Working around a broken slat became her problem. She angled her head to look at the broken bench as explanation enough.

"Oh, the bench."

That was it. No offer to switch seats happened. Why had she expected more? Cam liked to refer to himself as a practical man. It sounded better than the ways the frat guys described each other.

"Go on, what's the favor?" Already she regretted asking. Once he told her then, she'd be obligated to do it if she could. Isn't that what friends did for each other? It went double if the people were dating.

"Remember I asked you if you could get into staff files. Have you ever got into the grade books?" He lowered his voice on the last word. It could have been his attempt at discretion. Since the nearest living creatures were ducks, no real issue.

"Well," she hesitated, already disliking the conversation. "Most of that stuff is automated. You take a test in the testing center, and the grade goes into the teacher's grade book. Even the teacher doesn't touch it."

The teacher could change a grade if they wanted, but no need to tell him that. She'd entered grades before for an older prof who found the computer grade book overwhelming.

"Hmm, I was afraid of that." He released her hand to cradle his head between his hands and sighed loudly.

Part of her wondered if this wasn't bad acting, but she asked anyhow. "What's wrong?"

"Oh, nothing." An audible sniff, then a choking gasp signaling a possible onset of crying.

Couldn't be. He didn't even get choked up when the shelter dog commercials came on. Nothing was a typical male answer. "C'mon, tell me. What's wrong?"

A few more blubbery noises filtered out through his fingers. "I'll lose my scholarship if I can't get my art history grade up."

"Is that all? All you need to do is study. Ask for extra credit." It seemed like an easy enough solution. Her mind caught on the word scholarship. He'd never mentioned being on one before. Instead, he just bragged about how rich his family was.

"Yeah, that might be easy for you, but studying isn't my thing." He sat up long enough to give her the soulful puppy dog eyes. Her heart hurt the same way when she watched a shelter dog commercial, knowing she couldn't adopt the dog.

"I'm not sure what you want me to do. Your family is wealthy. Even if you lose the scholarship, it's no big deal." Not like, it would be with her. She barely scraped by with her scholarship and work-study job. Her mother was always quick to remind her that no money was coming since her father blew it on the cheap skank he chose over his family.

Cam's lips became a little trembly, and then he looked away. "I lied about my family being wealthy."

She wanted to ask why, but he kept talking. It was hard to hear him since he was facing away and the wind increased at that moment.

"Were rich...lost it...that's why the scholarship's important? I need you to change my grade."

She had no trouble hearing that last part. None at all. How horrible. Cam had pride and tried to hide it from her. He probably kept it from her as long as he could. Her hands passed over each other as she wringed them and a sigh escaped her lips.

"I can't do that. Each worker has an ID. Any changes come back to that person. Changing your grade would cost me my scholarship and my job." Knowing her refusal would upset him, she added, "It might even be illegal."

It might not be exactly illegal, but it would cost her dearly. No reason to put it to the test, especially for a male who couldn't come up with one grand gesture or work to solve his own problems. Her heart skipped a beat. The unreliable organ was probably anticipating the fallout from turning down Cam, not that she ever had before if you discounted the times, she turned him down for a date before they first went out.

Cam gazed at the pond. The ducks took his action as an invitation and started waddling toward him. The birds initially ignored them when they realized they weren't eating. Could be they expected him to pull something out of his pocket. His lips moved, but whatever he said was too soft to hear.

"Pardon, me. I didn't hear you." She hated asking, afraid her words might anger him. She wrapped her fingers under the bench hunching her shoulders forward expecting not a physical blow, but a verbal one.

Cam continued to stare off into the distance. "I asked who worked with you in the computer lab."

A peculiar question, but one she could answer, considering he inquired in a normal tone of voice. "You know. I've told you before, Noah, Mitch, Lauren, Prashant, Del, and Simon." It wasn't as if she hadn't talked about them before. Apparently, he hadn't been paying attention.

He looked back at her and grinned. "Of course, I remember. Isn't Mitch that geeky guy who has a crush on you?" His laughter punctuated the comment.

Before she had a chance to deny it, he elaborated. "Too nerdy to get laid. It must kill him to see you with me."

Her eyes rolled upward. Why did everything have to come down to sex? Mitch might exemplify geek fashion with his bad haircut and glasses. Still, he was a decent person. "Please, don't talk about him like that. He's sweet. He's even going to copy his notes for me."

This tidbit made Cam laugh even harder. Finally, he slapped his leg and leaned back against the bench. "He's got it bad. Doing little errands for you in hopes of endearing himself to you. Guys like him think that's the way to get lucky."

No way was she interested in Mitch. "He's just a nice guy who likes to help out people." Cam needed to talk about something else. It made her feel disloyal talking about the guy who was taking notes for her. Besides, she ran little errands sometimes—for Cam—and she usually did them to make sure he needed her. Her eyes widened with the realization of how much her behavior resembled Mitch's in always doing things to help.

Maybe he did like her.

"Yeah? How many other guys you work with knock themselves out for you?" His smug expression declared he already knew the answer.

Only Mitch. Del and Noah practically spit on her since she jumped over them in seniority. Technically, it was their fault since they often arrived late and left the staff office looking like a war zone. They spent most of their time gaming since the LAN network was incredibly fast and agreed to work third shift to avoid the supervisor. The man found out anyhow, and the assumption was she'd ratted them out after Noah invited her to a game session. Fewer hours and no longer working together served as their only consequence.

She shook her head at the idea of them being nice to her. If she suddenly morphed into an anime character, they might have some interest in her.

Cam's eyes rolled up skyward where several fluffy clouds drifted slowly by unaware of the drama below them. "What about Simon, that foreign guy, and Lauren? Lauren is that a guy or a girl?"

A duck waddled up to her feet and announced his arrival with a few earnest quacks. Frequently, it probably earned him a few chips, bread or pizza crust, or a French fry. Stella opened her purse to search for something to feed the opportunistic bird. Using her teeth, she tore open the cellophane of a package of crushed crackers, while wondering about Cam's sudden outburst of chattiness. This may have been as much as they talked since their first encounter. Why would Cam suddenly be interested in who she worked with and why? *Something felt wrong.*

Scattering the crumbs on the ground, she smiled as the duck thanked his appreciation, scooping up the bits before the other birds reached his bounty.

Instead of answering Cam, she looked toward the lake where the ducks were joining in a type of parade heading their way. In a few seconds, hungry ducks would surround them. Pointing to the feathered mass, she stood. "We need to go."

Cam jumped to his feet immediately and turned to walk up the path they'd come down. Stella had to make a few long-legged strides to catch up. Once they passed under the covered walkway, the birds stopped following. It was almost like there was some invisible fence blocking the creatures from the halls of learning.

Guilt stabbed at her when she thought of the birds hurrying after her sure they'd get something to eat. On the upside, they could use the exercise. The bell tower clock banged out the hour, hurrying students to their destination. *Hard to believe, it was that late already. All that time wasted on hiking across the campus and nothing to show for it.* "Cam, I have to get to my work study job."

Resting her hand on the messenger bag, she turned to speed walk to the technical science building. Cam's voice stopped her.

"Wait."

Could this be it? Finally, the grand gesture?

It only took Cam two steps to reach her side. He flashed his trademark smile and touched her elbow. "Hey, you never answered my question?"

Dear Sweet Goddess. She was tempted to say what question, but she was tired of the entire conversation, and her tone showed it too. "No, Simon is not hot for me. I never see him. Prashant doesn't say much, and when he does, it's something about everything coming out all right in the end. Lauren is a shy girl with thick glasses and an inferiority complex who barely says two words to anyone. Anything else?"

Cam held up his hands. "Whoa. Sounds like someone needs to go take a chill pill." He turned and jogged away without a goodbye or even a wave. Stella watched as a trio of girls stopped and watched him pass. Yeah, he did look good running, and he knew it.

The charm of dating one of the hottest males on campus had its downside. All the other girls lusting after him sucked. On the upside that made him more of a prize, but any time with Cam served as an emotional workout. The man picked up her insecurities, her need for affection, and confidence and, threw all of them high in the air as in juggling balls. Often her confidence would wing upward when she was with him, but when she wasn't, her insecurities came crashing down making her wonder if his interest had already moved elsewhere. Unfortunately, she could already feel his attention waning. Without him, she'd be alone on the campus as before. Sure, she kept busy with her homework and work-study job, but then there were those long weekend hours when no one came to visit.

CHAPTER TWO

S TELLA ADJUSTED THE paper to better analyze Professor Emeril's loopy handwriting. Out of the work-study students, she was the only one able to decipher his notes. Sometimes she wondered if he could even read them. Her knowledge of world history was good enough to enable her to fill in the illegible parts. In a math major's mind, Eurasia might become Europe, which was far from being the same thing.

As if he heard his name, Mitch pushed open the computer lab door. "Hey, you."

Stella looked up with a smile. "Hey, you, yourself. How was class? Did I miss anything mind boggling?"

Mitch pushed up his sliding glasses with one finger and shrugged his shoulders. "Not really. Same old. Same old."

A sheath of stapled notes fluttered to her desk. She picked up the thick pack. "Wow, pretty impressive notes. Thanks."

"Not really, I only wrote on one side." His backpack hit the floor as he sat down and flicked on his monitor.

Stella picked up the folder that had his work assignment in it. Other students thought the computer lab assistants just sat around and waited for someone to use the computers, but there was more involved than that. Noah and Del accused her of informing their supervisor about their gaming without realizing the obvious reason for their discovery was they never got their work done. It surprised her that they still had jobs.

"You only have notes to type into the SharePoint database."

He took the folder and groaned. "Not my fav."

His remark was typical Mitch. How well she knew him was surprising. Her eyes drifted over him. Cam declaring Mitch had a crush on her was probably a joke. Still, she considered the male hunched over the computer. Could it be true?

Mitch, unlike Cam, spent most of his time trying to *not* garner attention. He was as tall as Cam, maybe taller, but no one would know the way he hunched his shoulders and slumped in his seat trying to be invisible. She'd asked her roommate if she knew him after Mitch had mentioned Cece was in two of his classes. Despite Stella's detailed description of Mitch, her roommate denied knowing him.

If he had a crush on her, how should she handle it? Her fingers rested on the keyboard, her thoughts in disarray. Taking a deep breath, she focused on the messy notes she was transcribing. There was plenty of regular work for her once she finished the notes. Her boss didn't mind her helping the faculty out with light typing. Her reward consisted of a warm smile and a plain envelope. Inside the envelope rested a few crisp bills. Their denomination depended on how difficult the work was and how generous the professor felt. Mitch had cautioned her to set a standard rate to prevent the staff from taking advantage of her.

She didn't need things to be awkward between her and Mitch because they worked together. The slight patter of Mitch's fingers racing across the keyboard caused a stab of envy. No one on campus could type as fast or as accurately as he did. Too bad that wasn't a characteristic that girls wanted like rock hard abs.

The computer lab door swung open from Lauren's push. The reticent female didn't typically work with Stella, except when there was some test to proctor. A glance at the calendar listed a philosophy exam. "Hi."

A plexiglass wall separated Lauren from the student testing center. The girl nodded at her as she passed on the way to her desk on the other side of the administration section. Not known for her sparkling conversation, it was a challenge for Lauren to monitor the students. Most often, she only checked off as they signed in on the various computers.

The handsome, but not prepared, males sometimes tried to solicit more time or even actual answers. Somehow, they believed they had the right to such rewards that their plainer counterparts, who studied for the test, didn't have. In another testing center on another campus, maybe they would have received the benefit but not here. The outright flirting rattled Lauren so much that often Stella had to intercede.

At times, a buffed male would be lounging in a chair, sometimes with his hands propped behind his head, expecting Lauren to trot back with the needed answers. Instead, Stella would tap on the glass to get his attention, while mouthing the word, "No," or most often, "Try studying."

Mitch usually enjoyed the encounters. Even getting up to be able to see the shocked expression on the male's face. Occasionally, she had to go to the actual room because there were other students studying and knocking on the window would disturb them. The male in question maintained his smug expression until she whispered the same words she'd have mouthed. It made her wonder if Cam ever pulled the same stunt. If so, what were his results?

Her fingers hit the keys a little harder than necessary. Wasn't his inquiry about her changing his grade the same scenario? The only difference was she was sleeping with him, and he figured it was a done deal. Most men would assume as much.

"Angry typing, much?" Mitch called out to her, wiggling his eyebrows disrupting her tension.

The way she was going, she'd end up breaking the keyboard. "Oh, yeah. Never mind. Thanks for pointing it out."

Her fingers slowed, softening the impact of each finger on the key. The students trickled in to take the test. The murmur of voices alerted her that obviously a few were not following protocol. A large sign listing the rules had no talking as the first. Lauren was too timid to say anything. Normally, it wasn't an issue since the students didn't come in huge groups.

The talking continued loudly enough to carry through the Plexiglas. Getting up she weaved through the long tables crowded with monitors and CPUs only to find Lauren staring at the offenders with the same look of horror most people used for approaching death.

Since the voices were feminine, she knew it wasn't Lauren's usual kryptonite, the hot guy. Two female students with perfect hair and enough eye makeup to keep the cosmetic industry in business chattered loudly, ignoring the other students around them who were casting reproachful looks their way. Ah yes, she knew the type. The world revolved around them and they didn't give a damn about anyone else. Probably even argued with the prof about tests being out of style and an unfair measure of their ability.

No way could Lauren deal with them. They'd look through her and pretend they didn't even see her. Thankfully, Stella had her own experience with mean girls from high school. Both she and Leah medaled in mean girl avoidance and sly innuendoes that flew past the vicious females.

Opening the connecting door, a little louder than she should, she stood in the doorway. Everyone looked up, even the chattering girls. Leah's Nana once informed her how to handle difficult people. *Make an entrance, assume an attitude, show no fear, and make a statement, then leave.*

Her hand landed on the panicked Lauren's shoulder, as she said, "I'll deal with it." This earned her a weak smile.

Shoulders back, Stella flicked her long blonde hair over her shoulders. She nodded to the other testing students and approached the problem women with a confident air. "It has come to my attention that you failed to heed testing protocol."

The first girl pulled out a compact, checking her makeup. Her friend stared up Stella with a quizzical expression. Pointing to the sign, Stella enunciated the words slowly and loudly enough for the other students to hear. "No talking in the lab."

The girls looked at each other in surprise. One of the girls angled her head in Stella's direction, the calculation on her face obvious, and said, "You can't tell us what to do."

Oh, she wanted to play it that way. Stella expected as much. A slight motion of her hand signaled Lauren to cut the power to their units. Their screens went blank. The girls were too intent on Stella's reaction to notice their monitors, but the other students saw it.

One student voiced his observation. "Hey look, their computers were shut down."

Another student snickered. Bossy girl's face reddened as her mouth dropped open. Her head swiveled back to her friend, asking for help.

Stella placed her hands on her hips remembering from psychology that posture made her appear more intimidating. "You're done here. Come back when you can follow the rules. Better yet, maybe a blue book exam would suit you better."

One of the girls immediately stood up, teetering a little in her sky-high heels. Shouldering her expensive purse, she remarked over her shoulder. "We'll be back when the cute guys are working."

Her friend got up more slowly, returning Stella's glare with a malice-filled one of her own. "Don't think it's over, bitch. You may be head witch, here, but not for long."

Instead of answering, she merely watched the girls leave. Silence at the right time could be powerful too. Too many people made the mistake of thinking they had to respond to everything. Miss I'm All That thought she'd wounded her by calling her a witch. *Hah, she had no clue how right she was. As for being a bitch, well it took one to know one.*

A few of the students started clapping. A couple more thanked her. She nodded, accepting their appreciation and muttered, "No problem."

Keeping her back straight, she strode toward the open door, sanctuary. She preferred to be on the anonymous side of the Plexiglas. Closing the door behind her, she released a huge sigh. *Thank the Goddess that was over.*

Lauren popped to her feet and wrapped her in a huge hug. "Thank you so much, I could never have gotten them to leave."

Stella was about to admit her doubts about getting the two to leave when Mitch came over. Lauren still held her in an impromptu embrace when Mitch awkwardly patted her on the back.

The slight contact left behind a psychic handprint. Her eyes met his over Lauren's shoulder. Did Mitch follow the Goddess? Have a bit of magick in him? Technically, everyone possessed some earth magick, but few knew how to wield it. Often simple divination magic came under headings like hunches and lucky guesses. Others blessed with the ability to enchant often used their skills as a form of manipulation. Most who identified with the earth-based religions enjoyed spending time in nature.

His warm hazel eyes twinkled as he spoke, "You were glorious."

Glorious? No one had ever called her glorious. A bubble of warmth expanded in her chest. If all it took to be glorious was to kick two mean girls out of the lab, she might do it more often. The problem was if she did, she'd end up losing her job because one of their daddies would accuse her of harassment, terroristic threatening, or similar nonsense.

A huge smile blossomed on Mitch's face, animating his features. Goodness, he was even handsome when he forgot about trying to make himself invisible. A decent haircut, new frames, and more self-confidence and he'd be the one the mean girls came back to attempt to wrap around their manicured fingers. The thought dimmed the warmth spreading through her. None of them was worthy of Mitch.

A familiar scent rode the air. It didn't blend with the smell of dust, monitor wipes, or the metal smell of CPUs. Her nostrils flared a tiny bit as she tried to draw the aroma in. Sandalwood, she was almost sure of it. Sandalwood incense was a favorite for meditation, but there would be no incense in the lab. It could be sandalwood oil, which sometimes showed up in men's cologne and love potions.

Lauren's tight embrace finally relaxed as she dropped her arms. Stella shrugged her shoulders. "All in a day's work, I guess." Saluting the two of them, she clicked her heels together and walked back to her desk.

Their laughter followed her. Lauren's sounded nervous and forced while Mitch's was mellow. Just hearing his laughter made her feel good. The idea of him having a crush on her wasn't as preposterous as it once seemed. Her fingers went up to fuss with her hair, smoothing over the long length to see if any strands were out of place.

The only male in the work area was Mitch, and he could be wearing cologne. The distance between their computers measured a meter, which made it easy to pass folders without having to get up. In a matter of seconds, Mitch returned to typing fast, his head moving slightly between the paper and his computer screen.

Stella memorized chunks of info and then typed while occasionally glancing at the keys for reassurance that her fingers were where they should be, especially after she misspelled a word.

Work awaited her if she wanted to earn any extra money. As it was, everything she earned disappeared into the giant gaping mouth of the college. Nothing was cheap on campus, from snacks to copies. The on-campus stores took advantage of the students by hiking up the prices. Those with cars made runs to discount stores. Still others depended on a weekly check from their parents. Her mouth twisted to one side at the thought of parents. Hers had forgotten her. Dear old dad appeared to be in a hurry to recreate a new family with his young wife. Hard to believe when he emphatically told her having her ruined his life. Without her existence, he'd had left her mother years ago.

The baby tidbit came via Leah, who still lived in their hometown. Leah saw Stella's father more than she did. He'd recognized Leah and made a point of saying, "hello." He had to know her friend would convey the info to her. Maybe that's what he wanted. *Look, Stella, I'm happy now with my new wife and son.* A muttered curse slipped out.

Mitch stopped typing and regarded her with a furrowed brow. 'Hey, are you okay?"

Embarrassed that she'd drawn his attention, she grabbed for a convenient excuse. "I broke a nail."

Her eyes flicked down to her ragged, short nails that she'd regularly gnawed to the quick.

Mitch didn't call her on it. He lifted an eyebrow and returned to typing. He knew she'd lied, but he was too polite to pry.

A dozen keystrokes later, her maudlin thoughts caught up with her. Her mother never sent her money to tide her over. Even Cece's parents sent her an occasional care package filled with snacks, toiletries, office supplies, and a check. The best she got was an occasional pamphlet about the torments of hell if she should die today without repenting of her evil ways. No one could ever accuse her mother of being overly affectionate or loving. The occasions when she'd displayed a little bit of pride when Stella won a merit award disappeared about the time the divorce happened. Her mother's crutch during the entire ordeal was a small church she started attending. After the divorce, Stella stayed away from the house as much as possible due to the ghosts that hung out there. Not spirits that were unwilling to move on, but rather memories of happier times. If she stayed at home more, she could have provided emotional support for her mother, instead of leaving her vulnerable to the dubious care of The Last Days and Holy Resurrection Tabernacle pastor.

Stella had never stepped inside the shabby white building despite her mother's repeated attempts to get her to attend. At first, she might have gone, to keep peace in the house, but the judgmental messages placed on the marquee outside kept her feet planted firmly on the other side of the doors. Everything from *Repent Now or Burn Forever* and *Enjoy your sin today, pay for it eternally.*

The smell of sandalwood grew stronger as Mitch's shadow fell over her. He bent slightly to rest one hand near her keyboard. "Hey, what's going on with you?"

Her behavior must be odd if Mitch noticed. She meant to use a cramps excuse, which weirded out boys and stopped future questions. A slight turn of her head caused her to look directly into his sympathetic eyes. "Truth is I was thinking about my mother and how she hooked up with this fire and brimstone church. About the only communication, we ever have now is my monthly reminder that I'm damned to hell."

She wanted to call back her revealing words. Maybe Mitch belonged to a similar church. Instead of acting horrified, he reached for his chair and drew it to face hers before he sat.

His index finger pushed up his slipping glasses as he sat. "I understand. My older sister went through a stage like that when her husband left her. I think she thought if she prayed hard enough, he'd come back. He didn't. I always wondered why she wanted someone who didn't want her."

His insightful words allowed her to release the breath she'd been holding. "Maybe that's what happened to my mother. She hadn't been too religious until Dad left. We used to only show up at Our Lady of Sorrows for the major holidays, Christmas and Easter."

Mitch nodded, making her feel he heard her. When was the last time anyone had truly listened to her? She tried to remember. Talking with most people was a bit like a computer search. They responded to keywords that had something to do with them. Going away to school kept her distant from her mother's machinations, but it also limited any interaction she had with her best friend, Leah. Lately, she'd been the one cutting conversation short with Leah to be with Cam.

Mitch touched her hand. "Go on. What about your father? Is he still alive?"

Still alive that was a peculiar comment. "Yes, he is, very much to my mother's regret." *Did she want him dead too? It would be easier to forgive a dead father than one who chose to write her off.*

Her top teeth worried her bottom lip. Did she sound too much like one of the callers on a radio therapy show? Would Mitch feel awkward working with her in the future?

His hand went up to his glasses, probably to push the slipping glasses up, but he pulled them off instead and placed them near her keyboard. Stella blinked at the transformation the simple action made. *Talk about a Superman move.* Her eyes dropped to his chest wondering if he'd rip open his checked shirt to reveal a colorful spandex suit decorated with a giant S underneath it.

Using a bent finger, he rubbed the area between his eyebrows. "Be glad you have a father. Right now, things might not seem too great, but at least there's a future where the two of you can develop a better relationship."

His hand half hid his face, which may have been his intention, but it didn't disguise the pain in his words.

"What happened to your father?"

"Heart attack. He died when I was thirteen. We'd argued about me cutting the grass. I was going to do it. I just wanted to finish the level on my video game first."

"How horrible!" Stella placed her hand on Mitch's just as Lauren passed behind the two of them. *Let her think what she wants.* "I hope you don't blame yourself."

Mitch shrugged his shoulders and looked up briefly at Stella. His glassy eyes revealed his guilt-laden state. "My mother told me it wasn't my fault. His family had a history of heart disease. That along with too much fast food and no exercise caused it."

Stella almost felt like she was witnessing a drowning and didn't know what to do. "It would have happened no matter what. You're not to blame." Her hand squeezed his, realizing her problems seemed mundane in retrospect.

"Yeah, you're right. I guess. I just hate that our last words were in anger. Like most teenagers, I disappointed my father. I always wanted to do what I wanted to do and never what interested him. As a kid, we camped and fished together. As I got older, I was more into video games, especially the role-playing games. If I'd continued to canoe and hike with my father, he'd have been in better shape."

Whoa, he might be right, but she couldn't tell him that. "Mitch, listen to me." Her free hand touched his face to gain his attention. "You were a child while your father was an adult. As the adult, he made the decision to be physically fit or not. He could have exercised with your mother, a friend, or even by himself. There is no reason to blame yourself. In the end, Fate has her way."

Mitch's lips tipped up in a weak smile. "You suck at giving pep talks."

His words surprised a half-laugh that ended in a cough. Clearing her throat, she managed to reply, "Yeah, that's what I've been told." The warmth of his hand reminded her that they were still holding hands. His larger hand engulfed hers making her feel safe if only for a moment. It was a false security.

Security, safety, believing your world would keep spinning in its usual fashion were all things that she'd taken for granted not too long ago. Tons of parents divorced. Probably, over half the students at the university or maybe even more, which meant she had no excuse for feeling sorry for herself. *Suck it up, Stella.* Why couldn't her inner drill sergeant comprehend her feeling of rootlessness? In some ways, she was a jellyfish.

The current carried the jellyfish. A wave would sometimes hurl the gelatinous creature into an unwary swimmer. Without an actual brain, the jellyfish only reacted by wrapping its long arms around a leg. It might be holding on for dear life or assuming whatever it touched was dinner. In the end, it left a stinging sensation behind, a reminder of its brief contact. *Goddess, she hoped she wasn't like that. Hurting everyone, she touched.* Might do her good to watch her interactions if she could be so toxic.

Perhaps, feeling the same awkwardness after their shared emotional episode, Mitch released her hand while pushing back with his feet to propel the rolling chair back to his desk. "Time to get back to work."

She watched him pivot the chair and immediately return to typing as if nothing had happened. A thought nudged at her consciousness leaving behind the image of her scarring everyone she bumped against. "Mitch, did you ever play any video games after your father's heart attack?"

He continued typing, didn't even look up. Stella thought he hadn't heard her until he stopped typing and stared at the keyboard. Finally, he murmured, "Not a one." He remained silent for a few more seconds, then, he looked up. "Could you hand me my glasses."

CHAPTER THREE

ALL THAT TIME, he was only pretending to type. Grief could resemble a boa constrictor wrapping itself around the victim and squeezing out all hope. She certainly didn't have any sage wisdom to offer. Instead, she picked up his glasses and polished them on the edge of her shirt, before handing them over.

Flipping the page of her notes, she positioned her hands to start typing, but a prickling at the back of her neck distracted her. It reminded her of the time the bald man in a trench coat followed her around town when she was only ten. Her mother, busy shopping, handed her some money to go to a nearby ice cream shop only a few blocks away, and she knew how to cross the street safely. It should have been an uneventful trip until she noticed the man's reflection in a window.

Her first thought was it was a hot day, and he didn't need a coat. The ice cream shop was within sight when she decided he was following her. Breaking into a run, she'd dashed into the store. The man stood outside and glared at her through the glass emblazoned with the shop's name. Terror squeezed her heart for a moment as their eyes met. His cold eyes glittered, confirming she'd slipped through his fingers. She never told her mother about the man, somehow thinking she'd done something wrong to cause him to pursue her. Good chance her mother would have blamed it on reading too many mystery books. She remembered what it felt like, rather similar to the spot on the back of her neck now. Covering her neck with one hand, she swiveled her chair only to meet Lauren's baleful stare.

What was wrong? Stella's eyes drifted to the testing center. Most of the students had left. No problem, there, what could be her issue? She'd never had any difficulties with Lauren before, but her current glare declared she'd willingly plunge a knife into Stella's back. *Foolish, paranoia, she was getting as bad as her mother was. Think happy thoughts.* Currently, she didn't have a backlog of cheerful thoughts, but maybe she could do something that would make Cam happy and get his mind off her accessing academic files. Good Goddess, she couldn't change his grades. There had to be another way to show her love.

Cam had explicitly mentioned his upcoming birthday. A casual com-ment about how much he enjoyed gazing at the night sky stuck in her mind. It would also be something they could do together. Her intention was to get him a telescope she'd seen at the nearby pawnshop. With her luck, an astronomy buff could wander into the seedy little store, recognize the value of the Orion refractor telescope and snatch it up before she could.

Cam expected something. Instead of finding out his birthday by social media or even looking it up in the database, he'd told her. On their second date. If you could call it a date since it occurred at an off-campus Laundromat. Most of their dates were rather un-date-like, but then again most of the college populace either hung out or hooked up. The formal ritual of asking a girl out for a date had fallen by the wayside.

Her eyes shifted to Mitch, who stared intently at his monitor. She'd bet he'd be the type to ask a girl out on a real date as opposed to a general invite to a frat party. The man might even iron his clothes, comb the campus newspaper for ideas on what to do, and show up with a single rose. *Yeah, that sounded like Mitch.* Thinking about how adorable he'd look standing in the doorway clutching a flower, her lips twitched.

The man in question looked up. "What's with the goofy smile, and why are you staring at me?"

Caught. What could she say? Why was she staring at him and speculating what he'd be like on a date? Rubbing her open hand over her face, she stalled and wiped away her smile. *Think.*

"I, um, I was thinking of my second date with Cam. We went to the Laundromat." Her excuse sounded lame. Some might consider confiding her dating life to her male co-worker weird. Her roommate Cece had such a snarky side she kept as much as she could from her. Leah knew about Cam, but never acted that thrilled about him, which annoyed Stella. After all, she never made snide comments when Leah started dating Dylan. At least, Mitch would never gossip.

Mitch turned back to the monitor, snorted. "Whoa, why didn't I think of asking a girl out to view my laundry? I now realize my dating techniques are all wrong. Maybe I could follow up the next date with a trip to the grocery."

Stella wanted to protest, but at least three of their *dates* had been the grocery. Mitch's words made it sound stupid and lame. It wasn't like that. "Hey, now. The hum of dryers and the overwhelming smell of fabric sheets really set the scene."

She grimaced realizing she had once considered it romantic. The mother with the three screaming toddlers finally left leaving behind a silence broken up by the swish of a washer and the dual drone of dryers. Late on a Friday night, the place echoed eerily with its emptiness. It was then he mentioned his birthday, hinting broadly for something special. He probably meant sex, but since they were now already sleeping together, the telescope seemed her best bet.

Mitch slapped the desk, startling her. She turned to stare at him as he held up both hands dramatically.

"That's it. Why did no one ever tell me? If I rub my body with dryer sheets, I'll be irresistible to the opposite sex."

Her eyes rolled upward on their own. "You're not taking me seriously. I'm trying to explain what I was thinking. You make jokes about dryer sheets. I was attempting to think of a great gift for Cam's birthday. He mentioned his birthday on our second date at the"

"Laundromat." Mitch finished her statement. "God, he told you his birthday. So, you could go get him something, I bet. Something special, too." He added eyebrow waggle for emphasis.

Did every male use the same gesture to denote something risqué? "It wasn't like that." She denied the implications, even if it had been like that. Mitch never liked Cam and didn't try to hide it either. "Besides, what's so wrong about telling someone when your birthday is? It's not that out of the ordinary."

"Yeah, right." He turned back to the screen, giving her his back, which ended their conversation.

His words resurrected doubts. "What do you mean? I know you meant something?"

His silence and scrolling down the screen indicated he'd shut her out, which surprised her. Normally, Mitch wasn't moody. Finally, he muttered. "I bet you don't know when my birthday is?"

"Of course, I do. We've worked together for over two months. There's no reason I wouldn't know your birthday. We're friends." As she spoke, she made a mental inventory of everything she knew about Mitch. The sound of slamming file cabinet drawers indicated Lauren remained in a snit. The noise didn't make it any easier to think either.

She should know this. Her hand slid closer to her mouse. *A quick peek at the personnel records would help her faulty memory.*

"No fair looking it up."

He guessed her intentions. Damn. "Obviously, I'm a crummy friend. I can't remember your birthday. Sue me."

Swiveling his chair, he turned to stare at her. "The reason you don't know my birthday is I never told you. I never said anything because I didn't expect you to do anything for me. A guy who tells you his birthday expects a big deal. The fact that he told you on the second date makes it even more suspicious."

Her hand shot out and wrapped around his arm. "Not so fast, boyo."

He laughed. "What are you now, an Irish gangster from the thirties?"

He was right; she sounded bizarre. "It's your fault." Noting his raised eyebrows, she added, "Mostly." She dropped her hand, bit her bottom lip, and wanted to ask why it looked suspicious, but was afraid of the answer.

He inhaled deeply, and then let it out in a loud sigh. "I'm sorry I said anything, but can't you see Cam is using you."

No, not this argument again. She glanced at his lips pulled into a frown. Hadn't they already had this discussion before? Wait that was Leah. Stella denounced Leah's concerns calling her jealous, which was ridiculous since she'd been with Dylan forever. "Explain how mentioning his birthday is using me?"

"You didn't ask for it. He offered it, even mentioned he'd be open to gifts. Told you on the second *date*." He made a point of emphasizing the word date, implying their date was no more than laundry duty.

Everything was true. As a tech geek, Mitch knew how to manipulate data. Cam was everything a girl could want if you liked six pack abs, great hair, and a gorgeous smile. Stella almost missed Mitch's comment as she mentally searched for other attributes Cam might have.

"Wonder how many other girls he's mentioned his birthday to."

Her first response was to deny he hadn't told anyone, but how did she know? He could have made up flyers and handed them out to the various sororities. Mitch's logic was taking her down a path she didn't want to go.

He muttered, "Forget about it." When she fell silent.

Goddess, she wasn't sure, how they even got into this discussion but wished they hadn't. A lack of drawer slamming caused her to glance in Lauren's direction who still shot daggers at her. Strange.

She resumed typing as Mitch stood and walked out of the room. Good chance he left to avoid the tension. More likely, he went to grab a soda. Her fingers flew across the keys making up for the time she wasted discussing Laundromat rendezvous and the importance of telling birthday dates. Green and red squiggles appeared under various words indicating that while typing fast, it wasn't always accurate.

Thanks a lot, Mitch. Now I must go back and proof everything. It wasn't like she didn't already proof usually, but now she'd have more to correct. Her fingers slowed a bit as she tried to read each paragraph carefully, making sure she made sense out of the semi-illegible notes. The tiny clock at the right side of the screen reminded her that she had plenty of regular work left on her shift and no real time for her extra duties.

The pneumatic door springs caused the fire doors that enclosed the lab to close with an ominous clang, rather like the sound of the prison gates closing. She looked up to see Mitch brandishing two chip bags.

"Snack run?"

"Of a sort." Mitch shrugged and placed a bag of multigrain chips on her desk. "Consider it a peace offering."

The brightly colored bag drew her attention, especially since it was her favorite. Hunger whetted her appetite even more. Her fingers reached for the shiny sack as she considered her actions toward her co-worker. "Thank you. I'm sorry if I went all crazy over the birthday issue. You're right. No one goes around announcing their birthday unless they want a gift or a big party."

She certainly hadn't. Cam hadn't asked hers, and she hadn't offered. There didn't seem to be a point since they might not be dating then anyhow. Ripping open the bag, she picked out the first chip and allowed it to sit on her tongue, appreciating the mix of flavors and the tang of saltiness. She'd denied herself the delicious luxury for quite a while. The second chip she consumed faster and the third chip even more so.

The real reason she never told Cam her birthday was she didn't want to be disappointed again. Last year, her father, too involved with his new family, did nothing for her birthday. Her mother had the nerve to send a note about contributing to the crazy church in her name. More likely, it bought her penance, forgiveness, or something. Leah had sent her a present, but the campus postal service delivered it to the wrong dorm. She didn't get it until almost a week later.

That made her last birthday a particularly depressing day. Wrapping her fingers around the last chips in the bag, she shoved them into her mouth and crunched down hard, causing crumbs to slide down her face. The feeling of hopelessness threatened to return. Another bag of chips landing on her keyboard interrupted her visit to birthdays past.

Mitch gestured to the bag. "Looks like you could use another bag."

Chips packed her cheeks, most likely giving her a chipmunk appearance. She looked away from Mitch, in the direction of a nearby dark monitor that reflected her image. A wild-eyed woman on the verge of tears with plump cheeks and food crumbs dotting her face stared back. A tissue wiped away the crumbs. Chewing and swallowing slimmed her cheeks, but nothing could remove the lost look from her eyes.

Feeling thirsty, she reached for the water bottle she kept by her monitor. It wasn't there, another casualty of her meeting with Cam. The water bottle she usually brought sat back in her dorm room doing her no good. The fountain at the end of the hall between the restrooms would serve.

The deserted hallway gave her time to think as her footsteps echoed on the cement floor. If this were a movie, something sinister would jump out of one of the darkened doorways. Currently, her thoughts provided enough of a fright factor. Somewhere she'd lost her way, going from a confident female who was going to change the world into a distant individual most people managed to look through. It was no wonder she found Cam's interest so gratifying.

Three long drinks later and a wipe down with a damp paper towel rid her of most of her crumbs. It was time to return. Thank goodness, she worked in a facility most students seldom used, probably unaware that part of their tuition paid for use of the lab.

About the only time, students showed up was to print out papers. The younger profs encouraged online submission. This helped when paper completion happened two minutes short of the midnight deadline. Nope, no one to witness her minor meltdown, except for Mitch and Lauren, and Mitch would be cool about it. Lauren had mood swings, which meant it could go either way depending on the day.

Her back to the room, she held the door handle causing the door to swing close slowly and not announce her return. Fighting against the automatic assist that usually slammed the heavy door shut tested her bicep muscle. When she wasn't sure how much longer she could hold the heavy door, it clicked closed. She pivoted and ran into a solid, masculine body. Her nose buried in his chest, and she inhaled the variety of aromas. The predominant one was a sandalwood and a hint of dryer sheet along with a clean, underlying scent she identified as Mitch.

His hands wrapped around her shoulders steadied her. *Could it get any worse?* "Umm, sorry." She looked up into Mitch's face.

"I was worried about you. If you hadn't come back, then I'd have looked for you to see if you were okay." A blush painted his cheeks. His hands fell from her shoulders as he stepped back, allowing her access to her desk.

Tucking an errant lock of hair behind her ear, she moved around him. While her back was to him, she spoke, "That's sweet of you." Looking at him full on might cause her to choke on the phrase. Stray dogs had nothing on Mitch. He could convey sincerity and promise absolute devotion by softening his eyes. She wondered if anyone noticed other than her.

"Yeah, I'm sweet like that." He took a step toward her as she slid into her chair. "Are you really okay?"

The easy answer would be yes. *What was he asking her? Was she okay that her boyfriend was a bit of a user? Mitch had no idea how right he was on that one. Was she alright that her family put the dys in dysfunctional? Was she okay after her manic chip frenzy? That was probably the real question.* "Yeah, I'm okay. Maybe a little junk food deprived. I went a little crazy there."

"Good." His hand settled on her shoulder for a second, then left, as if he'd overstepped his bounds.

Stella wanted to tell him to put his hand back. For a moment, she'd felt a connection, a sense of belonging and understanding. Something she could never achieve with Cam no matter what the body part. Mitch stood behind her rather like a shield protecting her. The silence wasn't awkward, rather the opposite. Finally, he spoke breaking the bond.

"May first."

What was that supposed to mean? The date dropped out of nowhere made no sense.

Mitch continued in a voice too low for Lauren to hear. "It's your birthday."

"Of course, I know it's my birthday." He'd looked it up while she was gone. "Why did you look it up when I went to get a drink?"

He didn't make mention of her chip eating frenzy. Besides getting a drink, she was more on a search for her mental stability that she'd misplaced.

"I did look it up." The stray dog steals your heart look slipped over his face again. "But not today, the day we met."

The memories of that day filtered back. David, the tech lab supervisor, convinced the new staffers that some cosmic disaster equivalent to the apocalypse would happen if they ever used their access inappropriately. He'd certainly frightened her, but Mitch didn't seem to have any fears about peeking into her file. Could be that he realized David was all bluster and ignored the warning. Then again, the problem with tech-savvy students staffing the lab is that they were capable of devising ways to get around security protocol.

"Oh." That was the best she could do. She wanted to ask why, but she knew. Her birthday was important to him because he was interested. Mitch would have possibly devised a whole array of birthday surprises if the two of them ever were a couple.

He shrugged his shoulders and gave her a sheepish smile. "Sorry. I don't want you to think I'm stalking you or anything."

"No problem." She uttered her standard reply, never giving his behavior a sinister slant for a moment. Leah explained after her sister Nora's amazing rescue how her sister sensed her kidnapper's evilness before the incident. There was no evil in Mitch.

The sound of music drifted through the area. A band featuring a long guitar solo with the lead singer shouting a few unidentifiable words about every eight measures. Stella craned her neck trying to identify the source. Rules forbade students bringing their iPods into the testing center because they could insert answer info onto it. If grades were money, and they often were with scholarships, then college served as a training ground for future embezzlers. Every known way to cheat the system occurred at least once, and dozens more ways would pop up before the end of the semester.

Lauren's iPod lay on the counter ear buds unplugged. It could be a simple oversight, but Lauren sat beside it with the earplugs in her hands, daring Stella to say something. Pushing up out of the chair, she walked toward the testing center. Since no bent head worked feverishly to finish a timed exam, Stella couldn't complain about disturbing the students and refused to mention it bothered her. For some reason, she felt it was Lauren's intention. Why give her the satisfaction?

Sighing deeply, Stella realized now that she was in Lauren's area;

she'd have to make some comment on her appearance. "Any more exams?"

Lauren jammed the jack back into the MP3 player, silencing it. "No. That's it."

Stella glanced at the clock on Lauren's monitor. About twenty minutes left on the shift. The brief look at the screen identified a dating advice website. It didn't matter what site she was on since she was only supposed to monitor the exams. 'You could shut down and leave early."

Mistrust peeked out of Lauren's eyes while her lips pinched as if she'd bitten into a lemon. "That would cut me out of twenty minutes." Her gaze flicked back to Mitch. Odd that she'd look at Mitch. Technically, Stella oversaw Lauren, not Mitch.

"Not really, I can turn off your computer." Suspicion still flickered in Lauren's eyes. "Maybe you can ask Mitch to do it."

The idea brought a sly smile to her face. "I'll do that." She opened her messenger bag and dumped assorted snacks, water bottle, and iPod into the bag with one swipe.

To appear busy, Stella moved around the exam center, moving mouses to see if the screens would flicker to life. Lauren walked over to Mitch's station and bent down to whisper in his ear. Her actions surprised Stella because she didn't think the girl had that much boldness. She'd figured wrong.

On a hunch, she went back to Lauren's computer. An open file materialized with Mitch's name at the top. It included his schedule, his dorm assignment, his home address, his phone number, and his birthday, which was yesterday.

Talk about a major crush. No doubt, Mitch was supposed to find this little token of her obsession, then knowing how she felt would be equally smitten with her. A stupid middle school plan, although it might work. College could be a very lonely time as opposed to the big party most high school seniors envisioned. Instead of alerting Mitch to her find, Stella closed the page.

Yesterday was his birthday. What did she do? Nothing, when he'd saved her butt on more than one occasion due to a Cam emergency, which was usually only an emergency in Cam's eyes. She should do something.

Strolling back to her station, she wondered how she'd approach him. Hearing her footsteps or more likely it was the lights she turned off as she cleared each area, Mitch turned at her approach. The third shift used a very limited area. Although the lab was supposed to be open twenty-four hours, very few students burned the midnight oil, probably not relishing a walk back in the dark.

"Did you send Lauren over to whisper in my ear?"

Why would she do such a thing? "No, that was all her. I told her she could leave early and she doubted my generosity. I suggested even that you could close down her computer."

"Yeah. I'm not sure what I did to deserve the honor. Oh well, only fifteen more minutes." He made a face. "This utility scan should finish by then."

"If so, you got more done than me. I'll be taking work with me." Seated in her chair, she turned it away from him. Make it look casual. Staring at her monitor, she asked. "What did you do for your birthday yesterday?"

"Ha! I knew you would look it up. You're so predictable." A broad grin displayed the one incisor that lapped over the other.

The predictable label didn't appeal. She had no desire to confess where she'd picked up the information, either. "I asked you what you did. Maybe a cake?"

His smile disappeared as suddenly as it came. "My mom sent me a card with a strange letter in it."

"What was so strange about it?" At least, he had a parent who wrote to him. Her mother's scribbled words on pamphlets detailing her fiery end never counted as actual correspondence. Anything had to be better than that.

"Well, ah…" He stopped for a moment as emotions chased across his face, too rapidly to discern any of them. "I think my mom meant well. It started out with 'I'm so proud of you being in college' since neither one of my parents went to college, but then the letter sort dissolved into ranting really."

Maybe it wasn't so different from her mother's missives. "What do you mean?" The changing expressions said more than he did. None of them involved happiness, excitement, joy, or even the milder stepsister, contentment. "Tell me later, I think your file is done." She nodded in the direction of his monitor.

Stella gathered up the notes for her work tonight. A jump drive saved what she'd already finished. Technically, she should be able to open the file back on her own laptop, although too many times, she discovered what should have worked often didn't. No reason to take chances. If she pushed it, she might get a few of her extra money assignments done.

The computer clock glowed 8:59 as Mitch powered down his computer, and she could hear Simon before he even opened the door.

CHAPTER FOUR

T HE SQUARE CUBES that served as campus security lights threw down small pools of illumination at wide intervals leaving most of the surrounding in darkness. Small lights lined the path throwing a minimal light onto pedestrian feet, but not much else. They were a recent installation after a news story about sexual assault on college campuses. All it really managed to do was create even more shadows making almost everyone in a hoodie resemble a faceless serial killer.

Thank the Goddess that her colleague walked her to her door every night, a job that should have fallen to Cam.

Stella hooked her arm into Mitch's. "Let's do something fun for your birthday."

"Birthday was yesterday. You missed it." He covered her hand tucked into the crook of his arm with his. "What fun ideas do you have?"

Good question. It was a sizable campus with a variety of activities nearby. "We could go get a pizza, go bowling, even play miniature golf. Mainly, I just like to talk to you outside of work and class. We seldom get the chance, right?"

Despite her face turned up to his, she noticed two girls walking behind them. They rode the edge of their personal bubble eavesdropping. The two females whispered furiously. She didn't recognize them, but one looked a little familiar. She might have seen her somewhere earlier that day. Her head whipped back when she heard her name. The girls stopped, allowing them to move ahead on their own.

"Okay, sounds great. Let's turn here. I know a pizza place we can walk to." A warm breeze carried the aroma of car exhausts, fast food, and the sulfuric smell of a spent match.

"Think fast." A male voice shouted as a sputtering string of firecrackers landed near her feet.

Before she could even jump out of the way, Mitch swung her up into his arms and kicked the offending firework away. "Jerks. I ought to—" He growled the words.

Hoping to dampen what could be a fight, she added, "Get pizza," to the end of his sentence.

"You're right," he agreed before placing her feet back on the ground.

"I worried that you'd get hurt."

Stella rather missed being in his arms, but she'd never mention it. Falling for Mitch, who was nice and protected her, would make her a lousy girlfriend. *It's more than Cam usually did.* Her troublesome-self whispered, always busy pointing out the flaws in her life. They walked a few moments in silence their hands no longer touching.

She touched his elbow just barely to get his attention. "You never finished telling me about the letter from your mother and why it was strange."

"Yeah, that." He sighed. "It started out okay with how proud she was that I was going to college. She went on to having a crappy job because she never went to college. Then on to dad dying and not even having an insurance policy and how hard her life has been ever since his death." He shoved his hands into his pockets.

"Whoa, that must have cheered you up immensely." How parents felt the need to burden their children with their own issues always amazed her. "Had the experience, myself. I get my own version of that from my mom." Her eyes rested on his wrists that ended in his pockets. She was willing to bet they'd gone into the pockets, eliminating the possibility of their hands casually touching.

Mitch pointed to the fairy lights draped over the trees outside the pizzeria. Stella knew the place, never actually went in, but was aware that it was a very popular hangout. A shiver of apprehension danced across her shoulders. No doubt, word that she'd been out dining with Mitch would ripple across campus. Not true, she was out with a friend celebrating a missed birthday. Of course, whether it mattered depended on *if* anyone knew she and Cam were an item.

The warm temperatures made the outside tables appealing. Stella settled back in the plastic lawn chair. The fairy lights illuminated the area with the help of a neon PIZZA sign and a votive candle flickering on each table for atmosphere. The striped table umbrellas advertised an Italian liqueur. A few couples huddled their chairs close together while conversing in low voices, no doubt, murmuring about how in love they were.

Every time the eatery's door swung open; groups of chattering students spilled out along with the sound of televisions turned to a sports channel while other students elbowed their way inside. The loud, boisterous voices indicated more than a few had too much to drink. Mitch pointed to a table farther away from the door in the shadow of a large tree. Without discussion, they both moved toward the table.

Mitch picked up a menu and flourished it. "Our location makes it impossible to read anything. I'll go in and order since I doubt as busy as they are, they'll check to see if anyone is outside. Anything you don't want on your pizza?"

"None of those little fish things." She grimaced, thinking of tiny eyes staring at her while she bit into the slice. Yuk, it was enough to make her a vegetarian, but not quite.

Mitch laughed. "Got it. I don't like them, either."

His tall silhouette weaved around the other tables. How did anyone get service if the staff failed to look outside? A casual glance at the other tables revealed the whispering couples had no plates or pizza box on their tables. One couple had oversized sodas, but that could have come from the convenience store nearby.

The light from the open door had illuminated Mitch's profile briefly before he disappeared inside. Excellent sharp lines despite the glasses. Her father used to say a man's profile was his résumé. For some reason he believed those who had no inner purpose or character would be chinless individuals. Of course, his logic probably resulted from his own chiseled profile. In retrospect, considering how her father kicked her and her mom to the curb, a man's profile didn't mean squat.

A simmering spark of resentment flared. Just about the time, she thought she was over her father's desertion something happened, and the pain flared up again. Many middle-aged men abandoned their family when a younger woman beckoned. Often the younger woman ended up dumping the cheater, but it hadn't happened yet with her father.

Her lips pulled down as she crossed her arms and slumped into her chair. Mitch's shadow blocked out the surrounding light, as he leaned forward to look at her.

"Hey, what's wrong?" He slid into his seat, pulling it closer to hers. "I went inside and you were happy, but now you look like someone ran over your puppy."

Exhaling deeply, she pushed up in her chair and tried for a smile. Wasn't the whole purpose of the outing to cheer up Mitch who only got a lousy letter from his mother on his birthday? "I'm sorry. I'm not sure how it happened, but I started thinking about my father. I know I should be glad to have a father and all, but the way he left wasn't easy to deal with."

She reached for the votive candle, turning it in her hand, watching the flame flicker, almost die as the wax washed across it.

Mitch's larger hand pried the candle away from her. He positioned the candle closer to him before resting his hand on top of hers. "I know he left your mother for a younger woman. That's lame. How did this affect you?"

Her lips tightened, not wanting to tell the real story. "Of course, there were the endless arguments. I was the bone between the two of them. My mother pointed out how his selfishness would ruin my life. He'd scream back that she was the one who wanted children and he never did."

His hand tightened over hers. "Harsh. Did they know you overheard?"

Stella shrugged, not sure if Mitch could see the action in the dark. "I don't know. I doubt my father cared. He told me to my face that he'd never wanted children and I was the only reason he stayed in the miserable marriage as long as he did. In some convoluted way, I ruined his life, not my mother or him."

"Damn, that's hard."

Stella sighed heavily. "You're the only person I ever told, besides Leah, I mean. I would never tell my mother because that would set her off." The thought of her mother flying into a rage and threatening to drag her father back into court was a result she'd like to avoid. No good would come of it, especially if they wanted her to testify or something.

Even though it was dark, she knew Mitch was staring at her. His voice was soft when he asked. "You never mentioned it to Cam?"

An inelegant snort escaped her lips that she turned into a cough, pulling her hand from underneath Mitch's to cover it. *To think I almost said why would I tell Cam. Of course, you're supposed to tell your boyfriend all your personal issues.* She'd discovered a while ago that Cam didn't really listen. It wasn't too surprising. Her half-dozen high school dates weren't great listeners either, too busy trying to decide how they could get her into bed. Obviously, her father epitomized the disinterest men had for female problems.

"Um, no. I never told him. It never seemed like the right time."

It would have been the perfect time for Mitch to point out what a jerk Cam was, but he didn't. His silence made her wonder if it was due to pity for her over dating such a self-absorbed jerk or if he was bored with the whole conversation. Time to lighten things up. "Did you ask if you could get some birthday candles on the pizza?"

His silhouette reminded her of those black paper pictures her first art teacher enjoyed creating. At the time, Stella thought they all looked pretty much the same with the girls having ponytails and the boys with a few hairs sticking up awkwardly. Gazing at Mitch, she realized she'd be able to pick him out in dim light. Odd that she'd be able to do that. She hadn't really spent that much time observing him, despite work and their classes together, or had she?

His glasses slipped as he shook his head as if shaking off his silent stupor. A brush of his right hand pushed the glasses back in place. "I doubt this place has birthday candles. I didn't ask. I didn't want the fuss."

Didn't want the fuss. The words sounded artificial. It was something he probably thought he should say. Most people did want the attention even if it wasn't authentic. It made them feel special. Having a bunch of minimum wage employees interrupt their busy night to crowd around some stranger and force themselves to sing an off-key version of Happy Birthday was what he didn't want. Mitch wouldn't enjoy the curious looks of other diners wondering what was going on. Yep, she could do without that, too.

Still, it was hard to believe he did nothing for his birthday. "Do anything special for your birthday?" she asked, halfway fearing the answer. Back before her family life when into the toilet, her mother made the entire birthday week about her. Instead of having her favorite food for one meal, it was a week full of delicacies such as cheeseburgers, ravioli, and little hot dogs in pork and beans. The last dish made her roll her eyes at her early culinary tastes. There were small gifts beside her plate all during her birthday week leading up to the big day.

Looking back, she could probably trace the disintegration of her family to the breakdown of birthday traditions. When she was fourteen, her mother seemed preoccupied about something and placed a candy bar by her breakfast setting instead of gifts, something her health-conscious mother would have never done before. Because Stella was a big fan of sweet stuff, she gobbled the candy down with her cereal without comment, certain her mother would retrieve the bar. When she was fifteen, her mother forgot about her birthday until two days before the actual event and urged Stella to pick out her own gift, saying she'd pay for it. Her father didn't even make it home from a business trip that year in time for a lame birthday party with a handful of recycled candles on a frozen cake her mother hadn't thawed.

On her sixteenth birthday, her parents were deep into their fight mode. Her father was seldom home and argued with her mother behind closed doors when he did return. A two-and-a-half-inch wooden barrier didn't stop the words or the anguish from slipping under the door and wrapping itself around Stella. Neither one realized they'd both forgotten Stella's birthday. Thank goodness for Leah, who picked her up after a whispered call for help and ferried her back to her house. To her shock, Leah's family had decorated the house with a birthday banner and balloons. A cake with the correct number of candles graced the kitchen table. The memory brought tears to her eyes.

Mitch chuckled in a half-hearted way that caused her to shut down her own inner pity me show. It was far from a real laugh. That type of thing you do when you've done something stupid and there's no one to comment on how stupid it is, so you end up ridiculing yourself.

"Yeah, I threw a party."

Well, that didn't sound like the shy male she knew. "Really, who did you invite?" Part of her was miffed she wasn't invited, but she'd never admit it.

"Oh, the usual." He held onto the last word stretching it out. Holding up a fist, he began to count putting up his index finger. "There was me."

Well, she expected that.

His middle finger joined his second one. "Myself."

Oh, she knew where this was going. She wondered if she should stop him but didn't. He certainly had the right to feel sorry for himself.

His ring finger popped up. "The ghost of my father telling me how disappointed he was in me."

For a second, she wondered if his father's ghost did materialize. Stella believed in ghosts in theory but had never ever seen one.

His pinkie came up slowly. "Then there was my roommate's friend, I invited over for the night, without his knowledge, of course."

Roommate's friend and why would he invite this friend over without his roommate knowing. She knew Jake, his roommate, had a girlfriend because Mitch had mentioned the awkwardness of going back to his room and trying to pretend that they weren't doing it about six feet from his head. Dorm rooms were tiny unless you paid the extra two thousand to score a room in the newer dorms. Scholarship students never merited this.

She couldn't quite remember the name of Jake's girlfriend. It was a cutesy name. The type girls gave themselves like Candy, Treasure, or Precious. Did Treasure, or whatever her name was, cheer him up? Knowing Jake, Mitch was a definite step up, but still the thought made her uncomfortable. She wanted to ask but didn't. Instead, she folded her hands in her lap wishing there was something she could do.

Jumping to her feet, she announced, "I'll go check on that pizza." Suiting her actions to her words, she rushed to the door before he could say anything else. Inside, she worked her way through the crowd of standing students, wondering why they insisted on going somewhere that was so busy. The counter loomed in the distance rather like an oasis. Her goal was to get past the sea of half-drunk students, mostly male. No doubt a few would take the opportunity to grope her, one of the reasons she avoided crowded places. Inhaling deeply, she prepared to shoulder her way through the bodies with a few elbow jabs and sharp pinches for any gropers.

A bleary-eyed male a little taller than her turned to comment but stepped back allowing her to pass. He made sure to elbow the male next to him, who also stepped back. It was like the parting of the Red Sea. Of course, it would have to be renamed the parting of the drunken hoard. At the counter, she turned to see Mitch was right behind her with a fierce look on his face, daring anyone to touch her.

His expression shocked her. She'd never seen him look anything but friendly or thoughtful. Despite his leanness, his countenance promised retribution that even the most liquor-befuddled brain could process. Mitch was being protective. The idea thrilled her, sending a jolt of euphoria through her body. When was the last time a man protected her? It would have had to have been her father, but he'd quit defending her long ago.

It was probably politically incorrect to like the feeling, but she did.

Mitch made the few steps to the counter and spoke close to her ear, "I told you I would get the pizza."

His earlier message never penetrated due to her rapid bolt before she fell victim to uncomfortable details of his self-made party the previous night. The smothering heat wafting from the pizza ovens and an excess of human bodies almost made her wish she stayed planted in the cooler outside air. Perversity caused her to shrug her shoulders. A deft move allowed Mitch to slip in front of her and signal the help. Stella grabbed the sodas while Mitch picked up the pizza and balanced it on his fingertips. Stella trailed behind her friend rather like a tugboat following a larger ship. It certainly was easier getting through the crowd. If she always had someone like Mitch by her side, crowds wouldn't be too bad.

Once they reached their outdoor table, she waited until they both sat before, she launched her protest. "I told you this was my treat. It isn't much of a present if you pay."

Mitch opened the pizza box allowing a whiff of garlic laced steam to escape. He pushed the open box in her direction. Picking up a piece, she brought it close to her mouth, but instead of biting, she spoke. "This isn't over, Mitch McDougall. Thought you'd trick me. Not sure why."

She bit into the melted cheese and tangy sauce enjoying the taste and warmth. Mitch grabbed a large triangle and folded it in half. Catching her eye in the dim light, he said, "You are the present."

"What was that supposed to mean?" With Cam, it'd mean he expected her to do something kinky he'd read about in a magazine or heard on that stupid radio show that the male half of the student body listened to faithfully. The show revolved around two adult men trading bathroom jokes and salacious stories, which must have appealed to fourteen-year-old boys. Ironically, men believed their tales.

If she ever wondered who the smarter gender was, that show alone should make her feel superior. Mitch held up a finger as he chewed. Manners, so unexpected in a college student, but still appreciated.

Was he going to say something that would creep her out? Even if he had spent time with Treasure, she doubted he turned into a typical frat guy overnight whose twin obsessions were drinking and removing girls' thongs before they climbed on top of them.

Picking up his soda, he took a pull on the straw, probably helping the pizza go down. He set the drink down and touched the edge of her hand with his close fist. So gently, she almost wouldn't have felt it if she hadn't seen the action, reminding her of a butterfly kiss. Not exactly as if she experienced any of those, but what she thought one might be like.

"Being here with you is my gift. This is the first time I've been out with a beautiful woman since I started college."

"Seriously?" The whole idea was hard to believe. Mitch might not be a smooth-talking player, but hardly a troll. Her mouth twisted to one side, as she remembered most girls weren't hoping to score an intelligent male. Most preferred to be the smarter one. "C'mon, a guy like you could have any girl he wanted. Have you even asked anyone out?"

"Mmpft." The nonsense word was more of a reaction to having a mouth full of pizza and trying not to spit it across the table. Stella decided to take it as a *no. He hadn't asked anyone out.* A passing car's headlights brightened their corner of the terrace briefly, causing the groping couple to grumble, but spotlighted a tender expression on her companion's face that confused her.

His soft reply caused Stella to inch her seat closer to hear.

"College was never about parties or hooking up for me. I knew I'd have to hit the books to make it. Never really intended to do otherwise. I wasn't exactly a hit with the girls back at my old school, anyway. No fairy godfather bestowed on me the gift of irresistibility when I hit college, either. Besides the only girl, I really liked was involved with someone else. There really wasn't anyone else I cared about."

Out of the entire half-whispered conversation, she seized on one part. Mitch had a secret crush on a girl. Obviously, one with a boyfriend, but who could it be. The large lecture class, they both, attended was full of females, not that she paid attention to any of them. Her goal was to get there on time and take notes. He'd never talked to anyone, either. "Who's the girl? Maybe she's not very serious about the boyfriend. They could break up, ya know."

Here she was hoping for a couple to break up if it would make her friend happy. Couples split up all the time. Most were never together. They just hung out until someone more interesting caught their eye. A snippet of her earlier conversation with Cam slipped back and teased her with its implications. No, it couldn't be.

The flickering votive silhouetted Mitch's head and cast a tiny rosy circle on the plastic table. Enough light to see that the man angled his head away from her as he spoke. "I doubt they'd break up since she's planning on buying him a telescope for his birthday."

His words startled her almost as much as his resigned tone did. Sure, Cam hinted that Mitch liked her, but she dismissed it as one of his mind games. In Cam's mind, she gained more attractiveness if other men wanted her. Why it mattered if other men desired her baffled her since the man kept their relationship practically secret. The number of people who knew they were dating she could count on one hand. Cam, Mitch, Leah, and the cashier at the discount store where they shopped, but the last one may have assumed they were related since they were both blonde. Not sure, if it ever came up in conversation when Cam spoke to people.

At one time, she considered mentioning it. If Cam were someone else, she might have, but being acknowledged male eye candy on the campus made any mention bragging. After a while, she hesitated wondering if Cam shouldn't be the one advertising his hold over her. Her quandary about what terms to use for their relationship fell by the wayside with a constant barrage of classwork, work-study, and her side work of typing up lecture notes.

Mitch's abrupt mention of his own attraction to her caused her to blurt out, "Oh." She smashed her lips together sure she'd made a big stupid circle with her mouth.

Mitch's heavy sigh was louder than his words. "How could you not know?"

Easy, she wanted to answer, but she didn't. Memories of the endless thoughtful things Mitch did for her crowded her mind. He not only kept her caught up in class but put funny cartoons he'd cut out of the local paper on her desk. Half that time, he'd never known she was dating Cam. At first, she wasn't. Then, she was too unsure of Cam's player ways to admit to seeing him. When she finally did confess her infatuation to Mitch, there was a lull in their shared conversations and spontaneous gifts.

Had she been just using Mitch? Goddess, she hoped not. Would that make her little better than her mother, who her father accused of trickery. Her shoulders drooped as the pizza solidified into an uncomfortable mass in her stomach. "Why me? I'm not deserving of your affection."

Before he could answer, Stella stood to leave. Wiping away tears, she lunged away from the table, making an unsteady path through the tables.

A yelled comment about another chick who couldn't hold her liquor went right over her head until she realized the speaker meant her. She whirled, ready to face her nameless accuser and bumped into the solid form of Mitch.

He cupped her elbow and guided her onto the sidewalk. They had walked a few moments in silence before he spoke. "I didn't mean to upset you. I shouldn't have said anything."

More tears filled her eyes, threatening to fall. Was she crying for herself or Mitch? She wasn't terribly sure. "You didn't do anything wrong. It's me."

His hand tightened on her elbow as she stumbled on the uneven pavement. He kept her upright instead of allowing her to kiss the cement. "There's nothing wrong with you. I consider you perfect the way you are."

A grunt served as her reply. Even though it was a cliché, it was the first time anyone ever said it to her. One of the tears blurring her vision trickled down her face. Wouldn't it be wonderful to be that person he thought she was? "You don't know me that well, then."

"True," Mitch admitted. "But I'd like to know you better."

What was that supposed to mean? Stella watched her feet as they negotiated the buckled sidewalk. "Better you don't. I kinda like the idea of you thinking so highly of me." Her words made her sound like a diva, so she managed to chuckle, making it sound like a joke. It wasn't.

She wasn't sure when it happened. The whole concept that she was broken and not okay. Maybe it was always part of her. After all, she had the nerve to show up nine months after her parents did the deed. Of course, her father enduring a loveless marriage as well as spending thousands of dollars on her upkeep didn't help either. Upkeep made her sound more like a lawn.

Her mother's newfound religion wasn't much better, which resulted in her mother always warning her of eternal damnation. This bothered her mom more than it did her since it somehow reflected poorly on her mother's parenting skills. She wasn't sure if the real problem was her going to hell or her mother looking like a less than a stellar parent. It might be both. Then, there was Kevin.

Oh, she tried not to think too much of the almost unknown senior who awkwardly asked her out to the senior prom. It was unfortunate he chose the morning her father stomped out of the house with a suitcase. The traumatic departure continued out on the front lawn where mothers with kindergartners stood on the sidewalk with strollers waiting for their oldest to board the bus.

Her mother clutched a skillet in her right hand because his abrupt announcement caught her in the middle of unloading the dishwasher. Her mother baited him by telling him that running back to his skanky ho would result in some incurable STD and a painful death.

The nearby mothers took a step back while covering their attentive children's ears. Those with more than one child had more of a challenge as far as ear coverage.

Her father, halfway in his car, yelled back. "You ruined my life. Everything you touch you destroyed." Catching sight of Stella, he added, "I wish you'd never been born."

Most people at the bus stop probably thought he was talking to her mother. Apparently, that was the impression her mother received too, because she hurled the skillet at the car, dinging the door. Her father's face suffused with red, and he opened his mouth, but no words came out. Instead, he closed the car door and sped off.

Her mother, suddenly aware of her audience, dusted off her hands, announced to the listeners, "Good riddance." Her actions announced it was her plan to chase off her husband with a frying pan before work. Stella stayed on the front stoop staring at the departing car, knowing he'd been staring at her, wishing she'd never been born.

It was hard to stop thinking about it. So, when Kevin Hardesty asked her if she'd go to the prom with him, she didn't answer, barely even heard the words as she turned away afraid, she might start crying again. Apparently, not quickly enough, because it was all over school that the idea of going to prom with Kevin sent her into an enormous crying fit by the end of the day. When the gossip finally reached her via Leah, she wanted to find Kevin and explain. She never had the chance. He hanged himself that night from the local park swing set. The police found him near midnight when making their nightly rounds.

Though no note indicated he had killed himself due to her not going to prom with him, it didn't stop the rumors. Leah assured her she wasn't the problem. Bullying may have sent him over the edge. His stuttering made him an easy target. It also made it hard for him to ask her out, but he tried, and she cried. The image of her father screaming that she ruined everything she touched came to mind. Maybe he did mean her mother, then, but apparently, she was her mother's daughter.

They were almost at her dorm when she realized they had stopped talking while she fell into her memories and pulled the scabs off old wounds. "Sorry about being so quiet."

The lights were more plentiful around the building, illuminating the two of them. Most of the campus pathways lights were close to the ground that shone only on feet. It never revealed people's faces or even those hiding near the path. Mitch was more than kind to walk her to her dorm.

His arms wrapped around her, holding her tight for a few seconds. The closeness and warmth cause a tickling sensation in the back of her throat. Oh, Goddess, she was going to cry some more, but instead of silent tears leaking out in the dark, it would be big ugly gasping cries. The thought made her break free of his embrace and dart for the entrance. She shoved past another girl opening the door, ignoring her muttered complaint.

Her rapid race up the stairs had her holding her side as she reached her own door. The sobs welled out as she swung open the door. No roommate in sight, which was good. She didn't want to explain why she was crying. It was hard to understand herself. Mitch considered her perfect, a definite improvement on her father's opinion.

Dropping to her bed, she pulled the covers over her not bothering to remove her shoes and cried.

CHAPTER FIVE

T HE SOUND OF the door closing along with talking woke her. Stella blinked finding focusing difficult. Her fingers moved over her swollen eyes under the shielding covers.

A masculine voice she recognized as her roomie's current squeeze spoke. "Looks like ice queen tied one on. You said she was boring straight."

A snort, then a loud laugh rattled the room. How many people were in the room staring at her blanket-shrouded body?

"No way, she probably passed out from studying too much. I did hear a rumor she had a guy but never saw any sign of it."

"Looks like one person under the covers to me. Should I lift them to discover?"

Stella, curled in a fetal position, faced the wall holding tight to the polyester cocoon she had wrapped around herself. She squeezed her eyes shut to block out the brightness. Why couldn't she get a little privacy?

"Stop it." The hissed words pierced the mental fog enveloping her. "We're here just to get the weed and leave. Remember?"

A masculine mumble indicating nothing served as a response. A few footsteps and drawers opening and slamming, then a door shutting meant they were gone. Maybe. Stella counted to one hundred just to be safe. Slowly removing the blanket, she blinked in the glare of the light left on.

So straight, she was boring, huh? It wasn't a horrible thing to be. It sounded wrong, but there were worse things, such as getting kicked out of school for having drugs on the premises. Somehow, she'd have to get a new roommate. What excuse could she use without narcing out her roomie? Maybe she should use her roomie's excuse that she couldn't get enough studying done in her current environment. Hard for a college to argue against that one.

The swollen skin around her eyes pinched and stretched. Her face would be a mess tomorrow if she didn't use ice or even cold tea bags to take down the swelling. Standing, she stumbled in the direction of the small cabinet where she kept her food. Opening the door, she peered into the empty cabinet. "What the...?" Her surprise morphed into anger. Damn, another reason she needed a new roommate.

For the most part, she didn't have anything worth stealing, but apparently a box of breakfast bars, instant soup, and teabags must have disappeared with her visitors. Stella balled her hands on her hips. Probably just swept everything into a bag without even examining what they were grabbing. Difficult to imagine hot tea as a go to beverage to accompany the pot high munchies.

Pushing the door shut, she moved to the tiny fridge, not expecting too much inside. Stooping, she discovered a yogurt past its due date, a carton of takeout food that wasn't hers, and a tiny bottle of energy drink. None of it tempted her or was what she needed. She opened the even smaller freezer compartment for the two plastic ice trays. At least the ice would serve instead of the tea bags.

At last, something was going her way. She pulled out the first tray only to discover it was empty. "Seriously." She flung the tray toward her roommate's bed. Maybe the second one had ice in it. Her fingers lifted the light tray already knowing the answer before she tipped it up to the light. Empty.

The second tray followed the first as it flew across the room. Stella stumbled back to her bed. Too tired to do anything anyway. Tomorrow could be a mental health day. Goddess knows plenty of students took them. Mitch would cover for her at work, but she'd have to call him. The thought had her falling back on the bed.

How could she explain her bizarre behavior? The light was still on, but she didn't have the energy to turn it off. Rolling over, she freed her cover and pulled it over her, dimming the light. Tomorrow, she'd deal with everything.

Images of her impromptu date filtered into her dreams. *A white tablecloth stretched across the table with the absence of groping couples with their oversized plastic cups filled with who knows what made for a different scene. Mitch tucked his glasses into his shirt pocket as he smiled. His lips were moving, but she couldn't hear what he was saying. All she could see was how soft and inviting his eyes were as they came closer. She knew he was going to kiss her. The possibility tantalized as she leaned forward closing the distance the small table put between them. What type of kisser would he be? Music was playing in the background, the same trio of notes repeatedly, which sounded vaguely familiar.*

"Answer your stupid phone!"

The strident command shocked Stella into wakefulness as her phone stopped chiming. An object landed on her covers. Lowering the blanket, she discovered her cell phone.

Palming it, she turned it to check who her persistent caller was. Cam, of course, just as well she didn't want to talk to him.

Her eyes flicked up to catch her roommate staring at her.

"Damn, you look like crap. What happened to you?"

Stella didn't need this. There was so much she wanted to say to her roommate but wasn't up to the confrontation. Instead, she walked past her to go to the bathroom. Living in the cheap dorms meant she had to share the facilities with a dozen girls.

Inside the restroom, she rested against the wall confronted with the fumes of a dozen different shampoos, body sprays, and styling agents. For females so concerned about looking good, they could trash a bathroom. Stella walked over to a mirror where the custodian had taped a note. In all caps, it read ITEMS LEFT OVERNIGHT WILL BE CONSIDERED TRASH. It was a familiar message that most of the students continued to ignore since it hadn't happened yet.

The tired face with red puffy eyes and pillow lines could have been used in an ad about the tribulations of college life. Despite the lack of alcohol, she looked hungover. Not that she had all that much experience partying hard, but she'd seen her share of dorm mates stumbling through the halls with smeared makeup and the acrid odor of vomit clinging to them. The only regret she had been acting the fool with her best friend on campus. She hadn't always considered Mitch that way, but there weren't a whole lot of contenders for the honor.

Resting one hand on her abs, she pushed her finger into the soft skin feeling for bloating. PMS might explain the emotional cascade she'd undergone, but not entirely. Her stomach felt surprisingly flat. Turning on the spigot, she splashed cold water on her face. It helped a little.

She swung the door closed on her bathroom stall the same time two residents entered.

"Did you hear about Stella being wasted?"

On her spot on the toilet, Stella stiffened in horror. They were talking about her. Any association with drugs would cost her scholarship. It was the driving reason she needed a new roommate. Knowing Cece, if administrators found weed in their room, she'd blame Stella, denying any drug use.

"Well, Emily did mention it. Didn't believe it. It's right up there with the story about her dating that hunk of man candy, Cam Winters."

The sound of pelting water accompanied their laughter. Realizing they were in the showers, Stella flushed, pulled up her pants, not even bothering to fasten them. She held onto them rather like would be gangsters who insisted on wearing jeans ten sizes too big. The door beckoned as she darted for it before the gossipers stepped out of the shower. Would they be embarrassed? All she knew was she didn't want to face anyone who felt a stoned Stella was more likely than boring Stella going out with Cam.

Students in the hallway served as obstacles for her to weave around. Biting her bottom lip, she offered up a short prayer that her roommate was gone as her hand touched the doorknob. The miracle of all miracles, she was. No way was she in any shape to attend class. Grabbing her computer, she shot an email to her professor explaining her absence as the stomach flu. It was something that usually never rated a doctor's note or a visit to the campus clinic. Unfortunately, it was also the one most hungover students used, too.

Now, she'd have to call Mitch. She stared at her phone not wanting to make the call to explain. Instead, she texted, *Won't be at work. Cover for me. Thanks.* The phone chimed even before she could turn it off. A text from Mitch.

Are you avoiding me?

Well, yeah, she was avoiding him and everyone else on the planet. Mentioning it would invite more questions. What could she say? The idea of going away to a secluded spot in the woods without everyone speculating about her behavior appealed. She'd already informed her prof she had the flu. Mitch would probably take an extra handout in class for her if there were any. A chance conversation might occur with Dr. Fleming mentioning she had the flu. With all the possible outcomes, she needed to stick with the same lie.

No, of course not. I just have the flu.

That should satisfy him. He might tell her feel better, which was the favorite catch phrase when a person announced illness. It always sounded more like an order. You feel better. The underlying message was sick people are no fun. Get well or I'll drop you as a friend. Maybe it only sounded that way to her. Could be she was overthinking it. The phone chimed again.

You didn't act sick last night, A little moody, but not sick.

Sweet Goddess save her from intelligent men. The impulsive plea horrified her. *I didn't mean it. Don't rescue me from smart men.* Outside of Mitch, there had been a void of smart men in her life. It could be that hormones trumped intellect every time, even though all the males must have received reasonable grades for admittance. Their bizarre fraternity initiations, beer pong, and dares to bed as many females as possible didn't symbolize higher learning in any form. More than a few had convoluted plans to cheat their way through the year.

Moody, huh. He got that right. Nothing she wanted to deal with right now. She considered not replying, but that would have the considerate male stopping by to make sure she hadn't rolled out of bed gaining a concussion in the process. Argh, what to do? Her fingers tangled in her hair as she shoved a restless hand through her tresses. What a mess. The phone chimed again.

I'm coming over. I'll get you some chicken soup from the shop on the corner.

Her lips tilted up. He was a thoughtful man. The prospect of his arrival catapulted her out of bed. He couldn't come over. It would be hard to fake an illness with him there. Full sunlight filtered through the cheap blinds indicating late morning. A glance out the window revealed students heading to class, which she should be. Guilt rode her hard rather like one of those demons her mother continually insisted were hitching a ride on her. Apparently, demons were not big fans of walking since they were always busy hitching a ride on someone. There had to be some way to discourage Mitch. A little truth sometimes works.

I lied. It's my period. The cramps are super bad. Don't come over. Nothing you can do. Probably hate you because you're a male and don't have to go through this.

Periods, cramps, tampons all worked on men like how a cross did on traditional vampires. The idea grossed out the males, in general, since their bodies never offered up monthly gifts of blood. At the most, men knew they couldn't offer any helpful advice. Most usually clammed up or changed the subject. Would Mitch be any different?

Understood

Obviously, he was the clam up sort. Her stomach lurched. All her talk of flu might be having undesirable consequences. Then again, it could be the lack of food. Maybe she should have let Mitch bring her soup.

Her tummy gave another rumble. The clever thing would be to get cleaned up and go to the meal hall. If nothing else, she could probably get some fresh fruit and a granola bar. Breakfast would be over by the time she got there. Especially, since a shower was a must with her Medusa locks. Of course, that meant interacting with people.

Stella stumbled back to her bed and sat. Her shoulders drooped as she considered all she had to do. "Goddess, I can't handle it." Even eating required too many steps. Turning off her cell phone, she climbed back under the covers. The only good thing about her roommate was Cece would leave her alone and make no annoying efforts to see if she were still alive.

Sleep came fast, taking her under. She tumbled off her wakefulness boogie board and slipped into the ocean of sleep. Generally, she fought her descent into slumber, but not today. Her last conscious thought consisted of wondering why anyone would fight sleep. It was such sweet mindless place devoid of reality and the associated responsibilities.

A brownish mist circled around her feet. Dead trees decorated the landscape, throwing out long, black ragged shadows. No moon or sun in the cloudy sky made her question the shadows. The flapping wings of a bird drew her gaze upward. A raven or possibly a crow landed on a nearby tree.

The bird's dark eyes fixed on her. Most people considered the crow a symbol of death. Then again, in folklore any bird in the house indicated a future death, probably because a bird in flight represented the soul. Stella kept her gaze fixed on the bird trying to remember the most positive symbolism for the large bird.

Crows were highly adaptable and intelligent. Shamanic meanings included being fearless, magic, personal transformation, even destiny. For the most part, all good things, her mood lightened a little. Several other crows lighted on the tree, crowding it with their dark bodies. The birds shifted on the branches making room for new arrivals.

What did an entire flock of crows mean? Murder was the weird term for a group. The crow also served as a trickster in animal legends. Was it an elaborate con? If it were, she was clueless. What if the birds were ravens? All she could think of was Edgar Allan Poe's poem with the raven answering "Nevermore." In the end, she couldn't quite remember the entire poem. Just that something about a depressed writer whining about his dead true love. She wasn't sure if the raven's nevermore was telling him he'd never love again or what.

One of the birds cawed, causing the others to caw, flapping their wings until suddenly the tree lifted off the ground.

"Stella, Stella, I know you're in there." The male voice penetrated along with the pounding she thought at first was the sound of the tree carried away by countless crows.

Wakefulness trickled in slowly. The weave of the blanket filled her view; making her wonder if it was the sky. The cloudy brown sky turned a nauseating puke green. The pounding continued. A part of her knew she should investigate, but another part voted for ignoring it. Didn't things go away when you failed to acknowledge them? Pulling the blanket closer, she rolled toward to the wall and away from the sound.

"Stella, open this door or I'm going to the campus police!"

Police. Her eyelids snapped open. There was a reason she wanted to avoid the cops, but she couldn't remember why. Would have to answer the door. Eventually, she might remember the thing about the police. A groan escaped as she pushed into a sitting position. The blanket served as her protective shield as she half draped it over her head and across her shoulders. A combination stagger-stumble walk brought her to the door. Blinking several times, she tried to shake off the last vestige of the crow dream.

It might be Mitch with food. Buoyed by the hopeful thought, she threw the door open. A scowling Cam greeted her. What was he doing here? Her memory might be lagging some, but she was sure she as much as broke up with him when he suggested using her job to do some grade changing.

Cam's eyes took a downward sweep of her body and then returned to her face before speaking. "You look like shit!"

Her hand still on the doorknob propelled the door shut before the thought even solidified in her brain. Unfortunately, Cam's upraised hand stopped the door just short of closing. Her moment of indecision gave him enough time to push his way into her room.

Stella took a step back, sliding away from him. This was the man she loved? Did love? The angry male placed his hands on her shoulders and burned her with another disapproving stare. "God, you're a mess. I came over here to prevent you from doing anything else foolish."

Foolish? She backed away the way a person would from a rattlesnake. Did she even know him? The back of her legs hit her bed, destroying her balance and sending her wind milling backward. As soon as she hit the mattress, she scrambled back to her feet. No reason to send the wrong signals. Although right now, his sneer reflected the mattress dance was not under consideration.

He folded his arms and leaned back against the door. "I guess I shouldn't be too surprised you look like garbage. That's what happens when you go slumming."

Okay, she'd give a zombie a run for her money as far as looking like death five days old. The mirror already delivered the unwelcome news. What was this slumming nonsense? Sure, the college town might not be affluent, but it was no ghetto either.

Cam continued talking, not waiting for her reply. "You thought I wouldn't hear about you and Mitch's date the last night?"

Stella almost corrected him but decided against it. Sure, it wasn't a real date, but no need to tell him that, especially since it upset him so much. It was probably the most emotion she'd seen from the man when he wasn't watching sports channel. Could Cam be jealous? His face grew flushed as he spoke.

He did come all the way to her dorm to see why she wasn't taking his calls. As for the disbelieving shower girls, she hoped they caught a glimpse of him. The furrow in his forehead smoothed out as he flashed his potent smile. His lips were moving again. Stella shook her head to clear it.

His voice had an echoing quality like being in a tunnel. Slowly, she deciphered the words.

"I'll give you thirty minutes to get ready. Then, I'll swing back by and pick you up."

Cam was taking her somewhere. Where? "Are we going out to eat?" Crossing her fingers on one hand, she certainly hoped so.

"Lunch usually involves food." His lips twisted as he shook his head. Two long steps took him to the door. "Thirty minutes."

The door closed leaving Stella frozen for a few seconds. "Thirty minutes!" She grabbed her shower caddy, a maxi dress, underwear, and a towel. She sprinted to the showers. The row of bathroom mirrors reminded her from various angles how horrendous she looked.

The showers started out cold, which meant a twenty-second warm up period to make the water bearable. No time today, stepping into the icy water set her teeth chattering. Tensing her muscles, she endured it. Besides, it would help her shake off the lethargy. The sense of despondency that had fastened itself to her required extra loofah scrubbing. Call it exfoliating, but she was trying to rid herself of the feeling that nothing mattered.

The bathroom door opened, and two girls came in talking. Stella didn't recognize the voices, but that wasn't too surprising. A full schedule, work, and Cam kept her too busy for the social activities that might have gained her a few friends. Then again, she didn't have a whole lot of use for girls who only cared about boys, nail polish, sex, and shoes. Part of her wanted to warn them not to depend on men to fulfill them, using her mother as a poster child of what happens when a woman expects a man to make her dreams come true.

That type of behavior would make her a social pariah if she weren't already. Fingers in her hair, she lathered up. Ready to step back into the water flow for the rinse, she stopped when she heard Cam's name.

"Cam Winters was in our dorm. I can't believe it. I didn't think he made personal visits because girls just line up outside his apartment." Laughter greeted the remark.

Her teeth ground together as she imagined the speaker falling into a sinkhole that opened up underneath her. Her fingers continued to lather her hair as she continued to eavesdrop. How did they know he had an apartment as opposed to a dorm room? Ugly answers she didn't care for crowded her mind.

"The man must be desperate if he's knocking on dorm room doors." The females found this remark equally hilarious.

The sound of the door slamming indicated another woman entered. Stella stepped under the stream of water still able to hear their laughter and catch a word here and there. Her curiosity propelled her out of the water again. Conditioner, she needed to condition her hair. Time was ticking. Cam would probably be back in exactly thirty minutes too. It would help if gossip girl and friend cleared out, allowing her some peace.

An extra big glop of conditioner landed in her hand. Good. It would make her hair look greasy in a couple of days, but the extra conditioner would make her hair shine today. She needed something after the mess Cam witnessed. It was no wonder he didn't kiss her goodbye. Instead, he slipped out of the door like a cat burglar.

A third voice joined the gossip crew. It sounded somewhat familiar, but she couldn't place it.

"Sex is the last thing Cam would be here for. The man could stand naked on a corner and be mobbed by women who wanted to blow him."

The words made her want to vomit, but luckily, her empty stomach didn't comply. Sure, Cam turned heads with his underwear ad-worthy physique, sun-streaked hair and knowing smile, but still. Did the women on campus have no dignity? Her fingers slowed smoothing conditioner to the ends of her hair. Did she have no dignity? She and Cam had a relationship. Wasn't he taking her out? He certainly hadn't done that in a while. A grocery trip to the discount mart did not count as a date.

"I heard he was flunking out of most of his classes and even got Hilary to do his homework for economics, but found out she only looked smart."

The trio chuckled, then, went on to discuss their plans for the day before heading for the showers or toilets. The breakup of the group had Stella shimmying the maxi dress over her still wet body with no time to dry off or shave her legs. She needed to be gone before the girls popped out of the various stalls. Why was she running? She'd done nothing wrong. Inhaling deeply, she tried to calm down her racing heart. Any other girl would brag about Cam taking her out for lunch. Instead, she acted as if she were on some spy mission. No reason she shouldn't go out. She was as good as the rest of the females on campus. Her bold affirmation did little to convince.

A clear path greeted her as she poked her head out of the shower enclosure. A quick tooth brushing was all she'd allow herself before heading out. Makeup and hair, she'd do in her room. With any luck, her roommate wouldn't be there.

In her room, she set her travel alarm clock in front of the mirror. In and out of the shower in under ten minutes, but she didn't shave. She forgot her shower shoes too. That wasn't like her. Mitch occasionally teased her about her lists and obsessive organization. Her purple shower shoes were still in the caddy. Great, now she'd probably get athlete's foot or some other fungal bacteria.

Brush in one hand and blow dryer in the other, she smoothed out her natural blonde hair. The heat flushed her face, but even considering that the mirror reflected an attractive woman. If she owed her parents nothing else, they were both reasonably good-looking, which was probably the reason her father found it so easy to hook up. If Cam were only in the market for looks, then she'd fit. Hundreds of other girls on campus would too.

She shook her eyeliner, trying to decide if she'd go with a clean line or a little Cleopatra curve on the end. Straight line, she didn't have time to risk the curve and starting over when it smeared. What was so different about her that had Cam continually asking her out until she accepted?

A quick swipe of mascara finished her eyes. She fluttered them at her reflection lightening her mood a little. She could almost admit that Cam was dating her for sex, which wouldn't be too different from most males on campus. While that might be true, he could easily date women, hotter and better in the sack than she was.

The blush brush whisked over both cheeks, and a smear of lightly tinted lip-gloss finished her makeup. Could it be true about Cam flunking? She never could accuse the man of studying too much. The only sign of grade anxiety was when he asked her if she could change his grades. His argument sounded logical with the prospect of losing his scholarship, but as his girlfriend, her job should be to encourage him to study and bring his grades up, not help him cheat.

Her phone chimed the same time she gave her hair a final flip. Picking it up, she scanned the screen.

Thirty minutes are up. Waiting downstairs, outside.

Stella's eyes drifted back to her travel clock. Two minutes remained, but she wouldn't quibble. Instead, she grabbed her purse and headed out. Waiting outside meant none of the catty girls would see Cam escort her. On the other hand, she didn't have to do his homework, either, to score a date.

The tiny voice that she sometimes labeled *mother* whispered, "If you change his grades, he'd be yours forever." The idea was tempting. Sure, Cam wasn't the greatest boyfriend, but it was certainly better than being alone, wasn't it? Her sandals made a clopping sound as she hurried down the stairs. The stupid elevator took forever, forcing her into the dank stairwell that hung onto smells the way a dog guards a bone. The combined aromas of pizza, vomit, and body spray caused her to cover her mouth with her hand as an impromptu mask.

Her steps slowed as she approached the first floor. Cam should be outside the door waiting for her. Possibly leaning against the tree where all the disbelieving residents could see him. *Yeah, that's right. Bookish Stella hooked one of the campus hot bodies.* Today would be a great day. Obviously, the man was going to make their relationship more public, more real. Her lips lifted in an impromptu smile. The depression that had embraced her in a chokehold and held her down under waves of despair last night vanished as she faced the front door.

The majestic oak trees that provided shade and trysting spots for young lovers gave the dorm's façade collegiate charm. Her lips twisted as she recalled the college pamphlet. Yep, that sucker had all the marks of a Photoshop expert. Of course, at the time, she didn't care about the campus's appearance. All she knew was that she wanted out of the battleground her home had become and a full scholarship was the ticket.

A few students stood in the tree shadows. No Cam anywhere near the building. A quick tap brought her phone back to life and allowed her to reread Cam's message. If he was waiting, where was he? A breeze ruffled the dress around her ankles, cooling the damp sections that stuck to her body. Absentmindedly, she pulled the dress away as her eyes scanned the area. Two short toots of a car horn caught her attention.

The sound came from the side parking lot almost empty except for a handful of cars. Usually, parking space rated up there with premium concert tickets during midweek. The weekends were different since most students did their best to get away even if it meant visiting another college or driving home. Most managed to entertain themselves with the limited attractions of movies, restaurants and glow golf. A few used the weekends to run those former mom errands of laundry and grocery shopping.

The lack of cars made it easy to spot Cam's familiar red car. It looked more like a garish Easter egg to her, but he insisted it was an Italian sports car, an ancient one. Her hand went up in greeting as she hurried to meet him. Instead of getting out and greeting her, he stayed in the car. As she drew closer, she noticed he sported sunglasses.

It was almost as if he was hiding, and the sunglasses were part of his disguise. Stella squashed the suspicious thought as she hurried toward the car. It was a sunny day, which meant anyone would wear sunglasses. Yeah, that was it.

CHAPTER SIX

"**G**OOD, YOU'RE HERE." Cam glanced in his rear-view mirror before reversing. Stella kept quiet, busy fastening her seat belt. It clicked in place about the same time Cam floored it. The small car had lurched before the power kicked in, hurtling it down the narrow road. They careened onto the main road causing another car to swerve out of their way. Stella closed her eyes, sure of impending death. A honk, muttered curses, and Cam laughing assured her she lived instead of waiting a soul assignment in Summerland. Somehow, she forgot Cam's driving habits since her trips in his car were rare. *Wouldn't want people to see the two of them together.* Stella shook her head trying to rid it of the annoying inner voice. Why did her conscience develop such a cynical attitude?

"I heard that." Cam's head swung in her direction. The dark lenses hid his eyes, but his lips pressed together in a firm line. "How many times do I have to tell you this is a high-performance engine? I must rev it up occasionally. Can't drive around like your eighty-year-old grandmother."

Instead of pointing out, she didn't have a grandmother; she watched the scenery fly by. Strange, he never remembered. She'd mentioned it more than once. Her mother's parents died in a bizarre safari accident. Her father lost contact with his parents, which left her with no grandparents to fuss over her.

Groups of students in school T-shirts and colored face paint stood near the bus stop. There must be a game. The light changed, forcing Cam to slam on the brakes, propelling Stella forward until the seat belt locked, throwing her back into the seat.

The stop allowed her more outside world observation. A couple holding hands strolled in the direction of the bus stop. The tall, slender male angled his head toward the girl. His nod and subsequent smile were indicative of his attentiveness to his date. The girl tiptoed to kiss his cheek. The spontaneous display made her envious. Why couldn't she and Cam be more like that?

Lunch out was a start. In the end, she wasn't the type of female who inspired whole-hearted affection. Goddess knows her mother wasn't one either. The stiffness of her parents' relationship hadn't been evident until she started hanging out with Leah. At first, Leah didn't invite her over, preferring to meet her at other places. It made Stella think that her parents were even worse than hers were. The natural affection between Leah's parents, Adam, and Maura, surprised her since she believed married people stopped touching around the age of thirty or whenever they had kids.

The last thing she wanted to be was forty plus years old throwing things at her husband's car as he drove out of her life. Her eyes cut to Cam without thought. The smirk gracing his face wasn't for her. A more charitable person would call it a smile. It wasn't.

The way he drove with his shoulders back and his smug expression demonstrated he'd taken in his current surroundings and found no one nearby that he considered in his league. A tidbit of information from psychology class about people accepting or rejecting people in five seconds popped in her head. Something about a casual glance decided if a person was helpful, dangerous, or not necessary. At some point, Cam decided she was helpful.

Yeah, helpful, it wasn't what she wanted. She didn't expect some awe-inspiring love where a man would travel to the ends of the Earth to rescue her, but something a little better than being helpful. In some ways, she was little more than a maid service with side benefits. Still, he was taking her out.

The car picked up speed as they left the congested campus area. Stella studied the strip malls, churches, and an assortment of neighborhoods. Not having a car kept her close to the school. The scarlet and golden tree leaves hinted at a season change despite summer heat lingering past its time. The buildings became less and less as browning cornfields dominated the scenery, out of the city and its associated chain restaurants.

"Where are we going?"

Cam kept silent for a few heartbeats. For the tiniest moment, a scenario rolled out where he dumped her dead body in a ditch. Fear ran down her arm raising the hairs in the process. *Stop being stupid. He has no reason to kill me. Haven't witnessed a crime. Have nothing worth taking. In this case, I'm one of those people whose worth more alive than dead.* The sudden crime scene images faded with his reply.

"There's a diner this way I thought would appeal to you since it's small town and all."

Small town? She'd never mentioned being from a small town, a city, not an overly large city, but not a small town, either. He was confusing her with someone else, not a flattering thought.

"Oh." Not the best response, but considering everything swirling around in her brain, it had to be the safest.

A few left-hand turns onto narrow roads with almost no traffic demonstrated Cam knew the way. He may have known it because he'd been there before. An abandoned double-wide with a rusted truck chassis resting on cinder blocks marked the turn. Who lived there once? Better yet, why did they leave? The obvious answer would be better prospects somewhere else, rather like her father. Maybe the air inside the doublewide bore the taint of contempt and disappointment too, although, right now, it probably smelled of mold, mildew, and decay.

Why do people promise to love one another and then leave, after doing unspeakable damage? Of course, there may have never been any love between her parents, just a small flare of attraction mistaken for the real thing. How did a person know when they were in love? All she had to do was stand still for five seconds in the dorm lobby and she'd hear a girl announce her love for a current boyfriend. If she stood a few seconds longer, another girl would publicly plot revenge against someone she used to love. As words went, love got passed around more than a bottle of Jack. Women who barely tolerated one another kissed the air near each other while trilling their affection, waiting for the other to leave before ridiculing her.

Trust was a much harder word to earn. Few people believed in one another. Her eyes cut to Cam. Nope, she didn't trust him. Wished she could, but so far had no real reason to. If she could trust him, then maybe she could love him, but to do any of that she'd have to get to know him. It hadn't happened yet. The fact she never knew about his journeys to the country for small town dining epitomized how little he shared.

A small diner with a neon sign with a burnout N announced it *DI ER*, which sounded rather unappetizing. Underneath the neon, a narrow strip of plywood declared *Good Eats Inside* in sloppy blue painted letters. An older pickup truck and a dated sedan covered with religious bumper stickers sat in front. Cam drove across the pitted, gravel parking lot slowly and parked alongside the truck.

"We're here." He grinned at her, like announcing a glorious event.

Now, she didn't expect white tablecloths and tuxedoed waiters, but something more than this. Road Kill Café might serve as an alternate name or the 50/50 diner because you had a fifty percent chance of getting food poisoning. Stella had sat in the car for a second, before she noticed Cam standing in front of the car. Oh yeah, she needed to get out. If Cam liked the restaurant so much, it must be good. Her forced smile stretched her lips upward, but no joy inhabited it.

The hum of insects greeted her as she opened the car door. Black flies swirled in some abstract landing pattern before swooping down into the bed of the truck. Curiosity pulled her feet closer to the truck bed. Inside lay a buck with molting antlers. Congealed blood covered the area around the bullet hole hosting dozens of flies. The glassy, dead eyes stared at her, importuning her, asking her why.

A small shriek and a jump backward served as her only response to the unvoiced question. Cam laughed at her, making her wonder if he parked by the truck deliberately. Perhaps, he'd already seen the deer inside. Her excitement about their date had fizzled when she realized they weren't eating in town. Died a little more when she saw where they were, and she wasn't too sure if any enthusiasm survived.

"C'mon, let's go. I'm hungry." Cam gestured to the diner, probably hoping to hurry her.

Her feet moved, but she'd left her appetite back in the truck with the deer. Once she reached Cam, he draped an arm around her shoulders, which improved her mood somewhat. His hand cupped her shoulder and brought her in for a squeeze. "You're my girl, right?"

The words both cheered and puzzled her. Sure, last night, she had doubts if she wanted to be Cam's girl, especially if he wanted her to do things that went against her personal code of ethics. Today, though, after hearing those girls doubt that Cam could be interested in her. She wanted to be his girl, but a keen desire to parade him in front of the doubting Thomasinas didn't qualify as a reason for a relationship.

He squeezed her against his side, his fingers pressing down on her upper arm. "I didn't hear your answer."

It hurt. She'd probably have finger-shaped bruises tomorrow. "Yeah, I am," she muttered the words while working her shoulder trying to shake off his grip. He relaxed his hand, allowing it to ride lightly against her upper arm. It must have been a mistake. Forgot his own strength, that's all.

A cowbell clanged as the door opened. A tired, middle-aged woman attired in a garish orange smock paused in her discussion with the two camouflage-garbed hunters. "Hey, be with you in a minute."

Half dozen booths comprised the seating. Cam chose one closest to the jukebox. The waitress bustled to their booth as soon as they sat, placing paper napkin wrapped utensils along with paper mat menus on the table.

The woman cracked her gum, before grinning at Cam. "Haven't seen you in a while, last time you were with that cute little…" She stuttered to a stop and glanced at Stella, before finishing. "…cousin."

Yeah, cousin. Stella wasn't buying. Apparently, she wasn't the only girl he'd driven to the isolated diner. It made her wonder how long a while was. It could be two months, two weeks, or even two days if—she glanced at the server's nametag—if Doreen was teasing. Not feeling any special-ness. Wasn't being someone's girl supposed to feel different?

Cam settled for the Hungry Man platter. The bacon double cheese-burger with fixing's, French fries, onion rings, and hush puppies should not only fill him up but also give him indigestion. Her salad order received a censorious look from Doreen. Stella's desire to eat any meat had died when she spotted the buck. The grim line of the server's lips announced her oddity by not ordering something fried. No way could she explain how the deer's eyes made her reconsider her eating habits, at least for a day.

Order tucked into the pocket of her bright smock, the woman started the burger on the grill. Apparently, the place was a one-woman operation. It explained why she remembered Cam. Didn't look like the place merited too many customers.

Cam reached across the table, grabbing her hand that rested on the paper menu. "I know it doesn't look like much, but the food is good. It can be our place."

Yay.

He flashed his usual grin, before releasing her hand and sliding across the vinyl bench seat. She thought he might be moving to her side, which would be somewhat romantic. He stood and headed for the jukebox. He dropped in change and punched a selection before turning back to her. "It only seems right that we have our own song."

A bell when off somewhere in her heart, but that could have been the fries alarm, too. The man was trying. The rich, mellow sounds of The Temptations singing *My Girl* filled the diner, causing the two hunters to glance back at them.

One chuckled, while the other commented, "Yeah, I used to be an operator like that. Had all the girls swooning."

Cam held out his hand to her. He wanted to dance, right here in public, in the tiny area running in front of the booths. Okay. She put her hand in his and stood. He placed one hand on her waist and held her hand as they slowly box stepped around the room. She sighed a little, as he brought her closer. Close enough for her to rest her head on his shoulder.

When other girls were picking out prom dresses, her family disintegrated in full view of the neighbors. No time for romantic moments, especially with her entire attention focused on getting scholarship-worthy grades. Even though they were dancing cheek to cheek in the middle of nowhere, it still reigned as one of her best dances. A faster song came on, sending them both back to the table.

Cam shrugged as he sat. "Jukebox is some relic from the sixties. All they have are ancient songs."

Did that mean *My Girl* wasn't their song? It could mean that was the closest he'd come to expressing his feelings, and then again, he'd probably never heard it before. Most people didn't have a mother like hers. Before her religious conversion, her mother played the oldies station aloud and sang along energetically. In retrospect, her singing reflected the state of the marriage. Whenever her parents fought, her mother's singing lacked energy, or she'd only sing the angry girl songs. Near the end, she'd quit singing altogether. Occasionally, she'd whispered the lyrics to a melancholy song. Stella knew something was wrong then, but pretending she didn't was easier.

Doreen arrived with their food, placing a large steaming platter in front of Cam. The grease glistened under the fluorescent light turning Stella's stomach a little. The plastic bowl the server shoved in front of her barely merited the name salad. Strips of American cheese covered the wilted lettuce, without another vegetable in sight. As an afterthought, Doreen placed a bottle of ranch dressing on the table, not asking what she wanted. Ranch might have been all they had since it didn't look like the type of place to attract healthy eaters.

Cam bit into his cheeseburger with enthusiasm. Picking up her fork, she stabbed at her food, forcing herself to swallow the slimy cheese and overly salty meat. The appeal of the place must be the absolute assurance you'd never run into anyone you knew. The location would suit drug dealers, as well as men who were into secret dating. Then again, Doreen would remember whoever came in.

Between the burger and fries, Cam hesitated long enough to speak. "Did you think about what we talked about?"

"What did we talk about?" Her fork loaded with week old lettuce hesitated on its way to her mouth. Sure, she thought about it. Hoped he'd forget the whole idea.

Another record dropped in the machine. The Supremes crooned about *Baby, Where Did Our Love Go*. She had to wonder if Cam picked the songs in any order. If not, then Fate must have taken a hand in the serendipitous placement. Her expectations of today being an incredibly romantic day showed what a gullible fool she could be.

"You know." He gestured with a fry. "The grade changing to keep my scholarship. Got some friends that need grade changing too. Six of them."

Her fork dropped from her hand, pinging against the table and drawing an annoyed glance from Doreen.

"Something wrong with your salad?" The server snarled the words daring her to complain.

"No nothing," Stella squeaked, causing the hunters to chuckle.

"Yeah, that one has no backbone," Doreen told the hunters loud enough for Stella to hear. "Not like the redhead."

Part of her tried to track the conversation while the rest of her wrestled with the scope of the outrageous suggestion. She picked up her fork stalling. "Six friends, really?"

"They're on scholarships too." Cam explained as he bit into an over-sized onion ring.

Yeah, and they probably partied hard never considering the consequences. "I don't think it can be done. One person, maybe, but Financial Aid makes quarterly checks. You can't have a D, and then finish with an A."

Cam stopped eating; his eyes rolled upward. He rubbed the bridge of his nose with his index finger. "Don't give me an A, but something high enough that it averages out to a 2.5. That's all I need to keep my scholarship."

"Why should I do this?" Never mind that she did not intend to do so.

The music changed again to *Eleanor Rigby*, a Beatles tune about a lonely woman no one cared about, especially poignant lyrics. Could it be her life story?

"Looks to me like you're getting really chummy with Mitch. Did you know he has a DUI?"

Mitch defined straight arrow.

"I can tell by that look on your face you don't believe me. Go ask him. Back in the summer, in Michigan. Apparently, the awards board doesn't know, or he wouldn't have received a scholarship."

Her heart sank as the Beatles sang about all the lonely people. It gave her a sudden desire to kick the machine. The worn record caught, repeating, "Nobody came." What little she knew of Mitch's life, he probably thought nobody cared, especially with a father who checked out by dying and a mother who blamed him for the death.

This must be how a cornered rat feels. Sure, she could call Cam's bluff. The jerk made it up. An emotional push into the direction he wanted her to go. She shoved the salad bowl away from her, unable to stand looking at it for one more second. Cam's smug face made her doubt Mitch's innocence. Strange, it hadn't popped up yet. A misspelled name or a wrong number on a social could bury a file. It also might explain why Mitch worked so hard at the work-study job and classes. He had to get as much done in as little time as possible.

Doreen interrupted the silence. "Oh lookee, you gobbled down that hungry man platter. I do love a man with an appetite." She giggled girlishly. "Maybe a piece of pie might fill the hole you got."

The woman leaned over the table exposing her generous cleavage as she picked up the platter. Stella stood abruptly. "Excuse me." She headed for the door marked restrooms. The woman could crawl all over Cam as far as she cared.

Raw plywood created a makeshift stall around a cracked seat toilet. A chipped mirror reflected her shocked expression. Oh yeah, no surprise there. She thought today would be super romantic. Instead, she ended up holding a friend's future in her hands. She could save Mitch's life if she forfeited her own aspirations. Then again, maybe, she could get away with it. Leah would know what to do. She typed in Leah's number into her cell and then held it up to her ear.

No ringing. A glance confirmed what she suspected, no bars. Of course, there wouldn't be anything as practical as cell service in the middle of nowhere. Goddess, she had to get out of here. Placing the phone back in her purse, she rested her hands on the sink. What was she going to do?

A twist of the faucet sent water spilling into the bowl after an initial protest from the pipes, sounding like no one had made use of the bathroom in quite a while. If they did, they hadn't used the sink. Disgusting. The water flowed clear and cold after a few seconds of rust. Good. A few splashes helped combat nausea that the questionable salad and suspicious request had on her. Mascara pooled around her eyes, running in rivulets down her cheeks. Yeah, she looked the way she felt.

It didn't matter anymore how she looked for Cam, but she wouldn't give Doreen another ridicule opportunity. A damp paper towel removed most of her makeup. Inhaling deeply, she considered what she knew, which wasn't much. No decisions should rest on so little information. The reflected, slightly damp, female stared back waiting for an answer, a solution. "I need to get back."

Chin up, shoulders back, she marched out of the restroom only to find Cam talking to Doreen as he shoveled down apple pie. Doreen perched one hip on the wall separating the booth from the work area. She leaned forward, which put her almost on the table. Stella snorted, earning an irritated glance from the woman. Half-drunk sorority girls showed more restraint and class.

"We need to go," she announced as she reached the table.

Doreen cooed in an unnaturally high voice. "Did you hear that? She's giving orders like she's the boss of you."

Great. She didn't need this. Stella eyed the diner interior. The hunters had left, leaving no one to distract Little Mary Sunshine from what used to be her boyfriend. Now, Stella wasn't too sure, what he was. The man continued to eat, anticipating a catfight over him, no doubt. "I'll wait outside to give the two of you some privacy."

Her eyes stayed fixed on the car outside the glass window. Don't look back, even though her heart shattered a tiny bit with each step across the discolored linoleum floor. Outside, she leaned against the car. To get her mind off the present, she read the various bumper stickers on the nearby car. *Jesus Loves You, but I don't. God, Guns, and Glory make America Great.* Those were the less provocative ones. Many told people what they could do with themselves, their politics, and to get back over the border. Had to be Doreen's car.

Eventually, Cam came out, complaining as he walked toward her. "You didn't have to go and be so nasty."

She waited for the fob beep before wrenching the door open. Once she snapped the seatbelt in place, she felt a little more confident that she'd make it back to the college alive. Cam didn't act anything like the person she thought she knew. Mitch had hinted that Cam's appeal consisted of charm and good looks. Initially, she resisted such inferences. Didn't want to acknowledge what it would say about her. The grumpy Cam climbing into the car was very likely to leave her in the middle of nowhere. Stella would be wandering around in strappy sandals and a maxi dress in the land of chiggers, coyotes, and snakes. An involuntary shudder shook her.

"Are you cold?" Cam turned and looked at her, before reversing the car. "Looks like you've been crying. No need to, I have no interest in Doreen. Old ugly broad like her could use some charming now and then. I consider it my gift."

Seriously, he thought she was jealous. Even believed she ran to the bathroom for a cry session, incredible. He had more in common with a hollow chocolate bunny than an actual living person. For a smart girl, she'd made a major misstep. Hopefully, it wasn't anything she couldn't correct.

"Quiet, that's a change." Cam turned on the radio but only got static. He punched the CD player button, which filled the car with what Stella referred to as angry rock. A favorite among males, and the occasional female, who felt the world owed them something, but failed to pay up. His taste in music should have served as a hint, but she chose to ignore it, along with dozens of other clues.

They drove back in silence with the soundtrack of screamed lyrics concerning rage, hate, and retribution like Doreen's bumper stickers. The two of them would make a great couple. Every couple of miles, he tried to get her to talk. The first time he'd ever wanted her to talk.

The atmosphere in the car weighed heavy, making breathing difficult. It wasn't the air, but more the smugness, the certainty that wafted off Cam. He knew he had her trapped. The thought brought up the half-digested salad into her throat. She gulped the bitter reminder back down. Each moment with him was the equivalent of being stuck with a large hypodermic needle. The storefronts grew familiar as they worked their way through town. Ten blocks from campus, Cam stopped for a red light. She unsnapped her seatbelt, opened the door, yanked her dress to her knees, and jumped out.

"What the hell are you doing?"

She kept walking, not bothering to look back. Traffic tended to be heavy this time of day. Cam would idle through more than one red light. His impatience at having to wait tilted her lips up.

No time like the present to work out issues. If her day went on in the same fashion, Cam would be waiting at her dorm. With that in mind, she veered to her right into a strip mall. The clear glass windows of a Laundromat served as her closest sanctuary. Inside the humid building, she collapsed into a hard-plastic chair before calling Leah. Her friend could give her advice about the situation. The phone rang three times before she received a message about the number being out of order. Strange. Her finger hesitated over the three before she tapped it again. Leah was three on her speed dial. She used to be two, but she moved her down when she typed in Cam's number. Should have kept her at two.

Same message. Weird, it made no sense. She'd had the number for three years. Could be there was a phone foul up and would be working in a couple of hours. Mitch would be her next resort. His number was already ringing before she could think of an excuse. She couldn't just ask him if he ever had a DUI. It would sound like she trusted Cam more than she did him.

CHAPTER SEVEN

"**H**ELLO, STELLA. GLAD you called."
Relief and enthusiasm colored Mitch's voice at the same time, making her feel even more the Judas. "Yeah, um, I was wondering if we could talk."

His up tone flat-lined. "Never a good sign. Where are you at?"

Stella glanced at the window, reading the backward lettering. "Henrietta's Wash Tub. It's in the strip mall close to Bacon Street. Do you know where it is?"

"Yeah, I've done my laundry there before. I can be there in ten minutes. Okay?"

"No problem. You don't have to rush." She had no clue what he might be doing. He could be hanging with friends, but more likely studying. Even still, the man would willingly charge to her side, no questions asked. Guilt settled on her along with the damp, fabric-sheet scented air. A girl wearing a college T-shirt folded her laundry out of the dryer. Two small children raced around the row of washers, shrieking despite their mother's entreaties to "settle down." When Mitch came, they'd talk outside without the rumble of dryers or unintended eavesdroppers.

How did one approach this type of thing? Was a DUI considered a criminal record? She didn't know. Specific language in her scholarship forbade any drug or alcohol abuse along with directives that if she did, her scholarship would be revoked.

Mitch came through the door, windblown and breathless as if he'd run the entire way. His dark-rimmed glasses were missing, which gave him a more casual, appealing look. The co-ed folding laundry stopped long enough to smile at him. He didn't even glance at her; headed in Stella's direction.

"Your glasses?" She gestured to the bridge of her nose.

He pulled them out of his pocket and placed them on. "I didn't want them to fall off while I ran."

"Don't you need them to see where you are going?" She tried to imagine Mitch running blindly down the surrounding streets.

"No, just close-up really. That's why I wear them when I'm in the computer lab."

Another thing she didn't know about him. Computer lab and class were the only places she saw him. "Let's walk." She headed in the direction of the doors, glancing over her shoulder to make sure he followed.

Mitch caught up in two long-legged strides and cupped her elbow. "Sure, you want to walk in those shoes?" He angled his head at her feet.

"I'm good. As long as you don't walk too fast." The straps on her shoes rubbed against her ankle while her small toe, kept slipping through the toe straps. It stood out like some mutant growth. "I think I'll take them off. It's still warm enough."

Mitch wrapped an arm around her waist as she balanced on one foot and removed her shoes. Once her shoes were off, he dropped his arm, leaving her feeling a bit bereft, but she couldn't ask him to put his arm back, especially when she had to ask personal questions.

"You look very nice for hanging out in a Laundromat."

"Yeah, about that. I got all dressed up because I thought Cam was taking me out on an actual date. Turns out, he was just mad because some of the students were teasing him about seeing you and me together. He drove me way out in the country to a nasty diner that should be in a horror movie."

A menacing growl came from Mitch, but it didn't alarm her. She knew how he felt about Cam. She'd never given his opinion the weight it deserved.

"You know why he drove you to the country, don't you?"

"Because he's a jerk." The memory of her momentary panic at possible abandonment returned.

A satisfied chuckle answered her response. Happiness flashed in his eyes, crinkling them up at the corners. He cleared his throat. "You're right. He's a jerk in several ways. He chose the out of the way place to minimize anyone thinking you're dating."

She suspected as much, especially after Doreen's comment. There was nothing likable about the place to make someone return. The fact Doreen knew him, meant it was his usual take the naïve chick out on a date hole in the wall location. He probably used the same story about getting back to the date's small-town roots. It might have worked a time or two when the girl was from a small town. "Yeah, you're right."

Mitch stopped walking. Stella halted too. He held his hands over his heart while his mouth dropped open. His clownish behavior lightened her mood.

"Stop overacting. You were right all along. Are you happy now?"

Mitch smiled, reached for her hand. "I guess it would be wrong of me to admit that I'm very pleased. Rather petty, small-minded, and all that, but, on the other hand, I don't want to see you unhappy."

"Yeah." Her heavy sigh served as an exclamation point.

"Hey, I'm sorry. I knew you cared about him, but you're better off without him."

His fingers still held onto hers, feeling like a lifeline in a way, but he'd distance himself as soon as she dropped the bomb. Might as well do it now and quit prolonging their false intimacy. "Cam had a lot to say about you."

"The man seems to be obsessed with me. I am no competition for him." Mitch shook his head looking like he couldn't comprehend his rival's actions.

Be brave, spit it out, it will only hurt once, similar to ripping a Band-Aid off. "Cam seems to think you got a DUI in Michigan over the summer."

He dropped her hand just as she suspected he would. His eyes narrowed the same time his hands balled into fists at his side. "Damn it. I thought I got past that."

Well, talk about a revelation. No one appeared to be whom she thought he was. "Do you want to explain? This could ruin your scholarship."

His lifted eyebrows acknowledged the obviousness of her statement. "I know. It was a stupid thing to do. It was two years ago, not one. Illinois, not Michigan. I was underage too."

"Whoa, that's bad." Her hand covered her mouth before she made any more stupid remarks.

"Yeah." He shoved his hands in his pockets and walked looking down at the ground. "Every month that goes by and I'm that much closer to graduating, I think it won't catch up with me. How did Cam find out?"

Stella shrugged her shoulders. "He didn't say."

Large trees shaded the sidewalk the closer they came to campus. The root system buckled the sidewalk tripping the less alert walker. They both kept their eyes trained on the ground. Stella more to save her toes, but Mitch probably because he saw his future slipping away.

"I was at my cousin's wedding, my favorite cousin, Annalise. She always treated me like a brother she liked, as opposed to the ones she had."

"Go on," she urged. Mitch had never spoken of his cousin.

"It was a big deal wedding. All the stops pulled out. Even had an open bar and a champagne fountain."

No secret how the story would turn out, but there were missing pieces. "You aren't a drinker. When everyone is partying hard, you're at the computer lab working."

"True."

He looked up at her. The misery in his eyes touched her, froze her and caused her to despise Cam more than she ever hated any human being. Mitch continued talking, pulling her from her self-loathing mode.

"I thought I was a big deal too. Annalise asked me to be a groomsman. I thought I looked like a player in my black tux." He laughed. "Make that better than usual. I even had a date, a girl I'd started seeing. We'd been out a few times, and I thought it might be serious, especially since she accompanied me to the wedding."

Weddings, unrealistic expectation, and free alcohol, yep not a good combination. "What happened?" she prompted when he looked reflective.

"Yeah, that." He cleared his throat again. "Trina must have heard that weddings were a great place to pick up guys because she left with a different one."

A swell of anger at the unknown girl's perfidy resulted in her stomping her foot. "Ow!" Not the best idea when barefooted.

Mitch immediately bent to examine her foot. "It's not bleeding." His thumb tenderly brushed the leave debris from her foot. "Wiggle it." Her toes all flexed, as did her foot. "Not broken."

Passing students threw them speculative glances. "Get up, please." By the time, she reached her dorm there would be gossip that Mitch proposed to her. Not something, she wanted Cam to hear. It might force him to his next step, which wouldn't be good.

"You got drunk because she left you?"

"My intention wasn't to get drunk, but in the end, I guess I did. My mother had left the reception with her sister. I was supposed to help break everything down. What I ended up doing was climbing into my cousin's car, when I shouldn't have. I promised to drive it back to her house since she left in the limo."

Stella stole a glance at him. With his shoulders slumped forward, hands in pockets, his chin down, he could have modeled for dejection.

"It's weird the DUI never came out. How long do those things stick on your record?"

"Depends on the state. Usually eight years, sometimes twenty. A deputy who attended the wedding pulled me over. He recognized me. I think I babbled about my date dumping me. Didn't matter, though. I blew over the legal limit. My mother came and picked me up, which was another disappointment in her life. The next morning, we picked up the car and drove it to my cousin's house making up some excuse about it being too late the night before. My mother didn't want anyone to know what happened. I figured it would come out then, but never heard anything. Maybe being in a different state had something to do with it. I thought it was behind me. After that, I was super straight, no alcohol, no partying, no weed, nothing."

No partying? Her brows knitted together. "I never took you for an off the chain type."

A rueful smile greeted her remark. "Yeah, with good reason. Bad results. I couldn't afford anything else. The earlier charge resurrected like a zombie. Still, it puzzles me how Cam Winters would know."

The hum of the riding lawn mower in the distance explained the scent of fresh cut grass. Walnuts littered the sidewalk. Some of the nuts sported a solid green covering, while the majority had black splotches rather like Cam's soul if he had one. Stella's foot intentionally connected with one before, she remembered her bare toes. Sucking her lips in, she kept silent. Complaining about doing a stupid thing would only make her sound like a diva.

Mitch looked at her reddened toes and merely raised an eyebrow. Of course, he had enough on his mind and probably hated her a little right now. Association with her brought him into Cam's manipulative sphere of power, never a good place to be. Her nose crinkled as she remembered her breathless reaction to her initial spotting of the narcissistic man.

Student Life Agency hosted a mixer for the incoming freshmen complete with an inflatable obstacle course and free pizza. Most of the freshmen males showed for the pizza while the upperclassmen concentrated on rating the incoming females. The long shadow of a tree had hidden Stella as she watched Cam work his magic. A ray of sun broke through the clouds serving as a celestial spotlight. At the time, she giggled, thinking even the sun wanted to touch him. Luckily, he hadn't seen her reaction.

Meeting two weeks later, didn't smarten her up. It only made Cam more inaccessible. He'd already burned through all the available hot girls, not even stopping long enough to catch his breath. No wonder she blew him off initially, unable to believe someone like him would be interested in her. Now it seemed his interest came from her work-study position as opposed to her personality. "Do you think Cam went out with me because of my job?"

Mitch lurched, trying to disguise a stumble and eventually stopped. "Are you kidding me?" Both eyebrows rose with his inquiry. "First, you're hot." He held up his index finger. Before continuing, he coughed into his closed fist. "I mean I noticed your personality, your intelligence, your work ethic, but someone like Cam would notice—"

Her friend's politically correct retraction caused her to grin. "Yeah, yeah, I know what you mean. I never knew you thought of me that way." She used her right hand as a fan pretending to be overwhelmed by the notion.

His shoulders went up in a Gallic shrug before turning away. "What good would it have done? I considered myself content in the friend zone."

Students talking loudly about an upcoming concert approached in mass, forcing the two of them off the sidewalk.

"Who knew it was rush hour?" Stella quipped as she walked across the grass. Mitch had liked her, all along. She never knew, while she wasted her time on someone who was only grooming her for future opportunities. Now, thanks to her bad judgment, either she or Mitch would lose their scholarship. She couldn't afford to lose hers, but neither could Mitch.

"I was wondering," Stella started, unsure how to phrase her question. Her hand tucked a lock of hair behind her ear, a tell, Leah would have recognized it immediately. "You've been here longer than I have."

"True." His bent finger pushed up his slipping glasses. He angled his head to the right. "Almost to your dorm."

The aging building indicated she only had a few minutes left. Off to the right, in the side parking lot, a bright spot of red signaled Cam waited. *Oh, joy.* With any luck, she'd escape into the dorm without attracting his notice. Stella darted to Mitch's right side using his silhouette as her safety shield. "Um, you've been here probably as long as Cam has, right?"

"Possibly. I can't say I had that much interest in him. Why do you ask?" Their footsteps mutually slowed as they neared the front door. A female student cradling a clothes basket piled high with clothes gave them a cursory look.

Stella flashed a smile at her, not knowing her name. Instead of responding, the girl rested the basket on one hip as her free hand searched for her ringing cell phone. Glancing back over her shoulder, she measured the girl's progress as she talked. When she thought she was far enough away not to eavesdrop, she asked, "What kind of scholarship is Cam on?"

"What?" Mitch shouted the word and stopped. Stella realizing her Mitch-shaped shield was gone, hurried back to stay in his concealing shadow.

"Lower your voice. I don't want everyone to know." She hissed the words. "Sorry, I don't mean to sound harsh." Conflicting urges to both hide and peek, kept her rooted by Mitch's side, angling just backward enough to glimpse Cam resting against his car with his arms folded and his mouth twisted to one side. She knew the pose, his irritated one. His sunglasses might hide his eyes, but not his body language. A blonde attired only in short shorts and a glorified pushup bra that masqueraded as a top sashayed toward him with enough hip action to merit a future chiropractor visit. Ah Lily, from the third floor, hard not to recognize her. For once, the idea of him flirting with another girl didn't upset her. It gave her the distraction she needed.

"Okay, I asked," she leaned up on her toes, lowering her voice, "if Cam was on any scholarship?"

"Yeah, that's what I thought. Don't see how? An academic scholarship would involve showing up at class. We both know he doesn't do that. If he can't keep up his grades, then a sports scholarship is nil too. Why do you ask?" He pulled off his glasses to polish them on his shirt.

"Cam told me he was going to lose his scholarship because of his grades." The rushed statement sounded ridiculous when she said it. Why did she believe him?

"Hmm," Mitch lengthened the sound, perhaps stalling. "You believed him. Was he trying to work the heartstrings? Maybe you were mad at him?" The corners of his lips tipped up with the inquiry.

"Past mad. He was being a jerk and told me his life would be ruined if his grades didn't miraculously improve," She spat out the words with distaste, realizing how easy he manipulated her emotions. He had her going along with her concern for Mitch.

"What does he expect you to do? Help him with his homework or what?"

Her shoulders went up in *I dunno* shrug. No reason to tell Mitch and have him worry, too. He probably would insist on confessing to DUI. The type of noble, selfless action, she realized Mitch was capable of and Cam wasn't.

"What little I heard from my roommate, who had the bad luck to be Cam's roommate once, is that he comes from money. Already flunked out of one school. With a history like that, not sure why he's trying to pass himself as a scholarship boy. I'm surprised he's lasted as long as he has."

As much as she didn't want it to be true, she realized Mitch's portrait of Cam bore more resemblance to the actual male than her romantic one did. Even when she blessed him with good motives, he was still a selfish man who expected her to help him shop and do laundry. He probably had a harem of other girls doing his academic work. The fact he wasn't passing explained his need to get her to change his grades. They'd been together a couple of months, which made her wonder if she were a backup plan or the original plan all along.

Mitch's hand landed on her shoulder. Her focus moved up to the concern in his eyes.

"Stella, you'd tell me if you were in trouble. If Cam was forcing you to do something you didn't want to."

His words hit so close to home; she had to look away, aware her poker face was nonexistent. "Yeah, yeah, I would." Resting one hand on his arm, she leaned to his left for another peek. Lily's back blocked most of her view of Cam, but the fact Lily and the car remained meant Cam had to be there too. A couple inches of blonde hair showed above Lily's head.

"I need to go now." Rocking to her toes, Stella planted an impulsive kiss on Mitch's cheek. "You're a good friend."

Her fear turbo-boosted her feet, shooting her to the entrance. It didn't stop her from hearing the muttered words. "I wish I knew what was going on."

No, you wouldn't want to know. Her hand pushed open the stairwell door. Adrenalin coursed through her body pushing her up the stairs at a speed any other time would have astounded her. Her fingers pushed into her side trying to push out the muscle spasm. Her hard, raspy breathing echoed in the narrowed stairwell sounding a bit like a B horror movie. The metal banister grew moist under her sweaty hands. A large three loomed on the door ahead of her. Almost there.

A few more steps and she'd be in her room. Sanctuary. Well, of a sort, if her roommate wasn't there. The thought had her sliding down the wall, landing on the cold concrete step. That sucked. Was there no safe place for her?

Sighing deeply, she leaned back against the wall, the railing pushing her head out at an uncomfortable angle. She couldn't stay long in this position. In just a couple of minutes, after she mentally prepped, she'd go. Her roommate would either ignore her as usual or hit her with a barrage of nosey questions. Personally, her regular antisocial behavior would work in Stella's favor.

Her fingers tangled in the full skirt of her sundress she'd donned with high hopes earlier. She'd hoped the malicious skanks would see her with Cam, proving they were an item. Now, Cam disappearing from her life would solve a multitude of problems and improve her mental health in one fell swoop.

Why she ever fell for him puzzled her. Her hand gripped the banister as she pulled herself upright. Leah would listen to her and help her sort things out. After what her best friend had gone through, Cam's machinations would seem like child's play. Falling through time and battling a scorned lover determined to kill her and several others made Stella's situation just college drama.

Leah would help. Maybe she could get Leah's Nana to read her cards via the phone too. If she could get the entire Carpenter family behind her, then Cam's crazy idea wouldn't happen. The thought calmed her racing heart. It would all work out. She wasn't sure how yet, but it would. Stella took a deep breath, mentally calming herself. When did she talk to her friend last?

A cursory check of the hallway revealed a couple girls walking away from her, giving her a clean shot to her room without talking to anyone. Good. Burnt popcorn stink filled the hallway, crinkling her nose. When she first started school, she called Leah almost every other day. Even though Leah sounded happy whenever she answered, an awkwardness existed between the two of them.

Could be she interrupted her and Dylan? All she did was whine about college while Leah remained upbeat about her experiences. Leah stayed home and went to community college. Not much had changed in her life. No lame roommates or conniving men who pretended to be her boyfriend. After a while, they didn't talk as much. A couple of times, Leah called when she was with Cam. She hadn't answered, of course.

Her room door swung open, revealing her roommate in the process of leaving. "See you're finally up. You were pixelated last night and never even heard me come into the room."

Stella chose not to correct the assumption certain it would prolong her roommate's departure. "Yeah."

Stepping into the hall, her roommate made space for her to enter the room. Stella had her hand on the door to close it when her roommate spoke.

"The odd couple came by Joe Christian and Wanda Witch wanted me to tell you her cell number changed. She wrote it on the whiteboard."

Stella's roommate had tacked on the unflattering nicknames the first time Dylan and Leah visited. Their insistence on oversized emblems of their faith made it hard not to make wise cracks. Leah now sported a pentacle large enough to set off a metal detector, ironic considering she'd ridiculed the Jesus squad in high school for all their crosses. Then again, her boyfriend was part of the group. In their way, it could be a visual message that faiths could co-exist. Whatever it was, it made people remember them.

The white board near her bed served as her daily to-do list. It also tracked assignments and upcoming tests. Leah's strong emphatic writing brought a sense of normalcy with it. Ignoring her departing roommate, she moved close to the board. Dylan and Leah could still be on campus. If she called now, they might return. That would be glorious. She could do without Dylan, but unlike most males, he knew when to keep his mouth shut or make himself scarce.

Her fingers danced over the phone keypad punching in the numbers. A couple of jabs on the send button resulted in nothing. Why wasn't her phone working? Was it dead? The illuminated battery icon showed almost a full charge. It made no sense. She powered the phone off, and then on, hoping the action would make it work as it did with the computer.

Staring hard at the number, she slowly punched it in again, mouthing each numeral aloud. When she got to the end of the number, a sense of uneasiness assailed her. The last smeared number she thought was a three. It could have been an eight or a five. Next to, it was a tight, cramped memo. *Don't Wreck Yourself Again. Not Sure If I Could Take the Shock. ROTFL*

It had to be her roommate or her slacker boyfriend's writing. A closer inspection revealed the problem. There were only nine digits. Instead of the ten there should have been with the area code. Her idiot roommate erased one accidentally adding her sarcastic note. *Damn it.* She glared at the still open door. There was no Cece in sight.

Stella stomped over to the door and slammed it. The vibration caused her framed poster of the Green Man to tumble from the wall and crack.

Despair returned settling on her shoulders, pushing her down to her bed where she curled into a fetal position, dropping her phone by her head. It rang so close to her ear that it practically levitated her off the bed.

Leah. Her hand clutched the phone. Excitement sped up her heartbeat and pushed aside the lethargy that held her down. A glance at the illuminated screen showed Cam's name not her friend's or a new number. Her grip loosened, dropping the phone on the bed. It stopped ringing and then started again. Apparently, Cam would keep it up until she answered.

No other choice. She picked up the phone, powered it off before resuming her fetal position, and pulled the sheet over her head with nowhere she had to be, and nothing she really had to do. Her mind drifted between a consciousness and sleep. A gray, misty land inhabited by bare skeleton trees and whispering voices of people she couldn't see.

CHAPTER EIGHT

S OME OF THE voices became louder and familiar. Her father spat the phrase carved into her heart. "If you hadn't been born, then I would never have stayed with your mother and subjected myself to hell on earth."

A feminine voice, less familiar, but it evoked the combined smells of whiteboard markers, stringent bite of pine cleaning solution, and the mildewed scent she associated with high school gym lockers. "Stella ruined my life."

How did she do that? She couldn't quite remember. The girl's face flickered in and out of focus like a broken video camera. Something about her going out with Jacob whom the girl liked. Jacob something. Nothing ever came of it. She couldn't remember Jacob being that great anyhow.

"I could have won that full ride scholarship if it hadn't been for Stella snatching it away from me. Administrators probably awarded it to her because they felt sorry for her with her crazy ass parents." She recognized the voice of one of her high school classmates, Tricia, an ambitious overachiever whose academic zeal suffered when she started dating the soccer captain.

Did the school administrators feel sorry for her? Did they promote her as a candidate because her parents insisted on a public airing of their marital troubles? Tricia sounded like she hated her. She thought they were friends, not good friends, but school friends at least. People who saw each other every day and talked about trivial matters. Not the type of friends who called in the middle of the night for a ride.

All she ever did was cause heartache. A coldness settled on her. Her hand searched for the blanket as she kept her eyes tightly closed. No reason to look, she knew what she'd see, the world that had suddenly turned against her. The blanket provided an additional barrier between her and the outside.

Eventually, she found herself back in the land of fog wandering be- tween skeleton trees. Something large hung from a tree, twisting from a rope.

The blurred shape drew her while something inside her urged her to go another way. She knew she should, but her feet kept moving forward as if she'd surrendered all control of her body.

Her heartbeat lunged from its slow, steady pace to an all-out run, but her feet didn't comply. She shuffled toward the swinging object. Her body responded as if it belonged to a senior citizen as opposed to someone who hadn't reached her twentieth birthday. Inhaling deeply, she drew on her meditative practice to slow her heart and ease her building anxiety. It didn't help.

Her inability to draw a deep breath left her panting like a dog. As she drew closer to the tree, the shape faded, and then sharpened, startling her with the image of a hanged man. The wind tussled with the body, gradually turning it. Stella recognized the long, lanky body and the dark hair before the final twist of the rope revealed the face. The skin above the tight noose swelled due to the restricted blood flow, turning a bruised reddish purple.

The scream never came. Unable to push it past her panting, it lodged in her throat, making the simple act of taking in oxygen even more problematic. The grotesque image of her friend hanging held her gaze. His eyes opened, causing her to stumble back a few steps, tripping over a tree root and landing on her butt. Her hands took the brunt of her fall. Her attention stayed on Mitch's head. His lips moved.

"Stella, you did this!"

Her hand flew up to her chest, holding in a heart that threatened to beat out of her chest. "How did I do this? I care about you. I never want anything bad to happen to you."

"Care! Does this look like the act of a concerned friend? You had the ability to stop Cam, but you chose not to. The only person you care about is yourself."

Oh, she had contemplated doing nothing; certain Cam's threats were meaningless. Who knew it'd come to this? "I don't understand. Cam only threatened your scholarship."

"My scholarship, my reputation, my credibility, my only chance to get ahead. Sure, I've done things I've regretted. It looked like I would finally triumph over them until you came along disturbing everything, I'd built with your desire to have every guy at your feet."

"It wasn't like that." How could she make him understand? His eyes closed, and the wind twisted the rope, turning him away from her.

Stella woke with a jerk. Sweat drenched her tired body. Her muscles burned reminding her of her earlier attempts to take up running. After what her runner acquaintances called a light jog, she'd be nauseous, dizzy, and shaking, like now.

What happened to her? Bad dream, for sure, but it shouldn't drain her. What if it wasn't a dream, but was a glimpse of the future? It would mean her father was right. She destroyed everything and everyone she touched.

What if she caused Mitch's suicide?

There didn't seem to be any way out of her dilemma. It would help to talk to Leah. Lately, she'd been such a bad friend, not returning her calls until Leah might think she no longer cared about their friendship, especially when she didn't call after she'd left her new number. In the end, it was hard to know who could help her. Possibly her mother? A deep breath escaped her. College served as a buffer between her and her mother. Still, mothers were supposed to help, part of their job description or something.

An inner voice, she'd called intuition and her spirit guide, urged her not to call her mother. "I have to. There's no one else. Besides, moms are supposed to love you when no one else does. You can always go home when things are bad."

A brief memory of one of her fellow students dropping out of school when her ultra-conservative parents stopped paying tuition after she came out. "That's her parents, not mine. My mom will be there for me, even if my father isn't." Stella lowered her voice, aware of the ridicule her talking to herself would inspire.

Steeling herself, she readied herself for the call. Her mother never qualified as the warm and fuzzy type. When she fell and bloodied her knee as a toddler, her mother would wipe it with a burning antiseptic and put a bandage on it. No kissing it and making it better or rocking her until the tears stopped. Practical, that's what her mother was. The woman made lists, followed plans, and got things done. Well, she used to until her dad walked out.

The phone in her hand, she scrolled down to home listing. Her mother passed her organizational skills to her, which allowed her to rise to the top of her class and snag the coveted scholarship. Sucking in her lips, she tried to still the voices that warned her not to call. Seriously, what could happen? If her mother gave her bad advice, she didn't have to act on it. No reason to tell her everything.

Her thumb hit the call button, ending the dilemma. The familiar sound of her mother's voice brought reassurance. She seemed friendly, normal, not like the frenzied woman yelling at her fleeing spouse, nor did she sound like the woman constantly quoting paraphrased Bible verses. True, Stella would never qualify as a Biblical scholar, but she did know the line, God helps those who help themselves, came from *The Grapes of Wrath*, not the Bible.

"Hi, Mom. It's me, Stella."

Her mother chuckled. The sound brought with it a surge of warmth. When was the last time she heard her mother laugh?

"What's so funny? Would you like to share with the class?" she teased her mother already feeling better about calling. Dropping the blanket, she sat up, straightening her spine, her mother's mantra coming automatically to mind. Good posture made every woman look good. It not only made a female's figure look better, but also conveyed confidence.

"You, thinking I wouldn't recognize your voice or the cell number I pay for every month with the pittance I receive from your father. That's the good months when he pays on time and isn't plane hopping with his Jezebel of a wife to the various fleshpots like Vegas and Paris." Her voice became shriller, losing any warmth as she spoke.

Stella moved the phone from her ear, not needing it close to hear, as her mother grew progressively louder. She didn't call to talk about her father. His desertion and young new wife had been discussed to death in her opinion. Jezebel and fleshpots must mean she was still attending psychos-be-us church. Paris a fleshpot? Never thought of it that way.

"Mom, let's not talk about Dad. I have a problem that I wanted to run past you." Even as she said the words, she had doubts. It would be great if someone could be a neutral sounding, board. The practical mother she used to know could come up with a logical solution. Although, her mother's current way of solving problems involved allowing a Bible to fall randomly open and poking at a verse with her eyes closed, would not help her.

"Don't tell me, you're pregnant, you little slut!" The snarled words sounding like an alcohol-fueled rant. No wonder, she'd been so friendly at first enjoying a warmth that came from too many Long Island Teas.

"No!" Her answer came automatic, equally angry that her mother would call her a slut. Why did she call? All she wanted to do was hang up. Of course, she couldn't just hang up. That would be rude as if calling her a slut wasn't harsh. "Never mind now doesn't seem like a good time."

"Good time? Whadya mean a good time. There's never a good time. We're all going to die. Are you ready to die?"

Stella placed the phone on the bed as she shot both hands into her hair, cradling her head. Her mother's question echoed in her head. Was she ready to die? She could hear her mother still talking about ending up in a lake of fire. Ready to die, it would be like going to sleep if she did it right. A long restful sleep where she'd never have to worry about Cam or Mitch accusing her of ruining his life. Without her to threaten, Cam would have no leverage and wouldn't go through with his plans since no one could execute them.

The idea took root, calming her. She picked up the phone, ready to hang up, knowing she didn't have to worry about offending her mother if she were no longer around.

"Stella, you're not still part of that witchy nonsense. That's your problem. You need to get into a real church. I'll get Pastor Jim to recommend a few places near the campus."

Not caring about the furor her words would cause or maybe wanting to needle her, she said, "Oh yes, still involved. In fact, I'm head high priestess now. Every full moon, we strip naked, hop on our broomsticks and fly. Only after, we down a couple goblets of innocent babies' blood. We can buzz your house if you'd like."

Her terminating the call cut her mother's anguish cry of, "No!" short.

A stillness surrounded her as she contemplated her room. On her side, color-coded storage boxes stood in straight towers with neat labels. Clipboards with various lists hung from nails. Her need to control her environment took organizational to a completely new level. Apparently, it hadn't worked.

The open dresser drawers, wrecked closet, and the pile of odiferous clothing crowded her roommate's side proving that organization didn't always win the day. Cece, the name her roommate insisted on—despite the room assignment list declared it was Charlotte—for the most part, acted happy. If Stella discounted the times Cece was high, asleep, or out and out snarky, then she was happy. Probably happy then too, especially when acting like a total jerk. Cece's slacker boyfriend suited her too. Picking a boyfriend out of her league never worked, not that she had all that much experience, but she did now.

Pills. She needed pills. Maybe Cece had something she could take. Stella pawed through the open drawer, moving around half-eaten cookies, crushed crackers, wadded paper, thongs, unmatched socks, and a container of birth control pills. She held up the plastic container. "Nope, the best it would do would probably cause water gain if I took the whole package. You'd think she'd have something. Then again, the girl was all about getting high, not dying."

People died all the time from mixing drugs, often prescriptions, and alcohol. Being underage never served as an obstacle to getting drunk. Plenty of drugs on campus, too, but she didn't know any dealers. Asking around would cause some raised eyebrows and with her luck, a call home. Prescription drugs would be her best bet. She'd heard the nurse practitioner at the campus clinic wrote out prescriptions without even blinking an eye, especially on the weekends. Most of the students faked their injuries for a pain killer or muscle relaxer. She'd overheard two students talking about it while working in the computer lab. Enough pills created a floaty high, very relaxing. It made sense that taking all the pills with a fifth should do the trick.

Injury, what type should she have? An outward one wouldn't work since a lack of physical symptoms would be easy enough to disprove. *Focus.* The word reminded her of her father who often chanted the word to hone her critical thinking skills. "Yeah, thanks a lot, Dad." Her bitter words hung in the air.

Maybe she should compose a heartstrings-pulling suicidal note. No. Everyone had to think it was an accident, especially Cam. Still, she could look good. Do her best to have good posture as she stretched out in bed, which would please her mother. The absurdity made her giggle. Of course, she'd be on to her next life, hopefully, a better one. Wasn't clear on that aspect. With any luck, she might get a choice. Who knows she could come back as an animal—hopefully, a well-loved pet.

There had to be something she could use to get drugs. The idea of looking it up on the Internet beckoned, but someone could check her history. Mitch would still be able to trace her cyber footsteps even if she erased them. Knowing him, he'd blame himself. Didn't want that for the only truly decent male she'd ever met. Sure, Leah's brother, Ethan was okay too. Even Dylan, Leah's boyfriend, managed a spot on the decent male list, but Mitch held the only romantic possibilities. Not that much would come of it, now. If he'd discovered what a mess, she'd made he'd never speak to her. At least dead, he'd think positive thoughts of her. After a while, she'd be a faded memory, some girl he knew in college who overdosed on muscle relaxers. Yeah, muscle relaxers would work.

The scent of cinnamon drifted on the air as she opened the exterior door. The spice had her imagining students clutching mugs of hot apple cider as they chatted. Could be someone got ambitious and used the communal kitchen. More likely, the nutrition centers, as the school liked to call the cafeterias, were trying out some seasonal favorites. The thought of stopping in to see what it was tempted her.

Don't go there. You have a mission. Killing herself didn't seem like a quest, but everyone would be better off. Mitch wouldn't lose his scholarship. Her mother would get the insurance money, and with any luck, she wouldn't give it to her 'you'll die a fiery death' church. Her father could no longer blame her for ruining his life.

A huge maple tree with the scarlet leaves served as her landmark for the clinic. The modern concrete building did not fit in with the stately brick academic buildings. Adding a clinic for students' medical and mental needs had to have been an afterthought. Apparently, earlier students were healthier or toughed it out. No cars in the front parking lot and only an older sedan in the side lot. A dent marred the car in the side parking lot.

Car wreck, yeah that would work for a cover story. Constant pain from the car wreck last year. What hurt? People were always complaining about something hurting. Her back, yeah, that was good since back pain hurt no matter if you were standing, sitting, or even lying down. Couldn't question it either, since it was a matter of perception.

A male student staffed the front desk. He glanced up and immediately closed the computer screen with a blush, assuring Stella it wasn't anything academic. "Can I help you?"

"Yes, I'd like to see whoever is on duty about pain." She pressed her hand to her lower back and grimaced. "Back pain."

"Okay." He pushed forward a clipboard. "Sign in. Your medical card is on file?"

Medical card. Didn't even consider that. Hadn't come to the clinic before. "Yes." Her answer satisfied him since he only glanced at her name before vanishing behind the file cabinets. He returned in under a minute.

"You can go in." He gestured to a door behind him, not even bothering to look up.

Stella slowly walked in, realizing her choice would be a permanent solution to a temporary issue. At least that is what all the suicide prevention stickers had printed on them. Still, it wasn't a simple matter of being embarrassed because she sexted the wrong person. As for her life, it hadn't been good for a while. When was life a joy as opposed to some daily obstacle course she ran, hoping not to screw up too much? Somewhere in high school, back when she and Leah were a team, before Dylan.

A middle-aged woman with frizzy hair and reading glasses perched on her nose looked up from her computer. "What brings you here?" The tired tone of her voice announced her disinterest.

"Pain." She touched her back and repeated her grimace while wondering if she could fool a medical professional as well as she did the student out front. The white lab coat intimidated Stella, convincing her she could see through her hasty fabrication.

"Cramps?" The woman raised an eyebrow. The unspoken message conveyed that she had no sympathy for crybaby students who showed up with female complaints.

"No, oh no, ma'am. I wouldn't come to a clinic because it was my time of the month." She watched the woman's face shift from disdain to possible caring. Difficult to measure, but the ma'am helped.

"This pain, what causes it?" She gestured for her to continue, as she typed something on her computer.

Stella stretched her neck trying to see her name on a file. She wondered if her parents would obtain the file with her false accident on it. Even if they did, it would be too late to do anything about it. "Car accident."

"Recently? Were you a passenger or a driver?" She swiveled and typed a few more words.

Car accident. Would there be a record for that? Would it have done enough damage to get painkillers? "I was hit by a car." The woman's gaze snapped back to hers.

"On campus?"

The inquiry brought back the belief that campus accidents guaranteed free tuition if you were the pedestrian, not the driver. Stella considered it an urban myth, but maybe it wasn't. Plenty of students probably claimed accidents hoping for a free ride. "Oh no, it was back in my hometown. Messed up my bike, totaled it. It did a number on my hip and spine and put me in traction."

The woman clicked her tongue and shook her head, muttering something about a helmet or lack of one. Stella considered pointing out that a helmet would not have helped her spine or hip but didn't. Instead, she waited silently for the nurse's summation.

"You look fine now."

Seriously, her makeup smudged from crying made her look somewhat ragged. "I'm not. Constant pain with the weather change. Causes my back to act up." She pushed out a whimper that sounded far from convincing.

"Hmm. It's a gorgeous fall day." A disdainful look settled on the nurse's face.

Who said this woman gave out pills similar to candy? Stella staggered to the wall, putting a hand on it. "It hurts to stand. It hurts to sit, too." She used the same complaints her former neighbor used after breaking several bones when rear-ended by a semi. The woman always sported a visible pain patch. She needed pills, not a patch.

After an exam, in which Stella manage to moan, grimace and shudder, she received two foil wrapped sample packs of painkillers and muscle relaxers. Pocketing the proffered pills, she wondered if they'd be enough.

The practitioner wrote something down on a prescription pad then tore it off and handed it to Stella. It could be a prescription for more painkillers, which would mean she'd have to find a way to the pharmacy.

"This is an order for X-rays at the local hospital. Get this done as soon as possible and have them sent here. Dr. Lomax will want to look at them before prescribing any medicine. If you take one pill every eight hours, it's enough to make it through the weekend."

Enough to make it through the weekend. Not enough. "I will, ma'am. There's no chance of overdosing, is there?"

"Good question. Not too many students would be conscientious enough to ask. No problem as long as you don't take them all at once." She gave a slight chuckle. "I can tell you're not the type."

Stella nodded, keeping her face expressionless. Samples in one hand and X-ray order in the other, she exited the building. Cece usually spent the weekend with her boyfriend, which would save her from any efforts to rescue her. She'd pull up the covers over her head just in case. That way, Cece would leave her alone, thinking she was asleep.

Decision made she kept her gaze forward. Anything could distract her from her intention from a squirrel gathering food for the upcoming winter to the outstretched branches of the Pin Oak tree that marked the entrance to the library where a male walked down the steps. A peripheral vision caught the familiar figure striding down the stairs. Mitch. She'd probably interrupted his studies when she called him from the Laundromat.

If only he'd come over and tell her how much he needed her, she'd forget the plan. Her fingers tightened around the sample packages. The sharp foil-wrapped cardboard bit into her palm. Her eyes fixed on a sign about the upcoming billiards and beard contest. She came to college for this. The total of the educational experience included growing facial hair and hitting balls with a stick. There'd be beer, too, but that didn't merit a mention since it was a staple of college life.

Mitch continued down the stairs, staring at an open book in his hands. Her feet carried her away from an accidental meeting. Just as well, since her intention would result in a better life for the one person who cared about her. Weren't you supposed to sacrifice for those you cared about? If she used her father as an example, there came a time you quit sacrificing and did whatever you wanted.

Her stride quickened as she neared her dorm. Cece could never be counted on being predictable, which meant Stella needed to be dead by the time she returned when she wasn't too sure, how long it would be. None of those news reports gave details. The incredibly brief reports summed up one person's struggle with life and his eventual defeat in two sentences. Edward Norwood, forty-one, found dead in home, drug overdose suspected, with nothing about Edward's love of silent movies or his collection of model trains. Not a single line about how he bought dozens of Girl Scout cookies every year and gave them away. Not a word about Edward falling deeply in love when he was twenty-two, only to have the woman reject him. Excluded were the details that Edward hated his job and his boss was a jerk. Factors such as being behind on his rent and possible eviction never appeared in the paper. Stella shook her head slowly. No wonder the man committed suicide even if he was only a figment of her imagination.

A dark-haired girl approached with a smile and waved. Stella half-smiled. Unsure if she should put up her hand clutching the pills. Odd, on her last day of life, that someone would be friendly, especially since she found the females on the campus to be singularly unfriendly. Too much, like high school where you were either competition or a wing-woman. Competition in regards to grades, dates, or even popularity turned women against one another. No one had anything to worry about from her. While her grades weren't bad, they weren't stellar curve setting ones from high school.

As for being a wing woman, she didn't know enough viable males to serve as an introduction. The wing woman traditionally needed to be less attractive than the woman who was trying to hook the man. Mitch considered her very beautiful. His declaration baffled her since she saw the same face in the mirror every day of her life. It had changed over the years. Her plump cheeks thinned down into smooth curves while her teeth straightened thanks to braces. Not sure if she'd ever consider herself beautiful, but enough of the female populace saw her as a threat. The part, who didn't, because they were too involved with their boyfriend or school, didn't have a need for her friendship. Why kid herself, she wasn't known for her upbeat banter or perky attitude. Leah had served as her only real friend in high school.

The scholarship dictated her school choice, not friends or lack of friends. It didn't matter at first because of so much activity that first couple of weeks. Some girls even tried to befriend her until they realized she wasn't the party type and only came to school for an education. Maybe the dark-haired girl was one of them. Her wave could be her second stab at friendship. Could be she needed Stella somehow. How could she desert her potential friend?

As the female drew closer, Stella's smile grew wide as she racked her brain for a name without success. Instead of meeting her eyes, the woman drifted by yelling a greeting once she passed. Twisting backward, Stella saw her potential friend, who was going to need her in some fashion to delay her suicide, talking to another girl. Whatever. Why did she expect a friend when she hadn't had one the three months she'd been here?

Better to check out now before things got ugly. People checked out all the time in different ways. Her father chose divorce, which left an ugly scar behind. Her mother in one of her many rants about him mentioned death would have been kinder because she would have gotten both sympathy and insurance benefits.

Her hand landed on the exterior door. The first tug didn't budge it. Strange since it remained unlocked during the day. A second firm tug pulled it open and sent her staggering back a step. An errant wind blew across the campus, creating tiny funnels of fallen leaves and slammed the door she'd just opened.

Odd. That wind coming out of nowhere. Her third attempt opening the door produced nothing. Could be the lock tripped with the slam. Talk about a sucky day. Couldn't even get into the building successfully. Never mind the conscientious nurse practitioner who wouldn't give her a full bottle of pills. Her feet landed on the leaves with a satisfying crunch as she stomped around the building to the front rotating door.

The freshmen buildings still had the archaic spinning doors. Supposedly, it helped keep the lobby heated. The simple concept baffled drunk or high students as they walked in an endless circle never getting anywhere. Stella had chuckled when she'd witnessed a trio of smashed girls spinning around but never getting into the lobby. Their dizzying journey stopped when the muscular catcher for the softball team stepped in behind them.

The infamous door was empty. Success. She sprinted for it to get in before some joker came in behind her at a run, enjoying the prospect of a prank that'd send her around for a couple of loops. She stepped into the lobby after only a half turn. Orange and brown couches faced each other in conversational settings. Could be the colors reflected someone's idea of warmth for students far away from everything they held familiar. More likely, the furniture came from a faculty area remodeling. Freshmen always got the rejects. Administration and professors didn't have much investment in freshmen because so many never returned. The praise, awards, and new furniture went to juniors and seniors who enriched the school with their continuous tuition payments.

Her feet slowed as she walked to the elevator. She could take the steps but abandoned the idea, picturing herself stuck in some stairwell, unwilling to make the last few steps to her floor. The elevator door pinged open. Two girls both on their cell phones sauntered out without acknowledging Stella. Not too surprising since she doubted, they even glanced at one another.

On the elevator, she punched her floor button while considering all the symbols she'd passed. The leaves falling off the tree indicated a circle of life. Not everyone lived to be eighty-three. Most didn't. The rotating door made her wonder if she'd spent her entire life walking in a circle. Everyone who walked past her without a smile, a word, or recognition that she existed signified she might as well not be there. Then there were the people that her presence merely irritated from the rude waitress at the diner to the student worker she'd surprised at the clinic. She could probably live her life out with no recognition and the occasional jerk.

She couldn't destroy life for Mitch the way she had for her father. The elevator jerked a little. Her hand gripped the railing wrapped around the inside of the car. It reminded her why she preferred the stairs. The unit must be on its final cycle, too. The cable could snap, hurling her to the basement, ending her dilemma. The thought made her lips tip up slightly.

The fact the building contained only four stories meant, she'd only break something and be in pain. Not good, not something she wanted. When the doors swooshed open, she breathed a sigh of relief. Music blared from several rooms in an undeclared war of musical genres. Normally, she did her best to ignore it as she walked to her room. Today, she listened. A happy reggae beat greeted her. The inhabitant could be from Jamaica or simply embraced a Jamaican outlook. Two more strides carried her into the sounds of an angry woman wailing about the injustice of life. *Yeah, understand where the singer is coming from. The real question was why did the woman keep trying?*

The sound of strings and woodwinds had Stella stopping. The number on the door read fourteen. No name card under it meant someone who didn't want anyone knocking on her door and introducing herself or, worse yet, wanting to borrow something. Borrow translated into you'll never see this item again, except on a post in social media with the borrower wearing it. Yeah, whoever was in room 14 may have been worth knowing. Something inside her opened with a longing for a possible friend behind the undecorated door. If she stared at it long enough, it might swing open, revealing the missing cog in her support network. Stella turned; realizing her mental grabbing at straws only delayed the inevitable with no reason to stay and every reason to go.

Inside her empty room, the stink of Cece's unwashed clothes hung in the air, mingling with something dead, a mouse in the wall most likely. The janitor staff put out poison never making the connection that the rodents would not conveniently exit the building before breathing their last. Her nose crinkled, but she wouldn't have much longer to endure it anyhow. *Did people smell on the other side? If they did, what did they smell?*

A quick search of her roommate's side of the room netted her a half of bottle of vodka. It'd do. Her arm cleared her nightstand, brushing the lamp, radio clock, and her daily planner to the floor. She placed the bottle of vodka on the stand along with the muscle relaxers and pain pills. The pills she lined up like waiting floats in a parade. She popped the first pill in her mouth and took a large swig of liquor. The harsh burn of the liquid nearly had her spitting out the pill in reaction, but she held on. The room appeared the same, nothing changed. *Yeah, one pill wasn't going to do it.*

Three pills sat in her cupped hand. She forgot which color was a painkiller, but it didn't matter. She carefully placed the pills on her tongue before taking another swallow of the cheap liquor. College students favored the brand because of its potency and price. *This is horrible for my liver.* The random thought made her wonder briefly if any of her body could be organ donation quality. When she received her driver's license, she'd agreed to be an organ donor. Someone might as well make use of her body since she wouldn't be using it.

The thought made it easier to swallow the last four pills. A lethargy slid over her, relaxing her muscles, fogging her mind. Her hand wrapped around the bottleneck. Holding it up to eye level, it looked as if two cups remained. Cups were not the proper term her mind insisted. Must drink it all. Can't take chances. The liquor spilled out of the side of her mouth. Was her throat even swallowing? The tinkling of the bottle hitting the floor came from a distance as a fast-moving fog obscured everything.

CHAPTER NINE

W AS SHE ASLEEP, lying down, or even dead? *She never got around to cleaning up. Dead people never thought about makeup, did they?* A sensation of movement lifted her up. Underneath the fog, she could see silhouettes of buildings, occasionally something moving that could be a car. Was it moving, or was she? If so, was she flying? Would her arms be stretched straight out like plane wings the way she played as a kindergartener? The thought amused, making her want to mimic her younger behavior.

Her arms didn't work. *Weird.* Wiggle fingers. Nothing. Stella glanced down at her body, seeing more clouds drifting by as opposed to her body. *Was this death? Did she suddenly vanish when her heart stopped?*

She swallowed the ball, which had formed in her throat. *Did she swallow? Did she even have a throat? Dead was so much more confusing than she thought it would be. Where was Summerlands, Heaven, or Hell?*

A beige fog surrounded everything. Her mother's voice spoke, "This way."

Stella drifted closer to the source. Odd, her mother, could arrive so fast after her death, but maybe time moved slower on this side. The shadows of people moving like dark ants under the cloud cover attached to her mother's voice.

"We have to be quick before anyone sees us."

The rising hysteria had become practically second nature to her mother as her marriage worsened and finally ended. It was another reason why Stella applied to colleges that weren't a commutable distance.

Her spirit hovered over the four people scurrying across the campus. The clouds shifted revealing her mother, the shifty con artist minister, and two muscle-bound men who could have doubled as biker bar bouncers. Their appearance confused her. Wasn't sure why the minister came unless it was another attempt to save her soul. *Wonder how much mom paid for this house call. Make that dorm call. Salvation visit?*

"This door." Her mother opened the back-door Stella had so much trouble opening earlier.

Hovering above them, Stella watched the group snake up the stairs. Her mother led the group acting as a spy leading a mission.

Was this what dead would be like, constantly watching the living? It didn't sound like much fun. Her mother's behavior intrigued her. Would she freak out when she found her dead body?

They were at her door. Instead of knocking, her mother opened the door, demonstrating she'd never locked it. "Whoa, smells like something died in here."

Mr. Sleazy Minister grabbed her mother's arm. "Wait! Demons are inside. I must cast protection first." The man withdrew a vial from an inside pocket and shook it side to side. "Begone evil spirits. By the power invested in me, I cast you out." The man shook, then put out his hands and grappled with something.

Nothing. You think being dead would give me supernatural vision, and I could see the demons.

He pocketed the vial and turned to the waiting three. "It's safe. I see the possessed collapsed on her bier of filth."

Harsh, it would make sense if he were referring to Cece's bed, but I wash my sheets every week.

One of the bruiser guys stepped into the room and looked in the direction the minister pointed. "Passed out if you ask me."

The response earned a glare from the minister who mouthed the word, *possessed.*

"Yeah, yeah. That's what I meant. Possessed and passed out look so much alike.

The body interests me, considering it was my body. The bouncer first in the room knelt and picked my body up gently. I didn't feel anything, but I guess the dead never do. My arms flopped down, and my head lolled obscenely to the side. My mouth gaped open. What a mess!

The men left the room with the minister in the lead, holding a wooden cross in front of him. Did he think B-movie vampire girls inhabited the dorm? Of course, as movie vampires they'd wear revealing outfits or lingerie. If a student did pop out of her room, she'd be sporting a T-shirt, yoga pants, and no vampire fangs.

The muscle men's heads swiveled side-to-side checking the area around them as they moved silently down the hall. Her mother trailed behind, biting her lips and looking slightly dazed as if she were the one who'd taken a handful of pills and washed them down with alcohol.

If she were dead, her mother's behavior would be understandable.

Dead? She didn't feel anything. What about the white light and her dead relatives welcoming her to the great beyond? A glance down the hallway revealed a red exit sign. Somewhat appropriate, but not the light at the end of the tunnel. No relatives were in sight, except her mother, who was still alive.

What was the deal? Shouldn't they notify the administration? Call an ambulance. One man climbed into the back of the dark SUV, and then the other one passed her body inside. Her mother opened the front passenger door without a tear on her face. Her earlier confusion gave way to her trademark expression, a pursed mouth reflecting a rotten flavor on her tongue. It indicated things were not going her way.

Yeah, daughter committing suicide would do that to her. Not something to brag about. As the only child, Stella bore the brunt of carrying the family banner. Only children had to meet all the parents' dreams and expectations since no spare existed. She'd dropped it in the mud this time. No possibility of redemption either.

Leah's grandmother, Esmeralda Hare, would shrug her shoulders and say, "It is what it is."

None of that easy acceptance of events that fate dealt them for her family. Nope. Her family raged at the injustices, the tears in the life plan. Everything was personal, deliberate, and malicious. No doubt, her father would view her death to cast a cloud on his happiness with his new wife, Bunny or Barbie. Couldn't remember her name since her mother usually made up a different one every time, she ranted about her. She probably thinks the names are insulting as opposed to lame.

The black SUV got smaller as she went higher. The tree branches studded with a few remaining leaves made it hard to see the ground, but not impossible. The four-lane road that cut through the campus contained a black SUV. It could be them, her. Hard to think of the slack body as hers. How could it be when she was in the clouds similar to a passenger in an airborne plane?

The buildings, sidewalks, and roads resembled a topographical map. It reminded her of the one she made in fifth grade, except there was no oatmeal box-shaped cylinder buildings. There weren't any in her town either, but due to limited box supply, she'd improvised. Yeah, her family majored in improvising. Only once they improvised, they pretended it was always what they wanted, even planned for, until it wasn't. A watery shine drew her eye.

The local lake shimmered underneath her. The term lake gave the body of water more grandeur than it merited. A lifeguard stand and a thin strip of beach marked one end of the water. Originally, the park served as a community park that failed. A thick chain link fence encompassed the water for safety. Difficult to see from this high up, but she knew it was there. It wasn't enough to keep out drunk college students intent on an evening of skinny-dipping. More than one person drowned in the endeavor. Would their ghosts be hanging out there by the water's edge?

A small strip of something white fluttered in the breeze. Her narrowed eyes couldn't bring it into focus. Not a ghost or at least nothing resembling the transparent figures often seen in movies. Spirits usually chose invisibility, according to Leah's grandfather. People tended to freak out, which didn't mean ghosts weren't there. Obviously, no one noticed her hovering in the sky similar to a parade balloon.

The landmarks grew smaller until only splotches of color. Green over here indicated the forest. A spattering of dark dots meant houses. A winding strip of silver could be either the river or a highway. Clouds blocked her vision as she ascended to who knows where. The concept of heaven was one she denied years ago, especially the one populated with angels strumming harps. It made no more sense that angels perched on clouds, than fiery demons existed below the ground. If that were the case, wouldn't an astronaut catch a glimpse of a celestial city as he hurtled through space?

Of course, it didn't stop it from existing even if she didn't believe in it. Her knowledge of the afterlife consisted of her mother warning her she'd burn in hell if she didn't change her ways. Would she meet a Biblical saint in white robes, who'd question her life? It could be that some grand entity didn't resemble humans at all. What if there were huge dog statues outside the gates? That would be nice. A world ruled by canines. There would be plenty of trees, endless fields, and the occasional cat.

Her drifting upward stopped with a bump. Had she reached the edge of the atmosphere? She put up her hands to feel but encountered no obvious barriers. She felt nothing. Did her fingers still work? She held up one hand but saw nothing but a gray vapor. Was she disappearing? An unfamiliar voice sounded to her left.

"I think we should tie her up."

Whom were they tying up?

Her mother's voice added, "Do you have to? It seems like overkill, especially since she's unconscious." A hint of entreaty colored the request. Completely different from the way her mother made any request sound as if issuing a royal edict. Do this or be banned from the kingdom. To be fair, her mother's opinion usually proved right. Well, right about practical things. That was before the foundation of her world cracked. She didn't recognize the uncertain woman who sounded like her mother, but acted more like a victim.

"Don't be fooled, sister. The demons that possess her know many tricks. Tying her is a necessity. We'll also need to sprinkle her with holy water."

In the one brief conversation Stella had with her father since the separation, he'd asked if her mother were still seeing the strange minister. She'd assume he meant church attendance, not an actual relationship. Besides, calling someone sister wasn't too romantic. What was the deal with the water anyhow? As far as she knew, only Catholics felt the need to bless the water. Water as one of the four elements was naturally sacred.

Her mother's voice regained vigor as she argued. "I know we need to rid her of the demons, but a hospital would serve too, much better than this filthy shack."

"Sister, you forget yourself. Even being close to your diseased child has infected you. Perhaps we need to start the exorcism with you."

Exorcism. Whoa, she didn't want that! The ominous words hung in the air. Leah had told her about some church that performed exorcisms and killed people in the process. Their rationale was at least they saved the person from eternal damnation, if not death. Somehow, she needed to explain she wasn't possessed. Wait. Would it matter if she were already dead?

In fact, why was she still here? Didn't spirits move on to wherever they had to go unless their death was unexpected? Hers wasn't. Her preoccupation with the present and the transportation of her body must have prevented her from leaving. Somehow, she needed to move on to whatever the next realm was.

The arguing became softer as a beige fog revealed the skeleton tree forest. She'd been here before. This was it, huh. Her feet moved soundlessly toward the mist covering them each time they encountered the soft ground. She assumed it was dirt because of the trees. No moon or sun hung in the cloudy sky, but a weak light illuminated the scenery from behind, throwing shadows everywhere.

If this were the passage to the other world, where were the welcoming relatives? C'mon now, she had some. Grandma Laney and Grandpa Jim both died in a car accident when she was ten. Her grandparents' death turned her spontaneous mother into a control freak, someone who had to have everything planned. Her Aunt Gigi should be here too. Gigi, her mother's only sister, used to spoil Stella the way indulgent single aunts did with gifts from her various travels as an international flight attendant. She even brought the kimono Gigi gave her to college. A brain aneurysm took the vibrant, confident woman right before Stella's birthday. Her mother blamed third world health care because it happened when she was overseas.

No Aunt Gigi motioned her forward with a grin. No Grandpa Jim patting his pocket where he hid a supply of her favorite soft peppermint candy. No Grandma Laney held her arms wide open. No one. Loneliness swamped her, causing her to stumble, almost falling into the mist. Her hands caught on her knees before she face planted into the fog. If she tumbled into the mist, it would be the end. The thought had no basis as it popped into her head.

Only trees without a leaf or bud to mark the season dotted the landscape. Not that unusual, if they were dead. It felt like strolling through a botanical graveyard. A chill had her chafing her arms and peering into the shadows. No wonder her mother went all controlling since her relatives disappeared in a span of three years, leaving only her husband and Stella. It explained the obnoxious behavior of nosing into every aspect of Stella and her father's life. Her lips tightened as she considered the possibility that her father could have already cheated. Life sucked.

Death, however, was no picnic, either. Where was everyone? She couldn't be the only person who died today. Did each person rate a personal hell or purgatory? "Am I all alone here?" The words echoed through the trees mocking her. An echo indicated they bounced off a hard surface, possibly rock or even a ravine captured her words and threw them back to her.

Great. A huge gaping hole existed somewhere. She'd probably stumble into it and break her neck. The ground-hugging fog would make such an accident a certainty. Panic welled up inside her, making her want to break into a run. Logic prevailed. "I'm dead. What else can happen?"

The sound of something swaying drew her. The first sound she'd heard in this silent tomb of a place. Off to her left, a creaking noise rode the wind. It reminded her of the swing on Grandmother Laney's porch. A twinge ran across her shoulders.

"Someone walked over my grave," she murmured the words. Although not cheery, it helped hearing a human voice, even if it was hers.

"Stella, over here. I'm over here."

Someone was here. At last. She must have arrived at the wrong entrance. She hurried toward the familiar voice trying to decipher whom it sounded the most like. A masculine voice, but not old like Grandpa Jim's.

"I've been looking for you, Stella. I've been worried about you."

Someone cared about her. She broke into a jog. The only reason she committed suicide—besides escaping a terrible outcome—was that no one really cared about her. Her mother arguing with a crackpot minister made her wonder. Did she know anyone young who had died? There was that guy in high school who hung himself from the park swing set after his awkward prom date request. Not as if she could forget him, especially since some people believed her refusal spurred his actions. She hadn't said yes or no, just burst into tears.

Not a great memory, the only other person she knew who died was a transfer student in her math class. Someone mentioned he passed out walking home on a frosty night and froze to death after taking a handful of prescription drugs.

Maybe her version of the afterlife was only for people she knew that OD'd.

"To your right, Stella."
She peered into the darkness, trying to remember the boy's name. It

would be good if she remembered it. His voice struck a responsive card indicating somehow that they were more connected than she remembered. Karl, something. Kev. Yeah, that was it, Kevin. Confident, she had his name. She turned into the darkness.

The creaking sound increased as a wind buffeted her, pushing her back.

"Stella, where are you going?" A note of fear tinged the question.

The wind kept pushing her back as she tried to reach Kevin. "Stop it!" she screamed the words, not expecting anything, but the wind vanished. Turning back to her path, she shouted, "I'm coming."

A small orb of light appeared growing larger as she stopped by a massive tree with something hanging from it. A body. Not again. Her feet remained mired in the mist as the body slowly rotated. This time Mitch looked fresher, his skin intact. His hanging happened recently.

Her hands pressed on her temples securing her head to her neck. Instead of devils with pitchforks, Hell was obviously a place where all her mistakes followed, denouncing her as the fraud she was. "How did this happen? My death was supposed to solve Cam harassing you."

Her fingers moved up into her hair, gripping it, pulling it. Tiny shards of physical pain joined her mental anguish as her eyes stayed on her friend swaying from the tree. Odd. He was almost like a decoration, an especially terrible one. He didn't even look dead, except for his face, which was ruddy and bruised. Maybe he wasn't dead yet. She could still save him. That was her mission to save Mitch. She was here in this misty between worlds place to save him. Here she thought she had no purpose in life, but this was it.

Her fingers dropped from her head, as a purpose grew inside her, rather like the ball of white light, she'd often visualize when covering herself with healing energy. The thought propelled her to the base of the tree trunk. Her right hand rested on the tree as she searched for a reachable branch. All of them hung out of reach. Even jumping wouldn't make her tall enough. How did people climb trees?

"Damn, why'd I have to be such a girly girl growing up? I should be able to climb this tree."

Mitch's laugh sounded behind her. "I'd like to see you climb a tree, but to what purpose. How would it change anything?"

Didn't he understand she was trying to save him and didn't have time for idle chitchat? Her eyes continued to search the tree for a possible handy built-in ladder as she spoke. Not looking at him made it easier to concentrate. "I'm trying to save you. If I can get up the tree, I can cut you down."

Squirrels climbed trees all the time. As far as she knew, they didn't have claws. A jump propelled her almost a foot off the ground as she flung her wide-spread fingers at the tree trunk. Her fingertips caught on the rough bark. Her heart leaped. She'd be able to crawl up the tree just like a squirrel or some macabre creature from a cut-rate horror movie. A snap had heralded the breaking of the bark before she fell with a sickening splat. Her hands were buried wrist deep in the mist. Still, she could feel something thick and moist under her fingertips. She pulled her hands up immediately, examining them for evidence of what she touched. A few long scratches with droplets of blood outlining them and a broken nail were the only evidence of her failed attempt. Apparently, squirrels were much lighter.

"Stella, what do you plan to do once you get up here? Are you going to gnaw through the rope with your teeth?"

Mitch's body twirled slightly, allowing her to see his face. He managed a brow lift as he faced her. Strange, the same facial expressions he'd use when he was alive. The familiar gesture exerted an emotional tug. She had to save him. Getting up became problematic since she didn't want to stick her hands back into the ground covering mist.

If she could stay disconnected from it, or as much as possible, it wouldn't absorb her. She wouldn't become part of the gloomy backdrop. Probably not feasible, but all she had to go on was instincts. Her hands rested on her knees as she leaned forward, pushing off her legs to stand. "I'm not giving up on you, Mitch."

The words were as much for her as they were for him, a bit of a rallying cry. She wasn't sure how she'd save him unless she sprouted wings and developed scissor like teeth capable of chewing through the rope. Her feet shuffled back allowing her to get a better image of the tree. Huge. So big, that some of the thick branches dipped down to the ground.

Why hadn't she seen that before? She darted toward the low branches, not sure how she'd solve the cutting issue, but she had to try. The slender limbs touching the ground didn't look strong enough to hold her weight, but maybe they would. Her sudden speed burst should have carried her to the location, but the branches lifted, moving out of range again.

What? She blinked. Okay, she did take a bunch of drugs, and that might mess with her mind. There was also the possibility of torture in the afterlife. Trick playing trees could be part of the plan. The large, bare tree, she'd formerly regarded as simply dead, took on malevolent characteristics. She'd swear there were two evil eyes in the lines in the trunk, and a knothole created a slyly grinning mouth.

"Give it up. You're not helping yourself or me. We're both dead. You could have helped me earlier."

Her teeth sunk into her bottom lip as she listened.

"I know Cam had something on you. It had you running scared. You could have told me. Together, we could have worked something out." His

concerned eyes held hers. His right arm stretched out with the palm up and open. His crooked little finger stood out awkwardly away from the rest of his fingers reminding her of a kid not picked for the team, standing near the team, but not with them.

Working in the computer lab provided either chaos that required more than the three workers they had or dead time. Her nose crinkled at the expression and swiftly corrected it. Empty hours didn't sound that much better. During this period, they exchanged stories about their childhoods. His crooked finger resulted from climbing a forbidden tree and falling. Despite the pain, he didn't inform his mother because that would mean confessing his disobedience. Besides, he didn't know it was broken. The pain, he figured, was a type of cosmic spanking.

The injured finger had blackened before his mother insisted on taking him to the doctor. X-rays showed that the break had already started healing crookedly. The only reasonable thing was to break it again and splint it, but having already suffered through painful days and sleepless nights the idea had him whimpering. His strong reaction had his mother settling for antibiotics to help speed up the healing much to the doctor's disgust.

The finger identified him more than anything else could. It told her about his unwillingness to disappoint his family. His one DUI must have been devastating, the gift that kept on giving rather like an STD. Who knew Cam had a connection that allowed him to dig up the incident?

A silence hung thick between them. It served as an invisible cord connecting them, and a wall. The blankness required an answer, a reply, some explanation. A crow called in the distance, causing an involuntary jump and a backward glance over her shoulder.

"There are crows here?"

Mitch's outstretch hand dropped to his side, with a floppy rubbery motion indicating no bone, no muscle, and no life.

"I asked why you couldn't confide in me, and you talk about crows? I thought we had something. I felt like you trusted me."

Each word pierced her skin like an icicle, searching for her heart. When the tip found the beating heart, then it would freeze solid. Stop that, you're already dead, nothing to freeze. The impression of wings had her ducking her head as a stately owl glided past her ear.

"Surprised you heard him coming. Most don't."

Her mind grabbed onto the word, most. That implied others walked through this misty shadowland stopping and talking to Mitch, who swung in the breeze similar to an oversized windsock.

"There are others here?"

She turned slowly regarding the bare trees with a suspicious gaze, expecting zombies half hidden by the trunks. First a crow, then an owl, what next? A vulture or a shambling cow carcass to remind her of her deceased state?

"You always changed the subject when I got too close to something you didn't want to talk about. I allowed it when we were both alive because I was too worried about you liking me. The wrong word or action would cause you to scurry away rather like a wild deer. There were times I thought we made a connection, but I must have been wrong."

Both his eyebrows lowered into a V as the wind spun his body, causing his words to trail after him. "Must have had a good laugh with Cam about me kissing you."

An uncomfortable thickness formed in her throat. A gulp didn't remove it. She swallowed again to no effect. Regret lingered in her esophagus blocking it worse than a wad of unchewed peanut butter sandwich. Her right hand went up to her chest as she coughed. What if she couldn't breathe? A rising panic raced through her. The hairs on her arm stood up as her senses responded in a fight or flight reaction, she recognized from her physiology class. Who knew the same physical responses happened after death, too?

Think. Nothing can hurt you here since you're already dead. A raucous unfamiliar bird call drew her attention upward. Two large birds flew in a circle their skinny necks standing out in contrast to their thick-feathered bodies, too big for crows and certainly not eagles. The croaking cry came again, chilling her while drawing on a memory. Two similar birds had crouched close to the entrance of their gated subdivision tearing way at a dead doe. Her father had told her to look away as he made the turn, but she had looked back instead, curious to see what he didn't want her to see.

One bird had plunged his curved beak into the rotting carcass while the other cackled in anticipation. Bile had risen in her throat causing her to bolt from the car when it stopped in front of their house.

"Vultures," Mitch spat the word in disgust. "Means I don't have much time left. They show up this time every day to do their dirty work. A tidying of the premises."

Vultures ate dead animals. Her father had explained it to her after she emptied her stomach. It was nature's way. This revelation only assured her that nature had a dark side. A sudden screech preceded the vulture's downward plunge. Stella dropped to the ground and covered her head certain the birds would go for her eyes. Isn't that what they did in the movies?

"Get back! Stop it! Not again!"

Hearing Mitch's agonized cries, she dropped her arms. His body swung wildly as the birds took turns diving at him, ripping off flesh in the process. His legs kicked ineffectually at the determined scavengers. A large hole in his side exposing muscle, a rib, and what she thought, might be the liver. The only liver she ever looked at belonged to the cat she dissected in biology. A uniform gray colored all the feline's organs, making the lab difficult.

Her hand wrapped around a nearby branch. She swung it, using it as a sword, screaming as she charged the birds. They flew a short distance and huddled in a nearby tree, shrieking their complaints.

"Thanks. Appreciate your effort. They'll be back. It happens this way every day. Rather like the Prometheus myth. Instead of my liver, they devour all of me. Each day, my flesh returns and once again I become the human piñata."

His wound didn't ooze blood, but an organ slid a little, threatening to spill out on the ground near her feet. Thank the Goddess it didn't. Her gaze moved upward gliding over the missing chunks of flesh and ripped clothing. Dark splotches covered his face, and his skin tightened against his skull giving him the look of a dried apple doll with severe, mournful features. His thin barely there lips pulled away from his teeth in a parody of a horse grin.

She shouted over the vultures' vocalizing. "What can I do to help you?"

His breath came out in a wheezy gasp, "Too late...to...help... Did you care...for me a little?"

It wasn't supposed to be happening this way. Her death should have put everything back in balance. All would be as it should be, not like this. A pair of vicious, ugly creatures should not devour the only dependable male she knew. The birds' complaints rose in volume along with the noise of hundreds of beating wings. A flock of vultures darkened the sky, making the shadowy landscape into instant night. A sickening odor of death and decaying flesh landed with them as many perched in nearby trees and several on the ground beside her feet.

One pecked at her foot between the sandal straps, puncturing it. Blood decorated the wound exciting the birds. The dark harbingers crowded forward. She stumbled backwards in her attempt to escape.

"Run! I'll distract them." Mitch thrashed about sending a foot flying in the process. The birds lighted on it screaming insults as they shoved each other out of the way with their strong wings. "Hurry, Stella. You have to complete your soul's mission."

Soul's mission. What did he mean? "Mitch, I hate leaving you. The kiss mattered a great deal."

A large vulture's wingspan hid Mitch's face, cut off a reply that started with "Stella, I'll always—", and ended it with an ominous gurgle.

CHAPTER TEN

RUN, RUN, RUN, the words repeated in her mind. *Her feet carried her away from the sound of the feeding frenzy. The path veered to the right but hadn't she come that way? Why bother returning to where she'd already been. No door awaited her, allowing her the ability to go back to life for an instant do-over. Too bad, since suicide provided no solution at all. It only made everything worse.*

Another path cut through the bare tree woods a little further up to her left. A stitch in her side gave a moment for contemplation as she gulped air and shoved her fingers into the spasm. The trees resembled a clutch of black-garbed widows huddled together and away from the path. A dark glossy shrubbery peeked out of the ground fog. Strange. She hadn't seen this before. It looked like it could be alive, unlike the trees.

Even though she could no longer hear the vultures, it didn't mean they weren't there. No doubt, they'd be looking for the second course in a couple of minutes. Besides, bushes couldn't look ominous. Better hurry. She broke into a jog, heading toward the glossy leaf bushes. The ground mist cleared, exposing a gravel path and a rabbit. The black and white rabbit resembled an overfed pet rather than a resident of a haunted forest. It stood on its hind legs, almost reaching Stella's knees.

His nose twitched as his mouth moved. She expected it to speak. Leah had followed a rabbit to her grandfather in her time traveling experience. Could Leah's grandfather have sent the rabbit as a messenger? Made sense since the grandfather's last name was Hare. Weren't rabbits symbols of luck? How would anyone know she needed help since she hadn't shared her plans?

The rabbit's dark eyes brimmed with intelligence or so she thought. "Speak to me." Instead of the furry little mouth opening to complain about being late and missing tea as in the popular child's book, nothing. No words about turning left at the next hanging corpse emerged from his mouth. Its cheeks continued moving as if it had some massive wad of gum. No words. How frustrating! The first semi-normal creature was no help at all.

Know and be known. *The cryptic words materialized in her mind, pushing out any reference to children's books and forest creatures with no sense of direction.* Know and be known. *The words came again in clear bell-like sounds. The rabbit continued chewing without a glimmer of teeth showing, obviously not talking.*

Know and be known. *The words rose in volume the speaker shouted over her warring thoughts, fears, and reflections on childhood reading selections. The bunny gave her a reproachful look as if animals were capable of such a thing. It dropped to four legs and bounced off into the mist.*

The fog grew thick, rising quickly, covering the path and the direction of the rabbit. Her eyes searched for the hare as she lunged in the direction it went. Her only chance of leaving hopped away twitching its tail. A sense of urgency propelled her right into the glossy bushes, which happened to have thorns on them. The brambles held her tight as she struggled to free herself. What were the bushes doing in the path?

The more she struggled, the tighter the branches wrapped around her squeezing her tight, thorns penetrating her skin. The bush belonged in a horror movie where plants grabbed at people and sometimes ate them. She swallowed hard. As a light snack for some aggressive shrubbery, she'd never complete her soul mission, whatever that was.

What did they do in the movies when attacked by plants? Sure, problem-solving using hackneyed movie plots might not be the best plan, but what else was there? In the movies, the person usually had a machete to hack off limbs. Yeah, made the mistake of dying without taking a weapon with her. No wonder ancient burials featured weapons placed with the body. They knew something modern man forgot.

Death was not the great sleep nor was it a marble condominium in the clouds. Who knew it would be some never-ending scavenger hunt with meaningless clues? Know and be known, *how would that help her with this mutant plant? The glossy leaf plant looked benign, however, was anything but. Delicately grabbing a branch, she detangled the needle-like thorns from her clothing only to have another twig wrap around her. So much for stealth. The plant knew what she was doing before she did it. Leah's Nana, Esmeralda, always talked to the plants because she credited them with intelligence and understanding.*

"Um, plant, could you please let me go?" Her voice echoed in the stillness, sounding both loud and stupid. As a reply, the branches wrapped around her left knee tightened, the thorns penetrated the thin material, embedding into the sensitive skin behind her knee.

"Ow!" She glanced down at the limb wrapped around her knee like a tourniquet. "Just my luck to score the plant bully. Do you want to play rough, huh? Take this."

Her fingers grabbed a fist full of leaves, jerking upward. A high keen filled the air as the ragged edges of the torn leaves spurted black liquid. A spattering of black dots decorated the front of her dress. Creepy. Did the plant scream and could the liquid be blood, well plant blood? Never had that happen back in the real world. Her legs were still captive, but the grip eased off some.

Her hands hovered over the plant before plunging into greenery ripping wildly. The high-pitched screams stopped her for a moment. "It's you or me, plant," she growled the words through gritted teeth as she continued plucking. The thorns tore at her skin, causing numerous scratches and bleeding. Dark red blood slithered down her hands mixing with the black liquid from the plant.

In vampire movies, the mingling of blood would cause the sharing of consciousness. That's how they tracked Dracula by using Mina Harker's impressions of where the master vampire resided. Did she really want to know what a plant was thinking?

Stop. The plaintive plea sounded in her head. Without any actual thought, she did stop. The bare bush sported only a few leaves, a multitude of thorns, and oozing black liquid slid over it dripping into the vapor. Great Goddess, she killed it or close to it. The branches that held her tight draped uselessly on top of her feet. How long had she kept at it after the plant gave up?

Leaves stuck out of her balled fists. Her fingers unbent, revealing the torn fragments. She hadn't meant to kill it. It was either it or her. Her actions were instinctive. What anyone would do to survive, right?

She took one ragged leaf and held it up to the branch. The torn leaf adhered to the branch with the ripped part growing back before her eyes. Talk about regeneration. She repeated the operation with a half dozen leaves but then stopped.

No reason to give the plant enough energy to attack again. The rest of the leaves fluttered toward the ground from her outstretched fingers. Their slow, graceful tumble ended when she could no longer see them in the mist. A slight movement in her peripheral vision caused her to pivot to her left. The torn leaves were silently marching up the branches like ants on parade and reconnecting. The sight had mesmerized her for a second before she bolted back to the path.

A thick hedge blocked her original path. Another passageway opened, complete with glowing moonflowers lighting the way with their open white blossoms. Would it be smart to choose the easy path? Might as well have a neon sign with an arrow on it. A dangerous shrub behind her that could pull up roots and follow determined her choice. Best bet would be to get out of the angry plant's vicinity.

Besides the flowers didn't appear to have any murderous intents, but then she'd thought that about the bush. The mists obscured the path, and then pulled back enough revealing a few feet. The vapor floated higher encompassing her in thick fog, reminding her of cotton batting as it wrapped around her. Warm, soft, and possibly suffocating her, but that would only apply if she were still alive.

Her initial struggle only tightened the white blanket around her. Violence is never an answer. The mantra popped into her mind probably from an anti-bullying campaign. Yeah, right, easy to say when something isn't trying to absorb or possibly digest you. *Inhaling deeply, she took two deep meditative breaths, grounding herself. Her panic lessened as she used the meditation chant.*

Acknowledge it; let it go, be at peace. *She inhaled deeply once more aware that calmness flowed through her, relaxing her muscles, gliding over her skin, penetrating deep in her psyche. It reminded her of water supporting her, floating on a raft in the pool with not a care in the world. Didn't people use white light in visualization? Sure, her light had weight and texture.*

For a moment, she drifted above the trees, peering down at the white encased figure on the path. The mummy-like creature was she, but she felt no fear or even attachment to the form. In the distance, mountains welled up out of the mist projecting both grandeur and ominousness. An understanding slipped over her. The faraway mountains were her end destination. As soon as the epiphany occurred, she landed back in her mist-wrapped body. The whiteness no longer frightened her.

A slightly off-key singing drifted on the air. The song, an old rock ballad about not stopping, reminded her of something her mother might have sung before she found religion. The singer stumbled over a few lyrics and inserted dubious ones of her making. Just like her mother. The dark forest grew thinner, giving over to spindly pine trees and large boulders. A woman in leggings, a tulle ballerina skirt and a fuchsia off the shoulder top strummed a guitar. A green scrunchie decorated her asymmetrical ponytail, which bobbed in time with the few notes she picked out on the guitar.

Something familiar about the outfit and the woman tugged at her memory. At least, she wasn't swinging from a noose. A live person suited her much better than the talking dead. It inspired less guilt too. Perhaps feeling her scrutiny, the woman glanced up and grinned.

"I bet you think I'm a lousy guitar player. I am." A carefree laugh bubbled up full of joy and abandonment.

Stella caught herself laughing with her. What a relief to meet someone happy on this soul mission. "No worries. I can't play either, but I always wanted to learn."

"You still can." The woman offered the advice with a strong pluck. The discordant note hung in the air, confirming her inability.

"Yeah, I know, but..." She hesitated, not knowing if she should add,

but I'm dead. Who knew what people or souls did after they die? Plenty of people with agendas would tell you in a heartbeat. Personally, she didn't care for any of the final solutions.

The woman rested the guitar against the rock, pushed off, and stood. "Hey, I'm Roberta. Most people call me Bobby."

"Hi, Bobby." She grasped her outstretched hand and shook it firmly. The warm, solid clasp of a hand anchored her in the moment. Her lips tugged up in response to Bobby's almost constant smile. The journey wouldn't be too stressful if everyone else were this nice. Apparently, Bobby would give her some cosmic clue or insight to complete her mission. Her bottom teeth scraped over her top lip with just enough pressure to let her know both were there. No body parts falling off yet.

A person didn't just ask how long someone had been dead. Not sure, what protocol was in this nebulous place. "Cool outfit you got on there. Vintage?" Stella asked carefully.

Bobby fingered her puffy skirt. "Oh, vintage, if you mean banging,' it is. I got it the other day. It's part of my college wardrobe." She spun in a fast turn with her arms gracefully over her head. "The whole outfit makes me feel just like Cyndi Lauper, except I can't sing or play the guitar."

"Cyndi who?" Bobby might as well be speaking a foreign language. Should she know this person? The same feeling of bewilderment she normally experienced when the fantasy role-play gamers tried to talk about their avatars and adventures swept over Stella. They assumed wrongly because she worked in the computer lab that she must be interested in online RPGs too. Instead of chiming into the conversation, she found something to do in the lab.

Bobby blinked twice before breaking into an upbeat song about girls wanting to have fun. It sounded familiar. Maybe Stella had heard it on a television show or movie. Wait. Her mother used to sing it when they were at the park playground. She'd push Stella in the swing and sing while other mothers screamed toothless threats at their children as they climbed the slide the wrong way or threw sand at one another. At the time, she'd thought her mother made up the song just for her, especially since she only sang the chorus.

Bobby danced closer, still singing, and grabbed her hands, swinging her in a slow circle. The unexpected action caught Stella by surprise, but she found her balance fast enough not to stumble again as they reeled in some 80's flavored version of Ring around the Rosey. The nagging feeling that she should know this cheerful female reasserted itself. Obviously, it would help with the soul mission. Their spinning circle wobbled as Bobby leaned back a couple inches too far, taking them both down.

The soft green grass cushioned their fall. The mist had vanished, and the dark woods had turned into a green, inviting copse with sunlight streaming through the leaves. The rocks and the mountains remained, along with a laughing Bobby.

Odd that everything changed. Why did it change? Bobby dropped her hands and pushed herself up. "I wish you were my roommate."

"Really?" Happiness arced through her body that someone wanted her as a roommate. Being from different times could be a barrier. "I wish you were mine. The one I had was like a cranky iguana slithering in, making noise, eating my food, and them slithering out with some caustic jab."

"Yeah. She sounds like a winner. Didn't catch your name?" Bobby arched an eyebrow as she dusted off her leggings and picked a twig out of her skirt.

"Stella." She paused waiting for the inevitable wrong name. Estelle, Estella, even Estrella, a few even tried to change her name to Ellie, which she'd admit was more playful, but it wasn't her name. She watched her fellow traveler shape the words first, as she made her way over to what she knew would be a warmed rock. The uniform heat of the boulder encouraged Stella to stretch out putting her hands behind her head, staring up at the bright blue sky. Too bright, she closed her eyes, soaking in the warmth.

"Stella. I like that name. Not common, ya know."

"Yeah," she agreed, not opening her eyes. It'd be nice if she could just stay in this part of her journey. Once grade school started, there were very few visits to the park. Instead, her mother carted her around to half dozen classes where she learned manners, gymnastics, and languages. Being able to say, "Where is the American Embassy?" in Russian and Italian ended up serving no purpose. She could have been outside soaking up the sun instead of math tutoring to make sure she excelled in school.

"Probably because they didn't want their baby girls associated with that female traitor in that old play."

Stella opened her eyes, realizing she never gave much thought to her name. Once, she looked it up online, and it meant Star, which she thought was cool. "What female traitor? What play?" Her gaze scanned the immediate area for Bobby. Nothing. She jackknifed into a sitting position. Where was she?

"Bobby?" she called, hating the slight note of hysteria in the single word. Why did she think dying would be a long dreamless sleep? So far, it had been more work, worry, and downright creepiness than living.

"Here."

The voice came from below her. Stella peered over the edge of the boulder. An audible sigh of relief escaped her lips upon spotting her companion. Bobby had her face in a large patch of yellow daffodils crowded together. The flowers, which muffled her words, Stella would swear hadn't been there before. How could you miss all that yellow?

"I love Daffodils. They're my favorite flowers."

"They're my mother's favorite too, which surprised me."

"Hmm, why?" Bobby rocked back on her heels and stared up at Stella. "Why wouldn't she love daffodils? They're both beautiful and courageous. They come up before any other flowers. Sure, that spring is here. They are the optimist of flowers. Their bright yellow color makes me think of sunshine and happiness. They endure year after year." Throwing her hands skyward, she announced with enthusiasm, "The daffodil is my role model. Forget people. Maybe we should model ourselves after plants. Much less drama. Whadya think?"

Plants as role models? Well, that's something she never considered before. "Yeah, I guess it could work. A plant does what it is supposed to do until it dies. Daffodils would be better than most people I know."

"Exactly." Bobby's laughter bubbled out of her as easy as breathing. Stella envied her. Too much time went into weighing if she should laugh at something. Would she offend someone if she laughed? Was it politically correct? Should she laugh even though she thought it was rather mean spirited? In the end, the opportunity usually passed her by before she could decide. Wasn't laughter a reaction as opposed to a choice?

The bubbly blonde-haired woman stood and leaned against the stone just brushing Stella's leg. Greedy for human contact, she moved her leg the barest millimeter keeping the contact. "If daffodils aren't your mother's type of flower, what would be?"

Good question. "Something, dark, and broody, that does well in the shade. A navy or black rose bud that never blooms out fully."

"Sounds terrible. Is she really that bad?" she asked, screwing up her face in a grimace.

Depending on her mother's mood, sometimes she not only became the dark rain cloud, but the lightning and thunder too. "Not always. Mainly, she's sad, disappointed in life. My father left for another woman. Just walked out of our lives one day. Most people say they know it's going to happen, but my mom didn't. Why else would she react so negatively? Huge scene in front of the neighbors."

"Bummer. Should have known. Did she get up, dust herself off, and vow to make your father pay?"

Her cupped palms held Stella's attention as she analyzed Bobby's statement. Her jaw clicked as she worked it around. The clicking came from it not being in alignment. The dentist accused her of grinding her teeth at night. Try living with the constant pressure of two adults playing an oversized emotional game of Jenga. The blocks had to come tumbling down sometimes.

She yawned on purpose, fighting the desire to grind her teeth. "At first, she was bitter, and then she became all depressed. I even missed her bossiness. Then she joined some church that told her what to do and think. The pastor's a total douchebag. Hate him." She slammed her balled fist into her other hand in a hollow slap for emphasis.

"Do you not like this pastor, then?" Bobby turned a mischievous expression her way. Stella sent her a dark glance, earning laughter. "Well, did you consider maybe your mother needed someone to tell her what to do? Maybe she didn't trust her own judgment since things went so wrong."

It made sense. Not the type of sense, Stella liked, though. Her parents were supposed to be all-knowing people who provided stability in her life. Her father humiliated her by hooking up with a woman young enough to be her older sister. He'd turned into a stereotype of a middle-aged man trying to recapture his youth. Her mother turned to religion, perhaps imagining it would solve all her problems if she just followed the right rules and gave enough money to the church.

"No, never considered it. My mom used to have it together. She was an office manager that managed other people's schedules. Very organized. Prompt. Efficient."

"Sounds like a control freak."

"She was."

"What happens when a control freak can't control something?"

"They go crazy?" Her mother had lost touch with reality.

Instead of her usual smile, Bobby's expression took on the thousand-yard stare. She sighed deeply. "I'm not sure how your mother dealt. All the super organization was a coping mechanism. I read about it once. People try to control their surroundings, since they can't control life."

Oddly, this person who never met her mother might have a point. Stella's lips twisted to one side as she imagined her mother as a panicked engineer of an out of control locomotive. "There wasn't too much she could do. Everything happened all at once, too, losing her job, losing her husband, and then, I went off to college. Maybe it was easier to give the responsibility of her life over to some scheming religious huckster who saw a tool."

A discordant chord filled the air. Bobby had the guitar tucked under one arm again, strummed the chords, and sang slightly off key, "There once was a woman named." She paused, angling her head in Stella's direction. "What was your mom's name again?"

"Roberta, like yours." Didn't she mention this before or did she just think it? Couldn't remember what she thought or did. Was this part of crossing over, the forgetting?

"Hmm, strange." Her fingers plucked the strings creating a trio of notes, not harmonious ones. "Imagine she didn't go for any nicknames like

Robby or Bob, huh?"

The thought of her efficient mother sporting a nickname was unthinkable. Her father never used any endearments for her mother, always calling her Roberta, more like she was an acquaintance or co-worker he didn't know too well, or maybe didn't want to know.

A few more chords had sounded before Bobby settled on one, she liked and continued strumming. "Roberta, Roberta, where are you now? You journey far and long with no clear destination. Tired and weary, you closed your eyes and woke up to a world strange to you."

The words could have applied to her as well as her mother. "Hey, that's decent considering you made it up on the spot."

Holding the guitar close with one arm, Bobby cupped her right hand and polished her fingers on her shirt. "Yeah, I have a few talents. Making up stuff is one of them."

"No, it was more than made up." This throwback to the seventies described the situation perfectly. "I don't know a whole lot about my parents, but I did know they got married because my mom was pregnant with me. I ended up tying together two people never meant to be together in a loveless marriage."

A snort, slightly animal-like, came from her companion. "Seriously, who told you that BS?"

"Well, uh, my father right before he left."

Bobby grimaced. "The crap people tell their children in an effort to whitewash their actions makes me want to barf." She accompanied the statement with a gagging reaction. "Tell me you didn't fall for it."

Her silence served as answer enough. Bobby put her guitar down and wrapped an arm around Stella's shoulders. "Okay. Let's look at things realistically. They both had choices. Hadn't they heard of The Pill? *So, they got married, a choice they both made. At any time, they could have called it quits. They didn't. Then your father decides to jump ship. He somehow tried to place his guilt and shame on the only person who didn't have a choice in the scenario. Lame."*

The arm across her shoulder comforted her as much as the words did. When the same thoughts had occurred to her, she'd rejected them as an easy way out of the cesspool her family had become. Bobby could be right. If she were right, then her dying didn't help her family or Mitch. An impulse, a push, had her standing and looking off in the distance at the mountains. Her time here was up. Bobby didn't know because she continued chattering.

"I wouldn't put up with settling down and being the traditional wifey. No not me, I want to travel, explore, and have adventures."

Bobby was her mother. She knew it. This carefree, happy girl caved into pressure to be something she wasn't. The epiphany had her staring, cataloging the outfit, even her attitude. So different from her mother who could have popped out of a filing cabinet fully formed and attired in a washable suit and sensible shoes.

The glade darkened. Gathered clouds minimized the sunlight while an ominous dampness seeped out of the ground developing into a mist. Not a good sign. Time to go. She glanced back, wanting to remember the free-spirited version of her mother, but the outspoken Bobby had disappeared.

In the distance, the sun shone down on a slender path. Leaving no doubt, in which direction she'd go with no reason to look behind and no desire to repeat everything she'd already done. Bobby's mellow personality appealed, which was weird considering she'd never gotten along with her mother.

CHAPTER ELEVEN

*T*HE DARKNESS AND *mist increased, causing her to break into a jog. No low-lying briars reached for her feet. Still, no reason to linger or take chances. The universe, God, Goddess, whatever created this world, urged her to move on. A meadow with tall, waving grass starting to turn brown, indicating fall or approaching winter, stood in front of the mountains.*

Dust kicked up around her sandals as she walked. Exhaustion dogged her steps until moving became more like walking through a pool. It shouldn't be this hard. Sleep would be nice. Yes, that's what she needed.

A green mossy area beckoned in the sea of dry grass. Odd, it would exist, but it did. Her feet headed toward the soft looking mound when a voice sounded in her head. Don't stop. Don't sleep. You'll never awake.

What? Stella's determined march to the mound halted. She turned slowly looking for anyone or anything that could be talking to her. Never underestimate the plants or the wildlife in this strange, unknown landscape of nothing, except for the grass, soft looking moss, and mountains.

Did she think it? It didn't make sense because she wanted to sleep and wouldn't warn herself not to. Sleeping sounded wonderful. Sure, a feather pillow would be nice, but she'd settle for the moss. A large pillow stuffed inside a crisp white case appeared on top of the mound.

Exactly what she needed. Ah, sleep, wonderful sleep. Three strides carried her to the moss mound where she fell to her knees. Her fingertips glided across the ironed pillowcase. It felt real but needed further investigation. Her head rested on the case. The scent of fresh cotton and the lingering aroma of spray starch relaxed her. Nice. She rolled onto her back thinking how the pillow reminded her of the ones from home. The cases her mother painstakingly starched and ironed. Once she told Leah about her mother's need to iron almost anything, she could drape over an ironing board. Instead of making a caustic remark as she expected, Leah's lips turned up in an uncertain smile, the kind people give when they had no real answer and are unsure what's expected.

Yeah, she didn't know what she expected her friend to say. Truth told she liked the ironed pillowcases. So smooth and cool against her skin, her eyelids closed as she promised herself, she'd only take a small break, a tiny nap, that's all.

Get up! The shrieked words rattled inside her skull, forcing her eyes open with a snap. Now, she knew she didn't do that because all she wanted was to sleep.

Another voice choked with tears, more distant, called her name. Stella, Stella, my precious child stay with me.

Her mother, she was almost sure of it. Not the happy, carefree version, but the ironing one. Was she here? Sitting up, Stella looked around. No one, but the ground fog and darkness were closer than before and moving fast. If she stayed asleep, it would cover her in a matter of minutes. Not an outcome she wanted. The vapor swirled around as if dancing, retreating, and then swirling forward fooling her into thinking it wasn't moving fast. It was.

Decision made, she pushed up into a standing position. Her legs moved in rhythm with her swinging arms, like a race walker. The strappy sandals she'd donned earlier with high hopes of a romantic lunch with Cam did not serve. They alternated between separating her little toe from the rest of her toes and sliding across the terrain. Her feet slick with dust stuck out of the front of the sandals catching every broken stick and stray stone. Pain pulsed through her big toe as it encountered a pointed shard. Her lips mashed together as she held in her yelp.

Hadn't every childhood book and its movie counterpart featured dark woods where bad things happen? Leah's Nana explained that the dark represented the unknown, not necessarily evil. So far, the unknown hadn't treated her well. Frustrated with her sandals, she stopped for a moment, ripping them off her feet and throwing them into the tall grass. Without them, she could move faster.

The unwelcome sensation moved over her like anonymous hands touching her in a crowd, when her arms were pinned against her body, and she could do nothing about it. Afraid to look over her shoulder, she kept going forward, breaking into a light jog. Wincing whenever her feet stepped on a stone or stick, which was more than she liked. It sounded like someone was behind her, but she didn't want it to be true.

The sound of grass brushing against jean-clad legs came closer. Not Bobby, she knew that much. Please don't let it be Mitch, too macabre. The footsteps broke into a run making Stella erupt into a lope, scoping the area for a possible hiding place. Pain pierced her side making her wonder why her lack of athleticism stayed with her even after death. Labored breathing contributed to her dry mouth and inability to swallow. How long could she go on like this? Almost anyone could outrun her half-loping, half-limping gait.

Wasn't death supposed to be easy? Pain-free? Wasn't that why people committed suicide? What a crock! Someone needed to come back and explain that things weren't exactly peaceful on the other side. The grass crackled behind her, underneath a heavy footfall. Heavy breathing, not her own, reached her ears. So close. Help me now, Goddess. *An extra burst of energy sent her speeding down the trail. Must get away.*

"Stella."

Her name caught and stayed in the wind. A familiar, masculine voice, not Mitch. She stopped, even though everything inside her warned her not to and turned fearing what she'd find. Cam's bowed head greeted her as he rested his hands on his bent knees trying to catch his breath.

He glanced up, pinning her with his gaze. Before the same look would have mesmerized her. Now, it frightened her, making her back up slowly. Same artistically ruffled hair, primo bod, and model worthy skin, but it had no effect on her. No desire to look at him in awe, wondering how he could have chosen her. No, the mixture of lust and pride went missing. Maybe death did that to a person, but she remembered still caring about Mitch, even her mother.

Cam elicited none of these feelings, only the desire to get away from him before he contaminated her with his brand of evilness. Turning her back to him, she fixed her eyes on the mountains and continued her journey.

"What are you doing? Why won't you wait for me?"

Her pace slowed. Leaving him would be rude. The memory of his intentions to ruin Mitch if she didn't fix his grades resulted in her speeding up again.

"Wait, you worthless ho."

Seriously? He thought that would make her stop. A small rock on the ground beckoned her without a word. It fit into her hand exactly as she thought it would. Pivoting, she released it toward her intended target only to have it skim Cam's shoulder.

"Hell. Have you lost your mind?"

His comment made her angry enough to scan the ground for more stones. Why did he keep following her? Was she crazy? Some people would say she was since she killed herself. It would make sense to some, especially everyone in her mother's fire and brimstone church.

Crazy people did insane stuff. What was the definition of insanity? Dr. Poli, the chemistry prof, quoted Einstein's definition about once a week, something about doing the same thing and expecting different results. The quote could shame or enlighten those who never studied, but still expected to pass the weekly quiz.

Oh, she studied for the tests and aced most of them. Still, she expected Cam to be something he wasn't. He never showed any signs he was a stand-up kind of person, just the opposite. His hand landed on her shoulder; she tried to shake it off, but it remained, fingers digging into her collarbone.

She stiffened her other hand and brought it down on his wrist as hard as she could breaking his hold. Cam swore and stumbled backward.

Stella glared at him. "I'm crazy all right. Crazy to think you were a decent human. Insane to believe you cared about me. Totally whacked because I thought you'd let me into your self-centered world. I was wrong. Dead wrong. I'd had enough of you when I was alive." She stomped her bare foot on the dusty path and fisted her hands.

The patronizing smile indicated he considered her words a show, the type of emotional upheaval females were prone to. His smug expression sent her blood rushing through her body as if she were a cartoon thermometer. Any time, she'd blow her top, and it would all go spurting out, except she wasn't a cartoon and nothing about the situation was funny.

"I'm done with you. Be gone." She clapped her hands in front of his face; the same way she'd treat a stray she didn't want to follow her.

His eyebrows lifted as his mouth dropped open. Her not wanting him shocked him more than any words and it was probably hard for him to conceive of any female not wanting him. She expected him to declare her a lesbian to soothe his ego. The rebuttal she expected never came. His surprised expression never changed as he grew lighter and lighter until she could see the outline of the darkening glade behind him.

Stella blinked twice. No Cam. Impressions from his distinctive athletic shoes remained on the dusty path, but he didn't. An initial curl of unease slowly unrolled through her body. Did she do that?

Her gaze went to the path and Cam's footprints, the only evidence he was ever there. Her head slowly shook side to side. He could have left on his own, but Cam never did things that didn't benefit Cam. The fact she wanted him gone would be reason enough to stay. This soul search stuff would be much easier on her own. On her own. The words echoed in her head as she pivoted toward the mountains.

"All on my own," she whispered the words afraid she might be overheard. Strange, yeah, she knew it. Stranger was her constant effort not to be alone. As an only child, she didn't come into the world with instant playmates. Instead, her mother made play dates, enrolled her in programs while constantly reminding her to play nice, which she soon discovered meant tamp down her feelings and go along with what the other child wanted. Her early experience of trying to assert her preferences was slapped down fast.

Her easing fear allowed her to remember the repressed memory. Normally she hid the memory in a box wrapped with yellow and black tape bearing the label, bad memory. The scent of finger paint tickled her nostrils while the sound of children laughing filled her ears in preschool.

She recognized the pink housekeeping area. Pink to remind the girls that was their place, not the block center, or the car area with the rug printed with roads and cities.

Lilly, the beribboned daughter of a physician, elbowed Stella. "Let's play shopping."

Eli and Malcolm building a brightly colored city from blocks appealed more. Her slowness at replying earned her another elbow jab and redirection. "You can be the store owner."

Shopping was a tedious game, and being the storekeeper was even worse. It consisted of handing several items to Lilly while she complained they weren't what she wanted. Most of the time, Stella could never find anything that suited Lily, not a fun scenario.

Her mother wanted her to play with Lily, commenting that it would result in good connections. Spending more time with Lily sounded like torture. She tried to explain it to her mother, who laughed and told her to play nice.

With no freedom of choice, she'd handed Lily a faded dress that she'd discarded with a sniff. Her aggravation emerged in a sly manner. Stella knew her role. What if she changed it?

Lilly donned the sequined princess dress smoothing it over her body in front of the unbreakable mirror. Before she could complain about the dress, Stella spoke, remembering the attendant's words from the other day when her mother popped into an upscale fashion store.

"No, that dress does not suit. Take it off. Your skin and hair clash with it." She wasn't sure what clash meant, but she injected the same snootiness in her voice that the attendant used. Lilly erupted into loud sobs. It ended with the pre-school teacher scolding Stella and calling her mother.

Compromise was how to play the game, her mother explained after a lengthy timeout. The unfamiliar word must mean allowing other people to have their way. Often people were still mean even when they had their way. Her inability to tolerate stupid people made her a better, stronger scholar, but it left her feeling as if something was missing.

Patches of grass taking over the path ahead of her made her wonder if she'd veered off somewhere, but no clearer path presented itself. Of course, she had no clue where she was going or what would be there. The thought wasn't as horrifying as it would have been.

"The only thing that was missing was your own sense of self-worth." The remark startled her, although Leah had said as much.

Someone was walking next to her. Uncertain of the identity of the fellow traveler, Stella cut her eyes toward the stranger, trying not to be too obvious. An older woman with graying curls nodded in her direction. The woman's hand curled around a carved walking stick topped with a glass orb. The staff would be something Leah's grandmother would use, but the sizable stick measured close to six foot. Too big, even for the feisty Esmeralda Hare. Trying not to look or react, she took in her visitor's broomstick skirt and a flowing embroidered blouse, which told her nothing. The woman could be from almost any time and several regions. Her feet were bare too. Her green eyes reflected amusement. "Got any theories yet?"

"Are you my grandmother I never met?" She'd always wanted one. Someone preferably like Leah's who could give her counsel and gift her with a magickal charm or two.

The woman used her stick as a third leg creating a slightly odd gait. Stick, foot, foot, and stick again, the stick pulled her along. Stella slowed her pace out of consideration. The woman winked at her. "I saw what you did there. I'm not your grandmother, but a guide, even a mentor of sorts."

Stella stumbled to a stop. Her mouth dropped in surprise, then closed as she formulated a response. "A mentor! A guide! You're too late. I'm dead."

The rude words elicited a chuckle from the woman. "I'm glad you're finally finding your voice. We have much to talk about, you and me. Let's go to my house."

She pointed over Stella's shoulder. There was nothing behind her, but mountains. Five seconds ago, they filled the horizon. Doubting her senses, Stella pivoted slowly looking in the direction the woman pointed.

A small cottage with blue shutters and a purple door sat about hundred yards away. Some feathery wildflowers grew near the door, and an oversized Calico cat stretched out on a paving stone in the sun's rays. Smoke curled out of the chimney making it look almost storybook-like.

"Ah, you see it now. We only see what we allow ourselves to see." The woman nodded, planting her stick in front of her as she strode. "Your third eye is opening."

Stella placed her fingers on her forehead. The skin itched and twitched. Something was trying to break out of her skin. She'd heard plenty of talk about third eyes in Leah's house, but she assumed it meant something other than looking like a mythological creature.

The woman snorted, an inelegant almost bear like growl, and then faced her with a grin. "Name's Maja. If you don't know your mythology, I was the most beautiful of the Pleiades sisters. Some folks changed my name and story, but I prefer Maja."

Her shoulders went up in a casual shrug as if being a mythological entity was no big deal. Stella mentally cataloged her companion's attributes, trying to decide if any were god-like. Maja towered over Stella, but she didn't intimidate with her presence. Tall, slender, she must be strong to carry such a massive walking stick.

The sleeping cat awoke at their approach, stretched, arching its back and morphing into a much larger, more lethal feline. Stella's skin around her eyes stretched at the sight of the sleek, muscled leopard. The large creature bounded forward, which resulted in Stella stumbling sideways as the graceful cat placed his front paws on Maja's shoulders, greeting her with a swipe of his long tongue.

Maja's husky laughter at the display settled the issue of her divine origins. No regular woman could hold up under the weight of a two-hundred pound plus pet, especially one in motion, which would quadruple the mass. What was the formula for force again?

"Come, Stella, stop thinking about math formulas and have some tea." Maja pushed the leopard down and gestured to her home, walking faster and more upright than before.

Weird, but Stella tabled her desire to ask about it. You didn't question the immortals.

The leopard resumed its cat shape and weaved in and out of Stella's legs making her step carefully, unsure when she might find herself riding the large cat during an unexpected shapeshift.

Maja ducked as she entered the small cottage, making her wonder why the woman didn't whip up something larger. Inside, sunlight beamed through the windows in squares of illumination in the dim cottage, and a fire glowed in the fireplace. Intricate tapestries decorated the wall depicting stories she assumed were mythological in nature. Hard to tell in the light, but one featured a bear who turned into a man. Hope there wouldn't be a quiz later.

Two overstuffed wingchairs angled toward the fire made a comforta-ble conversation area. A cherry butler table nestled between the chairs close with a delicate china tea service atop. A floral area rug covered most of the cottage's stone floor bringing with it a coziness she didn't expect in this unknown world.

Maja filled a metal kettle and swung it over the flames before she settled into a wing chair. "It will be a while before the water is ready. Have a seat."

Why didn't the woman just blink them some tea? Taking the proffered seat, Stella folded her hands in her lap with her dirty bare feet crossed at the ankles and bent at a demure angle pretending she would be having tea with the Queen of England.

"Queen of England, ha." Maja chuckled, her eyes danced as she regarded Stella. "Got a few years on the gal. Let's talk about your world."

What world? "You mean the one I just left?" Who knew she had to differentiate between worlds? The cat jumped into her lap and kneaded her thighs, before lying down.

"Calisto likes you. High approval. He doesn't like many." The kettle

gurgled and hissed over the fire. Maja used a metal poker and hooked the metal arm that suspended the kettle and swung it off the fire. Her fingers wrapped around the hot metal handle without demonstrating any discomfort, while she talked as she poured a steamy plume of water into the china pot. "Your world, the one we're in right now. Your thoughts created it."

Nothing made sense. The drugs and alcohol must have colored her perceptions. Her right hand played with a tendril of hair, bringing it to her mouth to chew on, a nervous habit from her childhood. What if Maja was right? She couldn't be. "No offense, but I couldn't have made this world. I don't know about you so how could I imagine you."

The woman hooked the empty kettle back on the arm. She placed the tiny china lid on the pot before she heaved a dramatic sigh and fell back in her chair with both hands crossed over her heart. "Don't remember me. My heart is breaking."

"Oh, oh, I'm sorry. I do remember you. I just misspoke." Her initial urge was to comfort the woman, but Calisto's presence on her lap kept her seated. "I mean you're very important, and I. Ah," she stammered to a stop unaware of the proper protocol for when you insulted a Goddess or a demi-goddess, not that she'd had a conversation with any before.

"Be at peace, child. I know you don't know me. I inserted myself in your world because I thought you needed guidance to get where you need to go, to live the life you were destined to live." Maja reached forward covering Stella's hand resting on Calisto's back.

A wave of serenity swept through Stella, pushing out her anxiety, fears, and failures as it moved through her. Warmth wrapped around her as she relaxed in the chair listening to the low-throated purr of the contented cat.

"That's why I don't blink up a cup of tea like your television witches and divine entities do. I choose to save my power for the important things. Let's get to work."

Get to work. The words implied she needed to do something. She exhaled slowly balanced on a euphoric high. Her head rolled back on the chair, her face upward. Across the ceiling marched numerous monsters and imps with sly eyes and expectant faces. Their glowing eyes fixed on her waiting for her next breath, next step, or more likely her next stumble. Then they would descend on her, ripping her apart with their wicked claws and sharp teeth. A shudder shivered through her body as the warmth disappeared.

Maja removed her hand and scooted back in her chair. "Sorry, dear, but too much euphoria just leaves you floating around in the clouds and good for nothing."

Wiggling her hips, Stella slid down in the chair, without disturbing the cat, and lengthened the space between herself and the waiting creatures. How could Maja endure living with so many ominous creatures?

"Tea's done." Maja poured the tea into the cups with a dramatic flourish, which demonstrated years of experience. "One lump or two."

"Three." Stella croaked the words. Who cared if sugar rotted her teeth, padded her waistline, and caused premature wrinkles when demons hovered above? It'd be hard accepting a cup from her awkward position, but if she straightened up, she'd be closer to the fiends.

A plump scaly creature with tiny wings fluttered down from the ceiling, landing on the top of her wing chair. His shadow enveloped her, as did his sulfuric brimstone breath as his lips parted revealing sharp, yellow canines. As their eyes met, she drew up her legs to make herself as small as possible. Calisto bounded off her lap with a plaintive meow.

"Banish your self-doubt the way you did that Cam fellow," Maja ordered as she calmly stirred her tea.

Inhaling deeply, Stella's tight embrace of her arms loosened, allowing her hands to drop into her lap. She broke eye contact and brought her hands together in a light slap. "Be gone," she whispered. The shadow remained, along with the bad breath.

The sound of a heavy sigh filled the room. Maja placed her cup of tea back on the table. "Like you mean it." She clapped her hands together, sounding like thunder. "Desist, cease, halt, and flee from me now, I say." Her powerful voice filling the cottage caused the fire to leap. The shadow vanished.

Stella sat up in her chair. "Thanks. Appreciate it." An upward glance revealed plenty of monsters waiting, but their sense of gloating vanished along with a few of their brethren. Maja packed a punch.

"Oh dear, I only wanted to demonstrate. You have the strength if you only believe in yourself. You're so incredibly capable. In time, you'll be a guide." Her fingers lifted a delicate cup brimming with tea and offered it to Stella.

"Thanks." The fragrant steaming cup added normalcy to a scene that was anything but. "How can I be a guide? Do I guide souls through the dark forest?"

Maja sipped her tea with enjoyment as her eyes rolled upward. "Hmm, nothing a good cup of tea can't make better. My own blend by the way." She took another sip, held it in her mouth, before swallowing.

Stella emulated her host's behavior by bringing the teacup to her lips. The aromatic fragrance wafted on the air as she tried to place the spices. Ginger, cardamom, cinnamon, a citrusy tang, and a hint of something else she couldn't name wove together in a harmonious dance. The warm, sweet liquid flowed over her tongue, awakening the taste buds and leaving them bereft when she swallowed. The former feeling of comfort that had so *rudely left her returned.*

"This tea is magic."

Her host nodded in agreement before putting her cup down. "Some say that, but the intentions I endow it with is the real magick. Remember how you felt when Cam appeared, annoying you with his self-absorbed, critical chatter."

Her timber tentative, Stella replied, "Yes." Odd that Maja knew Cam's name but maybe it came with the territory, or she'd plucked it from her mind.

"Go back and examine your emotions. Describe them to me."

A moment that happened, less than twenty minutes ago, was already fading as she tugged at the threads to weave it back together. "I was..." she hesitated, reaching for the right description, "upset."

"Upset? That's what happens when two seeds fall into one hole, instead of one when I'm gardening. Were you only upset?" She probed gently, inflaming the sore spot Stella had already rubbed raw.

"No!" She jerked forward sloshing the tea over the rim of her cup. To avoid any more accidents, she placed the cup back on the table and stood. The emotions came pouring back, unsettling her with their impact and setting her in motion. Her pacing carried her across the width of the small cabin, giving her a chance to examine the tapestries in the shadows. One was a man bear or a bear-man.

Her attention jerked back to her anger at Cam. Her fingers closed into fists as she uttered a small growl. "Cam is the problem. The reason I'm here." Stopping, she stomped one foot, forgetting stone lay underneath the carpet. "I couldn't stand seeing his smug face, always critical, telling me what I should do, and pushing me. I'd had enough, couldn't stand the sight of him or his pompous attitude. I wanted both of them gone." She slammed her hands together as she growled the last word.

A few of the creatures hanging from the ceiling winked out of existence. Did she do that?

"Ah, such skill, such potential. I'm impressed in such a young mortal. There's a reason I chose you."

"You chose me?" The thought astounded her. All her life she'd worked hard to be good enough. Even if it was kickball or math bowl, she never wanted to be the person who sucked, the one who caused her team to lose. Playing it safe guaranteed she wouldn't make costly mistakes or huge triumphs either. Never the rabbit, always the tortoise. Why a deity would choose her baffled her. "Why?"

Maja rubbed a jewel-bedecked long-fingered hand over her face. "I see some of my younger self in you. Not enough confidence in your natural abilities. Our world is several layers thick with entities existing in each realm. Occasionally, the domains overlap, and you spy someone or something from another realm. It could be a glimpse of the future, someone from the past, a voice, a suggestion whispered just when you needed it. Has that ever happened to you?"

"More than once." She never told anyone, certain she was losing her mind. It would be enough for her mother to insist on an exorcism.

"Can you describe this experience?" Maja encouraged as she leaned forward in her chair.

Everything blurred together, making it hard to pick out individual experiences. Her breathing became frantic as she searched her mind for details, only finding mists like what she encountered in the dark forest. "I can't remember. Everything is getting foggy. Is it my time to pass over?"

Maja stood and wrapped an arm around Stella, tucking her close. "Listen, child, our time is short. Your job involves finding your own answers and not be influenced by outside forces. You're not crossing over. You'll go back to the life you left. You're not dead."

"Not dead," she repeated the words trying to take them in. Just about the time she accepted being dead, she found out she wasn't. "What happened?"

"You're in a comatose state due to the drugs, alcohol, and the desire not to live. Your body still lives, but your mind, along with your spirit, went on a voyage for answers," she murmured the words close to Stella's ear.

Did she find all the answers? Her death did no good. Excellent, since she wasn't dead. Cam would be a toothless threat if she alerted administration that he was threatening her, but first she needed to talk to Mitch. What seemed so hopeless didn't seem as bad now. As for her mother, she could accept she was like so many other people desperately searching for value and hope in all the wrong places. If only her mother found that younger, happier self. "I'm not ready. I need to know more."

Maja's other arm wrapped around her, pulling her into a tight hug. "Don't worry. I have a mentor for you. You'll recognize her when you meet her."

CHAPTER TWELVE

HOW WILL I recognize her, she wanted to ask, but a gut-wrenching pain doubled her over? Eyes closed, breath held, she rode out the spasm. She heard voices, an argument. Her mother's voice rang out over the man's.

"My daughter needs medical help now."

Mom. Her eyes wouldn't open. Her lashes were tangled and caked together with what her mother used to call sandman's sand, but she only labeled gunk. The high wail of a police car siren came closer and then stuttered to a stop. Someone bumped into her bed frame, jostling her, causing the rope to rub on her wrists. Great Goddess, they'd tied her up. Nausea that threatened before returned, causing a thin spray of vomit. Basic first aid knowledge had her turning her head to prevent it from sliding back down her throat.

"Stay if you want, Roberta, but I'm not getting arrested."

People ran by her, and a door slammed.

The mattress depressed as her mother sat beside her legs. "I'm not leaving my daughter."

A fierce pounding rattled the door. "Police. Open up."

The mattress creaked as Roberta stood, crossed the room, and opened the door. "Thank goodness, you got here. That horrible man and his thugs just ran out the back door. They tortured my daughter because of her religion. Forced me to watch. A regular hate crime."

Stella listened to her mother as she broke down in tears, confessing her love for her daughter and her stupidity in trusting the snake oil salesman posing as a holy messenger. Disgust, hate, even contempt should have overwhelmed Stella, but she kept listening for even a hint of Bobby, and then she heard it.

"I should have known the man was no good. He didn't even believe in musical instruments."

Someone sawed diligently away at her restraints. "Don't worry. We'll get this off you." Her right arm came free, leaving behind a deep ache in her shoulder blade. Rolling it eased the stiffness a little.

"She's conscious," a female voice exclaimed. "We need water to wash her face."

A cool damp towel covered her eyes, wiping away the gunk. Finally, she could open her eyes. The anxious face of her mother filled her vision. "Can you ever forgive me?"

After kidnapping and possible exorcism, theirs would never be a television family relationship. Still, she could forgive her mother and move on. "It's okay, Bobby. Everyone goes down a wrong path now and then, trusting people who don't deserve their respect, let alone trust."

Her mother's eyes grew wide as she stepped back.

"I think you need some water." The female officer brandished a bottle, propped her up, and dribbled the water down her throat. It felt good, relieving the dryness, but not quite up to the delicious hot tea, Maja brewed. Had she imagined it all? Some crazy dream brought on by too many painkillers.

The rope snapped off her left leg as an officer sawed through it with a lethal-looking blade. She wiggled her feet, lifting her rear from the mattress, testing to see if her leg still functioned. It still worked, but it hurt. The rope restraint around her right ankle dropped to the floor as a pair of medics rushed into the room with a gurney.

A medic knelt beside the bed and donned latex gloves. "I'm Sean. I'll be examining you to make sure nothing is broken before we put you on the gurney."

Stella nodded her head unsure if she were supposed to introduce herself at this point. Who knew how long she'd been tied to the bed? Her rank body odor wrinkled her nose and partially answered her question. Sean gently picked up her arms, examining them. "Several long scratches, the type you'd expect from briars."

"What? Let me see?" Her mother, trying to look around the medic, resisted her involuntary escorting out by an officer, and stared back as she left.

Sean continued his survey as the other medic made notes. "I'm going to roll you on your side to check your spine before lifting."

The other medic assisted in rolling her carefully onto her side, pressing her abused shoulder into the mattress. A small groan escaped as she surveyed the room, though it was a little hard to see between all the uniformed legs. The walls were dirty, with holes in the drywall a little larger than a closed fist. A card table with an oversized Bible and a wooden cross on top of it reminded her of one of the scenes from a vampire movie she'd watched. Abandoned metal chairs lying on the floor bore witness to the speed of the escape.

"Her legs are filthy, covered in dirt." The medic commented while a large flash went off. A scraping sound along with pressure on her left shin alerted her to an officer scraping dried mud into a plastic evidence bag. Scratches, dust, knowledge, it all had to be real. The Pleiades, the Seven

Sisters, she'd have to look those up.

"I need to see her! Please."

Mitch's voice had her twisting around to catch sight of his face. He stood in the door flanked by two officers. His tight lips expressed a determination she knew well.

"This is a crime scene. You could contaminate it." One officer explained, blocking Mitch's entrance by positioning himself in the middle of the open doorway.

Mitch held his ground. He must have called the police. Of course, he did. Despite all her mother's protestations to the authorities and fast forming regret, she might not have made it if not for Mitch.

"I'm okay. Meet me at the hospital," she told him.

"Which one?" His voice carried over the noise of the various individuals collecting evidence.

A medic answered for her, which was just as well since she had no clue where she was going. The two medics lifted and covered her with a blanket before strapping her in. The material, tucked tight around her toes all the way up her body, warmed her. The gurney clicked in place as they raised it and maneuvered it through the cramped fetid room.

Slanting sun cut through the bare tree branches as the medics backed out of the building. Strapped down, her vision was limited to blue sky with the occasional wispy cloud and bare tree branches. The crisp air carried a hint of burning in it. Nice to be outside. Alive.

Mitch's tall figure caught her eye. He waved, giving her a cautious smile, his worry reflected in the position of his hunched shoulders.

A small dark woman rushed forward and stuck a mike in her face. "Is it true you were the intended sacrifice in a Satanic ritual?"

Seriously? She wished they'd put the blanket over her head. Sean, the medic closest to the reporter yelled, "Get out of the way. You're compromising her medical care."

Mitch joined in, moving his tall form between the gurney and the reporter as the medics wheeled the gurney to the waiting ambulance. The reporter was part of the problem. Time to make a stand. "Mitch," she pushed the words past dry lips. "Tell the reporter I was not a satanic ritual sacrifice. Satanists do not sacrifice people or animals. That's all movie nonsense."

His somber eyes held hers as he nodded. "I'll tell them, but I don't know if it will do any good. The news is all about sensationalism and preying on people's secret fears. Reporters don't care about the truth."

"Thank you."

The female medic spoke to Mitch, "We've got to get your girlfriend to the hospital."

"Yes." He never bothered to correct the term, girlfriend. Then again, it wasn't like him to confide in a random uniformed stranger. *Oh, we just work together and occasionally share secret chunks of our lives. I would like her to be my girlfriend, but she brushes off my overtures to chase after some hot bad boy.*

Good thing he never mentioned it. In the end, it made her sound stupid, probably because she had been. Not anymore. The gurney snapped in place inside the ambulance while Sean attached a blood pressure device to monitor her pulse.

The female medic took her temperature while she chatted. "My name is Jill. Your boyfriend is a good one. He protected you from the reporters and knew exactly what you needed to have done."

"He did, didn't he?" She never really thought about it, but Mitch always seemed to know what she needed. Why hadn't she ever realized how attuned the two of them were. Too busy meeting Cam's various needs—make that demands.

Jill typed some info into a small mounted computer. "Yeah, it's hard to find a man who will treat a girl well."

Sean rolled his eyes and reached for the grab rod. "Jill, you better hold on and talk less."

The woman followed his advice but merely grunted in response to his comment. The ambulance's wail was intensely loud inside the compartment. The vehicle weaved in and out of traffic and occasionally gave a stronger blast. Despite the straps, Stella felt the sway of the gurney, but at least she wasn't jerked around as much as Jill and Sean. They reminded her of human laundry on a metal clothesline in the middle of a tornado. Only the tightly packed ambulance kept them from flying away.

"We're here," Sean announced as the ambulance slowed and bumped up into the driveway. The doors swung open and hands reached out to guide the gurney down. Questions flew.

"Blood loss?"

"Heart Rate?"

"Pressure?"

What she could gather from the comments was she suffered dehydration, shock, trauma to the joints from being tied, lacerations, and abrasions. No mention of her filthy feet.

Some of the people waiting looked up at her entrance, possibly cursing her arrival because it would mean an added delay until their exam. Another news reporter milling in the crowded lobby spotted her and made a break for the gurney. No Mitch was there to run interference although someone shouted for security.

Interference came in the form of Esmeralda Hare brandishing her wolf-headed cane. "Stand back or I'll turn you into a toad."

The male reporter stumbled backward. The cane, the threat, or Esmeralda's sudden appearance may have contributed to his reaction. Could it have been something else? Like Maja watching over her? Who knew? She did know the things weren't always, as they seemed. Even when she thought she was alone and friendless, forces she didn't understand were beside her.

Hospital personnel surrounded her and lifted her from one gurney to another. "Good luck, kid," Jill wished her before letting go of the gurney.

After being looked over by a half-dozen people with various titles, Stella made it upstairs to a private room. An IV rehydrated her while a monitor beeped in the background assuring everyone, she was okay. The nurse checked her pulse, wrote it down and gave her a weary smile. "I imagine you left a nightmare. Scary" The woman shivered for effect. "Nothing a couple of days of forced rest and being pampered by your family won't fix."

Of course, that would require a family who would do that. A little sigh caught in her throat as her father walked through the door looking haggard and much older than she remembered. He bent over and kissed her forehead before dropping into a nearby chair. "How's my best girl?"

The childhood nickname made her heart trip. What she would have given for such a casual endearment even a couple of weeks ago. That time was gone. "They tell me I'm alive. Good considering, I was unconscious for thirty-six hours without food or water. Where's Mother?"

"Umm, she had some paperwork to finish with the police." Her father stared down at his shoes. Under arrest was what he didn't say. Just as well, she didn't want to see her anytime soon.

Her father brushed his hand against hers. "Pamela thought maybe you could spend a couple of days with us."

Geesh. She fought hard not to roll her eyes. His new, much younger wife gave him official permission to allow his recently kidnapped and abused daughter to come home with him. What an invite. She hoped to avoid the dubious charms of Pammy but wasn't sure what other options she had. She'd turn down her mother if she weren't in jail. "Oh, I don't know. How about I get back to you."

A commotion near the door revealed Mitch, Leah, and the entire Carpenter family crowding the entrance. Her father picked up her hand and kissed it. "I understand. I'll get out of here so you can see the people you want to see."

"No, you don't have to go."

His shoulders pitched forward as he left without replying. He looked pathetic. A voice that sounded remarkably like Maja's spoke. "Don't feel too sorry for him. He made his choices and left a wave of devastation behind. It's his mess if he wants to clean it up."

So true. It was hard to think of her parents screwing up, but they did, making them seem a lot more human and not the least bit god-like. The Carpenters along with Mitch spilled into the room. The usually reticent Mitch made sure to take the only chair in the room, pulling it close to the bed.

"I apologize if I'm embarrassing you, but I figured I needed to get to the front of the boyfriend line with Cam being in jail and all." Mitch reached through the bed railing to rest his hand on hers. "Do I get to the front of the line? My heart stopped when I realized something happened to you?"

A few "ahs" came from Leah and Nora. Esmeralda grumbled, "Get on with it. We got important stuff too."

Feeling suddenly better, she turned her hand to grip Mitch's. "You're already at the front. You always should have been."

Mitch's eyes brightened along with his expression. Pure joy illuminated his face. How could she have ever thought Cam cared about her? He never looked at her the way Mitch did.

"No, no, no," Esmeralda shook her head as she walked toward the bed. "Make the man work, grovel, and keep him uncertain. Make him dance. Don't tell him he's number one. Sheesh, girls today." The rest of the family laughed.

Mitch mouthed, *thank you,* and topped it off with a wink.

Leah and Nora crowded the left side of her bed while Mitch relinquished his chair to Esmeralda, earning him a promise not to turn him into a toad.

"Nana," Leah added, "quit threatening to turn people into toads. You know you can't do that."

Instead of Esmeralda answering, her dapper husband Buell stepped forward attired in a double-breasted suit and tie. "I wouldn't bet on that. The woman can do anything she sets out to do. I wanted to hear more about this Cam character who sounds toad worthy."

"Me, too," Stella added, wondering if she had anything to fear from Cam. Mitch stepped closer to the group as he explained.

"Initially, I alerted everyone about your absence. I contacted campus security who went to your room. Cece, your roommate, swore Cam killed you and that she saw him and some other guys carrying you out and everything."

"That wasn't Cam." She interrupted the story, trying to put the pieces together. "Cece was probably high when she came back." No other reason in explaining why she'd connect Cam with the hired muscle and the black SUV.

"Yeah, we know that now," Leah, commented. She circled her hand. "C'mon finish the story. I never heard all of it. Just bits and pieces."

Mitch nodded, but his gaze went to Stella. "Is me talking about it bothering you?"

"No! Please tell. How else will I know?" She didn't feel the need to explain she'd washed down a handful of drugs with alcohol. Later, with a smaller group, although, according to Leah, more than half of her family had the ability to have already sensed it.

Mitch brushed her hair back as she leaned into his touch. Esmeralda cleared her throat, which started Mitch talking. "Cece rattled off Cam's address like she'd memorized it or something. Police went over there. No response. They broke in due to having probable cause. Boxed up DVD players, laptops, and game systems crowding the small apartment, but no Cam, and no Stella. They had to send a van for the stolen merchandise."

Ethan elbowed his way to the front of the group. "How did they know it was stolen? Could be the guy had a lot of stuff."

"Well, apparently some electronics store had been broken into earlier, and the items matched the description of what was stolen."

Did Cam burglarize the electronics store? If you'd asked her last week, she'd have defended him. So much, she didn't know about Cam. Bizarre, she'd known him for weeks and knew almost zilch. All she knew was that he excelled at manipulating women.

Nora scratched her head, considering the details. "Where was Cam when this happened?"

Mitch held up one finger. "Now, that's where it gets peculiar. He was busy breaking into the computer lab. In fact, he was in the lab and had a computer powered up, but couldn't get past the password. He had no clue the door was alarmed. When caught, he insisted Stella gave him permission to be there. The campus police had him in the car when the county police zoomed up and grabbed him. The truth is he didn't kidnap you or murder you, but he either robbed the store or accepted stolen merchandise, and did break into the computer lab. If that wasn't enough, he swung at one of the arresting officers."

"Out of curiosity, were the officers all men?" Stella asked, wondering if uniformed women would be able to withstand his legendary skills.

Mitch shot her an interested look, hoisting one eyebrow. "I don't know."

Leah pointed to Stella. "How did you find out where she was?"

"Ah, that. You're the only one who's asked. The police just took the address and went with it." Mitch ran a hand through his thick hair. "I remembered Stella saying something about her mom attending The Last Days and Holy Resurrection Tabernacle or something like that. Not too many churches named that in her town, two to be exact."

He stopped talking with two bright spots of red on his cheeks. Stella told him, "It doesn't matter what you did. The results are the only thing that matter. Okay?"

"Um, right." He managed a smile and then shrugged. "At the first church, I got a disconnected message. I called the second church. Whoever answered the phone informed me that both Roberta and the minister left to look at church property. It was some big deal because they took some other investors with them, even rented a black Escalade to view the property. She saw it when she came into work. I confessed I was one of the big investors and wanted to catch up with them. Did she know where they went? Somewhere around the college, and then she made a remark about the license on the rental being funny. I asked why. It read STD 234, which made it an easy one to remember."

"Very convenient," Maura, Leah's mother, commented working her way up from the back of the crowd to stand near the bed. She reached over the footboard to pat Stella's feet. "After you get out of the hospital, you're coming home with us. With Nora gone, there's a room practically with your name on it."

At last, a solution to her home problem offered in a casual invite "Yes, I'd like that."

Ethan interrupted, "Everyone knows we're taking Stella home with us. It goes without saying." He sauntered up to Mitch and elbowed him. "The story, man."

"I used a realty site to look for isolated properties, not close to anything. Something preferably abandoned, so there'd be no real interest in it and found about four probable places. My plan was to casually survey the sites, but my lack of wheels slowed down the process. It's hard to convince a friend to drive you to abandoned buildings. I tried using one of those online sites that supposedly helps you find information for a fee. Worthless. By this time, I knew Stella had been gone over twenty-four hours. I was getting desperate and hacked into the tax assessor's website. Not that hard, really. I found out the addresses for derelict buildings. Out of state owners held the first two buildings. The Last Days and Holy Resurrection Tabernacle owned the third. Bingo. I called the police and explained I was a friend of Stella's and had reason to believe she was being held against her will at that location. I had to get a taxi to take me out to the middle of nowhere, which is rather hard to convince a taxi driver to do when he's worried, you'll rob him."

Stella rubbed Mitch's hand against her face. "How could someone not trust you? You don't have a criminal bone in your body."

Mitch's face erupted into a goofy, so in love smile, the rest of the group elbowed one another. "If you don't count lying and hacking into databases."

"Let's go get something to eat," Maura suggested, catching everyone's eye as she left the room.

Ethan was the last to go. "I hope you know that's code for giving you two time alone. Use it well."

Stella's grip tightened on Mitch's hand. "I need to talk to you." She didn't want to mention it when everything appeared to be working out, but she still needed to.

Mitch reached for her other hand. "Go ahead, sweetheart. You can tell me anything."

The look in his eyes reassured her. "Cam blackmailed me. He threatened to get you in trouble because he found out about your DUI."

"Is that why you went out with him?" Mitch looked both concerned and confused as he played with her hand, using his index finger to outline her fingers and sending a jolt of electricity up her arm.

"Hmm." His actions made her forget the question for a second. "No, I went out because he kept asking me."

"That's all it took, huh?" Mitch continued to play with her hand not looking up. "If I'd known that then I would have taken that approach."

"Wish you had." Stella didn't add they could have avoided this entire mess, but maybe they wouldn't have. Her mother still would have kidnapped her. Only she may not have been out of it as much. They used drugs on her, too, ether or chloroform so it may not have made much of a difference.

Mitch's eyebrows lowered as his lips turned down. It didn't take clairvoyance to realize he blamed himself. "We could have had so much more time together watching movies, holding hands, eating pizza, and snuggling."

"Snuggling, I'm all for that."

He looked up and grinned, the worry gone from his eyes. She hated to put it back, but she wanted to have an honest relationship. "He wanted me to change grades on the computer, his and six friends. I think he was close to being kicked out for academic failure and probably taking money from the others."

Mitch snorted. "Yeah, I hear you actually have to show up in class to pass."

"Well, apparently Cam didn't hear it, and he failed to meet the right girls to do his homework. Kept getting dumb ones."

"You're smart. I know that. I had a peek at your grades. You're setting the curve in some of your classes."

Stella grinned. "Thanks." She threw him a significant look. "You'll lose your job if you get caught accessing privileged files."

"I did it from Lauren's computer."

They both laughed.

"What I have to tell you I'm not proud of. I took a bunch of pills and washed them down with vodka. I felt there was no way out. If I didn't do what Cam wanted, you'd have lost your scholarship."

"Stella," Mitch leaned over the railing gathering her in his arms, careful of the IV. "Screw the scholarship. You're all I care about. Besides, a failing student and felon isn't exactly Mr. Credible. I'm so sorry you didn't tell me. Remember you can tell me anything, no matter what."

She sniffed. "Okay, I'm a practicing Wiccan too."

"Oh that, you told me that before."

"I did?" She didn't remember doing that. "When?"

"Oh, never directly, but you always were the go-to person about any earth-based religion. I figured it out. I'm smart like that."

"On that note," Esmeralda trilled from the doorway. "I have someone I want you to meet."

A tall woman stood behind the diminutive Nana. The woman followed Esmeralda slowly, using a cane. A gray braid trailed down her back.

"Maja." The name escaped Stella's lips.

Esmeralda looked truly taken back. "You know Mary? Only her friends call her Maja."

"You could say we met in another place, another dimension."

A look of comprehension settled over Esmeralda. "Then you know why she's here. Don't you?"

Mitch looked from woman to woman. "I don't. Why?"

Stella's eyes teared up a little. "She's to be my teacher, mother, and grandmother."

Maja grinned. "I told you that you'd recognize your mentor when you met her. The teacher arrives when the student is ready."

THE END

RECLAMATION

PAGAN EYES, BONUS STORY

BY
RAYNA NOIRE

RECLAMATION
Rayna Noire
Copyright © 2018

To obtain permission to excerpt portions of the text, please contact the author.

All characters in this book are fiction and figments of the author's imagination.

CHAPTER ONE

L EAH STOOD AT the edge of the white tent, shading her eyes looking for Ethan. Her mother decided the house wouldn't do for the event. Too many people would want to attend the celebration, as her mother insisted on calling it. Macabre. Weird. Wrong, somehow, she understood on one level, but it didn't stop the feeling of being adrift.

The bright green leaves on the trees heralded spring, rebirth. Birds engaged in mating flew after one another, calling sharply, like some humans. One successful pairing wove a grass and twig nest in a nearby tree. Random splotches of color displayed wild flowers in bloom, but she had a difficulty seeing them for the tears flooded her eyes.

Nora came up beside and handed her the tissue box. "Any sign of Ethan?"

"No." Her answer was slightly muffled by the tissue. "Is Mother still doing the 'everything is great' attitude?"

Nora gazed at the small, winding path that led from the parking lot. "Trying. She's unraveling fast. If we don't get this ceremony going, she'll be an emotional puddle. Dad's trying to support her. I swear by Athena that he's falling apart, too."

The tissue obscured Leah's vision as she blotted her eyes. "I wasn't prepared for this, despite the stroke." Heaviness lodged in her chest. It felt like an anchor not only holding her in place, but also pulling her to the ground. Her hand landed on Nora's shoulder, hoping her sister could hold upright. It'd be embarrassing to end up prostate in front of so many of Nana's friends. Her grandmother had expectations of appropriate behavior, no reason to disappoint her, especially today.

The sound of running feet captured their attention. The vivid green of the new growth mingled with the bright sunlight. Streaming through the branches, it silhouetted the approaching figure. The runner slowed as he approached the festival tent, passing into a shaded area allowing identification. Ethan stumbled up to them, his tie askew and his hair windswept.

Nora reacted first. "Where's grandfather? Orin?"

Clayton, Nora's husband, appeared beside Nora. "You look distraught. Had some problems wrangling Buell here, did you?" He peered around Ethan to the empty footpath behind.

"No." He managed the word between breaths. Then, changed his mind. "Yes."

Nothing he said made sense. Leah knew her younger brother enjoyed being dramatic now and then, but this was not the place for it. Her hand dropped from her sister's shoulder and landed on her hip as she fixed a stern gaze on him. Odd, his boyfriend, Orin hadn't come with him, but that didn't matter now. "Quit playing. Where's grandfather?"

Ethan's wide eyes met theirs as he spat out the word. "Gone."

Nora reacted first. "What do you mean gone? How could he be gone? Your job was to get him here. He connects most with you."

Clayton jumped in, not even giving Ethan a second to answer. "Where did he go?" His brows lowered as he reached for Ethan's arm.

As if anticipating the move, Ethan stepped back out of reach. "He's not here."

"I know." Nora and Leah spoke in unison.

The forest went silent as if waiting for an answer to the question, too. Ethan thrust out his hands as he tried to explain, turning his palms upward. "Not here. Not in as not with me. When Orin and I got him in the car and were driving here, he shouted to stop. I did. He jumped out of the car, went running off between some buildings, then disappeared. We both got out of the car to follow. He ran into a blind alley where two building walls angled to form a V. No doors, no way out, no grandfather. Nothing. We even tried to go into the buildings. Obviously abandoned and locked up tight. I left Orin there in case he came back."

The heaviness returned to Leah's chest. Her hand clasped the amulet her grandmother had given her before her last time jump. It pulsed under her closed hand.

Nora shook her head slowly. "Where could he have gone?"

"Time portal." Clayton spoke the words before Leah could even form them. "He even showed me a map he made of all the known ones in this area. Had a time table and knew when they winked in and out of existence, too."

A certainty, a knowing, enveloped Leah. Her amulet pulsed as if agreeing with her. "Why today? It's grandmother's funeral. An odd day for him to go time hopping." A kernel of resentment grew as she considered all those who came to pay homage to Esmeralda Hare and her own husband fails to show. What was wrong with the man? The hand on her hip fisted as she considered the possibility of her mother slipping into a full meltdown. No Nana to threaten to turn everyone who didn't act right into toads. They all knew she'd never do that to family. She'd never perfected the spell.

With her grandfather gone, somehow keeping the family together fell on the grandchildren. Being an adult sucked.

Clayton held up one finger. "Of course, today. He couldn't imagine a life without Esmeralda by his side."

Ethan's gasping slowed as he finally caught his breath. He straightened his tie and asked, "Where do you think he went?"

Clayton's gaze went upward as he considered the possibilities. "I think he went to be with your grandmother."

A general murmur of agreement greeted the remark. Clayton's hand stroked his bearded chin. "That may have been his intention, but portals can be tricky. Better yet, what time did he return to since both are in their eighties?"

"Wonky, you mean." Ethan added, but cast a glance over his shoulder as if expecting the man in question to appear. "We know he wouldn't have gone back before he met her at the carnival."

Clayton disagreed. "We don't know that." He moved his hand in the air in a circular motion. "It's the time portal thing. Not dependable."

A long sigh drew attention to Nora. "Why should we worry if he went back to see Nana. It's rather romantic that he wants to spend time with her and avoid all those misunderstandings they had at first."

It all sounded good in theory, but Leah did not want to explain to her mother that not only did she lose her mother, but her father had vanished into another time.

Ethan quit looking at the path. His gaze snapped back to them with an even more panicked expression, if that were possible. "I have to go. Now!"

"Where?" Leah asked, aware she was not going to like the answer.

Ethan shoved his hands into his dress pants as he shifted his weight from foot to foot, a telltale sign of his nervousness. "Well, ya know grandfather has been more confused lately. I guess I noticed it more because we spend time together."

"Go on," Nora urged, her upper body leaning in his direction to not miss a word.

Clayton stepped close and wrapped an arm around her waist, providing physical and emotional support.

Ethan's eyes flickered side to side before he spoke as if what he had to say shouldn't be overheard by non-family ears. "He could go back in the past and mess things up. Might even see the young him romancing Esmeralda, get jealous, and decide to take the young him out of the picture."

The birds in the nearby tree flapped their wings and shrieked in the opposite mood to their earlier cooing. Did they know something or was it a normal aviary disagreement? The image of her elderly grandfather hiding behind a brightly colored tent took form in her mind. An erratic, ceremonial magician was the worst kind. "The young Buell Hare wouldn't know what hit him."

Nora spoke slowly, emphasizing each word. "None of us would ever exist." She glanced up at her husband. "Except Clayton."

The enormity of situation stopped all conversation as they stared at each other, taking in their corporeal forms, wondering if each sibling would gradually fade out of existence if something went wrong in their shared past.

Clayton broke the heavy uneasiness that wrapped around them all. "I can't imagine anything going right in the past, especially with a grief-stricken Buell determined to return to Esmeralda, possibly the young Esmeralda. She won't recognize him. It could sour the romance between the young Buell and her. I have to go back and get him."

He dropped the arm wrapped around his wife and tried to step toward Ethan, but Nora wrapped both of her arms around him and held on for dear life.

"I've seen the results of the time portal. You'll not leave me for twenty or forty years. We'll go together."

Ethan turned, leading the way while Nora and Clayton followed, holding hands. Leah naturally fell in line, but the three turned at once as if sensing her presence.

"Leah," Nora gave her the 'I'm the older sister, and you need to do as I say' stare down. "You have to stay to explain to Mother what's happening."

A valid point, but not one Leah liked. Why did she get to be the bearer of bad tidings? Great. The trio hurried down the path, disappearing between trees blinking out of sight due to the glare of the sunlight, rather like the time portal would cause them to vanish out of this era. What if Grandpa miscalculated, and instead of ending up at an old-time carnival, they all ended up on some medieval battlefield. The thought chilled her as she stared at the bright spot that swallowed up three of the remaining family members.

Both hands covered her face, as she prepped herself up for what she had to do. Behind her, she could hear the slight hum of voices, along with the crackle of so much psychic energy in one place. Her hands dropped from her eyes as she considered the possibility of Esmeralda's talented friends and sometimes rivals. An idea formed as she pivoted, ready to serve as the messenger. Better yet to present a solution, too.

With enough skilled witches, anything was possible or at least that's what she kept telling herself as she ran toward the tent. It was easy to spot her mother dressed in her grandmother's colorful carnival outfit from her early days. Maura, her mother, claimed it helped her to feel close to her departed mother. The guests, especially the older ones, remarked on how similar her appearance was to Esmeralda, as if the departed served as hostess to her own funeral. They'd chuckled, seeing the idea as amusing and not totally whacked.

Her father, in his dark suit, stood next to Maura, his arm encircling his wife's waist. He appeared to be a solid support if you didn't peer to closely at his face. Despite her grandmother's imperialistic ways, her father, Adam, adored Esmeralda. In some ways, she'd served not only as the matriarch to the Hare family, but also his, when his mother had run off with a traveling evangelist. If he ever needed advice about life, career, or family, Esmeralda would offer it. She offered it, even when not asked.

A woman swathed in purple stood holding her mother's hand. Traya was probably Nana's best friend and most avid rival. They had a strange relationship that consisted of competitive one up-man-ship. Once, she made the mistake of commenting that Traya couldn't read the cards as well as Nana. Esmeralda corrected her, pointing out that Traya was as talented, even though she may not have as much style. The remark had surprised Leah who knew her prideful grandmother insisted she was the best fortuneteller in the region. This had to be the highest praise she'd ever heard for Traya.

Nana would cut anyone off at the knees if they ever try to criticize Traya, although it was okay for her to make digs. Perhaps, that was how she'd be with Stella, her own best friend, once the two of them reached their eighties. What others might view as hurtful remarks would be a form of playful teasing. As she moved closer, the tears sliding down the woman's lined face displayed her sorrow. Her mother comforted Traya, instead of the other way around.

"I know it's hard. We both know Esmeralda won't stay twiddling her thumbs in Summerlands long. I suspect she's already here in the gentle breeze rustling the tree leaves, the joyful bird song, or the spring flowers."

A dog yapped in the distance, and Adam joined the conversation, saying, "Who knows she could even be that barking dog."

They all managed a weak laugh, knowing Esmeralda would never settle for something as subtle as a breeze. The barking dog would be more appropriate. Not a small yappy dog, but something that would command attention such as a sled dog, Saint Bernard, or even a wolf.

Traya held a tissue up to her eye, mumbled something, and moved in the direction of another group of people talking in whispered tones.

Her mother's eyebrows lifted when she saw Leah. Ah, yes, she knew the question without any words spoken. It wasn't so much telepathy, but more of the obvious.

Her father chose words over thoughts. "Is Buell here?"

Okay, the plan didn't seem very inspired with both parents looking at her in an expectant manner. What did they truly want? That Buell would appear, and they'd get this celebration over with and on to the wine and cakes? Then they all could separate and leave to grieve in private. Well, not just yet, she needed the community.

"Well, ah, no. We have a bit of a problem."

Her father's brows beetled before he even heard the news while her mother's shiny eyes and partially open mouth made her look vulnerable, rather like a baby bird.

Leah inhaled deeply, trying to arrange her words in such a way that her siblings' plan to bring Granddad Buell back didn't sound like a train wreck. "Um, Ethan and Orrin had Granddad, but he made them stop the car."

"Understandable," Her father murmured. He continued when his wife snapped her gaze from Leah to him. "Attending the funeral," his face flushed as he stumbled for the right euphemism, "I mean celebration would make it all too real."

Grateful for any delaying time, Leah interjected, "It is real." Although, her father normally made sense, he wasn't this time.

"Of course, it's real, Leah." His hand dropped to her shoulder, gave it a slight squeeze, imparting warmth and comfort at the same time. "I know you haven't lost anyone close to you before or experienced that kind of grief. It's almost as if a protective shield drops over you, causing you to not to accept the death. Often, it feels like a dream and all you must do is shake it off to make it go away. Once you wake, none of it will matter because everything will go back to being the same."

Leah watched Adam's lips move, hearing the words, but concentrating on how to explain her own plan on locating Buell. A blue butterfly with wings outlined in black hovered above her father's shoulder, near his ear. Butterflies often symbolized the soul. Could it be her grandmother signaling her? Her eyes narrowed as she concentrated on the butterfly. Did it have a message for her? Her father's voice faded along with the chirping of birds. A stillness replaced the sound. It felt more like a whiteness, a light that managed to be both light and cool, but no message. Esmeralda's distinctive voice full of energy and confidence didn't sound inside her head. Instead, an impression of contentment spread through her. Peace. For a few heartbeats, her consciousness floated in a sea of tranquility. Free of worry, no actions needed, a sense of well-being filled her.

"Leah, Leah, are you with us. Adam, I think she's slipped away."

Her mother's worried voice withdrew her from the calm place she'd entered. Blinking, she brought her parents' concerned faces into focus. A quick glance over her father's shoulder confirmed that the butterfly had flown away. Ah, yes, they expected something. Shouldn't they be able to sense it? Was she imagining things rather like the protective shield her father mentioned?

"Ah, the truth is," Leah paused wondering what happened to her great plan. "Grandpa didn't just stop the car. He ran off."

Her mother gasped and pressed her hand against her chest. "Adam, this is terrible. You know Buell's state of mind is compromised. There is no telling what might happen to him."

Leah's upper teeth embedded themselves in her lower lip. Her mother would not be thrilled that Nora and Clayton went after him. For all she knew Ethan and Orin joined the search, too. She, alone, was there to pass on the news. Didn't they kill the bearer of bad news in ancient times. She could understand why.

Her father tightened his arm around his wife. "There, there, let's not go thinking the worse. We need to assess the situation, then determine what we need to do. Maybe Buell just ran off. Grief-stricken people do that."

She knew her father was trying to calm down her mother, but she found herself shaking her head no. Her grandfather hadn't just gone for a stroll down the street. In his own way, he was just as dramatic as his late wife. Nothing as normal as visiting the neighborhood watering hole to drink a toast to his wife would satisfy him.

"Leah?" Her mother managed her name in a quivering voice, that gained strength as she continued. "You know something."

Well, she did. It wasn't going to make her popular to say the least. If she wanted to put her plan in motion there was no time to waste. "Ethan and Orin chased him into an alley with no way out. No doors. Nothing. Ethan is sure he slipped through a time portal."

The emotions shifted across her father's face, concern to alarm, then back to concern. As an engineer, he never wasted time beating around a subject or trying to solve any problem his family might have, even when they didn't want his help. He gave a slight nod of this head. "Sounds like a time portal to me."

"Exactly," she continued, anxious to get out all she needed to say. "Grandpa has even showed Clayton a map he's drawn up of the various portals in the city and a schedule of when they blinked in and out of existence."

Her mother stiffened her back and narrowed her eyes. "He planned this."

"Possibly," her husband agreed. "He was always obsessed with the time portals after using them for Leah."

They were talking too much, when she needed to put her plan in place. "Um, yeah. Anyhow, Clayton and Nora are going back to the house, I assume, to get the map and find Grandpa."

"What! Has this entire family gone crazy!" Her raised voice attracted attention. Maybe such a display at a normal funeral would cause people to look away politely. Not so here. It only drew everyone closer.

"What's wrong, Maura? Is there anything I can do?" Traya asked.

Her mother held her hand up. "Go on, Leah. I know there is more."

Leah found herself nodding. There was more, a lot more. None her mother would like.

"Speak!" Her mother barked the word like the time Leah pedaled her tricycle toward the busy road. Only in that case, the word, uttered in such an intense tone, had been *Stop*.

"Ethan explained that Grandfather has been forgetful—not quite himself. We assume that he's going back in time to be with Nana. He'll probably try for the early years when they met at the carnival. In his confused state, he might not recognize the young Buell."

Before she could explain more, her father spoke. "An extra Buell wandering around in a world where there is already a Buell will not work out well."

Traya put a finger to her lips for a moment, looking thoughtful, before dropping it. "A man of his magickal expertise could be dangerous in any century. Still, I think I have a solution."

"You do?" Leah asked in unison with her father.

"Let's find Ava. She's our resident medium. All, we must do is send Esmeralda a warning. She's always been a smart cookie. She'll know how to handle Buell no matter his age."

It sounded so simple. All they needed to do was send a message, and all would be well. There was, however, an issue of extracting Nora and Clayton from another time if they'd already jumped, too.

CHAPTER TWO

I T WASN'T HARD to pick Ava out of the crowd as Traya herded the small woman their way. She was dressed all in black. A few of the attendees had worn black more as a fashion statement than appropriate wear for a funeral. Loren, for example, sparkled in full drag queen attire, towering over the other guests. Her coven had gotten together and made photo t-shirts of their last group, shots of them all wearing pointy black hats and holding broomsticks. It probably made the guy at the t-shirt shop wonder. Then again, it was more likely they did it all online.

Esmeralda joked once that Ava wore black because people expected it of her. You seldom saw an old timey medium not wearing black. A few hacks did it for nefarious purposes, so they could move around a dark room pretending to be a spirit.

The tiny woman approaching them wasn't like that. She clutched a cane like the one Esmeralda had used. The way Traya towed her along, the woman had no chance to use her cane. They both came to a stop in front of Adam and Maura.

Ava held up her hand as she took a deep breath. "Okay, you want to send a message to your mother."

"That's right." Her mother nodded enthusiastically. "As soon as possible."

The medium took Maura's hand as she spoke." Grief is hard on anyone. It is especially hard for you, knowing how close the two of you are. Know that Esmeralda is in Summerlands. I'm certain she has sent you signals that she'd arrived."

The image of the beautiful butterfly came to mind. Maybe her mother missed it. It hadn't been one of those small yellow or white butterflies that were common in the area. No, it had been a large, brilliant blue one because Esmeralda would never do anything ordinary.

Her mother put up both hands and waved them. "Stop. I don't need the 'she is better off' speech. I need to send her a message. Buell has taken off into the past and could possibly wipe out most of the future Hare family in his current state of mind."

"Damn!" Ava steepled her fingers. "Can't you guys grieve the normal way? Drink too much. Eat way too much comfort foods. Look at photo albums and weep."

"We'll do all of that as soon as we get my father back—and possibly Nora and Clayton, who may have followed him into the past."

"Ethan and Orin maybe, too," Leah added.

Her mother turned slowly and gave her a look that would have melted a few. "What? What did you say?"

To think, only a few minutes ago she'd thought of the bearer of bad news being killed. "I don't know for sure. Ethan was all for jumping back in time because he has a special bond with Grandpa."

"That would be true."

Didn't Leah have a special bond, too. Didn't they travel back from the Burning Times together? "Anyhow, you know Ethan. Once he gets something in his head, there is no stopping him. If he goes, I believe we can assume Orin wouldn't sit and wait here."

"Oh, this isn't good." Ava added.

It was all Leah could do not to say, *really?*

"Ava, you've got to get a message to her." Maura wrapped her hands around the other woman's. "Right away!"

"I'll try," she agreed. "Keep in mind, it's not like you see on television. It isn't picking up a phone and dialing 1-800-Summerlands. Those of us in the business usually advise people to wait four months before seeking out contact."

"We don't have four months!"

Her father unwrapped her mother's hands from the medium who winced, which meant Mom must have been squeezing as spoke.

"I know. I'll do what I can. What I was trying to say, it's never a case of the departed not wanting to talk to you. It's more of them learning how to communicate. There are times when it's easier to communicate such as the wee hours of the morning with the atmosphere isn't being blasted with numerous electromagnetic messages from wireless devices and satellites."

She held up her hand before Maura could speak and dropped it as she spoke. "I know we can't wait that long. Also keep in mind, the spirits have an active life on the other side. They aren't just sitting around waiting for a call from a loved one. I imagine Esmeralda would be busier than most. She's probably organizing a group or two as well as meeting old friends. Normally, I like to meditate on the departed for an hour or more." The hand went right back up. "I know. Time." She pointed to a copse of trees. "I'll be over there trying to reach Esmeralda. I'll let you know what I hear."

Using her cane, the medium walked slowly to the trees. She sank to the ground, fanning her full skirt out like a blanket. It physically hurt Leah to wait. Who knew how much time passed in other dimensions as they stood around? "Mom, Dad, I know it would be great if Ava gets a message to Nana. I think we need to do more. Surely, with all this physic power here we should be able to watch grandpa. Maybe we could direct Nora and Clayton his way. Best of all, we could bring them all back."

Her phone chirped before her parents could respond. Her first impulse was to ignore it. There was enough going on. She didn't need to know any of the local gossip or what movies were showing at the theatres. After she signed up for the theater app, she was always getting updates. Still, it could be important. It might be her boyfriend, Dylan, telling her he was on his way or even Ethan.

The text said something about an image attached. She clicked on it to reveal a map in Buell's distinctive handwriting. He often joked he could have been a cartographer because he did love making maps. Near one portal was a yellow highlighter circle with a penciled in message.

We took this one.

Nora and Clayton sent them the map and the needed details.

They probably just left, which wouldn't reassure her mother at all. She chose to hand her father the phone. He studied it and handed it back to her. "At least, that is something."

Traya and her mother had their heads together discussing something. Once they separated Traya took off, hitting the various groups. Her voice carried. "Did anyone bring a crystal ball or a scrying mirror?"

There were some answering voices.

"I brought my travel one."

"I should have listened to my intuition."

"My spirit guide prompted me to bring mine."

"I have Tarot cards with me."

A thin, bald man worked his way through the crowd carrying a bowling ball bag. It was Larry, the chain-smoking psychic. Even though Larry could be accurate at times, her Nana regarded his smoking during a reading as not professional.

"Here it is." He placed the bag on the table, unzipped it, pulled out an ornate stand, and then a clear, quartz crystal ball. "What do you need me to do?"

Her mother starting to speak. "We needed…" Her words trailed off as she noticed Ava making her way over to them. "Just wait a moment. We might not need your help."

Ava walked even slower than usual. It didn't take any psychic skills to deduce that things had not gone the way she had hoped. Her mother's shoulders went up as she tensed, ready for whatever Ava might say.

The medium reached them and shook her head.

"Why not?" Her mother demanded in a strident tone, just a hair away from hysterical.

"I mentioned before the spirits are busy. As sensitive as Esmeralda is, I wouldn't be surprised if she didn't feel Buell's energy and recognized it on some level. If the grandchildren start showing up, that must make a disruption in the atmosphere, too. She's probably busy trying to figure out what is happening."

Maura pivoted toward Larry. "We will need your help. It's time for Plan B." Her eyes found Leah's. "What is plan B?"

CHAPTER THREE

L EAH SHIFTED HER feet and moved a little to get a better view. Larry sat on one side of the craft table that had been set up for refreshments. The cupcakes and individual bottles of wine and apple juice had been shoved together to make room for the ball. He stared at the clear ball, then up at the crowd surrounding the table. So far, nothing had happened. The ball hadn't even gotten misty as it should have. How could shapes form without mist?

He cleared his throat. "It's hard to perform with all of you staring at me."

It had to be a little bit like public speaking, but so much was on the line. "Everybody." Leah waved her hands. "You all could help if you directed energy to the ball. With most of the local Pagan community here, we should be able to find Buell, Nora, and Clayton" She didn't add Ethan and Orin, hoping they hadn't left. Maybe she should text him, but with so much going on, she hadn't even attempted to do so.

The mist grew in the ball, taking on form and color. The shape of a carnival tent appeared with an ornate sign shaped like a hand with lines and runes inscribed on it, announcing palm reading was done inside.

Traya leaned forward and pointed at the ball. "I recognize Esmeralda's tent."

A beautiful, dark-haired woman stepped out, put her hands on her hips, and glanced around in an assessing manner. "Would you look at her? She's so young." Traya declared. "I wonder what is going through her mind."

✧   ✧   ✧   ✧

ESMERALDA GAZED AROUND the carnival grounds. Where was that new roadie? He wasn't the usual type of man with little skills and ambition who was willing to take a manual labor job for a few bucks or to lay low for one reason or another. In that last regard, a carnival was an excellent place to lose or reinvent yourself.

A trio of fellow carnies strolled by, chatting and waved at her. She waved back and yelled, "Do you expect a big crowd tonight?"

"Big enough," one commented and laughed. "It's Sunday. Everyone had already been to church, so they're ready for a little sinning after every pastor told their precious flocks not to come to the carnival."

"Den of depravity," shouted another.

The third pointed to Esmeralda. "You're the worst. A regular witch of Endor."

Esmeralda smiled. "You're right if you mean I'm always right. Not sure, why all the hate. King Saul asked her for predictions. She gave them. They were right."

"What are talking about?" one of the carnies asked.

"Never mind," Esmeralda shook her head. "I keep forgetting how illiterate you guys are. I long for someone I can talk to. What I wouldn't give for a companion I didn't have to explain everything to."

"That's the reason you're still single. All that yapping. No man likes that."

Esmeralda waved her hand. "I ought to turn you into a toad."

The sizable man backed away, holding his hands up. "I didn't mean it. You're a beautiful, desirable woman. Any man would want to marry you."

A dapper man carrying a ladder walking by said, "I agree."

Esmeralda wiggled her fingers in a small wave before she ducked into her tent. Let the man think she was waving A knock on the wood board at the front of her tent surprised her.

A customer, already? She shrugged her shoulders, pulled out her Tarot cards, placed them on the table, and lit a white candle before calling out, "Enter."

She half-thought she'd use a red candle for the endless line of women, both young and old, seeking true love. It would be hard search in this town. So far, not only did she discover they were tight-fisted as far as crossing her palm with silver, but more than a few had threatened the carnies when they were at the local grocery buying supplies. The carnival tents would stay up, though, as long as the people still came, bad tippers that they were.

This customer felt different. It wasn't a woman that she knew, but an older man, tall to a degree he ducked his head as he entered too avoid the cross bar holding the tent up. He had a crown of silver hair, and when he saw her, his face lit up.

"Esme, I'm so happy to find you, finally. I had my doubts about the time portals. Still, here I am," he gestured to Esmeralda, "and there you are."

She shuffled the cards as she regarded him. "You appear to know my name or at least part of it. Something about you seems familiar. Yet, I've never met you."

The man reached for her hands, but she pulled them back. Something wasn't right.

"You're the love of my life. How could you not know me? I'm Buell Hare."

"Buell Hare?" The Buell she knew was tall and had similar eyes. He was also about fifty years younger. "Are you Buell's father or grandfather? He hasn't mentioned you, but we haven't talked about families in depth, yet. Did you come for a reading?" She shuffled the cards and turned over a card. "This is your indicator card, which tells who you are. The Magician."

"Highly appropriate since I am a ceremonial magician." He raised his eyebrows. "Why don't I tell you what the card means."

Esmeralda grimaced. "That's not how it works." She slapped the table. "You will pay me."

The enigmatic, elderly man grinned. "Just as feisty as ever. Does my heart good. As for the card," he tapped one wrinkled finger on the colorful pasteboard. "The man points up with one hand then down with the other as if saying as above, so below."

"Most people with eyes could see that. What else do you have?"

"Some people say the magician is the go between for the spirit world and the physical one. He also has all the elements on his table, which demonstrates his connection with the Earth. He has incredible potential and can manifest whatever he wants. Sometimes, his appearance is a prompt for people to go after what they want."

"It's a decent reading. Fairly grandiose considering it is your card. So, you're the link between Heaven and earth."

"Maybe, but what I consider myself is the link between your present and your future."

Peculiar. What was even more peculiar was he said it with so much certainty. The tent flap opened and a young woman with short, dark hair peeked in. "There you are, Grandpa. You're such a trickster." Looking back over her shoulder, as she stepped in, she called out. "Clayton, he's in here."

A man with curly hair and lively eyes stepped in the tent, too, making it a little crowded.

Her customer turned at his entrance. "Clayton, you didn't have to come. I can get back on my own."

Clayton caught the dark-haired woman's gaze and nodded his head. She murmured something. Then, the Buell she knew pushed into the tent. How many other people would fit into this tent?

"Buell?"

Both men answered. "Yes."

Well, this could be confusing. The older man would be leaving and possibly without paying. She stuck out her hand and gave him a significant look.

He chuckled and reached into his pocket. "I brought something just for such an occasion." He pulled out a few coins and put them in her hand.

Not bad. More than she usually got. He might be a bit odd, but she could overlook that. At least, his grandchildren worried about him. That said something. "Thank you. I'll leave you to your grandchildren."

Her Buell worked his way to her side and put his arm possessively around her waist.

The older man smiled at them. "Would you take some advice from me, son?"

"It depends." He pushed his chin up and moved his feet a bit a part. "What do you have for me?"

"Just this. Love is a precious jewel. Cherish it. Even more." His moved a tad to the left as he continued. "Even more important, cherish her."

The man gave them a final knowing smile before leaving. Esmeralda watched the tent flap close, leaving her and her Buell alone.

"What do you think that was about?" He turned his soulful eyes on her. "The advice was good."

"I agree. When he came in, he was so happy to see me, which was odd."

"I'm happy to see you every day."

She laughed. "According to the other carnies, my appeal will wear off because I'm too opinionated."

He snuggled her a little closer. "That happens to be one of my favorite things about you. I know all women have opinions, but few express them. That lets the male portion of the world assume their way is the only way. I love the way you slap back when people make that mistake."

The idea amused her. "If you like that, there's more where that came from. I imagine I could amuse you for days."

"Years." He dusted a kiss on her hair. "Decades. Eons. In some ways, I feel like I have always known you."

Esmeralda turned in his half-embrace to frame his face with her hands. "I, on the other hand, feel like I've been waiting for you. I didn't know what your name would be. Certainly, had no clue there would be more than one Buell Hare in my time, yet here you are."

He completed the embrace and tenderly cupped her chin. "Here I am."

CHAPTER FOUR

L EAH CAUGHT HERSELF sighing. Her grandparents could have easily starred in their own romance movie. She had no clue they were both so young and good-looking when they met. It was easy to see Nana was just as feisty when she was young. Before she could witness the kiss, Traya put her bejeweled fingers over the ball.

"I know Esmeralda would want some privacy." She nodded to Larry who had lit up another cigarette. "Put that out and change the channel. We need to know if they all get back okay."

Larry stubbed out his smoke and shot Traya an irritated look. "I see you know nothing about crystal balls. It shows you want it believes you need to see. What do you think this is *The Wizard of Oz*, and I can tune it into any person I choose?"

Instead of answering, Traya worked her chin back and forth as if holding in words, then she peeked through her fingers. The scene had changed, but it wasn't the carnival. There was a clearing with a few raw timber homes and a corral.

Larry stared at the scene. "I don't understand."

Within the crystal ball, Ethan strolled between the trees, giving all around them a thorough survey. The taller Orin was a few steps behind him.

Maura gasped. "It's our baby boy and friend."

Her brother would not have been happy to hear himself referred to as a baby boy, especially in such a large crowd.

Her father peered into the ball. "Time period is wrong. It's much earlier."

Inside the ball, there was a shout and both Orin and Ethan spun around as a bare-chested man in only a kilt charged at them with an ax. Maura mumbled some words and flicked her fingers at the ball. The crowd around the ball backed up, brushing off their faces and clothes.

Someone said, "Not cool, Maura. You splattered us with your spell."

Her eyes were on the ball where Orin helped up the angry man, minus the ax. She couldn't hear what they said, but apparently all three of them were okay. Guy fights in the past must be similar to current brush-ups where guys traded punches and ended up being good pals later. That's what Leah hoped happened.

Her father kept his eye on the scene. "It appears they are in the wrong country, too."

"Dear Sweet Goddess." Her mother moaned the words and swayed a little, causing her father to help her to a seat.

Here she always imagined her mother as the strong parent. Still, her mother dying, her father charging off into the past, along with two of her children and their significant others, was a heavy burden to bear. It had in all been a trying day. Her mother had only prepared herself for her mother's send-off, nothing more.

What where they going to do? She worked her way to her father's side and nudged him. He took a step back, realizing they might want to keep the conversation private from Maura. One of the women swept in and took Adam's place and probably did a better job at consoling, too.

Her hand dipped into her pocket to find her phone as she discussed the obvious issues with her father. "Grandpa sounded okay. Not confused like Ethan mentioned."

"I noticed that, too, although it could come and go. Maybe going back in time strengthened his memory, because in some ways he was younger."

"Possibly. Did you notice how protective his younger self was?"

"I did. I even wondered if this had to happen to cause his younger self to declare his feelings."

"Wow, Dad, you may have something there. Here I was worried that one of the Buells would cease to exist when they met each other. That didn't happen. We know Clayton took the map with him because he texted me a copy just in case. I have confidence they'll find their way back."

He reached for her hand and gave it a squeeze. "I do, too, honey. The real question is Ethan."

Impulsive, that's what her brother was. Even though he preferred to call himself spontaneous. "I bet Ethan decided to run right after them. He didn't have a map to consult."

"You're right. Then, Orin, followed, of course. On the bright side, as if there is one, Orin is bound to be giant no matter what time they're in. That, at least, might keep them safe."

Her father gave a little nod as if agreeing with himself. They all needed to reassure themselves that somehow this day would work out okay. If Nana was here, she'd bark out a few orders and have everyone scampering. In the end, things would work out. She wasn't there, and there was this Nana-shaped hole in the family. No one had stepped up to take the leadership role. So far, they were more like the United Nations, which translated to not making any decisions in a prompt manner.

They didn't have time to draw up a committee and Mother was too overwhelmed to take part. "Dad, we need to do something."

"I agree. You've been in the past before. What is time travel like?"

Obviously, her father was thinking along the same line she was. She should go. Grandfather was grieving. Clayton and Nora, although familiar with time travel, would be disoriented by their return jump. Two jumps in one day would be more so.

How could she describe time travel in a way that made sense? "Remember when we went to the theme park and Mom made you ride the twisty roller coaster with Ethan?"

"That wasn't something I could easily forget. It's like that?"

She sucked her lips in as she considered if that was a good enough description. "Somewhat. Imagine the ride much longer. Sometimes, it's total blackness and other times there is color when you get close to landing. It's like driving ninety-miles an hour with the scenery whipping past you, then you land, usually hard. I never landed on my feet."

He steepled his fingers together. "Sounds a little rough."

She made the mental correction. A lot rough. She pulled out her phone to examine the map and noticed a message from Ethan. She read it and passed it to her father.

I must go. Don't be mad. See you when I see you.

Her father exhaled hard. "I'll never understand him."

"You don't need to. I just need to find him." She toggled up on her messages to find the map. "Here's the map and schedule."

Her father took the phone and enlarged the images in spots. "Aha, I see what Buell has done. There's a math formula here for the cycles. When you enter a time portal, it's in a state of flux. This is why timing is so important."

"You sound like you know about this?"

"A bit. Sometimes, Buell and I did discuss it. Your brother jumped blind. He assumed a great deal."

"Got that." It still didn't answer the question of how they would find Orin and him. "Can we calculate where he and Orin are?"

Her father's gaze veered off to somewhere above her head. "I can to a degree. What time did you get your text?

She glanced down at her phone. "Two-ten. That's when I got it. Was there a time lag between when it was sent and when it arrived?"

Her father reached into his pocket for his own phone and pulled up the calculator function. "No, I would stick with that number because he texted you before he jumped. Even if it took a minute or less it should still be in the same time period frame. Buell told me something about the portals switched every ten minutes."

Her father must be confused. She wrinkled her nose not comfortable with correcting him. "Grandpa jumped into the past and waited twenty years for me to arrive in the Burning Times. Then we had twenty-four hours to make the jump back, not ten minutes."

"I know, sweetie. There were a lot of different variables. Buell didn't know as much about the time portals then as he does now, either. There are stable portals and unstable portals. Most are unstable, which is why they keep switching every ten minutes. They're all over the place if you know where to look."

The possibility of people stepping through into another century alarmed her. "Do you think some people accidentally shifted?"

"More than a few, I imagine. What are your suggestions about the jump?"

The surprise of being asked for her advice kept her wordless for a few seconds but not any longer. "Bring snacks. What passes for food in some of these times is not pleasant. An analog watch. Matches or a lighter. A printed copy of the map because my phone won't work."

He cleared his throat. "Then, that's what I'll do. Can I see your phone? I'll need to run home and make a copy of the map."

He may have thought she didn't hear what he did there, but she did. Her father was going to make the jump, not her. The person who had no magickal skills and not much psychic ability would wander back in time. Besides never time traveling before, her father didn't adapt fast. "No, you can't have my phone."

"What?"

She hunched over her phone and typed. "Okay. I sent the map to myself as an email. We can head out to one of the nearby office stores, pull up the email on their computer, and print it out. We can make several copies if you think we might need to pass them out to folks if we don't come back."

"I saw what you did there. The we thing."

"Like I didn't see what you did. You need me. This time, I'll be teaching you, and we'll all get back okay, thanks to your superior math skills, which you did not have the courtesy of passing on to me. The real question is what to tell Mom."

"We're getting ice?"

"Please. She'll sense you're lying. Tell Traya and let her handle it. I suspect she can be much more guarded than we can. Mom knows how to slip around any barriers we put up. Surely, you noticed that by now."

He scratched his head and managed a weak smile. "That explains a lot." He held up a fisted hand. "Let's do this."

Leah gave the fist a curious glance before bumping it with her own. "We got this."

CHAPTER FIVE

T HE SOUND OF something falling and a few muttered curses had the celebration guests turning to find the source. The older Buell Hare lay stretched out on the ground while Clayton and Nora had pushed up into sitting positions.

"Are you okay, Grandpa?" Nora leaned over and asked.

He groaned a little. "That first step back is always a doozey."

The news of their reappearance spread through the crowd. Maura came flying through the people. "You're back."

She dropped to her knees kissed her father, then worked her way to Nora and Clayton repeating the same action. "Adam, Leah, they're back," she called out.

Several people rushed forward to help assist the time travelers, but none of them were her husband or youngest daughter. They must not have heard her. No matter, they'd discover soon enough. She held her arms out and embraced Nora. "Thank the Goddess you're back."

Nora returned her hug with a tight embrace. "I felt your energy calling me home."

"For that, I'm grateful."

Maura turned to her son-in-law and held out her arms. He grinned, then stepped into them. "Clayton, I was betting on you to bring my daughter back, since you had so much experience with time traveling."

"I'd like to take credit, but it was luck and the map your father made that allowed us to step into the right spot. Your father is as familiar with the various time portals in the cities as most people are with fast food restaurants. He not only brought us back, but brought us close enough that no real walking was involved. We were hoping to return on the same day, not the next day, or even a year later. The timeline can be tricky like that."

"No matter." She gave him another squeeze before releasing her hold. "The important thing is you got back."

Buell held out his arms and declared, "You're passing out hugs and grateful greetings, and I get none?"

The somber man who had stumbled aimlessly through their home as if a tragic ghost these last few days after the death of his wife was gone. Instead, the father she knew so well stood before her with his customary twinkle that hinted, he knew something amusing no one else did. He looked weary, but instead of looking sad, his expression appeared more resigned.

She flew into his arms and kissed him on the cheek. "I was so worried. What were you thinking to go off like that?"

"I needed to say my final goodbye. My beloved left so suddenly." He shook his head. "Some might think we had decades together, but it is never enough. Not only did I want to see Esmeralda again, but I wanted to see myself, too. I was able to advise myself to treasure her."

"You always did."

"Maybe I did because my future self told me to do so. You realize your mother was a very strong-willed woman, and that would be hard for many men to take."

"Not you."

He nodded. "You're right about that. She was always the perfect match for me. It felt like we knew each other the first time we met. I have no doubt we will meet again in future lifetimes. It's a shame most people can't remember their past lives."

It was a shame. "It would probably keep me from learning things I already knew." Her shoulders went up in a shrug. "That's karma."

"True." He lifted his busy eyebrows. "Where's the rest of my grand-children and your husband? Aren't they excited to have me home?"

As if on cue, Traya moved closer and patted Buell on the shoulder. "Glad to have you back. Leah was a little overcome, fearing she lost both grandparents. Adam is helping her to deal with it. As for Ethan and Orin," Her eyes met Maura's, who shook her head slightly. "I believe they went for a walk. You know how young love is. Why don't you come sit down under the shelter and tell us what it was like to meet yourself in the past. Since you're here, I guess that blows that old conundrum that two versions of your self can't meet without one wiping out the other's existence."

Maura stepped back as Traya led Buell to the shelter. Where had Adam and Leah gone to? Even though the park was wooded, the trees were spaced far enough apart that they didn't hide anything or anyone. No sign of them, which made her uneasy as she followed the crowd up to the shelter.

❖   ❖   ❖   ❖

THEY CHATTED ABOUT watching the time travelers through a crystal ball. Grandpa shook his head and grinned. "Someone happened to bring a crystal ball with them to a celebration?"

Larry edged up on the group and raised his hand. "That would be me. Kinda got everything in my van since my landlord didn't renew my lease.

Told me he didn't want my kind around. Wasn't sure if he meant smoker or Pagan, probably both."

Grandpa pointed a finger in Larry's direction. "You're going to have to show me how that crystal ball works as far as viewing time travelers. I have a few, but I never could tune into different times."

Nora stood up, brushed herself off, and slowly surveyed the crowd. "I don't see Leah."

Traya who had made it up to the inner circle, waved, then spoke. "She went to go get ice."

Buell Hare staggered to his feet, turned slowly, and fixed an intent gaze on his wife's friend. Esmeralda always like to say that Traya had some of the best mental shields around. They were good, but a tiny tick by her eye, her tell, always gave her away in bridge. She and her partner were convinced Buell could see through cards, but it was the tell that did Traya in.

"Where's Dad?" Nora inquired.

"Ice, too." Traya answered, earning a suspicious look from Buell.

"I thought you said she was overcome at the loss of both grandparents—now ice?" He could not read her mind, but he could compel her. He focused on creating a mental hook to pull out the information, which resulted in Traya slapping his arm.

"You need to stop that. Esmeralda would not approve. Ava, the world's finest medium, is here. It wouldn't take me more than a minute to relay the information."

Traya was right about that. His Esme wouldn't be pleased. "I suspect she can see everything that is happening here, but you're right. She wouldn't be happy to have you whining when she just got comfortable in Summerlands."

❖   ❖   ❖   ❖

THE GROUP WORKED their way up to the shelter to get out of the sun. Maura's lips twisted as she surveyed the crowd. No one would call her husband, an adventurer. Normally, he played it safe. Still, when it came to family, he could be aggressive. Her eyes narrowed as she considered what might have happened. "I should have known!"

Her comment attracted the attention of all the celebrants, and her father asked, "What should you have known?"

"Adam and Leah have gone back to retrieve Evan and Orin."

"Did they get lost in the city? Even so, I expect they'll be able to find their way to the park. Probably just distracted, that's all."

"That's not it. They went after Nora and Clayton who went after you. I'm not sure why they did it." A tear slid down her cheek. "I don't want the rest of my family lost in time."

Buell's brows gathered together as he pondered the situation, then gave a slow nod of the comprehension. "Don't worry, daughter. Your husband is thorough and methodical. When he decides to do something, he thinks it through. You and I may have a wee bit of magic in our bones, but when it comes to magic of love, your husband has the full measure. Besides, he has Leah with him. She knows her way around a time portal."

His words made sense, and she wanted to believe, but it was hard. She gave a sniff and added, "You're right."

A few of her friends parted her on the back. Nora wrapped one arm around her and grumbled under her breath. "I could slap Evan for being so impulsive."

"Impulsive is who he is," Maura murmured. She knew her daughter would do no such thing. There had never been any violence between the siblings—some conflict, but no physical fights.

Buell made the executive decision to share the wine and cakes, especially the cakes that would melt away in the heat. Drinks were passed around along with the cupcakes and cookies. Then, started the unofficial remembering of Esmeralda. Each person had a tale. Some were funny, ending with the trademark line, "Don't make me turn you into a toad." More than a few had people reaching for napkins stamped *With Love to all My Witches, Esmeralda* to dab at their eyes. The outspoken octogenarian had been more generous with her time and money than she ever let on. The stories went on for some time, and the sun made its gradual descent in the west. A mourning dove settled nearby and serenaded the group.

One of the men pointed to the bird. "Do you think that's Esmeralda letting us know she arrived okay?

Buell shook her head. "My wife would never settle for such a dull bird to bring her messages."

Leah's voice carried in a moment of silence. "I don't see them anywhere."

"They should be here." Adam answered. "These are the coordinates. My math is right."

Everyone turned to find the source of the voices. They were coming from the crystal ball. Larry rushed over to it and placed his hands on his cheeks. "Oh, my! I must have left it on."

Maura elbowed people to get closer. She took one look and exclaimed. "They're safe!"

After staring at the ball for a couple of minutes, Maura slapped her own forehead. "If there is a problem to be fix, Adam is your guy, but I can't believe he left without telling me."

"As if you'd let him go," Traya remarked and earned a glare for her comment.

Buell had worked his way to the ball. His lips pulled down as he contemplated the figures walking through the woods. "I'm so sorry I've caused my family all this trouble." He covered his face with his hands.

Nora slipped between two of Nana's friends to reach her grandfather. She put her arm around him. "Don't worry. When it comes to math, Dad is unbeatable."

He dropped his hands. "That's exactly why I'm worried. All my formulas were untested. The two of you finding me was as close to Yule miracle as I've ever experienced."

The group that had hooted and laughed at Esmeralda's various antics minutes before turned maudlin. Tears ran down Maura's face as she sat by her father, clutching his hand.

In a flurry of feathers a brightly colored parrot landed on the table and pecked at the ball. In between pecks, it squawked. "Do something!"

Buell addressed the bird. "What do you want me to do?"

Instead of talking, it flapped its wings and flew in a circle around the people.

"All of the people. Of course. A ritual." Buell nodded in understanding. "We certainly have the right people for it."

The parrot flew away and rested high up in a large cedar tree. Buell whistled and motioned for the bird to come back. Instead, it very deliberately turned its back.

"That bird is so my wife. If she isn't the bird, then she is possessing it. What is she try to tell me?" He placed his hands around his mouth and yelled. "Please, come back to me."

The parrot flew back and landed on Buell's shoulder. He spoke with certainty. "Of course, I should have thought of it. The 'come back to me' spell. Sometimes, better known as 'Lover come back to me'. We'll need candles, paper, scissor, pen, matches, and honey."

Larry put up his hand. "I got that covered."

"You've got honey? That would have been one of the harder items to obtain. Not impossible. It would just take time to go to the store."

The parrot squawked, interrupting Buell's ramble. "Time to make the donuts."

"Donuts?" Traya raised an eyebrow. "I don't think there any donuts in the spell."

Maura held out her hand to the colorful Macaw. "Is that you, Mother?"

"Pretty bird."

Nora stroked the bird with one finger. "This bird has only so many words that it knows. Nana can only use what the bird knows. Time to make the donuts means get to work. Larry, go get the stuff please."

They chose both pink and red candles for love. Each person cut out a heart and set an intention in their minds to guide the travelers. A drop of honey on the heart signified love. Everyone held on to their heart as a drummer pounded out a heartbeat sound. The circle was created, and the directions called. Feet stomps, hands clapped, many spun in circles, while a few hooted wildly like owls.

Buell lit the two candles. Then raised his hands and spoke in a strong resonant voice. "Lord and Lady, God and Goddess, high spirits, air travelers, fairies, elves, listen all, I plead. From us are parted Ethan, Orin, Adam, and Leah. Where they wander, we do not know. We send out our love like a hook to reel them in. We set out our hearts and honey, and they are the bees. Return to me."

The group chanted, "Return, return, return," as each person stepped forward one at a time and used the candle flames to light their hearts. The flaming heart was placed on the empty cookie sheet to burn. After the last heart was lit and placed on the pan, Buell held up the pan and announced. "So, mote it be."

Silence followed. Many had their eyes closed and swayed, still caught up in the magic. Maura caught Nora's eyes, almost afraid to hope when a long, low thundering sounded. Near a copse of tall, silvery birch trees the air wavered and shimmered. Iridescent colors dances and wavered forming a circle. A rush of air came out of nowhere, ripping off a few hats in the process. Adam, Leah, Ethan, and Orin landed in a tangled heap between the birch trees.

Buell clapped his hands together. "Excellent! They must have shot through time!"

The travelers moved slowed as they untangled themselves and brushed off the dust of other times. Nora and Maura sprinted to reach them while Buell ambled at a more sedate space. They were talking all at once, a melee of voices, telling how they were snatched from the different places and times where they'd been.

Traya squealed. "Look, Esmeralda! We did it!"

The colorful parrot was nowhere to be seen.

✧   ✧   ✧   ✧

A WILD CELEBRATION followed. Not the kind where the police were called, but a memorable one all the same. The grove buzzed with magick and love. With the return of all the lost, the mood became jubilant. Every now and then people needed to be reminded just how powerful they truly are.

Dylan showed up late and waded through the celebrants in search of Leah. Finally, he found her sitting by her grandfather with a contented smile.

"Hello, Dylan. I'm glad you're here. Come sit on my other side."

As he sat, he asked. "This isn't what I expected."

"No?" Leah asked. "In what way?"

"Everyone is so happy."

Buell cleared his throat. "I realize you have your own beliefs. We believe—no make that, we know, Esmeralda is very much with us. She's always ready to lend a hand. When she died, for a moment, I thought I had lost all that was good about us. I hadn't. I reclaimed it. Now, instead of asking my wife her opinion on something, I'll try to think of what Esme would want me to do." He stopped for a moment and cocked his head as if listening to an unheard voice. "Oh, yes, dear. I agree. He would be an excellent addition I'll go talk to Larry about using your shop right away." And so, he did.

THE END

www.ingramcontent.com/pod-product-compliance
Lightning Source LLC
Chambersburg PA
CBHW050837030726

47503CB00007BA/2209